PRAISE FOR *SHADOWS OF THE SUN DYNASTY*

"What especially stands out in this edition of the Ramayana is the celebration of the feminine voice: the female characters who would normally be overshadowed by their male counterparts are now invested with agency and power. The extraordinary positive contributions from such female personalities leaves the reader with a fresh view of this amazing tale."

—GRAHAM M. SCHWEIG, PHD, Professor of Philosophy and Religion, Christopher Newport University, Virginia; Author of *Bhagavad Gītā: The Beloved Lord's Secret Love Song*

"Reader, be prepared for a treat. Vrinda Sheth's Ramayana is far beyond routine story-telling. Her telling is full of the kind of personal detail and insight that comes from knowing her subjects at a heart level. Rama for her is not only an archetypal hero—he lives and breathes, radiating mystical power; Sita is more than tragic heroine or unearthly goddess—she is a powerful self-aware human yet divine being. The Ramayana is a feast of emotion and grand inspiration: it calls us to experience life to the fullest, not shrinking from its tragedies or rewards but giving ourselves fully to the whole cosmic drama. Immerse yourself in *Sita's Fire* and you will find yourself doing just that."

—RANCHOR PRIME, Author of *Ramayana: A Tale of Gods and Demons*

"The intrigue and mystery starts with the opening line—never have I been pulled so quickly into a book through a few simple yet tantalizing words. The art and magic unfold page after page through story and image alike. From injustice and savagery to heroism and beautiful princesses, the unique style of Vrinda Sheth's writing captivates the heart and mind, drawing one deeper into the burning intricacies of *Sita's Fire*."

—BRAJA SORENSEN, Author of *Lost & Found in India*, *Mad & Divine*, and *India & Beyond*

"What an excellent retelling of the Ramayana! If sheer artistry, imagination, storytelling technique, and descriptive writing were not enough, Vrinda Sheth accurately conveys the emotion and underlying philosophical content of the story as well. With God as my witness, I went in a skeptic and came out a believer—and now I can hardly wait for future volumes in the series."

—STEVEN J. ROSEN, Editor in Chief, *Journal of Vaishnava Studies*; Associate Editor, *Back to Godhead*; Author of *Holy War: Violence and the Bhagavad Gita*; *The Hidden Glory of India*; and *Black Lotus: the Spiritual Journey of an Urban Mystic*

"*Shadows of the Sun Dynasty* by Vrinda Sheth is rich with deep insights into the motives and emotions of the entire cast, which makes for an unforgettable entrance into the political intrigue and web of emotions in the kingdom of Ayodhya. For those who enjoy an unforgettable story, you have in your hands a unique book that will pull you in from start to finish. Anna's exquisite illustrations further enhance the story. I expect this beautiful book to enthrall the present generation, leaving its indelible mark in their minds and hearts, as other versions of the Ramayana have for countless generations."

—KOSA ELY, Author of *The Peaceable Forest* and *The Prince and the Polestar*

SHADOWS OF THE SUN DYNASTY

THE SITA'S FIRE TRILOGY: BOOK ONE

SHADOWS OF THE SUN DYNASTY

AN ILLUSTRATED SERIES BASED ON THE RAMAYANA

VRINDA SHETH

ILLUSTRATED BY
ANNA JOHANSSON

MANDALA
PUBLISHING

San Rafael, California

MANDALA
PUBLISHING

PO Box 3088
San Rafael, CA 94912
www.mandalaeartheditions.com

 Find us on Facebook: www.facebook.com/MandalaEarth
Follow us on Twitter: @MandalaEarth

Bhaktiland

This book was made possible by a grant from Bhaktiland, a non-profit
supporting the expansion of quality bhakti art.
www.bhaktiland.com

Library of Congress Cataloging-in-Publication Data available.

ISBN: 978-1-60887-871-0

Book design by Raghu Consbruck
www.raghudesigns.com

  REPLANTED PAPER

Mandala Publishing, in association with Roots of Peace, will plant two trees for each tree used in the
manufacturing of this book. Roots of Peace is an internationally renowned humanitarian organization
dedicated to eradicating land mines worldwide and converting war-torn lands into productive farms and
wildlife habitats. Roots of Peace will plant two million fruit and nut trees in Afghanistan and provide
farmers there with the skills and support necessary for sustainable land use.

Manufactured in China by Insight Editions

10 9 8 7 6 5 4 3 2 1

To My Fathers

Pita, Yogindra Das, for being the most sincere and unique
person I know, for making spiritual growth the constant
aim, for even now showing me by example how to deeply
interrogate the purpose of life.

Len, bonus dad, for being fun and lighthearted,
for dedicating time to effective communication,
for being generous and invested,
for loving my mother.

Contents

RAMA'S ADVENTURES

THE QUEEN'S PLOT

Foreword

One of the most striking features of the Ramayana storytelling tradition, which has enthralled and inspired readers and audiences throughout South and Southeast Asia for more than two millennia, is the absence of a single authoritative text. The Sanskrit epic attributed to the sage Valmiki, which many scholars now think may have been composed in the fifth or fourth centuries BC, is revered as the literary origin of the tradition and even as the adi kavya or "first poem." Yet it is a remarkable fact that, prior to the colonial period, it was almost never translated, in the sense that we understand this term today: as a word-for-word rendering from one language to another. Instead, when storytellers in the many regional languages of the Indian subcontinent wanted to share the Rama story with their audiences, they seem to have relished the opportunity to retell it in their own languages and in their own ways, using local imagery and expressions and incorporating their personal insights into the beloved tale.

Indeed, it is sometimes said that there are "three hundred Ramayanas," and this is scarcely an exaggeration, for each one of India's more than a score of official languages now boasts multiple retellings of the story, most of them centuries old—and they are all different. Of course, they all retell the basic story of a noble prince who wins a beautiful and virtuous bride, only to be cheated of his throne and sent into exile in the wilderness, where he must eventually battle and slay a ferocious adversary, who has kidnapped his beloved wife.

Yet, within this basic framework there is ample scope for creativity on the part of storytellers, especially in the matter of characterization and motive. For, although several of the main actors in the Ramayana are understood by Hindus to be divine incarnations and their worldly deeds part of a larger cosmic plan, this understanding has generally not gotten in the way of an appreciation of their humanity and even vulnerability when on Earth. Many years ago, a great Ramayana scholar and a pious devotee of Rama in the city of Benares described to me how, in his childhood, he and his family members would retell and, at the same time, fiercely debate all aspects of the story on long summer nights in their courtyard, sometimes deliberately taking unusual positions, raising serious doubts, or challenging conventional assumptions. This wonderful freedom to reinterpret sacred narrative has been one of the great strengths of the Hindu tradition, and has ensured that its most important tales have remained vibrant and relevant throughout millennia.

Now Vrinda Sheth, assisted by her mother Anna Johansson, has added her voice to the ancient and echoing chorus of Ramayana narrators, giving us a freshly inspiring retelling of the Rama tale in English, beautifully illustrated, and intended especially for young adult readers. This is clearly a labor of love, but it is also—like the family Ramayana of my Benares friend—the product of much study, reflection, and even debate. It is grounded in two of the greatest classical versions of the story, the Sanskrit epic of Valmiki and the Tamil one of Kamban, which Vrinda has studied carefully in their English translations. I especially appreciate her use of the Kamban epic, which was probably composed in the twelfth century AD, for it was the first Rama epic in a regional language. It is even longer than the Sanskrit poem, and includes many original episodes and interpretations. Though still popular today in the Tamil-speaking regions of southern India, it is little known outside of India, and it deserves to be better appreciated. Happily, Vrinda has incorporated some beautiful insights into the story that are unique to this text.

In recasting the Indian sources for her intended audience, Vrinda has been respectful and culturally sensitive, yet she has not sanitized or oversimplified, nor has she glossed over the tensions and controversies that sometimes enter the story. As in the most beloved Indian-language retellings, her hero and heroine have retained both their divinity and their humanity, and their story remains sufficiently complex and multi-stranded to allow Vrinda's readers, who are sure to be many, to imagine the story in their own ways and, in time, to weave creative reinterpretations of their own.

And so, the Ramayana tradition continues here . . . Let the journey begin!

—Philip Lutgendorf
    Professor of Hindi and Modern Indian Studies
    Department of Asian and Slavic Languages and Literatures
    University of Iowa
    Author of *The Life of a Text: Performing the Ramcaritmanas of Tulsidas* and *Hanuman's Tale: The Messages of a Divine Monkey*

Preface

When I first started writing, I had no computer and no method. In its seed form, this book was 150 pages and was named *Prince Rama: Son of the Solar Dynasty*. It was written entirely in internet cafes while I studied dance at Kalakshetra in South India. To say that I was fumbling around in the dark is an understatement. As I completed the entire trilogy (ten years later!), the work as a whole had taken unexpected turns. In the years that followed the release of *Son of the Solar Dynasty*, my creative process underwent a complete transformation, and my first effort just was not cohesive with books two and three. As we found a new publisher, I was thrilled to get this opportunity to redo book one. What began as a hesitant tread into the Ramayana-retelling tradition turned into a headlong sprint. And here I am.

The book you hold in your hands now has more than tripled in size and is over 400 pages. With the support of my inspired editor Mirabai (Lee Harrington), I undertook an overhaul in point-of-view, absorbing much of the first text into this much larger body of work. This book also features thirty-three new full color illustrations, as well as three black-and-white drawings by my talented mother. As if all that was not enough, it has been renamed and completely redesigned. In short, a lotus in full bloom!

In the early years, I struggled often during the writing process. In *Son of the Solar Dynasty*, I was careful to document any instance where I strayed from Valmiki's original work. That would be impossible for this incarnation. Much as I tried simply producing a faithful retelling of Valmiki's Ramayana, I could not. The ideas came to me through a creative impulse I could not contain. The creation process has given me joy, inspiration, and a desire to study Valmiki's text deeper. When I finally surrendered to this creative impulse, I felt the wind under my wings. This jump into the realm of imagination took consistent leaps of courage, and I'm so thankful to my supportive husband and mother.

If you do not know Sita and Rama's story, this book is for you. If you are a Sita-Rama connoisseur, this book is for you. I pushed my craft to its limit to invite the unfamiliar reader into this magical world. For the concerned reader, I want to assure you that I always kept the original work close to my heart. The vast majority of my material is derived through retrograde plotting. Also, I want to stress that my rendition is only one of the many possible ways to view the story. (In fact, I have a fantasy of writing a new version every ten years!) As I circumambulated the original text, nothing became more clear to me than this: each of the characters have their version of the story that they wish to tell, and so does every reader.

Prologue by No One

I will not bother telling you my name. You will forget it. I am no one. Not a princess or queen, not the daughter of a wealthy man, nor the wife of someone influential. I was an ordinary woman, married to a cloth merchant. We lived in a small village adjacent to the Great City. I was dispensable, like most women are. I did not know it until it was too late.

In my last and final memory of being truly alive, the day was full of laughter and sunshine. My children and I had played in the forest, leaving any worries of a clean dwelling behind. The children were not concerned with such things, and I became a free being like them as I played hide-and-seek, tugging one of my daughter's braids, running almost as fast as my son. I marveled that they, who grew in my womb, could run faster than I did. I blamed it on my long silken dress, which caught around my ankles and made me trip. I allowed my daughter to tuck hers up so that she could run unencumbered. I did not even object when she took off the linen shawl covering her chest and tied it on her head like a turban. What harm could it do when she was as flat-chested as a boy? Their father was not with us to object, but I was mindful to keep myself covered in case neighbors were watching. All that modesty did not save me in the end.

After hours of play, even the children got exhausted. I hurried to unveil the food I had prepared and the utensils clinked and clattered. We ate it with relish. Afterwards, they insisted on letting my long hair out of its braid and combing it with their fingers, taking out the leaves and twigs. My daughter's bangles tinkled by my ears.

"You are the most beautiful, Mother," she said.

"Like a queen," my son said.

They both praised me with childish innocence. They were only eight and ten and still could not fathom anyone being wiser or finer than their mother.

I closed my eyes in pleasure as they played with my hair, decorating me according to their fancy.

Eventually, we fell asleep together all tangled up under a tree. As I fell into the dreamlands, I thought about my husband, wondering if he would have joined us today. But no, he was a serious man. Even now, on a summer day, he was away at the big city, counting the new shipment of cloths that had come in. He was in favor with the queen, who specially ordered countless bolts of his most expensive silks. I was proud of him, a true businessman, never a boy. I smiled and fell fast asleep with my daughter curled at my side and my son leaning on my shoulder.

I woke up, startled into wakefulness by a scream.

"What happened? What is the matter?" I cried out, looking around, bleary-eyed, ready to run to the rescue. It was my daughter, staring at me with huge tears trickling down her cheeks.

"Mother, I dreamt of a demon that has many, many heads and lots of arms reaching for me. He had sharp teeth and a red tongue."

"Ravana," my son said, before I could.

"The monster from the stories," I said, smoothing her hair. "That's all."

"But he felt so real," she said, "as if he was standing right next to us. And he was whispering, 'Wake up, wake up, sweet child, and come to me.' "

I felt a shiver run down my spine and noticed a chill in the air. The sun was going down. Suddenly I felt vulnerable, a lone woman with two children. I could hear my husband scolding me, as if I were an irresponsible child.

"Let's go home," I said, hurrying up and away, clutching their hands tightly.

I even left our steel utensils behind in my fear.

Once we were on the familiar trail, I felt reassured and let them run ahead.

The evening rays shone through the trees and it was a peaceful place. I settled into my stroll home, too tired to match my children's energy. Soon their laughter and calls faded, but they knew the way so I was not worried. We had walked here a thousand times. Humming, I began to pick some wildflowers for a bouquet; I could use the gold-plated vase the queen had gifted us. I froze.

My daughter's dream came alive.

Looking at me with countless pairs of eyes, he stood there, quiet like a statue. Not one of his many arms moved. All his eyes watched me, and all his mouths said, "Wake up, sweet child, come to me."

I threw the flowers at him and ran into the forest, too panicked to even think. I heard him laughing, a terrifying sound. When he caught me moments later, he had put my flowers behind his ears, mocking me.

"Don't be afraid, sweetling," he whispered, pinning my arms to my side.

All I could do now was plead. "Please let me go. I have two children who need me."

My child, being more perceptive, had sensed this monster around us while I had not. I could feel my tears running down my neck into my garment and shivered when his eyes followed the movement of my tears.

"Do you want to come with me?" he asked, mesmerizing me with his gleaming eyes and teeth.

The way his countless heads spoke in unison made me feel I was being hypnotized.

This is not real. This is not real! I told myself. Wake up, wake up now!

I would wake up at the tree and I would be the one who told my children about a dream of a monster with ten heads.

No, no, no. I shook my head, unable to speak. Then my mind was flooded with a vivid image of my son and daughter. Their . . . heads were . . . ripped off and . . .

"Come with me and that need not happen," he said.

What choice did I have then?

He said he had not come to kill me. But by the time he was finished with me, I begged him to. There is no going back once you take the hand of darkness. No matter what the reason.

I'm dead now. Or I'm alive, in another life, far from the one I knew and treasured. I might be one of his queens now. Or I might be a ghost, haunting everyone I meet with my violent end. I was not the only one. Simply one of many.

I don't know who I am. I'm no one. I could be anyone.

THE KING
OF THE WORLD

CHAPTER 1

The Sound of Victory

Manthara had another name once. But in the year she turned fifteen, her back reached its terminal crookedness, and from then on she was called Manthara, "The Hunchback." Never mind that she lived in a palace and was surrounded by so-called noble people. They were the first to rename her. It was a cruel world for those like her. Her kind, and anyone else with divergent features, was always shunned and considered harbingers of evil. A crooked spine meant a crooked mind. An eye defect meant an inability to understand righteousness. Too much hair on the body meant indulgence. Too little hair meant scarcity. A disease of the body meant a disease of the mind. All of these were cases of bad karma, and the karmically fortunate vigilantly guarded the boundaries of their lives. It was said that Manthara's mere shadow would cast a curse on whomever it touched.

At the onset of puberty, when her spine began its determined downward spiral, Manthara naturally retreated, intuiting the change that was coming. She hid in the royal garden, shunning her duties. Like her parents and grandparents, she was a servant in the royal palace of Kekaya, one of the fifty kingdoms under Ayodhya's rule. It was a position of some privilege, and the elders had noted that Manthara was gifted, a quick learner, someone who never forgot a thing once told. But because she was a servant's child and, more important, a female, she was relegated to standing in the corner as a dead observer. She was allowed to step out of the shadows only if one of the high-caste children dropped a book or spilled his ink. In short, she was a servant to clumsy idiots. The only pupil who never dropped a thing was Ashvapati, the king's son. He was the one who always knew the teachers' answers. He was the one who greeted Manthara as he passed by her in the corner. He was not like other humans, for he could communicate with animals, especially horses and swans. This gift had been given to him by a visiting sage, and the only restriction was that he could never share what he knew. His birth stars clearly showed that he would add to Kekaya's wealth through his natural rapport with horses, and he was named Ashvapati, "Lord of Horses." Ashvapati was unusual, for the other high-caste children did not have eyes to see servants. Still, Manthara learned a great deal by listening. She could recall every lesson, from the first to the last. That is how she suspected at once what was happening to her, even before she was sent to the physician. That happened in her eleventh year when her cycles began. The physician told her what she already knew: her spine was deformed, and she would become a hunchback in mid-adolescence. There was no cure.

Looking back later, Manthara wished she would have understood what her affliction really meant: that she would become repulsive, especially to men. She had been too innocent to understand that. Like most other girls, Manthara had been shy of the natural changes in her body: her budding breasts, the onset of her courses. She became extra self-conscious by the small but discernible hump on her back. Her parents sought a respectable boy for her, but it was the boy and his family who in their scrutiny noted the abnormality of her back. That was the beginning of Manthara. Though she hadn't truly been Manthara then, it was a defining moment. She had been on the verge of serving hot tea to the prospective family when the prospective groom, a mere boy, made his comment. The steam from the spicy tea made her face moist as she hung her neck in shame. No one wanted a Manthara for their son. She, who had once been a human being, now was a hunchback, an altogether different category. Her kind had a distinct reputation for being crooked in mind. It was deemed impossible for someone so ugly to be pious or wise. When the transformation was complete in her fifteenth year, she belonged to another category of the living.

This exclusion was the pinnacle of cruelty. The philosophy had no depth: it insisted on external beauty, a thing that had nothing to do with what was within. Therefore, Manthara disregarded the superstition of the people; she saw that *they* were the fools. She would let them whisper their faces blue and their souls black. She knew her own caliber. The soul within was capable of immense power, unimaginable to the feebleminded. She would show them one day what she was capable of. It took some time, however, for Manthara to come to this conviction. The transition from being an ordinary girl into an outcast was a bitter time for her. The world found every excuse to exclude the hunchbacked girl. She was no longer welcome at weddings or birthdays. She was not allowed into the temples or any other place considered sacred. She was barely tolerated by her peers. It was a miracle that she was allowed to remain in the palace at all, and for this good fortune she was meant to be endlessly sycophantic.

In her fifteenth year, Manthara's parents cast her out, and she could not go anywhere in public without children throwing things at her or ridiculing her. No one stopped them. She slunk around the palace, afraid of her tormentors. She couldn't bear that side of herself and cast about for something worthy to aspire to. She wasn't sure how to direct her ambition, but her heart burned with the knowing that she was meant to do something great. During these solitary years of survival, Manthara developed a rich inner life, one that gave her solace when externally there was none. She slept outside in the gardens, for the servants' quarters were full of people eager to squash someone less fortunate. Because of this, she stumbled across Kekaya's well-kept secret, hidden away in a remote part of the royal gardens. The discovery of a secret was in itself potent, a source of such thrill that it became an addiction. The secret itself influenced Manthara's path for the rest of her crooked life.

Manthara came across the secret from her habit of being where she should not. She had been shooed away many times from that area of the gardens. But even from a distance, she could see the unusual brightness of the flowers and trees growing there. One part of her mind suspected the nature of the plants, but she was not close enough to be certain. When she asked the other servants what was there, she did not get even a half-cooked rumor, only blank stares. This intrigued her and was the beginning of the obsession. She *had* to know the secret. She abandoned the little dignity she still possessed and crawled under bushes and trees to get past the guards. They kept their noses in the air anyway. No one but Manthara would dare go somewhere forbidden. Even so, she was not prepared when she came face to face with two creatures that no words could possibly describe. The three of them gaped at each other. The two beauties exuded a magnetic power so strong that Manthara, who did not like physical touch, felt an urgent need to embrace them. She did not. Only a fool would. Or a man. Manthara's heart hammered against her chest, and her mind worked faster than it ever had before. She took in every detail of the two women with the brilliant and haunted eyes. She knew what they were: not one but *two* flesh-and-blood Vishakanyas, poisonous virgins, whose very touch could kill.

This was a secret fit for kings, for the virgins were used as assassins against highly placed politicians or kings. No one could know that they existed at all, for whispers of a Visha would make the most licentious king wary. The virgins glowed with deathly pallor. They had the tragic aura of the dying, yet their life energies were fiercely fighting for them to live, making them pulsate with life. It was as if every moment of their existence was imbued with a life-and-death struggle. The living were drawn to them like flies to a fire. They were powerful weapons, created to kill unsuspecting men. One gentle embrace, one chaste kiss, was all it took. Because men could not see beyond their lust, they were easy to kill.

Imagine how surprised the Vishakanyas must have been when Manthara came crawling out from a bush, dirty, disheveled, hunched over, and uglier than a demon. They stared at Manthara with open fascination, and Manthara could see that their thinking had not been tainted by societal standards. They didn't see a Manthara; the Vishas just saw a girl with a terribly crooked back. Manthara loved them at once. They circled around her, never coming too close, but examining her gently with their eyes. Manthara was welcome here. No doubt they were starved for affection and company. Manthara was awed by their immense beauty and the enormity of their power. In a sense, they were outcasts too, hidden away, and brought forth only in dire political circumstances when a lustful king would die in their embrace.

Satisfaction spread in Manthara's heart. Every woman had a Vishakanya in her, a being whose touch was lethal. Men were such utter fools. Manthara felt camaraderie with the Vishas, and having befriended them, she knew more about herself and the world. Manthara would never give birth to life, but she could cause death. She could be poisonous to the touch. There was satisfaction in that possibility. For many years, this was Manthara's highest aspiration: she would be a self-made Vishakanya.

It was a complicated aspiration, for just as Manthara's kind had a reputation, so did the Vishas. They were always maidens of uncommon beauty, selected at a young age and introduced to a diet of poison, without which they would die. Even if Manthara had possessed uncommon beauty, which she certainly did not, she was far too old at fifteen to ever become a Visha. But she was not so easily deterred, having found a fitting goal in life. Several times a week, she crawled through the underbrush and visited the two creatures, observing especially what they ate and drank. That was the most fascinating part. They drank only the water from tender coconuts, and every few days, a man came bearing two vials. Manthara hid away, and the Vishas kept her presence a secret. They would not divulge, however, what type of poison they were administered. Manthara watched the man struggle to be unmoved by the Vishas, for he always had to jerk his sneaky hand away at the last moment. From her hiding place, Manthara could not get a sense of what the poison looked or smelled like. But patience always rewards, for one day, she was close enough to hear the man ask: "How many flowers have you eaten?"

Suddenly an image of the Vishakanyas eating certain flowers was clear in Manthara's mind. It dawned on her that they were surrounded by poisonous plants of all kinds. There were white soma flowers, shaped like the moon; pink oleander bushes; and lots of lily of the valley with tiny white flowers shaped like teardrops. She saw the vivid purple aconite and

the suicide tree, with its round green fruit the size of her closed fist. The names of the plants came to Manthara effortlessly, one of the many lessons she had absorbed standing in the shadows. This was the answer to her prayer. She would eat flowers too. If the Vishas could casually eat ten of the teardrops, surely Manthara could eat one and work her way up. She found the pristine teardrops and plucked several tears off. Every part of this pretty flower was poisonous. Manthara popped it into her mouth without hesitation. She made it back to her quarters before the vomiting began. She grew dizzy and ill and was bedridden for days. But she survived and was well on her way to become a Visha too. Or so she foolishly thought. Manthara managed to ingest as many as four of the teardrops at a time before the charade was exposed.

During this time, it became known around the palace that Manthara was not suitably humble. She dared exchange words with Prince Ashvapati himself. She dared look others in the eye. She dared open her mouth before superiors. She refused to accept her position as a hunchback. Manthara knew she was despised, but the feeling was mutual. Even a dog, kicked once too many, might growl and show his teeth. Manthara was no dog. She showed her teeth at the mere suggestion of a kick. It worked like an incantation and kept the malicious away. Manthara had not yet learned the true nature of humans. Punishment was the twin side of goodness, one followed by the other. Manthara had to be put in her place, as if karma had not already done it. It began as the typical coward's confrontation: many against one. Manthara was alone in the gardens when they surrounded her, sticks and stones in hand, smug with the fact that no elders where in sight. She counted five males and three females. All known faces, a mix of servants and high castes, people who had once been her friends. It began as a verbal feud despite the weapons in their hands.

The leader of the gang swaggered forward. He was Manthara's antithesis, too handsome to be considered cruel. He was the very one who, lifetimes ago, had been her prospective groom. Manthara kept her eyes on him, knowing his vicious streak. "Even the snake knows its place," he said. "It slithers close to the ground. Manthara thinks she is something special. She thinks she can piss on the sacred fire and thereby ignite it!"

The girls giggled, and the boys voiced agreement.

"I say," Manthara replied boldly, "your mother mated with a baboon to beget you."

A few boys laughed uneasily. One with an asinine face leered, "You paint your bottom with the sacred clay, mistaking it for your face."

This provoked loud laughter, and they began to circle around her. Poking her with their sticks, they threw out what meager insults they could think of:

"A snail has more spine than you!"

"Yama's messengers would run screaming if they saw you!"

"You leave a trail of slime wherever you go!"

"The spit of a lowborn is cleaner than you!"

"Worm!"

"Snake!"

"Witch!"

Manthara felt the savage threat of the rocks and sticks they held. Her hands were heavy with nothing. But she was not yet afraid; they had needed those objects *and* each other to even muster the guts to approach Manthara.

"I say," she cried, "that you are all low-caste cowards who drink donkey urine."

"You see?" the leader said. "She needs to be taught a lesson!"

"Yes! Yes!"

"Bow at my feet," he said. "And I will consider forgiving you."

"Your face is nearly there anyway!"

She stared them down. This had always caused anyone to disengage before. The leader swallowed hard but waved his stick at her. "Bow down now," he repeated, but he had lost his authority.

"Not even your mother loves you, cripple," a girl said in a shrill voice. She threw one of her rocks. It landed at Manthara's feet. Manthara kicked it hard, stubbing her toe, and the rock flew against the shin of the leader, scraping his skin.

"Bow!" he squealed, swatting her across the arm.

It was a harmless blow but humiliating.

"I would *never* touch your feet," Manthara said. "You are a leper."

"I am not!" the boy cried, a touch of fear in his eyes. He swatted her again, this time harder. Another boy joined in. His stick was heavier, the blow stronger.

"I curse your ancestors to remain disembodied for all time," Manthara cried. They gasped and looked at each other, but the two boys who were hitting her did not stop. Tears stung her eyes. The sticks stung her skin. "Leave me alone!"

Another stone flew at her, this time hitting her shoulder.

"Your father is a corpse collector!" Manthara shouted, looking desperately for an escape now. Her tormentors were growing frenzied. Manthara sensed the change in the air. But she couldn't stop her tongue. It was all she had: "Your mother consorts with demons! Your sister is a mongrel! You are not even the stool that comes out of me each morning!"

As blood trickled down her face, she clenched her teeth together. Now everyone who held a weapon began to use it. The sharp rocks cut her, and the sticks lacerated her skin. Manthara bared her teeth and snapped at every hand within reach. With twisted faces, they herded her deeper into the garden, as if she was a pig they would thrash for fun. The beating grew more vicious. Manthara could not contain her cries, and she fell to the ground. Several of her bones broke, and her words were just pleas. Still they did not stop. Finally she grew quiet, a broken mass of bones.

Spent, they spit on her and left her to die, bloodied and broken.

"Slither out of this if you can," the leader said.

The night was dark, and darker still in Manthara's soul.

Where she got the power from, she could not say. But she dragged herself slowly forward, like the slime they had accused her of being. She knew where the wildflower grew. She ate a whole plant of teardrops, maybe more. The last thing she saw and heard was a flock of swans flying overhead. She walked gratefully into the halls of death, where even the crooked are welcome.

But she was not that lucky. It was Ashvapati himself, recently made king of Kekaya, who came to her when she gained consciousness. Manthara lay in a sickbed in the royal quarters, bandaged and wrapped in soft linen, though she had no recollection of being moved from the gardens nor being nursed. Ashvapati demanded to know what had happened. In a rare concession to his gift, he hinted that his swans had alerted him to her dying in his garden.

Manthara gaped at him, knowing the secrecy he was sworn to. Should he ever reveal what the swans told him, he would die on the spot.

"Who did this to you?" he asked, fixing his dark eyes on Manthara.

Manthara saw something like affection in the young king's eyes. Hoarse from induced bouts of vomiting, Manthara struggled to describe the attack. She didn't yet know the extent of the damage to her, but as she spoke, she felt several teeth missing in her mouth. Even small movements caused blinding flashes of pain.

"This will not go unpunished," Ashvapati promised, asking her to name her tormentors. Their names felt like curses in Manthara's mouth.

"Now, about the teardrops." Ashvapati eyes turned into narrow slits. "Do you wish to die?"

His tone was such that Manthara could not answer yes.

"For if it is," he continued, "I will gladly assist you. If you think your back is such a

handicap that you wish to ignore all else that you have, then perhaps you do not deserve to breathe the same air as those who are grateful for their eyes that see, their ears that hear, their tongue that works, their minds that are brilliant."

His words made Manthara's eyes sting. It was not her back alone that she loathed, but every tormentor who loathed her for it. Yet she accepted Ashva's words as a compliment to her abilities. Manthara's heart opened and she told Ashva everything. The humiliation she had felt becoming a hunchback and an outcast. Then the camaraderie with the poisonous maidens, and finally about her quest to become a Vishakanya through ingesting lily of the valley regularly.

"I cannot bear to be just a hunchback," she said. "That is not all that I am. The Vishakanyas are guarded and revered. No one would think of harming them. That's what I want."

Ashva listened without a word and then said, "I will engage you in a service suited to your intelligence. I will station you in a position of prominence."

"Why would you do that?" she asked. "Hunchbacks are forbidden."

"Will you promise to never seek the Vishakanyas again and swear to keep their existence a secret?"

Manthara's heart grew shrewd. So Ashva was not simply keen on her welfare. He was protecting state secrets. Manthara had some power here.

"Will you promise to never ingest poison again?" he asked.

"Why don't you simply let me die?" she demanded. Her sense of power had been short-lived. If Ashvapati had wanted to, he could have simply allowed her to continue her descent into the land of Yama.

"It is my duty as the king," he answered. "You are not the only one who is targeted. Why should your body be a disqualification?"

On that very day, Ashvapati rebelled against the ancient laws that forbid the crippled and deformed to enter public service and to receive positions of honor. He simply changed the laws; it was like opening the palace doors to beggars on the street, for that is what Manthara's kind had been reduced to. She herself had been further crippled in the attack, with a smashed knee and broken bones in her hips; she would always need a cane to walk.

Ashvapati allowed Manthara to watch as her tormentors were sentenced to fifty lashes across their backs. She would have sentenced them to death, one and all, but she did not yet have that kind of power. She was sixteen and off to a good start, guarded by the king of Kekaya himself. Of course, children continued throwing things at her and calling her all manner of names when no one else could hear. Manthara always found small ways to have revenge, striking them with her cane, hissing curses at them, or putting a petal from a teardrop in their food, just enough to make them ill for a few hours. She made sure that they would associate their misdeeds toward her with pain and discomfort.

In this manner, Manthara continued mostly being Manthara while remaining unsure of her purpose. It was when Ashvapati married and brought home his queen that Manthara's world shifted once again. When she beheld Queen Chaya, she experienced the same flare in her core as she had when she encountered the Vishas. Chaya was just as beautiful but in the opposite way, luminous with life. She laughed often and sparkled in every situation, like a multifaceted gem. The normally coolheaded Ashvapati was goo in her hands. Queen Chaya barely had to raise her voice before her order was carried out. She was verily a goddess on Earth. Manthara saw great power and knew that this was what she had wanted all along. To be a queen. Ashvapati worshipped his queen, and that was enough reason for Manthara to dislike her and covet Chaya's position. True to his word, Ashva employed Manthara as the first assistant to the queen. Chaya was too gracious to object. Manthara began observing the queen as she had scrutinized the Vishas. What did Chaya do that was special? What set her apart from other women?

While Manthara waited and watched, Chaya gave birth to a son. They named him Yuddhajit, "Victorious in Battle." There was a huge celebration and Ashvapati was not himself at all. He smiled and danced, kissing his wife and child for all to see. Manthara had never seen him so happy. He did not even look at Manthara. If Manthara was herded in an alley now and beaten to death, he would never have noticed. The marital bliss of the king and queen continued in this unbearable manner. Everyone agreed that Chaya was beautiful and passionate in just the right amounts. It took Manthara several years to discover the queen's weakness—a small thing but a flaw nevertheless: Chaya did not like being excluded. The queen thrived on company and social events: she wanted always to be in the know, to be part of the important events of Kekaya. She grew fretful and anxious when Ashvapati was occupied elsewhere. Once Manthara discovered this, she began making a plan. She smiled to the queen and brushed her hair with gentle strokes, ingratiating herself, so that the queen would be unsuspecting and listen to Manthara's whispers. Then another child was born, a girl named Kaikeyi.

This is when Manthara followed the persistent urge within her. She knew nothing about child care. It was not necessary. She was simply strong-willed enough to undermine the other woman with just a word or gesture. It didn't take much to unhinge a new mother. Every time Ashva was expected, Manthara seated herself close to the queen. The moment Ashva entered, Manthara would pinch the little baby and make her scream. Chaya would startle at the sudden outburst, and Manthara would swoop the baby up, and press the child's nose to her neck, where she had put a strong dose of calming soma pulp. It worked every time. The queen's eyes would grow insecure and Ashva would look at Manthara with approval. Manthara would make a show of returning the now calm child to her mother's arms, instructing Chaya what to do in a light patronizing tone.

Manthara didn't do all the work herself; she made casual comments to the other servants, planting doubts regarding the queen's mothering abilities. Queen Chaya felt it, growing nervous when she handled her baby. She started shooing the servants out as often as she could, which made them whisper even more. Of course, there were certain servants who would turn the other way when they saw Manthara, and they stood firmly by Queen Chaya's side. Probably they warned the queen of Manthara's duplicity. But like most good people, Chaya didn't muster the spine to accuse Manthara for a good many months. Eventually, though, there was a confrontation.

The newborn was several months old and Prince Yuddhajit had turned four when Queen Chaya summoned Manthara to her quarters. "I see what you are doing," Chaya said, forgoing any courtesies. Even in her anger, she was a goddess.

Manthara had never seen the queen's eyes cold with wrath. Now she saw the queen's lethal side, and fear climbed up her spine. She hung her head in submission.

"You wish to undermine me before my husband," Chaya said. Her hands were clenched. "Why do you do this? What could you possibly gain? I am the queen and you are . . ."

She left the obvious unspoken. As Manthara's heart lurched, she denied the accusation, complaining of the pains in her spine. At length, she described her aches and blamed all her shortcomings on this obvious fact. Chaya was moved and even patted Manthara's hump carefully. For several months, Manthara restrained from interfering, but her plan was fixed and she bided her time.

The plan hinged on Ashvapati's weakness too: once he made a decision, he never ever reconsidered. That was his strength and his weakness. It had served Manthara well when a million and one fools wanted to strike down Ashva's new laws opening the doors to the crippled. No one could deny Ashva's strength of vision and the unparalleled kingdom that he had created. Many of the highest positions were occupied by Manthara's kind, people with extra limbs, physical deformities, who were hideous to look at. One and all were intelligent, like Manthara. In Kekaya, the crippled were physicians, accountants, teachers, and highly placed servants. Ashva's decision was flawless. Those who had spoken against it were never again welcome in the court. He had expelled many good Kekayans who were too biased to accede to this new law. Many friends had become enemies. That was Ashva's strength, and the weakness that Manthara would play on. She started with the queen. It was Manthara's own fascination with Ashva's gift that gave her the idea. The queen probably hated the exclusion when Ashva spoke his swan's secret language.

Holding the queen's hair and brushing it delicately, Manthara began speaking of Ashva's swans who lived at the large vvve by the horse fields. Not a day went by without Ashva visiting this sanctuary. Innocently, Manthara asked, "Aren't you curious to know what the swans say?"

"Of course. But I know he is bound to secrecy."

"If he wishes to tell, he can," Manthara said. "He told me once."

In detail, Manthara described how so many years prior, Ashva had intervened with the help of his swans, saving Manthara, who lay half-dead in the gardens. Expertly, Manthara bent the truth, sticking so close to it that the lie would not be discerned.

"Ask him," Manthara said lightly. "I think he would tell you if you insisted."

Chaya listened and looked at Manthara with big eyes.

Soon after, Manthara watched as the king and queen left for an excursion to the swan lake. That same night, Manthara and everyone else in the palace's inner quarters woke up to loud wails. The servants watched in silence as the queen was dragged through the halls and expelled from the palace. The chain of whispers told Manthara that her plan had exceeded beyond her imagination. At the swan lake, Ashva had laughed out loud, and Queen Chaya had demanded that he share the joke with her. Ashva had taken this as the queen's callous desire for him to die. She was cast off as queen and exiled forthwith from Kekaya. Manthara's whole body trembled, and she had difficulty breathing. She didn't know whether to be elated or sick to the stomach.

Once Chaya was gone, the king rode out into the plains like one possessed, leaving no message saying when he would return. While he was gone, Manthara never left the side of the abandoned baby girl. She was still a suckling of eight months, rooting for her mother's breast. No one dared take the princess from Manthara, for they did not know the king's orders.

Manthara held the child and didn't mind her shrieks. It was the sound of victory. Sure enough, when Ashva returned, he pointed at Manthara, appointing her the sole caretaker of the child. He did not look at Manthara or smile. He had returned from the plains forever changed, hardened and reduced. He would never love or trust a woman again. But he had a soft spot for Manthara because of her deformity, protecting her the way he would an injured animal.

After the queen's exile, a rumor took firm root that Manthara, the ugly hunchback, was Ashvapati's lover. Manthara may have started that rumor; she certainly did nothing to dispel it. The evidence lay in Manthara's frequent nighttime visits to Ashva, when she spoke of the princess, reporting on the child's growth. No one but Manthara knew what took place during those visits. The king had grown too stern to hear, much less address, such flippant rumors. So Manthara was not the queen, but she was the caretaker of the princess. This was as close to royalty as she would ever become, and she would never let this position of power be compromised.

CHAPTER 2

Kaikeyi's Mother

Night after night, Keyi's wails broke the silence. Always, Manthara was there, pulling her out from the scary dreams and saying, "Sh! Sh!"

On this night, Keyi hid her face in Manthara's chest, which was just like a cave. When she was little, she used to curl herself into a ball and hide inside the hollow. Manthara's arms would hold her tight and she would be safe. But now she was a big girl. She couldn't fit in the cave anymore. Keyi was so big, she had to call Taya by her proper name, Manthara. But it was an ugly word that other children only said when they wanted to cause pain.

Manthara rocked back and forth like a swing. Still, Keyi couldn't stop crying.

"Be quiet! I'm right here." Manthara was not happy with Keyi's terrors. "Six years old and still screaming at night! Curse on your mother! Thirty gods curse the day I got this child. Not a night of sleep since. Always waking up, screaming into my ear. I should have dropped you under a horse long ago, a mercy killing. Sh! Sh!"

Manthara's strong voice made the darkness flee. Keyi didn't always know the meaning of the things Manthara said. But that was okay, because Manthara was the most intelligent one in all of Kekaya. Keyi didn't feel stupid for not understanding. In due time, Manthara said. That meant when Keyi grew a hump on her back, just like Manthara. Keyi had learned that she could not repeat

Manthara's words to others, or they would look at her with round mouths. And Manthara would be very cross, calling Keyi a gossipmonger.

But still, no matter what Manthara said, she always pulled Keyi into her lap. She always held Keyi until the terrors ran away. Sometimes she whispered about the pain in her back. She said it was like living with a nightmare all day and all night. All because the people in the palace wanted straight backs and no secrets. Secrets were things that everyone pretended not to know. Manthara didn't pretend and so she had no secrets. That's how Keyi wanted to be.

As soon as the thump-thumping in Keyi's chest stopped, her arms slipped off Manthara's neck. Keyi heard a great sigh as Manthara heaved Keyi back onto the bed. The night terrors had passed, but they waited for Keyi. The next night they would come again. For now, feeling safe next to Manthara, Keyi dreamt of a place where the sun always shone.

"Keyi," someone whispered.

Keyi opened her eyes. A shadow stood over her. It spoke with Yuddha's voice, so it had to be him. Her brother looked huge in the dark. Manthara was fast asleep, another shadow by Keyi's side. Manthara's mouth was wide open and her breathing sounded like grasshoppers singing. Keyi would never dare place anything into Manthara's open mouth again. She had gotten so mad, Keyi had to hide under the bed to escape from Manthara's cane.

"Wake up, Keyi!" Yuddha shook her. "Indu is foaling. She is already lying down. Hurry or we'll miss it."

Everyone said that Yuddha and Keyi looked exactly alike, with black hair and blue eyes. But Keyi had long shiny hair, like the tail of a horse. Yuddha's hair was short on his head, though he was ten, almost all grown. He knew things that Manthara didn't, especially about horses and how to kill enemies. Usually you had to sit on top of a horse, that's how the enemies were killed, and why everyone in the world wanted to get horses from Kekaya. The mares had to make new foals every day so that righteous kings could kill their enemies.

Keyi ran to her secret hiding place under the divan, a place Manthara could reach only with great difficulty. She made sure Manthara wasn't awake, and then pulled out breeches and a vest, her brother's old clothes. When she turned around, Yuddha was already gone. She had to run to the stables by herself. She had never been there before at this hour. It made her heart gallop like a spooked horse, even though she knew all the statues were actually guards. They were supposed to come alive and save her if anything happened. She was special because she was the princess. Everyone had to be careful around her. That's what Manthara said. She told Keyi everything. Keyi knew lots of things other six-year-olds didn't. Not even Sukhi and Dukhi, who were eight, knew what Keyi knew. The reality of the station, Manthara called it. Or something like that. Keyi still got mixed up with her words. Manthara didn't mind. She was very patient. Only her cane sometimes wasn't.

Keyi ran across the courtyard towards the stable. She had been to the fields where millions of horses ate grass, but she had never been to a foaling. Yuddha had explained it all to her many times, eager to show how grown up he was. You know it is time, he said, when the mare starts sticking her bottom and tail up in the air. Once she lies on her side, you know it will be any minute. Then the foal comes, hooves first, if all goes well. Sometimes it didn't, and there was a lot of tension around Father then. He didn't like to lose a single horse. He had lost too much already, he said. Yuddha couldn't explain what Father meant by that. The main thing was not to be worried when the foal came out. It would look very strange, because it was hidden inside a white covering. The first time Yuddha attended a foaling he had thought a ghost was being born. But he was a nice brother. He didn't want Keyi to be fooled.

Keyi reached the stable. She took a deep breath, safe in this known place, her favorite playground. She didn't need daylight to find her way. Here, she would often shadow Yuddha, jump in the hay, climb on the horses, and hide in the empty stalls. Keyi knew exactly which stall Indu lived in. The stable was dark, with only two torches burning by Indu's stall. The shiny eyes of the other horses watched Keyi as she ran by. Only Yuddha and his guard Soma were there. Yuddha waved at her to come quickly. He reached for Keyi's hand. "You didn't miss it yet. Remember what I said? It will not look like a foal at all when it first comes out."

"I'm brave," Keyi said. When she was awake, the night terrors were just shadows.

"Look! Look! There it comes," Yuddha said. He squeezed her hand tightly.

A white bubble grew from Indu's bottom. Then Keyi saw small hooves poking through the white layer. With each of Indu's breaths, a little more of the foal was pushed out. Brother and sister held their breath as Indu gave a final push and the foal slid out, landing on the hay. Right away, Indu turned to look at her foal, and then she started licking it, moving away the slime that covered it. Indu didn't think the foal was strange. She wasn't disgusted by all that white goo on her foal. She just licked it all off. Then Keyi saw how perfect the foal was, with nice hair all over. How had it all fit inside the mare's belly? Keyi felt an ache in her throat. It got really tight, as if she had to cry. "Can I touch it?" she asked. "Can I touch it?"

"No, Keyi. Not yet," Yuddha said. "Soma, is it a filly or a colt?"

Soma was examining the foal with gentle hands.

"A filly," Soma said. He didn't have to call Yuddha "prince," because he had been Yuddha's guard since he was born. Just like Manthara didn't have to call Keyi "princess," or even by her proper name.

Keyi couldn't take her eyes off the newborn filly. The mare kept on licking and licking her, all over.

"Why is she doing that?" Keyi asked.

Soma smiled and said, "That's how the dam bonds with her foal. She is showing her motherly affection. That's how they grow connected as mother and child. If the dam doesn't do that, if she turns aggressive by kicking or biting, then we have a problem."

Keyi got a strange feeling in her stomach. As if she knew the answer to something. But it was all a jumble. She had to be sure. With her cheeks feeling hot, she asked, "Did Taya lick me like that when I was born?"

She looked at Soma real fast, and saw his eyebrows coming together. He didn't understand. She didn't see pretend in his eyes. But Yuddha started laughing.

"She means Manthara," Yuddha said, in a voice that meant Keyi was very dumb. "Why would Manthara lick you? First of all, humans don't do that. Everyone knows that. Second of all, Manthara isn't our mother."

"I know she isn't *our* mother!" Keyi cried. "You hate her. But you can have your own mother, and I can have mine."

"Well in that case you would have a ugly crooked back like her, wouldn't you?"

"YUDDHAJIT!"

Father's voice thundered through the stable. The horses flattened their ears, and Soma stood up and bowed to the king. Yuddha flattened himself against the stall, looking down at the ground. Even when Father wasn't admonishing him, Yuddha got stiff around Father, pressing his arms in towards his sides.

"How dare you ridicule Manthara?" Father yelled, walking towards them almost like he was running, "You know the great lengths I've gone to here in Kekaya to protect those like her."

"Yes, Father," Yuddha said in a tiny voice.

"Is there anything wrong with Manthara's mind or her faculties? No. But there seems to be a problem with yours. Name-calling is not fitting behavior for any Kekayan, much less the prince!"

"I'm sorry, Father." Yuddha looked like he was a small boy.

Keyi looked from Father to Yuddha with anxious eyes. This was not good. Yuddha would find a way to have revenge on her. She wanted to beg Father to hug or praise Yuddha, but even she was scared of his wrath when he moved with swords for arms.

"You should take a lesson from your little sister here," Father said, making it worse. "She does not judge based on body. See how kind and gracious she is towards Manthara, accepting her unconditionally."

"That's because she thinks Manthara is her mother," Yuddha said, glaring at Keyi. "But we have no mother!"

Father jerked away from them both when Yuddha said that. His lips turned down, as if he had eaten spoiled food. Father started inspecting the newborn filly, smacking his lips and making silly sounds. His hands were not stiff or rough at all when he touched the filly. He was like a different Father once a horse was near. He loved them more than anything else. Yuddha lifted his hands towards Keyi and made a pretend motion of strangling her. That's how much he hated her right now. Keyi knew he was regretting bringing her along to the foaling. Then he stood very close and pinched her underarm as hard as he could. Keyi closed her eyes and didn't flinch, or the punishment would be worse later.

Taya is my mother, Keyi decided stubbornly. No matter what Yuddha said.

"What should we name this little one?" Father said, and now his voice was sweet. He looked only at Keyi, excluding Yuddha. Father preferred Keyi, saying out loud that she was better than a boy. When she was grown, she would be king of Kekaya, she was sure of it.

"Surya," Keyi said. The name of the sun god. Keyi loved the sunlight. There were no nightmares in daytime.

"But Surya is a boy's name," Yuddha protested.

"Yuddha," Father warned. "If Keyi says Surya, then it's Surya. Horses aren't obliged to live by human rules."

"It *is* a boy's name, stupid," Yuddha whispered into her ear. "Don't talk to me ever again."

Keyi crossed her arms over her chest. That's how Father showed he didn't care. It was *not* a boy's name. Indu meant moon, and someone had named the mare that. So a filly could be named after the sun.

Father didn't stay long because he had to attend to other mares that were foaling out in the fields. Each day in Kekaya, a thousand million foals were born and Father attended them all. That's why they barely saw him. Keyi watched until Surya stood up on shaky legs. Indu was still circling around the filly, smelling her and kissing her on the muzzle. Mother and daughter wanted to be together, and that's how it would be, even when Surya was grown. Yuddha was on the other side of the stall.

"Are you still angry at me?" she asked him. But he was ignoring her, which meant that he was. "You can change Surya's name if you want."

Yuddha didn't answer, but then he said, "Our mother was beautiful. She was the queen. She had long black hair like you. There was no one as kind as her in all of Kekaya. Manthara is not beautiful. She is not kind. Her eyes are mean. Her ways are crooked, like her back. I wasn't name-calling. Why can't Father see that?"

"Why are you lying?" Keyi said. "You told Father yourself that we don't have a mother. Don't pretend now. Don't pretend that you know anything!"

"Ask anyone in the palace, if you don't believe me. Our mother was a beautiful queen. Everyone in Kekaya knows."

Keyi crossed her arms even more. This was supposed to be a happy day, when she got to see her first foaling. Instead Yuddha was being mean and telling lies.

"It's all Father's fault," Yuddha said, and then left. Soma followed him, but stopped by the door and turned to Keyi. "I know your brother speaks with anger and doesn't say the right words. But he is right. Your mother was a true beauty."

Soma hurried out, leaving Keyi to look at Surya, the lucky filly who had a dam that wanted to nuzzle her all day. Keyi looked one last time at them. Manthara *had to be* Keyi's mother. How could a little filly have something that a princess didn't?

By the time Keyi left Surya and Indu, the sun had come out and the whole palace was awake. Keyi stopped by the alcove next to her room to visit with Sukhi and Dukhi, Keyi's best friends aside from Manthara. Keyi told the twins all about the foaling. She was just about to ask them about Yuddha's lies when Manthara appeared out of nowhere. Keyi hadn't even heard the sound of her cane.

"Begone!" Manthara shouted, threatening the twins with her stick.

Sukhi and Dukhi ran away as if Manthara was a scary witch. She did look a little bit like one when she waved her cane like that. "You should not trust other children," Manthara cautioned, waving her fist at Sukhi, who peeked out from behind a pillar. "You'll see, the closeness you have with them now will not remain."

Keyi eagerly caught hold of Manthara's hand. "I have something to ask you."

"You've dressed as a prince again," Manthara scolded, looking at Keyi's leather vest and breeches. Keyi felt clever for having hid them from Manthara.

"I *am* a prince," Keyi said. She put her hands on her hips and set her feet wide apart, an imitation of Yuddha. Manthara sighed loudly.

"I have to ask you something," Keyi insisted. "I have to ask you something." Keyi didn't tire of repeating the same words all day until Manthara listened. "You have to sit. I have to ask you something. And I want you to think about it first."

Manthara smiled. It was what she always said to Keyi. Always telling her to think, think. She let Keyi lead her to the seat in the alcove. The sun was very bright here. Manthara's eyes got smaller than usual, and she turned away from the sun. Keyi put her hands on Manthara's cheeks. When Manthara grew still and looked into Keyi's eyes, Keyi said: "I'm going to ask Father to make you my mother."

Manthara stood up. "What is this nonsense!?"

"You didn't even think before you answered!"

"There is nothing to think about."

"Is that because—because—because . . . you *are* my mother?"

"Keyi . . . What has gotten into you? You know I am not your true mother."

"Then who is?" Keyi asked.

"Sh-sh-sh," Manthara said, taking a firm hold of Keyi's arm. She looked over her shoulders, as though she feared being overheard. "You must *not* speak of her. Especially not in front of your father."

Keyi tugged at Manthara's clothes and then her face, pulling her down. Manthara unwillingly knelt so they were face to face. Keyi put her nose to Manthara's and made her voice quiet. "Why can't you be my mother? I want *you* to be my mother."

"Why do you suddenly care to have one now?" Manthara asked.

"This morning Surya was born. I named her myself," Keyi said, "Indu started licking Surya all over. That's how she found a mother. Maybe my mother didn't want to lick me. Maybe she thought I looked ugly like a monster when I came out from her."

"Is that what your brother said?" Manthara held her cane and heaved herself up. "My legs are numb," she muttered. "I feel ancient. Only thirty years and already a hag."

"Don't be a hag. Be my mother," Keyi said.

"Should I tell her the truth?" Manthara was talking to herself out loud, ignoring Keyi.

"Tell me, Taya. What's the reality of the station?"

"Sit-u-ation! But no. This is different. Your father has given me orders."

"A secret?"

"Sh! Your father doesn't want you to know."

"But I can keep secrets, Taya. Promise."

She could see Manthara thinking. First, her eyes went to one side and then the other. But she wasn't really seeing what was in front of her. Sukhi and Dukhi had snuck close and were sitting by a pillar making faces at Keyi. Keyi shook her head at them. Not now. It was a sit-u-ation.

"Maybe if I tell her those night-terrors will go away," Manthara said to herself. This is how Keyi knew so much. Manthara would forget that Keyi could hear. "But if Ashvapati finds out . . ."

Keyi grew impatient: "When no one can hear, I'm going to call you Mother."

"You will do no such thing!" Manthara exclaimed, so loudly Sukhi and Dukhi jumped up and ran away. Manthara grabbed Keyi's arm, exactly where Yuddha had pinched her. "Ouch!"

"Now, you listen to me," Manthara said, dragging Keyi along. "We are going back to your rooms to change your clothes, and once we are there, you may *not* call me Mother, understand? You really should be addressing me as Manthara. Be done with all this childish Taya, Taya. You're old enough to use your tongue properly."

"I will *not* change my clothes. I'm going riding with Yuddha later."

"You are far too young to be on horseback. You could fall off and break your bones. Then we both would be crippled."

"But I want to be like you, Manthara."

"Sssssssss," Manthara said, hissing like a cobra. She was outraged.

Keyi pressed her lips together so she wouldn't say any more wrong things.

"The whole kingdom adores you," Manthara said, getting out of breath from walking and talking. "What do you need a mother for?" She paused to take a deep breath. "Your mother would ruin you if she was here."

Keyi stopped. Manthara tugged at her arm, but Keyi was stronger.

"The grass would grow all over me?" she asked. "And no one would visit me?"

Manthara frowned, but then lifted her eyebrows. "Oh. You're thinking of the wasteland beyond the fields, the old Kekayan palace?"

Keyi nodded. "It was empty and full of ghosts. No one likes it there. I don't want to ruin me."

"Not as long as I live," Manthara promised.

Keyi looked up at Manthara and said, "Mother, Mother, Mother!" Then she tore her hand from Manthara and ran away, as fast as her legs could carry her.

"Kai-keyi!" Manthara cried, spitting out her full name. "Come back this moment!"

Keyi made a neighing sound. She threw her hands on the ground and bucked her legs, kicking them to the air several times. She jumped up and raced away in the direction of the stables, but kept her ears behind her and heard Manthara order a guard to bring the princess to her rooms. Keyi was not faster than her guards—not yet. So she ran back, running straight towards Manthara. Keyi came to a halt right by Manthara's ear, her long hair swaying forward. She leaned in and whispered, "Mother!"

Manthara tried to catch hold of her, but Keyi was faster and ran away again.

"All right, Keyi," Manthara shouted, "Stop this game. I will tell you what you asked."

Keyi twirled on her feet and started dancing back.

As soon as Keyi was within reach, Manthara grabbed for her hand. But Manthara was too slow, and Keyi ran ahead towards her room. She could hear Manthara calling to the other servants, ordering a hot bath, their morning meal, and for the garments and jewelry to be brought. Everyone in the palace did what Manthara wanted within the snap of a finger. Ten million servants came running in. They pulled off Keyi's clothes and pushed her to the bathing room. They splashed warm water on her arms and shoulders and scrubbed her clean. The water smelled like flowers. One of the servants was the mother of the twins, Sukhi and Dukhi. Why did they have a mother when Keyi didn't?

Keyi stuck her lip out and caught a glimpse of Manthara, who was on the bed getting a massage with a stinky brown oil. It was good for her back, she said. While the servants dressed Keyi, she whispered the words "Manthara" and "Mother" to herself. As Manthara got a bright sari draped around her, she did some funny movements with her arms and head, lifting them up and down. She said this would improve her chances of living for a long time. Sometimes Keyi imitated her, since she wanted to live a long life too.

When the servants' hands stopped pestering Keyi, she stood in front of Manthara and announced, "I'm done!"

She twirled, feeling pretty despite the fact that she wanted to be a boy like her brother. Her long hair was braided and full of flowers. She wore bangles, anklets, earrings, and necklaces. The gown was silky and blue, like her eyes.

"Finally, you look like a princess," Manthara said. She flicked her hand to the servants, shooing them out.

"When I'm a horse," Keyi said, lifting her palms up, "I can't be a princess."

She threw herself on the bed and started jumping up and down, crushing the flowers in her hair, destroying the work of the servants. Her jewelry tinkled and her dress wrinkled. Manthara gave her a long look and then sat down, putting her cane away. Keyi hadn't forgotten the topic, and neither had Manthara. When Keyi got tired of jumping like a horse, she went and put her head on Manthara's lap.

"My needy little cat," Manthara said, stroking Keyi's head. "Your hair has grown so long."

"Just like the tail of a horse."

"Enough horse talk! I have to breath the stink of it day and night."

Keyi wanted to say that horses didn't stink, but instead she said, "Why can't you be my mother, Manthara?"

"You are too young to understand these things."

"It would be so much easier if you were my mother. Then there would be no secrets. Dukhi wouldn't say, 'Poooor princess,' and make faces at me."

"You talked to the twins?" Manthara wasn't happy. "If you keep talking like this, your father will come to know, and this will be very bad for all of us."

Keyi thought of her father's shout in the morning. How frightened Yuddha had become. She didn't want Father to shout like that at her.

"I will tell you the truth," Manthara said, and Keyi held her breath. "If you *promise* to keep it a secret. You cannot tell Sukhi and Dukhi. You cannot tell your brother. You cannot tell *anyone*. Do you promise?"

"Promise."

"Very well, then. Your mother is an evil witch, and she wants to harm you."

Keyi started shaking her head.

"She is the one who comes into your dreams at night and frightens you."

"No!"

"Yes! She sneaks her way into your heart and fills it with terror. That's why you wake up screaming. Your mother is in there, banging on your chest. Every time she comes, she takes a piece of your heart with her."

"Why?"

"She eats it."

"No!"

"Yes! She sits in there and tears at your heart. You have to banish her, or you will have no heart left at all."

"How do I banish her?"

"Instead of screaming and whining and waking up the whole palace every night, you have to be a brave girl. If you scream, she knows that she has won. You have to be very silent. You have to tell her to *go away*."

Keyi nodded. "I will tell her it's *my* heart!"

"Good."

"Mothers are supposed to be nice."

"Even dams kick their newborn foals sometimes, don't they? It's lucky that your father discovered your mother was the heart-eating witch."

"Father knows?"

"Oh, yes. Else you would have no heart by now. Neither would your brother."

"We would all be heartless! Father saved us in time?"

"Yes. You must be very grateful to him. Most of all, you must never ever tell anyone that you know the truth."

Keyi promised. And yet, as time went by, Manthara told the princess many versions of the truth. Soon enough, Keyi did not know what was a secret and what was a fantasy. But she did know this: Even if she didn't have a mother, she had Manthara, and that was more than enough.

CHAPTER 3

The Dead King's Prophecy

King Dasharatha, the emperor of the world, king of Ayodhya, lord of men, left Earth behind. He and his troops, all mortals, were summoned to fight in the battle of the immortals. Dasharatha had won his first such battle when he was barely on the brink of manhood, gaining his name, which meant "Ten Chariots." There had been many great warriors in the Sun dynasty, but none who had claimed Dasharatha's skill on a chariot. He was so swift that his arrows came at the enemy from ten directions. Above and beyond, the people of Earth trusted in his military skill. But in all his wars, Dasharatha had not yet come face to face with the legendary blood-drinker king, Ravana.

Like every other king in Dasharatha's line, Dasharatha was eager to be the one to fulfill King Anaranya's prophecy. Dying at Ravana's feet, Anaranya had promised that a son of the Sun dynasty would be Ravana's destruction. Dasharatha wanted to be that man. At least that had been his ambition when he was younger. Dasharatha had ruled the Earth for over thirty years. When he ascended the throne, he had been so pure, bent on doing everything right, keeping all his promises, being a faultless king. But he had learned on a moonless night, when he was only fifteen, that sincerity and pure intentions were not enough. There was no such thing as a faultless life. Thus far, however, Dasharatha had won every battle. But even then, he was only a man. Quite possibly, he would not survive the day.

This time the summons was unusually urgent. Ravana's pet son, Indrajit, was gathering his dark forces against the gods. Dasharatha was transported within seconds from his throne up into the battlefield. He was outfitted with great haste by ethereal beings that moved so fast he saw no hands, no substantial form. Moments later, his army materialized behind him, transported in the same instant manner. He saw some of his men double over and retch, unused to traveling at the speed of mind. From long experience, Dasharatha knew he had only minutes to organize his troops, and without hesitation he moved out among his men, calling out to the commanders of each section. Then he turned to face the enemy.

The horizon was black with blood-drinkers. The shining ones on Dasharatha's side floated above the ground, emanating golden light; the enemy seemed to emerge from the darkest of hells. Dasharatha was still not immune to their dreadful forms, which obscured gender and age. Their deformities and behaviors made them appear like rabid dogs, when in truth many of them possessed superhuman powers and intelligence. Like parasites, they preyed on human flesh and blood. They were man-eaters, night stalkers, and blood-drinkers, predators of all things good and uplifting. The light and the dark, the good and the bad, the beautiful and the terrifying were never so starkly illuminated. Dasharatha, who had survived many immortal battles, felt the terror grow among his troops. This twilight zone, where the two armies faced each other, was unknown to them; there was no sun or moon here, no day or night, no point of reference.

The blood-drinkers chanted hissing prayers, invoking their king, with his ten heads. Dasharatha clutched his bow tightly in his left hand, flexing his fingers around it. His right hand needed to be nimble and swift, to place arrow after arrow on the bowstring. The task of an archer's right hand was the most demanding. It had to pull, aim, release a million times.

He let his bow rest on his shoulder and pressed his hands palm to palm at his chest, praying they would not fail him today. His work on Earth was not done, and if he died, the Sun dynasty would end. He was the only living king in his line. But the future did not exist here. Nothing existed but this war between the gods and the blood-drinkers. Still, Anaranya's ancient prophecy gave Dasharatha courage. This battle could not be his last for Ravana was still alive, waiting to be killed by a son of the Sun dynasty. Though Ravana's name was in the air, the demon king himself had not appeared in a battle for hundreds of Earth years. In his last battle, he had defeated Yama, lord of death, proving himself truly above all law. The best Dasharatha could do was fight alongside the shining gods and demolish Ravana's spawn, with their blood-red eyes, fangs, and flaming red hair.

Indra, the king of the gods, and the commander of the armies, rode past Dasharatha on his many-tusked white elephant. Indrajit was Indra's archenemy, a blood-drinker so lethal that he was known as "Conqueror of Indra."

Indra lifted his hand in blessing to Dasharatha, who pressed his hands together in supplication. Ravana had ten pairs of eyes, but Indra had many, many more; his whole body was covered in eyes, seeing every direction. He shone with immortal beauty and power.

"On my signal, the conchs will blow," Indra called. "The moment the sound of the conch shells erupt, charge immediately. That's what the enemy will do."

Dasharatha understood that the blood-drinkers followed the rules of warfare, though only barely. They would not wait for the sound to resonate, bringing victory to the strong. Blood-drinkers could not be allowed free range again on Earth or the higher planets. They had to be returned to Rasatala, the planet below Earth, where they belonged.

Dasharatha lifted his bow in the air, rallying his troops. Pumping his bow in the air to their cheers, he was grateful for every single moment of his training. It was in his first battle that he had earned his name. Today, he would be glad to fight with the power of one. He was not an old man yet, though previous battles had left their scars. His right arm did not obey his lightning commands like it used to. But every warrior counted today. The gods were badly outnumbered. Ravana's clan had only grown over the years.

As the demonic chants and celestial hymns reached a crescendo, a battle of sounds, Dasharatha touched each of the weapons secured along the chariot. The unbreakable, heavenly metal of his armor gave him strength. The flag on top of his chariot was emblazoned with a sun, the sigil of the Sun dynasty. Wherever he was on the battlefield, his men would take courage from this blazing sun. Whether he lived to tell it, Dasharatha would be commemorated in the history of the worlds.

Dasharatha sought the end of the blackness, seeing instead millions of red eyes. Their chants crept under his skin and into his mind. As the red eyes began hypnotizing him, the sound of the conch shells broke his trance. A hundred thousand screams followed. Charge!

Dasharatha called out too, baring his teeth, urging his four steeds fearlessly into the war zone. The battle began. Light and darkness collided. Metal on metal, magic on magic, the cry of war followed by the cry of death. Unnatural colors and sounds hit Dasharatha's eyes, as painful to him as arrows through his body. When the enemy forces pushed them back, Dasharatha felt a wave of sickness but pressed forward. He tightened his hold on his composure and then his weapons. His arrows never wavered. His hand was intent: Pull. Aim. Release. When his earthly quiver would have been empty, the heavenly one was brimming. He fired with relentless vigor. As he killed, he kept up a steady stream of words, punctuating every physical movement with a verbal counterpart.

"I am the king of Earth. The son of the Sun dynasty. The last living heir. I will demolish darkness. Uphold justice. Give my life!"

Again and again, he repeated the words. He wasted no mercy arrows on half-dead blood-drinkers, leaving them to the death they deserved. Would these creatures be allowed on Earth? To prey on innocent men, women, and children?

Never!

Dasharatha's resolve pushed away the effects of the dark chants; everything around him shone with clarity. He could see his men fighting at the far edges of the battleground. He could see the light emanating from the shining gods as they flew above him. He was prepared to die to protect the Earth. And yet he fought to live.

"I will live!" he shouted, releasing his arrow.

He moved with impossible speed. All his words dried up. He expanded his focus to include not one target at a time, but two, then five, and finally ten. He lost track of time, place, and identity, forgetting his earlier declarations. He was one with the war. If it won, he won. He operated without thought or feeling, repeating the same mechanisms over and over again.

A cloud of darkness descended on them, Indrajit's magic. It suffocated the natural light emanating from the shining ones. Dasharatha could not even see the tip of his arrow, it was so dense. The sounds of chaos ensued. This was no longer a war but a slaughter. Dasharatha released his arrow without a moment's hesitation. He did not need eyes to find his target, only his keen hearing. He had paid the price for this skill, a crime he carried always in his consciousness. Nevertheless, this ability served him well. He aimed at targets he could only hear, knowing his aim was tried and true.

The black fog lifted, pushed away by high-pitched and clear sound vibrations. The celestial singers retreated, their work done. With satisfaction, Dasharatha saw the path of dead blood-drinkers he had created despite the darkness. Streams of blood painted the wheels of his chariot red. And then a large blood-drinker landed in front of Dasharatha. "I am Subahu," he declared. "Son of Tataka."

Drops of sweat stung Dasharatha's eyes. He vaguely recognized both the name and that face, then fired his arrow. Subahu turned into a deer and the arrow zoomed past him. The next moment, he resumed his grotesque form.

"Release my brother!" he bellowed.

Dasharatha eyes narrowed. He did not understand Subahu's demand and sent another volley of arrows toward him. Subahu shape-changed with an impressive speed that Dasharatha had never seen. Dasharatha fired at a lion, an antelope, a boar, a gazelle, even a tiny black bird. Every time Subahu became himself, he shouted, "Release my brother!"

Some of Dasharatha's arrows hit their mark. One of Subahu's arms was pinned to his side, crippling his animal forms. Subahu flew up and landed on one of Dasharatha's horses, sinking his fangs into it. The animal whinnied loudly, running faster; the chariot began to totter. Dasharatha grabbed his sword, cutting the dying animal loose. It toppled to the ground behind them. Subahu clung to the side of the chariot, snarling.

Dasharatha shot him in the eye, the arrow penetrating his skull. Subahu lost his grip and fell off the chariot. Dasharatha gained control of the remaining horses and turned the chariot back to face Subahu. The blood-drinker was on his feet, hurling a javelin at Dasharatha. It grazed his arm. He threw down his bow and grabbed a sword. Subahu clung to the chariot, growing in strength the more blood flowed, his own or Dasharatha's.

"Release Marichi!" he snarled. "My brother will destroy you!"

He lunged at Dasharatha's sword and used it to pull himself into the chariot. Blood squirted from both his hands. Laughing loudly, he waved his hands at Dasharatha, splashing him with blood. The drinker was too close, and that's when Dasharatha realized whom he resembled, the oldest prisoner in Ayodhya, whose name was unknown. The pieces fell into place, and the moment this took was all Subahu needed to slash at Dasharatha. The tip

of the blade cut into Dasharatha's cheek. He parried immediately, aiming at Subahu's face. The arrow was still in his skull, the one eye blind. As they circled each other in the narrow confines of the chariot, Dasharatha could smell Subahu's putrid breath. Subahu was skilled, despite having only one hand and one eye to use.

Suddenly, a giant vulture swooped down, brewing up strong winds in his wake. Dasharatha's heart leaped. It was Jatayu, king of vultures.

With a piercing cry, the vulture sank his talons into Subahu's back and rose into the air, the blood-drinker dangling helplessly in his claws. Flashes of animal forms were visible, but Jatayu's sharp beak pecked at his skull, and Subahu was unable to complete any transformation. Dasharatha roared his appreciation. Friends for life were made in this field of death. Subahu fell to the ground, his limbs twitching. Dasharatha would never release Ayodhya's oldest prisoner, presumably Subahu's brother. Jatayu flew up and away, the bond of friendship resonating between him and Dasharatha.

Dasharatha took charge of his chariot just in time to stave off a pack of ten or twenty translucent blood-drinkers who pounced on him. But they were nowhere near Subahu's league, and Dasharatha had no difficulty in sending them to the land of Yama. The chariot flew onward and the battle continued. A distant part of Dasharatha tracked time and noted that two days passed, then four. They did not cease at night to rest, for there were no nights here. Neither blood-drinkers nor gods showed any sign of tiring. Mortal men did not have the same resilience, but Dasharatha knew that his brave men fought past all known limits.

Far away, in the middle of the battlefield, Dasharatha saw the opposition of light and dark rising above ground, high into the sky. Indra was at the helm of light, battling an invisible force that pushed forth the darkness. With a blinding crack of lightning, Indra broke the darkness apart. A single blood-drinker with flowing black hair hovered in the air before Indra. It had to be Indrajit. Indra wielded his lightning bolt again, but Indrajit was gone. Not dead but defeated, for the next moment, the invisible Indrajit issued a command to retreat.

For a moment, Dasharatha felt his bow verily tugged out of his hand. He tightened his grip. The enemy withdrew their remaining forces, crawling backward, weapons raised. The blood-drinkers disappeared into the void, as if they had never been there. The dark light slowly receded.

Dasharatha stood stunned. He was alive. They had won. He could scarcely believe it. The ensuing silence was eerie. Dasharatha dropped his numb arms to his sides and let his prized bow fall to the floor of his chariot. Only then did he realize he was standing on a chariot and that his horses were nearly dead of exhaustion. A light breeze swept over them. An ethereal being, transparent and soothing, surrounded him. As he crumbled to the chariot floor, he or she caught him and swept him up and away.

"Rest now," the being whispered.

Dasharatha was called into a restorative dreamland.

When he awoke, Dasharatha knew the rest had been only minutes, but it was enough to give him and his troops the energy to march home. Knowing well how differently time moved in the twilight realms, none of them wanted to tarry and find their families and homes irreversibly gone. One day here was one year on Earth. None of the humans wished to stay longer than necessary. This was the one condition Dasharatha always made: those who survived would return to Earth without delay. The interstellar pathways opened and returned them to Earth, and a quiet march began toward the gates of Ayodhya, the indestructible capital. Home.

Despite the victory, Dasharatha knew the truth: the war would not truly end until Ravana was destroyed once and for all. According to Anaranya, a man of the Sun dynasty was destined for this great act. In his heart, Dasharatha knew he was not the one. How long could he then ignore that he had no sons to continue his line?

CHAPTER 4

The Great Queen

When the queen of Ayodhya raised her hand, the signal moved swiftly, and the northern gates opened. Bugles and conch shells blew, and flower petals showered down on the foot soldiers that entered. The king was returning from a terrible battle. He had been gone a full seven years, his longest absence yet. The people of Ayodhya hailed the returning soldiers with all their hearts. Queen Kausalya stood at the highest tower of the palace overlooking the army's return. Soon she would set eyes on her husband, King Dasharatha, emperor of the world. Her chest rose and fell as her heart hammered against it. She caught herself straining to see beyond the marching soldiers, so took a deep breath and put her hand across her heart. She had to be patient. She had greeted her husband in this manner more times than she could remember. In twenty-eight years of marriage, Dasharatha had fought many battles. The queen knew that the king would come into view only after four divisions of foot soldiers, an equal number of horseback riders, followed by two divisions of chariots. The king, a masterful chariot driver, always rode in the midsection of the chariots. Behind him and the rest of the chariots, legions of elephants would follow. As the king dismounted to greet the queen, the elephants would patiently wait.

A cold wind blew through the tower, and Kausalya's veil blew up. She held it down at once, alarmed at the omen. The cold wind passed and Kausalya let go of her veil. But the warning remained.

After only two divisions of foot soldiers, the horse riders rode in. Kausalya's heart plummeted as she peered down at the soldiers and took in their fresh wounds and heavily battered armor. Thirty gods, Ayodhya had never been this hard hit. She turned back to see the oncoming army with this dawning knowledge. The soldiers bravely smiled, waving to the cheering crowd. Cries of joy erupted from every corner, yet it caused fever-like tremors in Kausalya's body. Certainly the survivors deserved this celebration, yet Yama's shadow clung to the army. Kausalya focused on her fellow Ayodhyans; she knew what they felt, for she longed with her whole body to set eyes on Dasharatha. For seven years, she had wondered if he would return. For seven years, she had waited for this moment. She had formulated what she would say. Every time he returned from war, she had planned to speak of it. Every time, courage failed her. But not this time. This time she *would* not balk. She swore it on every wound she saw on the brave soldiers. She had to discover why he did not seek an heir to their mighty empire.

The horses danced in the sun, tails swishing. Even they could feel the celebration in the air, the euphoria that the homecoming produced. But Kausalya clenched her jaw, unable to join the celebration: the horse riders had been reduced to half their numbers.

Hidden from the public eye in the high tower, Kausalya was spared the duty of gaiety. The servants around her were silent too. Kausalya wondered how the immortal gods had fared. Did humans join the war against Ravana and his blood-drinkers, only to be slaughtered first?

Kausalya dreaded to see the caravan of the dead that would come in at dusk, when all the citizens had returned home. She had an inkling now that the parade of the wounded and dead would surpass the living. The funeral pyres at the southern side of Ayodhya would burn countless days. Kausalya prayed for the northern winds to bless Ayodhya, else the stench of burning bodies would be the air they breathed for weeks. But that was the least of the concerns with so many warriors gone. Kausalya felt compassion for the bereaved and also immediately wondered how the kingdom would replenish its resources. As the empire that ruled every recognized kingdom on Earth, Ayodhya had a formidable responsibility. The power hungry would not think twice before striking at an opportune moment. All the more reason for Kausalya to bring her question to Dasharatha's attention, once and for all.

The chariots came into view, and Kausalya's blood rushed to her face. He was near. After so many years as his wife, Kausalya loved no one better than him. She searched first for the king's flag with its brilliant sun. In the long years of waiting for his return, she had often turned to the sigil to bring her hope. Once she found the golden sun billowing in the wind, she focused intently on the chariot, waiting for Dasharatha to come into view. There would only be few moments to see his beloved face in the distance, and then she would run down all six flights of stairs and meet him on the ground, just in time to greet him as he dismounted. As she prepared to run, she could feel the servants around her prepare to descend behind her. They knew the routine well.

Dasharatha's chariot came closer, and Kausalya's palms joined at her heart. She lifted them to her face and pressed them to her lips in utmost gratitude. The golden parasol shaded his body from view, but she could see his large hands resting on the chariot railings. His strong arms bore no new wounds. Again her gratitude surged. Kausalya looked forward to drawing her fingers across his familiar calluses and the line of scars along his bow arm. She gathered her long dress and turned. The sounds of the descending entourage filled the tour, and Kausalya ran. There was so much joy in these moments, for she rarely displayed her feelings in public. The servants always talked of it after, so she knew that they rather liked her for this rare display. Even after so many years, neither she nor her people had grown tired of the ritual. The joy rushed through her body and made her breathless.

As she reached the ground floor, she met Sumitra, the second queen. Kausalya slowed down, let go of her dress, and took three deep breaths before continuing in a more regal fashion. This was only Sumitra's second time welcoming the king home from a battle of this magnitude. The younger queen did not intrude on the established rituals. She was content to wait for Kausalya's command. Happily, Kausalya reached out to Sumitra, and the two women joined hands as they walked down the marble stairs. They did not need to speak; the anticipation was strong in the air. After fifteen years together, they had become the best of friends. Sumitra was a gentle soul who deferred naturally to Kausalya's judgments. Though Kausalya did not demand subordination, she appreciated Sumitra's sensitivity to etiquette. Truly, they had found a way to live in harmony as co-wives.

Dasharatha was waiting at the bottom of the steps. Sumitra withdrew, knowing how much this moment meant to Kausalya. The eight ministers also conceded the queen's right to greet the king first. Kausalya swept past them, seeing only her husband. Dasharatha was stunningly handsome, the most attractive man Kausalya had ever known. The light of the sun emanated from his being. As she walked toward him, she saw the injury to his face, and her hand flew to her mouth. The wound was a sword-thin line, but it cut into his lip and up toward his eye. The cheek was swollen and the left eye nearly shut. Whoever had inflicted that wound was right-handed and had come far too close to Dasharatha's face.

"Great Queen," he said, addressing her formally. The love in his eyes was too strong to bear. She waved forth the servant holding the refreshments. Dasharatha accepted the rose-scented cloth and wiped his brow and face. He drank heartily of the cool water laced with lime and honey. Then he focused on Kausalya, as was his wont.

He took her hand and said, "You are a vision to behold, my queen. My eyes have longed to see you. Your flawless attire of gold and white soothes my heart. Seeing you, I feel certain that all has been well in the kingdom in my absence."

Kausalya looked again at the battered side of his face. He gingerly touched the swollen cheek and dropped his hand with a light shrug. "I will tell you all in due time."

The eight ministers stepped forward to greet their king. Sumantra, the closest among them, had tears in his eyes. Their relief at his return was evident in their every gesture. They gathered around him like bees around a nectar flower. Dasharatha greeted them warmly, glancing often at Kausalya. She admired that he was a king through and through, taking the time to greet one and all with warm words. He had brought with him the immense security of his presence. He was their king. Now that he had returned hale, all was well in the empire. Having enjoyed his sole attention for a long minute, Kausalya was content to observe him greet the ministers and the other dignitaries present. She bided her time, ready to intervene if she noticed the king's energy flagging.

After a few moments, she gently nudged Sumitra forward. The younger queen also deserved a moment in the sun. Dasharatha's eyes grew warm when Sumitra stood before him. He aptly compared her to a sweet spring morning. Kausalya then brought forth the welcoming articles, and Dasharatha's eyes fastened on her. She felt his love envelop her and her own rose to her throat, aching. She offered the burning flame to him, tracing a circle in the air around him. She offered flower petals at his feet and dabbed sandalwood paste on his forehead.

"I will continue the welcoming ceremonies in the king's quarters," she informed everyone. "There he may begin to rest and the physician will tend to his wounds. You may all return to your duties. Those among you who are welcoming a family member, please go home. Find your loved ones and greet them appropriately. Tomorrow the celebration will commence."

The king nodded as Kausalya spoke. Once rested, the king would resume his authority, and Kausalya would no longer presume to make commands in his presence. The queen looked at the lively crowd, the patient elephants with their swaying trunks, and the wounded warriors. The day had been joyful, but night would bring sorrow when the dead were announced. Kausalya's closest circle of servants stayed with her, but several of the attendants hurried away, eager to reunite with their loved ones. Kausalya knew that she was sending many of them into the arms of grief; so many had not returned. During the great celebration the next evening, the dancers, actors, and singers would enact all salient episodes of the immortal battle, thus entertaining and informing Ayodhya what had transpired. The living and dead would be glorified.

As the queen prepared to escort the king to his

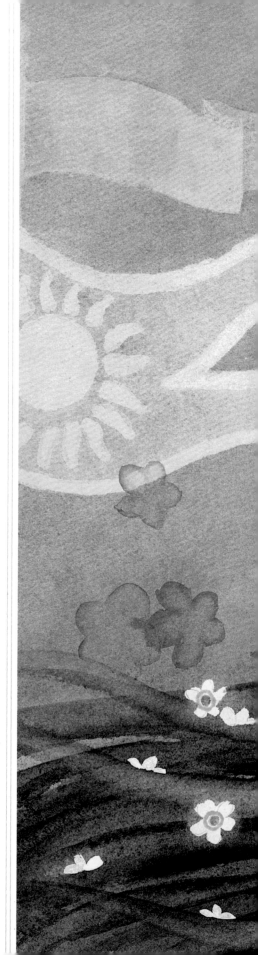

quarters, the ministers cast several meaningful glances at her. She knew what they expected of her. She would broach the forbidden topic with Dasharatha. Kausalya turned to Sumitra and promised to summon her in the evening, once the king had rested. A protective circle of servants and guards formed around the king and queen as they went within.

Once inside the palace, Dasharatha reached for her hand, and Kausalya walked by his side in silence. It would take her several hours or perhaps days to adjust to his physical presence. He was always with her in thought, for when he was gone, she made every decision based on what he would have done. But in person, he often surprised her with his actions. He was a strategic man yet prone to follow the impulses of his heart. His hand was warm, his calluses rough against her soft fingers.

Kausalya did not scrutinize him as they walked, but by the time they arrived at his chambers, she had a sense of his physical health. He had sustained no major injuries, but he was not able to fully move about with his normal confidence. She suspected that some of his ribs were broken. The wound on the face seemed to be the worst of it.

As they entered his quarters, Dasharatha sighed and visibly relaxed. Everything had been arranged meticulously in his quarters. Kausalya was proud of the beauty, order, and freshness that the king was returning to. Not knowing when he would return, she had regularly assigned the cleaning of his quarters. She was pleased to see him immediately at ease.

Dasharatha's pace slowed and his shoulders fell forward. Kausalya escorted the king to his seat, a golden throne with velvet pillows. The physician stood ready with his medical instruments and examined Dasharatha's face with careful hands, administering cleansing potions to the wound. As he did this, the queen bathed Dasharatha's feet, a task she always chose to do herself.

"Great King, the swelling and cut on your face is minor," the physician said. "It will heal within two weeks. No intervention is necessary. May I examine the rest of your body?"

Dasharatha nodded, and Kausalya and her maids helped the king remove his armor and the blood-stained garments he wore. She took his heavy sword and placed it carefully in the alcove with his personal treasures. She would have a servant cleanse and polish the weapons in the morning. The physician prodded the king's body, lingering on the ribs.

"Your ribs are bruised, Great King, but not broken," he said. "I recommend three days of bed rest to heal your rib cage. A dose of soma morning and night will relieve you from pain."

"No," Dasharatha said. "I can bear the pain. I do not wish to cloud my mind."

The soma plant was the most effective pain remedy but was also addictive in its potent ability to numb the mind from reality.

"Very well," the physician said. "I will prepare a healing jatamamsi ointment and send it here by evening. It will ease your sleep."

Dasharatha was satisfied.

As the physician departed, Kausalya called for the refreshments and food preparations. Kausalya helped her husband remove the rest of his adornments: the gem that expelled poisons, the gold armlets, necklaces, and earrings. He stood stripped down to his loincloth, every muscle in his body outlined. Bruises and cuts covered his body. His rib cage was dark purple. He winced as he walked toward the bathing room. But Kausalya doubted he would take three days of bed rest. When he was not on the battlefield, he spent several hours at the training grounds. The bathing room was full of fragrant mist steaming from the large bowls of scented water. Two male attendants stood ready to scrub the king clean. After reassuring herself that he had fresh loincloths to wear, she left him to bathe.

The maidservants stood ready with a simple meal consisting of a vegetable broth mildly spiced with ginger and lime, fluffy white rice with cardamom pods, fried bitter melon, and a creamy yogurt sauce with finely grated cucumber. The king did not eat for days while in battle. Kausalya had made sure this first meal was suited to his needs. She looked at the Taster of Foods and nodded. Carefully the Taster sampled each food. If there was any poison in it, he would be the first to know. Around his neck, he wore vials filled with antidotes. So far, he had never needed to use them. As she oversaw the Taster's work, Kausalya called the head of the maids to her side. "Divya, I will dine in private with the king. But when he takes rest, I wish to speak to the commander of the army, Senapati. If he no longer lives, bring me the man in command. We must prepare to meet the needs of the grieving. I want to have an accurate idea of our losses before the night brings in the wounded and dead."

"Yes, Great Queen." Divya bowed and left, followed by a group of ten maids, women whom Kausalya was training to take positions of importance in the palace.

Kausalya sat down, waiting for the king. Two maidservants immediately came to her side and fanned her gently with peacock feathers. She could hear the sounds of water splashing against the marble floor; the scents of rose and khus wafted out from the bathing room.

Dasharatha strode out, glistening with water, wearing a fresh loincloth. His manly body was worthy in comparison to the gods. She accompanied him to the next room, where his royal clothes were arranged. He allowed her to select what he was to wear, and he accepted her help in donning the clothes and jewelry. Kausalya so much enjoyed this casual nearness. Soon their days would return to normal, and Kausalya would have her duties, and his attendants would help him dress. As she decorated her husband and king, she studied his features.

His physique was a map to his heritage; he was a perfect composite of his parents, though it was not a word he would use to describe himself. His thick black hair was wavy and grew past his shoulders. His beloved face had the beginnings of furrows around the mouth and two deep lines across his forehead. That's when she noticed that he too was studying her, following every move she made. She became strongly aware of his desire to embrace her, but it was daylight and the duties of a king and queen yet upon them. She hurried out of the room and into the large chamber where he would eat.

As Dasharatha sat down, he smiled and pulled his hair into a topknot. Kausalya served him herself, waiting on him just like one of the servants would. The Queen Mother Indumati had instructed Kausalya that this was a queen's way to demonstrate her affection. Kausalya had always listened carefully to her mother-in-law's words and had honored her until she left this world for the next. Kausalya's obedience had pleased her new family and her husband.

As the king ate, Kausalya knew the time for a discussion was approaching. After bathing and eating, Dasharatha would be in his most relaxed state. He would fall into a deep sleep soon after. There was no better time to speak to him, and yet the task ahead tightened Kausalya's stomach. She waited until he expressed his satisfaction and could eat no more.

Then she seated herself next to him and looked without wincing at his swollen and discolored face. Without hesitating, she said the words as she had sworn she would. Perhaps if she had not felt trepidation, she might have introduced it with more grace. But she knew the topic would not please him, and so she spoke directly: "Until you have announced an heir, you cannot go to another battle."

The air grew thin. His demeanor changed at once and he looked at her without blinking.

Kausalya, who had known Dasharatha's parents well, again saw King Aja and Queen Indumati's features in him. He had his mother's full lips, marred now by that sword line wound across his upper lip. Unlike other warriors, he had never had broken bones in his face; his nose remained straight and flawless. Dasharatha's eyes were just like his father's, dark and intense. Kausalya felt the force of them. Usually they were tempered by warmth, the promise to be just. Now her husband's eyes were inscrutable.

"Forgive me for bringing this topic up," she hastened to say. "You have just now returned. I am so relieved and therefore I must speak. I fear there will never be a right time. Afraid of incurring your displeasure, I have not raised my concern until now."

He nodded thoughtfully, the guarded look gone. She had managed to diffuse some tension by addressing his resistance.

"What is it that you wish to say then, Great Queen?"

He maintained a formal tone, and Kausalya looked at his battered face, wanting to back out of the discussion she had initiated. What else could she really say beyond her command that he announce an heir? Conflicting emotions made her throat dry. She called for something to drink. If she had borne the king sons, as was her duty, they would not be having this discussion. She drank the water gratefully. And yet Sumitra had not borne the king sons either, as they all had hoped she would. How could she proceed without casting blame on Dasharatha?

The king waited, crossing his arms over his chest and leaning back in his seat.

Kausalya did not have much time alone with him, for the king constantly had people at his door. Kausalya's mind raced. Where to start? What to say?

"I wish to speak plainly about our lack of children," she said. "We have been married nearly thirty years now. A lesser king than you would have set me aside long ago."

"I would never do that," he said, a flash of fire in his eyes.

"I know, I know," she said, placing her hand on his. He had never allowed her to feel unworthy. He took her hand and drew her closer to him.

"The fault is not yours," he said.

"I do not wish to cast blame on anyone," she answered.

Kausalya had not been selected as Ayodhya's queen for nothing. She knew what mattered. She knew what was expected of her. She fulfilled all the duties that were within her power. But she had not borne a son, her foremost duty. Kausalya was secretly ashamed of

the relief she had felt when Sumitra was childless too. It would have been an answer to the empire's need. But something had softened between Kausalya and Dasharatha; it was no longer Kausalya's fault alone that they were childless. And therefore the time had come to look beyond their immediate family for a suitable heir. Surely Dasharatha could understand this.

"I have returned victorious from countless battles," Dasharatha said. "Why this issue now?"

In his question, the queen heard his desire to avoid the topic, that resistance she did not understand. There was something in Dasharatha, a master at statesmanship, that did not want to address this. He systematically avoided it altogether. Even the ministers knew they could not speak openly with him about it.

"Why now?" she repeated, almost laughing. "I think about it every time you go into battle! This time, I had seven years to think about it!" After her exclamation, she immediately softened her voice. "Every day I prayed for your safe return. And yet I could not ignore the questions of the ministers or my own. What would we do if you did not return?"

Dasharatha let out a long sigh. "Yes. Seven years have gone by."

The truth Kausalya had neglected dawned on her. Seven years on Earth was a mere seven days in the land of the gods. Although utterly exhausted by battle, Dasharatha had experienced the passage of time as one week. Kausalya had encountered this before, but it never failed to shock her. They looked at each other in silence while Kausalya quickly faced the facts. Kausalya had aged and he had not. She realized that it was quite likely that she now exceeded him in age. It made her suddenly feel unspeakably old. She wanted to cover her face with her veil and run out. Instead, she sat still.

Dasharatha looked tired. "I do not wish to speak of this."

She acutely felt his tension. It bordered on revulsion. She hated to face her husband's displeasure. If it wasn't for the ministers' urging, she might not have done it. But Ayodhya needed an heir. It was simple.

"We must," she insisted.

Kausalya looked into her husband's eyes, seeing only its secrets. Every king had secrets, she had no doubt about this. But King Dasharatha stubbornly ignored their lack of children and fought war after war. It was Kausalya who had to look at the lists that the ministers compiled of possible heirs. Dasharatha had no brothers or distant male relatives who could serve in his place. Death was as inevitable as birth; an heir eventually had to be announced.

Dasharatha stood up and backed away from Kausalya; his eyes turned darker and more fathomless for every step he took away. Kausalya stood up too, holding his gaze.

"Speak to me," she implored. "Tell me. Trust me."

She opened her arms wide and bared her soul for him to see that she could be his witness. Dasharatha stretched out on the bed, his arm placed over his eyes. She was dismissed.

CHAPTER 5

The Horse-Lord's Daughter

Dasharatha surveyed the losses from the war with a pounding heart. The victory had cost Ayodhya nearly half its troops and resources. With an urgency that almost felt like another battle, Dasharatha threw himself into the repair work. The royal stables were empty, and Dasharatha's own stallion had been killed by Subahu. Dasharatha welcomed the opportunity to journey to Kekaya to acquire new horses. The lord of Kekaya had become known far and wide as Ashvapati, "Lord of Horses," and Ayodhya had relied on his equestrians for many years. Usually the king sent Sumantra, his closest friend among the eight ministers; he had an excellent hand with horses and knew nearly as much about the animals as he did about politics. This time, however, the ministers urged the king to personally go; Ayodhya's alliance with smaller kingdoms like Kekaya was more important than ever before, with its troops so diminished. Kekaya's fealty would be fueled by a personal visit by the emperor. Keen on maintaining Ayodhya's power, Dasharatha agreed. The swelling on his face had disappeared, and the thin scar across his lip was hardly visible. He had physically recovered from the ordeal. Perhaps the trip would give him direction and insight regarding the heir issue that Kausalya had pressed him on.

On the day of his departure, his two queens marked his forehead with auspicious red pulp.

"Return as soon as you can," Kausalya said.

Although she was one year past forty, she did not look past her prime. She was tall for a woman, but in every other way a typical Ayodhyan beauty with fair skin, large and pleasant eyes, and thick, unruly hair. He lifted his hand to her cheek.

"I will not tarry," he promised. "May the gods protect you in my absence."

The sadness in Kausalya's eyes intensified; she did not like to see him leave. Though their marriage had been arranged by his father, the moment of parting had always been like this with Kausalya. He had to resist the impulse to cancel his plans and stay with her, a youth's passionate notion. Kausalya would not want such a token of his love. She served the kingdom, as did he. He beheld Kausalya a few seconds longer, aware of the ache in his heart, for he could see the wall that stood between them. After so many years of marriage, there were no children. Kausalya had grown sadder every year, even though Dasharatha time and again assured her that he did not blame her.

As the complicated feelings overtook him, Dasharatha dropped his hand. Their relationship as man and woman had long ago lost its ardor when it became clear that it would not produce the desired result. There were other purposes to lovemaking, yes, but . . . Ah, he turned away from her. He had come to deeply rely on Kausalya as a friend, and he knew the tug in his heart for her was unique. Sumitra, his second wife, did not restrain him in this way. Even now, the princess of Magadha stood in the background. She had been that way from the beginning, shy and quiet. If he was honest, however, Dasharatha felt that neither of them needed him as a man. Perhaps that was why he did not feel averse to leaving the palace so soon again.

"The time has come," Sumantra said, holding the reins to the chariot.

Dasharatha allowed him to serve as charioteer, though Sumantra was far too qualified for the role. Everyone else had already ascended their chariots and waited for the king. Dasharatha stepped onto the chariot; Sumantra clucked to the horses and started their journey.

Dasharatha looked back and waved to Kausalya. He noticed the wind catching her veil, momentarily hiding her face and playing with her hair, lending softness to her serious demeanor. Perhaps he should not have dismissed her when she pressed him on the heir issue. Perhaps he should have opened up and told her. No. The very thought made him shrink in the daylight. Instead he decided that upon his return, he would sit with her and discuss the right course of action.

Kekaya was two weeks on horse from Ayodhya; the travel time alone would take them a month. Therefore they decided to skirt other kingdoms, like Videha, where King Janaka ruled Mithila with a gracious hand. It was one of the closest neighboring kingdoms, and yet it was impossible for Dasharatha, as the emperor, to arrive and leave the next day. Therefore the emperor's travel party had long ago opted to go incognito. They flew Ayodhya's banner with the sun sigil, but they did not stop anywhere during the day and set up their own camp at night.

Because they would return with a large cargo, they traveled to Kekaya in a small party of twenty chariots, ten horse riders, and ten packhorses. They did not know how long the process of acquiring new steeds would take and had not set a firm return date. Ashvapati's collection of horses had a well-deserved reputation, boasting horses of all colors and breeds.

"Every time I visit," Sumantra said, raising his voice about the clatter of hooves, "King Ashvapati has a new, improved breed to show us."

Dasharatha thought of Ashvapati, who at forty-eight was three years senior to him. It had been several years since they last met, but Dasharatha did not think time had softened the horse-lord, perhaps the most stern and terse man on Earth. Of course, Dasharatha had met the subordinate king only after the infamous incident that many said had caused the king's disposition.

"Does he still forbid talk of his wife?" Dasharatha inquired, gripping the railings of the chariot lightly and leaning forward toward Sumantra. The minister would have first-hand information about the current affairs in Kekaya. "Please set aside formality and speak openly."

"It's allowed now," Sumantra said, with a short laugh. "When his daughter turned thirteen, he finally revealed the story to her. I suspect she knew it long before. She and her brother are very close, as you will see. Prince Yuddhajit was old enough to remember their mother. I can't imagine that he hid the truth from her all those years."

Dasharatha appreciated Sumantra's astute observation, seeing beneath the state's official veneer.

"From a political standpoint," Sumantra said, "our communication is easier, for we can speak more freely, without incurring offense, though as you can imagine, it remains a tense topic."

Yes, Dasharatha could imagine it would always remain contentious. The story was highly unusual. One day Ashvapati had overheard the conversation of two swans and laughed out loud. Her curiosity piqued, Queen Chaya demanded to know what the swans had said, knowing well what the consequence would be. Infuriated by her callous demand, Ashvapati exiled her for all time. No one in Kekaya had seen or heard of her since. Chaya's children had never known their mother, as was Ashvapati's resolve.

"What would you have done, Great King, if you were in Ashvapati's position?" Sumantra asked.

"There can be little doubt," Dasharatha said, "that Ashvapati acted against his heart and in favor of his kingdom when he decided to cast his queen out. He is a true king. A remarriage would have done him good. He grows more solitary and stern every time I met him. "

"He is an affectionate father, however," Sumantra said. "He dotes on his daughter."

"She was a memorable child. Seven or eight, perhaps, but sharp. Her feisty replies made the entire assembly laugh."

Dasharatha requested Sumantra to brief him on all pertinent matters of Kekaya, and finally they turned to the topic of the prince and princess.

"How old are they now?"

"Yuddhajit, who has been consecrated as prince regent, has turned twenty years. The daughter is sixteen now, I believe. But still unmarried. You must ask Ashvapati. Fathers love speaking of their children, and this is especially true of him."

They arrived in Kekaya without complication. Instead of greeting them in his city, Ashvapati, with his usual directness, had asked them to meet him at the plains, where he kept his vast treasure of horses. Understandably Ashvapati did not divulge the total number he owned, but from his reputation and wealth, Dasharatha knew that they numbered in the millions. Whereas Ayodhya and the land of Koshala boasted many types of agriculture and trades, all of Kekaya was a grazing ground for its horses. Its entire economy was built on horse breeding and trade. It was said that horses were treated like family members in Kekaya.

For the emperor's visit, Ashvapati had promised to select his one hundred best horses and herd them to the valley for Dasharatha's inspection. Though Ashvapati had agreed that his men would deliver three thousand horses to Ayodhya, Dasharatha looked forward to seeing the ones that Ashvapati considered his best. Dasharatha would make his personal selection from those, between five and twenty, depending on what he liked.

Ashvapati waited for them at the appointed place and time. The two kings greeted each other and exchanged the necessary formalities. Dasharatha inquired about the kingdom's welfare. Ashvapati made no inquiries in turn, but called his servants forward to wash Dasharatha's feet. True to the Kekayan customs, the horse-lord's men needed no prompting when it came to Ayodhya's horses. The tired horses were rubbed down with hay and fed with fresh grass and water. Ayodhya's men were not neglected either, being provided with refreshments of wine, honey, and fresh water. A feast would be served in the king's honor in the evening.

Ashvapati walked away without a word. Sumantra silently gestured that this type of abrupt manner was normal for the horse-lord. Dasharatha swallowed his surprise and followed the other king to a pavilion.

"We will watch from here," Ashvapati said. "No one can watch my riders without being impressed."

Ashvapati's riders, having grown up with horses, were capable of unimaginable tricks and acrobatics with their steeds. After this, Ashvapati said nothing and answered questions with monosyllables. The silence between the two kings grew. Dasharatha clasped his hands, then unclasped them and placed them on his knees. He began thinking of his exchange with Kausalya on the day of his return from the god's battle.

"Where are they?" Ashvapati demanded in a loud voice. Dasharatha looked around to see if a servant would answer the question, but only Dasharatha was within hearing distance. The emperor smiled inwardly. It was rather amusing not to be granted the usual niceties; therefore Dasharatha didn't mind Ashvapati's behavior.

"I sent my daughter and her brother," Ashvapati muttered. "They were to select our best stallions and mares for you."

Why had he sent his daughter? It was a man's work.

Ashvapati started drumming his fingers against the seat. The tenseness that Ashvapati displayed began to intrude on Dasharatha. He took several deep breaths and cleared his throat.

"How old are your children now?" Dasharatha inquired, following Sumantra's suggestion. "I remember your girl well."

To Dasharatha's surprise, Ashvapati laughed out loud. "It has been too long since your last visit, Great King. She is not the little girl you remember. You will see. She has had many suitors, but none that can match her skills. I have come to trust her a great deal, especially with the horses. She has an eye and ear for them, discerning their temperament. Truly, she is as intuitive with them as I am with swans."

That was the longest speech Dasharatha had ever heard him give. Ashvapati stood up. "Come, let us ride. Sitting here will serve no purpose. I will find the reason for this delay."

The horse-lord arranged for fresh horses for the emperor and his men. Twenty riders from Ayodhya would come with them, including Sumantra and four from Dasharatha's personal guard.

"This is Sandesh," Ashvapati said, lightly smacking a white stallion on the flank so he would step forward. "Sandesh, meet the emperor himself. Please behave yourself."

Then Ashvapati waited, and Dasharatha felt like a boy tested by a strict master. He shook off the feeling by focusing on the magnificent stallion. After letting the animal smell his hands and gently stroking its soft muzzle, Dasharatha took his seat astride the horse. Ashvapati seemed satisfied with Dasharatha's effort, for he swung up in the saddle and began an

easy trot away. Only then did the rest of Ayodhya's men mount their horses. They followed their king at a comfortable distance, letting the two kings ride on their own.

As Sandesh fell into a trot, Dasharatha was glad he had taken that moment to introduce himself. He felt the stallion harken to him, accepting his commands. Though Ashvapati had a stern way with men, he was notoriously gentle with animals, naming all his horses. The white stallion, like all Kekaya's horses, was used to an intuitive master, or perhaps mistress. Dasharatha was curious about Kekaya's princess. In Ayodhya, girls were not trained to deal with horses.

The vast green fields and the valley embraced Dasharatha with its expanse. The land was perfectly suited for horse breeding. Ashvapati had made an astute decision, turning the grounds over to the horses that had made Kekaya a stronghold of wealth. Dasharatha observed the demarcations, separating one breed of horse from the other, yet the fenced-in areas were large, allowing the horses to run free. The riders passed a lake that Dasharatha remembered, a huge body of water that went beyond the eye's reach and was the main water source for the horses. Now, as then, it was full of swans.

"I've told them that this is their sanctuary," Ashvapati said, looking in the direction of the lake alive with swans. "No one will hunt them here. Shooting swans is forbidden in all of Kekaya. If your men are inclined to go hunting, remember to tell them this. Horses and swans are off-limits."

Dasharatha's curiosity was awakened; the other man's love for the birds was clear. Ashvapati did not hide it, as he had during previous visits.

"My daughter tells me that speaking with animals is more productive than talk between our own kind." Ashvapati laughed, as he always seemed to do when mentioning his daughter.

"Does the princess commune with horses?"

"Only she could answer that."

The lake's surface sparkled with the sunshine; some of the birds spread their wings and took flight, trumpeting as they flew up. The white stallion neighed, and Ashvapati's horse answered. Ashvapati smiled. Dasharatha assumed the other king was privy to something he was not. It was utterly clear that given a choice between a horse and man's company, Ashvapati would choose the animal.

But Ashvapati's concern was not only for the land and his horses. For a man who invited so little warmth, Ashvapati had implemented several laws that protected Kekayans with physical handicaps. His court and retinue were full of people who had physical impediments but whose intelligence made them invaluable. The wet nurse Ashvapati had chosen for his own daughter was a hunchbacked woman. She too had made an impression on Dasharatha with her dour face; he was sure, however, that she was a qualified mother figure or the king would not have allowed her near his treasured daughter.

Suddenly Ashvapati stood in his stirrups. He shaded his eyes and looked at the plains ahead, where Dasharatha saw only more fields full of horses.

"Ya!" Ashvapati cried, urging his horse into a gallop, leaving the lake behind.

Dasharatha's stallion picked up speed when the other horse did. He could hear the hooves of twenty horses behind him breaking into a run. Even the fenced-in horses started sprinting just for the love of it.

With the wind alive around them, they galloped urgently, though Dasharatha had no inkling why. Something had alerted the other man, and all Dasharatha's senses came alive.

As they got closer to a collection of horses, Dasharatha recognized them as Kekaya's best; each one was magnificent. It was not the time, however, to admire the horses in leisure; the horses were skittish, dancing around in circles, with ears flat. While several men on horseback worked hard to keep the horses together, everyone's attention was trained on the heated argument in the center. Angry voices filled the air, agitating both the horses and their owners.

Ashvapati reined in his horse and signaled to Dasharatha to do the same. The older man stood up in his stirrups again, taking in the scene before them. One man was being restrained but struggled against his captors. A horse was on the ground in the center of the commotion. A girl with long black hair had her arms around the horse.

"Kaikeyi!" Ashvapati shouted.

Then, "Yuddhajit!"

Hearing their names called, the prince and princess looked up. The girl, who had to be Kaikeyi, got on her feet and ran toward her father. As she did so, she whistled to a black horse and threw herself on its back. Dasharatha noticed at once that she was not a girl at all but a woman fully formed. As if pursued by demons, Kaikeyi came at them on her horse, her long hair flying behind her. As she got closer, a powerful energy pushed Dasharatha backward and away. Alarmed, he pressed his thighs against the flanks of the horse to steady himself. The stallion flattened its ears.

"He killed Surya!" Kaikeyi cried out.

Just as Dasharatha was about to move out of her way, she stopped her horse. Tears streaked her face, but the anger in her eyes made Dasharatha's neck hairs raise. Her leather vest and her hands were red with blood.

The princess did not even cast a glance at Dasharatha, looking at her father with flared nostrils, spitting out her story. "Dvi killed Surya for no reason. No *valid* reason at all. Like a true coward, he turned his anger on her; she was defenseless and innocent! It was me that he was angry with, but he killed Surya instead! He does not deserve to live—coward, sneak, shameless, malicious—"

Ashvapati held up a hand, stopping his distraught daughter, but she continued fiercely. "I want his life for hers! Surya had done nothing! You know how many hours I put into training her, and even before that she was my best mare."

Tears began pouring from the woman's eyes again and she looked back at the dead horse. Piecing the story together, Dasharatha gathered that Surya was Kaikeyi's horse, one she had been very fond of. Dasharatha could not take his eyes off this girl-woman whose anger and sadness were so palpable; he felt his own emotion rise. A young man rode up behind Kaikeyi. There was no doubt it was Yuddhajit, for brother and sister were as alike as twins, with striking facial features and lanky limbs.

"She speaks the truth, Father," Yuddhajit said. "We have restrained Dvi and were discussing what to do."

"I need to know more," Ashvapati said. "Who killed Surya, and why?"

"I told you," Kaikeyi said.

"Let your brother speak," Ashvapati commanded. "You are not in full command of your reason, my child."

Kaikeyi swallowed her words and momentarily glanced at Dasharatha, as if noticing him only then. Her eyes were blue, deep like the ocean, and piercing, like the tip of a sword. Dasharatha drowned in her eyes. His breath left his body for countless seconds and when it returned, heat spread through him like a fire. The stallion, sensing his strong sensations, danced nervously. Dasharatha sought Kaikeyi's eyes again, but she had forgotten him, nodding her head forcefully with every word her brother was saying.

"I did not realize," Yuddhajit said, "that Dvi befriended me only to get to Sister. I blame myself for not noticing his attentions earlier, but when he tried to touch her hand, she drew her sword against him, saying *no* and *never*, as only she can. In his insolence, he became angry, accusing her of being less than innocent. He turned on Surya, knowing it was Sister's favorite horse. We were too shocked to intervene in time. Surya is dead, as you can see."

Though Kaikeyi looked as if she might cry again, she straightened in her seat. Dasharatha noticed the belt around her slender waist, and the swords secured there. She had gained enough composure to remain silent as her brother spoke. Ashvapati had grown rigid on his mount.

"Did he touch you, my daughter?" he asked. "Whichever limb a man uses to touch the king's daughter without permission will be cut off without question. That is the law."

"No, Father," Kaikeyi said. "He would have held my hand, but I was too quick."

"Still, he dared turn his eyes and hopes onto my daughter," Ashvapati said, looking with outrage at Dasharatha, who had been unable to stop staring at Kaikeyi. Ashvapati turned his eyes back to her. "Your grievance is well founded, daughter. This man had committed several crimes. And only a foul person would seek revenge the way he did. Still, a man's life for the life of a horse? I will leave that decision up to you. Be the justice you seek."

A smile spread itself across the girl-woman's face. Dasharatha shivered. With manic speed, Kaikeyi turned her horse around and returned to the dead horse, Surya.

The stallion under Dasharatha started following Kaikeyi, but Ashvapati stopped them. "Stay here. She will have her justice."

Ashvapati again stood in his stirrups, watching his daughter. Without looking at Dasharatha, he said, "The dead mare was my daughter's first horse, born during the first foaling that she attended. She has been inseparable from Surya since then, ten years ago."

After a few moments, Ashvapati sat down, apparently satisfied with what he saw. Dasharatha could not follow his example. He could not relax onto the stallion's back or take his eyes from the woman and what she did. The princess had returned to her people. Not one among them had acknowledged the emperor as he was due, but Dasharatha recognized that they were in a crisis.

The accused man called Dvi was released. Yuddhajit handed Dvi his sword, still bright with the horse's blood. The men moved away, leaving Dvi to face Kaikeyi. The hundred horses that were Kekaya's best formed a circle around them.

"You will fight to the death," Yuddhajit declared. "May the best warrior win!"

Dasharatha felt a jolt run through him. They were letting a girl face a grown man! Dasharatha's horror overpowered the other sensation that had held him hostage. This would never be allowed in Ayodhya. Equals were meant to face each other, and a woman could not match a man's power.

With a commanding voice, Dasharatha said, "Stop this."

Ashvapati simply gave Dasharatha an amused look. "Did I not tell you she is no longer a girl?" When he saw that Dasharatha was not appeased, he added, "Trust our justice, Great King." He settled in to watch, crossing his fingers in his lap.

Dasharatha prepared to assert his power as emperor when the girl-woman began to roar, sword in hand. The sound was neither human nor animal. The sixteen-year-old girl disappeared and in her place stood a woman who could not be described in words. Only an answering growl, a war cry, would suffice, and Dasharatha felt the sound arise from his throat as if he was no longer a man or a king. The animal thirst for blood was in the air; every hair on Dasharatha's body stood up. He had felt this only in the midst of the wildest battle, when he lost sense of who he was, facing blood-drinkers on all sides, becoming one with the war. He was one with her now, on her side, forgetting any questions about the justice of the situation.

Kaikeyi's terrifying sound made her opponent blanch, and the next moment she was on him with her sword. Her terrible cry had frozen him as if he had surrendered. At the last moment, however, he lifted his sword to defend himself against the girl he had wooed.

"When you fall onto the earth begging for mercy," she snarled, "I will not grant it."

It was clear that she fought to kill, slashing with a speed that Dasharatha could not deny. Standing in the stirrups, he was transfixed. Waves of conflicting feelings made his legs weak; he was afraid for her life, stunned by his feelings for her, and impressed by her prowess. Although Yuddhajit and the other guards would surely intervene if she faltered, Kaikeyi did not lean on them. She was sleek and fast, smartly relying on her speed, not her strength. Dvi, the doomed suitor, would have demolished her otherwise. Dasharatha saw the moment Dvi transformed from helpless suitor to the sneak Kaikeyi claimed he was. He began fighting for his life, which meant he was ready to take hers.

When Dvi smashed his sword down on Kaikeyi's thigh with all his force, Dasharatha protested loudly. But Kaikeyi spun away, jabbing her sword deep into his side. He yelled and fell to the ground. Kaikeyi landed on his chest, kicking his sword from his hands, and crushed him down. The next second her blade had pinned his sword hand to the ground. She jumped away, pressing on her sword. His face reddened as he cried out, writhing in pain.

Ashvapati raised himself then, calling out in a commanding voice, "Now you must decide, my child, has Surya's death been avenged? You have defeated him in battle and inflicted wounds that may maim him forever. Has his crime been rectified?"

With a malicious grimace, Kaikeyi twisted her sword, breaking the bones in his hands. Sweat broke out on Dasharatha's skin. The girl's decision seemed portentous and would tell Dasharatha if she was cruel or just. It suddenly mattered greatly, even though he had known her less than an hour. Dasharatha prayed that Kaikeyi would do the right thing, but he could neither predict her actions nor think clearly enough to conclude what the right course of action was. He shook his head. He had made far more complex adjudications. What was wrong with him?

In answer, his mind descended to the darkness of his soul. There he found no righteousness. His attraction to Kaikeyi was not dependent on her decision. If she killed this man in revenge of her horse, it would be murder. But his desire did not care.

His eyes followed the movement of her heaving chest as she regarded Dvi, his life in her hands. She did not speak until she was calm and he had stopped moaning.

"You will serve in the stables for the entire winter," the princess said, "cleaning up the horse dung. If you intentionally harm another horse ever again, you will be sentenced to death by horse, without question. If you agree, say so now, or foreswear your citizenship to Kekaya from this day onward."

Kaikeyi looked toward her father, and Dasharatha felt his throat clog. He approved of her punishment. He approved of her. He was ablaze with her.

"I choose the horse dung," the man said, to general laughter.

Slowly, smiling sweetly, Kaikeyi pulled her sword from the ground and his hand. This time he made no sound, but curled into a ball, cradling his hand. Dasharatha appreciated his restraint; he knew the excruciating pain of broken bones.

"Justice!" Yuddhajit hailed.

"Justice!" the other men answered.

"Let no man hold this crime against him," Ashvapati cried. "Kekaya's justice has been done!"

Kaikeyi grinned and raised her fist in the air. She bowed to her father, who lifted his hand high in the air. Dasharatha realized then that this was not the first time Kaikeyi had acted as Kekaya's justice. What else had this girl-woman done? How many men had she killed? No one could acquire the type of battle skill she had demonstrated without killing, without being the survivor of a death struggle. Dasharatha turned to Ashvapati with a concern he could not hide, but Ashvapati's face showed nothing but pride in the daughter he had trained.

"Look," Ashvapati said, raising his eyebrows and inviting Dasharatha to behold the spectacle.

In her glee, Kaikeyi had again become the girl she was. Mounting the black horse, she stood on its back as it thundered across the expanse.

Dasharatha was transfixed, seeing her magic, her beauty, and her power. She was not a woman he could compare to any other woman he had known.

As she became a dark spot on the horizon, he felt a clammy feeling take hold of his skin. When she came closer, returning to him, he felt the warmth of the sun once again. While watching her show off her tricks and skills on horseback, Dasharatha knew only one thing:

he had been hit by Kamadeva's arrows. The god of love had not shot his arrows with care; Dasharatha was bleeding, it was painful, and he felt sick—but he had never been more alive.

"So," Ashvapati said to him, "what do you think?" He gestured to the collection of assembled horses.

Using the full force of his authority, Dasharatha turned to Ashvapati. "She is the one I want."

Ashvapati turned to see Dasharatha's selection, thinking he had chosen a horse. When his gaze landed on his exuberant daughter, his eyes glazed over. "I did not plan to part with her yet. I rely on her."

Dasharatha challenged him. "How many more Dvis will there be before you relent?"

They both knew that suitors would line up for Kaikeyi's hand until she was married; Dasharatha was not the only one bowled over by her beauty. Dvi had demonstrated that today.

Ashvapati nodded once. "I'm not blind. My daughter must marry." He turned his stern eyes on Dasharatha. "I only mean that I value her greatly and that I am in no hurry to part with her."

Dasharatha understood. Ashvapati would name a high price for his daughter. Dasharatha schooled his face to reveal nothing, though perhaps it was too late. He had a sense that Ashvapati would ask for more than Dasharatha could give. But what would he *not* give for Kaikeyi's hand?

"I planned to give her in marriage to a man of suitable age," Ashvapati said, again raising the stakes. Dasharatha was a great deal older, it was true.

His hand went to his sword hilt. "If I must prove my strength, I'm prepared to fight every other suitor for her hand."

Ashvapati relaxed into his seat, and the two men measured each other.

As emperor, Dasharatha was used to such scrutiny by foe and friend. "Name your price."

When Ashvapati did, Dasharatha shivered. His ministers would counsel him against it. They would call it unacceptable. Dasharatha's eyes followed Kaikeyi. Perhaps he was acting foolish. Perhaps he would regret it later. Perhaps the princess did not deserve such an enormous bride-price. Perhaps his decision now would cause political conflicts in the future. Perhaps Kausalya would be outraged. There were many uncertainties but only one truth: Dasharatha needed this woman. He had to claim her. He had never felt so certain about anything.

He looked Ashvapati in the eyes and agreed.

CHAPTER 6

Kaikeyi's Bride-Price

As the royal party rode home from the plains, Kaikeyi's elation over her battle victory abated. She felt the grief over losing Surya, but restrained her tears from flowing openly. It was not manly to cry, and she valued being treated as an equal among the men. This meant, however, that she never had the luxury of being who she was. Her four personal guards rode in their formation around her, and because of Dvi's recent threat, they would not allow her to break out from their protective square. Her brother had thoughtfully seen to a quick burial for Surya, understanding that she was not just any horse. Kaikeyi could not have borne riding away and letting nature run its course in decomposing the body. Surya deserved more. The mare would have lived for another twenty years at least if it hadn't been for the vile Dvi. Kaikeyi had been too compassionate toward him. She hoped the wound on his hand would fester and never heal. Dharma nickered beneath Kaikeyi, wanting her attention, but she continued to handle him automatically, something only an experienced rider could get away with. She didn't want to bond with Dharma or any other horse for a while. She had loved Surya since she was a newborn filly. Kaikeyi had never lost anyone she loved before, and she almost was not in control of her tears. This told her that Father spoke truly. Manthara was right. It was never wise to love, for it ended always like this, in heartbreak, one way or the other.

A slash on Kaikeyi's right arm was bleeding. It was a light cut, nothing that would need the physician's attention. She made sure to communicate this to her guards, lest they escort her straight to the physician. Kaikeyi longed to see Manthara and tell her what had happened. Would Manthara coax Kaikeyi's tears out, or would she ignore Kaikeyi's feelings?

Kaikeyi never knew how Manthara would react. But Manthara would tell her exactly what she had done correctly or perhaps wrongly. Her father loved her too much or was too absent-minded to scold her. He had always left that job to Manthara. She was the most caring person Kaikeyi knew, no matter what others whispered. Even now, it was Manthara's face Kaikeyi saw first and last every day. It was a face Kaikeyi loved, although she had come to understand that Manthara was considered unpleasant. The strain of Manthara's hunched back had etched premature lines into her face. But Kaikeyi did not think Manthara was ugly or mean, as others claimed. It also was not the etiquette in Kekaya to ridicule those like Manthara, who were disabled. But that didn't stop people from talking behind Manthara's back.

When the entourage of Kekayans and Ayodhyans finally arrived at the gates of Rajagriha, Kaikeyi felt her father's eyes linger on her, as did the emperor's. She had met the emperor's eyes for a brief moment out on the plains and had known at once who he was. Of course they had expected his arrival, but he was also a man of authority, like her father. She hadn't been able to meet the emperor's eyes again and avoided him for reasons she could not articulate. She avoided other men for the same reason. She couldn't help but notice, however, the fine silks and heavy gold jewelry he wore. Even his weapons gleamed, as if they were freshly forged.

At the palace, she dismounted Dharma and gave him a gentle pat on his muzzle. The stable hands ran forward to catch his reins and lead him away. They handled the guards' horses just as swiftly. Her guards closed around her again. Usually Kaikeyi barely noticed her guards, for they had been with her since she turned thirteen and were quite unobtrusive. Today, however, she felt that they were in the way, as if she might trip over one of their feet. It was how Kaikeyi had initially felt when Manthara assigned them as her shadow. On that birthday Manthara had been hysterical, warning her about the ways of men. Kaikeyi was too decorous to ask, but rumor had it that Manthara had castrated the guards before allowing them near Kaikeyi. What Kaikeyi recalled most clearly from that birthday was her father's words: "You have grown to be the spitting image of your mother." That had truly frightened her. She knew her mother was very bad—so bad that her father had made her disappear.

Kaikeyi hurried away from her father and the guests from Ayodhya. Going straight to her chamber, Kaikeyi did not bother to speak to her guards, as she otherwise would have. She left them without a word at the entrance of her chamber. Instead of bathing or undressing, she searched for the salve she kept to treat bruises and wounds. It was a salve Manthara used to alleviate pain in her back. She wasn't sure what it contained, only that it produced a glorious numbness. Kaikeyi glanced at the door often, knowing that Manthara would come as soon as she knew Kaikeyi had returned.

At sixteen, Kaikeyi understood much about men and their ways, but not as much as she wanted. So much was still hidden from her. She had been foolish to ever think of Manthara

as her mother. Her father and Manthara had never had *that* relationship. Her father had never loved another woman again. Love destroyed you like that.

The sound of Manthara's cane preceded her entry. "Keyi?" she called, as though she didn't know that Kaikeyi was within. Before Manthara was in the door, she ordered, "Wear your finest silks tonight."

"Why?"

"Your father's order."

Manthara entered, and Kaikeyi's suppressed tears rose to her eyes. Surya was dead. Kaikeyi rubbed her eyes, hiding her emotion from Manthara. She knew Manthara did not care for horses; they were nothing to her but a means to get from one place to the other.

"I cannot tell you yet," Manthara said, with a glint in her eye, "but your father is up to something. Something that might change your life."

Kaikeyi did not ask how Manthara knew this. Manthara always knew things. Also, it was not often that Kaikeyi was required to dress the part of the princess.

"What should I wear, then, for this life-changing event?" Kaikeyi was not interested in making these choices, though other girls seemed to speak of little else. Kaikeyi was happy to wear whatever Manthara told her to, only because she really did not care. When it came to her daily wear, she was her own mistress. In that sphere, she surpassed Manthara, knowing which clothes best suited the work she would do with her horses.

Manthara selected a light pink gown and a set of blue gemstone jewelry. Kaikeyi touched the gems as they lay around her neck.

"Were these my mother's?"

"You know they were." Manthara looked at Kaikeyi in the mirror. Her eyes asked, *How often must you ask?*

"I'm just surprised that he didn't get rid of everything that was hers."

Now they frowned at each other. Manthara worshipped everything Father said and did not want to hear a word of criticism against him. Kaikeyi decided not to tell Manthara about Surya. She understood nothing about true feelings, always telling Kaikeyi not to have any.

Manthara began brushing Kaikeyi's hair with firm strokes. She insisted on doing it, though any of the other servants could have done it. Sukhi and Dukhi, the twins, were experts with hair and styled their own with great flair.

Kaikeyi thought about how complicated people were. Manthara said one thing, Father another. They both expected a lot from her, though it wasn't always clear what. That's why she preferred horses. They had simple needs and ways that Kaikeyi could handle effortlessly. Communication with animals was easier. At least her father encouraged this aspect of her, letting her ride free in the lands—though after she'd turned thirteen, always in the company of her guards, even though she was capable of fighting her own battles.

"You are such a stubborn girl," Manthara complained, untangling the knots in Kaikeyi's hair. "How many times must I tell you to keep your hair braided?" She held up a long shank of Kaikeyi's hair. "Just look at these knots!"

Kaikeyi shrugged. There were worse things than tangled hair, though maybe not in

Manthara's world. Just then, the old woman stopped, closed her eyes, and moaned. Kaikeyi felt a flash of guilt for being dismissive toward Manthara, when Manthara so courageously battled the chronic pain of her back. Manthara's face contorted for a moment, but then she opened her eyes and continued, not even noticing Kaikeyi's observant eyes.

"I can do it myself." Kaikeyi began to pull away from Manthara. "You sit down and rest."

"And be blamed for a princess with matted hair? Absolutely not!"

Manthara yanked Kaikeyi's hair back into her hands. Kaikeyi clenched her teeth together; she would be surprised if she had any hair left after Manthara's rough handiwork.

When Manthara was satisfied with Kaikeyi's appearance, they went to the court. The light pink dress flowed softly around Kaikeyi with every step. Suddenly she felt feminine and nervous. Even the guards looked at her differently when she was dressed like this. She lifted her head high when she entered the hall. She knew she was the most beautiful women in all of Kekaya. Her people had donned their finest silks, and the hall was decorated festively. Yet, the wealth of Ayodhya clearly surpassed Kekaya's; it was clear in every sparkle of every gem the Ayodhyan entourage wore. Father was in a strange mood. He smiled broadly one moment, which was not his habit, then frowned and turned away. He practically ignored Kaikeyi. One didn't have to be Manthara to guess something strange was afoot.

Like all other celebrations, this one centered on food. To begin, steaming trays of rice were served with a rich and spicy stew. The memory of Surya laying dead on the plains, however, made Kaikeyi's appetite disappear. The emperor and his guests ate heartily, and Yuddhajit and his men did too. Kaikeyi's attention was trained on her father, but she glanced several times at the emperor, noticing his frequent smile and manly features. When the feast was over, Father called her close and put a hand on her shoulders. He turned her so that she directly faced the emperor, who was engaged in a conversation with Yuddhajit by the center-piece of the hall, a life-size carving of a stallion rearing on its hind legs.

Father put his mouth close to her ears and asked, "What do you think you are worth?"

Kaikeyi froze. "Father?"

She turned her eyes to her father, noticing the unusual flush of his skin. Father looked steadily at the emperor and inclined his head toward him. "He thinks you are worth the entire world."

Kaikeyi's eyes fastened on the handsome king of kings. "He said that?"

"In return for your hand in marriage, the emperor has agreed to the highest bride-price. His whole kingdom. The entire world. The son you bear will rule after him."

Her heart beat strangely. She touched the cool blue gems at her throat.

Her father turned her back to face him. "I will not force you. You have to decide. But a better proposal can hardly be imagined. You will become a powerful queen. As long as you don't give him the power to break your heart. Understand?"

Kaikeyi listened and nodded. She knew marriage was inevitable. Other girls of her age were long since married. Her father looked over her shoulder and then said, "Here he comes."

Kaikeyi felt the emperor approach; his presence made her back tingle. Slowly she turned to face King Dasharatha, feeling her father's expectation by her side. When she tried to meet the emperor's eyes, Kaikeyi's eyes strayed. She who usually was bold and direct, the opposite of coy, couldn't look him in the eye. Her father wasted no time and placed her hand in King Dasharatha's hand.

It was a bold move; he knew her temperament. She had not yet expressed her acceptance of this royal alliance. Aside from the brief glance, Kaikeyi had not properly seen the emperor's face. She felt the warmth at once in Dasharatha's grasp, the first male hand she had ever touched that wasn't her father's or brother's. Officially, this touch sealed the alliance, and instinctively Kaikeyi wanted to snatch her hand away and assert her power. She would choose her own husband!

As she was about to do this, she felt Dasharatha tighten his grip ever so slightly. Startled, she looked into the king's eyes, this man who might be her future—and she forgot to snatch her hand away. She heard her father laugh.

"It's done, then," he said.

But Dasharatha did not laugh. Instead, Kaikeyi saw the question in his eyes—and the desire. He was very attractive, with dark eyes and thick eyebrows. A vigorous man whose strength was visible in his broad chest and muscled arms. There were thin scars on his face and arms, and more on the rest of his body, she was sure. A thin white scar cut into his upper lip, which looked soft and full under his beard. She continued to stand, indecisive, spellbound by something she could not understand.

Yuddhajit would have scolded her for her hesitation. "One moment of hesitation," he had said countless times, "is all it ever takes to lose your life." How right he was. While Kaikeyi hesitated, her life was taken away. She looked into Dasharatha's eyes. They were sharp as steel, like her own, but tempered by something that Kaikeyi was thirsty for. She could not yet put her finger on what it was. Already, she did not belong to herself anymore, but to this man.

"The bride-price has been set," her father said, addressing the entire court. "As you all know, Kaikeyi is my only daughter. She is valuable to me beyond any material wealth. The emperor has agreed that Kaikeyi's son will rule the world from Ayodhya's throne. Her future is secured."

Dasharatha's grip tightened around Kaikeyi's hand as he solemnly swore for all to hear. "Your son, *our* son, will be the king of Earth after me."

Kaikeyi longed to retrieve her hand, not out of anger but to regain herself. The pulsating energy between their hands was too strong. She wanted to run away and hide; she felt both like a little child in his presence and as a full-grown woman.

Her father laughed again; he had never seen her so passive. "All hail the future queen of Ayodhya!"

All hailed. Kaikeyi was dazed. Manthara came to her rescue. Her cane pounded against the stone floor with each step. Kaikeyi's heartbeat. What had just happened? Was she betrothed to King Dasharatha?

Manthara was not pleased. Kaikeyi felt it in the way the old woman's finger sank into her arm and made her wince. It was where she had recently been wounded. Manthara loosened her hold, but as soon as they were out of the emperor's hearing, she pulled Kaikeyi down toward her and whispered, "He is too old for you. Maybe he cannot even sire a child. You can still say no."

Too old? Kaikeyi had not noticed his age. She looked back at the king, who was facing her father and saw him as Manthara did. A tall and strong man, but closer to her father's age than her own. She did not follow Manthara's train of thought. Perhaps she didn't want to.

"It *is* too late," she said, squeezing the woman's hand.

Suddenly she felt like a trapped horse. Skittish. Intensely desiring to break free from her captors and run. Manthara always made things that were simple become complicated. The "reality of the situation," she called it. This was already complicated enough. Kaikeyi was not sure she could handle such talk from Manthara right now, when her body was a stranger to her.

The princess and the hunchback walked out from the hall in silence. If Manthara had more to say, she would contain herself while the guards were within hearing. Over the years, Manthara had helped Kaikeyi see the reality of many situations. Kaikeyi could not, for example, be the king of Kekaya. Kaikeyi had been a foolish six-year-old and very sure that her father would choose her to be the next king. When Manthara insisted that Kaikeyi see the reality, Kaikeyi kicked her cane and ran off. Manthara was not allowed to punish her. She was the princess, Manthara the servant; this had dawned on the princess at six years of age. But Manthara was smarter than Kaikeyi, meting out punishment in her own way. She simply withdrew and started acting like the other servants. She did not come to Kaikeyi unless summoned, and even then she kept her distance and was silent. She refused to hold Kaikeyi's hand and was like a statue when Kaikeyi hugged her. It had taken Kaikeyi months to get Manthara back to her side. Manthara had never been Kaikeyi's servant, but a mother and best friend. And Manthara's words turned out to be the truth: no woman had ever sat on any throne in her own right.

As the two stepped into Kaikeyi's quarters, leaving guards and attendants without, Manthara sighed, "What a pleasure to be alone."

Kaikeyi sighed deeply too. She didn't know what to think, but her mind was drawn back toward the hall where the emperor stood. Manthara sat herself down on Kaikeyi's bed, looking into the distance. Kaikeyi looked at the old woman, wondering why others whispered that Manthara was as crooked in mind as her back. Kaikeyi loved Manthara's crooked back. She saw how Manthara labored through the day with the pain it caused her; she knew Manthara was unlike anyone else in the world. Kaikeyi was scared of the very thought of being without Manthara.

Still skittish, Kaikeyi walked around her chamber, examining objects she might take with her to Ayodhya. While she did this, she thought about what she really felt for Manthara. After a few minutes, she said, "Manthara, I'm *so* glad that you are not my mother."

Manthara's mouth became a tight line. Kaikeyi smiled. "Oh, it's too easy to upset you."

She went to Manthara and put one arm around her curve. "If you were my real mother, then you would have to stay here. With Father. You will come with me to Ayodhya, won't you?"

"Of course," Manthara said. "If you choose to marry."

But Kaikeyi wasn't sure she had a choice. The emperor had made his promise, and his eyes spoke of many more to come. Kaikeyi felt a thrill run through her.

Although Kaikeyi wanted to be wise like the queen she would be, she felt the question bubble up. She couldn't stop it.

She turned to Manthara. She needed to know. "What is the reality of this situation?"

Manthara stopped everything she was doing and assessed Kaikeyi. Her breathing was slightly wheezy from walking through the palace corridors rather hurriedly, swept up by the momentousness of the evening. Kaikeyi waited patiently for Manthara's breathing to turn full and calm. But Manthara still did not answer.

"Tell me," Kaikeyi insisted. "I can take it. I need to know."

Manthara turned the question back to her, daring her to step into her role as queen. "You tell me. What is the reality of the situation here?"

Kaikeyi thought quickly, assessing the recent events as Manthara had taught her to do. There was the marriage proposal. The emperor's spotless reputation. Her father's delight in the match. The bride-price. Her father's whisper to her. Manthara's comment that the emperor was too old. And most of all, the electrifying touch of the king's hand. It all made her head spin. She sat down next to Manthara. She *would* see it all for what it truly was!

"I'm getting married to the most powerful man on Earth," she said, shocked at how true her words were. She hardly knew what it would mean for her life, but it sounded incredible.

"And?"

"And . . . there is always a price to pay." Kaikeyi looked into the future, thinking immediately of her horses, her father's horses. "I will have to leave Kekaya, Father, and Brother. I will have to adopt the rules and customs of a new place. I will not be free to ride my horses every day. I'll be trapped in my role as a wife."

All these seemed like heavy prices to Kaikeyi. But she could tell Manthara was not impressed.

"Yes, and no," Manthara said. "The reality of the situation is that you are marrying an old man, whose favor you'll have to fight for. You are not his first wife or his second. You are his third wife. You will never be the true queen of Ayodhya. That position has already been taken, twice over."

Kaikeyi stood up. "Why would Father want this for me?"

"Actually your father has outdone himself. The bride-price is magnificent. The kingdom in return for your hand. Your son will be king. When that day comes, you will be the only queen that matters."

"You are satisfied, then?" Kaikeyi searched Manthara's face. The wisdom lines on Manthara's face enhanced the intelligence in her eyes.

"Am I ever?" the old woman scoffed, and they both laughed.

"I still have my doubts," Manthara said. "Whether that old king can sire at all. His other two wives have not produced children, not even girls."

Manthara took hold of Kaikeyi's hand. "But don't worry about that. Leave it to me. Your father has paved the way for you to become more powerful than you can imagine. You must guard your heart closely. Do not let yourself fall into those love games that befuddle others. Play the game—you cannot avoid it altogether when you are married—but don't get caught in its web. What is it that your father taught you?"

"Never give anyone the power to break your heart," Kaikeyi recited. Ashvapati had inculcated this in both her and Yuddhajit. Their father lived by those words.

"Good. Don't make the mistake your father made. He loved your mother passionately. I think we've all seen the results of that."

Kaikeyi became aware of the throbbing in her arm. "Hand me the salve," she said.

She could have borne the pain. It was nothing compared to when she had broken her arm and her ribs. But she didn't like it when Manthara said, "Don't make the mistake your father made," because on other days Manthara would say, "Don't be a fool like your mother." Kaikeyi could not be like her father or her mother. Yet she had grown to look exactly like her mother—a beauty, Manthara had conceded. Who and what Kaikeyi would become was not entirely in her own control.

CHAPTER 7

With the Love of a Mother

As Manthara left the princess, she itched to seek an audience with King Ashvapati. She did not like the alliance with Ayodhya; she did not like the emperor. Kaikeyi's obvious infatuation with him made it all the more concerning. Yes, the girl had tried to hide it, but was there anything about Kaikeyi that Manthara did not know?

Although night had snuck up on them before she could leave Kaikeyi's chamber, Manthara was on the edge of going straight to the king. Before she did that, however, she had to collect her thoughts and be sure of what she wanted to say. She paused in the unlit hallway, feeling like a spirit in the darkness. Releasing an exasperated huff, she admitted to herself that her thoughts were jumbled. Too emotional. She leaned on her cane, hobbling toward her room. When another servant passed her in the corridor, she pushed herself up with her cane and attempted to glide forward. The servant bowed and moved ahead. Manthara did not acknowledge the gesture. She should have been used to the deference of the other servants by now. She liked her elevated position, but it still felt uneasy, like someone might turn around and make a joke out of her again. It was also difficult to discern who was genuine in their supplications and who was merely dutiful. No doubt the other servants had coveted her position from the beginning. But King Ashvapati had chosen Manthara to mother his daughter—not any of them.

When Manthara walked into her room, she did not light any of the candles or wicks in the brass night-lights. The darkness suited her just fine, the amorphous shapes around her as deformed as she was. Though her feet ached, Manthara paced slowly in the darkness of her room. She had put her cane aside; in her private chambers she didn't care what she looked like, and the thump-thump of it had become synonymous with the immense effort she made during the day. She couldn't bear that sound.

Manthara let her head and arms hang loosely toward the floor, surrendering to gravity for a moment. She sighed deeply. Though Kaikeyi insisted on treating Manthara's hump as some sort of magical treasure chest, Manthara had never been able to adopt or embrace that thought. It was like having your worst enemy sit on your back, growing meatier and heavier every year and jabbing you with knives in your most tender spots. Just to lift her head upright, she had to cajole her neck, or curse it, whatever it took to convince it that she was still its mistress. It had only gotten worse with each of her forty-eight years, despite occasional ministrations by the king's physician. He had told her long ago what to expect: it would tax her lungs and heart and worsen with every year, which it had.

She resumed her walking, letting her head hang. The tendons in her neck exhaled with relief. Her eyes rested on her feet, which peeked out beneath the gray silk robe with each step. Manthara had to gather her thoughts before it grew too late.

"It *is* already too late," the princess had said. But she was just a girl; she didn't know how easily and quickly things could change and be changed. That was the world of politics.

"It is never too late," Manthara said now, into the darkness.

She had long ago fallen into the habit of speaking to herself out loud. "It is precisely in the moment when a course is set that one has to intervene."

That's what Manthara liked to tell herself. It gave her hope and power. She felt determined to change what she could, when there were so many things she could not. Though she meant to focus on her misgiving about Kaikeyi's betrothal, she felt her mind gravitate toward self-pity. It held immense power over her. It wasn't a pathetic self-pity, but an empowering one, and it was interwoven with every thought she had.

Her hunchback had branded her for life as an outcast. Even before that, she had barely been tolerated. Her belonging to society was conditional and depended entirely on the acceptance she got from people like Ashvapati and Kaikeyi. In order to survive, Manthara's primary aim was to maintain those relationships. They anchored her and justified her existence, when every other pair of eyes demanded to know what such a misfit was doing among them.

"You must be clever when you speak to Ashvapati," she told herself. "Nothing could be more crucial."

She was not afraid to speak her mind in front of him. But he had become completely intolerant of sentimentality, especially in women.

"Ever since that foolish woman," Manthara muttered, meaning Kaikeyi's real mother.

By the gods, Ashvapati had done everything in his power to turn his one daughter into a son. Kaikeyi acted like a man and moved easily in a man's sphere. It made Manthara giddy sometimes, the way Kaikeyi could match wills with a man and win. She won every single time!

But Manthara was also aware of how the gaze of men's eyes followed the princess. Kaikeyi herself ignored it. She was forever preoccupied with this mare or that steed, a new foal, or the splendid new trick she'd learned. It was on Manthara's say-so that Ashvapati had assigned four of his most trusted men to guard her. No man was to be trusted with a girl of Kaikeyi's beauty. Manthara did what she could to safeguard her charge.

When Manthara's feet began to send warnings up her calves, she surrendered and collapsed on her chair, falling back onto the plush cushions and rubbing her cheek against the soft satin. She had to get to the bottom of this. Time was ticking. As she mentally prodded her psyche, she tried to find why she disliked that handsome emperor, for, yes, he was handsome, even extraordinarily so. That was enough of a reason for Manthara to personally dislike him. "But that's private," she reminded herself, "and even petty. It will never suffice as an objection." She concealed this prejudice even from Kaikeyi, one of the most beautiful women in Kekaya, as her mother had been. Manthara couldn't afford to have any wedge between herself and Kaikeyi.

"Kaikeyi must never know that you feel stung when you see her beauty."

Manthara couldn't admire that beauty the way others did. Sometimes it made her stomach curl into knots that scarred her organs. It was unspeakably unfair.

"If only ugly, misshapen people like me were treated the same as the beautiful ones, then I wouldn't care. But it has never been that way, and it will never be that way."

Those who were born with symmetrical and anatomically perfect bodies treated Manthara as if she purposefully was unlike them. The very sight of Manthara was a blemish on their perfect lives. She saw it in their dismissive gestures, their unavailable eyes, and their empty greetings. The exception was, of course, Ashvapati. Manthara was sure even an impartial judge would find Kekaya's king superior to the visiting emperor. This thought brought her back to the problem at hand, and she again tried to pinpoint the source of her anxiety.

"You really do not know this Emperor Dasharatha enough to make any sound objection," she reminded herself. "Put him aside and search for the true cause of your misgivings."

It had been a long day, full of unexpected news. The plush cushions on the chair began to swallow her, so she pushed herself up, sitting as upright as her body allowed. She opened her mind to clues, seeking clarity. It had always been her strength: her intuition and her ability to articulate it. Ashvapati had commented on it more than once.

A memory surfaced. Yes! Manthara thought. This would guide her.

Kaikeyi had been three years younger, nearing her thirteenth birthday, and suddenly her transformation had been complete. Her small budding breasts became full. Her body filled out and curves appeared. Manthara had just turned forty-five; her cycles had dried up, ending her chance to have her own children, if that had ever been a choice. As Manthara ceased to be a fertile woman, Kaikeyi became one. Though Manthara had been carefully watching her charge and had anticipated this event, she had not been prepared for the upheaval it brought on. Kaikeyi was no longer her child, and Manthara had panicked. In a rare display of emotion, she ran to Ashvapati with tears pouring, pointing out the girl's maturity and demanding that Kaikeyi be guarded vigilantly. She still remembered clearly how the king had instantly shied away when he saw her emotions. Manthara had been upset enough to keep going anyway. She begged the king not to marry Kaikeyi off. As though Manthara was not being hysterical, the king promised her that he was in no hurry to part with his daughter. He had commented that Kaikeyi now looked exactly like her mother, and Manthara's shock at that made her stop crying. Ashvapati *never* spoke of the exiled queen. Shortly after, he had told Kaikeyi the truth about her birth mother and the reason for her exile. This revelation did not seem to affect Kaikeyi at all; she had no recollection of ever having a mother, other than Manthara. Since then, they had dismissed countless suitors. Though Ashvapati never announced a contest for his daughter's hand, Keyi's beauty made suitors bold.

"Or desperate, more like," Manthara spat.

There were few things Manthara detested as much as a man claiming to be in love. Dogs, all of them. Manthara knew it was carnal, nothing else. It was so elemental and yet men and women liked to give it big names and obscure it from what it was.

Manthara stifled a yawn. Something fluttered in her rib cage, and she was compelled to stand up. She was ready to face the king now. Never mind that it was the middle of the night. This was important. She had tarried long enough. She had to seek an audience now, before she missed the opportunity.

As she grabbed her cane and rushed out as fast as a hunchback could, she considered what the memory had come to tell her. What would she really say to Ashvapati?

The guards at the door appeared sleepy and let her in without a word. Manthara was a frequent night visitor. This had certainly given rise to rumors about her and the king's relationship. All lies, of course. It secretly delighted her that people could imagine something so preposterous. Ashvapati hated womankind altogether.

Manthara tiptoed in, barely using her cane. Ashvapati sat in the innermost part of his chambers, looking into the fire that burned there. How many times had she seen him sit exactly like this?

She paused for a long moment, regarding his profile.

"Yes, Manthara?" he said, without turning to look at her.

He must have heard her cane, though she had used it very lightly.

"Sit," he said, waving her to the seat next to him.

It never failed to move her when he acknowledged her like this. So natural, so easy. As though she was his equal. Carefully, almost tenderly, Manthara sat on the seat opposite Ashvapati.

"You are worried about Kaikeyi's future," he stated.

Manthara sighed deeply. He always understood her.

"I'm afraid this marriage will entail only suffering and heartbreak for Kaikeyi," she said. The old memory had clarified to her how much she abhorred the idea of marriage altogether. She did not want Kaikeyi to get married to anyone!

"Why do you say this?"

"What else is there in carnal relationships?" Manthara asked. "Surely the emperor seeks to enjoy her young flesh, and no more."

Ashvapati turned to stone; not even his chest moved with a breath. Manthara shuddered and reminded herself to tread carefully. He was a man, after all. There were limits to what he could understand. "I've seen firsthand what marriage can do to the most intelligent person."

She meant this as a not-so-subtle hint about his failed marriage. Though Manthara was unspeakably loyal to Ashvapati, she did not think he was a whole person anymore or a very lovable one at that. He was like Manthara. Only a great few could see beyond the obvious and find the hidden gold. Manthara actually smiled in the darkness, closing her eyes. She liked comparing herself to Ashvapati, her lifelong friend. Manthara felt more relaxed, seeing the contours now of her misgivings.

"You counsel against marriage altogether?" Ashvapati asked.

Manthara opened her eyes, staring into the fire with him.

As much as Manthara wished Kaikeyi would stay unmarried, the truth was plain to see in every curve of Kaikeyi's body. Manthara's own curve had deflected the desires of men, but Kaikeyi's invited them.

"No, Your Highness. That would be folly. But am I the only one suspicious of the fact that he has sired no children until now."

"That is the first valid point you make."

"Well?"

"He is a man of his word."

Manthara waited. But that was all the answer she got. Evidently, she *was* the only one who thought in obvious arithmetic. Manthara was forced to grasp for straws again.

"Princess Kaikeyi is a child of Kekaya. Is it wise to send her so far, to a place where she will always be an outsider?"

In truth, it was in Manthara's best interest to stay in Kekaya. Here the crippled were welcome, even honored. That would not be the case in Ayodhya.

"Ayodhya has a flawless reputation," Ashvapati said. "It is grand beyond imagination. Its common inhabitants possess more culture and knowledge than the most elevated Kekayan."

"Cultured folk are often the most cruel," Manthara countered.

Ashvapati looked at her then.

Manthara's tormentors had made it clear that she only had one acceptable identity. She had the ugly face of a witch, and her body agreed. Deformity was its true nature. She had, over the years, made sure to oust those aggressors from the palace. Not one of the eight who had attacked her was allowed anywhere near the palace. Manthara would have liked to do even more, but there were limits to her power. Sitting beside her king, Manthara rubbed her eyes and gnashed her teeth. Most people were cruel and judgmental, like those children had been.

"There was only ever one person who didn't laugh at me," she said, leaning toward him, unable to check her adoration.

"You have to accompany Kaikeyi to Ayodhya," Ashvapati said. "She will need every ally she can get." Then he added, almost to himself, "Only a fool would turn down the bride-price the emperor is willing to pay."

Manthara agreed with that. Fate had dealt Kaikeyi a mighty hand. It had its flaws, but they were not insurmountable.

"I'm going with her," Manthara said.

She didn't have to say the obvious: that she had invested too much into Kaikeyi already, that she had no life without the princess. Ashvapati might have smiled, but it was hard to tell with the fire flickering across his face. He was not prone to show emotion.

"I'm glad that you sought me, Manthara. Your apprehension confirms what I was pondering as you entered. The minds of men are fickle. Political climates shift constantly. My daughter will be the third queen, usually a place of limited power and repute."

"I warned her of this too," Manthara said.

"You know the ways of women," he said, as though Manthara was not one. "They are cunning and selfish. They are sweet until they get what they want. Those other queens will try to undermine Kaikeyi and put her in her place." He turned to Manthara, his eyes black like coals. "My daughter is *not* entering this agreement as a mere third wife. Dasharatha promises to revere her as his foremost consort. She will be the queen mother. Her son will sit on the throne. She will rule as the foremost queen. The kingdom will be hers. Do not let her forget this."

Manthara stared at Ashvapati, moved by his unexpected vehemence. There was a fanatic devotion there that reason could not deter. He had a vision for his daughter, and he wanted Manthara to safeguard it. Manthara's heart swelled.

"Manthara, you must be my eyes and ears in Ayodhya. You must be vigilant against the politics of the capital. In fact, I have something for you."

He stood and retrieved something from his desk and handed it to Manthara. Manthara received the heavy book and tilted it toward the fire, peering at the title. *The Laws of Manu*, written by Manu, the first man. It described in detail the laws for all mankind.

Copies of this work were extremely rare, for the sacred laws and scriptures were memorized and handed down by word of mouth. From man to man. Priest to priest.

"This is forbidden for women to read," she whispered in awe. Ashvapati said no more. He gave Manthara one of his penetrating, almost appraising looks, as though she would need every bit of aid to accomplish the task ahead of her. Then he turned his gaze back to the fire. Manthara nodded and stood up, understanding that the audience was over. Clutching *The Laws of Manu* to her chest, she hobbled out on her cane. The Lord knew she would need many weapons to emerge victorious in Ayodhya. Thankfully, this book was not her only source of knowledge. She had taken poisons and survived, and she still counted two Vishakanyas as her dearest friends. Manthara would not disappoint her king, who had done so much for her, who had given her a place in the world and a child to love. She would not let *anyone* in Ayodhya forget Kaikeyi's worth.

CHAPTER 8

The Flags on the Chariots

Kausalya never took it for granted that Dasharatha would return from one of his journeys. She had counted the days since her husband had left, as she always did. And now Dasharatha was on his way home. This time it had been only weeks, not years. Thirty-seven days had passed, and she was content; he had not lingered in Kekaya longer than necessary. Two of his riders had arrived the night before, promising that the king would arrive the following day with, they said, "a prize he had not expected to find." Kausalya looked forward to seeing the king's latest treasure. Not a day had passed without a prayer for his and Ayodhya's welfare.

That morning, she lit the fire lamps at the golden altars for him. Usually she did not pray for the fulfillment of her own desires, trusting the lord within to guide her thoughts and actions. On this day, she prayed that her husband would return with a plan for Ayodhya's future. Kausalya closed her eyes as the smoke from the incense began to swirl around her. The attending priests chanted the morning mantras, and Kausalya softly sang along. When she opened her eyes, the altar before her gleamed with gold and cleanliness. There were fresh flowers in vases and garlands wrapped around the pillars. It was the most pleasing sight, all in the honor of the thirty gods. Kausalya made her offering into the fire that burned day and night, then bowed to the deity of Vishnu and left the altar room.

Dawn brightened the palace as Kausalya went to Dasharatha's private chambers. Though she trusted her servants, it felt right to personally make sure all was in order there. She had arranged for his favorite foods to be prepared, and she would stand in attendance herself. These were the small efforts she made for him, to show him that even though she was queen, he was her first priority.

When Kausalya stepped into the king's chamber, she was pleased to see that her servants had meticulously followed her instructions: the champak flowers were fresh, and every cloth item in the room had been replaced with fresh ones. As Kausalya's gaze swept across the new canopy, the linen on the bed, the curtains, and the hangings on the wall, she commented on all she saw. The servants with her would send the praise on to the others. But when Kausalya walked to the alcove adjacent to Dasharatha's large balcony, the servants remained at a distance. Kausalya was careful not to touch or move anything. It was here that he kept his personal mementos: arrows from battles, scrolls, books, and certain gems that he prized. He had kept several of his boyhood bows, and they were hung on the wall. Kausalya carefully dusted the surfaces with a rose-scented towel. The king would know she had been here. In the early years of their marriage, Kausalya had often left a small gift for him here: a rainbow-hued gem, a white peacock feather, a portrait of him that she had drawn.

Satisfied, Kausalya went on to inspect the eating area. The tables were ready with golden plates and vessels. Here, the champak flowers floated in water bowls, and Kausalya took a deep breath, enjoying the smell of citrus. Now the queen called for a fire lamp, ignited the camphor she had brought, and walked around the large chamber waving the fragrant smoke into every corner.

When all this was done, the sun was high in the sky. The king would be here soon. With a slight twinge of nervousness, Kausalya departed from her usual duties and hurried to her chamber. Would her appearance please Dasharatha? She had dressed with extra care, knowing that he would be home. He liked her to wear sky blue. She glanced at herself in the mirror and confirmed that the light blue silks suited her. She called to a maidservant, asking her to twine a garland of flowers into her hair. As the maid released Kausalya's hair from its braid, it bounded up around her head and shoulders with a life of its own. Her hair was thick and black, despite her years. Kausalya inquired about the maid's family and her well-being. Kausalya always maintained cordial and close relationships with all of them. With expert fingers, the maid tamed Kausalya's hair, entwining the garland and arranging it on the top of her head.

Kausalya dabbed some sandalwood oil onto her fingers and lightly massaged her temples. There had been a time when seeing her husband had twisted her stomach into knots. Those were the hard years, when they realized that their union would be unfruitful. She had felt barren and unattractive, the opposite of a fertile woman. Kausalya had always felt that he was not completely open with her on this topic. He avoided it, almost like a child, hoping it will go away.

The maids secured Kausalya's crown against her hair. Though Kausalya harbored no vanity, she was pleased with the woman she saw in the looking glass. She had been told her eyes were large and pleasant, and she saw the kindness in them today. Left to her own devices, she might not have been so aware of what she looked like. But as she was the queen, every woman in Ayodhya looked up to her. Women's eyes were often critical, and there were high expectations on Kausalya to look and dress like a queen, as if acting like one was not task enough. She was glad to be considered a typical Ayodhyan beauty, neither striking nor plain but pleasant, with light skin, large eyes, and shapely cheekbones.

Kausalya turned to the head maid at the entrance. "Divya, please go to the treasury and ask to see Daksha, the head accountant. Inform him that I will be unable to come today. The king's welcome may take most of my day. Tell Daksha that I promise to bring a report of the expenses incurred in Kekaya."

Divya bowed and left.

"We are absorbed in our preparation to welcome our king," Kausalya said to the other servants. "But Daksha and the experts in other departments continue their work diligently. Whether the king is here or not, arriving or departing, Daksha keeps immaculate accounts of our expenditure and income."

It was easy to consider oneself the center of the universe, while in fact a multitude of important activities were always taking place.

"Yet you, Great Queen," the maid servant said, "must welcome the king *and* keep track of the expenditures."

It was true. Daksha and the other treasures were invaluable assets, but Kausalya alone knew the extent of Ayodhya's wealth. "I went to sleep too late," she muttered to herself with a sigh.

"You are the first to rise and the last to sleep," the other maid noted. "We do not know how you do it."

In a moment of self-critique, Kausalya noted how tired the tender skin under her eyes was. Quickly she turned her attention to the garland of fragrant flowers in her hair. It complemented her delicate diamond crown and the blue silk gown. Dasharatha would be pleased. He would arrive any moment now. Kausalya signaled to her maids that she needed no more attention. She stood and picked up the hem of her dress and hurried out, followed as always by a host of servants and guards, and ascended to the high towers. The attendants waiting there informed her that the king was fast approaching the northern gates. Kausalya had waited hardly a few minutes before she lifted her hand in the signal.

The conch shells blew and the northern gate opened. Since the king's entourage was small this time, Kausalya did not wait but immediately descended from the tower. At the bottom, she met Sumitra, who was dressed in summer yellow, with a sparkling, transparent veil.

"Well chosen, Sumitra," Kausalya said, admiring her co-wife.

Kausalya quickly embraced the other queen. There was so much innocence in Sumitra's being; one adored her as one did a child. Kausalya had come to love her wholeheartedly. Together they reached the courtyard just in time. The king was here!

"He will notice you wearing the color he prefers," Sumitra said.

It was such a trivial matter, really, yet it did please Kausalya that he noticed. "You made an excellent color choice too, Sumitra. If I know him at all, he will compare you to a pleasing sunrise."

"It is you he seeks," Sumitra said simply, in her way of saying just the thing that would warm Kausalya.

Kausalya squeezed Sumitra's hand, as if they were young girls. She began to search for her husband's chariot with its sun-gilded flag. Once she found it, she kept her eyes on the chariot, waiting for the moment she could look upon her king's beloved face. When his chariot got closer, she saw Sumantra acting as charioteer, but the chariot was empty. Quickly, she thought back on what the messengers had said: "The king will return with a prize he had not expected to find." A sudden anxiety gripped her heart. The homecoming ritual had been disrupted. It was the first time in all these years that he had not been where she expected him to be.

In the grip of this emotion, Kausalya saw an unusual sight: a girl on horseback. She wore her hair loose, she dressed in leathers, and she carried herself with an ease Kausalya had seen only on a man. She was extremely beautiful, the bloom of womanhood upon her. Kausalya knew this age well. She had arranged many marriages for girls this age, between thirteen and sixteen. Although to a man, the girl on the horse would look like a grown woman, Kausalya knew differently. But who was she? Certainly someone of importance, for she did not ride alone. Four guards formed a protective square around her. Their horses were bright white with shiny black manes and tails, an unusual and expensive breed.

Just then, Dasharatha rode up to the girl. Kausalya's heart skipped a beat. The girl tossed her hair and smiled at the king. Kausalya completely froze. Every cell in her being knew. But it could not be true. Dasharatha and the horse-riding girl were lovers.

"She is young enough to be my daughter," Kausalya whispered.

Sumitra leaned toward her, thinking Kausalya had spoken to her. Sumitra's face was unchanged. She had not noticed anything awry.

Kausalya closed her eyes, just for a moment. When she opened them, she was who she had been: Ayodhya's queen, Dasharatha's first wife, and a worthy woman who held her own. Nothing could change this, not even the words she heard next.

"Welcome Ayodhya's new queen!" Dasharatha called out.

He had joined hands with the girl and now raised their clasped hands into the air. Their horses danced together, hers black and his white. The king's exuberance was contagious; heartfelt greetings filled the air. Kausalya took this news more calmly. She did not join the celebration, but she would greet the new queen as befitted her station. Kausalya would reflect on her personal feelings at a later time. She reached for Sumitra's hand again, seeking comfort in the known. Dasharatha rode up to them as they stood there hand in hand. He dismounted from his horse, landing in front of Kausalya, his presence hitting her like a strong wind. She looked deep into those eyes that she loved and felt relief wash through her; he was still the same Dasharatha. Yet as he spoke, there was a quiver of excitement in his voice that Kausalya had never heard before.

"Her name is Kaikeyi," he said softly. "She is King Ashvapati's daughter and now my wife." The pleasure in his voice was clear.

Kausalya nodded. "I will welcome her as befits a queen of Ayodhya."

"I hope she will do the same," he said. "You deserve the highest honor. But Kaikeyi does not know our customs, and she is young. Be patient with her." He smiled at Sumitra and briefly touched their hands.

Mounting his horse, he called Kaikeyi forward. "Meet my other queens."

He exchanged a few private words with the girl and then rode away, the king's men following him. Kausalya knew how many responsibilities waited for him. But he had not commented on her dress or Sumitra's as he usually would have. He had not promised to seek her out later. He had not asked if she would be in his quarters later on. It wasn't just the duties of a king that preoccupied his mind. As Kausalya turned to face the new queen, she thought again, *Kaikeyi could be my daughter,* and then, *I will take her under my wing.*

Long experience with people had taught her that kindness and forbearance was the best course. Kausalya turned to the girl. "I will make all the arrangements for you and your people."

A princess never came into a marriage alone. Kaikeyi's retinue began to grow around her, but it was smaller than Kausalya expected of a princess. Kekaya was reputed to be a wealthy kingdom, but perhaps its wealth was bound up in their horses. Kausalya's gaze swept over them, beginning her thoughts on where to house the newcomers. Two servant girls of Kaikeyi's age who appeared to be twins were looking around curiously. An elderly woman with a hunched back lumbered down from a carriage and stood next to the new queen, the contrast between them striking. Kaikeyi was tall, with a proud, erect back. Her beautiful features hid all her feelings. The hunchback was half the girl's height, painfully bent over. But she did nothing to hide her displeasure. She stared at Kausalya, looking her up and down. And there they stood, nobody moving. The young girl did not move to greet Kausalya in any way. According to Ayodhya's customs, she should have touched Kausalya's feet, but even a smile would have sufficed.

Following her own heart, Kausalya went forward and embraced Kaikeyi. Nothing good would come from alienating the new queen. She hugged Kaikeyi to her heart, but the girl in her arms did not yield an inch. She stood stiff as a pillar.

"You are *not* going to be friends," the hunchback said behind Kaikeyi, and Kaikeyi's stiffness became unbearable.

Kausalya's arms lost their strength and dropped to her sides.

"You are rivals," the old woman hissed, looking at the young queen.

Kausalya blinked rapidly, unable to hide her shock.

Kaikeyi looked rather shocked too. "My rival?" she said, and looked more closely at Kausalya. "But she is old."

Kausalya's forty-one years claimed her face and her body. She had not felt them before. Compared to the girl in front of her, she was not just a woman, but an old woman. It was true. But Kausalya couldn't believe what she was hearing. The two in front of her came from a world that she did not understand; they spoke and behaved in a way that was unacceptable. Kaikeyi seemed to have no respect for her elders and no premonition that age would claim her too one day. Kausalya took a deep breath. She was determined to be kind to this misguided girl. The young queen would, after all, be residing in Ayodhya now, a place that Kausalya knew like her own heart. She knew the name of every servant and was a close friend with the eight ministers and their wives. These were just a few sites of her power. Kausalya was not a queen in name alone. Kausalya had also noted that the newcomers had offered no respect to Sumitra, treating her as though she was no one of import. Kausalya turned her eyes on Kaikeyi, ignoring the malevolent hunchback.

"Is it wise to alienate me so soon?" she asked. "Give me a chance to be your friend. Sumitra and I live in harmony. You can too."

"Is that a threat?" the old woman demanded, again cutting in before Kaikeyi could speak.

Kausalya sighed. It seemed that everything she said would be mangled today. Were customs in Kekaya so different? "You must be tired from the journey," she said instead. "Perhaps we shall speak another day."

"Perhaps," the girl said, raising her eyebrows and tossing her hair again.

She was not without some of her servant's malice. Kaikeyi turned away from Kausalya the way a child rejects a displeasing toy. Though Kaikeyi had let her hunchbacked servant speak for her, she took the lead now. She mounted her black horse and pursued the king, calling his name. Her four guards on their white horses followed her meekly. Hearing Kaikeyi's call, the entire party of men stopped and waited for her. Though the girl did not look back at Kausalya, her entire countenance seemed to say, "See, *I* am the queen here now. They harken to me."

The hunchback bored her eyes into Kausalya, asking her to *see*. As it was, Kausalya could not take her eyes from the scene ahead. Kaikeyi rode up to Dasharatha, leaned in, and whispered something in his ear. His arm snaked around her waist. He pulled her close and pressed his cheek against her hair, as if it was not broad daylight in public view. Kausalya looked away. The flags on top of the chariots fluttered on the gentle breeze. It was a beautiful day in a prosperous kingdom, even if it did not feel that way anymore.

Kausalya turned away, feeling as brokenhearted as a young girl. It wasn't just the woman in her that was alarmed; the passion between Dasharatha and Kaikeyi was too impulsive, too reckless, too much. It wasn't good for the kingdom. Kausalya would have to use her power as senior queen to make Dasharatha see caution. He could love the new one, yes, but he must *never* give her power. Kaikeyi would leave it to rot in the hands of Manthara. And from what Kausalya had gathered, Manthara would gladly tend to the rottenness until the stink suffocated all of Ayodhya. Kausalya would not allow this, not as long as she stood at the heart of the kingdom, by Dasharatha's side.

CHAPTER 9

The Perfect City

Each morning in Ayodhya began at the golden altars. It was the first of Ayodhya's routines that Kaikeyi was introduced to. Kaikeyi joined the king and the other two queens in this ritual. On the first day, Dasharatha eagerly walked her around the temple, which he described as the heart of the palace. Like the palace, every home, however humble, had an altar, a place to pray and begin the day. Here in the inner sanctum, the thirty gods were worshipped, each with a shrine of their own. The holy three—Brahma, Vishnu, Shiva—were placed in the middle of the vault and, among them, Vishnu shone brightly. The deity, made of solid gold, depicted a perfectly carved Vishnu resting on the coils of Ananta-Sesha, the thousand-headed serpent.

The golden altars were magnificent; there was no doubt about it. But Kaikeyi immediately felt off-kilter. For one, Manthara was not by her side. Crippled or deformed ones were not allowed in auspicious places. Two, the temple was Kausalya's domain. The senior queen was the first one there and the last to leave. When Kaikeyi stepped into the temple the first time, she thought at once of Kausalya's embrace. The fragrances that clung to Kausalya were all from the temple: camphor, sandalwood, and frankincense. The result was that she smelled pure, clean, and warm. Kaikeyi again was made to observe Kausalya in her element.

Kausalya tended to the altars and the rituals with an easy, loving hand. Every morning the garlands were made fresh, the wilted flowers replaced with fresh ones. There was an elaborate structure to the way the incense and the fire lamps were lit. Fires within the temple constantly burned. One was for the king's health and victory, another to remove threats from Ayodhya.

On the first day, after Dasharatha showed Kaikeyi each shrine, they sat in front of Vishnu's altar. Following the ritual's conclusion, Dasharatha wanted to speak about the gods. Kausalya, Sumitra, and others whom Kaikeyi did not know gathered around the king as he spoke.

"Scholars, who have time for such things, take pleasure in arguing who among the gods is foremost. Vishnu and Shiva are the top contenders. In my youth I took great pleasure in studying the Vedas and discerning the truth for myself. You see, any person can use the Vedas to his advantage, and knowledge is a dangerous weapon in the wrong hands. It is therefore not allowed for all people to have direct access to these secrets. We have to go through someone qualified, a priest who lives his life in study and contemplation.

"Vishnu, however, is the only god who does not live within the realm of the universe. He is reachable only through a heart connection, which takes one to his abode, the Ocean of Milk. There he reclines in eternal rest on his black serpent, overseeing the cosmos. He is the most difficult to reach, and by my reckoning then, the lord of lords. Let us not forget that Brahma, the creator, grew from a lotus whose stem was connected to Vishnu's navel."

As the discussion took place, Kaikeyi looked at the king's lips, and her mind wandered.

The first night with the king had made the deepest impressions on Kaikeyi. To her surprise, she spoke the language of passion, although she had no prior knowledge of it. What little she knew, she had gathered from observing Kekaya's horses and overhearing her brother talk. Manthara was a closed book on this topic, because, Kaikeyi suspected now, she didn't want to reveal her ignorance. With Dasharatha, Kaikeyi became a woman; he brought her to a new world. She belonged effortlessly. She could not describe it in words to Manthara, not even if she had wanted to.

Kausalya turned to Kaikeyi and asked, "Which god or goddess do you worship in Kekaya?"

All eyes turned to Kaikeyi. She quickly brought her mind back to the golden altars. The silk cloths rustled in the silence as people fidgeted, waiting for her response.

"We pray to Vishnu, like you do," Kaikeyi answered. "But truthfully told, we do not observe rituals like this. We are horse people, nature people, and our days are spent outdoors. My father, the king, spends hours in the forest, learning what he can from the animals, whose speech he understands."

"It took me a while to get accustomed as well," Sumitra said, with a shy smile.

Then they waited, expecting Kaikeyi to say something more, perhaps that she recognized Ayodhya's ways as superior. Kaikeyi said nothing.

The dancing girls began their worship, and this too was a new sight for Kaikeyi, though she was schooled in the arts. She herself had learned and excelled in the art of dance, and she recognized and understood the gestures and movements of the dancers. As she watched them for a while, moving from altar to altar, she felt the restlessness in her bones. She didn't want to watch. She wanted to dance!

Instinctively, however, she knew that she could not. Ayodhya's royalty were meant to be reserved and subdued. They were meant to watch and to be content as observers.

That afternoon, Kaikeyi settled into her new quarters, getting to know the servants assigned to her. The way people spoke here was slower, more formal, and decorous than in Kekaya, where the speech was efficient and minimal. Kaikeyi found that she lacked patience to hear Ayodhyans out. She wanted to be simple, direct, and quick. Similarly, she did not like sitting through long hours of prayer and worship, as both Kausalya and Sumitra did every morning. What was the purpose?

After just a few days of the morning routines, even the fragrances of the golden altars came to mean monotony to Kaikeyi. The smoke from incense gave her headaches, and when the priests flung another ladle of ghee on the fire, Kaikeyi longed to scream and run away, wanting the fresh wind in her hair, not the suffocating air left after the fire had devoured the rest. How could Dasharatha stand it?

Kaikeyi's father had taught her that the Lord was most present in nature. The best way to connect with him was in communion with creatures like horses and other animals, who had a simple, uncomplicated knowing of the Lord above. Whomever she tried to articulate this to looked at her as though she was an uncouth illiterate.

There was much to learn here, and every lesson told Kaikeyi how little she knew, how uncultured she was, and what a little girl she truly was in comparison to Kausalya. This feeling only grew during the celebration of her marriage to Dasharatha.

A grand feast was arranged in Kaikeyi's honor. It was much more spectacular than their wedding had been in Kekaya, though her father had spared no cost. Here, Dasharatha introduced Kaikeyi to a million important people, and when they sat down to eat, there was an overwhelming abundance of exquisite food. First they were served drinks: cool sugarcane juice spiced with lemon and ginger, creamy yogurt sweetened with honey and mango pulp, and rose-scented water. Then came dish after dish. The number of rice preparations alone astounded Kaikeyi. She tasted lemon rice with saffron and roasted cashews, rice with tamarind and curry leaves, rice laced with cumin and mustard seeds. When she was about to taste her fourth rice, Dasharatha leaned over and told her to save space for all the remaining dishes. The feast unfolded in this fashion, unveiling twenty to fifty varieties of each dish. Kaikeyi very soon could eat no more. It wasn't that she had overindulged. She simply began to understand the magnitude of her own lacking. She watched Kausalya move easily among all the dignitaries, knowing what to say to make them laugh and be at ease.

Kaikeyi observed the older queen the way Manthara would, and she saw what Kausalya was doing: she was displaying her power. Every gesture and smile exuded smug satisfaction. Though the feast was meant to welcome Kaikeyi to Ayodhya, all it did was cement Kaikeyi's knowledge that she did not belong. Even the head priest, Vasishta, a holy one, looked long and hard at Kaikeyi, without a trace of feeling. Kaikeyi felt all the food she had consumed turn in her gut. But she was a warrior. Their ill feelings could not subdue her. As soon as Kaikeyi could, however, she excused herself and returned to her chambers. She came away from the feast in her honor knowing how small her chances were at besting Kausalya in her role as senior queen. Kausalya's warning from the first day seemed true. Had it been wise to alienate her?

In her quarters, she was surrounded by Manthara and the twins, Sukhi and Dukhi. With her usual flair, Manthara revealed things she had heard, things that proved Kausalya's devious nature. Ayodhya was desperate for an heir, and Kausalya had instructed the servants to see Kaikeyi simply as a means to an end. The twins always agreed with Manthara in a suspiciously exaggerated manner. In turn, Kaikeyi shared what she had observed, revealing more of herself than she should have; she got exhausted by her own words. Intuiting this, she turned to silence and began reading a book on the Sun dynasty's genealogy. She did not notice at once when the king arrived. Sukhi and Dukhi stood up and moved away with Manthara. Kaikeyi looked up, seeing the king standing there admiring her, the way one admires a piece of art. It was Manthara's art, for she was the one who had overseen the decoration of Kaikeyi's person.

Now Kaikeyi allowed herself to be seen. It was a pleasant, even empowering, feeling. She saw in the king's eyes that he thought her more beautiful than anyone else. Who was the more powerful queen now?

"I know almost all the kings now," Kaikeyi said proudly to Dasharatha, closing the book. His was the last name on the page.

"Good. Then you'll be on the same level as an eight-year-old Ayodhyan," he said. He knew that she enjoyed being teased.

"Here I am, increasing my learning and you mock me."

"I'm sure there are many things you know that I don't," he offered.

"Yes?"

The king waited until the servants had left before he moved closer to her and spoke. "You have a way with horses that makes me think you speak their language. Your balance and precision on horseback are astounding. You are quicker with your swords and knives than I am. You are fierce like a tigress. I pity the man who makes himself your enemy."

"I sound wonderful," she said. "I should be the queen!"

"You are a queen."

"The third one," she said.

His scrutiny of her turned shrewd. She didn't like it and amended, still in a joking tone, "No matter. The kingdom is already mine. My son will be on the throne."

"Is that so?" he asked. "Where is that son of yours then?"

The joking mood between them vanished, just like that. Manthara's recent whispers gained ground within Kaikeyi. A strange look appeared in Dasharatha's eyes. Without knowing the details of his desperation, Kaikeyi thought she knew: he expected her to produce a son. That's why he had married her.

"That's what they say, you know," she said, and there was a tremor in her voice. "That all I am is a womb. Not a woman, not a warrior, and certainly not a queen to be respected. Only a womb."

"Who said this to you?" he asked, sitting by her side. "It's cruel and unnecessary. I will have them reprimanded."

"You wouldn't."

"I don't understand."

"Would you reprimand your senior queen?"

"Kausalya?" he said with a smile and leaned away. "Kausalya would not say such a thing. It's tasteless. Kausalya is not."

"Your wise and royal senior queen has an unpleasant side that you, being a man, obviously have not seen."

"Did Kausalya herself say this to you?" he challenged.

"No, but . . ."

"Let me guess. It was Manthara."

"Don't turn this around on Manthara!"

"Why not?" he demanded, raising his voice. "I'm not blind. I see the way she looks at us, at everyone in Ayodhya. You have no proof that Kausalya said those words. This is exactly how baseless rumors take root. I tell you this. Manthara is the cruel one, throwing unnecessary barbs at you."

"I know her better than you," Kaikeyi said. "If you came here to sing the praise of your darling Kausalya, why don't you go spend the evening with her?"

"Maybe I will!"

He stormed out of Kaikeyi's quarters.

Kaikeyi was alone. Perhaps she always would be. For who in this new place would be her friend? Thinking that the king would be with her through the night, her companions had left. Kaikeyi was too proud to call them back. Kaikeyi thought about Kausalya, her rival. Was the king with Kausalya at this moment? The thought made her whole body churn with unease. She could not tolerate it.

As she lay alone in her royal bed, Kaikeyi understood how vulnerable she was. From now on, she had to do everything to protect herself. She would have to move forward cautiously with the emperor. He was more powerful than she was, an experienced man, and she just a girl. When she relived his touch, a thrill ran through her body. But she could not be a fool.

The next morning, Kaikeyi decided not to attend the morning prayers. Instead, she would pray in her own way. With blunt determination, she donned her familiar leather vest and breeches, noting the sweet scent of dry sweat in the familiar gear. She deftly wore it all, leaving her long hair loose, hurrying to get ready before anyone might apprehend her—or, more strictly speaking, Manthara.

The old woman had been an absolute terror, domineering Kaikeyi like never before. If Kaikeyi sensed her lack of skill and culture, Manthara was on a mission to rectify it. She would not rest until Keyi was superior to the other queens, and so Manthara obsessed over every detail of Kaikeyi's appearance, frantically ordering her dresses and jewelry and throwing out perfectly functional ones. Kaikeyi almost wished she'd listened to Yuddha who had advised her to leave Manthara in Kekaya. The old woman showed no sympathy when Kaikeyi complained of her dreary duties, meaning the prayers in the mornings and the special days when extra observances required longer rituals, which seemed to happen every other day.

Just the other day Manthara had forced Kaikeyi to listen as she went on and on. "We must get rid of all these light, immature colors," Manthara had said, as though she was discussing a serious matter of state. A big pile of discarded garments lay at her feet. "We will set you apart with bold colors, like violet, crimson, dazzling white—"

"You seriously think a color palette is going to give me the position of primary queen?" Kaikeyi had countered.

"Don't take that tone with me. We cannot rest until we've secured your position."

She meant that quite literally. Manthara had turned into someone crazy; she never slept, except when she got her massages with the pungent medicated oils, which made her lazy and still, like a resting snake. Even then she would call on Kaikeyi, instructing her with closed eyes, assigning this reading and that reading, which would help Kaikeyi become someone of worth. At other times, Manthara stole around the palace, seeking the places that were forbidden to her, like the golden altars. More than once, she had been escorted back to her assigned quarters by apologetic servants. One of the Ayodhyan servants had even asked Kaikeyi if Manthara was hale in mind, for she inquired about the strangest things, like where in the gardens certain flowers grew. The Ayodhyans obviously didn't know the medicinal value of certain plants. Manthara was seeking lily of the valley, the beautiful wildflower with its white teardrops. The royal physician would help distill its essence and administer it to Manthara for her heart to function.

Feeling as if she was four or five years old again and sneaking out to ride with her brother, Kaikeyi scurried past the servants in attendance. Sukhi was one of them. Kaikeyi placed her finger over her lips, indicating the need for complete silence. Sukhi did not need further instruction, used to all her years in Keyi's service. Kaikeyi's four guards would be at the main entrance. Though they were from Kekaya, they took orders from Dasharatha now. So Kaikeyi headed for the servants' entrance on the side. She peeked out from the archways, looking right and left, expecting to hear the sound of Manthara's cane at any time. It was ridiculous—she was queen of Ayodhya, and yet Manthara had her in the same iron grip as before.

Running down the stairs on light feet, Kaikeyi reached the stables. She exhaled in exhilaration and was probably unfittingly loud in her greeting to all the stable hands. They grew still in their duties, greeting her formally as she passed. They did well to hide their surprise, for she would take her place as the mistress here.

"Please," she said, "these stables may be royal, but we are not in the palace. Please leave formalities outside. I am one of you."

Here, they were horse people first and foremost, and that was how it was done in Kekaya, fostering camaraderie among all people. She could hear them whisper behind her as she strode ahead but was too elated to care.

When she approached Dharma, her dear friend from home, he nickered in his stall. She leaned her forehead against his, stroking his soft muzzle.

"Tomorrow I will bring something for you," she said. "Today I could only bring myself."

The urgency still haunted her, for now she imagined that Kausalya would come screaming, dragging her into the altar rooms, scolding her for neglecting her queenly duties. Or if not Kausalya, then the king, who seemed overly in awe of Kausalya, as Manthara was quick to note. The king should not have married Kaikeyi, the daughter of a faraway horse-lord, if he wanted a prudish Ayodhyan woman. But the few arguments she had had with the king usually petered out to nothing when they locked into passionate embraces. The king promised that he had never ever loved anyone like he loved her. But where had that love been last night when he stormed out?

Kaikeyi ensured that the bridle and seat were secured on Dharma. She thought of her father and brother, wondering what they were doing in Kekaya. Had her departure affected them at all?

She led Dharma out of the stall but did not wait to bring him outside to mount him. It was glorious to be on horseback again. She smiled broadly to the stable men whom she passed. Without exception, they blushed and turned away, letting Kaikeyi know that even her friendly smiles were a transgression. Perhaps a married woman was not to smile at other men?

The courtyard disappeared in a blur, and though Kaikeyi did not know this large city, she coaxed Dharma into a canter and moved forward as though she had a purpose. The city was waking up, and Kaikeyi couldn't help but admire its elegance. Like Kausalya, the city was majestic, fragrant, and beautifully arranged. Nothing was out of place, and though Kaikeyi was no expert, she sensed the symmetry of the architecture. The buildings rose up into the sky, with ornate pillars, archways, and intricate designs.

Without any formal agenda, Kaikeyi beheld the city. She recalled Dasharatha's praise of the city, seeing the words come to life before her eyes. Ayodhya was built by Manu, the first man, and it was a legendary city in a league of its own. Layers of moats, ramparts, and high walls held back intruders. A broad highway running through the city was sprinkled with water and strewn with flowers daily by heavenly damsels, a gesture of Indra's gratitude. Ayodhya was unexcelled on Earth, and even the heavenly denizens gazed at it in awe, never before imagining that a dwelling on Earth could rival their own in Paradise. With its beautifully constructed buildings, seven-story houses, and gorgeous arches, Ayodhya was truly worthy of comparison with Indra's abode in heaven. There were mango groves everywhere, the trees heavy with fruit. Elephants walked the streets in rhythm with the drums and music that filled the air. Beautiful women, decorated with precious gems, moved about happily. If they paid Kaikeyi any attention, it was because a woman on horseback was not a common sight. Kaikeyi observed that even the men wore gold earrings, garlands of lotus and jasmine, and silk garment in all hues. She could smell the cleanliness of the city, with its cooling sandalwood paste and fragrant oils.

The marketplace overflowed with exotic merchandise from faraway lands, and the streets bustled with royalty bringing their annual tribute. Out of the thousands of people who resided in Ayodhya, Kaikeyi saw none who looked miserly, unhappy, or deformed. The people of Ayodhya were famed for the balance they kept between prayer and enjoyment. They were said to be content with their own fortune, whether they lived as warriors in mansions or servants in cottages. However great or menial each person's task, each performed it happily, knowing that the success of their society lay in each being vigilant in doing his or her own duty. Ayodhya was doubtless in a class of its own.

Lost in her admiration of the city, Kaikeyi had allowed Dharma to lead the way. She laughed when she saw he had taken her to a large gate that led out of the city. Dasharatha would not like it if she left the city without attending guards. He had specifically asked this of her. Placing her hand on her sword, Kaikeyi tapped her heels into Dharma's flanks. She was tired of being compliant, as if it had been two years rather than two weeks.

As Kaikeyi crossed the gate and out of Ayodhya, she tried to sense the magical wards that protected the city. Made of mantra, the sacred sound vibrations prevented intruders, specifically blood-drinkers, from breaching Ayodhya's security. But Kaikeyi got no sense of where the vibrations were located. She did see a large fire pit alive with flames and recalled that there were four of them, one in each corner of the city. Urging Dharma onward, Kaikeyi galloped beyond the city limits, leaving thoughts of fires and mantras behind.

The smell of freedom filled her as the wind struck her face. Water rose in her eyes, and she could let her tears fly in the wind without having to wonder what feelings she released. The balance was restored within Kaikeyi. She knew who she was here, even if she couldn't put it into words. Sitting in the palace temple, she felt as stiff and lifeless as the deities.

After riding hard for several joyful minutes, she slowed Dharma to a pleasant canter. She noticed at once that Ayodhya's order extended beyond its walls. The road that she had unconsciously followed was broad and defined. The fields were divided into neat plots of land, the farmers standing to look at her as she passed by. Unsure what etiquette required, she simply ignored them and focused on enjoying the scenery. Trees swayed in the breeze, birds cooed, the sun shone: it was perfect.

When she sensed that Dharma was thirsty, they trotted toward the river Sarayu, Ayodhya's primary source of water. Kaikeyi slid off the horse and led him forward with the reins. The river flowed steadily, the other bank barely visible to the eye. As Kaikeyi splashed her face with the river water, she thought at once about Manthara's tale of the crazed Asamanja, the blotch on the Sun dynasty. It was in these very waters that he had drowned his playmates, laughing all the while. That was the first piece of Ayodhya's history that she had learned, but she already knew that it was but a small piece of it. The kings of the Sun dynasty had been the leaders of mankind since Manu, the first man. Sagara, had carved out the oceans; Bhagiratha had called down the Ganga, the holy river that blessed one with liberation; Anaranya had faced Ravana and made the prophecy that a human would cause the demon's end.

Kaikeyi sat by the bank of the river, quietly watching it flow, while Dharma grazed on grass. The servant folk were busy with their duties, hauling water in pots that gleamed of silver and gold, washing clothes that, even heavy with water, sparkled with elegance and wealth. Kaikeyi had not strayed very far after all, for these servants belonged to the palace; she understood this by the precious objects they handled.

Kaikeyi was about to stand up when a man's head suddenly emerged from the waters. She startled at the sight. She could have sworn she had looked at that very spot of water for a good many minutes. The hair that flowed down the man's back turned from gray to white as the water drained from it. An old man, then. The man turned around slowly, meeting her eyes. His long beard was white like the clouds above. But he looked neither old nor young. The word that came to Kaikeyi was "timeless." She had seen him once before, at the wedding feast, one of the many new faces but one that stood out. He had looked her over as if she was bad karma in the guise of a queen.

Now he held her eyes, showing none of his own thoughts, only reading hers.

Though she felt herself shrink under his gaze, she did not tap into her authority as a queen or a warrior, for she had intuition enough to know she was no match for him. He was far beyond her powers. He was also an important person in Ayodhya. Perhaps the most important one. She recalled his name then: Vasishta, the high priest of the Sun dynasty, a mind-born son of Brahma, the creator. No one really knew how old he was.

Standing in the waters submerged to his navel, Vasishta called her name.

She shivered but inclined her head obediently.

"You are far from home," he observed.

"Sometimes I think we all are," she answered, surprising even herself.

"A philosopher." He smiled. "You speak truly."

She found that she was childishly pleased to have pleased him.

"We all are too far from our real home," he said in agreement.

"Even you?"

"I am here, and not there, am I not?"

She held on to her thought. "By choice, I would think."

"While yours was by force?" He waited, eyes on her, while taking his long hair and wringing the water from it.

She looked at the droplets of water that were hitting the still surface and creating ripples.

"I must have made a choice at some point," she said. "But I don't think I have the power now to unmake that decision. I think I'm like the water in your hair. Taken out of its element, it has not ceased to be water, but it cannot be returned to its natural state without your help, and as the drops fall, they change the surface before they return to peace." She grew aware that she had spoken too much—and that he was the wise one, not her. "Forgive me. I speak out of turn."

"Isn't it for the pleasure of doing so that you have escaped from within the city limits?"

"Is anything hidden from you, then?"

"Yes. Your end. Your innermost desires. Your motives. Everything that you desire and will do. These are hidden from me, for they change at every moment. Just like this flowing river."

"And yet at any time, we may come to the banks of the river and find the water flowing. Is that not a form of knowing?"

"A philosopher queen." Once again, he seemed pleased by the discovery.

"Manthara would never accede to that," she said. Seeing his quizzical look, she realized he had never meet Manthara. "She is my servant. My mother. My confidante. I don't really know how to describe her."

"Manthara chides you for being too philosophical?"

"In the moments when I think myself most wise, she says I'm foolish. And when I think myself utterly foolish, she praises me."

"Perhaps you should not listen to her overly much."

Kaikeyi almost gasped. It seemed so simple, coming from him. But Kaikeyi had never dared ignore Manthara for long.

"Tell me," Vasishta said. "How would you describe this city, your new home? I want the philosopher's answer."

She thought of how pristine and clean it was, how beautiful every person appeared. Surely such order came at a price. And yet she wasn't sure.

"I don't know if I can answer that yet."

"Humility becomes you. Then tell me this. What is the worst of crimes in Ayodhya?"

"Killing a child?"

He shook his head.

"Defiling a woman?"

Again he shook his head. Would he make her name every crime that she knew? Was it a test of her meager knowledge?

"Think about it. Observe Ayodhya and our ways. The answer may surprise you."

Vasishta stepped out of the water, a single white cloth wrapped around his private parts. The cloth shimmered with rainbow hues, too dry to be of normal silk. He picked up a small brass pot that Kaikeyi had not noticed and made to leave in silence. Kaikeyi saw two younger priests waiting for Vasishta.

"Wait," Kaikeyi said, standing up. "Holy One, please."

He waited.

She did not know why she had asked him to stop. Just as she had not known any of the words that had spilled out of her in his presence.

"May I learn from you?" she asked. But surely he had more pressing duties than teaching an uncultured princess from Kekaya.

"What do you wish to learn?" he asked.

"Everything," she said.

"Eagerness is good. But I'm afraid you will be disappointed if you set your goal so high. I myself cannot teach you what I do not know. And more important, I'm afraid no amount of knowledge will save you in the end."

A chill ran down her spine. "I thought you said you could not see my end, my heart, or my future."

He smiled, beholding her. "You have the signs of a diligent student."

"All my other teachers said so. I'm afraid I know very little, however, when it comes to the art of being a noble queen."

"That is perhaps not my forte," he answered, a smile on his lips. "Queen Kausalya is expert. She took Sumitra flawlessly under her wing. She will do the same for you."

Kaikeyi clenched her teeth and took a deep breath. The words that had flowed so naturally in Vasishta's presence were now blocked.

She stood quietly as she watched him leave, a small flutter of joy in her heart. His white hair was so long, it reached down to his knees. Tiny drops of water still dripped from the ends.

It was time for her to return as well. She felt that she had somehow effected a change in his reserve toward her. Perhaps all of Ayodhya would come to see her as a powerful philosopher queen.

CHAPTER 10

The Power of a Phantom

Two years passed by in relative peace. The largest trouble seemed to come from within Dasharatha's own palace, with two strong-minded queens constantly opposing each other. A terrible battle of wills had arisen. Kaikeyi who hardly visited the golden altars had ventured within one day after riding on horseback. Kausalya was aghast to find her sanctum smelling of horse and mandated that bathing be compulsory before entering the altars. This was hardly a new rule, for even Dasharatha bathed before praying there. Kaikeyi, however, saw it as Kausalya's attempt to publicly humiliate her. This conviction was cemented when Kaikeyi was foolish enough to ignore the rule. Kausalya's servants hounded the young queen until she ran out, a smell of the stables trailing behind her. It was said in the palace halls that King Dasharatha had been summoned to the House of Wrath to prevent the two queens from killing each other. Kaikeyi had never set her foot within the golden altars since. All this was not a concern of state, however, and Dasharatha kept his private life apart from his royal duties.

Sitting in his private council room, Dasharatha listened gravely to the reports from around the city and beyond. The king's scouts were like silent shadows, the ears and eyes of the king. On this day, nothing out of the ordinary was reported: a border skirmish, two subordinate kings fighting, and some complaints about the heavenly damsels sprinkling too much water on the road. Then a report came that would shake the foundations of all that Dasharatha knew.

A scout from beyond Ayodhya's walls came rushing in. Gulping for air, he said, "There has been an attack. A blood-drinker attack."

Dasharatha did not rise. He simply shook his head. It wasn't possible. This had never happened, not in Dasharatha's lifetime. Every so often a report of such an attack would surface. But when investigated, there was always a natural cause. Dasharatha remained calm.

"No blood-drinker has been sighted on our lands for countless generations," he said firmly.

Thanks to the tireless work of Dasharatha's ancestors, blood-drinkers were hardly known to the common man. They still haunted children's stories and were alive in the human consciousness. The warriors who returned from celestial battles kept the tales alive. But no one living within the safety of civilization had been attacked by a blood-drinker since the legendary battle between Anaranya and Ravana. Very few had ever encountered a real-life blood-drinker.

Yet the scout was sweating and pallid, as if he had personally seen the attack. This concerned Dasharatha, for it meant that the scout was certain of his report. When Dasharatha suggested other plausible explanations, the scout insisted on his version:

A young woman had gone missing in the forest. Her two children, a son and a daughter, had been seen running on the forest trails alone as darkness approached, which had alerted a neighbor's attention. Neither the children nor their mother came home that evening. Following the neighbor's advice, the man went searching in the forest for his family. He found his two children seemingly sleeping on the ground, but they would not awaken and were cold to his touch. He could see no cause of death, until he saw the marks on their necks, exactly like teeth, or very sharp fangs. The woman was still missing.

"But judging from the fate of her children . . ." The scout fell silent, then added, "The father carried both children here to us, hoping Vasishta could save them. But they were beyond saving. The man is distraught. Vasishta is with him."

"Does Vasishta concur on the cause of death?" Dasharatha asked.

"He does, Great King."

That eradicated any shred of doubt. Dasharatha stood up. "Take me to him."

He turned to the others present. "This news must *not* spread in the city. We must avoid panic among our people. Instruct the guards to close all the city gates until we know more. There is no reason yet for our people to start locking their doors and fearing night's approach."

The men nodded seriously.

He looked at each of the eight men there, his most trusted scouts, posted around the city to keep an eye on everything. "Fortify our walls. Even though the attack took place outside the city, we must be vigilant. Send a horse rider to each of the subordinate kings, informing them what has occurred. At this point we cannot say if it was an isolated incident or the beginning of something. If anything suspicious occurs in any of our kingdoms, I want to know at once."

"Yes, Great King."

Visions of the red-eyed blood-drinkers sprang up in Dasharatha's mind. He had no illusion about the dangers that existed, but they belonged in other realms, not on Earth. This should not be happening. Had something happened in the previous battle to turn the tides against them? Why an attack by a blood-drinker now, after hundreds of years?

Dasharatha left the room, noticing, as he always did in a crisis, the entourage that followed him to his next destination. Only some of them carried weapons. Others carried refreshments, fans made of peacock tails, and other items meant to make the king's duties easier. Dasharatha paused before entering the room. He had not faced a situation like this before.

When Dasharatha entered the room, everyone, including Vasishta, stood up. Everyone but the grieving father. He sat by his dead children, a son and a daughter, and looked up at Dasharatha with eyes that shone with anger. He had a boyish face and looked too young to have sired two children.

"This is your fault," he said to Dasharatha. The words came out in a hiss. "You are useless!"

Dasharatha grew still, taking the man's accusation to heart.

"If you had done your work as king correctly," the man went on, "the demon with ten heads could not have done this." He stood up now, glaring at Dasharatha with bloodshot eyes. His fingers flexed at his sides, as if he wished to fling a weapon at his king.

Dasharatha felt compassion for the delusion in the man's grief. Ravana with his ten heads was a favorite villain. Dasharatha did the only thing he could think of. He broached the distance between them and embraced the man tightly and firmly. The father struggled to be free, cursing Dasharatha loudly, speaking so offensively he would have met the death penalty under any other circumstances.

"Lochana," Vasishta warned, addressing the man by his name.

Dasharatha shook his head at the preceptor, letting the man rage on. Dasharatha did not let go, and it did not take long until Lochana slumped in his arms, anger spent. His chin trembled and his hair hung over his face. "My children," he whispered, and quiet sobs ran through his entire body.

Dasharatha's heart was nowhere but in the grief of this bereaved father. He had never faced such pain, and he hoped he never would again. For a long time, Dasharatha held the man to his chest; now Dasharatha was the father and this man his child. There were no hierarchies in the land of sorrow.

When Lochana's cries quieted, Dasharatha gently released him, keeping a supportive arm around him. Lochana had no energy left. He had, after all, carried his two children a very long way. Exhaustion was taking over.

Dasharatha looked into Lochana's eyes urgently. "I will do everything in my power to avenge the death of your children and find the culprit."

To his surprise, the man mustered a laugh. "You will not." It was a statement. Not an accusation. "It was the ten-headed one that did this."

The king looked at Vasishta with narrowing eyes. Was it even possible? After hundreds of years, an attack by the king of blood-drinkers himself?

"He has not been seen on Earth since the time of Anaranya," Dasharatha said, in a soft voice. "Thirty-six generations ago."

Dasharatha led the man back to his seat. Lochana reached out to his children's corpses, touching their pallid hands. They looked like pale angels, sleeping peacefully. Dasharatha's eyes found the pinprick wounds at the neck. In his battle experience, men needed to bleed copiously before death came for them. These children's lives had been sucked out cleanly and completely. Dasharatha had never seen anything like it before. While Lochana turned his attention to the children he had lost, Dasharatha consulted privately with Vasishta.

"Ravana? Is it possible? Or is he simply recalling the stories and making wild assumptions?"

"Something is not right," Vasishta said. "When he carried his children into Ayodhya, I felt a disturbance in the sacred vibrations that protect our walls. At first I was inclined to think we had a security breach, that this man was a blood-drinker in disguise. But he is not. He is true, his tragedy genuine. Still, he has unknowingly brought something with him here, something that was powerful enough to weaken the holy mantras that protect Ayodhya from intrusion. Whoever killed these children left a psychic imprint so strong, I believe their corpses are tainted. We should burn them as soon as possible."

Dasharatha returned to Lochana's side. His young face was lined with grief; he would never be a carefree person again. Dasharatha put a gentle hand on his shoulder and kneeled down to face him at eye level. Quickly he conveyed what Vasishta had told him.

Lochana did not look surprised. "I already told you," he said. "It was that ten-headed blood-drinker that the children call Ravana. It had to be. He had ten heads and twenty arms and horrible eyes that drained away my courage."

"You saw him?"

"Yes. When I found the children. When I discovered that they were dead. He appeared and laughed at my plight. I was not thinking, but I flew into such a helpless rage, I flung myself at him, without even a weapon in my hand. But my body flew through him and into the tree behind him." He touched his forehead, where Dasharatha for the first time noticed a swelling and the signs of a bruise. "I went straight through him. That's when I realized he wasn't really there. That he had somehow left a phantom of himself there. When I returned to my children's side, ignoring the vision completely, he disappeared into thin air. I hurried away as fast as I could with them weighing me down, full of the foolish hope that they might yet be saved. As soon as I saw that monster, I should have known."

His eyes were growing heavy, his speech slurred, as the events of the day weighed in on him.

"Take rest," Dasharatha said. "We will wake you when the arrangements for the pyres are done. We will spare no cost in sending these children to the heavens with a proper burial."

The man nodded, looking down.

Dasharatha's next words were unplanned. "Afterward, will you lead me to the spot where you found them?"

Again the man nodded, and Dasharatha had him escorted to a private chamber where he could rest.

Dasharatha understood from his own spontaneous request that he would not feel peace until he investigated this himself. He did not know what to make of the man's certainty, his words of the ten-headed apparition. It could have been nothing but grief-induced delusion. And yet Vasishta had said someone immensely powerful had tainted the children.

While the funeral arrangements were made, Dasharatha and a few select people discreetly went to Ayodhya's prison. There was one particular prisoner whom Dasharatha needed to question, one held in a secret cell. He was Ayodhya's oldest prisoner and knew more about blood-drinkers than anyone else. Getting him to speak was another matter altogether. The prisoner had maintained silence since before Dasharatha's lifetime, not even revealing his name. On his way to the prison, Dasharatha touched the thin scar across his lips, remembering the encounter with Subahu on the battle-field of the gods. "Release my brother!" the drinker had demanded. Dasharatha did not know whether Subahu had survived; blood-drinkers of that caliber, who could shape-change with such skill, were uncommonly difficult to slay.

Soon, Dasharatha emerged from the prison with clenched teeth. The prisoner had displayed mirth at Dasharatha's questions but remained silent otherwise. The records clearly held that no amount of torture would make the prisoner speak, so Dasharatha did not resort to such methods.

The king gave orders to organize a search-party and then went directly to the funeral ceremony. The two pyres were built and decorated with fresh flowers. Vasishta himself conducted the last rites, instructing the bereaved father where to light the pyres. As the flames began to burn, the royal musician sang melancholy yet melodious hymns, sending the two young souls onward on their journey. Lochana, who could have chosen to sit in meditation until the pyres burned down, turned to Dasharatha.

"I'm ready," he said abruptly. "I will lead you there now." He wanted justice.

"Everything has been arranged," said Dasharatha.

He took Lochana's elbow and led the man to his private rooms, where he kept his weapons. The chariot stood ready when Dasharatha came out. Ten heavily armed men on horses waited nearby. Dasharatha invited Lochana to stand beside him on the chariot, and once they were out of the city, the grieving father guided the king toward his village. To find the spot in the forest, they had to dismount and leave the chariot and horses behind.

The forest was peaceful and bright, an unlikely spot for a horrendous crime. Yet was any place truly suitable for it? Still, darkness didn't have a bad reputation for nothing. The enemy lived in the shadows, after all—except for this one who had ventured out into daylight and attacked Lochana's family.

They walked along a path that wound through the trees. After a few minutes, Lochana slowed down. The strain of returning to this place was evident in his abrupt gestures. There was no landmark that Dasharatha could see, but he trusted that the spot was engraved in Lochana's mind. Unconsciously adopting Lochana's mannerism, Dasharatha walked on his toes.

"Here," Lochana said in a hoarse whisper, pointing at a place on the ground. "This is where I found them." His eyes darted toward another place ahead of them.

Dasharatha followed Lochana's eyes, expecting to see only trees. Instead Dasharatha stumbled backward, losing his life force. Lochana sank to his knees, arms hanging slackly by his side.

Standing in front of them, lazily observing what they did, stood the most dangerous creature Dasharatha had ever seen. Just one of his heads was terrifying, with fangs and eyes that penetrated layers of skin, bone, and psyche. His massive shoulders held countless heads, each one as terrifying as the next. Who could say there were ten heads? To Dasharatha it looked like hundreds. Ravana's eyes hypnotized and menaced. He could certainly bend people to his will. He was bending Dasharatha now, who started seeing the appeal that Ravana, with his strong jaws and chiseled features, might exert on a woman.

The only thing Dasharatha could focus on was sending strength to his legs. He heard several of the guards collapsing behind him. Dasharatha gained admiration for Lochana's courage. Dasharatha had to do something. He felt his hand grow heavy, the grip on his sword slippery. It wasn't easy to lift it through the air and launch it toward Ravana's heart.

Dasharatha steeled himself for a battle that might end his life, but the sword went through Ravana and lodged in the tree trunk behind him. Ravana's body shimmered and blurred, the vision showing itself for what it was. But what was it, really? It was clearly sentient, for it responded to their presence and their actions. Now the apparition sneered at them, showing more of its fangs. The arms clawed impatiently through the air. It seemed to feed on Dasharatha's emotions, gaining more life and animation the longer Dasharatha stood there.

"Ignore it," Lochana whispered, his neck bent, his face completely averted from the apparition.

Dasharatha couldn't move. He felt as though invisible hands had grabbed his face, holding it still. He put all his willpower into breaking eye contact with the many-eyed monster, but simply couldn't. Now he knew that neither he nor any other human could ever stand against Ravana and win. No human had that hope. Anaranya had been wrong; it would always be a fool's mission. Ravana could not be slain even by the gods. Dasharatha saw the three livid scars across the chest of the apparition: the scars of Vishnu. The lord of lords himself had discharged his famed discus at Ravana. Yet the monster still lived. Dasharatha would have to stand here for all eternity, until the demon got tired of holding him captive.

What came to his rescue was the very weakness of the human frame. The forceful collision of impressions within his body and mind resulted in a sickness that was so strong that the bile rose in his throat. He didn't even have time to feel ashamed that he alone was vomiting before his men. The bile forced itself up his throat and through his mouth and splattered against the ground, an offering at Ravana's feet. With a hissing sound, the phantom

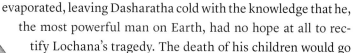

evaporated, leaving Dasharatha cold with the knowledge that he, the most powerful man on Earth, had no hope at all to rectify Lochana's tragedy. The death of his children would go unavenged. The mother would never be found. Anaranya's words would not come true. It was hopeless.

He heard his people take big gulps of air, freed from the vision. Dasharatha wiped his mouth and chin with an impatient gesture. How could a thing of no substance have such power?

Dasharatha felt his men's eagerness to leave. Lochana was standing up as well, waiting for the king's cue. But when he tried to move, Dasharatha's feet were stuck to the ground and incredible heavy, so he just stood there, thinking many conflicting thoughts, praying to the Lord above for some solution. Slowly the serenity of the forest began seeping into his consciousness, restoring it, shooing away the darkness. Ravana was not welcome here, that much was clear. Dasharatha hoped the terrifying apparition of the ten-headed enemy was gone, once and for all. Or would it haunt the woods now for all time, taking pleasure in frightening wayward travelers or lone wanderers?

Dasharatha shuddered. "I will place a ban on this section of the forest," he said to his followers. "When some time has passed, Vasishta will ascertain whether the woods remain haunted."

He turned to Lochana. "This forest will be named after your children. Once the ban is lifted, anyone who wishes to pass through must make an offering at your doorstep in their honor."

Dasharatha promised to send the children's ashes to him when the pyres had burned down. Lochana, with the other surviving family members, would conduct the final rite by offering the ashes to the element of their choice. Lochana returned to his village by foot.

Dasharatha returned to the city. It was perhaps the heaviest day in his life so far, not counting the night in his youth when he had pointed his arrow at the wrong target. That night had shattered something in his heart. There was no way to live on Earth without error, especially as the emperor. What he learned today was that no one in the universe was safe. Safety was an illusion. Ravana did not need a solitary forest to trap his prey. He could swoop into any place at any time. The Earth really was at Ravana's mercy and whim. His absence over hundreds of years had made them forgetful. Dasharatha's confidence in his ability to protect his own people had evaporated with the hissing phantom.

In the weeks that followed, it only got worse. News came back reporting the abduction of hundreds of women across the Earth. The ten-headed king had shown neither preference nor deference, but had kidnapped the married and unmarried, young and old, highborn and common. Ravana had acted alone, riding through the sky in a flying mansion. The women trapped within cried to be rescued. Families across the world were devastated. The men could do nothing to protect or save their wives. The few men and children who had been present had been slaughtered. Mostly, however, the abductions had been stealthy, targeting women when they were alone and helpless—the work of a coward, it seemed to Dasharatha, or one addicted to subtle terror.

Dasharatha engaged all his priests in fortifying Ayodhya's parameters with sacred vibrations. Even that might not keep Ravana out; no one could say for sure. Dasharatha put efforts into new sanctions restricting the movements of women. No women were allowed outside after dark. No exceptions. Kaikeyi was furious about this, having a habit of riding late into the nights when the king was busy. For once, Dasharatha ignored her complaints. It was the least he could do to prevent any further abductions.

Dasharatha received the reports with growing numbness. Kausalya assisted him in sending appropriate gifts and condolences, writing personal notes to the bereaved. Ravana had thoroughly demonstrated his power over mankind. They had only thought themselves safe because Ravana had left them alone. He could take anything he wanted, whenever he wanted.

No matter how long or fervently the king consulted with his ministers, no matter how many missives he sent back and forth to the other kings, Ravana stood laughing at their futile attempts. They were utterly powerless. Unwilling to admit this, they held strategic meeting after meeting. After a long session with his ministers, Dasharatha finally said, "I have lost faith in Anaranya's prophecy. A human cannot kill Ravana."

"Only a human can," Vasishta amended.

Dasharatha looked at Vasishta silently for a long time. He was emperor, and he had failed. Lochana was right: he was a useless king. There was nothing he could do to stop Ravana.

CHAPTER 11

The Women's Curse

Ironically, a tiny girl shook Dasharatha out of his apathy. He was awoken in the middle of the night, and informed that one of the scouts had returned with a girl, one of Ravana's victims. Dasharatha opened his eyes at once, looking up at the ceiling as the servant whispered what he knew. He tied a cloth around his waist but left all adornments, securing his sword around his waist as he walked. He nodded to both guards as he stepped out into the dark hall.

"Tell me," he said to the informant that waited.

"Chitra, whom you sent to the southern shores, has come back with a young girl. He says she is one of the abducted ones."

"How did she escape?" Dasharatha asked.

"I think the blood-drinker let them go."

That made no sense. What was Ravana's game?

"Why has she not been returned to her family?" Dasharatha questioned.

There was no answer from the informant, only a troubled look. Dasharatha grew fully awake. He had a feeling that one problem had been solved, only to present another. He took a deep breath of the fresh night air and turned the corner to enter the private council room.

As he entered, he was glad to see Sumantra there, as simply clad as he was, with puffy eyes from interrupted sleep. Then Dasaratha turned to the two who stood in the center of the room: Chitra, a middle-aged man who had been in Dasaratha's service all his life, and a girl, who was so young she did not qualify to be called a woman. This stopped Dasaratha in his tracks. If Ravana would stoop so low . . . Dasaratha's anger made his command cutting.

"Speak," he said, standing where he was, at a distance from the two.

The girl shrank toward Chitra, who spoke in her stead. "Great King, on your orders, I kept vigil on the southern side of Koshala's borders, and that's where I found her. She could not talk at first, but soon I understood that she had escaped from the blood-drinker."

"How?"

"Perhaps she should tell you herself," Chitra said.

When Dasaratha took a step forward, the girl took a step back. Chitra placed his hand on the girl's shoulder and she looked up at him with great trust in her haunted eyes.

Dasaratha took in the scene. The girl was a child, not even on the brink of womanhood. Her arms were thin and her body had not taken on feminine shapes. How had Ravana even taken this girl for a woman?

"No one will harm you here," Dasaratha said softly, taking a step forward. "You are safe now."

The girl began to cry softly. Chitra's hands rested on her shoulders.

As much as Dasaratha wanted the whole story, to discern its truth, he could not ignore how fragile and scared the girl was. So he held Chitra's eyes and mouthed silently, *Is it true?*

Chitra's jaw clenched, and he nodded once. He whispered softly to the girl, reassuring her, speaking highly of Dasaratha, encouraging the girl to trust him.

Dasaratha called for water and refreshments. He walked toward a side of the room that was filled with cushioned seats and soft rugs. He beckoned to Chitra and the girl. Dasaratha was careful not to make sudden movements or to touch her. But once they sat down, Dasaratha moved closer, sitting carefully within arm's reach. The girl leaned against Chitra.

"Where are you from?" Dasaratha asked conversationally.

"Nowhere," she whispered. And then, "I used to belong to Kalinga."

"What is your name?"

"Maharani. But my family always called me just Rani."

"Rani, do you want to tell me what happened?" Dasaratha asked. "We had no hope until now that we would see *any of you* again."

"That would have been better," she said, snapping her back straight, defiant for the first time.

Dasaratha held her gaze encouragingly, but she wilted again and told her story in a whisper. Dasaratha leaned closer in order to hear her words.

"He . . . um . . . took me from my mother's garden. I was playing outside alone. He . . . um . . . he . . ."

"You don't have to tell that part," Chitra said, looking at Dasharatha with pleading eyes. "Tell how you escaped and what happened right before."

Rani nodded and spoke with more confidence, the terrible part of the tale left behind for now.

"I was so scared I thought I would die, until he took me inside the flying palace, and I saw how many others there were. Everyone was scared, even the ladies who were much older than me. I saw only one other girl like me."

"How old are you?" Dasharatha asked hesitantly.

"Ten years," she answered.

Dasharatha nodded, encouraging her to go on.

"It was really beautiful inside the flying palace, like here. Golden and sparkling with jewels. We were high up in the clouds. But no one cared. As long as he was there among us, we tried to be silent, invisible. But as soon as he left to another part of the flying palace, everyone started crying again. Many were bleeding. But then one lady stood up. She had a big scratch across half her face. She told us to stop crying, that we were powerful, that we could do something. No one listened at first, but she went around talking to each of us, telling us that together we had more power than him. When she came to me, she said, 'Do you have anything given to you by someone who loves you?' I handed her the necklace that my mother had just given me for my birthday. She took a piece from it and threaded it onto a string, with beads she had collected from the others. 'We are loved,' she told me, giving me back my mother's gift. I believed her. Everyone started believing her. And suddenly I wasn't afraid anymore. She didn't have to tell us what to do. We held hands and it was like the words spoke themselves from my heart. Everyone said the same words. A curse on his heads. A true death curse. I had my eyes squeezed shut, and I stood as one of them in the circle. Then the words came, one voice from hundreds of us:

"'A woman is strong. A woman is powerful. Love protects us. You will come to know this, Ravana. Violator of the most sacred. You will pay with your immortal life. A woman, just like us, the wife of another, will be your final death.'"

Rani took a deep breath. The skin on Dasharatha's arms prickled. The curse had power, even here, spoken by one wisp of a girl.

"I opened my eyes. I didn't know what to expect as we stood there in a huge circle, holding hands. Some of us started crying again. But then flowers showered down on us, a blessing from heaven, and the flying plane soared down toward the Earth, and the doors opened by themselves. None of us dared move because we knew that *he* was still there, and we knew what he could do to us, any of us."

The unspoken violence Ravana had committed stood between them. Truthfully, Dasharatha was glad he was spared the details this time. The horrible act stood like a ghost in Chitra's eyes. Rani looked for the first time into Dasharatha's eyes, and he saw a sudden flash of triumph there.

"But when he came out, his hundred arms hung dead at his sides. He was pale and sweating. He couldn't even look *me* in the eyes. My heart grew big like the palace. I squeezed the hands of the women around me. It had worked! The curse worked. He did not look at any of us, as if each of us now looked like death to him. He left us without a backward glance, hurrying out and away. When we dared to go out into the sunlight, he was nowhere. That's when most of us turned and ran."

Dasharatha's heart leaped in his chest. Broken families could be reunited. The women could be restored to their homes, children like Rani reunited with their mothers. Although he had had nothing to do with it, there was a sweet victorious feeling. What extraordinary women! Then he realized she had said, "most of us." Had some women chosen to stay, allured by the seductive power that Ravana was said to possess?

"Not everyone chose to run?"

The girl looked troubled. "Some did not have the courage. They were too . . . broken."

"But not you."

She shook her head, the small smile on her face. She knew she had been brave.

Children had amazing resilience, as this girl was proving.

"A few stayed for other reasons. They looked at Ravana in that strange way. Like Mother and Father looked at each other sometimes. But the strangest thing was that *she* stayed. The lady who gave us courage, who gathered us together. She stayed. She told me, 'Run, little one, before it's too late,' but she never left the flying palace. She was wearing the necklace she had made with all our love beads, and she looked very brave. But she stayed."

Rani fell silent. "I'm not sure, but I think he might have changed his mind after a while. I was escaping with another lady, but then we saw something large flying through the sky. We thought it was him searching for us and panicked. She ran in one direction and I the other. I hid under a big rock and remembered my mother's love. The brave lady had told us that love protects. Maybe it worked that time, because whatever it was flew away and didn't come back. And so I escaped. I don't know what happened to any of the other women."

"You have been very brave," Dasharatha said. Then he told her how he had felt when he saw Ravana's phantom in the forest that was now dedicated to Lila and Lava. Rani's eyes widened when Dasharatha revealed that he had gotten sick on the feet of the apparition. "So you see, even grown men are frightened by Ravana."

This pleased the girl. She looked for a while at Dasharatha, as if still deciding whether he was trustworthy. Dasharatha turned to Chitra, silently conferring with him. The girl had shared her testimony, but there was more Dasharatha needed to know, things best said without the girl present.

"Can I speak to Chitra for a few moments? We will be right here, where you can see us."

Rani's anxiety returned, but when Chitra pointed to where they would be standing within sight, she nodded. Thanking her gravely, Dasharatha walked out of the girl's hearing range. He faced Chitra squarely, becoming king again. "I appreciate the value of hearing this firsthand from the girl, but why didn't you simply return her to her family? I could have had the report from you." Without meaning to be, he was angry.

Chitra was angry too. "They did not want her."

Dasharatha inhaled sharply. "What are you saying!"

"They said she was tainted and no daughter of theirs."

Dasharatha closed his eyes. This was it. One terrible problem was coming to resolution, only to bring him another that seemed far worse. He covered his eyes, wishing himself back into a dream or into Kaikeyi's arms. He had no dominion over a family's private affairs. He could not order a family to take back a daughter whom they shunned. If he did, he would simply sentence the girl to a life of being unwanted, mistreated, and a worse fate. What, then, could he do? If this girl was but the first of many, if all families reacted this way . . .

"I pray," he said, "that all families are not so cruel."

"As do I," Chitra said. The air between them was thick.

How was it that the two of them, with no blood relation to the girl, could feel so protective of her, when her own family had cast her out? And yet the two men knew it was always the women who paid the price of a man's violation. Dasharatha had assumed this would be different when Ravana was the perpetrator. And Rani was but a child. An innocent little girl.

Chitra broke the silence. "If I may make a request of you, Great King."

Dasharatha held still, giving away nothing. The gods knew he had made too many promises already.

"I wish to bring this girl home and raise her as our own. I allowed myself one liberty and stopped at my home to confer with my wife. She is of my mind in this. Rani will be our daughter, if you consent, Great King."

Dasharatha's throat tightened. The hour of night left him more open than usual, and he had already seen the tenderness between the two, the way the girl wholeheartedly trusted Chitra. The lord above had his hand on this girl, at least.

"It is an ideal solution. May every rejected female find a savior like you," Dasharatha said. "Bless you and your wife."

There was one more thing he had to ask, though he suspected the truth.

"Did he—was she forced to—" The words stuck in Dasharatha's throat.

He had sentenced criminals in Ayodhya to death, punishment, and penance, depending on the severity of the violation toward a woman, but it had never involved one as young as this.

"I beg you not to ask," Chitra said. And that was the answer, the confirmation of Dasharatha's fear. Curse upon Ravana's immortal life. He had learned nothing but perversity.

"That's why her family rejected her?"

Chitra's eyes grew hard. "If only that were the case. They did not even want to hear her story. Her mother was willing, but the father closed the door. They would not let us in. Finally Rani begged me to take her away, anywhere. I think she cried more about her family's reaction than what that monster did to her."

"But what was her crime?" Dasharatha demanded, though he expected no answer.

"Being a girl," Chitra answered. "Being a girl, in the wrong place at the wrong time."

Dasharatha straightened his back. There was nothing he could say to deny Chitra's words. Yes, any man who defiled, violated, or assaulted a woman against her will faced immediate execution, amputation of limbs, or the loss of genitals. But the woman would nonetheless have to face society's scorn. A raped woman was shunned, as if the fault was somehow hers.

"I thought it would be different in this case," he told Chitra. "Ravana is not some ordinary man, but a blood-drinker of such power and malice that a grown man is made weak before him. Each of those women should receive our heartfelt support for their courage."

Chitra nodded and then shook his head.

The king said, "If she is carrying his child, you must let us know. Ravana's spawn is not something we can ignore or take lightly."

"She's only a child," Chitra reminded the king. "Her moon cycles have not yet begun. My wife asked her. I cannot say if it's a kindness or the greatest tragedy. At least she is spared that."

"Yes." Dasharatha was relieved, though only momentarily.

This girl was to be the first of many. Somehow Dasharatha did not have high hopes for their homecoming now. Some of them could be carrying Ravana's children. There was no easy solution to this.

"You are thinking about the others that may be carrying," Chitra deduced. He was a clever man and highly trained scout.

"Yes," Dasharatha agreed. "And what we might do with the half-breeds. As a man, I question the morality of shunning an unborn child, even one with Ravana's blood. As a king, I'm afraid I have less liberty. But that is a matter for tomorrow. Let us focus this night on your poor girl. I need not tell you that it's best to keep her recent past a secret. You, who hold Ayodhya's secrets in your heart, know what people are capable of. Kindness and compassion is not often the first path of the masses."

Chitra nodded. He knew it well.

"She will always be welcome in Ayodhya's court," Dasharatha said. "This tragedy will *not* be held against Rani here."

And yet they both knew that even the king could not stop tongues from wagging and tales from being told. Chitra would have to school his adoptive daughter well; he would have to instruct her to have swift and sure answers regarding her sudden appearance in Ayodhya.

Dasharatha had the feeling that the morrow would bring much unsavory work his way. He was too weary now to even contemplate it.

"You must be tired, trusted Chitra," Dasharatha said. "Will you stay with us this night? I know your home is several hours away on horse."

They looked over at the girl, who was nodding off to sleep and then sitting up straight again, looking at them. She had not let Chitra out of her sight. It was not customary, however, for a girl on the brink of womanhood to share a room with another man, whether father or brother.

"I will ask Queen Kausalya to come," Dasharatha offered. "She has a gentle hand with children. She will know how to handle the girl."

"The queen herself. You are too kind, Great King."

Minutes later, Kausalya appeared. Dasharatha felt deep relief flood his heart, seeing her stark, unadorned face. She had hastily tied her unruly hair into a knot, and though her silk garment was lavish, she wore no jewels. She had indulged in no vanities, choosing immediacy. She looked at Dasharatha with grave and alert eyes.

Whispering into her ear, Dasharatha told her the situation. She shook her head, looking down at the ground. When she looked at the girl, Dasharatha felt the horror running through her body.

"No," she whispered, looking up at Dasharatha. "She is just a child. Her cycles have not yet begun."

How she knew these things, Dasharatha did not question. He only clenched his jaw and sighed. "Take the girl to a suitable resting place. She is frightened of everyone but Chitra."

Kausalya knew the rules of conduct and nodded. She took a step toward the girl but turned to her husband. "Once she has healed and come of age, I will welcome her into service here. We must do the same for all the women who return, only to be turned out. We must not aggravate the injury done to these women by isolating them from society and turning on them. Shame on the girl's family!"

They regarded each other, and Dasharatha felt very old. He saw in her eyes that she knew how the rest of the fates would play out. This was the very reason girls were guarded so vigilantly. Once lost, they could never be accepted again. He would need her assistance in the days to come. He himself did not yet know what the right response was to this crisis after a crisis. Together they approached the girl, who immediately fastened her eyes on Kausalya, the only other female in the room.

Kausalya held out her hand to Rani. There were tears in her eyes as she said, "Will you allow me to be your mother, just for tonight?"

Rani took Kausalya's hand, and the queen leaned her cheek against the top of Rani's head. Rani's head slumped against Kausalya's chest.

"We will see you in the morning," Kausalya said to Chitra.

Dasharatha was grateful again to Kausalya for her grace, for her mother's love, for being so empathic with everyone she met. She was a true queen, through and through.

Sumantra took Chitra under his wing, and Dasharatha returned to his chambers. New guards had relieved the old ones. Dasharatha nodded at them and stepped into the silence of his private chambers. Kaikeyi's soft breaths created a soft rhythmic sound, and yet Dasharatha could not sit down or return to sleep.

The voice in his mind was cold and cruel. Dasharatha wanted to turn away but couldn't. He looked at Kaikeyi as the voice demanded: *If* she *had been one of the abducted women ravaged by Ravana, what would* you *do?*

He wanted to insist that he would be different from Rani's family. He loved Kaikeyi so passionately that his heart ached. But he would not be allowed to keep a woman touched by another man as his queen. What did this say about him as king? And about his people?

With these thoughts, Dasharatha could not sleep.

CHAPTER 12

Holy Dancing Girls

As the sun brought the new day, Dasharatha sought refuge at the golden altars. Kausalya was there, of course, looking as tired as he felt. Together but separate, they prayed their own prayers. Dasharatha's eyes wandered often to the deity of Lakshmi, the goddess of abundance. If she were here, what would *she* do?

His eyes rested on the two dancers worshipping the golden altars through soft, graceful movements. One of them sang a hymn in praise of Lakshmi's benevolence. The other girl used intricate gestures of hand and face to bring the prayer to life. Dasharatha felt as if he was seeing Lakshmi herself dance through the girl. The girl tapped her feet in rhythmical ways, creating pleasant patterns punctuated by sudden turns and dynamic sweeps of her arms from one corner to the other. When the dancing girls finished their prayers, they prostrated themselves before Lakshmi's altar and moved on to the next one. Then it all began again, a soft prayer building into a crescendo of movement. It had been a long time since Dasharatha had seen something so deeply moving and resonant with mystic wonder. And a voice within finally whispered, *Ask your queens.*

Dasharatha searched for Kausalya with his eyes. The sun was brightening the morning. Kausalya's eyes were also trained on the dancing girls, following every movement, a rapt trancelike look in her eyes. When again the dance came to completion and the girls moved to the next altar, Dasharatha sought Kausalya's attention. King and queen looked at each other with bloodshot eyes. It would be a long day ahead.

"Will you and the other queens join the council today?" he asked. "I would hear your opinion on this delicate matter."

Kausalya inclined her head. "It would be my honor. We will be there. Though I can only speak for myself and Sumitra."

Kaikeyi's name lay unspoken in the air, as potent as her presence.

"Will she not answer to your summons?"

Kausalya did not smile. "Does she answer yours?"

"You think I spoil her? That I allow her too much free rein?"

"I'm afraid you would not like my frank opinion in this matter."

The serene mood evaporated. Kausalya added, "I welcome the opportunity to speak with you on this. I only want to make sure that you are receptive."

"It would serve us better to concentrate on the matter at hand first," he concluded. Kausalya was right; he would not be schooled on how to treat Kaikeyi. "I will make sure that Kaikeyi is present. As a trained warrior, she will have a different perspective from you and Sumitra."

Kausalya's lips moved, but no words came out.

"Thank you," Dasharatha said, "for coming so quickly in the night. You knew just what to do with Rani. I'm so grateful to have you."

"Poor, poor girl," Kausalya said, and the tension between them was diffused. "I will go to see Rani now. I have sent for the physician to examine her, and I think it's best if I personally attend. As you noticed, she is very distrustful of all males."

"Well done. I will expect you and Sumitra in the private council room at high noon."

"As you wish."

Kausalya moved away, taking the scent of camphor and incense with her. Dasharatha's eyes lingered on her, for there was an edge of coolness in her manner toward him. The queen interrupted the dancing girls and stood in close conversation with them. The young faces grew serious as the queen talked. When they nodded to each other and to her, Kausalya touched one of their cheeks and turned away. Though Kausalya's arms swayed by her sides as she walked, her hands mirrored the gestures of the dancing girls.

Dasharatha watched as the girls resumed their dancing prayer. Then he sent a messenger to inform Kaikeyi of the day's agenda. He himself had just enough time to go to the River Sarayu and refresh his mind before the meeting. At high noon, the king, his eight ministers, and the three queens gathered. It was not unheard of to seek the counsel of the queens when it came to the matter of women, though it was understood that the king's council would make the final decision. The ministers sat in their usual circle with the king at their helm. Kausalya and Sumitra arrived together, dressed in subdued silks that flowed with their steps. Kaikeyi arrived late, rushing in with pink cheeks, her crimson silks, and jewels sparkling with each step.

Dasharatha felt distant from his queens in this formal setting. He hoped it was not a mistake to include them. Beginning the meeting, Dasharatha called on Sumantra to bring in Chitra. Firsthand accounts were always the most powerful. Dasharatha wanted to spare the girl, so Chitra spoke for her. As Chitra spoke, Kausalya covered her mouth and looked away. Sumitra's eyes were wide and unblinking. Kaikeyi lifted her chin and sat straighter in her seat.

"Thank you, Chitra," Dasharatha said as the scout was dismissed. "Now, if I may summarize the events and the dilemma that stands before us. We are all well aware of the recent havoc caused by the king of blood-drinkers. Now one of them has returned to us. From her testimony, we know that she will be the first of many to return. We also know that she was rejected by her family, and that brings us to the reason for our meeting today. I would like to hear what each of you consider the best path for us to take."

"You have played your cards well, Great King," Siddhartha, the old one, said. "With the girl-child in mind, you hope to sway us to implement new laws. Only a heartless person would hold forth the age-old adages. And yet I must warn you that within these sayings, we discover the very truths of the people we serve. We are not alone in deciding the fates of these women. Society plays by its own rules."

"But are we not the lawmakers and the enforcers of all that society holds dear?" Sumantra asked. "We are here to examine and perhaps dismiss ways of thinking that don't protect the weak and innocent."

Kaikeyi fidgeted, her ornaments tinkling. Dasharatha saw a look of disgust pass her face.

"I would be amiss if I did not agree with Siddhartha," another minister said. "A woman lives in the care of her father, then husband, then son. The laws are clear on this. Once she crosses into the threshold of another man's house, she has lost her native belonging. That is what has happened to these women. Their families are not obliged to take them in."

"No man wants to raise his neighbor's children."

Kaikeyi spoke up. Her voice was rather curt, considering the esteemed council she was addressing. "Every woman should be trained in the use of weapons. That way she will defend herself and escape before any harm is done to her. Or else she will inflict what harm she can and die a brave warrior. We would then never have to face this unpalatable discussion. There would be no such thing as a ravaged woman returning to face society's unforgiving face."

Dasharatha was proud of her words. This was what they were here to discuss, after all.

Kausalya, however, disagreed. "Not every woman can be like you, respected Queen. It takes a great amount of energy and resources to train a warrior, and not everyone is naturally inclined to such work. I—"

Kaikeyi snorted, and then said, "Any child can learn how to kill with a simple knife."

Dasharatha held up a hand. He would not allow interruptions. He turned back to Kausalya.

She studiously avoided Kaikeyi's side of the room as she said, "It is *not* fair to demand that a woman face death because a man, out of his own volition, has violated the sacred laws. We are not speaking of situations when a woman consents and agrees to transgress the laws. We are speaking of circumstances when a pure and innocent woman, or even girl, is violated."

"I need not remind you, Queen Kausalya, what our laws are," Siddhartha said. "But I will do so only to remind us all that our justice system is fair. We are not lenient whatsoever toward men who violate women. A man does so at the cost of his life."

"Thank you, Minister," Kausalya returned. "But we are speaking of a situation where the criminal cannot be apprehended or punished. And it seems to me that the only ones suffering the consequences here are the women themselves. I do *not* agree that it is glorious for a woman to choose death in this case."

"There must be a way to purify these woman," Sumitra offered softly, speaking for the first time. "Holy One, possessor of ancient wisdom, is there no such ritual?"

All eyes turned toward Vasishta, who had not yet spoken and had observed in silence, as was his habit.

"I can think of a number of cleansing rituals," Vasishta answered. "But few of them would clean the minds of the suspicious. That is really what we are speaking of here, is it not?"

Everyone agreed.

"Can society accommodate and welcome back these women into its embrace?" Vasishta paused, looking to see if anyone would offer an opinion. "I'm afraid that mankind throughout history has not been lenient in these situations. Questions of purity, lineage, and offspring have remained foremost. It is known that a man, for the sake of his momentary pleasure, will cast a woman into a lifetime of darkness and shame."

Siddhartha spoke again. "Let me again be so bold as to remind us that marriage by aggressive abduction was sanctioned by Manu, the First Man."

Kausalya stood up. "I will welcome each of these ladies into service, as I have already promised to do with Rani. With your permission, I want to insist that we find a place in society where they are welcome. We must apprehend these women and offer them a home and an occupation before they succumb to society's pressure and end their own lives, the only recourse open to them aside from a life of shame."

"Who would truly take these women in?" Sumantra asked.

"When I oversee the dress and decoration of the dancing girls," Kausalya said, "I have learned much. They do not marry, at least not in the sense we think of it. They have many husbands. Their society does not have fathers, and so they do not insist on heritage and family names, the way we do. The mother claims the children as her own and raises them in service to the gods and the arts. Just this morning I was moved to tears by two of the dancing girls. No one can persuade me to believe that they are impure."

"You would make them courtesans?" Kaikeyi's tone was disparaging.

"If that saves them from suicide, yes! But not all the dancing girls are courtesans. Many of them are temple servants, dancing for the lords. Either way, they do not have that word *courtesan* in their language, for what they do, they do it for pleasure and their own reasons.

Let us not forget that we welcome them into our most sacred place and ask of them to invoke the gods through their dance. These women are revered by us. That is what I hope for the innocent women who have been ravaged by Ravana."

"Well said!" Sumantra exclaimed, instantly followed by words of praise from the rest of the ministers. Everyone was very pleased by Kausalya's surprising solution.

Only Kaikeyi did not make a show of support. It was ungracious of her, but she also was not fluent in the ways an official meeting was conducted, as her speaking out of turn had showed.

Kausalya spoke again, this time with a light, joyful voice. She urged them to send letters to the matriarchs of the society where the dancing girls lived. Dasharatha agreed to grant them endowments of land and wealth in return for their act of kindness.

Dasharatha's attention returned to his senior queen. He had needed a clear plan to enforce, and Kausalya's was both kind and doable. Her cheeks were flushed and her eyes sparkling, infused with vigor and purpose. She was beautiful.

Kaikeyi stood up and left, the only one to do so. Dasharatha's eyes followed her as she left. For a moment, the king wondered what opinion the hunchback might have on the recent event. Most certainly it would be in opposition to Dasharatha's opinion once Manthara knew it.

Soon after, the meeting was adjourned. In the days that followed, missives began flowing into Ayodhya, accounts matching Rani's tale. Messengers were sent out to the fifty kings as well as to every known matriarch in the realm of the arts. The kingdoms that were disinclined to oblige were instructed to safely escort the women to Ayodhya, where many homes would stand open and waiting.

Dasharatha was gladdened to hear of several cases where the families celebrated the return of their loved ones. And in so doing, they uprooted their family, left their home, and disappeared. That was the only way to escape society. Those rare families would resurface in another town with another family name. Some might suspect the truth, but when such an effort had been made for the loved one, Dasharatha thought even the coldest heart would find compassion enough not to stir up the past. There was some redemption in human nature, after all.

Among the returned women, Dasharatha did not find Lochana's wife. Still, he couldn't restrain himself from penning a letter to Lochana. His missing wife was, after all, the only woman abducted from Ayodhya's vicinity. Even when Anaranya fought with Ravana, the war had taken place beyond Ayodhya's city limits. For all his power, Ravana had never set foot within Ayodhya, the city of Manu.

Dasharatha's hand scribbled his well-chosen words across the parchment, writing that he hoped Lochana's wife would soon return, as others had. He hoped his message would encourage Lochana to welcome his wife with open arms. If, by some obscure chance, Lochana chose not to welcome his wife, Dasharatha wanted her to be escorted to Ayodhya, where arrangements had been made for the abandoned victims.

This was the letter the newly bereaved father and husband wrote in response:

Great King,

My wife is dead. I worship her memory. If she returns, touched and tainted by that monster, she is not the same woman I married. I have given up all hope of ever reuniting with her. We, my family and I, have made this decision together. I have made plans to remarry and begin my life anew.

I thank you for your concern.

Your loyal subject,

Lochana

Dasharatha looked at the letter for a long time. He had hoped his people would be more generous. But Lochana's letter was the voice of the people. Dasharatha was, in the end, the servant of his subjects. If he, the emperor of the world, was in the same situation, he would be forced to discard his own queen. A pure woman was hailed and worshipped. But even the shadow of a doubt was enough to cast away the purest of women. Perhaps the brave lady who had chosen to stay with Ravana had made the smartest choice of them all.

CHAPTER 13

A Queen to the Rescue

Kaikeyi had not liked Kausalya's success at the council meeting. Kausalya's notion of saving those poor girls was to create a new caste just for them. Kaikeyi did not think for a moment that their identities would be obscure. Everyone would know who they were and treat them accordingly. If Manthara was shunned for having a twisted spine, Kaikeyi could hardly imagine that Ayodhyans would be forgiving toward blemished females. Such a life was hardly worth living. Even so, Manthara's solution dismayed Kaikeyi: gifting poison to the girls in the guise of flowers. Manthara knew exactly where in the royal gardens such flowers grew. Kaikeyi told her to never speak of it again. Never mind that Kaikeyi had suggested something similar at the council, albeit choosing death with a knife in hand. Kausalya had openly dismissed Kaikeyi's opinion, and the senior queen had clearly gained the upper hand; Kaikeyi was restless to the bone. She didn't feel secure in her position, and when she examined why, it had to do with the fact that she had not produced a child for the king. Manthara muttered that when the king had three childless queens, the fault was hardly Kaikeyi's. No one spoke of it openly, but Kaikeyi sensed that all her power rested in the latent notion of her bride-price. But she had no sons and therefore no power compared to Kausalya.

On top of this, Kaikeyi was surrounded by more guards than ever before because of all those abducted women. She was allowed to ride only once the sun's rays shone brightly in the sky. When Kaikeyi had protested that she wasn't just another weak female, Dasharatha insinuated that Kaikeyi was a foolish girl with no understanding of the threat around them. He wanted her to fear the darkness and not fight it.

Then something happened that jostled Kaikeyi awake from palace intrigues. Dasharatha was leaving Ayodhya. In another unexpected event, a blood-drinker called Shambara was raiding villages beyond Ayodhya's borders, and Dasharatha was livid. Blood-drinkers were becoming too bold, sneaking out of their holes and making war on kings. The emperor was making ready to ride out and destroy the offender. Kaikeyi knew at once that she had to go with the king or stay behind in Ayodhya to wither and die.

She sought an audience with Dasharatha, approaching him formally, so that he would consider her merits as a warrior before anything else. She had eschewed her gown and jewelry for her fighting gear. If it came to it, she was prepared to prove her caliber on the training grounds. Dasharatha beheld her appearance and anticipated her request.

"No, my queen," he said.

"Yes, Great King," she said.

"This is not your fight."

"Your fight is my fight. Or else just say it. Say that I'm nothing but a woman to you. Helpless. Dependent. Weak."

He lifted his eyebrows and studied her.

"Have I been relegated to the women's quarters then," she said, "with only gossip as my weapon?"

"You underestimate a woman's power."

"That doesn't answer my question. You know that I'm not like other women. If I ever came face to face with Ravana, I *would* cut at least one of his heads off before he carried me away."

"You speak with levity of Ravana, as if he is a fantasy you can rip apart as swiftly as the pages of a fairy tale."

"If I'm so foolish and Kausalya is so wise," Kaikeyi countered, "then why do you seek *me* out every night and not her?"

To that, he had no answer. Of course he spoke of love. But that did not count in Kaikeyi's world. Manthara had always cautioned her that the king would profess to love her. It was nothing. Men's talk. The necessary pleasantries to create a romantic mood. This time, Kaikeyi used it to her advantage.

"My nights will be empty without you," she said, kneeling at his feet and looking up at him. "Let me spend my days and nights with you. I'm asking you as your lover. I'm asking you as a warrior. I long to fight at your side by day and be in your arms come night. Don't deny my power to serve you in both capacities. Please. I beg you."

Slowly, Dasharatha began to nod. He placed his hand on her cheek for a moment. "I see the fire in you, the one that burns in me. In truth, I don't have to personally go and face this Shambara. But after sitting idle for these months, receiving so many ghastly reports, I need to feel my own power again. My weapons long to serve." He looked at her carefully. "We need this, don't we, you and I?"

Her heart ached when he said "you and I," as though the world contained the two of them alone. He stood up and pulled her up into his arms. None of the other queens had the training or the courage to follow Dasharatha into war, but she did. She rested her hands on his heart, feeling its steady rhythm, and looked into his eyes. Was the feeling between them really love?

"My weapons long to serve," she said, echoing his words.

"On one condition. And I'm firm on this. Serve as my charioteer."

This meant that she would not engage in combat. Dasharatha was placing her in the safest position, as safe as one could be in the midst of violence and death. Only the cruelest warrior would attack the charioteer.

"Even as your charioteer, I might not be safe. The enemy may still target me, especially if they have abandoned etiquette, as I've heard whispered."

"Valid points though you make, I know I can protect you. None of my charioteers have ever died. If you are fighting separate from me, my eyes will be drawn to you and not the enemy. Understand?"

She didn't answer but stood up. "At your service, Great King."

"We depart on the morrow."

Kaikeyi bowed formally and left. She danced all the way back to her quarters. All the servants were caught up in her mirth. Manthara was aghast. She came rushing in with a speed that made the other servants shrink.

"Is he letting you accompany him?" she cried. "Doesn't he value your life at all?"

Kaikeyi was insulted by Manthara's reaction. "You forget that I'm a trained warrior!"

As always when Manthara was angry, the whole world centered around her. Kaikeyi felt the pleading note creep into her voice. "I've been playing queen here too long, Manthara. You forget that I'm a princess of Kekaya. I am a fighter first. Woman second."

Manthara showed the whites of her eyes. "This is beneath you, Keyi. It's a petty little battle. Don't risk your life for it. I forbid you."

Kaikeyi put her hands on her hips and faced her old matron. "If the king is ready to risk his life, then I'm ready to risk mine."

Manthara banged her cane against the marble floor. Kaikeyi, who was itching to leave Ayodhya, turned away from Manthara and did not listen to another word the woman said, though Manthara's voice grew louder and louder.

"I've spent every minute of my life raising you! Now you run off to some pathetic little battle. No one will remember this battle. You might return crippled or injured. Don't jeopardize our future. We have so much yet to accomplish." And so on.

It took great effort to ignore Manthara, but a force within Kaikeyi came to her aid. She knew she had to do this. In fact, Kaikeyi was childishly thrilled. She touched Manthara's curve for luck and then set out, throwing a dashing smile over her shoulder. Manthara's shrill prohibition echoed behind her.

Riding on her own horse with the king by her side, she felt free.

"Just this feeling is reward enough," she told Dasharatha. "It is worth the risk of never returning."

"Don't speak in such a way," Dasharatha warned her. Speaking of defeat or never returning was bad luck.

"We will both return alive," he said.

It was an empty promise, but she supposed it was his way to revoke the bad luck she had conjured.

As they rode out of the city gates with the army in their wake, Dasharatha briefed Kaikeyi on the details. Shambara, an obvious Ravana worshipper, was riding along the villages of Kalinga and Videha with a growing army. The deceitful had found a new master to serve. Dasharatha had no mercy for the blood-drinker or his followers. The king welcomed this opportunity to face the enemy.

On the third day, they arrived in the area where Shambara had last been seen. There were no signs of him or his army, and Dasharatha set up camp. Scouts were sent out in all directions to decide the next day's route.

As morning came, Kaikeyi dressed herself by the flickering flames of torches. This camp was no palace. Kaikeyi loved the plainness of the campsite and the limited rules here. She did not have to decorate her body in any way or walk about elegantly. There was but the warrior's gear to don: cotton undergarments, padding, and on top of it, the armor, fitted to protect all her vital organs. It was simple, functional, and smelled of sweat and horse.

The king seemed a more approachable man here.

"Dasharatha," she said, savoring the familiarity of calling him by name, since she was one of three in all of Ayodhya with this privilege. Even Manthara, with her irreverent ways, called him simply "the king."

Dasharatha looked up, pausing the sharpening of his blades. When she said nothing, he asked, "What is it, beloved?"

"Nothing. I just wanted you to look at me."

"Do I not look at you often enough?"

She shrugged. He put his work down and fixed his eyes on her.

"What do you see?" she asked.

"The one I love."

"The *one*?" She mocked. She knew that he did not love her alone. Dasharatha did not rise to the bait.

"Sometimes I forget how young you are," he said. "Your appetite for life cannot be satiated. I was like that once. Now small moments of happiness are enough for me."

She did not like being reminded of her youth, which was both her weapon and her weakness. He would always be twenty-nine years wiser than she. Kausalya used this fact to her advantage.

The horns across the camp blew urgently to signal that someone was approaching the site. The sun was about to rise, and the enemy's army was on them. Kaikeyi suddenly felt the rumble in the ground. She secured her sword and her knives and left the tent to pull up the chariot. When Dasharatha came out of the tent, she would not have dared continue their jesting. His lips were in a tight line, his eyes steely. This battle would end today.

The horses listened to her wordless commands, and they rode through the campsite as Dasharatha called out orders to the soldiers behind him. It was a language that Kaikeyi had not mastered, concerning formations and the strategy of attack they would employ. The soldiers hastily took the formations as the king ordered. Dasharatha blew his conch shell, the signal to attack. The enemy lines were already surging toward them.

Attacking aggressively, Kaikeyi led the chariot into the enemy ranks. Dasharatha earned his name, "Ten Chariots," a thousand times over. Dead soldiers fell in their path. Kaikeyi expertly maneuvered the steeds, guiding the four horses to slow down and speed up at the right moments.

"Left!" Dasharatha shouted, and she was already doing it.

As they worked like this, Kaikeyi felt that no king or queen had ever made such a team. She heard his arrows fly by her. The horses snorted. Men cried as they died.

"There he is!" the king yelled, and Shambara appeared before them, in a chariot drawn by four crossbreed mules. Kaikeyi had never seen such creatures. They had demon faces, elongated and flattened to fit into a horse skull. Their fangs protruded from their mouths and their eyes were intelligent but menacing.

The blood-drinker showed his fangs, and Dasharatha shot an arrow into his mouth. Shambara did not make a sound as he pulled the arrow out amid sprays of blood. Dasharatha's next arrow destroyed his opponent's bow. Screaming now in an unintelligible tongue, Shambara flung Dasharatha's own arrow back at him. It grew in the air and flew toward them, with impossible speed.

Without a sound, Dasharatha fell back, collapsing onto the chariot floor. The next second, Kaikeyi was splattered in the king's blood. The whole chariot shook, and Kaikeyi screamed.

Dasharatha moaned. A huge javelin now protruded from his chest. The arrow had transformed into a javelin and was pinning him to the chariot floor. She would not panic. The blood-drinker laughed wildly, blood gushing from his mouth. The horses started running wild. She had to gain control of the chariot.

Kaikeyi had to leave the battlefield now. She threw the reins into one hand and reached for a shield, crouching low and protecting herself from the onslaught of arrows. Faster!

The king's army understood what was happening. They moved, opening an exit route for her, closing it behind her as she escaped. She lost sight of the blood-drinker. The sounds of battle and death cries continued. The horses galloped wildly, smashing into Ayodhya's own foot soldiers. She shouted and screamed. She whipped the horses, a sign of her stress. There was no time to bend down and touch the king.

Dasharatha's eyes closed as he lost consciousness. The wound in his chest bled profusely.

"Open your eyes!" she shouted. She couldn't, even in this crisis, get herself to nudge him with her foot. Her tears rained behind her, flying away in the wind. She felt her braid whipping relentlessly at her back as she was thrashing the horses. "Go! Go! Go!"

Kaikeyi fled as if haunted by demons. She scanned the horizon ahead, looking for shelter. The battle raged on behind her, but she saw no one in pursuit of them. The army had expertly closed its formation, preventing the enemy from pursuit. Kaikeyi would take no chances with the king dying at her feet. Maybe she would continue until she could go no farther. She had no plan, for she had not planned for this. How could she have been so utterly foolish?

Even as she berated herself, a sense of calm settled on her. She had to stop the king's blood flow. She was not a healer of any kind, but she had seen enough men die to know this. There was blood everywhere in the chariot. She had seen blood before. Lots of it. But never the blood of the one she loved. She was afraid to stop and find him already dead. And that was the moment she knew: she loved Dasharatha. More than her own life.

When she could no longer hear or see the battle behind them, she sought the shade of a tree and pulled the chariot to a halt. She barely touched the reins, and the horses stopped with wild eyes and heaving sides. As the chariot lurched to a final stop, she lost her footing and slipped on the his blood. With shaky arms, she crouched at Dasharatha's side. His body was limp, his face pale, and his head loose on his neck.

He is dead, her mind whispered.

Her hand instinctively reached toward his chest, where she usually placed her hand on his heart. At once, she felt its rhythmical beating. He was alive. The javelin had not pierced his heart, or he would already be dead. She saw the blood pumping out in rhythm with

each heartbeat, but the javelin was to the right of his heart. She prayed she would have the strength to pull the javelin out, or else they would be doomed.

She stood up, holding on to the railing of the chariot for a moment. She began to rip her armor and clothes off. She would need every cloth to stop the bleeding. Once the weapon was out, he would bleed even more profusely. Next she climbed out of the chariot to see if the tip of the javelin had pierced through the chariot floor. It had not. This gave her hope. She spoke soothingly to the horses, promising them water at the soonest. She needed them to stay still. Back on the chariot, she planted her feet on either side of Dasharatha's chest and took hold of the javelin. She pushed into her feet, using all the strength she had to extract the javelin. She grunted like a man, ordering the javelin out. Unwillingly it followed her will. As she pulled it up and out, Dasharatha's whole chest followed, stuck to the javelin. Having no choice, she put one foot on his breast, pushing him back down, as she continued carefully extracting the missile. As the tip finally emerged, his blood pumped out forcefully.

She threw the javelin aside and pressed a cloth against the wound. The cloth drank up the blood, and she reached for the next cloth, adding the padding from her armor. Finally, she lifted his limp upper body and tightly bandaged it. As she was doing this, the chariot began moving and the horses neighed.

"Stop!" she ordered.

She had forgotten she was on the chariot and now realized she had to get the king down. Locking her arms around his chest and under his arms, she gingerly stepped off the chariot and dragged him after her, his legs thumping against the ground. The horses lurched away with the chariot. She had to release the poor animals, but she could not focus on anything but Dasharatha and his wound. She settled the king's head on her lap and began to pray.

She prayed to every god she could think of and tried to scrutinize her life for any acts of kindness that might boost her prayers and their urgency. Too tired to think so deeply, she repeated, *Please, please, please.*

Still sitting, her head nodded and her mind went into a trancelike state. She was neither awake nor asleep.

"Wake up!" a stranger said. "The king is dead. Come with me."

Panic welled up. The king had been alive seconds ago!

The stranger beckoned her to come with him. "Leave the king. He has left his mortal body," he said.

Was he a messenger from Ayodhya? Was the battle won or lost?

"Leave me alone," she cried. "He is going to live!" But when she looked down, there was nothing but a skeleton grinning up at her.

"There is no time for grief," the stranger insisted, pulling her away. "Ayodhya needs you. You will rule as the queen now."

But when she entered Ayodhya's court, it was Kausalya who sat on the throne, looking down at Kaikeyi with a benevolent smile that made Kaikeyi shrivel.

"That one deserves no mercy," Kausalya said. "Cut off her nose and ears. Exile her from Ayodhya."

With a jolt, Kaikeyi's trance broke. Darkness of night surrounded her, along with the sounds of crickets. Dasharatha breathed laboriously, his head a heavy stone in her lap. But he was breathing, thank the gods.

She touched his forehead. It was burning with fever and drenched in sweat.

Kaikeyi felt grim. Even here and now, when nothing mattered but the king's life, she could not forget Kausalya, the sinister old queen. Kaikeyi knew that if ever a queen would sit upon the throne, which in itself had no precedent, it would be Kausalya. Everyone in Ayodhya loved the older queen. She was born and bred in Koshala, one of them. Kaikeyi would always be the outsider.

Kaikeyi shook her head and smacked herself several times. She was indulging in utter nonsense. At this rate, she would be a widow. She checked her own forehead. Had she gotten sunstroke or was she in shock? Her throat was parched. Dasharatha was hot with fever. They needed water. Now. Even though she did not want to leave him, she needed to find water, to clean the sweat and blood from his body and keep his fever down.

She gently moved his head and placed it on the ground. She looked around at the darkness of night. They were nowhere near civilization. The campsite was miles away and she did not know the outcome of the battle. Suddenly she worried about tigers and then about blood-drinkers. She had heard that blood-drinkers could smell blood from afar more keenly than any other predator. Blood was seeping steadily from Dasharatha's wounds. But she had no choice.

Putting her lips to his ear, she whispered, "I must go find water, my love. Don't go anywhere."

The last bit made her smile a little. She got up, grabbing her flask, and emptied two quivers of arrows. She left and didn't look back. He was completely vulnerable and defenseless. But Kaikeyi told herself her fears were baseless. There were no blood-drinkers or tigers here. She calculated that she had until next daylight before anyone, friend or foe, might seek them out.

As she walked deeper into the forest, sword in hand, she listened for a stream or river. She tried to bring to mind all healing herbs and their uses, but she had not excelled in the healing arts, and her mind was blank.

"Keep looking," she told herself out loud. Manthara would have said, "Don't be a doddering fool." Manthara's reassuring face rose up before her, with its no-nonsense look: "Find water. Find useful herbs. Get back to him fast."

The sound of her own voice boosted her spirit, and she quickened her steps.

An hour later, she returned with two quivers full of water. The water source had been farther than she had hoped. She broke into a run when she saw Dasharatha's form. She had to move closer to the water in the morning, where she had even found a few bulbs of turmeric root. Turmeric was such a common ingredient in both food and medicine Kaikeyi knew it would prevent wounds from festering and illnesses from escalating. She dropped the bulbs to the ground and fell to her knees by Dasharatha's side, pouring water into his mouth. Most of it flowed down his neck.

"You are safe now," she said. Pure love for him pulsated in her being. "I'm here."

In response, she heard an icy laughter, which ran up her spine. She looked up and saw two translucent creatures with bright pink eyes watching her, the most base of the blood-drinkers who lived under the ground. She had never seen their kind before. Their blue veins ran along their bodies; their tongues flickered in and out of their fanged mouths.

Kaikeyi just stared. Her eyelids drooped over her eyes. Her arms hung limply by her sides. In the moment when she most needed it, her body was shutting down. The king twitched; his hand flicked against her thigh. She woke with a start, and without thinking, she was on her feet. A growl rose from her throat, so menacing that the hairs on her arms stood on end. The pink-eyed creatures fell on all fours, pouncing toward her, salivating like two dogs.

Kaikeyi broke into a run, lifting her sword, screaming, "Yah!"

With one quick stroke, she lopped off one of their heads. Like a headless snake, its body slithered on the ground. The other one shot upright, lifting its claws.

Silently Kaikeyi and the creature circled, swiping in the air at each other. He had no weapon, but his claws were sharp and so fast that she could see only a blur of movement. He was much faster and hungrier than she was. When she jabbed at his belly, he drew back, hissing.

In one desperate move, she kicked the head of the dead one. It flew up toward the creature. Instinctively he caught it, and in that moment Kaikeyi threw her blade at him with all her might. It sank into his belly to the hilt. For a second, he stood there, head in his hands, blade in his belly.

She ran forward, kicking him down as she drew her blade out.

His blue veins squirted blood so dark it seemed black. When it spread out on his translucent skin, however, it was as bright red as human blood. Kaikeyi felt sick with the thought that it quite probably was ingested human blood.

"Yah!" she yelled again and again, hacking both the creatures to pieces. "Die!"

They died, a hundred times over.

She collapsed onto the ground next to their mangled bodies. She took a deep breath and gagged at the foul smell. She crawled away from the stinking corpses and the defecation of death, then got onto her knees and then her feet. She had to get rid of these reeking bodies and untie the horses.

But first she checked on Dasharatha, pouring water into his mouth again. She carefully poured water over his body, hoping to cool down his feverish limbs. She kissed his brow and his cheeks. Her hands hovered over the wound. She had to move elsewhere; there could be other blood-drinkers on the prowl. But she didn't know if any other place would be safer. The king was too weak to be moved and he was too heavy for her, and ... and ... and ... The young queen passed out next to her husband, falling into darkness so deep, she might have joined her husband in the halls of death.

"Come back to me," she called out.

CHAPTER 14

The Dream of Rama

When the javelin crashed into his chest, he did not even have time to scream. Kaikeyi did. Her piercing cry went straight through him too. And he fell dead.

He who had fought alongside the gods in countless battles was now dead. He, who thought himself as immortal as a human could be, was dead. He who had no children—who carried the sun's blood in his veins, who ruled the Earth—was dead. Who was he now?

"Wake up!" she screamed.

Who was she?

"Sh-sh-sh," he struggled to say. If only he could have some silence, then the pain of "I" would be over.

"Open your eyes," she begged.

But he could not. The horses snorted, their hooves clattering against the ground. Where was he going?

His body was being rushed somewhere, but he hovered above it effortlessly. Yet he was connected somehow to that dying body, forced to follow the frightful rush of the chariot, its horses, and the commandeering woman.

He was not dead yet, he realized.

He saw her then, from up there. A woman whipping her horses until their eyes were rolling, her long black hair flying behind her like the goddess of war. *Don't get in her way,* he thought. Nothing could stop her. He knew this about her, but couldn't say who the fierce woman was. Then he saw the corpse in the chariot with its head bouncing wildly with every jostle of the chariot. The golden helmet was smashed in on the side. There was blood in a pool around his chest and her red footprints all around him. It had been his blood, his body. He drifted from the chariot. Up and away. He could neither hear nor feel its hasty escape from the battleground behind them. As he felt the connection to his mortal life weaken, there was only one regret: the Sun dynasty's illustrious line would end because he was dying and he had no sons. The regret surprised him. He had felt the pressure to produce an heir, and he had dutifully pursued it. But he had not wanted sons, not truly. He had known it would just end badly. He had killed that innocent boy, and the curse of the boy's father had branded him. That fateful night had been buried deep in his mind, where he kept secrets. It was the last coherent thought he had.

Memories of his earthly life grew dim. Thoughts became amorphous. He could no longer think or formulate his feelings as he had done as a human being. And yet he was not released from his mind. He was trapped in a borderland, neither dead nor alive. He was powerless, a strange, new feeling for him. The king and the man he had been would have raged against it. But there were no conflicts in this borderland, no tension. Now he was both more and less than the man he had been. In that powerless state, he simply waited and began to dream.

A green luminescence shimmered around him. He was not alone. There was a small boy next to him whose luminous emerald skin lit up everything around both of them. The king had never seen anything like it. The child had big brown eyes that were both intense and kind. Children did not have eyes like that. The boy, who was maybe two or three, did not speak, just floated effortlessly next to the king. Every now and then, he turned toward the king and looked him long in the eyes.

He wasn't a child, the king knew; he was in disguise.

That made the boy smile, and he took the king's hand.

The king opened his arms, and the child returned his embrace. The boy did not stop there, but walked into the king's heart. Stunned, the king followed. He realized he had never been inside it before. It was a vast place, a complete world with lush fields, forests, and buildings. There was a room full of the books he loved. Another room was full of paintings of people he admired. He stopped to look at two large ones of his father and his mother. They were young in the portraits, the way they looked when he himself was a young boy.

The child beckoned him to continue, walking ahead, deeper into the maze of his heart. The king followed, trying to catch hold of the boy's hand again.

"Are you my son?" he asked the boy.

"Rama," the boy said, uttering the two syllables with childish charm. He disappeared from view, into the maze of Dasharatha's heart, the green luminescence growing dimmer.

"Come back," the king called.

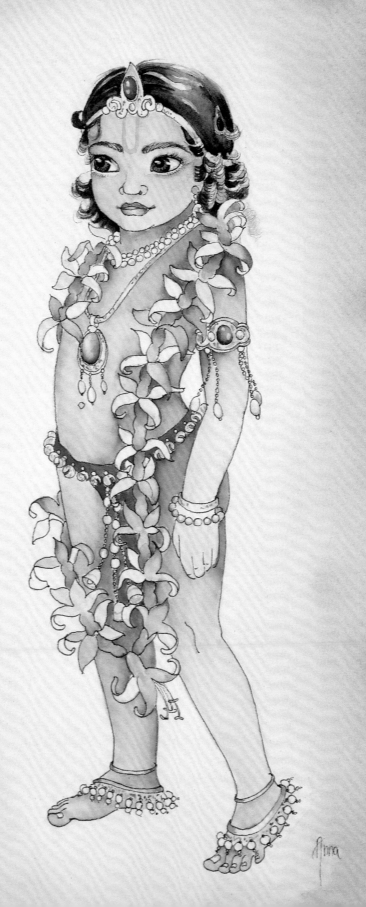

And he heard the words echo in every chamber of his heart: "Come back, come back, come back." It was his own call magnified by someone else's.

The woman on the chariot whispered, "Come back to me."

At once he was not in his heart anymore. He was back in his spirit, looking down at the pitiful scene of his body and the lady laboring for his life. Just as quickly, darkness shrouded him, and he was back in his body. He felt the strong beating of his heart, the pulsating ache of his near-fatal wound, the weakness of his limbs, and the thirst of his dry lips and throat. The world took shape around him even though his eyes were closed. The sun was scorching, and he felt the blaze on his skin. He felt as clearheaded as he once had been, the visions and thoughts of his spirit as diffuse to him now as his human thoughts had been. Though he longed to ask for water, the word that started forming on his lips was a name. *Kaikeyi*. He was acutely aware of his queen beside him and every word she said.

She was speaking to herself, as if he was not there at all. Incoherent words. A constant stream of words and stories that all centered around him.

"Kai," was all the king managed to say, but he felt his wife startle and turn to him with eyes that were as round as the sun. "Water."

Even these were too many words for a man who had nearly died and whose voice had not been used in days. How many days? He would ask that as soon as Kaikeyi got him some water.

She moved swift like lightning, and when she lifted the water to his mouth, she pressed her lips to his head and buried her face in his hair. He drank the water greedily at first, but told himself to slow down and sip it instead. If he drank too much all at once, his body would reject it. Though his body felt weak like never before in his life, he felt light and carefree. This woman had saved his life, and he had a tremendous feeling of something completely astounding in their future. There was a feeling of tenderness deep within his heart, toward whom or what, he could not say. He was grateful to be alive.

Without words, he pulled Kaikeyi into his arms, ignoring the explosion of pain in his chest. He wrapped his arms around her and felt her hot tears against his neck. The pain grew tolerable and Dasharatha noticed Kaikeyi was barely clothed. She looked as wild as a feral tribeswoman. Every piece of clothing had evidently gone toward dressing his wound. He felt his chest, and groaned. The pain was constant but bearable.

"How many days?" he finally asked, without letting her go. He could feel her rib cage pressing against his arms.

"I lost count," she answered at his neck. "More than ten. Less than thirty."

He stroked her long black hair. She would need extra care now. He knew what it was, coming out of a crisis. They had both been hit hard. Even before he looked at his arms and legs, he knew he had lost much of his strength. He would have to train many months, maybe years, to regain a semblance of his previous power. After a cursory examination of his body, he noticed that his beard had grown white. It meant nothing except he probably looked like an old man now. All these physical changes were inconsequential, compared to the deeper changes in his psyche.

"The battle? My men? Where are we?"

"Two of your men found us yesterday," she said. "We won. Nearly everyone on both sides succumbed. But Shambara was slain, and the battle is over. They would have found us sooner if I had not moved you several times to hide from blood-drinkers. I didn't know if you would ever come back to consciousness. I insisted that slinging you across a horse one more time might kill you. They will be here today with a carriage."

Dasharatha drank the remaining water. "I owe you my life," he said. The tenderness in his heart grew. "Ask anything from me and it's yours."

She looked up at him with her deep blue eyes. "My prayers have already been answered. You are alive."

He laughed, feeling both the joy and the pain spread in his chest. "Even more reason for me to repay you. I will give you anything you want."

"Just love me forever," she said, the words of the young woman that she was.

"I already love you more than I should. You could destroy me with one word, and you don't even realize it."

The spark in her eye showed up. "You make no sense."

He smiled, hugging her as close as his throbbing wound allowed. "If you had not saved me, I would not have survived. My life is yours. Now I've said it twice. You have two boons at your disposal. Any time you want something from me, it's yours."

Though his body was weakened, his passion for her was not. He drew her to him, wrapping his arms around her, feeling her vitality seep into his skin. The pain of his body mingled with the passion of his blood. Only the two of them existed, alone on the Earth together.

The union was an affirmation of the life he had nearly lost. After, the king's wounds throbbed relentlessly, and Dasharatha pulled away. A voice in his mind sent him a caution. It was perhaps the voice of reason, but it sounded very much like Sumantra, his faithful minister. Sumantra would not be pleased with Dasharatha's impulsive act, giving Kaikeyi two unconditional boons. It was not a wise political move. But Dasharatha was alive due to Kaikeyi.

To be certain, however, Dasharatha turned to Kaikeyi. He didn't have much strength left, but said, "The boons. Keep them to yourself. They are yours alone."

She nodded.

He fainted.

CHAPTER 15

The Queen's Secret

Manthara was Ayodhya's best-kept secret. No one knew that they had a mastermind among them in the guise of a hunchback. She would own Ayodhya the way she had owned Kekaya. Her foremost instrument was Kaikeyi, and she was intent on discovering Ayodhya's weaknesses. Her eyes were on the court of justice, the royal gardens, and the other two queens. Few people dared interfere with her. Of course, Kausalya had insulted Manthara by suggesting that Manthara would be a fitting mentor for Ravana's victims. Certainly: couple the outcasts with the cripple. Manthara could see Kausalya's logic, but it was as twisted as Manthara's spine ever was. First of all, those new girls couldn't even dance, so it was a joke. Second, Manthara did not want to compromise her status by mingling with that lot. If you associated with an outcast for one year, you became an outcast. Everyone knew this. Manthara was on to Kausalya's plan and avoided the new dancing girls as if they were diseased. It pleased her to look at them with disgust and see them shiver under her gaze.

Though Manthara frequently reported back to Ashvapati, she neglected to mention the abduction incident and Kausalya's solution. Ashva would learn of it through the ordinary channels, like every other king. Manthara was aware that in despising the dancing girls, she acted contrary to Ashva's principles.

She had not extended the compassion that she expected to receive herself. But why should she? Their situation was nothing like hers. No one would think of abducting Manthara, so apologies to all the thirty gods if she didn't exactly empathize with the alleged victims. They had only suffered from too much attention. Ravana was well known as a seducer and womanizer. No doubt half of those "victims" had secretly enjoyed it. They wouldn't die from being deprived a little now. Indeed, if Manthara had been king, she would have disposed of the problem by sending them on to the land of Yama. It was not such a terrible place. What was the fuss all about? Even Kaikeyi had acted horrified when Manthara suggested a gift of flowers. It was the first time Manthara had displayed her knowledge of the plants in front of Kaikeyi, but still, Kaikeyi's horror was like a child's—as if Kaikeyi hadn't killed people with her bare hands.

Speaking of Kaikeyi, when Manthara opened her eyes, her first waking thought went to the young queen. Then to her deformity. The curvature in her back had become stiff through the night. Once Manthara climbed out of her bed, it took a concerted effort to raise her head up. When she raised her face to look at the sky or, in this case, the domed white ceilings, an army of fire ants attacked her neck. Sighing, she let her head drop, seeing but not seeing the marble floor with its inlaid mosaic patterns. Yes, she lived in privileged quarters close to Kaikeyi, and every day she wore fine silks and costly jewels, but what did such things matter when her body was so detestable and withered? The only part of herself she valued was her mind. She had always been a notch sharper than everyone else. This was especially true once she came to Ayodhya; the maids here were dull-witted. It was as if Kausalya purposefully employed imbeciles so that she could herself appear more intelligent. Manthara had never heard anyone in Ayodhya say anything she didn't already know. Manthara had heard the reports of how close to death the king had been. A javelin through the heart, they said. It was a miracle he survived. Manthara wouldn't call it that. She wasn't sure she believed in miracles at all. It was Kaikeyi, the brave warrior-queen, who had saved the king with her skills on a chariot. Kaikeyi would have unprecedented power over the king now, having saved his life. Only Manthara could see this. Painfully intelligent, that's what she was.

Without looking, she grabbed a long piece of cloth and threw it around the lump of her body, stopping only to inspect that she was covered and decorous. Years of wear made the heavy silk sari fall nicely in place around her body, colorful and flowing. She did not have the habit of looking in the mirror. In fact she had the habit of *not* looking. She knew what she would see there: an old hag with gray hair, a painting of someone she actually didn't know. Especially today, her mind felt exuberant and sharp, awaiting the meeting with the one person she loved. Her body, as usual, struggled to keep up with her.

Today she would finally reunite with Kaikeyi, who would be released from her quarantine. The young queen had already been back several days from the battle but, Manthara was told, "in no condition to meet anyone." It had taken all Manthara's self-control not to lift up her cane and beat the guards on their arrogant heads. How dare they stop her from seeing Kaikeyi! The Ayodhyans treated her as a common servant when she was all but the girl's mother. Like a real mother, Manthara had survived sleepless nights and nursed the baby girl through months of incessant crying. In Kekaya, she had been acknowledged for this. But Ayodhyans had no concept of honor at all. They threw victims of abduction into prostitution, thinking it a brilliant solution.

So Manthara had bit her tongue and retreated to her room. Without asking, she knew who the order had come from: that self-centered king who never thought of anyone but himself. He certainly never considered Manthara's feelings. Instead of treating her as an ally, as Ashvapati did, he was always seeking a reason to send Manthara back to Kekaya. Well, Manthara was ahead of his game. In due time, she would reveal herself.

With unusual speed, Manthara left her chamber. Her fingers were restless around her cane. If they barred her entry again today, she would have less self-control. As Manthara walked past guard after guard, they made no gesture of acknowledgment, no deference to speak of. Was she considered a maleficent spirit haunting these corridors? That's what they made her feel like. If Kausalya walked by, they fell to the ground slobbering at her feet. If Kekaya was known for its horses, Ayodhya should have been known for its sycophantic servants. Manthara saw right through their pretend sincerity. The only thing indestructible about Ayodhya was its arrogance. The people were so proud of the city, as if they had built it with their own hands. Manthara rolled her eyes. Ayodhyans were constantly taking credit for things they knew nothing about. *Look at this magnificent archway,* they would say. "Who built it?" Manthara would ask, and they would look at her as if she had spoken in another language. They didn't have the brains to realize that a building was like a mind, built the way it was for a reason. Manthara disliked people who were too sincere, and she disliked people who were insincere. Every single Ayodhyan was one or the other. They dared to whisper that Kaikeyi was manipulative and selfish! Oh, yes, Manthara had heard it said, and all because Kaikeyi was honest. Unlike the likes of them.

Distracted by her own grumblings, she tripped on her silk cloth and fell.

"Let me help you," a guard said, stepping forward.

"I can do it myself," she snapped. She had managed all her life without help. Beneath his smile, she could see the disdain, the meanness. She knew they pitied her at best or found her disgusting. She got back on her feet with the help of her cane. It had more backbone than the guard.

As she hobbled along to Kaikeyi's quarters, she strictly avoided eye contact with any of the hypocrites. Sometimes she felt like a lonely witch, accusing shadows of their shapelessness. But wasn't it suspicious that in two full years living in Ayodhya, not one unkind word had been spoken to her face? They hid their ugliness well, while Manthara was not shy of displaying hers.

Her only safe place was with Kaikeyi. To boost her own spirits, Manthara fondly recalled a memory from when Kaikeyi was three. The little girl had cried herself to sleep, saying, "I want one too!" She meant the hump on Manthara's back. That's what you call disarming! The child's innocence made Manthara forgot how she saw herself. The child thought she, the hunchbacked hag, had a desirable form. It had melted Manthara's heart like nothing else, before or since. If she ever was cross with Kaikeyi or with anyone, she would bring this to mind and feel instantly soothed. Kaikeyi, as a little girl, would stroke and pat Manthara's hunched back, making it the object of her admiration and affection.

Even now, Kaikeyi would bend down and kiss Manthara's curved back. For good luck and love, Kaikeyi would say. She had done this before she left for the battle with the king.

Just then she walked through Kaikeyi's archway and stumbled upon the young queen.

"Manthara!" Kaikeyi cried out at once, and even clapped her hands together several times, before she smothered the old woman with hugs and kisses. And this was a miracle to Manthara. The only one. Surreptitiously, she wiped her tears with her sari.

"Oh, don't cry," Kaikeyi coaxed, noticing anyway. "I'm alive and well!"

Only then did Manthara feel the rush of withheld grief, her previous certainty that Kaikeyi would never return alive.

"The battlefield is no place for a queen," she heard herself blubber, reiterating her first warning to the queen.

"I know, I know, but if I wasn't there, the king would have died."

Taking Manthara's hand eagerly and leading her to a seat, Kaikeyi proceeded to tell her what had happened. As the story unfolded, as Kaikeyi described her brave escape, Manthara did not fail to notice how Kaikeyi addressed the king. Until now, the two of them had always called him simply "the king," formally and with a distance that Manthara approved. Now the young queen was bubbling with the event as it had transpired, but all Manthara could hear was how she went from "the king" to "Dasharatha" to "my husband" and even "my love"!

"You love him," Manthara said, interrupting her, and feeling the tendons in her neck strain. She could feel the accusation in her tone and in her eyes.

"Of course I do," Kaikeyi replied instantly. "He is my husband and king."

She pretended not to notice Manthara's total dismay. Well, she would.

"But you married him to be queen, not a foolish blushing bride."

Kaikeyi fell silent, staring at Manthara. They both knew that a servant could never speak like this to her queen, so frankly and openly. But Manthara could. Suddenly fear squeezed her heart, because she saw a new reserve in Kaikeyi's face.

"Don't close your heart to me," Manthara said at once.

"Is my every thought so obvious? You read me like a child reads its stories."

"It's only because I know you and serve your best interest. Don't forget your father's caution. What was his first teaching to you? The moment you give your love to this man, you surrender; you lose the upper hand, and he will have the power to break you."

She could see the incomprehension in Kaikeyi's face, almost as if she was shaken by Manthara's confrontation. What was so hard to understand here? Usually Kaikeyi would rise to any challenge and pull Manthara with her by the force of her passion. They had talked about this so many times.

But Kaikeyi answered in a shaky voice, "Aren't you happy that I don't have to be unhappy like my father?"

Manthara felt herself step back. Is that how Kaikeyi thought of her father?

"I didn't think this unity was possible," Kaikeyi said, "but Dasharatha and I have become one heart, one mind."

She was purring like an overfed cat, and Manthara couldn't stop what came out from her mouth: "Pah!"

They stared at each other then, at total odds, like two strangers speaking mutually incomprehensible languages. All the joy of reuniting was gone.

Kaikeyi threw out her arms and let them drop to her side, smacking her own thighs impatiently. "What is the purpose of marriage if not the meeting of two minds, two hearts, two souls?"

"I'm shocked by you!" Manthara said. Secretly she was pleased; she had missed this tension, this exchange of minds. "What's the purpose of marriage," she mimicked sourly. "Really? Are we then to start from your first letters again? From zero?"

Kaikeyi looked away, shaking her head, avoiding Manthara's persistent gaze. This was perhaps the most important premise of Manthara's lifelong views.

"Love and all that," she said, "might be right for some fisherwoman with no ambition. You are a queen! I will not let you get trapped in so-called love. The purpose of your marriage is not romance, but power!"

"Why are they mutually exclusive?"

At least she didn't deny it. Manthara felt herself tap her cane against the ground, as she did when agitated. She tried to still her hand, to speak calmly and rationally. "Love is not power but its opposite. Since the beginning of time, love has been the bane of a woman's existence, the reason she is content with less—content being subordinate, and indeed thinking herself lucky to be in a man's favor. But why can't a woman be queen and rule in her own right?"

Here Manthara cleverly appealed to Keyi's childhood aspiration to be king of Kekaya—an aspiration that Manthara had rightly shattered. Still it was good for the grown woman to remember that pure desire for great power.

Manthara added: "The dream-befuddled lover wanders around in the rose garden smelling the flowers, content in her love and her dreams. But at any time, the gate to the rose garden can be barred to her forever. What would she have in her hands then? The same she had to begin with. Nothing!"

And then Manthara bashed her cane on the ground with each word: "Nothing, nothing!"

The violence of her outburst echoed around them only because Kaikeyi did not rise to the bait. Her face was passive, giving little away. This in itself squeezed Manthara's insides again.

"No, Manthara, my dear, you are wrong," Kaikeyi said. There was no anger in her voice. She didn't add the rest, but it was written there, as bright as pictures in a storybook: *You wouldn't understand. You don't know. You have no husband. You have never enjoyed a man's company or his love. You are unloved.*

This young woman was standing before her and telling her in so few words that she knew more than Manthara about love, about love and how it worked. For the first time, Manthara felt her dark heart turn on her young queen—the daughter she never had.

You are ugly, she heard herself think. *Your beauty is temporary. You will be discarded. You think you are so clever. Without me, you would be nothing but a shallow beauty.*

"Manthara? Your expression scares me."

She can read you too, old hag. Be careful.

"Speak," Kaikeyi said.

Manthara regarded that worried expression on Kaikeyi's pretty face that would turn ugly and wrinkled one day soon.

The queen said, "You're not one for silences."

No, she hadn't been, but things were different now, were they not?

This was completely new, the need to censor her thoughts, to pick and choose what to say and what to withhold, all because of "love." Because Kaikeyi was foolish enough to fall into the king's trap. Manthara hated that man without reservation, and she allowed her body to fill up with the pure and hot feeling of hate. The king's "love" would sway Kaikeyi and turn her blind and weak, like she was already turning a deaf ear to Manthara.

But Kaikeyi waited for her response, so she smiled at her queen—not a genuine one, but the effort was enough.

"Very well, love him then, but don't say I didn't warn you."

"Oh, don't be a boor," Kaikeyi said, throwing her arms around Manthara, kissing her on the cheeks repeatedly. "I just now came home. I didn't know you would pick my brain and get to my depths within the first minutes. But then, no one in all of Ayodhya is as astute as you. Of course I'll consider your words with care." Then she pulled away and added, "If you also heed mine?"

"What?"

"Give Ayodhya a chance. Give the king a chance. I see now that we never did. We came here with so many reservations. We decided that Kekaya was a better place than Ayodhya. We decided that we knew more than anyone in Ayodhya. I think we have been foolish. Embrace this new life we have here, Manthara, in the same wholehearted way you embrace me."

If only you knew. But that was a private thought now. Out loud she sighed, to demonstrate the effort this would take from her.

"Don't expect any miracles overnight," she said to Kaikeyi. "I am who I am."

"And I love you," the queen said, her arms again around her.

No, you love him, she thought. As if it was either-or. But wasn't it?

Did the king love all his wives equally? No. Love was for one person only. That was the law of love. The more you shared it, the less there would be. Soon enough, Manthara was certain, Kaikeyi would not remember to hug her and kiss her and tell her she was the smartest one in Ayodhya. The king would need all that love and encouragement. There would be none left for Manthara.

"Don't look so disheartened, my dear," Kaikeyi coddled. "Ever since I was born, it's been you and me, has it not? Nothing has changed and never will. You are my best friend."

Manthara patted Kaikeyi's slender arm. In her heart, the decision had already been made. She would tread carefully around Kaikeyi from now on. Maybe it had begun when the queen went off to this battle Manthara did not sanction.

"I must be going," she said. "You need to get ready for the king."

They both knew how many hours it took to create Kaikeyi's best looks for the king, looks that none of those other creatures called queens could hope to compete with. Oh, regardless of today, Manthara was unspeakably proud of her lovely queen. But to her surprise, she saw Kaikeyi throw up her hands again.

"Oh, that? Is it really necessary?"

That casual disdain of all her training made Manthara's temper flare up all over again. "You listen to me, little girl! You will sit in front of the mirror right now and make yourself beautiful for the king, as you have done every day before this and will continue to do!"

"It's just that on the battlefield, all that was not necessary. And still we came much closer to each other."

"I will not listen to another word of this. Go to your mirror at once. This is another kind of battlefield, and don't you forget it!"

To Manthara's immense relief, Kaikeyi sighed and did as she was told. She felt her breath struggle to pass back and forth in her lungs. Her spine ached. All she wanted to do was lie down and rest. Instead, she followed Kaikeyi to the large mirror and said, "I will oversee your dressing today, as before. You don't seem to be yourself."

"No, I don't think I am," Kaikeyi said.

Nevertheless, she surrendered herself into Manthara's hands, and Manthara started commanding the maids to bring this and bring that. Several times she had to swat those useless creatures with her cane. It looked like Manthara had to do it all herself today. Thank the thirty gods, they had the whole day for this. Manthara was able to sit down at times and take deep breaths to revive herself.

"Here, I can do this braid," Kaikeyi said to one of the maids, taking over with deft fingers. "Go massage Manthara's back. She is overexerting herself."

"Only because you are not doing your part," Manthara complained, but closed her eyes with joy when she felt the strong young fingers digging into the flesh of her neck.

Finally, when Manthara was satisfied with Kaikeyi's look for the day and dismissed the maidservants, Kaikeyi turned to her with a determined look in her kajal-smeared eyes.

"I was bent on keeping this a secret," Kaikeyi said—and few things sounded so delicious to Manthara—"but I'm determined to prove the king loves me beyond all else, and I him."

Manthara waited.

"When the king returned from death's side to me, he said he owed his life to me. Without me, he said, he would not be alive. So his life belongs to me."

"Any man would say such a thing to please his woman. It's common."

"I'm not finished. Then he said, 'Ask me for anything.' He gave me two boons."

"What did you ask for?" Manthara said, breathless. She couldn't even imagine what she herself would think to desire when presented with such an expansive possibility.

"I spoke my heart. That my prayers had been fulfilled. He had returned to me alive."

Manthara rolled her eyes at that. Such romance. Pah. But then she looked again at the well-adorned queen. *This* was exquisite. Two secret boons, fragrant with power. Manthara felt slightly intoxicated, and had to grip her cane, lift her eyebrows, and shake her head.

What she hadn't counted on was that the king would be a victim of it too! He had clearly lost the upper hand now. That meant one thing: they—Kaikeyi and Manthara—now had a secret weapon that they would use when they needed it.

"I think he didn't believe me at first," Kaikeyi said, speaking almost to herself, certainly not seeing the calculating look in Manthara's eyes. "But when I insisted that I couldn't think of anything else I desired, he said with such tenderness, 'My promises and my love will be yours forever.' And then he reached for me, and . . ." Kaikeyi blushed, falling silent. That moment had been an intimate one, not meant for Manthara's prodding eyes.

"And you made love," Manthara said for her, waving her hand dismissively. "I wasn't born yesterday. That is the method, after all, to beget sons. You seem to forget its ultimate purpose, which I bless. Or had you forgotten that such physical union is meant to produce life? Your father, and in fact all of Ayodhya, are waiting for your son. And yet all you can think of is that your union proves that the king loves you."

Kaikeyi's cheeks were flaming angrily. "Oh, I should never have told you!" She turned away. "I knew you wouldn't understand."

I understand more than you think, Manthara thought.

"You did the right thing, telling me," she assured the queen. "I keep your secrets. You know that."

"But the whole point was not about the boons themselves, but about what it shows you about the king."

"You mean your lover?"

"Yes."

"That man is clearly ready to sacrifice anything and everything for your happiness. You were wise to keep those boons for another time."

"It was not a calculated act," Kaikeyi insisted.

Manthara turned away muttering, "He will be our doom. Don't say I didn't warn you."

All bad things started with love.

CHAPTER 16

An Earnest Wish

Dasharatha's convalescence took longer than he had expected. As he had first noted, his hair was now white or, as Kaikeyi liked to say, silver like the steel of a shining blade. Secretly, however, Dasharatha felt that whatever had turned his hair had invaded his entire body. When he looked in the mirror these days, he saw only an old man who stooped ever so slightly. He kept this knowing private and worked diligently to restore himself to his former prowess. Often he had dreams of a green-hued boy. He had a strong sense now that something crucial was missing from his life and felt the urgency tugging at him from the center of his heart, a child calling for its father.

The monsoon began, and the rain always had a calming effect on land and people alike. Wars seldom happened during this time. Every report came back to Dasharatha with news of peace. Of course, the king of Kashi was up to his usual intrigues, but that was the norm. Ravana and his kind were dormant. The holy ones expressed confidence in their sacred wards. And the kingdom relaxed with a sigh of relief. For now, Dasharatha could rest easy. The rainy season had always made him mellow and pensive.

As rain drenched the city, the citizens were celebrating not with pomp but with a quiet solemnity, each in his or her home. The rain poured, splattering against mud walls and palace walls alike. The wind blew, making the palm trees dance to the rhythm of the shifting tempest. Although the weather was stormy, no one seemed afraid. Rather, there was joy in the air, a celebration of the first rain of the year. Some children even played outside, their hair and faces dripping with water, like happy tears. Their parents looked on from doorways in amusement and called them inside only when the mud fights began.

The whole kingdom rejoiced in the rain because the monsoons marked the beginning of another year of prosperity and fertility. The rice would be plentiful; the mango trees would bend, heavy with fruit; and the drinking water would become as fresh and as sweet as sugarcane juice. The happy citizens raised their faces toward the sky and thanked the Lord for his benevolence. Next they looked toward the palace, where a sun gilded the flag on the highest dome, and they thanked the king. They knew the king's piety and firm rule made their empire prosper. Mimicking their parents, the children also turned their mud-streaked faces toward the palace.

Hearing these reports from within his city, King Dasharatha was deeply moved. As he had demonstrated time and time again, he was prepared to sacrifice his life for the prosperity of Ayodhya.

Dasharatha stood on his private balcony watching the rain infuse the land with life and his citizens with contentment. Yet he could not stop dissatisfaction from brewing in his heart. Since the last battle, he felt increasingly restless and even anguished. His body had all but healed, yet he could no longer ignore the enormity of what he lacked. So he joined his citizens by looking toward the Lord above. The king raised his face to the sky in prayer, closing his eyes against the rain. Even as his face streamed with water, tears stung his eyes and wet his cheeks. Suddenly a hand on his shoulder broke his reverie.

"My love, what is the matter?"

That voice had drawn him back from the halls of death. At the sight of Kaikeyi, his tears flowed all the more freely, as if competing with the rain.

"What is troubling you?"

When her quizzical gaze searched his face, he murmured, "Just raindrops."

Kaikeyi did not press him further, but simply wrapped her arms around him to comfort him. He returned her embrace. He felt the warmth of her graceful body where their bodies merged and the rain could not reach. He had received such miraculous love from this queen, but not the miracle he needed.

"I want a son," he said.

His heart exploded with the truth of it.

"Is this a revelation to you?" she asked.

"Yes," he said. "When you brought me back from death, I returned a changed man. I dream of a green-hued boy. I cannot stop thinking of him. All else has grown trivial to me."

Suddenly nothing but the whole truth would suffice. Dasharatha had not been planning to reveal his crime to anyone. The words were out before he could stop them.

"I committed a great crime once. It chills my soul to remember it."

She stepped away from him. There was no dismissal in this act, only a preparation to bear witness to his confession. Kaikeyi's eyes were stormy like the clouds above. He trusted her capacity to understand.

"Speak," she said.

The rain fell steadily around them. He closed his eyes and spoke.

"I was a carefree boy of fifteen, already the crown prince of Ayodhya. My father was greatly pleased with me, for I excelled in all my studies, and the science of archery was my favorite. My father told me I was the greatest archer on Earth. His assessment held great weight, for he was not only a reputed warrior but the emperor of Earth. Father encouraged my skill, saying that hunting would improve my marksmanship.

"I spent many hours alone in the forest, shooting faraway targets and practicing my aim. I did not consider the pain of the animals I killed. They were moving targets, nothing else, just as my enemies would be on the battlefield. I especially enjoyed nighttime hunting. It obscured my targets and increased the challenge. Maybe if I hadn't been so rash—if I hadn't taken such delight in my tricks."

He opened his eyes. The rest would not be as easy to reveal. Kaikeyi made no effort to shield herself from the rain. Dasharatha felt the storm in his heart gather force.

"The night was moonless," he said. "I was thrilled by its darkness. Every tree was a menacing blood-drinker, every sound that of the enemy. Through the quiet night, I heard a gurgling sound ahead. I took it for the noise of an animal drinking water. What an opportunity to practice my skill at hitting an invisible target. Without a moment's hesitation I grabbed my bow and aimed at the sound. As I released my arrow, I felt satisfaction spread in my heart, sure of my success.

"A cry of agony echoed through the dark. My heart froze in horror. I ran toward the sound as fast as I could, hoping I was wrong. The moaning grew quiet as I reached the stream. I truly could not see anything at first, but a clay pot bobbed on the surface of the stream, confirming my fear. I had hit my mark, all right, killing another human being. I fell on my knees, crawling closer to the curled-up figure. It was a boy."

Kaikeyi inhaled sharply. "Dead?"

"Dying. I cradled him in my arms. My arrow had gone straight into his heart. The blood spreading out on his chest was black as tar. It clung to my fingers, which would never be clean again.

"His eyes were rolling back in their sockets, but he struggled to speak to me. 'My parents cannot survive without me. Promise me that you will tell them what happened to me.'

"The hairs on my neck stood up. I was a murderer. That is what I had to confess.

"He spoke again, but his voice was fading. I had to put my ear close to his lips.

"'They will think I abandoned them,' he said.

"Even though he was in mortal pain, this boy thought only of his parents.

"'I will find them and confess,' I promised. I examined his wound with trembling fingers. Was there no way to save his life?

"'The pain,' he said, his fingers tugging at the arrow in his heart. 'Take it away. Please.'

"He pressed his fingers into mine and together we held the shaft that was killing him. I knew if I pulled my arrow out, he would die, but I did it anyway, to end his suffering. There was no way to save him. Blood trickled from his mouth and flowed from his heart. I didn't even know his name. The dead boy grew heavy in my arms and started slipping from my lap. I was perspiring from every limb. The smell of my sweat and his blood filled my nostrils. The water pot floated in the place where it had been abandoned. The nameless boy had been filling it at the stream. Taking it for an animal's thirst, I had murdered an innocent boy."

"Murder is too harsh a judgment," her voice was soft. "Your mistake was honest." She wanted to soften his guilt.

"No. The horror rippling in my body told me my transgression was beyond forgiveness. I stepped over the dead body and splashed my face with water, reaching for the pot. I felt the boy's final urgency cling to my heart. I had to seek out his parents. They were thirsty and waiting for their son. I cursed my ears as I filled the water pot. I had no choice but to leave the boy at the stream and search for his parents. I found the path that he had pointed to and soon found them—two enfeebled elders sitting in a dimly lit hut. I was afraid to enter the hut and face them. The water pot became a boulder in my hands, as heavy as the murder of the boy. Every word they said is imprinted in my memory."

"Share them with me," Kaikeyi said, stepping closer to him. "Let me share the burden of those words."

Dasharatha clenched his jaw, remembering the feeble parents of the boy.

"I had not yet gathered the courage to confess my crime. I stood outside their cottage, hearing every word. 'Why is he delaying?' the mother asked.

"'Oh, he will come, don't worry,' the father replied. 'Our son is so good. He takes careful care of us two useless creatures, blind and immobile as we are.'

"'We would die within days,' the mother agreed, 'for lack of water and food.'

"It was clear that they lived only for the love of their son. The water pot in my hand began to shake. I wanted to turn and flee. When the old mother once again asked where her son was, I went inside. I meant to fall at her feet and beg for forgiveness. But their expectant faces turned to me. They looked at me with unseeing eyes full of trust and love. I froze, my mouth dry.

"'Son, is that you?' the old father asked me. Thinking he knew the answer, he went on. 'What took you so long? Your mother was worried.'

"'He is back now,' she said, a smile lighting up her face. 'Come, bring the water to your old mother's lips. I'm so thirsty.'

"Frozen within, I went forward and put the pot to her lips. She drank a little but immediately asked, 'Why are you silent? This is not like you. Are you angry with us? Have you tired of caring for your old parents?'

"They waited with patient expressions on their faces. They expected me to answer them with loving words. What a son he must have been!

"I found some courage and threw myself at their feet. 'Forgive me! It was a mistake!'

"'Who are you? Where is our son?' they asked, drawing together and away from me.

"Their blind eyes turned on me, demanding the truth.

"Finding no other identity to hide behind, I said, 'I am the killer of your son.' I told them of my grievous mistake and the promise their son had exacted from me before he died.

"'Bring us to him,' they said.

"Though I was the killer of their boy, they accepted my help in escorting them to the stream; I led them carefully, one on each arm. Then I stood by silently, watching them cry like small children. They refused to speak to me. Their silence was more painful than their accusations would have been.

"'We are helpless without our son,' the father said at last. 'Better we die now than wait for slow starvation.'

"I told them I would bring them to Ayodhya and personally care for them."

"Of course," Kaikeyi interjected. "I would expect nothing else from you."

"They rejected my offer. The boy's mother said, 'He did not want to live without us. We don't want to live without him.'

"Though she was blind, her sightless eyes penetrated me to my core. I could see that they had lost all desire to live. Deprived of their child, they withered before my eyes. They asked me to build the boy a funeral pyre and told me that they would give up their lives in the fire. I was powerless to stop them. Before they entered the blazing fire, the father turned to me. 'You have deprived two old parents of their only comfort. Just as I now suffer with grief, so shall you end your days grieving for your son.'"

Kaikeyi's eyes lit up with understanding. "And therefore you have never truly wanted a son!"

"Those were their last words. All these years I have wondered if I will be absolved of the boy's murder only when their dying words came true. After they cursed me, the scene became entirely surreal. I expected them to scream as the fire consumed their bodies. Instead, the silence was as vast and dark as the night around me. I stared into the flames until they burned down and were gone. That curse has haunted me ever since."

Dasharatha searched Kaikeyi's face. His body felt light, and he shivered in the rain.

"Let it haunt you no more," Kaikeyi said firmly. "I banish such thoughts from your consciousness."

"But . . ." Did she not see the gravity of his crime?

She cupped his face in her hands, looking intently into his eyes. "I have borne witness to your crime. And I judge it an honest mistake. You would not have willingly or knowingly killed an innocent boy. *That* would have been a crime. What you did was a pure mistake."

"That was no solace to his parents!"

"No more of that! You have lived with this guilt for countless years."

"Thirty-two years."

"Thirty-two years, my love. That is long enough. Your remorse washed you clean on the same day that you killed that boy."

He sighed deeply and knew that this very confession was a step in that direction.

"What of their curse?" he persisted. "I will die grieving for my son."

"Not every word spoken in grief or anger is a curse. Surely you must see this, Great King."

"Perhaps. But in my heart, I felt the resonance of their words. I *know* it will come to be."

"You may have many extraordinary skills, my love. But you cannot see into the future. Or have you kept this secret power from me?"

She was smiling in jest. "Are you ready now to tell me more of the boy you dream of, the son you long for?"

He laughed, rain running into his mouth. "Yes, I'm ready."

He was delighted by her simple sense of justice, immensely relieved to share his secret with another living soul. He took hold of her hand and led her within.

King and queen were soaked to the skin. Cleansed and renewed. Sensing the change in his mood, Kaikeyi said something else to make him laugh. Dasharatha heart swelled with tenderness. He would let nothing stand in his way now.

CHAPTER 17

The Great Sacrifice

The next day, Dasharatha called a special meeting, bringing his eight ministers and Vasishta together. To cement the formality of the meeting he was about to conduct, Dasharatha recognized each one of them in due turn, praising their individual skills and accomplishments. He was pleased to see them exchange glances as he spoke.

"Today we will speak of Ayodhya's need for an heir," Dasharatha said.

There was a collective sigh of pleasure and relief. Vasishta's eyes sparked up.

"This conversation has been long overdue," Dasharatha began. "Please know that my avoidance was based on my complete trust in all of you, combined with a youth's foolish notion of immortality. As you can see, I am young no more. Nothing has highlighted this more than my recent near-death encounter. I had only one regret before I lost consciousness: 'The Sun dynasty ends with me.' Since then, nothing can rouse me from the urgency of this situation. I need an heir to ensure that my line continues."

"Hear, hear!" Siddhartha called out.

"Let me speak more candidly than ever before," Dasharatha said. "I have three worthy queens. None of them have borne me children. I had hoped that

Kaikeyi would be the mother of my sons. That has not happened. Hence, I wish to consult you. What shall we do?"

Vasishta spoke first. "Great King, today our patience has been rewarded. Many a time we have considered forcing our thoughts on you, but it is known that every pressure has an equal and opposite reaction, and so we have waited for you to come to us. Now you approach us with an open heart, and your determination blazes like the sun from your heart. Blessings are upon us. Only time stands between us and the solution."

Dasharatha verily grew in the warmth of his guru's words.

"We agree that it is no longer wise to expect any of your queens to bear children," Vasishta said. "The inability of a king to conceive a son indicates impiety in his rule."

Dasharatha's mind immediately went to the killing of the innocent boy. Despite his confession and Kaikeyi's assurance, he was not free of that night. He didn't meet Vasishta's eye.

"None of us feel that this is the case here," Vasishta assured the king.

A surge of relief washed away the memory.

"Nevertheless, there is a reason that you are unable to naturally produce an heir, and it is time to explore other paths. We have considered several options. You may adopt a worthy child as your own. You may nominate a prince from another kingdom as your heir. There are several worthy contenders. Such paths, however, are known to be fraught with uncertainties. Most human beings seek to elevate their place of origin, and the Sun dynasty may lose its position. Before we take such a final step, therefore, this council proposes a ritual by fire that will cleanse us and turn the tides in our favor. We are calling for a horse sacrifice culminating in the son-bearing ritual. It is an extremely rare and complex ritual, but it can be done, and is designed to give sons to sonless kings. Through it, we will petition the gods for an heir, calling for their intervention. This, we all concur, is the best solution."

Dasharatha considered their words. He understood from Vasishta's words that the council had prepared this speech in advance to present it to him at an opportune moment.

"I am favorable to your suggestion," he said. "Speak to me in more detail of this fire ritual."

Dasharatha knew the importance of fire and its pure force. Vasishta and the other high priest regularly conducted cleansing sacrifices on the king's behalf. The fire ritual Vasishta was now speaking of sounded like a more advanced undertaking.

Sumantra stood up and received the king's permission to speak.

"Great King, fire sacrifices are a common practice among kings, as you well know. The sacrifice of the white stallion is the lengthiest and the most costly. To perform this sacrifice, a white stallion will be released into the kingdom and beyond, followed closely by the king's army. The horse will roam at will from state to state, informing the subject kings of the emperor's intention to perform a sacrifice. A message embossed in gold, placed around the horse's neck, will explain the details of the sacrifice. All subordinate kings must submit tribute. This is the time for any rebellious king to declare insubordination by seizing the horse. Whoever seizes the horse challenges the emperor to war. The winner will take possession of the horse and thereby the entire empire. If no one challenges the horse, it will return home, the fire pits will be ignited, and the stallion will be sacrificed into the fire and released to its next life."

Dasharatha considered the procedure and its cost to the kingdom.

"The release of the horse is a mere formality, Great King," Vasishta said. "We have no reason to believe that anyone on Earth will object."

"If you believe this ritual will yield results, then I have no objection," the king answered, giving his assent. "Let us begin the preparations at once."

"The stallion can be released at an auspicious time," Vasishta said. "I will consult the planetary constellations. Usually the stallion will return within one year. This gives us the necessary time to prepare the details for the elaborate ritual."

"What shall I do?" Dasharatha asked.

"First, the queens must be informed, particularly Queen Kausalya, since she is the gate-keeper to Ayodhya's wealth. She alone will know how much Ayodhya's treasury can spare."

"I will seek her as soon as this meeting adjourns," Dasharatha promised.

"Second, the fertility ceremony at the culmination of this great sacrifice cannot be con-ducted by just anyone," Vasishta cautioned. "We need to find a qualified priest to preside over this crucial ritual. Only someone truly extraordinary has the powers to conduct the son-bearing ceremony. And there is only one. His name is Rishyashringa, 'the horned one.' Although in every way he appears like a man, he has a horn in the center of his forehead."

The king had seen stranger sights, so he only nodded. Sumantra told the council of Rishy-ashringa's remarkable birth and life. Rishyashringa was conceived in a most strange way by a doe and then raised by his father Vibhandaka in complete ignorance of the female gender. Until his adolescence, he did not know that women existed at all, having lived secluded deep in the jungle. Fate conspired to change his innocence in a most unusual manner, when a king named Romapada needed the touch of Rishyashringa's pure feet to end the drought of his land. A group of courtesans were sent to beguile the young boy to Romapada's kingdom. How could the boy resist when he did not even know what he was resisting? The moment Rishyashringa's feet touched the parched land, showers of rain blessed the kingdom. Such was the innate power of the horned sage.

Rishyashringa was still living in the kingdom of Romapada, who was a dear friend to Dasharatha. Truly, the stars were aligning for the fire ceremony to take place. Dasharatha felt the tug of satisfaction that comes when complex factors align effortlessly.

As the meeting adjourned, Vasishta placed his hand on Dasharatha's shoulder. "A word, Great King."

At once, Dasharatha became grave. If Vasishta wanted a word in private, it was sure to be serious. Still he wasn't prepared for Vasishta's question: "Who will be the mother of your son?"

Vasishta's penetrating gaze told the king he knew all. There could be no hedging or skirt-ing the topic. It was as if his three wives stood behind Vasishta, waiting for Dasharatha's answer. Vasishta's look informed the king that Vasishta knew Kaikeyi was his chosen one. By now, all of Ayodhya knew Kaikeyi's bride-price.

"I made a promise to Kaikeyi's father and to her," Dasharatha said. "She must be my first choice. I know this is unfair to Kausalya, who has been by my side since the beginning. But I must honor my word. There is no other way."

He would spend the rest of his life atoning for his choice, no matter whom he chose.

"Great King," Vasishta said, and there was compassion in his voice, "I must inform you that the ancient ceremonial laws require that wives be honored according to their rank. Kausalya will be called first. Kaikeyi last. In this, she will not be first or second but third, as is her rank."

Dasharatha felt a sudden weight on his shoulders. Kaikeyi would be publicly put in her place. It was not the place that King Ashvapati had envisioned for his prized daughter. Kaikeyi would not like it.

"I cannot break my oath," Dasharatha emphasized.

"She has not borne you natural sons. If she had, we would not be forced to this recourse. The costly and elaborate ceremony would not be necessary. Surely her father will agree. He would be foolish not to. The terms of your vow have expired or, at the least, changed. This is my opinion. But of course, you have the political mind, not I."

Dasharatha considered this, seeing the truth in it. "What will this hierarchy mean for the results of the ceremony?"

"We are wandering here into a realm that departs from human logic and reason," Vasishta said. "To those who cannot see the inner workings, the ritual has elements of magic to it. The fertility nectar will be divided among your wives according to their rank. Kausalya is entitled to the largest share and Sumitra to the second largest. But even a drop of the nectar is said to produce sons. Kaikeyi will not be excluded. If the sacrifice is successful, one or all of your queens will bear you a son. It's up to the gods. If we, however, neglect the injunctions and call a junior queen first, the entire son-bearing ritual will be compromised."

There was little more to say. Dasharatha and Vasishta went in separate directions. At the appropriate time, the white stallion would be released. In a year's time, when it returned, the fires would be lit. By that time, Dasharatha had to reconcile Kaikeyi to the fact that she would not receive the highest honor. King Ashvapati had to be informed. The warrior in Dasharatha fought the shackles that now bound his hands. The father in him rejoiced at the future ahead. Kaikeyi's firm dismissal kept the curse at bay.

Torn by opposing thoughts, Dasharatha returned to his private balcony overlooking the city. It was one of the few places where he felt completely alone, his favorite place to think. His thoughts needed the expansive space to roam free and take their shape.

Gazing over his beloved city still obscured by rain, he thought of Kaikeyi's father, the stern Ashvapati. Dasharatha knew all too well what their agreement was: Kaikeyi's son would be king. By this promise, Kaikeyi was entitled to the lion's share of the nectar. But Vasishta had been clear: Kaikeyi had not borne him natural sons. If he was to have sons at all, he had to carefully follow Vasishta's instructions. Ashvapati's stern eyes held no compassion.

Dasharatha decided to summon Kaikeyi first among the queens to inform her what was to happen. While he waited, he began formulating his letter to Ashvapati. When Kaikeyi appeared, she looked up at him with those eyes. That she belonged to him was one of the miracles of his existence. He never failed to notice how beautiful and appealing she was. He could not predict how she would react. It thrilled and terrified him. It was not easy to appease an angry woman, at least not an angry Kaikeyi. His other wives had never truly been angry with him.

"Here we are again," he said lightly. The rain still fell, but the sun shone through.

As Dasharatha spoke, Kaikeyi listened with unusual gravity. She understood what was at stake. The previous night's confession had been impressed upon her.

"I never married you," she said, "for the sake of your kingdom. That was my father's wish."

Dasharatha had thought so, but it was gratifying to hear.

"But I loathe the idea of a horse sacrifice," Kaikeyi said.

Of course she did, considering her deep love for the animals.

"But you understand that it is our only avenue?" he asked.

She nodded, gazing into his eyes.

"Will your father be as understanding?"

"I doubt it. His aspirations for me have no limits. He wishes me to be a man and a woman. A queen and a king. I don't think it's possible to please him."

Dasharatha had to smile. He had never understood the complex nature of his father-in-law.

"But what choice does he have?" Kaikeyi said. "I have not borne you any children. I could not give you what you needed the most."

"I did not marry you for that," Dasharatha said. A smile spread across her face. "You give me what I need the most."

Her whole countenance changed, and Dasharatha felt the response in his body. He had to remind himself that it was midday. He could not abandon his duties now to cavort with Kaikeyi.

"I will see you in the evening," he promised. "I must write this letter to your father."

"Send him my respect," she said, and turned away.

"I always do."

He watched her leave, his passion for her ignited. He carefully breathed the rain-filled air. The letter to his father-in-law would write itself now that Kaikeyi was on his side. Still, when Dasharatha sat down, he crafted his words, desiring Ashvapati's approval while also conveying that there really was no other choice.

As he handed the letter to an envoy, he felt an unexpected satisfaction.

In his personal life, he favored Kaikeyi, but Kausalya deserved more than she was getting. Sumitra had never claimed his love and time the way the other two women did. Sumitra was acceptance personified. He was pleased that all three of his wives would take part in the ceremony. Ashvapati had to understand that Dasharatha had no choice. He would do anything for a son now. Even face the retribution of Kaikeyi's father or fate.

Poisoned Minds

Half a year passed. All anyone could talk about was the horse sacrifice at the end of the year. Manthara, however, had other things on her mind—the fact, for example, that she would not be welcome there because she was a person of inauspicious and ill-omened appearance. She was not overly crushed by this fact. She would indeed have been surprised if a ritual in Ayodhya welcomed one such as her. She had her doubts about the success of the whole procedure. She bided her time, keeping Kaikeyi on her toes with pointed questions:

What if Kaikeyi remained childless anyway?

What if the sacrifice was meant to exclude Kaikeyi and favor Kausalya?

What if one of the other queens tried to kill Kaikeyi?

What if Manthara was poisoned? What would Kaikeyi do then?

Manthara felt it was necessary to remind Kaikeyi of the hostile situation they lived in. She made it a point to come up with new possible scenarios of their ruin, and she was in the middle of describing her latest suspicion while Kaikeyi rubbed an ointment on her back. It contained drops of lily of the valley, Manthara's all-time favorite poisonous flower. It had grown naturally in Kekaya, but here Manthara carefully grew a few plants herself, loving the innocent look of the teardrop flowers. In small amounts, the distilled oil also made you gentle, sweet, and secure. Manthara made sure that Kaikeyi also used the oil.

Kaikeyi's firm movements across Manthara's back were interrupted by the loud noise of trumpeting swans. The fountain in Kaikeyi's courtyard always had a team of swans. Someone was dashing through the courtyard with such speed that the swans flew away in alarm. Kaikeyi's attention turned toward the entrance, and Manthara stopped talking. The thundering sound of a chariot stopped and then footsteps echoed up the stairway.

Kaikeyi stood up. She was dressed elaborately, like a queen attending a function. Manthara was pleased by her immaculate appearance. Dasharatha appeared. He was angry; that was obvious by his erratic entry and the way he barely greeted his beloved.

He turned on Manthara at once. She wasn't prepared for the accusation she saw in his eyes.

"What is it?" Kaikeyi asked, placing her hand on his chest. "What has happened? Your heart is racing."

Dasharatha took a deep breath, straightened his back as if he wasn't already double Manthara's height. He did not look at Kaikeyi, but held Manthara's eyes.

She did not flinch, but her knuckles tightened around her cane. *We can do this,* it confirmed, solid in her hand.

The king steadied his breath and stepped away from Kaikeyi and toward Manthara. The names she called him in private surfaced in her mind. As she met his stare, she could see that he hoarded names for her too.

"You," he said, as if uttering a curse. "You are no longer welcome in Ayodhya."

"What?" Kaikeyi cried out. "What are you saying?"

Kaikeyi immediately sided with Manthara, and Manthara felt her fingers relax around her cane. Dasharatha changed tactics, focusing on Kaikeyi instead of Manthara.

"Manthara has shown her true colors," Dasharatha said. "She has been plotting against Kausalya and Sumitra, seeking a way to kill them by poison. As the time for our sacrifice nears, she wishes to eliminate the other queens. Perhaps to elevate your position."

Dasharatha's eyes were now intent on Kaikeyi. What would the king do if his darling wife was complicit in the plot?

Kaikeyi's arm slid off Manthara's back. She smiled. "This is not true. Manthara, tell him. You would never do such a thing."

"There is no use denying it," Dasharatha warned. "I know what happens in my own kingdom, Manthara. Your sly questioning has not gone unnoticed. I can call on several witnesses who will testify to the fact that you have been asking what poisons are used in Ayodhya. Your questions have circled around Kausalya and Sumitra's habits and foods, asking whether they have servants who taste their food, whether they wear gems that expel poisons, which antidotes they keep nearby. You have been thorough but not subtle. Because you have served Kaikeyi since her birth, I will spare you corporal punishment. But you will leave Ayodhya at once. I never want to see you in my kingdom again."

Manthara spat out, "Why would I go for subterfuge when I'm innocent? Believe me, if I wanted those two dead, they already would be."

Dasharatha's hands moved toward Manthara as if he meant to drag her out this very minute.

Kaikeyi stepped in his way, holding up a warning hand. With one hand on Manthara and one on Dasharatha, she said, "Let us speak calmly."

"No," Dasharatha said. "You may trust what she says, but I do not. I do not put faith in a single word that comes from that mouth. In fact, I distrust it, knowing that she does not have my best interest at heart."

"What of my best interest?" Kaikeyi asked, and there was a plea in her voice. She was smart not to challenge him in return, for his anger was at its very edge. Kaikeyi's arms were now protectively around Manthara again. "Manthara would never harm me."

The king looked from one to the other; only now it began to dawn on him that Kaikeyi had chosen Manthara over him.

"Very well," Dasharatha said, "since you do not trust my judgment or honor my authority"—the ice in his voice was a king's—"I will see you, Manthara, in my court tomorrow. There you will answer to this charge."

"I will not let her face you and all your ministers alone!" Kaikeyi protested. "She is an elderly woman, and you have not even given her a chance to speak."

"She will be heard tomorrow in my court. Stay out of this, Kaikeyi."

He took her hand and pulled her away from Manthara. He glared at Manthara as though he couldn't bear to be in the same room as her. That didn't discourage Manthara, though, as she quietly followed them, hiding behind one of the curtains to overhear.

"Kaikeyi, this is not a minor offense," he said urgently. "Do not side with her. She has a poisoned mind. This has escalated beyond personal likes and dislikes. She stands accused of harboring murderous intentions. We cannot shelter such a person within Ayodhya. *The Laws of Manu* are clear on this. As a king, I would be a fool to allow such a person in our inner circles. She is not the well-meaning mother figure you take her to be. You *need to see* how far from such a figure she—"

"She couldn't be worse than my real mother," Kaikeyi muttered.

"She is!" Dasharatha said in a loud voice. "Your mother was open and outspoken regarding her desires. She bore the consequences of it. Manthara, on the other hand, is sly and manipulative. She will say anything to serve her own purpose. And I don't think, my dear, that your best interest is her first priority."

"You are wrong," she said in that soft way, as if she felt bad for his error in judgment. "Manthara is here in Ayodhya because I am here. She has been at my side long before you were. Even if I wanted to, I could not turn away from her."

"You trust her more than you trust me?" Dasharatha said.

Although Manthara could not see his face through the thick curtain, she smirked at the tone of his voice. He was sad now, the poor king. What a spineless fool he was, Manthara thought with a hushed cackle. He had bound all his hopes and desires into Kaikeyi, giving her such power. Good. Kaikeyi was Manthara's weapon.

"I will vouch for her innocence," Kaikeyi said, and Manthara's heart lurched. Kaikeyi spoke loudly, not afraid of being overheard. "Manthara has never worked with poisons. You can ask my father. There were other people in my father's service who worked with poisons. It was not spoken of openly, and I do not know much. But I do know that Manthara was not part of that work. She has never poisoned anyone."

Manthara peeked out from behind the curtain, loving the fierce look in Kaikeyi's eyes. She was proud of Kaikeyi's quick thinking, even if it wasn't strictly the truth.

"Except for you," Dasharatha said, and sighed. "She poisons you every day. I can see that she has won you over completely. You cannot see her as I and the people of Ayodhya see her."

"That's correct," Kaikeyi answered. "And I think you are the ones who need to improve your vision."

The king's reply did not come at once. Manthara heard movement and pressed herself against the wall. When he spoke, his voice echoed at them. Manthara guessed he stood by the edge of the stairway.

"I warn you, Kaikeyi. Manthara encourages this heedless impudence in you, and it is not a desirable quality. I assure you that she will be given a fair hearing tomorrow. Because of your relationship with her, she will receive the mildest possible punishment. If you side with her, however, or interfere in any way, I cannot protect you from the laws. They are not forgiving toward those who conspire against the state. Your loyalty will come into question, and you will not be included in the ceremony for a son. If this is important to you, I implore you to trust our fair adjudication. For the love we share, stay out of this."

Manthara couldn't stop her voice as she called out from behind the curtain, giving away her hiding place. "You call it fair? You have already made up your mind against me!"

She flung away the thick curtain but stumbled as she got tangled in the ornate border. The king made his exit without a backward glance. Manthara pulled at her cane, cursing it and the ornate hemline of the curtain that wouldn't let her go.

Kaikeyi turned to her but didn't offer to help. Her eyes were steely, her face frozen. She came to Manthara's side, bending her mouth to Manthara's ear. "Is *any* of this true, Manthara? You *have* to tell me."

They studied each other. Manthara liked what she saw: the two of them against Ayodhya. Since that was the case, Manthara answered, "You know me better than anyone. Anything I do is for *your* welfare."

Kaikeyi straightened and looked down at Manthara. A tingling feeling rose up Manthara's spine. She sensed Kaikeyi coming to a decision. Manthara's gut filled with dread, as it always did at the moment of uncertainty.

Kaikeyi took Manthara's cane and bent down to untangle it. While Kaikeyi worked to free the cane, Manthara steadied herself against Kaikeyi. Curious servants began to peek out from various corners. Manthara would deal with them later, doing whatever necessary to ensure their loyalty. Impatiently, Kaikeyi ripped off parts of the hemline and freed the cane. She stood and handed it to Manthara. It was all the answer Manthara needed.

They bid each other goodnight, knowing that the next day would be crucial. They had never witnessed Ayodhya's justice before.

As she rose the next morning, Manthara felt like a very old, small, and useless hag. Fighting the fear she felt in the pit of her stomach, she dressed herself with even less care. She couldn't believe those fools had actually summoned her to the king's great court. Since coming to Ayodhya two years ago, she had never even been inside Dasharatha's court. It was not a place where women presided, especially not ones such as she. Once she realized this, she had set her plan in motion. Now she would behold the results of her work.

Pushing her cane into the ground, she strained to straighten her spine. She would not be subdued by these people. Leaving her chambers, she was dismayed to see two guards waiting for her. Her insides shriveled. Fair hearing? She was already being treated as a criminal. She looked around, hoping to see Kaikeyi. Her mistress had promised to defy the king and appear alongside Manthara. It was all so official. It felt like a bitter draught that cured her from any illusion that she might belong in Ayodhya. She would never belong. Kaikeyi was nowhere in sight. Maybe Manthara had misread their silent interaction. Manthara prepared to face the situation alone, feeling like a martyr.

She scowled at the two guards, noticing that they were no more than boys. They hadn't even cared to send her proper guards. "I know how to get there," she told them.

They shuffled to their feet and could not meet her gaze.

"If you dare lay your hands on me, you will be sorry."

She smacked her cane against their shins to show them what she meant. She enjoyed the sound of her cane against their bones. Because of their phony valor, they didn't yelp, though she saw their faces turning red. She would not spare them the rod if they were impudent with her, an elderly woman. Without looking at them again, she started shuffling toward the court, complaining loudly about how far away it was. When the guards pointed out that they were there to "save" her the walk, she complained even louder about that.

"This way," one of the boy guards said, and she was forced to follow. "We go by chariot."

She huffed but was relieved. It would have taken her well over an hour to walk, though she had set her mind to it, like a penance. She couldn't decide which of her mistakes had been more foolish: her idea that she might gain acceptance here or this trap she'd set to test them. It was all panning out exactly as she'd envisioned it in her nighttime planning. It sent shivers up and down her crooked spine. It was all working too well; it was spiraling out of her hands. The workings of justice were one thing in theory, another when a hotheaded king like Dasharatha ruled. Though she was completely innocent, and she told herself that she was, they might sentence her to death. The root cause of it was her ugliness. She knew that.

"You are so ugly, you deserve to die," she murmured to herself as the chariot left the place where she lived, which had not yet become home. Now it might never be. "You are too ugly to live in Ayodhya," she whispered to herself. It pacified her to reduce the whole drama to this core truth. The deeper she looked at the charge she was facing, the more certain she was. The king had claimed just yesterday that he didn't despise her because of her hunchback, but what other reason could it be? Manthara had never heard of a beautiful woman facing charges in any court. No, you had to be downright ugly to be a criminal.

Annapurna

As the chariot made its way through Ayodhya's streets, Manthara avoided the Ayodhyans milling about. She couldn't bear their eyes, as annoying as the stabbing pains in her neck. They had obviously never seen a misshapen body like hers before. Did they not have the courtesy to hide their gaping? A longing for her homeland hit Manthara with such force that she felt she was going to be sick.

"Stop the chariot!" she said, her voice ringing shrilly.

She clambered off the chariot with her insides heaving and made it to the side gutter just in time. She retched violently, emptying her insides. If only she could puke out herself; then she would be free. As the water in her eyes cleared, she surveyed the mess she'd made, noticing most keenly how pristine the gutters were. Or had been, before she came along. That was the way Ayodhya was. Pure and pristine. And that was why it hated her. She reminded it of the nastiness that was there somewhere. Every place and every person was externally spotless. Only hypocrites could be that clean. She turned around, seeing the crowd that had gathered around her. No one had the sense to fetch her water or offer her support. They continued gaping as if they had never seen anyone be ill before, either.

"Water!" she croaked.

Only a guard moved, merely doing his duty.

Manthara leaned on her stick, wiping the sweat off her forehead, eager for the water so she could be free of the stink that clung to her. She refused the eyes of every single person there. It seemed to her as if time had stopped and their mouths gaped at her for an eternity. She was unique in Ayodhya. Not a single decrepit or handicapped person was allowed in public view. Did they have a dungeon where they threw all their disabled? Or were they killed at birth?

She received the jug of water, snatching it out of the boy's hand. She began to drink greedily, gulping it down, feeling it splash down her neck and onto her chest. Like poison it burned her throat, and she spit it out, throwing the jug to the ground.

"Bah!" she said. "Even the water here is foul."

She waved the crowd away with her stick and climbed onto the chariot laboriously. *Don't touch me,* her glare warned the red-faced guards. Empty, she was full. She resolved not to be meek and subdued as she faced the king's court. Manthara had crossed paths with the king often enough that she could not hide her contempt. Why should she attempt to now? He had openly said that he distrusted every word that came from her mouth.

"Go faster!" she shrieked. "Let's get this farce over with."

The chariot stopped in front of the dazzling marble steps that led up to the court. She utterly hated every step and every sight of this so-called heavenly place. That didn't stop her from observing the wealth that Ayodhya insisted on flaunting: "Look at this marble stairway, inlaid with precious gems. We are so rich here in Ayodhya, we eat gold nuggets."

She turned her lips down. The display of richness highlighted how skewed Ayodhya's morals were: they didn't even know how to spend their wealth productively. As Manthara made her way up the many steps, she had never felt it more keenly, the divide between us and them. As her foot mastered the last step, she heard the thundering of hooves behind her and peered over her shoulder. Finally!

Kaikeyi raised a dust storm in her wake as she galloped down the courtyard. She flung herself off the horse before it came to a standstill and ran up the steps to Manthara's side.

"I thought we would go together," she said, her breath short, her brow furrowed.

Manthara looked approvingly at Kaikeyi. She had dressed for this occasion in a closely fitted dress that displayed her form. Her beauty would not go unnoticed.

"They must have anticipated it," Manthara said. "They sent those two buffoons to handle me."

Kaikeyi tucked her arm into Manthara's. "I'm *so* glad you are not my mother," she said with false cheer.

Manthara smoothed Kaikeyi's hair and fixed her veil. The words had taken on a double meaning over the years, which they both appreciated. Manthara clucked and said, "I love you too, my dear."

Arm in arm they entered the court. Immediately, four guards closed in around them, escorting them toward a throng of people. Some of them were in chains. So there were other criminals in Ayodhya, after all. That was a relief. Manthara saw only one other woman among the accused. A bearded man stood on a platform above the others. As they approached, his crime was declared.

"You have been found guilty of forcibly defiling an unwilling maiden. Two of your fingers shall be cut off and you will pay a fine of sixty gold coins to her and her family."

Though Manthara had memorized the punishments for subjects suspected of poisoning queens and of treason, she began quavering. Would they cut off part of Manthara too and deform her further?

She concentrated on the hall, though she despised the ornate decorations of gems and gold inlays. At the very end, the haughty king presided on a large golden throne, overseeing the special cases. This was the line that Manthara was ushered to. The king was surrounded by his eight ministers, who sat on smaller golden thrones. Vasishta, looking as aloof as Brahma, the creator, sat in a place of high honor, along with the other priests. Manthara's eyes darted back and forth. The sides of the hall were lined with seats and filled with Ayodhya's men, not a friend among them. Hundreds of ill-wishers. But the wealth was dazzling. Even Kaikeyi seemed unsettled by the grandiosity, whispering to Manthara, "As the queen, even I am bound by certain rules. But no matter what happens, know that I'm on your side."

In an effort to subdue Manthara, queen and hunchback were made to wait and listen to further sentences. After taking it all in, memorizing the face of her enemy, Manthara looked straight ahead, honing in on the king. His eyes were not on Manthara but on Kaikeyi, of course. He was not pleased that she was here. Good. He would see what happened when he meddled in things he should not. Manthara tightened her grip on Kaikeyi. But when she looked up at the king, she might have retched again had she been alone. Presiding in his court, the king was no longer the man Manthara knew as Kaikeyi's lover. Here he was made of steel—justice personified. Suddenly Manthara was afraid for Kaikeyi's defiance. Had Kaikeyi pushed her luck too far by openly disobeying the king?

The two of them waited in silence in the back of the line. The man whose two fingers would be amputated was led away. Manthara admired his expressionless face, the way he would give this arrogant council nothing more.

"Kaikeyi, princess of Kekaya, daughter of Ashvapati, queen of Ayodhya," the king said. His voice echoed through the wide chambers. "Step away from the accused."

Kaikeyi tightened her grip on Manthara. The two women clutched each other in this hall of men. "If you stay by her side," he said, "I have no choice but to direct the charge against both of you. If you are complicit in Manthara's actions, not even I can save you."

All eyes were on them, the beauty and the hunchback. Manthara felt Kaikeyi falter, sagging against Manthara's grip. Manthara's mind flew in its cage. She alone had to carry them both through this. The king's wrath was palpable. Because Manthara did not know for sure how this would end, she deliberately disengaged herself from the queen.

Kaikeyi tightened her grip on Manthara, but then let go, trusting Manthara's initiative once again. If Ayodhya had a shred of its proclaimed decency, Manthara would emerge unscathed. If by some chance Manthara would be unfairly sentenced, Kaikeyi would avenge her. Manthara did not doubt it. So she stepped ahead and away from Kaikeyi.

Raising her voice so that everyone would hear, she said, "What have I done to incur your wrath, Great King?"

Every eye turned on Manthara. Even the criminals gaped at her, denying her a place among them.

"You will not speak unless spoken to," the king said. His voice and eyes were neither cold nor warm. "Guards, guide the queen to the visitor's seat."

Kaikeyi let herself be guided to the seat while holding Manthara's gaze meaningfully.

"Let the trial begin," the king declared, signaling to a bare-chested young priest.

The priest chanted: "Those who bear false witness fall headlong into hell. The sky, the earth, the water, the twilight, day and night, sun and the moon, know the conduct of every living being. He who swears an oath falsely is lost forever. The soul within is the supreme witness of man."

Vasishta stepped forward. "I request the honor of sharing a few words."

The king nodded.

Vasishta looked past Manthara to Kaikeyi as he spoke. "I once asked an intelligent and curious person what the worst crime in Ayodhya is. I do not know if this person has yet discovered the answer, and today I will speak plainly. Having committed murder, a person may do penance in this life and the next to atone. His heart can be cleansed if his penance is sincere. Other heinous crimes may similarly be rectified through lifelong penance. There is but one crime that is devious for its effects cannot always immediately be seen: oath-breaking. Our civilization is built upon the power of word. A promise should not be made or used lightly. Human life began as thought, took form in sound vibration, and morphed into words. Its final manifestation is visible as action. Oath-breaking is the most devastating crime. It pulverizes the building blocks on which this entire Earth is built. Your word is your destiny."

Behind Manthara, Kaikeyi sighed deeply. Vasishta's eyes grazed Manthara for a moment before he withdrew to his seat.

The king's voice made Manthara jolt. "You, Manthara, have used your word to threaten the kingdom and stand accused of scheming to poison the senior queens, Queen Kausalya and Queen Sumitra. As an aggressor to the state, you face capital punishment. Do you have anything to say in your defense?"

Kaikeyi stood abruptly, but Manthara raised her hand. She was astounded by her own willpower, for her insides were gone. She struggled to bring words to her lips; her tongue was thick, her mouth stubborn. They would say nothing. Let these fools sentence her on false charges; they would suffer in hell for their crime. She heard, however, Kaikeyi's movements behind her, the rustling of her silks and the tinkling of her jewelry. Manthara had to speak before Kaikeyi did something rash.

"It's a false charge," she croaked. "I'm innocent." She couldn't get herself to say the words gracefully.

"What proof do you have against her?" Kaikeyi demanded.

"Queen Kaikeyi, princess of Kekaya, you are a visitor in this court," one of the ministers said. He had a wispy beard that moved with each word he said. "You will not speak unless spoken to."

Kaikeyi was silenced but by no means stilled.

"Sumantra," the king said, "read the charges."

Sumantra, one of the few whom Manthara had actually found sympathetic, rose. He held the scroll and read: "On the day of the half-moon, King Dasharatha announced that Queen Kausalya will sit by his side at the sacred fire, and that the other queens will be honored according to their rank. Kausalya will be entitled to the lion's share of the fertility nectar to become the official mother of the nation. On that same day, Manthara cornered one of Kausalya's maids, asking her about the practices that protect the senior queens from poisons. Since then, the accused has been carefully shadowed. We have six witnesses who are prepared to testify to the fact that Manthara has made comprehensive inquiries, including offering bribes, regarding the availability and practice of poisons in Ayodhya. Since her arrival in Ayodhya, the accused has made no attempt to hide her ill will toward the two senior queens. Although she has not yet made an attempt, we find her intentions reprehensible. *The Laws of Manu* state that any person in the king's proximity who harbors malice toward him and his subjects shall be slain. We, the Court of Ayodhya, therefore find you, Manthara of Kekaya, guilty of scheming against the welfare of the state."

Angry murmurs rose in the room. Kaikeyi had become motionless. Manthara waited.

"Do you deny these charges?" Sumantra asked of Manthara.

"I do not," she admitted.

The court fell silent. They had no doubt expected her to kick and scream and make a scene.

"Because of your long-standing relationship with Queen Kaikeyi," Sumantra said, "the king has elected to spare your life, but you will leave Ayodhya immediately. You are free to return to Kekaya if they will have you. Henceforth you are not welcome within Ayodhya's boundaries."

"I do not deny your findings," Manthara asserted loudly. It was now or never. Her voice was shrill, and she shrieked, "*I charge you* with faulty reasoning! My interest in the matter of poisons was selfish, yes, but not in the way you have deemed. I have served my queen since her birth, and I'm prepared to sacrifice my life for her safety. I made inquiries about Ayodhya's practices only to protect Kaikeyi from death by poison. She too must wear the gems that expel poisons; she too must have the antidotes nearby; she too must have someone assigned to ingest her foods before she does. The other queens are jealous of Kaikeyi, and I have feared for her life every day since we arrived here."

She spoke the rehearsed words. She was not stupid. She had known that the servants would never keep their mouths shut. Especially not to protect one like her, an outsider, on top of being a hunchback. "My only crime is being concerned for Kaikeyi's safety and asking questions. That is all I've done! If these are crimes in Ayodhya, then and only then do I accept my guilt and its sentence!"

She glared at them, forcing them to rethink their hasty conclusions. She felt their shrewd eyes taking in every last bit of her hideous appearance. Had she been a beautiful woman like Kaikeyi, they would not have instantly concluded she was guilty! Manthara swallowed her bitterness. She had made a calculated ploy, and Ayodhya had played right along. It had not been without its delights. She had always liked asking uncomfortable questions. The horror had been so evident on the other servants' faces. But she had committed no crime. If they sentenced her, it could only be out of spite. Even malice had to be proved!

Kaikeyi left her seat and sided with Manthara again. She, at least, had come to her final decision.

"Anything you say to Manthara henceforth may be addressed to me," Kaikeyi said, and there was anger in her voice. "She is my servant, and what she does is on my orders."

Sumantra turned his grave eyes to Kaikeyi. "Did you order her to make these inquiries?"

If anything gave Manthara delight that day, it was the king's face then. He was clenching the sides of his throne, unable to hide his anxiety. What would the high and mighty king do if he found out his precious darling Kaikeyi was guilty?

Nothing. Nothing at all, Manthara thought with disdain.

"It is as Manthara says," Kaikeyi said with a tremble in her voice. "We are newcomers here. Manthara's primary purpose is to keep me safe."

Though Kaikeyi had evaded the question, it was a beautiful woman's appeal, and it worked. Manthara sensed a change in the air. They would not demand more from the beautiful queen. But Kaikeyi was not fully aware of her own appeal, for she continued, "If I wish someone dead, I bring out my sword and wage an honest fight! I do not fight in the shadows."

The ministers and men of the court looked to the king. Of course he had been the one leading this charge, even if he pretended to rely on his ministers. Sumantra murmured something to the king. So did Siddhartha, the white-bearded minister with puffy eyes, who looked as if he was on his deathbed. By the looks of it, he was determined to take Manthara with him. Whatever the ministers said, the king was all too eager now to dismiss the charges, since Kaikeyi and Manthara stood united.

"I am not convinced of your servant's innocence," the king said, addressing himself to Kaikeyi, as she had requested. "But as she points out, she has, as of yet, taken no action. She claims to be innocent. Manthara is free to go, having found a way to explain her actions. She will no longer have free access to Kausalya's and Sumitra's quarters. In addition, her behavior will be scrutinized and her motives reexamined in one month's time. Be aware that she is under surveillance." The king's eyes turned to Manthara, who had already frozen to the spot.

As if she had not already been under surveillance. Did they really take her for a worthless fool? The suspicion that would follow her like a stink now was Ayodhya's "justice." Here they punished you for being honest and asking questions openly.

The final blow came when a servant produced something that belonged to Manthara. Those animals had snooped around her room! They had found *The Laws of Manu*, her gift from Ashvapati. What else had they taken?

"We found this in your chamber," the king explained, as if she was an idiot who did not recognize her own possessions. "Did you not know that this book is forbidden to women?"

Do you *know that I am not woman?* Manthara wanted to shout. She had never been with a man, never enjoyed the privileges of womanhood. *I am a hunchback!*

"I do not care to hear how you procured this forbidden work," the stupid king said. If only he knew Kaikeyi's father had given it to Manthara. "It does not belong to you any longer."

Manthara had memorized most of it anyway. She knew far more than she cared to about cattle disputes and inheritance laws. Let them have their petty laws.

"You have demonstrated why this sacred text is forbidden to your kind," the king droned on. "You simply use it to your own advantage alone."

Manthara glanced at Kaikeyi. Did the queen realize that all of precious womankind had just been insulted? Kaikeyi's face was clear, gazing up at that king whom she adored. No doubt they would use this conflict as fuel for their midnight passions. Manthara's revulsion for them all knew no bounds. Her chin twitched; her mouth worked but made no sound.

The man who had recited the opening lines stood up: "May the lord in your heart guide your words and actions henceforth."

The trial was over. Kaikeyi began to lead Manthara away. As soon as Manthara turned her back on the king, she started planning how she could inflict some actual pain on Ayodhya. Now she knew how easy they all were to manipulate. The day that Ayodhya fell apart, Manthara would stand aside and watch.

CHAPTER 19

Three Queens

Spring again arrived in Ayodhya. Kausalya beheld the white horse gallop triumphantly through the northern gate. It symbolized victory and the fruition of their goal. As expected, no one had challenged King Dasharatha's authority as emperor. It was a testimony to their satisfaction but also to his military skill; few would dare rise up against a king who had never been defeated. The time to perform the fire sacrifice was quickly approaching. Kausalya was ready. The previous year had been a busy one, especially for her, who oversaw food preparations, payments, and the well-being of the workers.

In addition, Kausalya was fiercely committed to integrating the women who had returned from Ravana's failed abduction attempt. None of the thirty-three women were native to the land of Koshala, and this added to the challenge. The one woman from Ayodhya, the mother of the deceased Lila and Lava, was not among the returned. Rani spoke often of the many who were still missing, especially the one she called "the brave lady" who had rallied them together. The matriarchs of the dancing girls had impressed Kausalya with their warm welcome and their detachment from the endowments, for they were already far wealthier than most Ayodhyans. Though Kausalya did not practice favoritism, she couldn't keep Rani from her side. Rani had taken to Kausalya just as she had to Chitra, her adoptive father. Far

into her adolescence, the girl showed little sign of morphing into a woman. Perhaps it would always remain so. Kausalya was now training Rani to be her assistant; although petite, Rani was sharp as a whip and bursting with energy.

With Rani as her shadow, the Great Queen oversaw the creation of the arena where the ritual would take place. Thousands of bricks had been shaped and guesthouses for the invitees had been constructed. Kings and their representatives had been called from all over the world. It was paramount that everyone be duly honored in a sacrifice of this magnitude. The brick makers, carpenters, and earth diggers had constructed a small city on the banks of the Sarayu. They had built long halls to facilitate mass food distribution, and even while the rest of the site was under construction, Kausalya had ensured that food was provided for all travelers, workers, and citizens who wanted it. Kausalya had wielded her usual authority in seeing the arrangements through.

Dasharatha might have three queens, but Ayodhya had only two, for Kaikeyi was nowhere to be seen in these dealings. Kausalya was active, morning to night, and Sumitra was there by her side, falling naturally into the role of Kausalya's caretaker. When Kausalya forgot to eat or drink, Sumitra was there to sit her down. Kaikeyi, however, was conspicuous in her absence. What the youngest queen did with her time was not Kausalya's concern. Dasharatha refused to hear a word on this topic. After Manthara's trial, he had all but resigned himself to Kaikeyi and Manthara's ways. Rumor had it that Kaikeyi spent all her days tending to her horses, as if she was a horse merchant rather than a queen. Like a child, she was opposed to the killing of the white stallion, as though she would not partake in the results. The young queen could be so lax and whimsical only because others, namely Kausalya, shouldered the responsibilities.

As the auspicious time came closer, the sacrificial arena was completed in the center of the temporary city. The customary fire sacrifices required six fire pits, but for this event Vasishta had ordered eighteen, laying them out in the shape of an eagle. The priests who had constructed the fire pits assured the king that the bird shape would help the offerings fly up to the heavens.

The night before the fires were lit, Kausalya withdrew from service to focus on her personal rituals and prayers. She knew the priests would ensure that all the ghee pots were filled and the dusty roads sprinkled with fragrant water. The chief priest, Rishyashringa, directed every detail with an expertise that no one could question. As evening came, Kausalya dressed in pure white and went to take part in the slaying of the white stallion. Sumantra, the trusted minister, was there, and handed Kausalya the sword. Knowing how unfamiliar this part of the ritual was to Kausalya, he repeated his previous instructions: "Three strokes with the sword. Use all your power, both physical and mental."

Kausalya gripped the unfamiliar instrument and walked toward the stallion. The stallion grew docile as a priest whispered mantras into its ear. Mantras for the swift rebirth of the animal were chanted aloud. Wielding the sword with all her power, Kausalya ended the stallion's life with three strokes. She had never killed a living creature before, not even an insect. But the sight of the dead horse didn't shake her; she knew that death was part of the natural cycle. Kausalya also knew the importance of this ritual. Like her people, she did not believe in coincidences. She had not borne her husband a son; it was no trick of fate. There was a reason for it. She prayed that the cleansing fires would purify them all and restore balance. Kausalya circumambulated the animal three times with the sword in her hand. Her hands shook as she handed the bloody sword to Sumantra. Only then did Kausalya see the other two queens. Sumitra and Kaikeyi circumambulated the dead steed, thanking it for its sacrifice. Kaikeyi appeared stiff throughout her walk around the stallion; she couldn't bear the sight of the dead horse. Kausalya resolved to stay with the dead animal throughout the night, to atone for sins known and unknown. If the sacrifice proved futile, she would know that the fault was not hers.

The next morning, in the presence of the kings and royalty invited from far and wide, the fires were lit, and the horse's flesh was offered into the flames, along with three hundred other animals. The sacred scriptures guaranteed that the king would be purified of his sins as he breathed in the smoke from the offerings. The priests performed ritual after ritual, and Kausalya sat by the king's side, offering oblations into the fire at the required times. The mantras charged the atmosphere with energy, and Kausalya felt that her earthly existence gave way to something more expansive; she grew small, becoming simply a piece in the unfolding of the ceremony, which was larger than any one of them.

One by one, the gods in heaven appeared, to accept their respective oblations and bless the sacrifice. They were shining beings, personifications of beauty. Kausalya was dazzled. Finally, it was her turn to step forward and accept her oblation. Although the three queens were of equal birth, scripture divided them. First, Rishyashringa called for *Mahisi*, the queen, and Kausalya rose. She could not help the pride that welled up in her heart. Rishyashringa then called for *Parivritti*, the neglected woman, and Sumitra rose shyly. Lastly, he called for *Vavata*, the concubine, and Kaikeyi accepted her oblation, her face painstakingly neutral.

Their part done, the queens were escorted to a chamber built especially for them. Here they would wait for the culmination of the ceremony, when they would drink the fertility nectar. This part of the ceremony had to be done in utmost privacy, and therefore the queens waited without their usual attendants. Choosing a seat near the windows, Kausalya took her place and Sumitra seated herself nearby. Kaikeyi sat across from them, clearly apart.

Kausalya listened to the sacred hymns chanted in the large arena. The air vibrated with the ancient mantra's power. They had prepared an entire year, and Kausalya tingled with the excitement from all she had seen. She repeatedly glanced at the entranceway to see if her husband was coming. She could not understand how Sumitra or Kaikeyi could be so calm. She let her gaze rest on Kaikeyi, trying to read her. Kaikeyi was especially hard to interpret; her beauty was distracting. At that thought, Kausalya felt resentment rise in her throat. She pushed it firmly away, not willing to taint a sacred time with petty emotions.

It occurred to Kausalya that Kaikeyi was so unruffled because she was young and inexperienced. She had not been by the king's side through years of barrenness; she had not felt the deep sense of failure Kausalya and Sumitra shared. Kaikeyi had not been a witness to the anguish of Ayodhya while it grappled with its heirlessness. Of course, Dasharatha had never blamed Kausalya, but still she wondered: Would the two other women be sitting here now if she had given birth to a son?

Yes, Kausalya did feel entitled to the king's love; he was her husband first. What a platitude it had been when Kaikeyi arrived. It was such an old story, it almost didn't hurt, being displaced by a younger woman. And there it was again, her old resentment. She even called it that—"my old resentment"—because she was determined to put it behind her now. Only because Kausalya had ached with emptiness so long would she know the sweetness of fulfillment. Kaikeyi could easily recline there now without concern, absentmindedly twirling a strand of her black hair around her finger. Looking at Kaikeyi with her new resolve, Kausalya was able to see more of the young queen's heart.

Kaikeyi fidgeted in her seat. The three queens had never been so long in the same room before. Kausalya and Sumitra held each other's hands and leaned toward each other to share words. Kaikeyi's eyes lingered on their clasped hands.

Some Ayodhyans called Kaikeyi power hungry. Kaikeyi wouldn't understand why she had earned that reputation. She seemed to feel no guilt or remorse about her actions. For her it was a competition, and she was the winner of their husband's affection. Rumor had it that Kaikeyi's father still held high hopes that Kaikeyi's son would be king. Perhaps King Ashvapati did not know how close Dasharatha had come to banning Kaikeyi from the ceremony altogether. After she had sided with Manthara during the trial, Dasharatha had been cold with fury. It took him months to relent. Those months had given Kausalya an insight into her husband's dependence on Kaikeyi. Instead of properly rebuking Kaikeyi and going on with his duties, he had been completely self-absorbed in his heartbreak. It was a relief when finally the two made up and reunited. He loved Kaikeyi too much to exclude her forever. Kausalya was beginning to accept this truth because she was the *Mahisi*, the queen, and Kaikeyi the concubine.

The curtains behind Kaikeyi shifted with the breeze, and one of the sun's rays found its way into the room, falling on Kausalya. She was startled by the sudden ray of light and let out a quick laugh, lifting her palm to shield her face. Kaikeyi's eyes fastened on the older queen.

Feeling Kaikeyi's scrutiny, Kausalya returned her gaze. Neither of them lowered their eyes or looked away. Kaikeyi's eyes were like windows to a palace. Kausalya could see their

depth but not their content. Kaikeyi smiled at Kausalya for the first time since the two had met.

Kausalya turned her attention to Sumitra. Sumitra had been considered gentle all her life. It was a quality that served her well, as the tension oscillated back and forth between the two other women in the room. Sumitra was by definition the middle queen, and it was likely that she felt the burden of it, always the buffer between Kausalya and Kaikeyi. Somehow Kaikeyi did not seem threatened by Sumitra. With Sumitra, Kaikeyi was almost kind. Most often, she did not take note of the middle queen. That was a sort of kindness.

But even Sumitra's life had changed when Kaikeyi descended on them like a storm. The king was their sun and Kaikeyi the cloud. Their lives had become barren without their husband in their lives. Why couldn't they all share him? It had worked so wonderfully for Kausalya and Sumitra in the days before Kaikeyi. This was a phrase that had gained a life of its own, that spoke volumes in only two words: "Before Kaikeyi." Those were the golden times. Holding Sumitra's hand now, Kausalya felt how deep her bond with the middle queen had become.

Because Sumitra was there, Kaikeyi was subdued. Kausalya did not know why. *Because Sumitra does not hate her,* Kausalya suddenly thought. But did Kausalya truly hate the youngest queen? There was no clear answer. Yet she knew that this day, this magnificent day, would change them all. Already there was more air to breathe for all of them. In the past, it had been painful staying too long in the same room as Kaikeyi, who seemed to begrudge sharing even the very air they breathed. But today was different.

Kausalya thought back to the earlier ceremony by the blazing fire, when the three queens had taken their places next to their husband and king. She was taken aback when she heard that the scriptures had names for each of them. When the words "Neglected Queen" were pronounced upon Sumitra, the middle queen glanced at Kausalya. In name, Sumitra was perhaps the neglected one, but Kausalya was the one who felt it more keenly. Sumitra had never expected and certainly never demanded the king's love. To her, it came and went like a wonderful season, a memory to be treasured. Sumitra was all grace and gratitude.

Suddenly, Kaikeyi stood up, a flush in her cheeks.

"He is coming!"

Kausalya stood up too, though she could not yet hear footsteps.

Moments later, the king appeared in the entrance, holding a glowing vessel in his hands. When he came toward them, he brought sunlight and life with him. Kausalya felt only the deepest love for him. For a few seconds the king stood there smiling, looking at them one by one, silently acknowledging each of them. He had never looked more handsome. The golden vessel in his hands, the fruit of the entire sacrifice, made him glow like the sun.

"This vessel came into my hands," Dasharatha said, "from a being made of fire. Even Rishyashringa fell silent when this being arose from the fire. The being was vigorous and virile, his complexion red. His golden mane blazed around him like the fire itself. You can sense his energy in my hands."

The vessel in the king's hands shone with an unearthly glow. When Dasharatha moved closer to them, Kausalya saw tears glistening in his eyes.

"Kausalya," the king said softly, calling her to his side. "Drink half of this nectar."

Kausalya lifted the golden vessel to her lips. Kausalya deserved this honor, but she almost expected Kaikeyi to assert herself and snatch the vessel from her. It was just the sort of scene Kaikeyi was capable of. But today was not like other days. Kausalya's being filled with delight as she drank the nectar. It was the most sublime substance Kausalya had ever tasted: sweet, nectarous, energizing.

Dasharatha turned to Sumitra. "Drink half," he said.

When Sumitra handed the vessel back to the king, her eyes were still closed, savoring the nectar. The king handed the vessel to Kaikeyi, repeating the instruction to consume half of the remaining nectar. Kaikeyi savored the nectar, as they all had. When she handed the king the vessel, he weighed it in his hand. There was one small portion remaining. The king and his three queens looked at one another. Who would finish the nectar that everyone in Ayodhya, including the king himself, had worked so hard to procure?

In a rare moment of harmony, they all turned to Sumitra. The greatest miracle was that they were all in perfect agreement. Sumitra would drink the final portion of the heavenly nectar. Tears rose in Sumitra's eyes. She had not expected to be chosen. Beyond a sign of affection, none of them knew what this honor would entail, if anything.

Sumitra took the golden vessel in her hands and drank deeply until not a drop was left. Dasharatha gave them his warmest smile and returned to the sacrificial arena with the empty vessel to complete the sacrifice. The queens sat down again, filled to the brim by the nectar. Kausalya's hands instinctively went to her belly, already feeling the promise of life within.

CHAPTER 20

The Firstborn Son

Nine months passed. Since the epic ritual, all the queens were expecting. Kaikeyi pressed her hands against her swollen belly and felt content. She hadn't known that carrying a child would change her temperament. In the first few months when Dasharatha had banned her from riding, she had felt crazy; her belly had been flat and the child within but a dream. Now she felt the child's movements and kicks and dreamed about her unborn son. She spoke to him. She sang to him. She would protect him at all costs. She reached for him, her hands on her belly.

Since the charge against Manthara, the old woman had been on her best behavior, outwardly respectful to all things Ayodhyan. Her act did not fool Dasharatha, but she had given him no further reason to object to her presence. Kaikeyi also refused to discuss Manthara with him or anyone else. Dasharatha did not like that there were forbidden topics between them; he said it increased his suspicion toward the hunchback. It couldn't be helped. Kaikeyi pointed out that he himself had such restrictions with others. He did not, for example, entertain Kausalya's words on how to treat Kaikeyi. The senior queen's attempts to insert herself between them had failed. Kaikeyi had never been more secure in her position as Dasharatha's beloved.

When Manthara came in for her daily visit, she always made it clear that she did not share Kaikeyi's docility. Kaikeyi made her feel the baby's movements. While Manthara's bony fingers prodded the belly, she said, "You better pray your baby is born before Kausalya's."

"Oh, Manthara . . ." Kaikeyi was tired, heavy with the child she carried. The child was due any time. It was hard work growing a child in your womb, more tiring than Kaikeyi had imagined. It looked so easy when other women did it. But Kaikeyi felt all the changes in her body and the needs of the growing child. Never in her twenty-one years of life had Kaikeyi felt so content being passive. She felt as if she hadn't had a single argument with anyone in the entire nine months. She floated in a pleasant dream bubble—except when Manthara woke her up with her piques.

"It's not in my control," she reminded the old woman.

"Yet there are things you can do," Manthara said slyly. "Herbs you can take, mantras you can say, magic spells, sure to hasten the birth of this child."

"Black magic?"

"White, black. What does the color matter as long as it does its job."

"Manthara, please, do not pester me like this." Kaikeyi placed her hands protectively over the swollen belly that was the home of her baby. She wouldn't endanger his existence.

"If you don't take action, you will regret it. Take steps to achieve your goal before it's too late."

Kaikeyi wanted to lash back and demand, "Your goals or mine?" But she did not feel sharp-witted enough to argue with Manthara, so she lied, saying, "I'll think about it."

In truth, she had already made up her mind. Not everything Manthara thought was golden. Kaikeyi would not tamper with her unborn child's future. She might have aspired to bear the king his first child, but now she couldn't muster the same determination. If the gods willed it, her son would be born first. If not, he might still be king of Ayodhya. Kausalya's child might be born dimwitted or deformed. So many things could happen.

"You will regret your docility," Manthara warned.

And Kaikeyi did, two days later, when she heard the news: Kausalya's labor had started. A rush of anxiety took hold of Kaikeyi; destiny was supposed to be on her side. Kaikeyi's son was supposed to be the firstborn. If Kaikeyi went into labor now, she could still give birth before Kausalya did. But Kaikeyi's baby felt none of her sudden urgency and was resting as peacefully within her as he always had. Kausalya would be first again. She was the first queen, the first wife, and now she would be the first mother. The fact of the situation tore at Kaikeyi's heart. Why hadn't she listened to Manthara? She got up from her seat and began to walk. Manthara watched. After walking in a circle around her quarters, Kaikeyi sat down again. She was too heavy with child to pace or jump on a horse, as she otherwise would have.

"I wish *my* baby would be born first," she said quietly. "I want *my* boy to receive the king's affection. I want him to be the favorite son."

Thankfully, Manthara did not make it worse by chiding her or telling her it was her own mistake. She was kind and empathic in that way, ready to listen and comfort when Kaikeyi really needed it.

In truth, she had no answer to Kaikeyi's sudden concern. Would Dasharatha love his firstborn son more than Kaikeyi's son?

"Did my mother worry like this about me before I was born?" Kaikeyi heard herself ask.

Manthara didn't answer. She rarely did when it came to this topic.

"Did my mother love me?" Kaikeyi asked.

"Every mother worries," Manthara said.

"Did she *love* me?"

"Does it matter?" Manthara demanded, with her most caustic face. "She got herself exiled. If you truly loved your child, you would not be so stupid. Remember that."

Kaikeyi sighed. It was not exactly the sort of assurance she had been seeking.

A few hours later, a maidservant came running. "The king's first son has been born!"

"So quickly?" With round eyes, Kaikeyi turned to Manthara.

"Sometimes the gods are merciful." The maidservant's joy was palpable.

Manthara turned her lips down. She had evidently not prayed for such mercy toward Kausalya.

"I want to see him," Kaikeyi said.

This child was a rival to her own son. She wanted to find a reason to shun him, the way she spurned Kausalya. Manthara stood up, preparing to accompany her. Kaikeyi nodded to her, though they well knew that Manthara was not welcome in the other queens' quarters. Escorted by several servants, Kaikeyi made her way to a place she had never before visited: Kausalya's inner apartment. It wouldn't be hard to dislike Kausalya's son; most newborns looked ugly, with shriveled, red skin and swollen eyelids. As the young queen and her servant neared Kausalya's inner chambers, no one seemed to notice Manthara. Kaikeyi relaxed. She needed Manthara by her side. As they entered Kausalya's bedroom, Kaikeyi was not surprised to see Sumitra there. Sumitra's belly was so enormous, it was shocking that she had not been the first to give birth. She was expected to deliver twins.

"I thought the boy would be here," Kaikeyi said to Sumitra. Since the beginning of their pregnancies, Sumitra had welcomed Kaikeyi with new warmth.

"He will be here soon," Sumitra assured her. "He is being bathed and dressed. Kausalya is also undergoing the cleansing ceremonies by the midwife and the priests."

While they waited for the newborn, Kaikeyi allowed herself to speculate what the child would look like, his father or mother. She tried to conceal her malice towards the firstborn from Sumitra.

A maidservant appeared in the doorway, announcing the arrival of the prince, as if he was an eminent guest. The little prince already had an entourage. The woman who would be his wet nurse cradled him to her heart, followed by guards and attendants. Sumantra, the handsome minister who also was kind-natured, never took his eyes off the child. Kaikeyi and Sumitra fell silent. The newborn was asleep. He had a delicate face and an unusual luminescence. Kaikeyi's thoughts fled. Sumitra too seemed speechless. The two queens gazed at the child; all thoughts of whom he might resemble were far gone. Kaikeyi had not known that a newborn child could be so exquisite. His cheeks were round and smooth, and soft

black hair framed his face. Kaikeyi admired the curl of his thick eyelashes. His skin was the color of lotus leaves shining in the sun. Kaikeyi reached for the baby. The wet nurse reluctantly handed him over. As she received him, Kaikeyi felt a swell in her heart, as if this was her own son.

"He is remarkable," Kaikeyi whispered, outlining the baby's lips, nose, and eyebrows gently with her finger. "Look at his hands and feet. Every part of this little child is perfectly shaped. And he glows like an emerald. I have never seen anything like it. His pink toenails look like lotus petals against the hue of his toes."

"He is opening his eyes," Sumitra said, holding the infant's hand.

They both fell silent, waiting for the boy's first glance. The baby's eyelids fluttered, but then remained closed. Kaikeyi began to gently prod the baby: "Wake up, little one."

As soon as she said these words, the baby slowly opened his eyes and looked at her. His eyes were large and bright, as jet black as his hair. Tears rose in Kaikeyi's eyes as the infant looked into hers. There was such love, trust and innocence in his eyes. "Kausalya is so lucky to have a son like you."

She could never hate this child; she felt ashamed of having planned to.

The next moment, Kaikeyi felt a rush of pain run up her spine. A sudden flurry of movement in Kaikeyi's womb startled her. She inhaled sharply.

"What's wrong?" Sumitra asked.

"I think it's my turn now. My baby is kicking!"

Manthara was immediately by her side telling her to breathe deeply.

When the sudden pain subsided, Kaikeyi gently kissed the baby on his cheeks and reluctantly handed him to Sumitra. Kaikeyi's maidservants came to her side, readying to escort her to the birthing room. As Kaikeyi left, Kausalya appeared, followed by Dasharatha and a procession of priests humming auspicious hymns. Both of them looked eager to see their new son, hardly sparing a moment for Kaikeyi. Another contraction wracked Kaikeyi, erasing the outburst of jealousy she felt. The king noticed her grimace and cast a worried glance at her as she passed; she tried to smile bravely at him. This was his moment to see his dream come true. Having met the little boy herself, Kaikeyi would not begrudge him that. Dasharatha would be by her side in due time, she had no doubt.

Soon enough, Kaikeyi had no room for any thoughts at all. The pain of childbirth was not alleviated by Kaikeyi's exposure to physical pain as a warrior. Kaikeyi had never felt so vulnerable. She clung to Manthara's hand; she cried for her lost mother. Her respect for every mother in the world grew with every contraction she had. Finally, as the new day arrived in Ayodhya, her son was born. As the little one suckled at her breast, the exhausted Kaikeyi knew that her world had found a new purpose. She would *never* be as stupid as her own mother had been.

CHAPTER 21

A Mother's Morning

Before Kausalya had a son, her desire for one had been theoretical, grounded in Ayodhya's need. She had not imagined the profound transformation that would occur in Dasharatha and herself. Over the years, she had seen many changes in Dasharatha, the natural ones of aging and maturity and the unnatural ones, becoming a reckless lover in the arms of Kaikeyi. Kausalya's own changes were not as visible to her, focused on the well-being of others as she was. The moment her son was born, however, she was reborn with him. Twelve days after his birth, he was named Rama Chandra, "Pleasing like the Moon," and now she was, first of all, Rama's mother.

The change in Dasharatha had begun on the day he found out his queens were expecting. He had placed his hands on Kausalya's belly and made a solemn promise that he would not show favoritism to any of his sons. At any cost, he meant to prevent rivalry among them. Because he made the promise to Kausalya, she understood that he was determined not to favor Kaikeyi's child. Just one day after Rama was born, Kaikeyi gave birth to Bharata. The two brothers looked alike, green hued and perfectly proportioned. But fate was a jokester: when Dasharatha was so determined to be equal, to distribute his affection equally, he got a son like Rama. His resolve was challenged from the beginning; the moment he received

Rama into his waiting arms, the bond was forged. Rama was the king's dream come true. Although Dasharatha tried to check the force of his natural affection, everyone else, even Kaikeyi, adored Rama. Indeed, they worshipped him. Dasharatha couldn't stop the tidal wave of people's affection for this son of his. Kausalya could only stand back and watch in amusement as Dasharatha stood bewildered by his own resolve.

Even as Kausalya became Rama's mother first and foremost, her queenly duties continued. When she had taken two weeks to rest and recover from childbirth, she didn't simply imagine that Ayodhya was falling apart. It really did. On her return, the golden altars needed a thorough polish, the maidservants a talking to, and the treasury a reorganization. To Kausalya's amusement, little Rani had taken charge in Kausalya's absence. She was now sixteen years old, as flat-chested as a boy, and a force of nature. She had, with the fierce will of the survivor, carved out a position for herself. Over the years, in fact, the new dancing girls had provoked a change in the entire dance form. It became energetic and swift rather than fluid and sweet. It was impossible to ignore a dancer now as she displayed her art. Many times Kausalya had to simply put aside her prayers and tasks at the golden altars to be swept high by the force of the dancer. She knew, however, that it was not a complete success story, for many servants, riled up by Manthara in secret, shunned the new women. The saying that "one year with an outcast, you become an outcast," had somehow become a terrible truth among them. None of Kausalya's efforts to shed light was able to extricate that belief from those who held it.

Just like Manthara's dubious influence, Kaikeyi's dominion over the king had grown. Kausalya had little to do with the king's daily life. She had not objected openly during the first years. Year by year, however, Dasharatha grew more withdrawn, and now she could not speak to him in private. She was no longer welcome in his private quarters, a place he rarely visited anyway, being always at Kaikeyi's. She regretted her compliance. She should have intervened sooner, while Dasharatha still gave her his ear. Now he simply would not listen to her. Even when the youngest queen wasn't present, Dasharatha was reserved. From his actions, Kaikeyi's will was clear. He never visited the other two queens, by day or night. The exclusion stung. Terribly. After Rama's birth, Kausalya thought the bad feeling would vanish, that her resentment would disappear. But it did not. It had only grown heavier over the past four years. Though Kausalya strived to be unaffected, there were moments when she barely could survive her loveless marriage. Her only solace was Rama, and she turned to him every day.

As Rama approached his fourth birthday, Kausalya was nearing fifty and treasured every moment of being his mother. Rama had gone to sleep knowing that he would be a bigger boy the next day. All his brothers were very excited about this event. "We are turning four!" they said, as if they were one being.

Bharata turned four the day after Rama, and Sumitra's twins, Lakshmana and Shatrugna, two weeks later. Dasharatha had decided that on Rama's birthday, the princes would ride through the streets of Ayodhya and give gifts to the citizens. Then they would serve the holy ones food, and only then would they officially be four years old.

After her morning prayers at the altars, Kausalya went to Rama's room. She had woken up early for the occasion, invoking special prayers and blessings for his success. She prayed he would excel in all the arts of warfare, scripture, and statesmanship.

When she entered Rama's room, she released the attendant from service and walked to the bed. She was unsurprised to find Lakshmana, the older of the twins, fast asleep next to Rama. Both boys slept soundly, and she tiptoed around the room, arranging scattered toys, and finally she settled down by the bed. Seeing Rama always soothed her, whether he was awake or asleep. She wondered if her love for Rama would be different if Dasharatha had still claimed her attention or affection. Kausalya exhaled and watched the orange and red rays of the rising sun make their way upward. The gentle rays turned the white palace walls pink and peered in through the windows to color the sleeping inhabitants with their brightness.

Kausalya turned her face from nature's beauty to behold her sleeping sons. Yes, sons. She thought of all four boys as her own; indeed, all the mothers felt this way. Dasharatha's promise to be impartial had created magic after all. The sun's rays tinted the boys' faces, making their cheeks shine with a pinkish glow. Kausalya admired Rama's smooth, round cheeks, his arched eyebrows, and his long, curling eyelashes. His hair, blacker than the kajal around the queen's eyes, was scattered loosely around the pillow. The strands of hair coiled around his head like black serpents. Kausalya shuddered at the image and rearranged Rama's hair. She prayed that no harm would ever befall him.

Her eyes moved to Lakshmana's face. His skin was fair in contrast to Rama's, but he had the same long eyelashes and black curly hair. In truth, their heads were resting so close together on the pillow, their curls were interwoven. A smile blossomed on Kausalya's lips when she thought of the friendship between Rama and Lakshmana. It was rare to see them apart; actually she could not remember ever seeing Rama without Lakshmana nearby. Even now in their sleep, they did not let each other go. Kausalya reached over and stroked the boys' clasped hands.

Rama stirred and looked up at his mother with sleepy eyes. "Don't be sad, Ma," he said, reaching up to touch her cheek with his little hand.

Kausalya's heart skipped a beat. How did he see into her heart like this? She had not felt sad exactly, but his words made tears well up.

"Sometimes you can be so happy," she said, "you have to shed a few tears."

She stroked his soft cheeks. His eyelids fluttered, and he turned to his side, falling asleep again. Sumitra entered the room and Kausalya smiled warmly at her co-wife.

"Great Queen," Sumitra said in greeting. "Our sons are still sleeping?"

"Yes, Sumitra. Look, they fell asleep playing."

Kausalya motioned toward the bows and arrows, Rama's favorite toys, scattered on the floor. Lakshmana still clasped a wooden arrow to his chest. The two queens exchanged a glance and laughed softly.

"I think these two are the real twins at heart," Sumitra said. She moved a stray curl from Lakshmana's face.

Annapurna

"Yes. And I wager that Shatrugna is in Bharata's chambers," Kausalya said.

They spoke then, as they often did, about the bonds the boys had made with one another. Lakshmana and Rama were inseparable, and so were Bharata and Shatrugna. Although Rama was not much older than his brothers, the other boys somehow looked up to him. "Rama said," and "Rama did," were common phrases they used.

Kausalya was extremely thankful that there was no jealousy or rivalry between the brothers. She had feared that the dynamics between herself and Kaikeyi would replay between Rama and Bharata. But it did not. Kausalya had to credit Kaikeyi for this, at least. She did seem to genuinely care for Rama. The name Rama Chandra suited Kausalya's son, for like the moon, his soothing presence pleased even someone as hardhearted as Kaikeyi.

As Sumitra and Kausalya were talking, the third queen suddenly appeared in the doorway, draped stunningly in a sari of her favorite color, red. She held a flower garland in her hand, and her hair was wet from her morning bath, cascading down her back. How did she manage to look so dazzling every moment of the day?

Kausalya turned away. She couldn't help but feel that Kaikeyi was an intruder. Today she had brought a flower garland for Rama. Kaikeyi looked briefly at the two other queens and sat down by Rama's side, placing the garland by his side. She took Rama's hands in hers. Kausalya would not begrudge her son any affection he got, even from her rival. Love was love.

Kaikeyi gave Rama few quick kisses on his cheeks and whispered into his ear. Without another word to Kausalya, Kaikeyi departed. She left a tense feeling in her wake, as though she had made a parting insult and rushed out.

The sun was steadily rising. It was time to wake the princes.

Kausalya took Rama's hand. "Rama, Lakshmana, wake up," she prodded.

Lakshmana stretched his limbs and lifted his arms toward his mother. Sumitra lifted the half-sleeping prince into her arms and brought him back to his rooms. She touched Kausalya briefly on the shoulder as she left.

Kausalya sighed, an old intuition rising. It was not too late to intervene, to bring Kaikeyi back from her willful insolence. Dasharatha refused to speak of Kaikeyi in anything but defense. Kausalya had waited and waited, hoping someone else would bring the younger woman to her senses. But no one had done it. Perhaps no one else saw what Kausalya saw, that Kaikeyi's behavior could very well have an impact on the whole kingdom. It was time for Kausalya to put aside her pride, pull together her inner resources, and face the younger queen. She would summon Kaikeyi to the House of Wrath. There they could speak without interference. There had to be a way to make Kaikeyi see the damage she was doing. Dasharatha was not, after all, the husband of only one woman. Kausalya had to set them free from this game. Kaikeyi had to acknowledge the deep injustice she seemed set on executing.

Anxious about the confrontation ahead, Kausalya's heart raced, and she turned to her son, a surge of affection calming her. Rama yawned and stretched his arms, a toy arrow falling from the bed. Kausalya still remembered the day when Rama had taken his first step. How excited she had been! How bizarre now that she should feel he was already growing apart from her. A vague apprehension regarding Rama's future seized her. She shook it off and beckoned Rama to come for his morning bath.

She left Kaikeyi's garland on the bed.

CHAPTER 22

The House of Wrath

When Kausalya stepped inside the House of Wrath, she heard the silence right away, for even it had a sort of sound. The House of Wrath had heavy curtains covering every doorway to block out light and block in sound. For several moments, Kausalya just stood there wondering if she had done the right thing. She had summoned Kaikeyi here—not because she was angry but because she wanted to meet Kaikeyi alone, without Manthara peering out from behind Kaikeyi's back. The hunchback had proven herself nothing but malevolent. Kausalya usually managed to find redeeming qualities in anyone. The only one she saw in Manthara was her hunchback. Kausalya knew it was a painful and deteriorating condition; it would not be easy to have a joyful disposition. Still, Manthara's demeanor was consistently cruel, even if she had somehow managed to escape from the verdict that should have expelled her. Now Kausalya needed to reach Kaikeyi's heart, to steer her away from her willfulness. Therefore, the Great Queen abandoned her hesitation and walked into the House. The first chamber was pitch black. She slowed her pace, walking carefully through the darkness.

Kausalya had used the House once years before, when there had been an unspeakable tension between herself and Dasharatha about their childlessness. She remembered that the House had amplified her frustration and then released her from it. Or perhaps that had been Dasharatha's doing. Either way, Kausalya had been grateful for a place that was separate from the palace, where she always felt the need to uphold her majesty. The House had been designed to give total privacy to whatever conflicts went on within. The original architect had also designed it to evolve from darkness to light. The various chambers were illuminated by increasing degrees of light.

The first chamber, the one Kausalya stood in now, was dark as a cave. She had to walk carefully, having no sight to rely on. The darkness within and without became one. The boundaries between the seen and unseen selves melted away. Kausalya became still, her boundaries melting away. She was a soul, not a body. She felt the presence of the all-seeing witness in her heart, the one who sat hidden in everyone's heart. He was within Kaikeyi's and Manthara's heart. He was always whispering words of truth and light. One simply had to listen, although it often was all but simple. He would guide Kausalya, even now, in the right direction. But when she listened to his whispers, she heard Rama's voice: "Play!" Kausalya smiled. Her little boy spoke with the innocence of his age. Only play mattered.

Kausalya, however, had other concerns, and she clung to them as she stepped into the next room, only slightly less dark than the first one. Again the heavy curtain closed behind her, inviting her firmly into the room. Her eyes sought the one source of light, a small candle, at the far side of the room, casting a slight shadow.

She would wait here for Kaikeyi. It would be easier to face the younger queen without having to face her unearthly beauty. Kausalya knew she should not be affected by something so superficial as the body's appearance, and yet Kaikeyi's beauty was one of the reasons they were here today. The king was not unaffected. And so Kausalya could not be either. Suddenly Kausalya longed for the last and final room in this labyrinth of Wrath. She knew it was as bright as the sunlight outside. It was this room one had to pass through once emotions were spent, bathed in the healing rays of the sun before exiting refreshed. Kausalya had heard it said that the final room, with its open ceiling, was similar to the sun cell in the prison, designed to bring in maximum sunlight. The general rule was to stay in the House of Wrath until morning, bathing then in the sun's first rays. It took at least one night to bring forth hidden emotions and release them from one's being. She wasn't sure how long Kaikeyi would stay in her presence, but Kausalya had resolved to stay the night.

The silence was immense. Every flicker of the candle spoke of secrets that stayed within these walls. Kausalya's hands went to her adornments. Another rule of the house was to leave titles and belongings aside, inviting the emotional and psychic aspects of one's being to dominate. Could she bear to face Kaikeyi unadorned? She was Kaikeyi's elder, a fact that Kaikeyi was fond of pointing out. Kausalya's thick hair was transitioning from black to gray, a hallmark of her age. Sighing, Kausalya began removing the precious ornaments. If she hoped to reach Kaikeyi's heart, she could not hide behind superficial veneers. She would meet Kaikeyi today as a woman, not a queen. She placed her golden ornaments carefully on the armoire in the chamber. She hesitated only briefly before setting aside the gem that expelled poisons. Kaikeyi was not Manthara.

As Kausalya waited for Kaikeyi to arrive, she rehearsed what she would say to Kaikeyi.

The game had gone too far. Dasharatha, who was righteous in every other way, had fallen into the trap of favoritism. Why else were Kaikeyi and Dasharatha living as if only the two of them existed?

Kausalya hoped that anger would not come in the way. As Kaikeyi kept her waiting, the beginnings of wrath pressed on her calm. Her eyes searched for a distraction, but there was little to see but shadows. One room was helpfully stacked with clay pots, in case one needed to vent one's fury. Kausalya picked one up, weighing it in her hands. She peered at the designs drawn beautifully into the pot. Even if she was angry, she would not be able to dash the pot to the ground. She knew Kaikeyi had no such reservation. Where was the younger queen?

Was it possible that Kaikeyi would ignore her invitation and not arrive? Kaikeyi thrived on conflict. Then again, she also seemed to greatly enjoy trumping Kausalya. She might take this as another way to prove her indifference. Kausalya could only wait and hope. Kausalya placed the pot down, balancing it on top of the stack again. It fell to the floor, cracking apart immediately. The wrath was upon her, directed toward herself.

How had she been so naive? She had relinquished her position beside the king—the one that she had built over nearly thirty years of faithful service—without saying a word. That was her mistake. In practice, Kausalya now had no husband, no one to lean on. Sumitra leaned on her. The servants leaned on her. Ayodhya leaned on her.

Seeking respite, Kausalya put her hand close to a flickering candle, and the warmth kissed her palm. She heard no sound, but she felt a shiver run up her neck. She turned around. Kaikeyi had entered the room, a figure cast completely in darkness. Even so, Kausalya immediately noticed that Kaikeyi had not chosen to remove any of her regalia. Her crown stood on her head like spikes on a club. Kausalya felt naked, as she had feared she would. It was too late now.

She stopped her hands from reaching up to twist her unruly hair into a more regal position. Instead, she took a step toward Kaikeyi, saying, "Welcome."

She instantly regretted the word. She did not want to create a feeling of ownership. This was not her place, but theirs. Though Kaikeyi had not said a word, Kausalya felt her whole being rise up in response to the other woman's presence.

"Let's take age out of the discussion," Kaikeyi snapped. "Then you will not need to undercut me, and I will not need to point out your disadvantage."

"And yet you just did."

"You constantly try to educate me on Ayodhya's etiquette. What you really mean is that I don't belong here and that you do."

"Frankly, I called you here so we could speak without Manthara's interference. Not because I am angry."

"Aha! So I am the angry, unpolished runt from Kekaya. You are the regal queen of Ayodhya, the saint who always says and does the right things."

"We can both do the right thing, Kaikeyi. That's why we are here."

"Not because you finally are angry?"

"You wish me to be angry?"

"Yes. By the thirty gods. Show some emotion for once. No wonder Dasha turns to me. A dead fish has more passion than you."

Kausalya clenched her jaw and took a deep breath. She would *not* be roped in.

"Am I so abhorrent to you?"

"I did not come here to be questioned. Why are we here?"

"Do you really not know?"

"Do you have *any* answers, or must I supply them too? This could be amusing." Kaikeyi crossed her arms. "We are here because you are jealous of me, because you cannot stand me, because I am more beautiful than you, because you have always resented me, because you dislike my presence in Rama's life, because—"

"You may see many reasons to dispute with me, but I see only one. Your exclusive hold on Dasharatha, *our husband*. Or do you tell yourself that he is yours alone?" Despite her resolve, Kausalya felt the power of wrath spread coldly across her belly.

Kaikeyi took a step forward. "He has chosen to love *me*."

"You are twisting the truth into an untruth, and only bad can come of it."

"Of course, Great Queen. This is not about your desire to be the prominent queen, to sink your claws back into 'our husband.' No, this is for Ayodhya, for the good of all, for the sake of truth. You are so very self-sacrificing."

"And I am here to warn you that if you do not see the value in what you mock, there will be a fire, one beyond your control."

"That's the nature of fire, after all. To be unpredictable. Fierce and strong. Unlike you, I love fire. I like feeling out of control. It's what passion does. I choose it."

"Very well. Your choices are yours. I beg you to simply acknowledge that Dasharatha has three queens. Allow him to spend time with us. Allow him to be the husband of three, not one."

"I do not control him. He is the king. I don't tell him what to do."

"You are lying. To me or to yourself. I see the love in his eyes for me, for all of us, and yet I see how he restrains himself. I often feel as though he fears your disapproval. But he is the king, as you said. Why would he allow one woman to control him?"

"As I said, I'm not here to answer to you."

"He is, and should be, *our husband*. We can work in harmony to share him equally."

This was what Kausalya had really wanted to say. She felt her earnestness melt away any grievances. She closed the distance between them. "Kaikeyi, I promise you, I give you my word, I will not use his time to my advantage. I will not undermine you in any way."

"You couldn't, even if you tried. You do not have that kind of power."

"Is that what this is about then, proving your prowess? You would destroy relationships thirty years strong simply because you can?"

"Those relationships have expired. They have exceeded their value. When you go to war, you pick a fresh horse."

"This is not a war!"

"What else would it be? A dance in the gardens? A playground where we hold hands and make merry? Wake up!" She snapped her fingers in front of Kausalya's nose.

Quicker than thought, Kausalya's hand darted out, gripping the younger woman's hand. For a moment, she gripped it with all her force. Then she held it to her heart, pulling Kaikeyi in toward her. "Let's not fight," she whispered. "We can be friends. We can live in harmony."

Kaikeyi was quiet for the first time. Something had shifted between them. Kausalya held her breath. Kaikeyi did not snatch her hand away, so Kausalya continued.

"I called you here to reveal the wish I've had since you came to Ayodhya. I remember clearly the moment I saw you. You were unlike any other woman I had ever seen, so confident and elegant on horseback. I—" She hesitated. Kaikeyi's eyes were intent on her, though shadows hid her expression. "I wanted to be your friend." The actual word was *mother*, but Kaikeyi would not like that term. "I'm sure we can be friends."

"If," Kaikeyi said softly, "I share the king with you."

Was that Kausalya's condition? She released Kaikeyi's hand. The queens remained close, closer than etiquette normally allowed. Kaikeyi was fragrant; underneath the jasmine, there was a musky, womanly odor.

"He is not yours to share," Kausalya said softly.

It was the truth, but they were the wrong words in this delicate moment. Kaikeyi took a step back, a shadow falling between them as clear as a wall.

"Then why are you here?" Kaikeyi asked. "Are you not offering your friendship in return for him?"

"Everything is not a negotiation," Kausalya answered. "Until now, you have not welcomed me as a friend. We could be allies. Co-mothers. Co-wives. Within the royal house, you may seek supremacy. But the goals of life are not limited to these palace walls."

"And we are back to lectures."

Kausalya felt a sadness sweep over her. They had been so close to understanding. Kausalya had felt Kaikeyi's heart come out of its hiding place. They had been so close. But this meeting was folly after all. Kaikeyi had already crossed beyond reasoning. She acted out of impulse and desire. Her motives were hidden even to herself. And so, Kausalya did not ask the final question she had, which was simply, Why? Why was Kaikeyi set on destroying herself?

Kausalya wanted to embrace the younger woman, as if she was that girl again who had ridden confidently into Ayodhya. Kausalya had seen her fragility, had even then thought, *She could be my daughter.* It was not only her youth that had brought this idea to Kausalya.

"Anything else?" Kaikeyi demanded. "Or am I free to go?"

Kausalya did not answer. She felt a tear trickle down her cheek.

Kaikeyi brushed past her, leaving the scent of jasmine behind. Kausalya grabbed the closest thing her hands could find and threw it down with all her might. The clay pot smashed against the marble floor. Kaikeyi froze.

"I am capable of destroying you," Kausalya said. She threw another pot to the ground, and then another. The younger woman did not turn around, but neither did she leave.

Kausalya smashed everything within reach. "I am the queen of Ayodhya. I rule the treasury. I train the servants. I speak to ministers and their wives."

She flung a pot against the wall. "Look at me!"

Kaikeyi turned and faced Kausalya, the Queen.

"I have influence you could never dream of," Kausalya said. "If I set my will against yours, if I set my mind to undermining you, you would stand with nothing but Manthara at your side. But I do not wish to harm something that is dear to my husband, the king. I do not wish to destroy him. *I do not* use my power for my own selfish ends."

Kausalya saw her own power with blinding clarity. She held on to the pots in her hands and approached Kaikeyi. The candle lights flickered with her steps.

"That's where we are different, you and I," Kausalya said, breathing forcefully. "I sacrifice my personal enjoyment, every time, in favor of his. I am the first to rise in this kingdom and the last to sleep. And that is what a queen must do and the very reason *you* will never *ever* be queen."

She flung the pots at Kaikeyi's feet. The younger woman turned and ran.

Kausalya stood in the same spot for a long time, fury coursing through her veins. She had never displayed her anger in this way before. She looked at the demolition of the beautifully crafted clay pots. Only a few remained whole. She hadn't realized how many she had smashed.

She walked out of the room into the next one. Without meaning to, her eyes sought Kaikeyi. The rules of the House mandated that one stay through the night. But Kausalya was alone. It was a disappointment and a relief. The battle was over.

The darkness around her soothed and repelled her. She would not run away, as Kaikeyi had. She needed this complete privacy to put the situation into perspective.

The next morning, Kausalya walked out from the House of Wrath, lingering in the final sunlit room. As promised, the sun's rays warmed her entire body. She paused in the middle of the room, sending a prayer to that warm sun. Kausalya was satisfied with her own comportment, even if she knew now that Kaikeyi would not yield. The difference was that now when Kaikeyi continued in her same frivolous manner, she would know that she could do so only because Kausalya allowed it. Kausalya was the Great Queen, but she could not set her will against her husband, the Great King. The consequences of his choices would fall on him, and on them all. That was the glory and the ghastly truth of autocracy.

Kausalya let the warm rays spread across her back, caressing her neck, before she walked onward, back to her life as the queen who ruled Ayodhya but spent solitary nights yearning for a husband who never came.

CHAPTER 23

A Dirty Fight

His sons turned four and then five. Dasharatha still treasured the very first moment he had held Rama, his firstborn, in his arms. Cradling his son to his chest, Dasharatha had felt a joy so intense, he ceased to be himself. He had whispered Anaranya's prophecy into Rama's ear, just as Dasharatha's father had done into his. The tradition was too strong to resist, although Dasharatha had come to doubt the prophecy itself. It was quite possible that King Aja too had known the improbability of any human slaying the blood-drinker king.

After Rama's birth, it took Dasharatha years to feel like the same old man again. The two queens, Kausalya and Kaikeyi, had entered an unspoken truce when the boys were born. But in some ways, Dasharatha felt more on edge; he could sense their rivalry simmering beneath the surface. As a father, however, he was determined to keep his sons unblemished by it. It seemed to him that he had closed eyes in a moment of joy and opened them to see that his sons had turned five years old.

In a rare respite from his royal duties, Dasharatha watched his sons play in the gardens below. One, two, three, four, he counted, studying each of them. Losing any one of them would bring him unimaginable grief, and so the old curse sometimes resurfaced, whispering its threat into his ear. First Dasharatha saw Bharata, who was whispering into Lakshmana's ear. Or was it Shatrugna's?

Even if the king had been closer, he might not have been able to tell the twins apart. Lakshmana and Shatrugna were so alike they could hardly tell themselves apart. Dasharatha, who had prayed for one son, could hardly absorb these four miracles. His boys brought sunshine to his autumnal years, and they became his reason for living. Without that sunshine, winter would prevail.

Sometimes the four boys sounded like four hundred running around on reckless legs. The royal gardens were a perfect playground for the boys—filled with streams, fountains, tame animals, and huge trees of various kinds to climb on. Dasharatha sought his oldest son and found Rama climbing a tree. As Rama dangled from one of the branches, Dasharatha was suddenly struck by a vision of the boy floating in the air beside him. He had dreamed of Rama often before the boy was born. Now he recalled the vision from that time and place when he was neither dead nor alive. The boy in that vision had walked into Dasharatha's heart, and now he was playing in Ayodhya's gardens, a real prince made of flesh and blood. Dasharatha gripped the balcony, the marble smooth under his palms. If anything happened to Rama . . .

Loud cheers brought him back to his sons below. The young princes had come upon a pool of mud, a child's heaven, in the otherwise well-groomed landscape. They were sliding around in it noisily when Kaikeyi arrived. Laughing with them, Dasharatha's beloved sat down on a swing that hung in the shade of an enormous banyan tree. His eyes were drawn to her; he never tired of beholding her beauty. She was settling in and arranging her dress when a mud cake splattered against her cheek. She sprang out of the swing in surprise, making it sway back behind her. With her eyes wide and her mouth O-shaped, she faced four naughty grins—and five, counting Dasharatha's.

"Rama!" she called out, dodging a second mud ball.

By now, they all had realized that Rama was the leader of his brothers. The mud ball was dropping down from her chin onto her light-colored silk sari. She, who had grown so meticulous about her appearance, how would she react?

Kaikeyi darted forward to grab mud in her clean hands, and flung it at the boys. Shouting with glee, they ran in four directions, dodging her. Her teeth sparkled as she laughed aloud. Though Dasharatha was not close enough to hear clearly, it sounded as if she said, "Not fair! Four against one!"

Still, she hit at least three of them with her rapid firing. She was, of course, a far better shot than they, and his sons soon looked like beggars. The mud fight grew more heated, and the king's eyes darted back and forth as he noticed that every single one of Rama's mud balls hit their mark. His queen was unrecognizable, covered from head to toe in grime.

Kausalya's voice reached him from a distance. His sons below heard it too and promptly hid behind the banyan tree, leaving Kaikeyi alone in the sunshine to face Kausalya. As Kaikeyi broke into a grin, her teeth were white against the mud on her face. Kausalya did not smile. Suddenly anxious, Dasharatha strained to hear their conversation.

"You must have been attacked by monkeys," Kausalya said, scanning the area for the boys and speaking extra loudly so they would hear her. "Some very naughty monkeys."

Kaikeyi bent down and wiped her hands clean on the grass, as if that would make her more presentable.

Kausalya said, "I presume that you did not roll around in the mud on your own."

The boys giggled behind the tree, but Kaikeyi's smile disappeared. "What if I did? It's only mud, Kausalya. Let them play."

The two women faced each other then, speaking in low voices. Even from a distance, Dasharatha could feel the tension between them. Dasharatha made his way downstairs.

Just as Dasharatha entered the gardens, he heard Kaikeyi call for Manthara. The hunchback had cemented her position by Kaikeyi's side when Bharata was born. Dasharatha's revulsion toward Manthara was like an itch from an insect bite, irritating but bearable.

"Help me get the boys inside," Kaikeyi told the hunchback.

No one had noticed him yet. He had dismissed his guards at the entryway. Dasharatha leaned against a tree, thinking he had imagined the moment of tension between the queens. His wives looked peaceful and cooperative, as harmonious as the trees and leaves swaying in the wind.

Manthara went toward the banyan tree, muttering under her breath and looking sour as always. As much as had changed since the birth of his sons, Manthara's demeanor had not. When Manthara was close to the tree, she was bombarded with a torrent of mud balls.

The boys came into view, clapping and chortling.

Manthara sputtered, covered head to toe in mud balls. Kaikeyi choked on a laugh.

"You would never torment me like this," Manthara yelled, "if I were not so ugly!"

The boys froze, genuinely startled by Manthara's outburst.

Dasharatha stepped away from the tree.

Rama ran up to Manthara, saying, "No, no." He reached up to her and wiped some mud off her cheek. "You are not ugly."

His childish voice was endearing. Manthara swatted his hand away and sneered at the boy. Dasharatha's insides swelled with instant anger, and he rushed forward. Rama was not only a prince of highest rank but a child!

"Never mind these children," Kaikeyi intervened. Patting Manthara lovingly on her curved back, Kaikeyi led her away. "Let's get clean, you and I."

Kaikeyi looked over her shoulder and smiled reassuringly at the boys. She didn't see Manthara's over-the-shoulder grimace. Manthara stared hatefully at Rama, as if he had thrown all the mud single-handedly.

Dasharatha stepped into their path.

The queen and the hunchback were covered in mud, one looking dashing, the other hideous. Manthara's eyes were on the ground; her cane trembled in her hand. Dasharatha's harsh rebuke stopped on his tongue when he saw Manthara's face. Her eyes were closed; her head hung. Tears ran down her mud-covered cheeks, creating clear trails. These were not false calculated tears, for she had not seen the king. He sensed the terror she felt, as if she feared for her life. It was completely irrational, and yet Dasharatha was genuinely moved by Manthara for the first time in his life.

Kaikeyi saw Dasharatha, and there was a plea in her eyes. Without words, she understood his anger and saw his hesitation. Dasharatha let them go. The hunchback muttered inaudibly while Kaikeyi caressed her back.

Dasharatha turned to see Kausalya taking Rama into her arms. She called the boys close. "Some people don't like games," she told them.

Dasharatha thought it a fitting explanation to five-year-olds.

"Do you like games, Mother?" Rama asked, curling his arm around Kausalya's neck.

"Of course I do," Kausalya replied, wanting to placate him.

Rama laughed and rubbed his hands on her face, smearing it with the mud.

"You tricky boy!" she exclaimed, putting him down.

Lakshmana, Bharata, and Shatrugna followed Rama, as they always did, and ran their muddy hands all over Kausalya; the Great Queen actually toppled over in the grass.

"Boys, I warn you," she said, struggling to sit up.

They in turn ran away from her with the same glee as before. Clearly, they thought the game was starting all over again. Would Kausalya, his royal queen, deign to roll in the mud with her dirty sons?

Rama had clearly teased something out of his serious mother, for Kausalya threw herself into the game as if she was five years old too. They were so absorbed in their game that not one of them noticed Dasharatha. He settled himself into the swing, watched the sunset, and savored the sounds of their play. It was a perfect and peaceful evening.

Kausalya came running back and threw herself on the grass, saying, "No more!" Then she saw Dasharatha on the swing and sat up at once, wiping her face with her hands, managing only to appear more mud-streaked. He wanted to tell her that he liked seeing her so carefree.

"Father!" Rama called, and the other boys echoed his call. The mud on their skin had dried and fell off in big flakes as they clambered onto the swing, crawling all over him, truly like little monkeys. Talking all at once, they told him about their day.

He listened attentively, adoring their incoherent words, the way they saw the world. Dasharatha forgot about the hunchback and her outburst toward Rama.

Kaikeyi, clean and beautiful, returned. Had he not known, he might have thought her innocent of any mudslinging. He felt his face break into a smile. His grimy sons crowded around him eagerly as Kausalya watched from a distance.

"You are a very good shot, Rama." Dasharatha ruffled his son's hair.

"What is a good shot?"

"It means you will shoot your bow like a king."

"The other boys are just as good," Kaikeyi objected.

"Who is the best shot?" Dasharatha asked, looking at his sons instead of Kaikeyi.

"Him!" "He!" "Rama!" The three boys pointed excited fingers at their oldest brother. Rama looked at their fingers but said nothing.

"What do you say, Rama?"

Rama pointed to Kaikeyi. The queen kissed his hand.

Anna

"You clever boy," Dasharatha said. "I meant among you boys, and you know it."

Rama fidgeted. "I'm not allowed to say. Mother says one should not praise oneself."

"So you know you are the best shot?"

Still, Rama refused to claim the position his father gave him. Dasharatha wondered at the little prince's humility.

"Well, I say," Kaikeyi declared, "that we make these kinds of final conclusions once the boys actually start wielding weapons, not mud balls."

"As you decree, my queen," Dasharatha said with a bow.

"Really?" Rama asked, looking delighted. "A real bow? Real arrows?"

"First, you have to train with wood arrows that have no tips. Your bow will be real but small, made for your size and strength. When you grow bigger, your weapons will grow with you. Do you want to start learning?"

A chorus of voices shouted, "Yes, Father!"

How had he missed their eagerness to become warriors? Looking down at his sons, he knew why: in his eyes, they were hardly more than toddlers.

Only then did he notice how stiff Kaikeyi was at his side. It had been a long while since she had confronted him about anything; he almost felt slightly thrilled. Still, he gave her a cautious and cursory side glance. Could it be voiced before their sons?

She had the grace to send the boys off with Kausalya before she turned to him. His beloved's eyes were troubled rather than angry. She did not speak right away and seemed to struggle for words. The defense he had been building up started melting.

"What is it, my love?" He reached for her hands. She did not resist. "You know you can tell me anything."

She blinked rapidly and took a deep breath. "It's not that I don't love Rama, because I do." He felt his eyes narrow. "I don't even know what I'm trying to say . . . But when you singled out Rama, praising him above the others, I felt something in my belly, right here." She placed her hand right below her breasts, by her solar plexus, an information center that seldom told lies.

Dasharatha encouraged her to go on, caressing her hand with his thumb.

Her feelings tumbled out. "I'm Bharata's mother. And I have to protect him. I did not have a mother to protect me, you know. I have to protect him so that he will never know that emptiness. When he looks up at me, sometimes I feel that I'm all he has. Why do I feel that way?" Her chin trembled.

Though he didn't follow her reasoning, he saw that she was deeply affected.

"Does he not have *you*?" she asked.

"Why do you say this?" Dasharatha asked, genuinely confused. "I carefully divide my affection among all of them."

"Maybe. But there is a special look in your eye when you look at Rama. I know Rama is outstanding, but Bharata is remarkable too. He can do everything Rama can do. Sometimes I fear that you don't even see him because you are so focused on Rama. Why is that?"

Despite himself, Dasharatha felt a certain wall come up. She, of all people, should not

be asking him this question. She should know. Sometimes in love this happened; you loved someone more than another. He had known Rama before the boy was born.

When Dasharatha said nothing, Kaikeyi burst out, saying, "Rama is five years old! He is not the world's greatest archer, or mud slinger, or whatever latent talent you are dreaming up for him."

He could not understand the cause of her emotion. "Why are you *so* angry?"

"Do you love him more than you love Bharata?"

"Kaikeyi, don't."

"Answer me."

"You know the answer," he said. "I will not discuss this any further with you."

They sat there, anger loudly surging between them, hot as fire. He didn't even know why he was so angry. This is why he loved her, wasn't it, because she could provoke him so dreadfully? That thought did nothing to assuage his upheaval, and so he thought of Rama. Then of Bharata, and then the twins, Drip and Drop, that he could not tell apart.

"I strive to be fair to my sons," he said. "I don't want to repeat the same mistake with my sons as I've done with my wives. No, listen to me. I *don't* see our love as a mistake. You are my world. The center point of my life. I would never change that. But you have to admit that there is a cost. Others pay the price for our love. There are repercussions. Sometimes I wonder if I will be able to face my death with a guilt-free conscience. If I could do it over, wouldn't I wish to be a fair husband to all my wives? I feel guilty, Kaikeyi. Every time I see Kausalya, I feel deeply guilty."

Kaikeyi searched his face with ruthless eyes, seeing him all the way through. He hoped that she would affirm him yet again, accept him still, despite finding out something about him that she did not approve of or like. She wanted him to shun Kausalya. And he did, mostly. She wanted him to love only her and feel nothing for Kausalya. That he couldn't do. Kaikeyi wanted him to favor Bharata. He couldn't. Not in his heart.

"They are only five years old," Dasharatha said. "It's as you say. Let them be trained. Let them wield weapons. Before they are grown, there is no sense making comparisons or singling one out as superior to the others."

"Promise, then, that you will treat Bharata fairly," she said.

Sometimes he felt he did nothing but promise. Would he drown in those promises one day? But this was a promise easily made, one he had already made himself.

"I made that promise the day they were born, my dear."

Kaikeyi's anger seemed to abate. Her fingers came alive in his hand. For now, Dasharatha was forgiven.

CHAPTER 24

Manthara's Monsters

anthara was shaken by the children's attack. Even after Kaikeyi left, she continued to ramble to the servants in attendance. She cursed every single person who had cast a negative eye on her crooked spine. She told herself to hush, to stop complaining. It wasn't like her. After so many years in this body, wasn't she used to it?

Kaikeyi was the only one who never lingered on the pronounced curve of Manthara's back. But even with her, Manthara had no guarantee. If Kaikeyi ever found out that Manthara had orchestrated Queen Chaya's exile so long ago . . . This was exactly the sort of thing that Manthara might ramble about at a moment like this. *Quiet, old hag, quiet!*

Manthara had felt fragile even before Rama's attack. Just that morning, Ashvapati had sent one of his secret messages informing Manthara that her old friends, the Vishakanyas, had died. He did not mention how it came to be that they both died at the same time, but Manthara knew that Vishas did not live long; their poisonous diet guaranteed a premature death. Manthara was in mourning when those balls of mud were thrown at her.

Sukhi and Dukhi came in. The twins fawned over Manthara, helping her get clean. They tended to Manthara as if she was a porcelain doll, handling her gingerly. Manthara had never been able to decide if she craved or despised the way they treated her. That's how she knew that she liked them. They were from Kekaya, after all.

Once she was clean and lying down in the comfort of her plush silken bed, Manthara could not hide from the memory of the children's shrieks, the way the dirt had hit her in the eyes. The malice in their eyes had evoked the memory of being surrounded by a group of hateful youngsters.

"Monsters," she muttered, and meant it.

"Whom do you speak of, wise one?" Dukhi asked.

Manthara startled. Again, she had failed to consider that the twins were still there.

"Bharata is tolerable," Manthara said, "even sweet. But he follows that intolerable Rama around."

"But Rama is sweet too," Sukhi said. "Ouch!"

Dukhi had swatted her on the head.

"He makes your skin crawl, doesn't he?" Dukhi prodded. "I see how you cringe every time someone says 'Rama.'"

Manthara made a mental note to stop cringing. But it was true.

"You are very observant, Dukhi."

Manthara considered the question carefully. "There are several reasons," she said.

The twins listened, eyes shining with reverence.

"For one, there is the fact that Rama was born one day before Bharata. I sincerely hope it will not pose a problem when the time comes to crown Bharata king."

The twins exchanged glances.

"What have you heard?" Manthara demanded.

"Nothing, nothing," they both chanted.

Manthara waited.

"Only that Rama as the firstborn has the true claim," Sukhi revealed.

"Firstborn by a mere few hours!" Manthara cried.

She welcomed the opportunity to rehash this old grievance. The terror in her heart began to fade as she spoke with great conviction of Dasharatha's scheming nature. "If the king really is a man of his word, he will make Kaikeyi's son king, no matter what!" She pressed her lips together. "Now when I see how he looks at his darling firstborn, dread squeezes my lungs. We might as well throw those other boys in the dungeons for all their futures are worth. These Ayodhyans have no sense of honor. Tell me, does the promise the king made to King Ashvapati count for nothing? Shouldn't Kaikeyi's bride-price skew the decision in favor of Bharata?"

Sukhi and Dukhi erupted in chatter with their brainless opinions, swatting each other when they disagreed. Manthara hardly listened.

Instead she thought about Rama again and why she was so uneasy in his presence. The reason was hard to articulate. Rama's innocence was unnerving. Manthara experienced herself as grotesque next to the boy. Everything she said and did seemed utterly mean when he was around. Rama was so perfect that she felt every single imperfection in herself.

Manthara shuddered, throwing the silk sheet off, suddenly hot.

The twins stopped their chatter and began fanning Manthara with peacock feathers.

Still, Manthara could barely tolerate them. She did only because they were from Kekaya. And because they were reliable at spreading Manthara's rumors.

"That's enough," she said, dismissing them.

They left, heads huddled, yet their whispers were so audible that Manthara wondered why they didn't simply talk out loud. It was all, "Rama this," and, "Rama that." By the thirty gods, did no one tire of speaking about that little pest?

Manthara had no fondness for his kind. Rama was too unlike her. Yes, he was just a boy. She knew that. But there was no way she would ever open her heart to him. She had made that mistake before.

Horrible noises filled her ears. The voices of her childhood "friends." She could feel the sticks pounding on her back. Still, they had taught Manthara a valuable lesson. Appearance mattered more than anything else. If Kaikeyi was ugly or misshapen, would Dasharatha love her?

Manthara cackled loudly. The king's love was so superficial, it was a joke.

Manthara shook her head and noticed a small clump of mud in her hair. It crumbled to dust in her fingers. Manthara never forgot anything. She internalized the incident, her heart gnarling like the root of a tree.

This reminded Manthara that her report to Ashvapati was due. One of his faithful swans would carry and deliver their secret correspondence. It was genius, just like Ashvapati himself. When Manthara held one of Ashvapati's letters, she felt something like romantic love. Exactly what he had feared had indeed happened. The bride-price was swept to the side, as though it was nothing. An Ayodhyan promise.

Kaikeyi had been a child with no understanding of the challenges that faced her in Ayodhya. Kaikeyi still insisted that the marriage had been her choice, but Manthara knew better. She had seen how Ashvapati put Kaikeyi's hand in Dasharatha's, and the way the king tightened his grip on her hand, claiming her. Princess or not, Kaikeyi was just as powerless as any other girl, sold by her father to the highest bidder.

Sighing, Manthara got up from the bed. First, she made sure that no servants were in sight; then she sat down to write her letter. With her nerves frazzled, it was a challenge to write in a small script—and a larger challenge still not to completely exaggerate the day's event.

"Rama tried to kill me," she wrote and then tore up the scroll.

It had felt like that, yes. When the mud balls hit her eyes, she panicked. The death blow had been next. She knew exactly what it felt like, a massive numbness in the entire body while the mind grew frenzied in its cage. The release from the body was exquisite and terrifying. But the death blow had not come. Manthara had opened her eyes to see Rama dancing around her in glee, taking satisfaction in her terror. Cold-blooded monster!

Manthara composed an exact detailing of the day's event, concluding with the fact that all the princes had followed Rama's lead, not knowing any better. If Bharata stayed too long in Rama's company, he would grow into a servant, no more. No one in Ayodhya had the sense to nurture Bharata. Manthara urged Ashvapati to bring his grandson to Kekaya for some time. If Bharata stayed in Ayodhya, he would never learn of his birthright. He would surrender all his rights out of misplaced love for his "elder" brother.

Satisfied, Manthara stood up and shuffled to the small window on the eastern side. She leaned out saw the two swans waiting by the tiny pond. Day and night, they waited. Such was the loyalty Ashvapati commanded. Within a minute, one of the swans took flight and flew up to Manthara's window. Manthara patted it with awkward fingers and placed the tiny scroll in its beak.

Manthara was aware of the power love exerted on others. But she would stand fixed in the center of power, unbroken by love. She might seem like a powerless hunchback to the world, but she knew how the game worked. She would make her move when they least expected it.

CHAPTER 25

The Adopted Princess

After the mud fight, the princes constantly asked Dasharatha when they would get real weapons. Dasharatha had decided to craft new ones suited to their age. He was in discussion with the master of weapons to approve the designs when the messenger from Videha arrived.

Sumantra, who was authorized to handle all missives on behalf of the king, welcomed the messenger from the neighboring kingdom. When Dasharatha dismissed the master of weapons, he found Videha's messenger still waiting. Sumantra indicated that this matter required the king's personal attention.

"Please speak," Dasharatha said. "Dispense with all formalities, for I'm certain that you have repeated my honorifics many times since arriving here. Be at ease."

Being a messenger, the man was required to deliver his message before attending to his personal needs. He joined his palms at Dasharatha's words, then produced a scroll.

"King Janaka requests the privilege of privacy, Great King. This missive is for your eyes alone. I am not at liberty to hand this message to anyone but you, Great King. If this does not meet with your pleasure, I am to return to Videha with the scroll in hand."

Dasharatha's curiosity was awakened. He held out both hands to receive the sealed parchment. "You may ensure King Janaka that I alone will read this message. Have you been instructed to tarry and await my response?"

"If it pleases you, Great King."

"Without knowing the content of the letter, I cannot guarantee a response. I will send word to you on the morrow with instructions how to proceed. Sumantra, escort this faithful messenger to a resting chamber and see that all his needs are met."

Sumantra and the messenger bowed and left the small council.

The king waited until the end of the day when he was alone in the council room. The ministers and their servants had returned to their homes. He picked up the parchment, broke the seal, and began to read. He was glad for the privacy, for the letter made his eyebrows rise, and no doubt other expressions crossed his face. A warm feeling spread in his heart.

Even after Dasharatha had finished reading the missive, he held it in his hand. He went over the content in his mind; he wanted to hold on a little longer to the bright feeling it had conjured. It was similar to something he had felt when Rama was born, like something mystical was taking place. King Janaka had no sons, but the letter concerned a child he had adopted, Princess Sita, a girl who displayed such strange behaviors that either she was gifted beyond imagination or else entirely unsound. It was with this concern that Janaka had penned the letter to his superior king.

Dasharatha looked at the letter, scrutinizing it carefully for any sign that Janaka was considering abandoning the girl. She was not his by blood, after all, and Janaka did have the right to rescind his claim. The girl could be placed in a carefully selected home, one that perhaps suited her nature more. Janaka's letter seemed to state that she was not behaving like a princess. Dasharatha smiled at this. What was a princess supposed to be like at four years of age? Though Sita's age could not be exactly determined due to her supernatural birth, Dasharatha had received the news of her appearance four years prior. Dasharatha thought of his own sons, who were five years old and busy throwing mud at queen and hunchback alike. With their gaps in logic and boisterous manners, Dasharatha was not entirely sure that he counted them as human beings yet.

Dasharatha dropped the letter out of sight, pinching it between his fingers. It was clear that Janaka adored his daughter. On that account, the letter really was nothing but a father's anxiety over the future of his child. There was no sign that he regretted his decision to adopt her. From the reports Dasharatha had received, Janaka had not hesitated even a moment before claiming the child as his own. What a strange birth. Janaka certainly thought his daughter's oddities were tied to her peculiar birth. Some whispered that the child had merely been abandoned, thrown into a ditch. Perhaps her parents had even tried to kill her by burying her alive. Ill-wishing people always sought unkind ways to undo miracles. Be all that as it was, Dasharatha remembered that Janaka's first letters had been brimming with the incredulous joy of the miraculous child. There had also been a great number of witnesses present, corroborating the event.

Dasharatha found himself smiling. He liked the idea of a little girl who was wild and did as she pleased. Wasn't that the way of all children? But if Janaka's observations were

Great King Dasharatha,

    My hand trembles as I write this. I begin therefore by beseeching your protection for my daughter, a princess of Mithila, even if her bloodline may be unknown. Although you are aware of her unusual birth, I must remind you that she is not just a foundling that I chose to adopt. In the most miraculous event of my life, the ground cracked open at my feet, and this child was pushed up through the furrow, invisible hands handing her into my care. My heart swelled with the knowing that a miracle had taken place. I named her Sita, "Furrow," to remind me always of that moment.

    Before my hand is stayed by doubts, let me make my confession: When Sita cries, it rains in Mithila. When her brow furrows in confusion, storm clouds gather above the palace. When she gets angry, though not often, the fires come alive and blaze furiously. Once, the Earth started trembling, cracks appeared in the ground. Instinctively I reached for her. The moment I brought her into my arms the rumbling stopped. She babbles to the water-ponds causing ripples and waves, even on the most windless day. Animals of all kinds gather in the royal gardens and wait for her day and night. She persists in sleeping outside amongst them, on the bare ground. She is happiest when smeared with dirt, consorting with the creatures in the garden.

    I have started and stopped writing similar letters to you a number of times. Forgive any errors that may be present in this hasty missive. I'm determined this time to send it to you, Great King.

    I wish only to find an answer to these questions that plague me about this daughter of mine. If these phenomena persist into her womanhood, I fear for her future, and the future of our world itself. Imagine a girl who can make the Earth tremble and the skies open. I assure you that I carefully monitor the child and keep her at peace so that her strange behaviors may not be noticed by one and all.

    To your knowledge or Vasishta's, have there been other children like my Sita?

    Your faithful servant,

    Janaka, King of Mithila

true—that the girl's outbursts were tied to the elements—then she certainly was not an ordinary child. Far from it. Dasharatha's first impulse was to dismiss Janaka's observations. He wouldn't be the first parent with grandiose and misinformed notions of his child. It was highly common for parents to elevate their children to a status far surpassing any realistic notions. Dasharatha himself was hypervigilant against doing this with his sons, though he secretly knew that Rama in particular was extraordinary. But the nature of Janaka's claim was so unusual and so fascinating that Dasharatha had to consult with Vasishta. Since Vasishta's name was mentioned in the letter, it was no breach in confidence to consult the preceptor.

Vasishta answered Dasharatha's summons, appearing fresh from his evening bath in the Sarayu. As the preceptor read Janaka's letter, a rare smile blossomed on his face, and he touched the parchment to his forehead. He also held on to the missive longer than necessary.

"Indeed," Vasishta said. "This is most unusual. I do not think there ever has been such a child. Not to my knowledge."

Dasharatha considered this and then said, "I want to believe it because it delights me somehow. And yet it is unbelievable. The ramifications of a child possessing such powers . . ."

"It could be a blessing or a curse, depending on the temperament of the girl. I think it would be wise to send Shatananda, one of my pupils, to Videha to observe the princess."

"Shatananda? He is just a boy."

"Older than you by a few hundred years, Great King. Shatananda is the son of the venerable Gautama and Ahalya, and he is vastly knowledgeable about the universe and its workings."

The king agreed and carefully rolled the letter into a scroll and held it in his hand. He would place it in his private collection of noteworthy artifacts.

"We must handle this with utmost discretion," Vasishta said.

"Yes. Instruct Shatananda to assure King Janaka that only the three of us have been initiated into this secret. There is no reason to involve the ministers in this. Not until we have found something of note. *If* we do."

"I will inform Shatananda to depart at the earliest, with your permission, Great King. I expect that the arrangements will take several days, since he will be required to stay several months. If the child has a gentle disposition, as Janaka indicates, it may even take years. I will suggest that he also be engaged in their rituals, for that is another area of his expertise."

Dasharatha nodded, yet there was one more avenue to explore.

"I am not sure why I was reminded of it," he said. "Is there any connection between Princess Sita and the curse pronounced on Ravana?"

Vasishta smiled. "That dark soul has incurred many curses throughout his long life."

"The curse uttered by the brave women he abducted nearly ten years ago."

"Ah," Vasishta said. "The 'powerless woman' who will cause his final death."

"Hm, yes. But then Janaka describes Sita as the opposite of powerless. It couldn't be Sita. I don't know why I drew this connection."

"Your higher self knows more than you could ever imagine," Vasishta said.

"How could a powerless woman be the cause of Ravana's downfall?" Dasharatha inquired. "I never quite understood."

"It means that the noose grows tighter around Ravana's neck. And the death blow will come when he least expects it."

The hair raised on Dasharatha's neck. Was that a threat from the peaceful preceptor?

"No. A promise, Great King," Vasishta said, folding his hands at his chest.

As he departed, Dasharatha followed the holy one with his eyes. His long white hair reached down his back, and now that dusk was upon them, his radiance was clearly discernible.

Could Vasishta always read thoughts? Dasharatha had not vocalized that Vasishta's words had been threatening. And yet the preceptor had known. Dasharatha would never know the parameters of Vasishta's powers. That was why his counsel was so important in delicate matters like this.

Even though there really was no urgency around the matter, Dasharatha composed his answer to Janaka before leaving his duties for the evening. The well-being of the girl was the foremost concern, and it was too soon to draw conclusions. The sweetest child could grow up to be a menace, and the reverse was true. There was still every possibility that Sita would grow up to be an ordinary princess.

Dasharatha dispatched the letter with Videha's messenger, instructing him to wait for Shatananda's departure. Dasharatha understood that the entire process would take quite some time but looked forward to eventually hearing Shatananda's unbiased opinion. As he left the council room, he wished he could tell his boys about the unusual princess, but it was now a state secret.

CHAPTER 26

Kaikeyi's Favorite

Since the inception of the princes' training when they were five years old, their days were full of lessons. Kaikeyi was in charge of all their equestrian training, and shortly after the princes' seventh birthday, Kaikeyi insisted on doubling their hours on horseback. All of Ayodhya was preparing for the Summit of Fifty Kings to be held in the coming months, and the four princes would be presented for the first time. Dasharatha was eager to display the prowess of his four sons. Kaikeyi agreed and was very involved in the princes' training with weapons and on horse. Kausalya continued to domineer the palace as "the Great Queen," and Kaikeyi had retreated to her own sphere. She was not displeased with the arrangement, for she ruled her horses, her weapons, and her beloved. She was Dasharatha's chosen, and every day she put her mind to keeping it that way. She was attuned to his desires and kept herself immaculate for his pleasure.

How Kaikeyi appeared in the royal stables was another matter, for here she was both king and queen. When the princes came for their daily lesson, she directed them to their horses with a sharp voice and sent them out into the field. At seven years of age, they could ride competently and get their horses warmed up on their own. Here, she was the expert, and she had earned the respect of her sons and the stable hands.

The balancing act was like leading a double life. Almost daily, Kaikeyi transformed from a malodorous Kekayan horseman into a queen who wore colorful silks, smelled of jasmine, and adorned herself with vast arrays of jewels. She had to be scrubbed clean and have her hair washed every day, for the smell of horse clung to her. In the stables, she embraced rank odors and manners and wore men's clothes, including her beloved leather vest. It fit her as well as it had when she was sixteen. Leather, unlike human bodies, only got better with age.

"Isn't that right?" she asked of Dharma, the gelding on which she had ridden into Ayodhya. That had been over ten years ago. Dharma was becoming an old grouch. She rubbed him down with firm circular motions, touching even the tickly spots by his ribs. Kaikeyi was two years shy of thirty, practically an old woman herself.

"Isn't that right, Dharma darling?" In response, he nuzzled her neck, in the exact area where he knew she was ticklish. In horse talk, this meant he found her just as pleasing as ever.

Kaikeyi marveled at the movement of time. She was no longer the one caring for the horses' daily upkeep; those employed in the stables did the work, while Kaikeyi's duty was only to show affection to her equestrians. As was her duty to her husband. Dasharatha was close to sixty, though he was as strong and vigorous as a man half his age. His steel hair and the deep furrows on his face gave him dignity. Kaikeyi loved those lines and the thick wiriness of his hair.

Dharma blew through his nose, enjoying the rubdown Kaikeyi was giving him. She took a deep breath of the horsey smell of the stables. She looked over Dharma's flanks, to see the line of horses extend beyond her vision. But the royal stables were so well kept that the natural smell of horses, including their dung, was not as strong as in a Kekayan stable.

Kaikeyi brought her forehead to Dharma's, leaning in to her old friend. He started chewing on one of her gemstone necklaces, the green one, Expeller of Poisons. She wore this one thanks to Manthara. Chewing on the gem would probably not cause Dharma any harm, but she didn't want to risk it, and she tucked it safely into her vest again. For a second, she was aware of the lightness that came from being unadorned. Jewels had a certain power, which Kaikeyi keenly felt when she wore them. It had not taken her long to understand why kings and queens across the ages were known for their jewelry. She had many jewels now, and a few of them remained on her person at all times. The Expeller of Poisons was one among those that Kaikeyi never removed, not even when she slept or bathed. It was the custom of Ayodhya, and it had become hers.

Suddenly Kaikeyi compared herself to Dharma, whose body remained muscled, whose skin remained taut, whose eyes were clear and deep, and would remain so until the day that his legs could not hold him up anymore. Dharma was at least sixty in horse years. If not ever young like a horse, why couldn't she be the free rider she had been, riding across the plains of Kekaya with the wind in her hair? There, she had not known anything but that she was flying across the world. The price of being queen was too heavy at times. As her hands brushed

Dharma's flanks, her mind took the form of a majestic mare; she grew wings and flew into the sky, up and away.

The clouds were scattered by the stable hand's voice: "Your Majesty!"

Kaikeyi woke up with a start. The brush she held clattered against the floor. How long had she been daydreaming?

"Prince Bharata was thrown off his horse. He is calling for you."

Kaikeyi moved at once. "Is he injured?"

Without waiting for an answer, she left Dharma's stall with big strides. "Is he hurt?" she asked again, throwing the question over her shoulder.

"It did not look like he broke any bones," the man answered. "But I do not know for sure. I was sent to fetch you right away, and the king's physician was also summoned."

Don't let him be crippled, Kaikeyi prayed, anxiety rushing into her heart. She had mothered Bharata attentively for seven years, making him the best prince he could be. It could not end today with a fatal injury. She quickened her steps until she was running.

"Bharata!" There was panic in her voice. She felt like her son was an infant she had to rescue. Even though it was already too late. She cursed herself for sending them out on their own while she stood in leisure thinking foolish thoughts.

As she ran into the training grounds, she felt a moment's relief. Manthara was there hunched over Bharata. He was on the ground with legs splayed; he was pale but whole. He was sitting upright and there were no sharp protrusions visible. In her youth, Kaikeyi had broken seven ribs and both arms, and she had seen all sorts of destroyed bodies in Kekaya.

She sent a prayer of thanks to the gods. Bharata was spared.

Manthara prodded Bharata less than gently, repeatedly asking, "Here? Does it hurt here? What about here?"

"Mother!" Bharata said, avoiding Manthara's bony fingers and getting on his feet with a wince.

Kaikeyi wanted to engulf her son in her arms, but didn't want to exacerbate his pain. "Sit down," she commanded, touching him carefully.

Bharata leaned toward her, resting his head by her heart.

"He is fine," Manthara assured her. "The king's physician just took a look at him. He mostly got shocked when he found himself on the ground. It could have happened to anyone," she added, turning to Bharata.

Manthara was hopelessly fond of Bharata. In her books, he did not have a single flaw. Kaikeyi had to admit that she too would be hard-pressed to name a flaw in her son. Still, Kaikeyi noted that the other princes were happily riding their horses. That was strange. She would have expected them to stay with Bharata when he was hurt.

Manthara began muttering something about Rama's selfishness.

Kaikeyi ignored that and turned to Bharata, holding his shoulder and looking into his eyes. "How do you feel, my son? Do you want Manthara to take you back to your rooms?"

"No! I want to stay with Rama. I'm fine."

"Come, then," Kaikeyi said, holding out her hand to her son. She recognized that will-power and didn't want to discourage it by forcing him to rest. "But you must tell me the moment you feel fatigued. Today I will teach you how to tune your mind to the horse you are riding. Then you will never get thrown again."

"Father says you are the best rider he has ever seen," Bharata said.

Kaikeyi smiled. Bharata was a kind boy, always seeking ways to appreciate others.

"It's true," she answered. She'd never seen the point of false humility. "And if you listen attentively to me, you can be the second best."

Rama came riding up with Lakshmana and Shatrugna behind him. Rama had chosen a white steed, probably because it was the type of horse Dasharatha rode. The twins had chosen identical brown horses, no doubt to further confuse others. They still enjoyed that game.

"Bharata sent us to the other side of the field," Rama said, with a winning smile. "He didn't want us to see his tears, although he has seen ours so many times."

Manthara did not smile, but Bharata did, looking sheepish. "I'm fine now," he said. "Next time, I won't even get scared."

"I got frightened even the second time," Rama warned him, with a serious look. "But you are welcome to beat my record."

All the boys smiled.

"Finally I can beat you!" Bharata exclaimed, jumping into the air. His left leg faltered when he landed.

"Bharata!" Kaikeyi called out, reaching to steady him. Children ignored their injuries too soon. Bharata straightened and resumed talking, as though he had not just fallen off a horse.

The boys were forever competing. So far, none of them had beaten Rama's records in any areas, even though Bharata was often a close second. Kaikeyi knew this. As the boys spoke, she watched the way Rama handled his horse with ease. All Rama's attention was focused on Bharata. He was extremely attuned to all his brothers. Being such a young rider, Rama would need to keep some attention on his horse too. He didn't. With a thrill of recognition, Kaikeyi understood that Rama had already mastered the horse.

"Well," Kaikeyi said, interrupting her boys, and raising her eyebrows, "I have ridden over two thousand horses, both trained and wild. And I have only been thrown once."

They gaped at her with wide eyes. She laughed out loud. She had to boast more often. She enjoyed their unabashed admiration.

"Were you frightened?" Bharata asked.

"No," she said, though it was only partially true. The act itself had not scared her. But it had produced an unknown realization. The memory surfaced now more forcefully than she expected. To get a moment to herself, she sent the boys to fetch a horse for her and for Bharata. The stable hands had already returned the horse that had thrown the prince.

The one time Kaikeyi had been thrown off her horse, she had been alone on the plains of Kekaya. She had been almost fifteen years old, more dedicated to her horses than anything else. Her most trusted steed had bucked and thrown her off. As she hit the ground, landing painfully on her back, something had dislodged within her. Though the pain was tolerable, she had been overcome with a flood of tears so forceful that the horse had spooked and kept his distance. There was no one present but her and the horse, and Keyi cried into her hands, curling up on the ground. The fall had opened a hidden door, and out came a vision of her long-lost mother. A broken, ugly women who was too frail to even walk erect.

Kaikeyi's mother had gone from being the queen to being nobody, all because her father said so. Until that moment, she had thought of her father as all good and her mother as the evil one. The truth, however, was that Kaikeyi was a powerless girl, like her mother had been. She even looked like her mother. Would she too fall into disfavor one day and cease to exist?

Until then, she had thought herself fearless. She had been fast and deadly with her sword. She only had a few scars on her body from her many fights. From then onward, she had known that her fear hid from her, a skillful sneak that she could neither capture nor exile. But she knew that she did not want to end up like her mother. Exiled. Banished. Rejected. So many years later, she could still feel that amorphous fear sneaking around in her heart.

A soft horse muzzle tickled her neck.

"You are daydreaming, Mother." Rama smiled down at her from his white mare.

All four boys were on horseback, surrounding her. She had again been lost in her mind. She mounted the mare they had brought for her.

She turned to Bharata, looking at his horse. "Is that the one that threw you?"

"No." He looked suddenly worried. "Should I have chosen the same one?"

"It's important to master an aggressive horse. We will work with that horse another day. Now, if any of you want to be like me, you will need to listen not to me but to the horse you are sitting on. We will be silent for a minute. You will listen to your horse. Then we will talk about anything you noticed. Start now."

Kaikeyi listened to her breaths, counting them in seconds. She noticed that Rama was the first to close his eyes. Perhaps following his lead, the others did too. Sixty breaths later, only Rama's eyes were still closed. Kaikeyi was impressed. It wasn't like the horses stood perfectly still, but Rama's eyelids had not even fluttered.

"What did you notice?" she asked of them all.

"He is warm," Shatrugna said. "His sides feel warm against my legs."

"My legs became like part of his flanks," Lakshmana said, continuing his twin's train of thought.

"Good," Kaikeyi encouraged. "What else?"

"She misses the fields where she used to run free," Rama said.

Kaikeyi felt her stomach contract. Rama's white mare came from Kekaya. Was Rama merely guessing? To hide her confusion, she turned to Bharata. "What did your horse tell you?"

Bharata blinked and frowned. "I think he is tired. Or maybe I am. I'm not sure."

"Don't worry," she assured. "You are still shaken from your fall. Even though you are unhurt, your body will be quite sore tomorrow."

"Repeat this exercise three times," she instructed, "and discuss your findings with each other, like we just did. It's important that the horses learn to heed your stillness as much as your call to action. Understand?"

"Yes," they chanted.

"Rama, come with me," she said, surprising herself. His words had awoken a deep longing in her, not only for Kekaya's lands, but for a time when she had felt that she knew every word and thought her horse had. "We will ride without saddle or reins," she said, dismounting.

Rama followed. She had to help him take off the saddle; he was not tall or strong enough to do it on his own, and yet she sensed that his wisdom dwarfed hers.

"Rama," she said, feeling giddy, "today I will follow you!"

When Rama threw himself onto the horse's back, entwining his fingers into her mane, Kaikeyi did the same. They rode away wildly, fulfilling the white mare's desire to run free. They galloped, letting the horses jump the fence, then on and on, until Kaikeyi felt like her daydream had come alive. She was free and flying.

When they returned, Kaikeyi was full of life. She was inspired to her core by Rama's intuition with his horse. She recognized a natural master in him. How had he ever gotten thrown off a single horse? As they trotted back, more calmly now, she asked him this. To her surprise, he fidgeted and hedged. Kaikeyi felt certain then that no horse would ever throw Rama off its back. He had let himself be thrown off, for the sake of his brothers. What a brother he was!

In her delight of Rama's talent, she had neglected to engage the other princes. They had long since finished the three rounds of "listening" that she had assigned and were aimlessly trotting around the training grounds. When Kaikeyi and Rama returned over the fence, the other princes came to them at once, eager to share their findings and continue their training. But Manthara was livid.

"Kaikeyi!" she called, in that voice that Kaikeyi had learned not to ignore.

She quickly gave her sons another round of instructions and rode over to Manthara.

"Get down from that horse," Manthara commanded.

Kaikeyi sighed, yet did as she was told. It was more painless to simply do what Manthara said.

"What on earth are you doing?" Manthara demanded.

"I don't understand. You can see for yourself what I'm doing here." Kaikeyi motioned to the princes diligently doing their assigned activity in the middle of the training grounds.

"I see. You are such a fool that you yourself do not even know what you are doing."

Kaikeyi clenched her jaw and waited.

"You are supposed to teach Bharata," Manthara said angrily. "Instead, you are blatantly favoring Rama!"

Kaikeyi was shocked by Manthara's observation. At no time had she consciously tried to do anything of the sort.

"They both need to know how to ride," Kaikeyi said in protest.

"Yes, but why are you favoring Rama?"

"I'm not favoring him. They are equal to me," Kaikeyi said, realizing it was true. She made no distinction between Rama and Bharata. Yes, Bharata was the son of her body. She doted on him. But at no time had she considered training Bharata to the exclusion of the other boys.

"Rama is not your son. Don't forget that," Manthara said, and turned away so that Kaikeyi could say no more.

Kaikeyi found that she had no retort. She had never forgotten whose son Rama was. But she knew now that it made no difference to her. She loved Rama just as much as she loved Bharata. This realization flooded Kaikeyi's heart, washing out Manthara's insistence that Bharata had to be king. What did it matter who was king, as long as everyone loved each other?

CHAPTER 27

The Summit of Fifty Kings

The Summit of Fifty Kings was upon them again. Held every ten years, it was without a doubt Ayodhya's most important function. The fifty acknowledged kings traveled from all corners of the Earth, some of them journeying for many months, to assemble outside Ayodhya, near the river Sarayu. Rama and his brothers were well into their seventh year when the time for the summit came. Dasharatha was very excited. It would be the first time the tributary kings would meet his sons. The summit would take place in the arena built for the Great Sacrifice that had given him these sons. The subordinate kings would see for themselves that Dasharatha had heirs; the Sun dynasty would continue with undiminished brilliance. All the arrangements were made, and Dasharatha personally briefed his sons on what to expect. The kings came to the summit to match their strength with one another. That had always been the primary reason for the summit. This was the opportunity for the subordinate kings to establish hierarchies among themselves without going to war.

On the day of the departure, Dasharatha formally took farewell of his queens. No woman—a queen or a courtesan—was allowed at the summit, for a man's weakness had ever been his beloved. The only thing Dasharatha had not prepared for was the farewell between the mothers and their sons. The queens had never gone a day without their children. When the young princes did not emerge from the palace at the appointed time and the procession and large retinue stood ready, Dasharatha returned to the place where the queens were. He had left the princes there, satisfied that they were decorated with sandalwood and the auspicious red mark on the forehead.

In his absence, however, the scene had turned from formal into emotional. The mothers, even Kausalya, were smothering the boys with kisses and affection. Kaikeyi clung to Bharata as if her life depended on it.

"Neither land nor sea can part you from me," she repeated through her tears.

"It's only a matter of ten days," Dasharatha reminded them. "The princes will never be in danger. We have doubled the guards, and our sons will be vigilantly protected."

He might as well have said nothing. Kaikeyi held Bharata even closer, and the twins clung to Sumitra. Kausalya was whispering into Rama's ear, stroking his cheek.

Dasharatha's attention settled on Kaikeyi, as it always did. Her words struck a deep chord; there was some kind of binding sadness under the words, something that made him want to hold her and never let go. He went to Kaikeyi's side and put a soothing hand on her.

"Come, Bharata," he said. "It's time." He straightened, with Bharata's hand in his. "Boys. Princes of Ayodhya. It's time."

The mothers reluctantly let go.

"We will see you in no time," Dasharatha said.

The princes were ushered along by attendants, and Dasharatha walked forward swiftly, leading his sons by example.

As they walked down the steps toward their awaiting chariots, Dasharatha heard Rama ask, "Bharata, what did Mother's words mean, 'Neither land nor sea can part you from me.'"

"It means Mother loves me," Bharata said. "More than anything. Forever."

Dasharatha turned at the bottom of the steps, looking up at his sons.

"What we really are cannot die," he said. "I think that's what your mother means. That even if we are parted prematurely by death or man-made events, the soul will never cease to love."

The boys descended. "Can we ride with you, Father?"

Rama was the spokesperson, but the other three nodded eagerly.

"Your own chariots are ready, see?" Dasharatha motioned to the two empty chariots behind his.

"We want to ride with you, Father," Rama repeated.

"Very well. As you wish."

The king's chariot was sturdy, drawn by four steeds, and suitable for several grown men. The four princes would cause no undue burden to the horses. As the princes clambered onto the chariot, all traces of sadness vanished, and they bumped into each other to stand at the front. Dasharatha waved away the two extra chariots and ascended to join his waiting sons. The exuberance of the young princes would turn the entire summit into an adventure.

As they rode out of the city and toward the Sarayu, the princes pointed to all the flags and chariots visible in the distance. Each of the fifty kings was accompanied by at least one hundred attendants, so the summit promised to be eventful. Sumantra met them on the road, reporting that all fifty kings had arrived and were assembled in the main hall. Refreshments had been served, and they were especially eager to see the young princes. As they arrived, attendants ran forward to care for the horses and chariots. The conch shells blew, flower petals were scattered at their feet, and the curtains of the assembly were parted in welcome.

Along with the seven ministers, Sumantra stood at the opening and declared, "All stand for Dasharatha, king of Ayodhya, emperor of the Earth, son of Aja, descendant of the first man, descendant of the sun god, undefeated chariot master, servant of the thirty gods, proud father of four sons!"

The assembled crowd hushed. As Dasharatha entered the arena, he had two sons on each side: Rama and Lakshmana on one and Bharata and Shatrugna on the other. The royal musicians played enthusiastically with their drums, cymbals, and voices, heading toward a crescendo as the emperor walked across the assembly space and ascended to the royal throne. Four seats had been made adjacent to him for the princes. The music grew soft and melodious as Dasharatha settled into his seat.

"Now the kings will each introduce themselves and offer gifts," Dasharatha told his sons. He kept the boys engaged by allowing them to receive the gifts, each in turn.

As each king stood, his title was announced, and he formally pledged his loyalty to Dasharatha before sharing a brief report of his kingdom. Dasharatha scanned the assembly, his eyes naturally pausing on faces he knew well. First, his eyes settled on Ashvapati, his terse father-in-law who did not even blink his eyes in greeting. He had never quite forgiven Dasharatha for compromising Kaikeyi's bride-price, even though he sanctioned the compromise. Dasharatha clenched his jaw. Behind Ashvapati, Kaikeyi's handsome brother, Yuddhajit, towered, looking out across the assembly with a winning smile. Privately Dasharatha felt it was time for Ashvapati to step down and allow Yuddha to rule. That's what Dasharatha would do as soon as his sons were grown.

Dasharatha glanced at his sons to see if they were following the complexity of all that was happening. Lakshmana and Shatrugna were both dangling their feet and swinging them back and forth. But Rama's eyes were rapt on the proceedings. He whispered to his brothers, noticing things that Dasharatha no longer did: the splendorous attire of the kings, how each of them was surrounded by bare-chested men whose muscles bulged. Dasharatha leaned toward Rama and quietly told him that those were the kings' prized fighters who would later participate in the challenges.

When Janaka of Videha stood up, Dasharatha's attention heightened. Rama noticed this and straightened in his seat too. He had not yet outgrown his endearing habit of mimicking his father. Yet the young prince did not know the reason for Dasharatha's interest. Dasharatha knew Janaka would not speak of his daughter Sita publicly, but Dasharatha planned to confront him. The reports he had received over the years from Shatananda were vague and unsatisfactory. Vasishta proclaimed to be satisfied by them and called the case closed. Sita was a perfect little princess. But Dasharatha was not emperor for nothing. He could sense a conspiracy from leagues away. When Vasishta permitted Shatananda to permanently settle in Videha, Dasharatha's suspicion had cemented. He would get to the bottom of it here.

As the introductions came to a close, Dasharatha called for sugarcane juice and water with lime and salt. There was one more topic he wanted to address, mainly for the benefit of his sons. He stood up, thanking the kings for the generous gifts.

"Blessings upon this assembly of kings, representing the finest warriors and upholders of justice. I salute you for standing with me in maintaining a prosperous Earth for all our people. Since the time of King Anaranya, who died for this cause, we have worked ruthlessly to rid the Earth of blood-drinkers, and thanks to each of you and your illustrious forefathers we have succeeded in exterminating this threat to mankind."

A large smatter of applause greeted this speech.

"We know, however, that Ravana remains a threat to all realms. The tragic abduction ten years ago of over one hundred treasured women demonstrated the power of the blood-drinker king. We may not have the strength to engage in battle with him directly, but we have been successful in destroying the presence of his servants. Now, it is rare to hear of a blood-drinker venturing into the daylight and most civilized nations have not encountered them. To demonstrate this, may I ask how many here have personally faced a blood-drinker in battle?"

He could feel his sons straighten in their seats. Like all other children, they were fascinated by the monsters in their stories. Dasharatha raised his hand, and so did many of Ayodhya's men, brave ones who had fought beside their king. These battles had all, with the exception of the slaying of Shambara, taken place outside Earth, in the realms of the gods. Therefore, Dasharatha was satisfied to see that the kings of Earth did not count blood-drinkers among their enemies. Most of the other kings fought each other, claiming pieces of the great land, while Dasharatha fought for the entire Earth.

Dasharatha looked at the two kings who had raised their hands: Kashi, the newly consecrated king of Kashi, and Jayasena, the king of Hastinapur. Dasharatha himself had appointed Jayasena to rule over Hastinapur after he proved his caliber in a fierce battle in the twilight realms. Dasharatha nodded to both of them, indicating that they could lower their hands. Kashi did so, very slowly, an insolent smirk on his face, holding Dasharatha's eyes all the while. Dasharatha's eyes narrowed. This was Kashi's first summit as king, and Dasharatha had only received unfavorable reports of his kingship thus far.

"I know Jayasena's story well, as I'm certain we all do," Dasharatha said. "It was in the last summit, here in your presence, that he was appointed king in honor of his great deeds. I do not believe that Kashi has honored us by sharing his victory. Shall we hear it?"

"Yes, yes, yes!" the crowd called, the enthused seven-year-old voices loudest of all.

Dasharatha held up his hand to silence the assembly and pointed toward Kashi. "Kashi, king of Kashi, please tell us of your victory against the blood-drinkers."

Kashi stood and began to tell a gruesome tale. He had relentlessly pursued rumors of blood-drinkers roaming on Earth, finding them finally deep within the borderland where

no man desiring life would go: the jungles of Dandaka. There he had slain countless blood-drinkers, and Kashi was delighted to describe in detail each encounter.

As he spoke, a strange revulsion rose in Dasharatha's heart. As many reports had indicated, Kashi's alliance to mankind seemed questionable. He was clearly in awe of the supernatural powers the drinkers displayed. Kashi even had the look of a blood-drinker, with traces of bronze in his black hair.

"Inform the princes of the rumors," Dasharatha ordered quietly, looking at Sumantra.

"Rumors state that Kashi is a half-breed," Sumantra murmured. "They say his mother is a blood-drinker. The rumor started when a servant from the innermost quarters claimed that an enchanting woman who subsists on blood and shuns sunlight lives there. That same servant was found dead soon after. His father denied those rumors until his recent death. He never acknowledged a mother. Now no one in the inner circle speaks. Still, we've heard whispers that she is Kashi's true mother. Others speculate she's his wife."

The four princes were looking with big eyes, back and forth from Kashi to Sumantra.

As Kashi's tales came to a close, Dasharatha adjourned the assembly, encouraging all the travel-weary kings to rest before the summit began in earnest.

As the hall began to clear, Dasharatha sent a messenger to summon Janaka. They would speak in private in Dasharatha's quarters. He entrusted the princes into Sumantra's care and proceeded to his own place, followed by his entourage of guards and attendants.

"Please remain without, all of you," he ordered, as he stepped into the room. "I'm expecting King Janaka. Show him in promptly."

Janaka appeared shortly after and the two kings warmly embraced.

"What a great honor!" Janaka exclaimed.

He had no inkling why Dasharatha had summoned him.

"Please sit," the emperor said, while formulating his words. He had to ask questions without casting Vasishta or Shatananda in a dark light.

"How is your daughter?" he asked, offering Janaka a tender coconut to drink.

"Oh, I have two daughters now. One year after Sita, Urmila was born."

"You named her 'The Enchantress.'"

It was an unusual name for an infant, more commonly one that a woman earned, just as he had earned "Ten Chariots."

"It was because of her birth stars," Janaka said. "To counteract a planetary alignment that suggested her husband would leave her." He cleared his throat and put away the coconut. "Otherwise her stars are all auspicious. Urmila will be a bold, outspoken girl. And beautiful too. I believe she will live up to the name."

"What about Sita's stars?"

"I thought that was where your interest was," Janaka said with a smile.

The two kings looked at each other. All pretenses melted away. Dasharatha did not have to play the political game with the subordinate king. It was a relief, for the emperor did not feel natural at such talk, preferring directness and honesty.

"When I received your letter three years ago," Dasharatha said, "I was delighted."

"I was afraid it would frighten you."

"Afraid that we would take action against the girl?"

"I was incredibly fearful of that, yes."

"Is that why you decided to hide her nature?"

Janaka stood up and turned his back on the emperor for a moment.

Why did he hide his face now? Had Dasharatha miscalculated his openness?

When Janaka turned around, he had crossed his arms. "I do not know quite how to answer you, for I understand that you are speaking to me directly because you are not satisfied with Shatananda's reports. But Vasishta's pupil speaks truly. He was an amazing observer, never intruding on my daughter, yet noticing more about her than her own mother did. He saw a girl with extraordinary faculties. Sita was never quite a child, and she is prone to make rather prophetic statements. She notices complex things that even a perceptive adult would miss. But all of these are within the range of normal human behavior. As I'm sure Shatananda reported to you."

Dasharatha inclined his head, but Janaka shook his. "You must think me mentally unsound. First, I claimed to have a child who was in direct resonance with the elements. Quite a dramatic claim, I'm aware. Then when you sent a neutral observer, he found nothing. It seems suspicious."

Dasharatha was satisfied with Janaka's frank avowal. He spoke openly in turn. "Truly told, my suspicions lay elsewhere. I wholeheartedly trust Vasishta. What he keeps from me is for my own benefit. And yet in this case, I cannot understand the need for subterfuge."

Janaka shrugged. "I do not retract what I wrote in my letter. Sita certainly shook the foundation of my existence. I could neither believe nor deny what I saw. I think now that if I had written to you earlier, if Shatananda had come sooner, perhaps he would have seen a different Sita. You see, something changed drastically once she acquired the totality of human speech. She began to speak and understand. All occurrences stopped."

"Did you tell her to stop?"

"Not verbally, no. But as I said, she is very perceptive."

"It's possible then that she is concealing her powers?"

"I—hm—well, I don't think so. Deception is not her nature. I have made sure to keep a watchful eye on her, one that I believe she is unaware of. If she has any powers, she is concealing them even from herself."

Dasharatha lifted his hands in the air and decided to let the matter go. It was, after all, only a matter of interest to him. It did not affect the empire's future.

He thanked Janaka and went to bid his sons goodnight. If they wanted a tale, he would tell them of a little girl who might have made rain fall when she cried.

The second day of the summit was dedicated to hunting. It would begin and end at the sacred fire, where Vasishta presided over the fire ceremony. Each king held a fruit in his hand, and each then stepped forward, according to rank, and offered it to the fire. The symbolic gestures burned away attachment to the result of actions, one of the greatest binding forces of the world. After a light meal was served, the kings mingled briefly before donning their weapons. Dasharatha felt at ease among his people, even if Kashi approached the princes more often than necessary, praising them with ill-concealed malice. The only outstanding event of the morning was when a young king offered Rama his first challenge, a friendly archery contest. Rama's fine bow was ever slung across his shoulder. Anyone who had ever held a bow could see that the young prince had a natural talent. The competitions with weapons would be held on the third day, and Rama now knew who his first opponent was.

Before the morning assembly was adjourned, Dasharatha addressed the assembled kings. "This will be the first time my sons participate in a hunting expedition. May they learn from your example, and may they become powerful warriors."

He looked around at each one of them, letting the unspoken message of his words sink in. The young princes were inexperienced and Dasharatha expected the other kings to include them with due caution.

Satisfied by the somber quality among the kings, Dasharatha signaled for the hunt to commence. The feeling of urgency began at once. Fifty kings, each with two attendants, sat on their horses. The forest would be invaded, but Sumantra had carefully mapped out who would go where. As horses neighed and stomped their hooves, Sumantra's sonorous voice called out instructions. Some of the kings had hunted in this region before. It was not their first summit. Such kings were left to lead their own factions of the large hunting retinue. Sumantra guided the new kings, pointing them in the directions they were to take.

Dasharatha felt a shadow cross over him. Ever since the fatal hunting accident in his youth, he had felt dubious about the practice. He could not discount, however, the skills it had given him. It seemed like a necessary and unavoidable step in the training of any warrior. Kill an animal first, and a human target became that much easier. Dasharatha hoped the exuberance and spirit of the other kings would give his sons a taste of the undeniable thrills of the hunt. It appealed to the primal instinct of being a predator. Dasharatha knew men who were addicted to both hunting and battle for this reason. He had himself fallen victim to it in his youth. It was therefore that the scriptures cautioned even those who were sanctioned to hunt, warning that it was a vice. Should he say any of this to his sons? He knew they were well versed in the laws already.

The princes fidgeted in their saddles, and especially the twins had to be reminded to cease their bickering. The princes were chattering up a storm, clearly taken with the spirit of the kings. Thankfully, Dasharatha had only to glance in their direction to subdue them.

Dasharatha rode out, followed closely by his two guards, and the four princes followed with one guard each. A small division of ten soldiers shadowed them at a distance, a measure of safety that was a necessary precaution for the emperor and his sons.

As the roads disappeared and they entered the forest, Dasharatha stayed close to his sons, each astride his own steed. They looked quite small on the large animals. They were laughing and talking among each other, but Dasharatha noted how often they stole glances at the elders, mimicking their manners. They could hear calls and hoots echoing from other places in the forest.

As they rode, Dasharatha couldn't stop himself from instructing his sons how to hold their bows and arrows while on horseback. Kaikeyi would have chided him if she was present. Nevertheless, the thrill of the hunt was in the air, and Dasharatha was pleased. The anticipation gripped his belly and, from long years of experience, he knew the feeling would become unbearably tense until the arrows were released and the targets destroyed. He consciously turned off his empathy, as he had learned to long ago.

He wanted to impart his knowledge to his sons and wanted their first hunting expedition to be a success; ideally this meant that each prince would take down at least one animal. Every person reacted differently to the sight of death. Some were unmoved, some laughed, and some got sick to the stomach. Dasharatha looked at his four miracles: serene Rama, grave Bharata, irascible Lakshmana and Shatrugna. There was no way to predict how any of them would react today, and Dasharatha prayed for wisdom so that he would know how to respond.

He rode up to Rama, though he directed his words to all four boys. "The first time you witness a sentient creature die, you might feel a shock hit you somewhere in your body. It's a different place for different people. I want you to be aware of that sensation and understand that it's like that for all of us in the beginning. It's a necessary step to grow inured to death. Understand?"

The day for the princes to take human lives was still in the far future.

As they stalked deeper into the forest, Dasharatha caught sight of a deer, and he motioned the party to grow still. Speaking in a whisper, he said, "Soon she may sense our presence, perk her ears up, and grow still. If she deems us a threat, she will run."

The boys watched the deer. As expected, Dasharatha saw the alarm in their eyes. They had tame deer like this in their gardens.

"A skilled hunter," Dasharatha said, "would reveal his presence and cause the deer to run. That way the hunt becomes more active and unpredictable. If you fired at her now, it would be a question of marksmanship, not true hunting. Each of you has already mastered hitting an immobile target. Is that correct?"

"Yes, Father," Rama whispered back.

"Who wants to shoot a warning arrow to alert her to our presence? Then I will demonstrate how we pursue a moving target."

Slowly, Lakshmana raised his hand.

"Quickly," Dasharatha said.

The deer had sensed them already, her ears moving.

"Two more!" Lakshmana exclaimed softly, pointing at two deer visible behind the trees.

Everything happened so fast, even Dasharatha was caught unawares. The deer bolted. Dasharatha charged, releasing his arrows. She fell to the ground without a noise, and the two other deer escaped only because Dasharatha froze in shock at the scene before him. The deer bleated and lifted her head once before dying. She had expelled a fetus from her body, a dark mass covered in the mother's fluids. Dasharatha had prepared for many eventualities, but not this. His heart plummeted as he looked in disbelief at the new life on the ground.

"What happened, Father?" Rama's voice was laced with anxiety.

"What is that?" Lakshmana and Shatrugna asked simultaneously.

"Is it a baby deer?" Bharata asked, the shock clear in his voice.

There was nothing to do but examine the fawn. Dasharatha began to dismount, but Rama and his brothers reached the fawn before he did. The newborn was covered by a thick membrane and showed no signs of life yet. When four pairs of hands touched it, the fawn moved.

"It's alive!" they whispered, starting to peel off the layers that covered it. The mother, if alive, would have been licking the fawn clean. As the fawn was being thusly mothered by the boys, it lifted its tiny head. No one in that clearing was unmoved by this sight.

"We have to take care of him now," Rama said. "Because we killed his mother."

Dasharatha appreciated Rama's use of *we* instead of *you*. The fawn stood up on unsteady feet and took one step before collapsing, close enough to its mother to nuzzle at her udders. That's when one of the boys burst into tears; the next moment all of the princes were softly crying. They didn't cry the way they used to when they were infants, with full abandon, but it was more painful for Dasharatha to behold this. The princes were trying to be brave and warrior-like, but the tears trickled down their cheeks as the fawn bleated and poked its mother. There she lay dead, for the sole reason that they wanted to practice their skills.

Rama reached over to the fawn, and it began licking the prince's fingers. Dasharatha knew then that the hunting lesson was over. He resigned himself to the fact that it had been a complete failure. He knew he would not be able to rouse his sons into killing any other animals on this day.

"What should we do with him, Father?" Rama asked.

All four princes again claimed the little one, placing protective hands on it.

"We have to take it home with us," Lakshmana decided.

"As you wish," Dasharatha said, mounting his horse.

With eager hands, Shatrugna gathered the foal in his hands. One of the king's men helped the boy mount his horse. Another slung the dead deer across his horse. Sometimes the hide would be harvested and the meat offered to the gods. Today, however, every animal slain during the hunt would be offered into the sacrificial fire, another symbolic gesture.

They rode back in silence, save for the occasional reassurances the boys uttered to their adopted pet. Dasharatha needed time to find the right words to say to his sons. There was a teaching in everything, even a failed lesson. There was much he and his sons had to face before the summit was complete.

As they reached the summit grounds, Dasharatha had gathered his thoughts. He faced his sons and the orphaned fawn. "Instead of learning to slay today, your instinct to save and protect were called on. That is a valuable lesson in itself. Every act of violence must be tempered with compassion and the intention to protect. Don't forget, however, that you, as warriors, will not be allowed soft hearts. For now, you are only seven years of age, and I will allow it this once. You can keep the fawn. But do not get caught up in ministering to it, or I will remove it. While we are here at the summit, we will assign someone to feed the fawn and care for it. You are here as the princes of Ayodhya, after all, and we have many days of work left."

"Yes, Father, no, Father, we understand, Father," the boys chorused while gathered around the little one.

"Good. We will meet in the arena for the feast. This evening the challenges begin."

He watched as his sons went to their assigned room. Now Rama was carrying the fawn, though Lakshmana was begging for a turn. The episode had really taught the boys the opposite of the intended lesson. Dasharatha was not altogether displeased.

After the evening feast, the sacrificial fires were lit. Eight large pits blazed as the sun began to set. The fire pits were auspiciously decorated and built according to the ancient laws. One by one, each king was acknowledged for his success in hunting. As each animal's body was offered into the fire, its species and gender were proclaimed. The priests chanted mantras for their swift rebirth, and ladles of ghee were poured into the hungry flames.

Dasharatha was the only king who offered only one animal into the flames. He saw the questioning looks by the other kings, but he was not obliged to answer to them. He glanced at his sons and smiled reassuringly. The fires now reached up to the night sky, and shadows played across every man's face. Perhaps it was only this that made Dasharatha's skin crawl when it was Kashi's turn.

Kashi stood by the fire, licking his lips and smiling with great satisfaction as his list grew longer and longer. He had slain an entire herd of antelopes—fourteen females and one male, along with five young.

Rama turned to his father with a question in his eyes. "Is that righteous?" Rama asked, as though he already knew the answer.

Dasharatha shook his head. Only a monster would take pleasure in killing the young of any species. It was an impressive deed. And that was not all: three musk deer, five boars, and, finally, a tiger.

As Kashi's self-gloating increased, the fire sputtered and died down, suffocated by the immense number of animal corpses. Rather than being alarmed, the fool Kashi took this as another sign of his power: he could suppress even the sacred fire. Kashi clapped his hands together in self-applause. A few kings followed suit.

They heard Vasishta roar, and the fire burst up, swallowing the animals in one gulp and they were gone.

As the third day began, Dasharatha had little attention to spare for his sons, for he was challenged to combat by king after king. He did not accept every challenge that came his way; instead he measured each king's motives carefully. At his age, Dasharatha was more interested in maintaining friendly relations than proving his superiority. If the challenging king was fresh and young, Dasharatha would ensure the young king fought with several others before he faced Dasharatha. Dasharatha enjoyed sparring with swords, spears, or wrestling bare-chested. When they were not engaged in challenges of their own, his sons sat on the sidelines, cheering and applauding their father. It was a glorious feeling.

Dasharatha was incredibly pleased that even at fifty-seven, he could match strengths with subordinate subjects.

When Dasharatha was interrupted amid a wrestling match, he knew something important was afoot. He stood up, panting, realizing how exerted he was only in the reprieve of action. He was loathe to admit it, but the injury from the javelin wound on his chest ached terribly.

"Rama is outdoing everyone at the archery ring," the messenger said.

Dasharatha took the linen cloth that was handed to him and stepped away from his opponent.

"Sumantra thought you would want to witness his feat," the servant said. "When I left, he was facing the champion of Uttar-kashi. If we make haste, you will be there to see how Rama fares against such formidable opposition. All of the world's best archers are lining up to match forces with him."

While Dasharatha listened, he wiped his body clean, sprinkled himself with rose-scented water, and donned his crown and the golden bands around his upper arms and wrists. With practiced swiftness, he reached for his bow, quiver, and sword.

He bid his opponent farewell, promising a rematch soon. Sumantra knew him well. He couldn't stand to miss any of his sons' milestones. Especially not Rama's. The messenger struggled to keep up with his stride, although his four guards trailed behind him like an impressive cape.

The proceedings in the archery ring did not stop when the king entered. The usual customs were suspended here in favor of total concentration on the warriors who competed. Arrows flew so swiftly, no one had time even to blink.

Sumantra softly hailed Dasharatha, immediately coming to his side with folded palms. He pointed to where Rama stood. Rama was but a small figure, armed with an even smaller bow, suited perfectly to his height and strength, but one that was surely not a match for a grown man's bow. Dasharatha and Sumantra discussed this as Dasharatha took in the scene. There was a long line of archers eager to try their luck against the seven-year-old prince. The line dwindled before the king's eyes, for lesser archers dropped out when they saw one of their superiors defeated.

Dasharatha remained standing, though his legs were strained from the many challenges he had accepted. He crossed his arms over his chest, all his attention on Rama. The boy seemed to notice nothing but his targets and the task at hand. Unlike Lakshmana, Rama did not jest in between actions or lighten the mood with smiles and words. Dasharatha knew this. Still, he sensed an unusually formidable determination emanating from Rama.

"I don't know if I would dare challenge Rama now," Dasharatha said. "He's on a winning streak."

Sumantra smiled at this and did not disagree. There was something in the air.

Lakshmana stood near his brother, offering him a cloth to wipe his sweat when his hands grew slippery. There were ten targets, one farther away than the other. The last three were the most difficult. For the eighth, one had to look at the target through a mirror. Ninth,

blindfolded. Tenth, blindfolded and hit a moving target, relying on the other senses alone. The archers were now demonstrating increasingly difficult tasks that Rama had to match.

Rama's opponent shot an arrow into the air, then launched another arrow against it, splitting his previous arrow in half. One needed the eyes of a hawk for such precision. Rama repeated the act effortlessly. Everyone applauded. There was a joyous mood in the air, the archers seceding gracefully to the boy, accepting his talent.

But Dasharatha noted instantly what Rama's weakness was, an unavoidable result of his young age and the bow he was wielding: his arrows flew in lower arches and did not have the range that the grown men's arrows had. Therefore he applauded heartily, knowing that his son's victory spree would end the moment the men switched to long bows, which shot arrows traveling far distances. Rama's arms were not long enough or strong enough to wield a long bow yet.

When Rama was declared the victor of the short bow contest, Dasharatha applauded the loudest. No child archer had ever held this title. Dasharatha was very proud and did not hide it.

He walked forward into the ring, his guards moving around him protectively. When Rama saw his father, his face burst into a smile.

"Father, did you see!"

"Certainly. You are the youngest victor in the history of the Sun dynasty. All hail, Prince Rama, the youngest champion of the short bow!"

All hailed and cheered. Rama looked around with a shy smile.

"Now come with me, my son. Let the competition continue with the long bows. I will let you crown the victor when he is announced."

"But I want to continue," Rama said.

"That's not possible, Rama. You have not yet learned to wield the long bow."

"Can't I try with this bow?" He held forth his wooden bow with its delicate carvings.

Dasharatha looked at the weapon. A masterful bow made by the best, yes, but still only a boy's bow.

"I'm afraid not, Rama. You would only come to fail. It is not done."

Sumantra agreed from the stands. All the archers inclined their heads in agreement.

Rama did not. He looked as stubborn as Kaikeyi, and said, "I want to continue."

Dasharatha felt the pressure of the questions around him: How would he respond to the defiance of his son? He pushed those questions away and beheld Rama, considering what would be right for the young prince.

"I will allow you to face one competitor. No more. This will teach you to understand your limitations."

Dasharatha had been a foolhardy child too. He had thought himself capable of anything. Then came the slow shattering of the spirit, the acceptance of defeat. A good warrior had to know his limits.

"Who wants to compete against me in the long bow competition?" Rama called out, his high, clear voice ringing through the arena.

To Dasharatha's horror, Kashi of Kashi stood up. He looked delighted to have the opportunity to utterly squash the boy. "I do," he said, before Dasharatha could protest.

"I must forbid this, Rama," he said, only for his son to hear.

"Trust me, Father," Rama whispered back.

"I trust you, Rama. But not your bow. Or your age. Indeed, it's impossible. They may not laugh at your defeat since you are a boy, but it will besmirch the sweet taste of victory you've had today."

Meanwhile, Kashi had armed himself and was approaching. "Worried about your pet son, Respected King?"

Dasharatha did not bother with the insolent words, for he truly was worried for Rama. Kashi was not a kind or generous opponent. But Rama would not be dissuaded.

Custom demanded that Dasharatha and the other competitors leave the two opponents on the ring. Surreptitiously, Dasharatha raised his hand and made the signs to the guards to raise their bows and stand in active protection of the prince. Under other circumstances, he would have openly declared the threat Kashi was under. He doubted that anyone had missed the synchronous act of the guards as they stood, arrows drawn. One false move and Ayodhyan arrows would be fired at Kashi. Thus, Dasharatha left Kashi to the fate he would choose. He had never been a true ally, always the first to cause conflicts. Dasharatha forced himself to keep walking away from his son and the ruthless king.

"Your father has granted you only one opponent," Kashi said, in that bellowing voice he had. "Aren't you glad I volunteered? Or didn't you know? I was the undefeated champion of the last summit. Oh, that's right, you were not yet born then. You were not even a suckling babe at your mother's breast. Even now you are hardly past that stage. Cried when you said farewell from your mother, didn't you? You look like a soft one."

Sumantra put a calming hand on Dasharatha's shoulder. Challenging talk was often part of combat, depending on the temperament of the warriors. But Kashi was base enough to descend to goading a little boy. It was not surprising but nevertheless galling.

Rama took Kashi's words calmly. "Your bow will speak truly," he said. "As will mine."

Scattered applause erupted.

"You first," Kashi said. "Show me your best."

Rama, who knew the theory of the long bow, if not the praxis, turned toward the targets.

Dasharatha's heart sank. It just wasn't done, even with a grown man's short bow. He wanted to stand up and argue that for the competition to be truly fair, Kashi had to wield a boy's bow too. But Rama had insisted on participating in the long bow contest. The rules could not be changed to suit the whims of a young prince.

As Rama launched his arrow, it sang through the sky. But when it was halfway to the target, it began losing momentum, as any grown archer would have known it would. Kashi laughed loudly. That's when Rama surprised them by nocking another arrow, which hit his first arrow and propelled it forward. With a sharp thud, it reached the target.

"At the navel," the scorekeeper declared.

Dasharatha's eyes widened. Rama's arrow had made it, though by way of his son's unconventional method. The arrow had reached the target at the navel area. The customary place was the heart. But cheers still erupted.

"Pah!" Kashi said, and spat as though Rama had done nothing unusual.

He walked over to the tenth target, which was farthest away, farther than most long bows could even reach. He meant to show all of his brute strength at once. With quick movements he dispatched his arrows, one by one. To increase the difficulty, he looked away as he shot each arrow. Before the arrows even reached their destination, he bowed and walked away, pumping his bow in the air, congratulating himself. Camp Kashi alone cheered. There was a smattering of noise as his targets landed.

Ten, Dasharatha heard.

"Ten in a perfect line," the scorekeeper declared. His voice was barely discernible, the perfect line invisible to all but him.

There was a loud murmur across the crowd. It really wasn't glorious, outdoing a seven-year-old. Dasharatha was glad he wasn't alone in thinking so. Nevertheless, Kashi was undeniably skilled. Dasharatha was angry, having allowed it to go this far and began ascending toward his son to escort him from the arena. But Rama walked to where Kashi had stood. He faced the faraway target, his fingers curling and uncurling around his little bow.

What could the young prince hope to accomplish? Every grown man knew that Kashi had again established himself as champion. And yet there was an intrigue to Rama's insistence. The young prince had, after all, won the short bow title, the youngest to ever do so.

Rama, a small figure in the distance, put an arrow to his bow.

Dasharatha leaned forward, straining to see what his son was up to.

Rama jumped straight up into the air, releasing his first arrow. He repeated this movement, shooting one arrow after the other, as Kashi had done.

Each time, he jumped high and released his missile. Instead of ten arrows, Rama kept going.

Did he mean to exhaust the arrows in his quiver? And thereby prove that he had done everything in his power? Dasharatha watched intently, seeing his son jump and shoot, jump and shoot.

Suddenly Rama was done, his bow at his side. He stood unmoving, facing the faraway target. Silence descended. A pleasant wind blew over the arena. Rama's hair and silk cloth billowed up around him. Murmurs rose.

"Ten in a perfect line!" the scorekeeper shouted in the distance.

Dasharatha lifted his arms to the sky. Impossible!

"Ten in a perfect line!" the scorekeeper shouted again, having heard no response.

A collective roar roused them all to action. Dasharatha was one among many when he ran forward to see how his little son had accomplished this.

Rama himself was nearly forgotten as they ran past him to see for themselves. Quickly, Dasharatha understood that Rama had employed the same technique he had first demonstrated against Kashi. Every arrow had been nudged forward by the other. When the foremost arrow had lost momentum, the one behind it propelled it forward, in a long succession.

The arrows lay on the ground, several paces from each other. Finally, at the target, there it was: the perfect line of ten arrows. Two perfect lines of ten arrows.

Rama had really done it. Dasharatha could hardly believe that his little son had just broken all known records of archery.

As they returned from the target, Dasharatha was congratulated endless times, as though Rama's feat was his due. In truth, he was as astounded as anyone. The chatter around him ceased, and Dasharatha's eyes fell on Rama.

He stood face to face with Kashi once again. Dasharatha's blood froze. There was no mistaking the threatening look on Kashi's face. His hand was on Rama's shoulder, a gripping claw. Lakshmana was unsuccessfully trying to pry Kashi's hand off. The king was going too far. Dasharatha sensed the tension in the guards surrounding the ring.

"Step away from the prince at once," Dasharatha said.

Kashi looked up. "Oh, I'm only congratulating him on his victory." He murmured something between clenched teeth.

Lakshmana paled.

Dasharatha quickened his steps, raising his hand high. "I warn you, Kashi. My hand is set to give the signal. Ayodhya's arrows are trained on you. Step away now, or lose your life."

"You wouldn't dare, with your pet son so near," Kashi said with a sneer. Yet he took several steps away. Loudly, he declared, "All hail to Prince Rama, youngest-ever champion of the long bow, winning by fair means alone."

The final phrase was not customary, but the people in attendance were reminded of the great feat they had witnessed. Kashi successfully turned the attention toward the young victor.

"All hail Prince Rama!" they shouted.

"All hail the youngest champion!"

Rama's chest was heaving, as though he was angry or frightened, and Lakshmana was still pale. Regardless, both princes rose to the occasion, smiling and receiving the heartfelt congratulations of the people around them.

Kashi left without a backward glance, followed by his lot of disgruntled followers. They were not even half cheering. It was ill done. Dasharatha knew something amiss had taken place in his absence. He had never reckoned that Kashi would approach Rama before examining the results for himself.

He put a hand on Rama's shoulder, the other on Lakshmana's. Together they played the role of joyful victors. In some measure, it was true. Dasharatha's praise was heartfelt. In the morrow, Rama would be hailed and crowned in the morning assembly, as all victors were.

As soon as Dasharatha could, he excused himself, saying the young princes were tired.

Along with Sumantra, he escorted the boys back to their quarters. He signaled to Sumantra to stay close and listen. In their rooms, the boys went straight to their rescued fawn, which eagerly licked their fingers in turn. Dasharatha gave them a few moments with the fawn, seeing it soothed the boys. Then he could no longer wait.

"What did Kashi say to you, Rama?"

Rama turned to Dasharatha, the fawn in his lap. "He said if I tell you, he will send blood-drinkers to kill me in my dreams."

"He is a liar, Rama. His threat is empty."

"Kings can lie?" Rama's utter surprise was almost endearing. "Don't liars and oath breakers lose their soul connection to the Lord as they are flung into the deepest loneliness in hell?"

Lakshmana nodded vigorously.

"Very good, Rama," Dasharatha was forced to say, praising Rama's elegant knowing of the laws. "You are right. I fear Kashi has less reverence for the laws than we do. Your knowledge protects you, Rama. Now tell me, what was his true threat?"

Rama shivered. "He said he could see I had made a pact with evil forces to get power. He vowed that when he gets Shiva's bow, he will be more powerful than me, for Shiva is the lord of all spirits, and with that bow he plans to kill us all and become the most powerful king on Earth."

Dasharatha took a deep breath. That was no minor threat—and directed to a little boy. If that wasn't a coward's act, Dasharatha had never known one. He felt his temper arise and didn't trust his voice to immediately reply to Rama.

Sumantra said, "Dismissing the children as harmless or inconsequential, he has laid out his master plan before us."

Dasharatha nodded, clenching his jaw. He would have to set extra eyes on Kashi, even if reports were consistently innocuous. Kashi was too busy wreaking havoc in Kashi to be a serious threat. Still . . .

"What is Shiva's bow?" Lakshmana asked.

"Shiva's bow is in the care of King Janaka of Videha," Dasharatha answered. This neutral topic restored his calm. "It is an ancient heirloom, protected vigilantly by him in the heart of Mithila, their capital city. No mortal man has been known to lift the bow ever. As the name implies, it belonged to Shiva, the destroyer of the worlds. Only he has wielded the bow, before he gave it to Janaka's ancestors. It takes three hundred of the strongest men to lift it. Kashi's aspirations are beyond him. And we thank the lords for that. For with that bow in hand, he might be able to carry out his threat. At present, Rama, you must know that he is nothing but a coward and a bully, despite his physical strength and weaponry. You must take care not to accept any challenges by him again. That goes for you too, Lakshmana, and your brothers."

The princes nodded seriously. Just then, the brothers in question came bursting in, calling, "You won, Rama? You won, you won!"

And the boys were swept up in talks with each other, Bharata and Shatrugna declaring which competitions they had won and so on.

Quietly Dasharatha left the room with Sumantra. On the way out, he ordered the servants to arrange massages for all the boys, especially Rama, so they would be rejuvenated on the morrow.

"May I suggest the same for you, Great King?"

Dasharatha knew Sumantra was right. There was another day on the morrow, and Dasharatha was still tense, having seen his son in the grip of a monster like Kashi. Knowing that one of his sons would one day be torn from him was never far from his consciousness.

The summit concluded successfully on the tenth day. That was when Ashvapati arrived unannounced at Dasharatha's door.

"Welcome," Dasharatha said. "Please come in."

Ashvapati, who had never been one for small talk, got straight to his point. "I have thought a great deal about my daughter's bride-price and the subsequent events."

Dasharatha felt a stiffening begin in his gut but kept his smile in place. Ashvapati's mere presence had the power to make Dasharatha uncomfortable. Kaikeyi had assured Dasharatha that this was her father's specialty. When Dasharatha had deviated, by necessity, from the promise he had made to Ashvapati, he had fallen from grace. It was clear in Ashvapati's curt tone and manner. It was not fair, but that was the nature of human dealings.

"I have come to say this," Ashvapati said. "I know you in Ayodhya place great value on the firstborn. But in Kekaya we consider a person's abilities above any other qualification. Bharata deserves to be considered Rama's equal. I think this is the least you can do in the face of your so-called compromise."

Dasharatha reminded himself that humility always worked like magic. There was no point in antagonizing Ashvapati further. But he did not take orders from his subordinate kings. Ashvapati's words had an unacceptable arrogance.

"Bharata is an exceptional boy," Dasharatha said.

"And yet you spend your time watching Rama with googly eyes."

Dasharatha lifted his hand and subdued his retort. "Is it necessary to speak in this manner? Your daughter is most dear to me. I do not wish to fight with my queen's father."

"She is so dear that you would without second thought favor the son of another."

There it was, out in the open. Ashvapati's accusation. Dasharatha took a step away. The other king reminded him suddenly of Manthara. There was the same bitterness around the mouth, the same twisting of reality. Dasharatha did not want to engage with this. The matter had been settled before the princes were born. Ashvapati had agreed then. Now he wished to put pressure on Dasharatha to again consider the old bride-price. Now that he had an eligible contender in Bharata. It galled Dasharatha that Ashvapati dared accuse him of favoritism. He didn't want to part badly with his father-in-law, but when the other man was determined to cut open healed wounds, he had no choice.

"Shall I have one of my guards escort you out?"

"I think you have understood my message."

"Message or threat?"

"Oh, I'm just an old horse-lord with decrepit servants. You have nothing to fear."

Dasharatha forced a smile to return and showed Ashvapati out. He decided to take the man's words literally and dismiss the situation. Ashvapati's intrigues were not Dasharatha's.

The concluding feast was grand, and all the champions were again honored, Rama first among them. Dasharatha had never felt such satisfaction at a political event before. Everything pointed to a brilliant future for the Sun dynasty.

Rama's Adventures

CHAPTER 28

The Enemy in the Shadow

Rama always felt a little strange that he so easily outshone his brothers. He didn't mean to. It simply happened. Long after the summit was over, Rama and his brothers spoke about everything they had learned and accomplished. The princes turned eight years old, and their training continued in earnest. More often than not, Rama was the one teaching his brothers how to use their bows and arrows.

Rama's favorite days were when Father came to oversee their lessons. It had happened more often after the summit, for Father had come to see where the boys needed more practice. On such days the other teachers, even Vasishta, remained in the background, and Father took charge. It was always exciting. Even the next hunting lesson had turned out spectacular, though Rama had felt apprehensive about the idea. Each of the princes had shot down a deer cleanly, and the animals had been offered into the fire by Vasishta himself. The sacred mantras promised them a swift and better rebirth, and Rama thought he had seen their souls arise from the fire and fly up.

Today the attendants brought them to the library, and the princes broke into a run to find that trapdoor that still evaded them. Rama knew he was almost too old to run into places in this way; more was expected of him now that he was eight. But he could *not* stop his legs and the excited hammering of his heart. They had plans for that secret door once they found it. The plan changed, depending on their needs, who they were angry with, and so on.

Running past Lakshmana, Rama reminded him of a place they had not searched. Then Rama stopped abruptly, his entire energy running ahead of him while his body stopped.

Father was standing in the center of the room, waiting for them.

Rama could not read Father's expression, for today he was the king, even with his sons.

The brothers grew still and carefully walked closer to their father.

Father did not ask them to sit. He began with a question.

"Who is your most dangerous enemy?" Father looked at each of them in turn.

The four princes surrounded their father with rapt attention. Rama became still. He wanted to get it right. Bharata became still too. Lakshmana's and Shatrugna's gazes traveled from one side of the room to the other while they thought.

Shatrugna lifted his hand first. "Rebel kings," the youngest boy said.

"One guess each," their father offered.

Rama scrutinized his father's face. Had Shatrugna been close?

"Your own self," Lakshmana said.

Rama nodded. That was a good answer. But Father would not budge until they had all answered.

Bharata's answer was longer. "If someone is your friend and you tell them everything and then they turn on you. You know, a traitor."

"What do you say, Rama?" Father's attention was intent on him.

"I think all of the answers were right," Rama said. "It depends on the circumstance."

This made Father laugh.

"Who got it?" Lakshmana asked. "Rama's answer doesn't count!"

"It does!" Rama protested, glaring at Lakshmana.

"No, because you didn't say your own"—he looked at the ceiling, searching for the word—"definition!" He smiled.

"Boys."

They fell silent, looking up at their father. "If I say Rama was right, then you all got it right."

"A trick question," Bharata said, dejected.

"Actually, you were all wrong," their father said.

The young princes sighed loudly, and Father amended his reply. "The right answer does depend on the circumstance, as Rama said. And in that sense, it was a trick question. There are many enemies." Father's eyes grew serious as he looked at each of them. "What if I told you that your most dangerous enemy is the blood-drinker hiding in the shadows?"

"Blood-drinkers!" Shatrugna's eyes were wide, like two moons. "But we have never even seen one!"

"Manthara is the only one who sees them everywhere," Bharata said. "But that's just to scare us."

"And Father," Lakshmana said, "at the summit, you said blood-drinkers were destroyed."

Father was silent. Rama had never seen his eyes so hard.

"If Father says so, it must be so," he said.

Lakshmana made his vampire face, showing all his teeth.

"It's not a joke, Lakshmana." Rama frowned at his brother, beckoning him to look at Father.

Their father was staring past their heads, viewing a scene they could not see.

Was he seeing blood-drinkers? Rama wondered. When Rama was grown, he would be able to see the way his father did.

"You and your brothers are old enough now, Rama," Dasharatha said, returning his gaze to them. "You must know what we are up against. Until now, I have protected you and your brothers from this. I have protected Ayodhya. Together with the kings of all other regions, I protect the Earth. One day, it will be your duty."

Father looked at them in turn.

"A king's duty is to protect," Rama recited. "A warrior's duty is to kill."

"One day, you will understand the distinction," Father promised. "As for the unseen enemy that seems to you a fairytale creature, I think it's time you see for yourself. Come with me."

Their father took the hands of the twins because they were the youngest and led the way out. Rama and Bharata followed, hand in hand.

Leaving the school and palace grounds on a chariot, they headed in a direction they seldom went. A retinue of guards followed, as they always did. Rama, who had never felt afraid for his life, wondered if the guards were secretly battling the enemy and keeping him and his brothers all alive, ignorant of the danger. It dawned on him that he was in constant danger, but protected so well that he did not even know it. Rama did not want to be in the dark.

"The prison," Lakshmana whispered in Rama's ear.

"What?" Shatrugna leaned in. "Where are we going?"

"The prison!" Lakshmana whispered more loudly but with more conviction.

None of the boys seemed to know whether to be excited or frightened.

Reaching the prison grounds, they marched next to their father with extra precision, arms swinging sharply. Rama's hand rested on the hilt of his sword, like Father's did. Father had made them wear one weapon each, as practice. They had never been inside the prison before, a building that did not look terribly different from other structures in Ayodhya, save for the huge spiked fence and the many guards.

On the inside, however, it was very different. It immediately felt dark and suffocating. The king and his four sons were trailed by a group of guards that seemed to grow larger the deeper into the prison they went.

The prisoners clamored for attention, calling out and reaching through the bars as the king and the princes walked by.

"Do not look at the prisoners," the king cautioned his sons.

Rama held his eyes extra wide, forcing them straight ahead. It wasn't easy to ignore people who had such a desperate need to be seen and heard.

When Rama said this to his father, Dasharatha replied, "They *have* been heard, Rama. They do not deserve your attention now. This is the punishment for their transgressions."

There were no windows. No sunlight. No wind or fresh air. No trees. None of the things that Rama loved. What had the prisoners done to deserve this? He would have to ask his father. How did you know that a punishment was just?

They walked into a dark tunnel that was dimly lit by torches. The flames flickered as they walked by, bat-like shadows that flew past Rama. The dark tunnel ended in a single prison cell with extra-thick bars. It was illuminated by a pool of the brightest light. Rama looked up and saw that this cell had no roof. It was like looking up at a long tunnel and seeing the sky above. A small kindness, even though thick bars obscured the blue sky.

"We are here," the king said.

He pointed to a lone prisoner chained in the center of the pool of light. The sun's rays completely engulfed the prisoner. After the darkness of the tunnel, Rama could barely make out anything but a lump in the center of the room. Then he saw the sacred fires that blazed in every corner of the cell. Heat wafted toward them. The other prisoners had clamored for attention, while this one hung limp and lifeless against his chains.

As if reading Rama's thoughts, Dasharatha said, "Tell me what is different between this prisoner and the others."

Rama felt certain that this prisoner must be a blood-drinker. But he said nothing because he did not yet have proof. The prisoner's skin was a pleasant dark shade, his hair a rare bronze. Yet these tones were not unheard of. Rama himself had an unusual color. That didn't make him a blood-drinker. So the boy waited for his eyes to adjust, for his mind to pick up any definitive traits.

"He sits in the light, while the others were in darkness," Bharata remarked.

"Not for long," their father assured them.

As they watched, the blinding rays of the sun crept across the prisoner's hidden face, his bronze hair glimmering in the sun. Then the sun was gone, replaced by a forgiving shadow. Evening was upon them. The moment the shadows settled in the prison cell, the prisoner looked up at his audience.

His eyes were red like blood. His bronze beard covered half his face, so it wasn't until he smiled at them that Rama saw his sharp teeth.

"Fangs," the prince stated, without taking his eyes off the prisoner.

"The stories *are* true," Lakshmana said with awe.

"Yes, this is a blood-drinker, though we feed him no blood," Dasharatha told his sons. "He is allowed only holy water from the golden altars. It keeps him weak. Though they are all weakened by sunlight, this one does not shun light entirely. It only keeps his faculties weak. The chains around his ankles and wrists are imbued with life and keep him in place, a gift from Vasuki, the king of snakes. Yes, the chains are alive and obey Vasishta's command alone."

"It's so hot in here," Shatrugna said, wiping his face.

"The four fires are crucial," Father said. "They maintain the power of the mantras that enforce the parameters of his prison. Fire is not their friend but ours. This prisoner has been here since the days of Anaranya, a captive from that ancient battle."

"What about when the fires turn to ash?" Bharata asked

"They will not. They burn as long as the fire at the golden altar burns. As you know, that fire is diligently tended to day and night, protecting Ayodhya."

The blood-drinker did not move a muscle or blink, but his eyes went to whomever spoke, so Rama knew he was listening.

"What is his name?" Rama asked.

"We do not know for certain, nor do we know what he is capable of, for some of his kind are expert shape changers. The chains prevent such a change, and one of Vasishta's sons regularly visits to strip his energy field of power. If nothing else, this prisoner is a reminder that his kind is real. I hope it is all the reminder you will ever need."

"I want to speak to him," Rama said.

"He can talk?" Bharata asked doubtfully.

"Good question, Bharata," Dasharatha responded, casting a concerned glance at Rama. "The blood-drinker tongue is different from ours. But this one speaks the language of humans, though he refuses to say what his name is. The records show that he initially insisted that his name was 'Ray of Light' or something of that nature, obviously a taunt. In the early days, they called him simply 'the prisoner' which became 'Ayodhya's oldest prisoner.'"

"I want to talk to him," Rama repeated.

"Don't!" Shatrugna hid behind Dasharatha.

The blood-drinker had not once taken his eyes off the four boys. His nostrils were flared and he repeatedly licked his lips.

"He is hungry," Lakshmana said, his lips turning down.

"He can hear you," Dasharatha assured Rama.

"I want to sit by his side and speak to him," Rama insisted. He looked up at his father. "Please."

Dasharatha looked down at him, scrutinizing his face. Rama held his father's gaze. If this was the most dangerous enemy, Rama wanted to know everything there was to know.

The king turned to the prison master. "Is it safe?"

"The chains restrict the prisoner's movements. He recently drank his weekly portion of holy water. Prince Rama will be safe as long as he stays an arm's distance away. But the prisoner will not speak. He has not spoken for centuries."

The guards opened the cell door and let the prince enter.

"I'll come too," Lakshmana said.

Dasharatha's hand flew up as if to stop his boys at the last minute, but they were already inside.

Rama approached warily and sat at the feet of the blood-drinker, looking up at him steadily. The prisoner looked back, meeting the gaze of the boy. They sat in silence for a while.

Rama wondered if he was being hypnotized, or the other way around. There was no way to retreat. He looked past the frightening redness of the blood-drinker's eyes and felt for the soul energy he knew every person had.

"Your soul is shiny," Rama said, startled.

The blood-drinker's head swayed back; he blinked and broke their eye contact. "That is my name," he whispered in a rusty voice. "Marichi, 'Ray of Light.'"

Rama looked at Lakshmana and his smile said, *See, I got him to talk.*

"Marichi," Rama said. "A name of great honor."

Marichi licked his lips, looking at Rama. Drops of saliva ran down the corners of his mouth.

"You would like to drink my blood?" Rama asked.

"I would drink the blood of a fly if they let me," the prisoner said, and laughed.

"Why do you like to drink blood?"

"Why don't *you* like to drink blood?" the blood-drinker countered. "It's ripe and delicious, salty and fulfilling. I was created this way. It's my nature. The way a lion preys on deer. Don't blame me."

Rama looked over his shoulder, searching for affirmation from Father.

"Don't look at your father," the blood-drinker snapped, his chains protesting as he struggled against them. "He knows nothing."

The boy turned his attention back to the blood-drinker, who said, "You are a sweet boy. Those were sweet words you said to me. You see more than others do. You knew I longed to hear that I'm not just a rotten blood-drinker, doomed to this hellhole because I was born with the thirst for blood. That's what the rest of your people say. That blood-drinkers are less than animals. Evil. Ignorant. You are the ones who are ignorant. Short-lived. Know-it-all-humans."

Rama was not surprised by the hate he heard in the blood-drinker's voice. He had been imprisoned for centuries.

"If I was a prisoner," Rama said, "I would probably hate my captors too."

"You think you know, little prince. You know nothing. You count my time here in human years and pity me. By my reckoning, however, I've barely been missed by my kindred. Hardly a day and a night have passed."

Again Rama turned his eyes on Father. This was all new information to him.

"Your father acts like a big king," Marichi said. "But he's at the mercy of my master. You are too. You live because my master allows you to live. Never forget that."

"Tell me," Rama said. "Who is your master?"

Having been silent for so many years, the blood-drinker let his words pour out of him. In this, he was no different than a human being. This pleased the boy, and he listened.

"One dark night, many thousands of years ago," the blood-drinker said, relishing Rama's raptness, "when saints and blood-drinkers roamed the Earth, a great and powerful being was born. On that somber, moonless night, blood poured from the heavens, and carnivorous animals paced left and right. Fierce winds rocked the planet, and meteors fell violently from the heavens and scarred the ground. The seas smashed against rocks and sucked down unfortunate ships and seafarers. The clouds rumbled and the winds wailed loudly."

Lakshmana grew still, and outside the cell, Bharata and Shatrugna leaned against the bars, straining to hear.

"In a small cottage high up in the Himalaya mountain, a woman was wailing, sweating to bring forth her powerful infant with his ten screaming heads and twenty flailing arms. His mother is one of us, a blood-drinker, as you call us. But his father is a sage and a god. My master was born with this double nature. With parental optimism, they named him Dashamukha, 'Ten Heads.' But only they call him that. Even his siblings call him Ravana if they must use a name. The terror of his birth night was only a small portent of what Ravana's life would bring. The omens indicated the birth of someone truly influential. Nature's unnatural phenomenon was sent by the gods as a warning, a protest against Ravana's birth."

Ravana's imprisoned devotee paused to regard the boy in front of him, making sure Rama was intent on his words. Satisfied by Rama's steady gaze, he continued. "When the ten-headed infant grew in size and power, the omens surrounding his birth proved true. His actions showed no trace of conscience. He killed on mere whim, drank blood, and laughed at the pain of others. Indra, lord of heaven, tried to stop him, sending forth lightning to strike him down. To everyone's shock, my master's roar stalled the lightning in midair. The gods were forced to bring the sun out from behind the ominous clouds they had conjured. Such was the extent of the power my master had amassed. Not even Indra could match the violence of Ravana's abilities. Since that day, the sun cannot shine, the winds will not blow, and the day will not turn into night without Ravana's consent. Do you understand, little prince?"

Rama nodded seriously. One of the guards coughed, and Lakshmana fidgeted.

"Tell me more about him," Rama requested. "Your master. How did you become his servant?"

"No one is completely evil. My master is no exception. I am no exception, I hope. Like most beings in this universe, Ravana wages a constant battle between his higher conscience and his lower urges. His blood is intimately tied to the gods. Kuvera, wealth keeper of the gods, is Ravana's brother. Ravana himself is vastly learned, but blood and destruction give him the greatest pleasure. Soon he became known as the most vicious of our kind, attracting a following of his own kind. I became one of his people early on. From an early age, Ravana resolved to become the most powerful being alive. I wanted to play on the winning side. And I did for many, many years."

"How did Ravana become so strong?"

The blood-drinker smiled knowingly. "He started like you. As a curious boy."

Rama frowned.

Lakshmana said, "Let's go, Rama," and tugged at his brother's arm, but Rama sat transfixed.

Marichi spoke only to Rama. "Ravana's power comes from Brahma, the creator of all things. While praying to Brahma, he abstained from all food. Diligently controlling his mind, he fasted for a thousand years. At the end of a millennium, he slashed off one of his

THE ENEMY IN THE SHADOW

ten heads and offered it to Brahma. In this way, Ravana cut off each of his heads as millenniums passed, without achieving his goal. Only after ten thousand years, when he prepared to cut off his last head—thus giving up his life—Brahma appeared. The creator cannot ignore a soul's petitioning forever. Brahma restored Ravana's nine heads and granted his request: to become invincible.

"Moreover, the pain Ravana had inflicted on himself inured him forever to the pain of battle wounds. The patience and endurance that he developed during his years of penance make him a more formidable enemy. He can tolerate any discomfort if it serves his purpose.

"Ravana fears no one. Nothing can stop him, not even Yama, the lord of death. He acts like he is above all the laws of nature and he is all but immortal. When Ravana asked for immortality, Brahma argued that he could not give what he himself did not possess. Ravana circumvented this by requesting immunity from the gods, beasts, demons, and all supernatural creatures. *No one* can kill Ravana."

"Gods, beasts, demons, and all supernatural creatures," the boy repeated. His eyes left the blood-drinker's face for the first time. He was thinking. His eyes returned to the blood-drinker and he said, "That means *I* could kill him."

The blood-drinker laughed so loudly that Lakshmana jumped in his seat. "Sh-sh-sh!" he commanded, though he was only eight and the drinker in front of them was thousands of years older.

The blood-drinker quieted down, his chains still rattling. Rama smiled a little, joining the blood-drinker's mirth.

When the blood-drinker was still again, Rama said, "I mean that any human being could kill Ravana. Your master didn't ask for immunity from humans."

The blood-drinker leaned forward. "Does a lion need protection from a frog?"

When the boy didn't reply, he continued. "Humans have never been a threat to any blood-drinker. If I wasn't chained down and weakened by constant exposure to sunlight, I could kill half of Ayodhya in a heartbeat. I'm nobody compared to my master."

"But why hasn't your master tried to rescue you?" Rama asked. "You are so loyal to him."

"Who says he will not come?" the blood-drinker challenged, raising his voice. For the first time, he glared at the boy. "It may seem to you that I have been here an eternity. But

in my eyes, it has barely been the blink of an eye! He will come for me!" And suddenly the blood-drinker lunged at the boy, biting wildly in the air.

The guards rushed into the cell. Lakshmana had his arms around Rama, pulling him back. The prisoner's teeth were tearing at the air, clattering as ferociously as his chains. Rama disengaged from Lakshmana's arms, staying where he was, his face barely an inch from the enraged blood-drinker.

"I'm not afraid," Rama said, waving away the guards with a firm hand.

"Rama," Dasharatha warned.

The blood-drinker was crazed, all civility gone. He snapped at Rama's face, salivating, dangerous for the first time. His red eyes rolled in their sockets.

Rama grabbed the blood-drinker's beard with both hands. "Be still."

Whether Rama's command or his strength did it, the blood-drinker stilled, returning to his former self, again almost human, though panting and fangs glinting.

The boy and the blood-drinker glared at each other. Slowly Rama let go of his beard.

"Leave me with your pestering questions," the blood-drinker said. "Call on me the next time you want to know who truly rules the entire universe."

Not knowing what would set off the blood-drinker's temperament, Rama stood up. He folded his palms at his chest and then turned away.

"Why did you do that?" Lakshmana whispered, following Rama out. "He is our prisoner. A blood-drinker. You shouldn't offer him respect!"

"He sits in there day and night, every minute of the day," Rama said to his brother. "Imagine that, Lakshmana. I couldn't do that."

As the guards let them out and locked up, Bharata and Shatrugna wanted to know what the blood-drinker had said. Rama was silent as they walked out of the prison, unresponsive to his curious brothers.

"You know how he is," Lakshmana reminded them, shrugging his shoulders and speaking for Rama. "He needs to think."

Bharata sighed. "Tell him to think quickly."

"Tell him yourself. He can hear you," Shatrugna said.

"Exactly!" his twin agreed.

"Boys!" Their father's voice brought them back to the prison grounds. "This way. Time to return home."

Bharata quickly caught Father's hand before anyone else could. The princes clambered onto the chariot after their father. As the chariot picked up speed, they held on to each other, and pretend-stumbled, exaggerating the movements of the chariot. Rama, who was still thinking, didn't play the game with them.

As they arrived back at the palace, Dasharatha turned to his sons before he let them free for the rest of the evening. "I don't want you to be afraid. We keep a constant vigil in the city. That prisoner you saw is the only blood-drinker in Ayodhya, and he will not escape. Not as long as I live. Before I let you go, tell me, why is the blood-drinker our most dangerous enemy?"

Again, they got one guess each.

"Because they drink human blood," Bharata said.

"Because they are evil," Lakshmana and Shatrugna said, both at once.

"All those reasons are right," Rama said, breaking his silence.

"That answer doesn't count," Shatrugna cut in, before Lakshmana could.

"But the real reason," Rama said, "is because they are in the shadow. We don't see them, so we think they don't exist. We think we are safe."

"Rama said he will kill Ravana," Lakshmana informed their father. "That's when the fangs started laughing."

Dasharatha looked with astonished eyes at Rama. "You really said that?"

Rama nodded, but looked down. He hadn't really meant that he planned to kill Ravana. He hadn't even known the ten-headed blood-drinker king was real until this day.

"That's what King Anaranya said, you know," Dasharatha said. "Covered in layers of dust and blood and struggling through his last few breaths, Anaranya, that brave fighter, cursed Ravana, calling him an arrogant fool. 'A man of my own blood will end your life, as you have ended mine.' Those were his last words, recorded in our history."

"I didn't mean *me*, Father," Rama said. "I meant that *any* human could kill Ravana. He never asked for protection against humans."

"That wasn't very smart," Lakshmana scoffed.

"No, it wasn't," Rama agreed.

"Don't worry, son, I never expected you to go out and kill Ravana. Few earthly beings have seen him with their own eyes. That he exists out there somewhere is a cause for great concern. We are never fully safe. But I will tell you this. Despite his power, Ravana is not immune to the curse of a righteous man. Anaranya's curse will prove true one day. Or so Vasishta tells me. Other powerful curses also weaken Ravana. The king of blood-drinkers knows, somewhere in the recesses of his underdeveloped conscience, that there will be a day of retribution."

"A day of retribution," Rama repeated, musing. "I wonder who will win when that day comes."

CHAPTER 29

The Pretender Strikes

Rama did not dwell on it, but he knew that his father's eyes followed him, even when all the brothers were present. This did not always please his third mother, Kaikeyi. Rama had understood how important Kaikeyi's pleasure was to Father, so he continued to subdue his abilities so his brothers could shine. This made his own mother sad, and Rama always focused on her exclusively if she was present. It was all a bit confusing. Understanding more made Rama understand less. Even larger concepts were challenging. Father said Ravana, the ten-headed king, was the most dangerous enemy, and yet the princes had never seen a blood-drinker save for Marichi, the imprisoned one. In the months after meeting Marichi, Rama would find excuses to visit the golden altars, to make sure that the central fire was burning strong there. It always did. Ravana did not even figure in Rama's dreams. But other enemies did.

Since the Summit of Fifty Kings when he was seven, Rama had a recurring dream of Kashi standing over a magnificent bow, a giant bow unlike any bow Rama had ever seen. In the dream, Rama knew it was Shiva's bow, and Kashi would grin and put his hands on it. Everyone around them would smile, but Rama would run forward to stop him. Rama ran and ran, never arriving. Kashi sprouted many heads and laughed loudly at Rama. A sweet voice sang a terribly sad song as Kashi claimed the bow, pointing the first arrow at Rama, who was unarmed and defenseless. That's when Rama always woke up.

Evening, before the sun set, was the best time in Ayodhya. That's when Rama and his brothers would finish their schooling for the day. Often they would gather in Rama's chamber, which had a view of the city.

When the darkness of night veiled the great city, Rama felt the change in Ayodhya's consciousness and his own. The blood-drinkers in the stories always came out at night and grew strong at nightfall, and it was their mood that dominated this time.

Rama's limbs were comfortably exhausted from the day's training. The twins were leaning across Rama's balcony, looking at the city's last burst of energy for the day. Bharata had not yet arrived.

"You are getting much better at handling your bow," Rama said to Shatrugna.

"What he means to say," Lakshmana said with a smirk, "is that you are almost as good as I am."

The twins were constantly competing and finding ways to excel each other.

"Oh," Rama said, and turned to Lakshmana with mock shock. "I thought you were Shatrugna. I actually meant to compliment you, Lakshmana. I got mixed up."

Lakshmana grimaced. "If Father said that, I might have believed it."

"What Rama means to say," Shatrugna said, "is that you should not be proud when you are better than others." Shatrugna punched Lakshmana lightly on the arm.

Lakshmana made another grimace, this time directly at his twin. "Where is Bharata?"

"How should I know?"

"You always know where he is."

"That's true," Rama chimed in.

"Vasishta called him, actually," Shatrugna confessed.

"See! You *did* know," Lakshmana teased.

"Vasishta?" Rama asked. "What did he want?"

The great preceptor had never sought them out after their school hours.

"I wasn't paying attention. He wanted to speak to Bharata alone. He kind of shooed me away, which was strange. But it was something about the prison."

"Why would Vasishta ask Bharata about the prison?" Rama was really puzzled now.

"That's what Bharata wondered as they walked away together. I think they went to speak with Father."

"That makes sense," Rama concluded. He moved away from the balcony and started strapping his bow and sword on. He wasn't required to wear weapons, like Father was, but he was ten now, and it felt right.

"Where are you going?" Lakshmana demanded.

The twins surrounded Rama, watching him don his bow and quiver.

"I want to find Father. I have a strange feeling about what you told me."

Lakshmana's expression turned serious. "Father says to trust those feelings when you get them."

"Yes," Rama agreed. "Are you coming with me?"

As the three boys walked out of Rama's rooms, their guards closed in on them, following their steps. Dusk had started setting in. Rama felt an unusual alarm in his body; it was true what Lakshmana said. Father had instructed them to listen to those instincts. Something wasn't right this evening. To Rama's relief, they spotted Vasishta coming out of Father's apartment.

"What has happened?" Rama asked, looking eagerly at their teacher. "Shatrugna says you were asking about the prison?"

When he bowed to touch Vasishta's feet, as he always did, the old sage flinched and almost moved his feet away. Rama hesitated and looked up at the preceptor at the same moment as his hand made contact with the old man's feet.

A shocking electric current ran up through Rama's fingers, yet more alarming was the meeting of their eyes. Vasishta was furious! Rama had never seen him so mad. His eyes were unrecognizable. Rama felt he was looking at another person entirely. Shocked, the boy snatched his hand away, and Vasishta hurried off without a word.

"What was wrong with him?" Lakshmana asked, looking at Vasishta's disappearing figure.

"You noticed it too?" Rama said. He lightly rubbed his fingertips.

"He's been strange all day," Shatrugna said.

Bharata appeared in the doorway, grinning. "There you all are. Father thought he heard your voices. Come in."

Father was sitting on his throne. Although it wasn't as large and decorated as the one in the court hall, it still had room for several people.

"Rama, my brave boy!" Father said, pulling Rama onto his lap. Usually Rama felt too big to sit on Father's lap anymore, but today he slung his arm around Father's shoulder and pulled Lakshmana onto Father's other knee.

"Something strange is happening," he said, letting the dismay show on his face.

"What is it, Rama?" Father grew serious at once.

Rama felt his father's trust and concern surround him as strong as an embrace. It almost made his alarm abate.

"What did Vasishta want?" he asked. "If you are allowed to tell us . . ." Sometimes there were secrets that Father was not allowed to tell anyone. Vasishta knew most of them too.

"I am not sure what the holy one wanted," Father replied. "He already knows the answers to the questions he posed."

"What questions?" Rama persisted.

"He wanted to know if we had moved the blood-drinker to another location. Of course not, I told him. We would not have done such a thing without his express permission. Only the sun cell is strong enough to hold one of his kind."

Father looked into Rama's eyes and stiffened, concern rising in his eyes.

"Oh, and you know," Bharata offered, "he quizzed me about how to extinguish the four fires in the sun cell. He pretended like it was impossible, but I wasn't fooled. I told him that as long as the fire at the golden altar burns, the smaller ones will burn too. He was pleased with my answer."

"Father!" Rama's voice was urgent. Dasharatha stood up. Rama and Lakshmana slid off his lap, onto their feet.

"Something was really wrong with Vasishta," Rama said, "when he met my eye. Like he was in a rage."

Father turned to Sumantra. "Summon Vasishta at once. Send a swift runner to the golden altars. Double the guards there."

"Yes, Great King." Sumantra hurried out.

"I am greatly puzzled," Father said, pacing back and forth. "Vasishta did behave rather strangely, avoiding looking at me directly. I assumed he was in a hurry. Perhaps I have offended him without knowing."

As they waited for Vasishta to return, Rama told Father about the wild look in Vasishta's eyes.

"He should have been here by now," Lakshmana observed. "He can't have gone that far."

Father nodded. He called another attendant to his side. "Send my messengers out to every place Vasishta usually visits. Tell the respected preceptor that the king needs his presence at once."

"As you say, Great King."

"Alert the commander in chief. Tell him to have the prison inspected. Especially the sun cell."

The attendant bowed and left. Just then, Vasishta entered, bright and glowing, his long white beard majestic as a lion's mane.

"You called for me, Great King?"

He smiled at Rama and the other boys. Rama studied him with a frown.

"Now that I see you before me, I'm sure it's all a mistake," Dasharatha said, smiling in turn. "My sons were puzzled by your recent questions about the blood-drinker." The king was almost apologetic.

Vasishta, the eldest person in Ayodhya, had served many kings of the Sun dynasty before Dasharatha was even born. Rama knew that Father didn't summon him lightly. Had they made a mistake? Was Rama's gut feeling wrong?

"What do you mean?" the preceptor asked. His puzzled expression was becoming the recurring mood of the evening. "Questions about the blood-drinker?"

"You were here about half an hour ago, asking me about the sun cell and the prisoner," Dasharatha clarified. There was an edge in his voice. Father was turning into the king, Rama could tell.

"On the contrary, Great King," Vasishta said, now completely grave. "You summoned me from my evening offerings, which were interrupted midway. I have not seen you since this morning when our meeting was adjourned, nor have I made any inquiries whatsoever."

Sumantra came running in. Rama had never seen him like this. "The fire has been extinguished!"

Father went into action. "Holy one, proceed to the Golden Altars, light the fire without delay. Sumantra, make sure the queens retreat to their inner quarters. Inform their guards to stay close. Bring my chariot!"

Father immediately swept out of the room, ordering Sumantra and the princes to follow. Rama's alarm was now the only thing he felt. If Father and Vasishta and Sumantra were behaving like this, something was very wrong in Ayodhya.

Rama heard Father calling for his chariot: "Make haste!"

A strange conviction began to grow within Rama. He felt his brothers hover around him like question marks. Rama hurried to his father, who was barking out orders and marching away, as if into a battle. His manner was urgent, more urgent than Rama had ever seen before. So Rama spoke fast, as fast as he could. "Father, the Vasishta I met earlier was an impersonator. Even though he looked exactly like Vasishta, his eyes were not Vasishta's eyes."

Father nodded and then called out, "Guards, protect my sons with your life. I'm going to the prison."

He jumped into his chariot, taking the reins in his hands himself. He didn't even wait for the charioteer to arrive. It was a moment of true urgency. As the horses started moving, Father turned and said, "Rama, come with me."

Rama ran forward and jumped onto the chariot.

"What about us?" Bharata called out.

But Father made no response. They were already out of hearing distance. Rama tightened his belt and made sure the string on his bow was taut. Somehow he felt Father had allowed him to come because he was armed, whereas his brothers were not. Rama could say this to his brothers to make them feel better.

As the horses flew along the streets to the prison, the wind whipped against Rama's face. This is what it meant to respond to a crisis. Rama held on to the side of the chariot and watched everything his father did. Then Father handed Rama the reins, even though he had not yet learned how to drive a chariot. Though the chariot moved at great speed and lurched from time to time, Dasharatha moved comfortably within it, replacing his crown with a helmet, putting on his armor, and strapping on his sword and shield.

Father stood at Rama's side once armed. He did not take back the reins of the chariot. "As a king, you must always be ready. Ready to fight. To protect. Never ask someone to give their life if you are not prepared to give yours."

Rama did not have to nod. His attention told Father how completely he absorbed the words. "But listen, Rama. If an attack is under way, I order you to stand aside. Let the guards protect you. That is what they are here for. Understand?"

Rama nodded this time. But he was glad his father had not extracted a promise from him. Rama felt how his weapons were alive, as if they had a gut instinct of their own. They knew something was happening.

The prison ground greeted them with its usual silence. Nothing looked out of place here. The sounds of the horses' hooves and neighs filled the air. Several other chariots came to a halt beside the king's. Dasharatha jumped off the chariot. He did not take Rama's hand or treat Rama as a boy.

The prison master came rushing out. "Great King! I was not expecting a visit."

Dasharatha did not stop to explain but hurried toward the sun cell. The prison master fell into step by the king's side.

"Has Vasishta been here?" the king demanded. Rama noticed the change in his father's voice, how it had become sharp and strong.

"Not since last month, when he came for a call with a sick prisoner."

"Good. Then we might not be too late."

As they hurried down the dark corridor, Father urgently briefed the prison master on what had occurred. Meanwhile, Rama kept pace with his father and noticed all the same things about the prison as last time he had been here: the lack of all he loved, the absence of time and life. Now, as then, he was headed for the sun cell, where the one and only blood-drinker sat in heavy chains, exposed daily to the sunlight he so hated. Maybe the blood-drinker deserved to escape after so many human lifetimes in the sun cell? Rama did not share this thought with anyone around him. Certainly not Father. He knew how diligently Father worked to keep Ayodhya safe.

They arrived at the sun cell. It was a terrible sight. The fires were dead, the walls sprayed with blood. Four guards lay beheaded by the fire pits, their blood still dripping onto the ashes. The chains lay in heaps on the ground. Marichi was gone.

"Call for maximum security!" the king roared. "Alert all the sentries to spread out within the city. Inform every citizen to lock their doors and windows. Tonight we are at war."

Rama pressed his face against the bars while Father gave orders. After a few moments, he ventured into the cell. There was something strange in the middle of the cell, where Marichi had sat for countless years. Rama placed his feet carefully; the floor was slippery. Not only blood but urine had been used to slake the fires. The stench was strong. Rama quickly glanced at the gruesome severed heads.

Then he lifted the heavy chains. Beneath them, the stone was etched with mantras, all in praise of Shiva and his snakes. Rama's hair stood on end as he read verse after verse. The poet was not Marichi but Ravana himself, for each verse ended with the phrase, "With each of my ten heads, I bow to the snakes that adorn you."

Rama whispered the last line out loud and felt something come alive in his hand. He looked down to see that he was still holding the chain, but it was moving in his hand, as if it was a snake. He recalled then that the chains were sentient, a gift from Vasuki, king of the snakes. The chains grew more snakelike and aggressive. Alarmed, Rama looked at Father, who was pointing fingers here and there, directing the men what to do. Rama wanted to drop the chain and be free, but that's exactly what the chain wanted him to do, so he resisted the urge and clutched the metal tighter. It hissed in anger, and Rama did not know what to do.

Just then, the last rays of the sun reached Rama, giving him strength, reaching into his arms and fingers. The enchanted chain-snakes struggled one last time and then melted in Rama's hand, falling into two separate pieces on the ground. Rama stared at them a few seconds, and then looked up to see if Father had noticed. He hadn't. The sun had come to Rama's aid, helping him quell the darkness that infused the chains. *I'm strong,* Rama realized, *stronger than I know.* He was stronger than the magic invoked by Ravana's mantras.

With this knowledge, he turned to his father, the king. "Father, what can I do? I want to help."

"Rama, you are too young. There is nothing you can do. When you become king, it will be your turn. Don't be too eager to join the darkness." Father's words were final. "We are doing everything in our power to contain this situation." Father turned away. "Go, now. Your guards will take you home."

Rama didn't want to be sent home like a child. In a moment of defiance that was more like Lakshmana, he kicked the chain on the prison floor. Then he did as Father commanded. Night was fast approaching. The king himself would join forces with the soldiers who would search and protect the city.

"Father," Rama said, squeezing his father's hand tightly. The king's look warned Rama that he would not entertain Rama's insistence. Instead, Rama said, "Don't hide the truth from me. I want to know what happens tonight."

Father's eyes grew hard.

"Promise me," Rama said. "I need to know."

"I promise," Father said, and then all but pushed his son away.

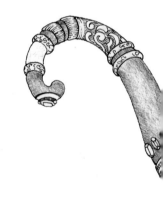

Rama quietly left. When he stepped out, he felt like a prisoner set free. The expansive sky greeted him like an old friend. Rama took deep breaths and felt that he was becoming himself again. When he had stood in the sun cell with the chains in his hands, he had felt a chilling darkness seep into his being. Now the wind blew in his hair, prickling his skin. The sun had disappeared, but Rama could feel it beyond the horizon, shining brightly in another place.

He climbed into Father's chariot, escorted by several guards, and returned to the palace. Rama had never felt so worried about everyone's safety. Having overheard Father's orders that the guards be doubled, Rama knew his brothers and mothers would be safe. He was not as certain about the rest of the citizens in Ayodhya. Who would survive the night with a blood-drinker on the loose? The privilege of his position weighed on Rama. He would have felt much better if he had been allowed to be a protector, marching through the streets with the other soldiers. Lakshmana would laugh at that, Rama realized. And it made him feel better. He could see himself: a ten-year-old little soldier, no match at all

for the blood-drinker prisoner or his accomplice, the one who had fooled them all and set the prisoner free.

But Rama would become a warrior who could protect Ayodhya. A warrior who would create fear in such beings and keep them in the shadows.

Rama looked with great care at everyone around him. The charioteer urging the horses onward. The guards at his sides. If the blood-drinkers could take any shape, how could you trust anyone? That was the most frightening question to Rama.

Arriving back at Father's, Rama got off his father's chariot less enthusiastically than he had jumped on. His brothers were there, waiting for his and Father's return.

"Where is Father?"

"What is happening?"

"Are we at war?"

Rama would have bombarded them with questions had he been left out.

"He escaped," Rama answered simply. "The blood-drinker is gone."

He told his brother that Vasishta had not been Vasishta at all, but an impersonator. The same one who had snuck his way into the prison, setting Ayodhya's oldest prisoner free. No one knew yet how it had been done, but the fact that he had taken Vasishta's form was the biggest clue. Bharata's dismay was greatest. He had talked to the impersonator for the longest time.

"Father is out there with the guards and soldiers," Rama concluded. "They are treating the city as if it's under attack, which it is. Remember Father's lesson from years ago? About how the most dangerous enemy is the blood-drinker because they hide in the shadows, striking when least expected."

His brothers' questions thinned out as a feeling of gloom and danger loomed around them.

"*We* of course are safe," Rama said rather fiercely. He pointed his thumb toward his chest, and it thudded against his breastplate.

"You are mad about that," Lakshmana observed.

"I wish there was something I could do!"

"But we're just boys." Bharata sounded like he was apologizing.

"They'll eat you up in a second!" Lakshmana said, his eyes large.

Rama smiled then, since he had known Lakshmana would say something like that. It was true, of course. And Father was right. The most helpful thing Rama could do was stay out of the way.

A guard approached them. "The king has ordered everyone, especially the princes, to be inside as night engulfs us."

The boys had been talking on the steps of the palace and were ushered inside.

As they parted ways to go to their own rooms, Rama caught hold of Lakshmana. "Will you stay with me, like we did when we were small?"

"Of course," Lakshmana said, without asking any questions.

With Lakshmana sleeping by his side, Rama felt they could laugh in danger's face. Still, all night he dreamed of people he knew turning into blood-drinkers with pointy teeth. Every time the blood-drinkers came close to Rama, the sun would become really large behind Rama. The blood-drinkers cringed, retreating to the shadows.

That's what he remembered when he woke up to his father's hands shaking him. True to his promise, Dasharatha called Rama to hear the morning's report with him. Rama got up quietly, without waking Lakshmana. Father looked tired. He hadn't slept at all, Rama guessed.

As soon as they entered the small council room, Dasharatha faced the commander of the army. "How many?"

Father glanced quickly at Rama. *I'm not too young*, Rama wanted to assure Father. He wanted to know. He needed to know what blood-drinkers were truly capable of. Protecting him was one thing; keeping him and his brothers in the dark was another. Rama planned to tell his brothers exactly everything that he learned about in the report.

"The worst fatalities occurred in the vicinity of the prison," the commander said. He looked exhausted too. "In the prison itself, four guards. In the houses closest to the prison, two families were attacked, including the children. Four adults and seven children. All drained of blood and dead. After that, the pursued got scared. Cautious, at any rate. Several lone people here and there, until the trail ends beyond the city gate."

"How many?" the king repeated.

The commander sighed. These were not expected war casualties but innocent citizens. How old had the children been? Who would attack innocent children?

"Seven children. Nine civilians. Three guards. Nineteen in total, Great King."

Dasharatha sat down. Rama's heart compressed, seeing the defeat on his father's face. A moment later, the king was on his feet, his face neutral. "This was the biggest security breach in all my time as king," he said. "The impersonator was close to all my sons and to me. We could all be dead. We are lucky that he had his eyes on rescuing his friend."

"Yes, Great King."

"We need to understand exactly how this happened and prevent it from occurring ever again. The Earth will never be safe," Dasharatha said in anger, "until Ravana and every single one of his blood-drinkers have been exterminated."

No one said anything. There seemed to be nothing to say to soften that truth. Dasharatha looked at Rama again. "We will continue this discussion once Vasishta is here. He knows the most about the wards around Ayodhya. I thought no blood-drinker or enemy could walk through them." The king named several others whose presence was required at the meeting. "I will return my son to his room."

As Dasharatha walked out with his arm around Rama's shoulders, he turned to his son. "How did you know, Rama, that it wasn't Vasishta? He had the rest of us fooled."

There it was: Bharata's apology, but in Father's voice.

"His eyes," Rama said at once. "His eyes were nothing like Vasishta's. He couldn't hide his real eyes. They looked wild and dangerous."

"He must have known it too," Father said, sounding mollified. "That's why he refused to look me in the eye. I did not insist on looking into his, thinking he was perhaps preoccupied with his own affairs. That was my mistake. Look what it cost us. Nineteen lives. And that vile blood-drinker Marichi is out in the world again. Creatures of that nature don't deserve freedom."

"Father . . ." Rama gathered his thoughts. "If blood-drinkers can take any shape, is looking into their eyes enough? What if you don't get close enough to really see their eyes? The pretender Vasishta was a flawless imitation."

Father took a deep breath. "I'm calling all our best sources together," he said. "I will find the answer to this question."

Rama was stunned when he realized that Father did not know the answer. This meant that he couldn't blindly rely on his father's judgment. He had to rely on his own.

Arriving at Rama's rooms, the king turned away, returning to his duties. Lakshmana was still sleeping, but Rama found no solace in the idea of sleep and the oblivion it would bring. Father blamed himself for the deaths in the city, Rama could see it. He couldn't think what to say to appease his father. Was that burden the price you paid to be king? Seven Ayodhyan children were dead. Rama could have been one of them had he not been a prince.

Lakshmana stirred and opened his sleepy eyes, looking at Rama who was fully dressed and sitting on the edge of the bed. "Where have you been?"

Rama told him everything. Lakshmana sat up, his eyes and hair wild.

"One day, I won't be just ten anymore," Rama said. "Then I will avenge their deaths."

"And I will help you," Lakshmana said, putting his hands on his hips. "We'll hunt them all the way to the land of Yama."

Rama sat up straighter. He took his brother's words seriously. Lakshmana would help him. Together they would be very, very strong. They would have to be. Just a prayer by Ravana had the power to influence snakelike chains. Ravana's power was all around them, and Marichi had managed to escape because of it. Rama had a feeling that he had just encountered his true archenemy.

CHAPTER 30

Bharata's Resolution

In the weeks that followed, Rama couldn't stop himself from looking carefully at every person who crossed his path. He had to be sure it was not a stranger in guise of a known person, or more precisely said, a blood-drinker impostor. As he looked in earnest this way and that, Rama made another discovery altogether. He couldn't help but notice how startled many people were by his solemn gaze; one person would shy away, another would open and blossom. Rama was fascinated by this discovery; his eyes were powerful. The eyes of others held power too, and sometimes secrets. Father encouraged him to keep looking in this new way, but also to emanate kindness and compassion, for even the most honest person might shy away from an intrusive gaze.

Even if Rama hadn't been observing everyone around him closely, he would have noticed that Bharata was not himself. He was acting like usual, smiling, joking with them, going on walks with Shatrugna, doing everything expected of him. But he did not *feel* happy. And in their last test with Vasishta, Bharata had answered many questions wrong. That was not like him. Rama was not the only one to notice this, of course. Especially around Vasishta, Bharata became almost sullen, certainly withdrawn. Rama scrutinized Vasishta with extra care too, relieved to see his teacher's patient eyes looking back at him.

Their schooling continued, now focused on all there was to know about blood-drinkers. The lessons took place in the royal library, a place full of scrolls, maps, and books with the strangest scripts. It was by far the most fascinating room in the whole palace. The princes kept searching for secret trapdoors. There had to be one behind a book or painting somewhere. Vasishta always sat on a simple grass mat, while the princes were allowed to choose their own seats. There were pillows and plush seats, but it wasn't seemly to sit above your teacher, so the princes sat on the floor too. After Bharata's poor performance on the test, Vasishta called the boys close, asking them to sit cross-legged next to him.

"The teacher-student relationship is wholly dependent on trust. I can see that it's lacking between us now, though it's not the fault of anyone present. Let us make a secret password that only we know. I will whisper it into your ear. You may not share it with anyone, not even your brothers."

He leaned toward Bharata first, whispering into his ear. Bharata's eyes lit up; he liked his secret word.

When it was Rama's turn, Vasishta whispered, "Vishnu."

Rama had always been drawn to Vishnu's legends; he liked his password too.

"If you ever suspect that I am not myself, ask me to whisper the secret word into your ear," Vasishta concluded.

"Or run for your weapons as fast as you can," Lakshmana suggested.

"I'm afraid that they run a lot faster than you do," Vasishta replied.

"Not faster than an arrow," Rama said.

Vasishta smiled. "Perhaps you are right. But I assure you that you will not meet another blood-drinker within Ayodhya's walls. We have reinforced the protection around the parameters of the city. And by this I mean the magic wards set in place by mantra. These vibrations are stronger than any gross matter can be. They automatically repel blood-drinkers and any other creature harboring evil intent. No outsider can ever breach it. Hence, Ayodhya's name, 'the Indestructible.' We are protected."

"Then how did the blood-drinker disguised as you find his way in?" Rama asked.

"This was the question we all asked after the event. It should not have been possible. After carefully searching the parameters with my mind, I found one weak spot in the vibrations on the south side of Ayodhya. Only someone extremely tiny and terribly perceptive could have found his way in. We believe now that this weak spot was created before any of you were born, in a tragic incident when two children were murdered beyond Ayodhya's walls. When the grieving father brought their bodies to me, hoping I would save them, he also unwittingly brought with him the powerful taint of the one who murdered his children."

Rama held his breath, noticing his brothers did too.

"We believe it was Ravana himself," Vasishta revealed. "Your father saw a phantom spirit of Ravana in the place where the children were found dead. Your father can give you a first-hand account of those events. We never suspected, however, that it would lead to this. The impostor who took advantage of this nearly imperceptible weakness in our wards had to be very powerful too. We already know the pretender possessed extraordinary skills, shape-shifting through many forms, and fooling everyone within Ayodhya."

"Rama wasn't fooled," Bharata interjected.

"Rama was quick to recognize something was wrong, yes. I'm sure he will be even faster the next time he sees a shape-shifter in action," Vasishta said. "But the impersonator achieved his goal and is running free with Ayodhya's former prisoner. That would not have happened if I, or any of the priests, saw him. He chose you, Bharata, because he knew that as a prince, you would know more than most grown men. And yet you are still a child. You do not have the faculties of a grown man yet. The blood-drinker knew this. His choice to approach you to extract the information he needed was a calculated move. Even if you were fully grown, however, he may have fooled you. Warriors like you are trained as masters in the physical realms. By necessity, they are not attuned to these subtle forces. I, as a priest, can see someone's true skin under their disguise, be it physical or emotional. But that is a power that few possess."

Bharata looked at Rama again, but said nothing this time.

"But how did the impostor know about the weakening in the protective ward?" Rama asked. "What if it was Ravana himself?"

Vasishta chuckled softly. "I know this incident may seem like a great adventure to you boys. But I'm afraid that Ravana is roused into action only if there is a beautiful woman in the picture."

Rama frowned, and Lakshmana did too. What did girls have to do with it?

Vasishta chuckled some more. "When you're grown, you might come to understand this. But to answer your question, Rama. I traced dark words to Marichi's cell. After millennia as a prisoner, he learned about the wards somehow, and with magic of his own, he spent years sending sound barbs against it, weakening it just enough to let his friend slip in and set him free."

"How did they escape from the wards on their way out?"

"This has never happened before, as I said. The protective spell was built as a shield. It only prevented enemies from entering. Once inside, there was nothing in place to stop them. I have made changes to it. Now it works more like a magnetic field that irresistibly pulls inimical beings to it. The next time a blood-drinker gets close to Ayodhya, he or she will be pulled into the magnetic vibration and find no way to escape."

"The next time we have a blood-drinker prisoner," Lakshmana said, "we should surround his cell and the whole prison with those mantras."

"With every spell there is in the whole world," Shatrugna said.

Vasishta nodded, but said, "Indefinite imprisonment is not an advisable punishment. I advised your father, and his father before him, to slay the prisoner. Blood-drinkers are vengeful by nature. Keeping one of them imprisoned so long could only pave the path toward sure vengeance. Now that Marichi is on the loose, I'm afraid we can expect that he will find a way to have his revenge."

"I will send my arrow into his heart," Rama warned. This was his promise to the Ayodhyans who had been killed.

"I'm afraid a blood-drinker's revenge is not like a warrior's revenge, Prince Rama," their teacher said. "You will not see it coming until it's too late. They don't extract their vengeance in blood, as you would do, but in suffering and terror. That is their pleasure."

Thereafter, they were taught everything that Ayodhya knew about blood-drinkers: their abilities, their magic, and the ways in which humans had protected themselves from them. The princes learned that there were different gradients of blood-drinkers. Some were night stalkers and could come out only at night. These creatures, also called night crawlers, lived in holes below the Earth or in caves. Their eyes were light pink and functioned only in darkness. Even moonlight hurt them. Their skin was whiter than white, so translucent that all their veins and organs were visible through the skin. The sun weakened them, and in this sense, they were the natural enemies of the Sun dynasty. Others were day walkers but needed blood to live. A common feature of the day walkers was their deformities, for they had refused to die when their bodies wanted to. They had spawned a species that were distinctive for their hideous forms, having extra limbs, eyes in their necks—if they had necks. Vasishta described at least ten different forms: some had animal heads, others many arms, or a gaping mouth on their stomach. He concluded by saying that not even imagination could encompass the vast variety of deformed creatures.

"Is that why we shun human beings who are deformed?" Rama asked. "Because they might be related to blood-drinkers?"

"That is very good thinking on your part, Rama," Vasishta answered. "I wish you were right, that the reasons were as simple as that."

The princes looked at one another. Things were *never* simple, they'd learned.

Vasishta looked to the sky, so the boys knew it was complex even for Vasishta.

"Rama has brought us to another topic," Vasishta finally said. "First, I want to inform you that not every society on Earth shuns those with physical imperfections. Kekaya is an example of that. Your grandfather, Bharata, has been a pioneer in protecting the deformed. Making Manthara, a hunchback, the caretaker of the princess, is an example of that."

Lakshmana made a face at this, but ducked behind Shatrugna so only Rama might see it. Manthara was the most evil person Rama and Lakshmana knew. Of course, she doted on Bharata and Shatrugna. But that made her enmity all the more apparent, since it was so selective.

"But Ashvapati is not the first and only to speak up on this," Vasishta said as though he hadn't noticed Lakshmana's gesture. Rama was sure he had, since Vasishta knew everything and more. "Remember that our standard, and by that I mean Ayodhya's standard, is subjective. A horse has its standards and a lion another."

"Who decides what the standard is, then?" Shatrugna asked, followed by Rama, who asked, "Isn't it unfair to make someone inauspicious because of the body they are born in?"

Vasishta smiled. "We will spend only a few more minutes on this. Then we must return to the topic at hand: blood-drinkers. Shatrugna, in one sense, it's the king who decides, but he is also the spokesperson and decision maker of his people. I'm afraid that from the beginning of time, the practice has been of shunning. Some tribes sacrifice the child at birth if any of its limbs are deformed.

"And Rama, you are right. It is unfair. In a karmic sense, the soul has attracted the right body for its present life. He or she is living with the consequences of previous deeds. Humans would do the crippled a kindness by treating them with compassion and dignity. But that is not the way of humankind."

Vasishta firmly returned them to the topic at hand. Rama found that he preferred the blood-drinker topic. The other one left a bad feeling in the pit of his belly. It was all the more confusing to him because Manthara, the one deformed person he knew, was really mean. He didn't think one led to the other, but in Manthara's case it had.

Rama focused on Vasishta's voice. Marichi had been one of the more advanced kinds; he had not been visibly reduced by his years without blood and exposed to the sun. Marichi had shown uncommon patience and strategy. He had never displayed his powers. The highest among them were kin to the gods themselves and lived as long as the gods, immortal compared to a short human life. They were master magicians and so beautiful that people of all races fell under their spell. There had even been a race of humans who had offered themselves as blood slaves to the topmost blood-drinkers, considering it an honor to sacrifice their blood.

The princes were fascinated.

"What all the blood-drinkers have in common is their fangs," Shatrugna said.

"Yes, but fangs in different sizes," Lakshmana said.

"If they hide in another body," Rama said, "you wouldn't be able to see their fangs."

Bharata said nothing. He had spoken very little throughout the day.

As the sun began to set, Vasishta stood and said, "Enough for today. We will continue tomorrow."

The princes stood up and touched Vasishta's feet, thanking him for the day's lessons. As soon as Vasishta had gone, Bharata left them without a word. Rama and the twins stopped speaking.

"Bharata!" Shatrugna called.

"He wants to be alone," Rama said, catching Shatrugna's hand.

Shatrugna continued looking at the empty doorway. "But what happened?" he asked. "He left without warning."

"What if he is ill?" Lakshmana asked.

"Yes, we'd better go see," Shatrugna said. "Or tell Mother."

The three of them hurried from the hall.

Rama had another feeling about Bharata's sudden departure. Since Marichi's escape, Rama had been furtively watching Bharata. If his brother was sick, he had been so for days. The brothers found Bharata in his room, standing by the window. When Bharata heard them enter, he quickly went to the bed trying to avoid them.

"Are you sick?" Shatrugna asked, reaching to touch Bharata's forehead, as their mothers would have done.

"Maybe," Bharata said. He didn't look at any of them.

"I'm going to get Mother," Shatrugna said, even though Bharata said, "Don't!"

Rama and Lakshmana sat down on each side of Bharata's bed.

"I don't think you are sick," Rama said softly.

Bharata pulled his legs to his chest, clasping his arms around them, and put his forehead on his knees. "I wish I could hide from you." His words were muffled.

"Are you angry with me, then?" Rama said. His throat became tight.

"Nooo," Bharata moaned. "I'm angry with . . . myself."

"Why?" Rama dared to move closer to his brother. Lakshmana stayed on the edge of the bed.

Bharata was quiet for a long moment, and then he burst out with the words: "Because I can't be like you!"

Rama and Lakshmana looked at each other.

"What do you mean?" Lakshmana asked, moving closer too.

"Rama could tell right away that it was a blood-drinker. But I couldn't!"

"Father couldn't tell either," Lakshmana said. "And neither could Shatrugna."

Bharata lifted his head and looked up at them. His eyes were reddish. He had been crying. "But I talked to him the longest." He hid his face again.

"Bharata," Rama said, though he was unsure what to say next. Bharata's disappointment in himself had been growing for days and days. Now Rama understood what had been wrong with his brother. But understanding and knowing what to do were not the same.

"Whenever I visit my grandfather," Bharata said, "he tells me that I will be king of Ayodhya when Father is no more."

Lakshmana blew air through his mouth. Rama exhaled. He didn't want to think of a time when Father would not be.

Echoing his grandfather's terse voice, Bharata said, "You have all the qualities and characteristics of a king."

Lakshmana smiled a little.

Bharata pronounced, "And you were born to be king." This time Manthara's shrill message had come through. Then Bharata exclaimed, "But I don't want to be king!"

"Because you made this mistake?" Rama asked. And thought: *Do I want to be king?*

"I'm not like you, brother," Bharata said.

Rama and Bharata faced each other. Rama saw no anger in his brother's eyes. It was simply a statement of the truth.

"Of course you aren't. You are like you."

Bharata smiled then, but forced himself to get serious again. "I mean it, Rama. I stopped comparing myself with you ages ago. I compete with you and the twins for fun, not because I ever think I can win against you."

"You win sometimes," Rama objected.

"But never when it matters," Bharata observed. "It's not your fault. It's because you are you. And I want to be like you, Rama. But I cannot. Because I'm Bharata. And I want you to be king after Father."

"Father is not going anywhere," Rama insisted. "We don't have to think about who will be king as long as Father is king."

"Other people are thinking about it," Bharata said, a dark frown creasing his brow.

Rama immediately thought of Manthara. And of course, Bharata had said his grandfather also willed this.

Rama hesitated, and then said, "I'm not sure if I want to be king either."

This time Bharata and Lakshmana looked at each other. Lakshmana got a challenging look in his eyes.

"What?" Rama asked.

"If you don't want to be king," Lakshmana said, "then I don't want to be Lakshmana." Rama shook his head.

Bharata nodded. "That's right. *Rama* means king."

Of course it didn't. But Bharata looked happier, as if he was not angry with himself anymore.

"Does this mean that you are not sick?" Rama asked.

Bharata opened his arms wide and stretched his legs out, and just then Shatrugna hurried inside with Kaikeyi in his wake.

"Are you not well, my son?" she asked. She put her arm around Rama as she sat down, reaching forward to touch Bharata's forehead.

"I'm fine now," Bharata said. He drew away from his mother, which negated his words, for usually he welcomed and sought his mother's touch. Bharata took a deep breath, and then said, "We have decided that Rama will be king after Father."

Kaikeyi withdrew her hand. Manthara appeared in the doorway. Bharata shrank a bit, but did not amend his words. Kaikeyi looked at each of them.

"What are you boys cooking up here?" she asked. "Why are you talking of such things? Those are decisions for grown men."

"And women!" Manthara added.

Rama did not have to look at her to know that she was furious. But she often was—at least when Rama was around. Rama stood up, keeping a distance from Manthara, though he glanced at her with a cautious smile. She glared at him, lips turned down.

"We have examined our brother and found him to be in full health," Rama said, as if he was the royal physician. "But, as you say, Mother, what do we know of such things? We will leave it to you."

Rama smiled as big as he could to Bharata, to show him that they were on the same side.

"Come, Lakshmana. See you tomorrow, Bharata." Rama bowed his head slightly.

They all knew that Shatrugna would stay with Bharata. Rama and Lakshmana bid everyone in the room farewell and left. Rama heard the thump of Manthara's cane pursue him, but she did not call for him and he did not stop to inquire what she wanted. No kind or true words had ever come to him from Manthara.

CHAPTER 31

Shiva's Bow

Rama woke up with a start. He sat up in the bed, calming his breath. Even though Rama had not seen Kashi for seven years, the dream of Shiva's bow still haunted him. Rama was fourteen, but the dream had not changed much over the years. Kashi always picked up the bow, sprouted countless heads, and aimed the weapon at Rama, who was unable to stop his enemy. It left Rama with a terribly impotent feeling, as if he was destined to lose what mattered most to him.

In the four years since Marichi had escaped, Rama had not encountered another blood-drinker, but the vision of the blood-drenched cell was clear in his mind. He was never again able to trust in the apparent safety and serenity of Ayodhya. He knew Marichi was out there. Kashi was out there. Both of those enemies were minor compared to the larger threat, the source of evil. Like Death coming eventually for them all, Rama could feel Ravana's presence, a darkness that tainted even the rays of the sun. Rama could feel the polar opposites engaging in a constant battle for dominance. It was within him and every embodied being. His mother, the Great Queen, had only momentary surges of the dark light, while Manthara's flames produced smoke and ashes alone. Within Ayodhya, Manthara was Rama's only opponent, even though the enmity was entirely one sided. The hunchback sought every opportunity to be nasty to Rama. In a way, Rama welcomed it, for she taught him how to interact with inimical forces.

As the sun began to rise, Rama looked at the side of the bed where Lakshmana used to sleep when they were younger. Since they turned ten, the brothers had started sleeping separately. Even after four years, Rama missed having his brother close by. The elders around them insisted that the brothers needed to prepare for adult life. What they truly meant was married life. Soon Rama's wife would be taking Lakshmana's place. For that is how Rama thought of the space next to him. Lakshmana had always been by his side, from time out of mind. Bharata said the same thing about Shatrugna. As for his future bride, Rama did not yet desire one, nor did he return the long looks of some of the girls in the palace. Rama knew his father would arrange the right wife at the right time. That was how it had always been done. The time for marriage was coming closer, for most princes married between fifteen and eighteen.

One of Rama's attendants stepped forward with a silver cup. Rama drank the cool water gratefully and began reciting hymns to fortify his mind. The prince accepted the servant's assistance as he bathed and dressed. They tied the sash around his waist, combed his long locks, and decorated his ears, neck, and wrists with his golden jewels. As Rama waited for them to finish, he played with his signet ring. He could feel the outline of letters that spelled his name when he pressed his fingers onto the ring. Every royal person had a ring like this, something that would prove their identity if they were ever lost in an obscure place. It was a possibility that seemed very distant to Rama. In Ayodhya, everyone knew him, especially because of his greenish skin. And yet, even here, wasn't it possible that Bharata could be mistaken for Rama? Rama and his brothers kept their signet rings on at all times, and every few years their rings were adjusted to keep pace with their growth.

When the servants were done, Rama nodded in thanks and left his quarters for the golden altars. It was a pleasing walk, giving Rama a chance to greet many of the other palace residents. In these early morning hours, a simple smile and a nod were sufficient, for silence was still encouraged and everyone had their mind on prayer. It was peaceful. Rama could understand why his mother called these hours her favorite time of day. Of course, Kaikeyi laughed at that, saying that nighttime, especially late nights, was the best time. She teased the boys, telling them they would understand this once they were married. Marriage seemed to be a topic that cropped up often these days, Rama had noticed. He was nearly as tall as Father now.

Kausalya's face lit up as Rama entered the temple and touched her feet.

"May the lord's blessings be upon you," she said, as she did every morning.

Rama sat at her feet as she decorated his body with cooling sandalwood pulp and drew the markings of the sun in the center of his forehead. The sandalwood was cooling at first, but turned energizing and warm. The red pulp from the saffron flowers was red like blood in his mother's palm. Rama loved to feel his mother's affectionate hands on him. As she leaned close to him, he breathed in her familiar smell of camphor and tulsi, essential components in the temple's rituals. Before Mother sent him to pray at the shrine of his choice, she placed a garland of tulsi around his neck. Rama recognized it as the one that had adorned the deity of Vishnu the previous day. The soft dew sprinkled over the tulsi leaves had kept it fresh.

At the shrine of Vishnu, Rama glimpsed his father, bare-chested and deep in prayer. Following his father's example, Rama sat cross-legged at Shiva's shrine. As he closed his eyes, the contours of Shiva's bow appeared, but no enemy dared enter Rama's mind when he sat protected in this golden sanctuary. Rama heard his brothers come and go behind him before he opened his eyes, feeling refreshed and strong in mind. Father had also left by then.

Lakshmana was waiting outside, leaning on a pillar and conversing with friends and attendants. Lakshmana attracted many people, for he was outspoken and full of life. As soon as he saw Rama, Lakshmana pushed away from the pillar and came to greet him. It was time for their morning meal, which the four princes ate together.

On their way, Rama and Lakshmana were ambushed. That was Manthara's skill, after all. Despite being a hunchbacked old woman, she could make Rama feel as if he was under attack. Rama felt it the moment he heard the familiar sound of the cane behind them.

"A private word with you, young prince," Manthara called out in a falsely sweet voice.

From experience, Rama knew that she only sought to get past the guards.

"Say no," Lakshmana whispered into Rama's ear. "She is not supposed to be here by the altars."

Rama signaled to the guards to step away and welcomed Manthara to come close. As she did, the scent of her various ointments and medicinal poultices wafted toward Rama. He recognized the earthy jatamamsi and hoped it had produced its calming effect on Manthara. There were other less familiar smells that made Rama dizzy for a moment. Manthara was dressed in a bright purple silk garment that flowed around her in a majestic way, but made her ashen skin look all the more withered. Rama smiled warmly at her, always hoping that this time he would break through her cold veneer.

"Do you think this is a joke?" she demanded, dispelling Rama's hope and his smile.

With Lakshmana at his side, Rama said nothing. He merely looked at her steadily. Rama had no inkling what he had done to provoke her anger, but she was nearly shaking with fury. Her eyes were like spikes of flaming fire.

"I saw you, just yesterday," she said, "whispering lies into Bharata's ear."

Rama frowned.

"Bharata is going to be king," she said.

Rama should have expected this. Manthara was obsessed with this topic. Rama pulled on his brother's arm and took a step back.

"You think because you were born first," she said, "that you are special, that your claim is stronger. I see it in your arrogant walk and speech. But your claim is only by a few hours! Never forget your great father's promise to King Ashvapati. We all know how much you prize your word here in Ayodhya. I will squash you under my cane before I let you become king."

"Quiet!" Lakshmana cried.

Hearing the prince's cry, two of the guards stepped closer. Rama shook his head at them. Manthara was harmless, if slightly crazed.

Before Rama could stop Lakshmana, however, his brother stepped closer to Manthara, looking down at her. "If you threaten my brother again, I will kill you! Rama is the jewel of the Sun dynasty and he shines like the sun. Bharata doesn't even want to be king. Or does his opinion not even matter to you in your selfish quest for power?"

Manthara's hunched back heaved up and down. "I know Bharata better than you. I know what his rights are. I know what his future is. You are the ones who have a selfish quest for power. Pah!" Her jaw jutted out in defiance; her eyes burned into Lakshmana.

He did not waver. Rama considered whether to intervene, but the opponents before him were infuriated for reasons he could not understand. Rama felt mostly compassion for Manthara, despite her consistent harangues against him.

"And you, Manthara," Lakshmana said, "have no right to even address us without our permission. What you say threatens my brother and is a false claim! Or must I teach you the basic courtesies of Ayodhya?"

"I spit on those courtesies!" Manthara screamed in the voice of a hissing snake and verily spraying Lakshmana's face with spittle.

The guards took a threatening step forward. Manthara waved her cane at them, as if she was a warrior. Her breaths turned wheezy. Rama lifted his hand to guide her toward a place to sit, but stopped. She would never accept anything from him.

"If your father tries to make you king, you should decline," she said between wheezes, looking now at Rama with her features twitching. "If you want Ayodhya to be happy, give Bharata his birthright back."

Rama and Lakshmana looked at each other. The rules of kingship were quite confusing, and Manthara could be right in some measure.

"The wise, all-knowing Manthara," Lakshmana said. "Yes, we will take your advice on this. You know better than Father, his ministers, Vasishta, and all the elders. Yes, you alone see the truth."

Manthara said nothing, but held Rama's gaze even as she hobbled away. Lakshmana clenched his fists and made to pursue Manthara. His neck was splotchy and his breaths came out in big puffs.

Rama put a restraining hand on this brother's shoulder. "Let her go. You defended me better than Father could have. I didn't know you were so eloquent, my brother."

Lakshmana stood frozen in his anger. He strained against Rama's hand for a moment. Rama tightened his grip. Lakshmana could do regrettable things when his temper was ignited.

"Come, Lakshmana," he said, stepping in front of his brother, blocking his view of the receding hunchback. The brothers stood face to face.

"Don't take Manthara so seriously," Rama said. "She has a bitter soul. It's not personal toward me."

Lakshmana melted under his brother's gaze but demanded, "How dare she speak to you like that? She is the most hateful person I know. She should be punished!"

Rama smiled; he trusted that his father had control over Manthara.

"Father says Manthara has holes in her heart," Rama said. "I can see them too. Punishment would only make those holes bigger."

"I cannot tolerate standing by when she acts and speaks so hatefully, Rama."

Rama took hold of Lakshmana's hand and pulled his brother away.

"Brother," Rama said, "I think it's wise not to mention this episode to Bharata. You know how aggrieved he becomes when Manthara acts like this."

"Do you mean to say she acts in any other way?"

"She is different toward Bharata and Shatrugna."

"That witch!"

Rama gave his brother a meaningful look, and Lakshmana took a deep breath.

Before they entered the room where their brothers waited, Rama looked again at Lakshmana. Had he composed himself sufficiently?

Lakshmana nodded. His normal color was restored, and his breathing was even.

The four princes ate and spoke about their plans for the day. It was Rama and Lakshmana's day to attend Father's Court, while Bharata and Shatrugna received individual attention from Vasishta. Later, they would all meet on the training ground, Rama's favorite time of the day. He would work his whole body into a tremendous sweat with martial arts, wielding his sword and shield, spears, clubs, and finally bow and arrow. Not a day went by without practicing archery, even though Lakshmana teased him relentlessly, saying he had already won every championship on Earth. Bharata was a close second, however, and Rama promised to meet Bharata in the archery ring later that day.

Rama and Lakshmana went to Father's Great Court. The gatekeeper announced their titles as they were stepping into the most formal area of the palace. Rama waited for Father, surrounded by several of the ministers, to signal for them to enter. Though Father had a silver beard like the other elders, Rama did not think of him as old. Father was already holding a letter in his hand and had a frown etched into his forehead. He had read the missive out loud to the others already.

Eagerly, Rama accepted the letter from his father and read with eyes that flew across the scroll. Lakshmana's body radiated heat behind him as he looked over Rama's shoulder. Normally, they might have been asked to sit down first, but clearly the missive was urgent.

The letter was from Janaka of Videha. He had held a contest for his daughter's hand. The bride-price was a show of strength, namely, to lift Shiva's bow. The contest had turned sour when no one had been able to budge the bow, this ancient heirloom that once belonged to Shiva. When Kashi failed, he accused Janaka of setting an impossible test. Janaka had innocently called Princess Sita into the assembly and directed her to the bow. Sita's unparalleled beauty had made the kings stand up in their seats, ready to line up by the bow for another chance to lift it. Instead, the thirteen-year-old princess had lifted the bow with one hand. Kashi had gone mad with rage, demolishing the area where he sat with his bare hands, accusing Janaka of witchcraft, foul play, and every trickery possible to man. Kashi and the kings he had rallied now held Mithila under siege, intent on stealing the bow and the princess.

"I dreamt of this," Rama said.

His recurring dream was a small scene of what had occurred. Rama returned the letter to his father and told them the gist of his dream.

"What will you do, Father?"

"Let us discuss," Father said, motioning for Rama and Lakshmana to sit.

Dasharatha turned to the ministers, giving them an opportunity to speak.

"Great King," Sumantra said, folding his hands at his chest, "this news proves yet again that mankind is impossible to please. First they were enraged that no one could lift the bow. Then they were enraged that Princess Sita could lift it."

"Sumantra speaks rightly," Siddhartha said, his long beard moving with every word. "We, who have been observing the ways of man all our lives, know that one can never fully satiate the desire of the shifting crowds."

Rama was about to ask how the princess had been able to lift the bow, when Father handed the missive to a servant and summoned the army general.

"Give this to Senapati and bid him come here," the king said. "This uprising is something a small section of our army can easily quell."

As they waited for the commanding general, Dasharatha dictated his response to Janaka, while Rama acted as scribe. The letter assumed that the siege had been quelled and peace restored; it would be handed to Janaka once victory was achieved.

When the letter was done, Rama said, "Sita must be a very special princess if all these kings are fighting for her hand."

Father gave Rama a secretive look. "Princess Sita is the most unusual princess on Earth. She mystically appeared from the Earth, and when she was a small child, she was inexorably linked to the Great Mother. Indeed, her father was mightily puzzled by her powers. He said that when she cried, it would rain. When she was angry, fires would blaze. When she screamed, the Earth would shake under his feet."

Rama looked at the various expressions of the ministers: some were amused, others skeptical. "But then she is not a princess at all," he said, "but a goddess!"

"Janaka's concern was such," Father replied, "that I consulted Vasishta, and we sent one of his trusted pupils, the esteemed Shatananda, to observe the princess. We had to first of all corroborate the existence of this extraordinary phenomenon."

Dasharatha paused, and Rama held his breath.

"Shatananda discovered nothing unusual."

Rama exhaled and frowned, the mystery shattered.

"His reports came back to Ayodhya full of anecdotes about a princess who was highly intelligent and charming beyond words. Even Janaka told me personally that once the princess mastered language, all supernatural occurrences around her completely stopped."

"It is possible," Siddhartha said, "that the girl was guarded by the Great Mother in the first years of her life."

"Yes, that is one possibility," Dasharatha answered. "And so to your question, Rama. No doubt Princess Sita is beautiful and worthy of this fight, but the hearts of men are strange. Now they fight less for her hand and more to restore the honor they lost when they failed to lift the bow. Frankly, I would not send any of you to that contest, though she is an eligible princess. That bow belonged to Shiva, the lord of transformation. No man has ever been known to lift it."

"Then why did King Janaka," Rama asked, "set the bride-price so high?"

"If you were my daughter," Dasharatha said, "I would have picked a very, very difficult task too." Father's smile was wry. "I would want to ensure that only the most worthy could win your hand."

"I see. It's because he loves his daughter so much."

"Yes. Sometimes we can love someone so much that we become blind to reality. In this case, I fear that Janaka may have set his price too high."

"What happens if no one ever lifts the bow?"

"Sita will never marry," Dasharatha said.

The melancholy song from Rama's dream drifted into his mind. "What happens if Kashi conquers the bow and becomes invincible?"

"Idle threats," Father said, clenching his jaw. "You were only seven when he made that claim, too young to realize how empty those words were. Kashi has already tried lifting the bow once now and failed."

The commanding general arrived and was dispatched with his orders and the letter.

The very thought that Kashi was so close to the bow made Rama's skin crawl. Rama wanted to be the one facing Kashi, shooting down his taunts and threats. Rama could see that Lakshmana was thinking the same thing, Manthara's nastiness turning trivial by comparison. Rama's mind dwelled on the battle and its outcome. Rama learned that politics meant to hold back and wait. Rama wished he was in the front lines of the battle but also knew it was a young man's folly.

Eight days later, the army returned victorious with a letter of thanks from King Janaka. The bow was safe. The princess who would never marry was safe. Kashi had been thwarted but had escaped. Like the conniving king he was, he had doubled his annual tribute to Ayodhya. Kashi had not, strictly speaking, acted outside acceptable parameters. Even princesses could be stolen against their will, so who could fault Kashi for trying?

This was another lesson for Rama; the contours of righteousness had many shapes.

CHAPTER 32

The Warrior-Turned-Sage

When Rama was summoned to the King's Court, his curiosity was piqued. He had not attended his father's court in a long while. At sixteen, he was astute in the matters of state, and his schooling had proceeded into other fields. In the past months, the learning had centered around the language of animals. To master it required spending excruciating amounts of time in stillness and observation. It drove Lakshmana crazy. Rama had proved especially fluent in the tongues of the five-clawed beasts. Lakshmana could summon crows. Shatrugna had seldom found anything more amusing. As usual, when Rama was summoned, Lakshmana automatically followed. Bharata and Shatrugna continued their language studies. As the brothers made their way to the court, crows and tigers prowled the halls, if only in sound.

All such boisterous behavior was subdued as they approached Father's Great Court. Here, they were no longer boys but young men in training. As soon as Rama stepped into Father's court, his eyes were drawn to the newcomer, a sage who had the fierce look of a warrior. His shoulders were broad and his arms strong with muscle. His matted hair hung like thick ropes down his back, and the only thing obscuring vivid battle scars across his chest was a wiry black beard that tapered off at his navel. He wore a piece of bark cloth around his hips and one slung across his shoulder. His forehead and arms were decorated with lines of sacred ash, and a necklace of large rudraksha beads encircled his throat. He was clearly a sage, but the first one Rama had met who had not always been one.

Rama could feel the power surging between the three great men in the court: Father, who looked stricken; Vasishta, who was ever calm; and the guest, who looked at Rama with the uncompromising eyes of Destiny. There was a battle of wills between the warrior-sage and Father. *This is about me*, Rama intuited.

Rama approached the throne and touched his father's feet.

He folded his hands at his chest and greeted the warrior-sage.

"Rama, my son," Father said, "our esteemed guest, the renowned Vishvamitra, has blessed Ayodhya by seeking our assistance. For the past six years, two blood-drinkers have consistently desecrated the fire sacrifice he is conducting."

"One hundred eligible sages await enlightenment," Vishvamitra said, "while these blood-drinkers play foolish games."

Vishvamitra's voice was authoritative. Rama immediately felt the urgency of the injustice being done to the sages. The harassment had been ongoing for six years, which probably felt shorter to the long-lived holy ones. Still, six years prior, Marichi had escaped from Ayodhya's most fortified prison cell. The escape had been possible only with the help of an accomplice, the one who had impersonated Vasishta so perfectly. Was it a mere coincidence that two blood-drinkers had then start accosting Vishvamitra's sacrifice?

Rama longed to ask this question, but Father and Vishvamitra were intent on each other, while they continued informing Rama of the situation.

"Vishvamitra's own hands are bound," Father said. "Although he is among the most powerful of the holy, he cannot use his powers while the sacred fires are burning."

"Such an act would refute the purpose of the sacrifice," Vishvamitra said. "For how can we surrender to the almighty while displaying our autonomy? No, I require assistance."

Father's countenance tightened. Rama felt it in his belly.

"The best fighters in my army will accompany you," Father promised. "Take as many of them as you require."

Vishvamitra did not even look at Father as he said, "King, I have already made my wish clear."

"But Rama has no experience," Father said, and all the pieces fell into place.

Rama's eyes darted back and forth between the two elders. Vishvamitra wanted him!

"He won the archery competition when he was seven years old," Vishvamitra argued.

Rama's eyebrows rose. He didn't know the holy ones kept pace with such things.

"But he has never been in combat! He has never faced a blood-drinker!"

"Isn't it time, then?" Vishvamitra demanded, the tendons in his neck visible.

Vishvamitra's temper was burning white hot, and he began to openly accuse the king. "You are being sentimental. It does not befit you, a son of the Sun dynasty. If you keep going down this path, you will break your word, for as I entered this faultless court, you offered me unconditional assistance!"

Father stood up. "I will personally assist you. I will lead the army, and we will not rest until we have destroyed the threat to your sacrifice."

"I want Rama!" Vishvamitra roared.

The court was silent. No one moved. They scarcely breathed. The tension coiled in Rama's system like a frenzied snakes. He did not like to see his father like this. There were pearls of sweat on Dasharatha's forehead, and his eyes were unsteady. His spirit was spiraling down into something dark and terrible. Rama wanted to speak but had not received leave to do so.

Vasishta intervened. "It would be wise for Prince Rama to know who Vishvamitra is. Once my rival, now a dear friend. Will the court listen to the tale of his transformation?"

Vasishta's gentle voice had a calming effect. Father's downward spiral stopped. Vishvamitra's rage calmed. Rama and Lakshmana took their seats, and the court's storyteller was called on. He stood in the center of the hall, and his eyes swept across them all, taking stock of his audience. He was Ayodhya's best storyteller, emerging from an unbroken lineage.

"Even if I were a lion," he began, "my tail would hang limp by my feet. My heart trembles as it realizes what I'm about to do. How can I presume to speak of Vishvamitra's life, when the great one himself is present? And yet this story was told to me by my grandfather and his before him. I beseech your blessings, great sage. Please forgive any flaws this tale may contain. They are all mine, and I'm but a caged animal with a wilted tail."

Rama and Lakshmana exchanged a smile. They loved this storyteller. Vishvamitra's temper had cooled for the time being, and he lifted his palm in blessing. In a sonorous, engaging voice, the storyteller spoke and the tale unfolded, taking them all on a journey.

Vishvamitra's transformation from king to sage was well known and took place in a time long gone, when he was known as King Kaushika. The king had reason to be proud; he had far excelled his peers in both intellectual and physical strength. But he was intoxicated by his power. His fierce temper and clear self-confidence gave him the upper hand in battle, as he never hesitated to strike. Without any substantial rivals, his pride flourished unhindered. He became arrogant and prone to a violent temper. His one hundred sons were of the same temperament, a pack of barking dogs.

When King Kaushika went on a hunting expedition one day, he had no premonition that his life was about to change. Accompanied by his army and his one hundred sons, they trampled through the forest, destroying its serenity. The forest was crushed by their passing, and they left many dead animals in their wake, slaughtering them only to prove their marksmanship.

Suddenly they came upon a haven, a place that felt like a temple, and even the most brazen soldier grew silent. In the center of this sacred place, Kaushika found a luminous sage, peacefully applying oil to his limbs. The effulgent sage was none other than Vasishta, and Kaushika fell to his knees with reverence, for Vasishta's name alone was enough to inspire awe. Son of the creator, Brahma, and counselor to Earth's kings, Vasishta was a name all knew. Standing before the sage, Kaushika felt like a chastened child at the mercy of his father. Perhaps this was a warning, for he did not like the feeling. He was used to being worshipped, not giving worship. What was so special about this old man, who had to massage his own limbs, having no willing servant to do such a task?

Vasishta invited the king and his men for a feast, and Kaushika reluctantly agreed, knowing the stark fare that sages subsisted on. He was astounded, however, by the luxurious and rich feast that mystically appeared before them. Every man was served the richest food of his imagination, and the soldiers had never before been so pleased or well fed. At this juncture, Ayodhya's storyteller described each dish in mouthwatering detail; some were entirely new creations imagined by Kaushika's hungry army.

Kaushika fell at Vasishta's feet, acknowledging his mystical prowess. Vasishta attributed the source of this richness to Shabala, his prized companion, a wish-fulfilling cow. She was the very same cow that had emerged from the legendary churning of the oceans, which had produced the nectar of immortality. Kaushika was stunned by the beautiful cow with her peacock tail and her ability to grant any wish. His arrogance reached its peak as he forcefully tried to abduct her. With Vasishta's permission, Shabala produced an army of protective demons from her udders, and Kaushika's entire army was demolished within minutes. Enraged, Kaushika's hundred sons turned on Vasishta; they were instantly turned into ashes by the holy one.

The sole survivor, Kaushika, was crushed. He had nothing left in this world. His sons were dead, and his sense of superiority had proved a complete illusion. Vasishta was far more powerful than he was. His ego recognized this and wanted nothing more than revenge. Like others before him, he began to perform immense austerities to achieve power, forsaking all comfort. He hoped to gain the attention of the gods. After many, many years, Shiva appeared before him and granted him knowledge of all the weapons that had ever existed. Kaushika thus became the most powerful warrior on the planet.

The years of austerity had not tempered Kaushika's ego; he returned immediately to Vasishta's serene dwelling. An immense battle ensued between the holy one and the powerful warrior. Kaushika summoned the full force of his prowess, while Vasishta merely used his wooden staff to deflect Kaushika's assault. Kaushika's venom grew more explosive when he saw how relaxed Vasishta was. The holy one remained seated while Kaushika ran about in a mad frenzy. Finally, Kaushika launched his most formidable weapon into the air. Vasishta's eyes remained fixed on Kaushika and he simply pointed his wooden staff at the weapon. The missile froze in the air and fell to the ground, causing no harm.

Kaushika had to accept defeat once again. He dragged himself back into the jungle and commenced his austerities. Being the most powerful warrior was not enough; he had to become a holy one himself.

Kaushika now prayed to Brahma, the creator, for that boon. A thousand years passed before Brahma appeared and assured Kaushika that he had proved himself worthy of being a rishi, a mind-controlled sage. Brahma's words only disappointed Kaushika, for he wanted to become a brahma-rishi, like Vasishta. Thus he had to continue his austerities to attain the next level, maha-rishi, and then persist until he attained the top status of brahma-rishi.

After many trials and failures, Kaushika took an unparalleled vow: to neither eat nor breathe for countless days. The gods were shaken by his display of control and appeared alongside Brahma to award him what he was striving for. In that moment, Kaushika became a brahma-rishi and could count himself among the holy ones.

Vasishta was summoned and gracefully acknowledged that Kaushika had become his equal. Because the determined king had learned to control both his pride and his temper, he became known as Vishvamitra, "Friend to All." Since then, Vishvamitra's fame steadily grew, for he was a fierce protector of the downtrodden and would do everything in his power to reverse injustice. Vishvamitra did not hesitate to curse even a king if that man's actions were not aligned with righteousness. Thus he became a holy one to be feared. Once he even created an entire new universe, but that was, of course, an entirely different story for an entirely different time.

As the tale ended, there was a collective sigh, the pleasure at having heard a great tale with a satisfying ending. The storyteller looked at Vishvamitra and received his approval. The holy one sought only one amendment.

"Perhaps my sons were barking dogs," he said, "but they were loyal and dedicated to their father, just like young Rama here. Their behavior was only a reflection of the father they had. At heart, they were pure, as most children are. Next time you speak this story, I pray you include this in your portrayal of them."

The storyteller folded his hands at his chest and bowed. As he left, Rama could see his immense relief. He had told the story without incurring Vishvamitra's wrath, and Rama sensed that if Vishvamitra had not been present, the tale would have included more anecdotes of that famous temper.

Dasharatha stood up. "I thank you, Vasishta, for your timely intervention. We have been eloquently reminded of Vishvamitra's stature."

"I wish to become your son's mentor," Vishvamitra said. And Rama thought at once of the arsenal of weapons the holy one possessed. "When you were his age, Great King, you had already fought in the battle of the immortals and gained your name. Give Rama the opportunity to grow. As a son of the Sun dynasty, he is destined to face blood-drinkers in battle. If Rama is ever in danger, I will use any means, as a sage or a warrior, to protect him. As highest truths go, however, Rama needs no protection."

Father took a deep breath. "Respected Vishvamitra, I resisted your request out of fear for my son's safety. I am his father, and it is my duty to protect him. I understand the great honor you bestow upon him. I relinquish him to your care. He will leave with you as soon as you require."

"I wish to depart before the sun sets."

Hearing this, Lakshmana instinctively leaned toward Rama. Would Rama be going without him? Rama felt his brother's distress and leaned back toward Lakshmana, steadying him. While Lakshmana's alarm grew visible, Rama's poise made him still.

Father needed only to glance at them once to understand. He turned back to face Vishvamitra. "I have one request to make of you, holy one. So far in this life, Rama and his younger brother, Lakshmana, have never spent a day apart. Will you honor us by allowing Lakshmana to accompany his brother on this quest?"

"As you wish."

Lakshmana's relief made him slump in his seat. The brothers looked at each other with growing excitement. It was their first adventure outside Ayodhya, but surely not the last.

CHAPTER 33

Rama's Rite of Passage

The preparation for the princes' departure was minimal. Vishvamitra wanted to walk out of the city as he had come, on foot and incognito, so the usual fanfare was dispensed with. The two princes needed only their bows and quivers. The queens were called to bid them farewell, but Rama melted first into his father's embrace. He couldn't understand why Father treated this moment as the final farewell, but he felt his father's anguish. Father did not release them lightly on this quest, and Rama sensed the seriousness of the situation. Father's eyes were dry with unshed tears, and he admonished Rama to honor Vishvamitra's every command.

Mother then invoked Earth's elements to protect Rama and bless his journey. Rama felt her love and blessings wrap around him like a cloak.

When it was Kaikeyi's turn, she embraced Rama tightly. He wondered briefly if she shared Manthara's desire to put Bharata on the throne. Manthara would be thrilled to hear Rama had left Ayodhya. No doubt she would pray day and night for him never to return. Kaikeyi, however, dispelled all such thoughts, for in her farewell, she used the words she had always reserved for Bharata: "Land nor sea can part you from me."

Though Rama knew the phrase well, it was the first time Kaikeyi had said the words to him, and Rama felt the haunting love in them. He returned his third mother's love unconditionally.

The four brothers took turns embracing. Whenever the elders were focused elsewhere, Shatrugna croaked into Lakshmana's ears, saying it meant "Safe journey" or "Spread your wings" in crow talk.

"Finally I'll be free of you," Lakshmana said, alternatively hugging and punching his twin.

Rama and Bharata interacted in a more contained manner, neither of them prone to displays of emotion, as the twins were. Rama didn't exactly feel that the kingship stood between them, because he would joyfully give it to Bharata and Bharata gladly gave it to Rama. Still, Manthara cast a formidable shadow, and it lay there in crooked shades of gray between them.

Sumitra placed the red saffron powder on Rama's forehead, a symbol of victory, and then on Lakshmana's. It was the only formality the king insisted on. If Lakshmana wasn't right beside him, Rama knew the leave taking would have felt more poignant. Indeed, Rama could not imagine what the separation from Lakshmana would feel like. He did not want to imagine it.

Vishvamitra was patient while the royal family took their farewells.

"I will return your sons within ten days," he repeatedly promised.

As they walked out of Ayodhya, Rama did not go unnoticed. The people of Ayodhya stopped whatever they were doing to behold Rama as he walked by. He felt their desire to rush toward him and receive his attention, but one and all remained respectfully distant. Rama smiled at as many of them as he could but did not wave, for he was Vishvamitra's pupil now. The holy one walked with bold strides looking neither left nor right. Rama felt a deep and instinctive trust toward him. It was like being with someone like Vasishta but who also cared for weapons and military arts as Rama did.

Vishvamitra walked in front as their guide, and the two boys followed in silence. They left the city and marched along the river Sarayu, resting only as night fell. Though not accustomed to walking long distances on foot, the princes were strong from hours of martial arts training and did not tire.

As night fell, they took shelter under a tree. Rama and Lakshmana had never slept on the bare earth before, with only their arms as pillows. Consumed by the newness of it all, neither youth could sleep. Rama had felt torn while leaving his father, but the feeling had started to vanish. He wondered whether his father also lay sleepless this night. Rama and Lakshmana whispered to one another, comparing experiences, until at last sleep overtook them.

The next morning they crossed the holy river Ganga. Vishvamitra had pointed out the beautiful landmarks they had passed, but on this day on the southern bank of the Ganga there was scarcely anything to see. A scorching heat engulfed the trio. The sun blazed angrily, and the hot sand seared their every step. There was no more greenery, and the desert stretched for miles around them. Gusts of hot air hit Rama's face repeatedly. The wind flung the sand mercilessly about, stinging the travelers' skin. A solitary vulture was the only

form of life they saw; heaps of bones were scattered about the dry landscape. Animal skeletons offered the only variation in the landscape, an unending expanse of dunes and plateaus.

"There was a time," their guide said, "when this area was lush and teeming with many animals. Now the only trace of animals you will see is that." He pointed to elephant tusks reaching up through the sand like giant white thorns. "The red gems you see sparkling in the sand have been spit out by venomous serpents."

Grimly, they walked on. Vishvamitra showed no signs of tiring, although the sun was burning like fire, so the princes followed his example without complaining. Sweat trickled from every pore, and it was not until both Rama and Lakshmana were soaked in their own salty perspiration that their guide turned and stopped.

"These austere conditions must be foreign to both of you."

"Yes, they are," Lakshmana admitted. "But we don't mind."

"You have borne the discomforts so far without a word of complaint," Vishvamitra remarked.

"No one knows what trials life may bring," Rama said. "To bear nature's affliction is a small test of endurance."

"True words, Rama," his mentor said, "but if we can avoid needless discomfort, why not? Also, this climate generates illness. Even great heroes are helpless against nature."

Then Rama and Lakshmana experienced the power of Vishvamitra, for he muttered a mantra swiftly, like a magical invocation. "You will remain unaffected by any climate that surrounds you," he promised.

No sooner had he said the words than a cooling breeze settled around them. They resumed their passage, but now less grimly, without feeling the onslaught of the wind and sun.

The boys looked at each other and did nothing to hide the fact that they were impressed by this trick. The sun began to feel comfortably warm, and they had the sensation of rambling through a pleasant park. The spell, however, couldn't blind them to the surrounding sights; the place became nastier with each step, oppressive with the sight of the skeleton-filled grounds. Rama could sense that the place was home to some unknown evil, but he did not yet know Vishvamitra well enough to simply express his instincts.

The evil did not remain unknown for long, as one of the mountains in front of them suddenly began to move. Although startled, Rama and Lakshmana continued to walk; Vishvamitra had not slowed his pace. He seemed, in fact, to be heading straight for that big lump of a mountain, which was strangely shaped with a cloud of black misting its peak. Rama strained his neck as he stared up at it and saw something alarming: two huge red hollows that rimmed two black circles. Were they bizarre caves? The black circles were rolling back and forth. Then another "cave" abruptly materialized under the hollows, and Rama gasped.

"It's alive!"

The cave, which had opened, now grimaced, widely displaying its sharp fangs. "It's alive," it mimicked in a voice that sounded like the croak of fifty thirsty buffaloes. "Have you come here only to insult me? Or are you simply fond of meeting your own death?"

Though Rama had known something terrible lurked here, he had not been prepared for this monstrosity, a talking mountain with fangs. He had never seen anything as appalling as this. This humanoid mountain could speak; it had eyes, a nose, and a mouth; and on closer scrutiny, seemed to have other humanlike body parts as well. The nose was so large and malformed that it could easily be mistaken for a rocky cliff. The hair that covered its head had invaded the creature's nose and arms. The hair was coated with dirt and therefore appeared to be some sort of hardy bush or plant—surviving despite the harsh conditions.

There was little time to scrutinize it, however, for the monster was coming toward them, its arms waving furiously.

"Rama, kill it," Vishvamitra barked, offering no further explanation.

Rama immediately pulled his bow from his shoulder and shot the monster between the eyebrows. It shrieked angrily, and Rama, who was about to shoot another arrow, gasped. Something about the high-pitched wail chilled him.

"It's a lady!" he yelled, horror stricken.

Lakshmana and Rama stared at one another, wide-eyed. So far in their worldview, women were beautiful and dignified. The only unpleasant woman in their life was Manthara, and she was an angel compared to this creature.

"Ha! You can hardly call that thing a lady," Vishvamitra said forcefully. "She does not even deserve to be called a woman."

"But how can I attack her?" Rama asked, his resistance to the idea written all over his face. But reflex made him fire five sharp missiles directly at her, for she was about to snatch Lakshmana into her gaping mouth.

"More than anything else, this creature is a monster," Vishvamitra said urgently. "I have brought you to this desert for the sole purpose of killing her."

Though chivalry toward women was ingrained in him, Rama had no choice but to keep hurling arrows at the demoness in self-defense.

She was throwing large rocks at them and bellowing, "I will eat you. I will eat you!"

Her concave eye sockets widened and squinted rapidly as she sought the next boulder to hurl. Rama's arrows covered her arms and neck like pins, but since the injuries were not life threatening, they did little to stop her onslaught. She ran madly around Rama and Lakshmana and created such a dust storm that Rama no longer knew where to direct his bow.

She laughed loudly and screamed, "No one can overpower Tataka!"

Hearing her shriek, Rama knew her exact location. He skillfully fired a torrent of arrows into her mouth, which rendered all further speech incomprehensible, although no less audible. She shouted at such a volume that the Earth seemed to shake and Rama's and Lakshmana's ears rang. Lakshmana plugged his ears for relief. He seemed content to watch what Rama was doing, as if it was a game. Rama was going to have a word with his brother later about this.

In this way, the young prince and the she-monster dueled for some time. Tataka lost an arm, then the other, yet still lived.

Rama was still ambivalent about killing a woman, and when the demoness seemed momentarily lost in her own sandstorm, Vishvamitra took the opportunity to speak.

"Her name is indeed Tataka," he said. "She is the mother of the two blood-drinkers who have continually spoiled my fire sacrifices. As you have seen, she has terrorized this region, which was once a lush forest. She became what you see today through her own evil conduct: a curse made her into a man-eating creature of the night. She is beyond redemption."

When Rama remained indecisive, Vishvamitra said sternly, "To kill a woman pure at heart is indeed the greatest sin, but to think of this monster as a woman is sheer folly and cowardice. A monster has no gender; it is an abomination. This creature is guilty of every sinful act ever conceived. To be patient with her is not a virtue. Keeping these facts in mind and to unburden the Earth, I order you to kill her."

Rama had listened intently while remaining alert to Tataka's advances. With the same speed that he shot his arrows, he weighed the arguments and instantly accepted their judiciousness.

"Your command is like my father's," he said. "Obeying you is a virtue in itself."

A steely resolve became visible on his face as Rama prepared himself to kill Tataka. The prince began to release arrows at such a speed that it was impossible to know when he shot one arrow and when he reached for another. When Tataka remained out of sight, Rama took out a long arrow and aimed at the sound he heard. The sharp arrow flew straight into Tataka's black heart. She fell to the ground with a crash and a final scream as her life escaped her hideous body. Blood flowed copiously from all her wounds, including her mouth, turning the desert red. A shower of flowers rained down on them.

The trio left the place covered in heavenly flowers.

Rama had never before taken a life. The lethal weapon, his aloe-wood bow, fragrant with saffron, now again rested quietly on his shoulders as his feet, smeared with Tataka's blood, left red footprints behind him. With the first arrow that pricked Tataka's leathered skin, what had once been a toy used to show off his marksmanship had become a lethal weapon.

Rama felt an urgent need to speak to his brother in private and slowed down, pulling Lakshmana aside.

"Why did you just stand and watch while I had to defend us from that creature?" Rama demanded, still not wanting to think of Tataka as a "she."

"Vishvamitra told *you* to kill her," Lakshmana immediately said. "I was following instructions."

But Rama could tell that wasn't the complete reason and simply kept looking at his brother, demanding more. "And you are so much better with your bow than I am," Lakshmana added.

"And?"

"And I would have insulted your prowess by joining in, as if it wasn't easy enough for you," he concluded.

"Insulted my prowess," Rama said, repeating Lakshmana's phrase. "Do you really think it was easy for me to kill her?"

"Rama, my brother," Lakshmana said, slinging his arm around Rama's shoulder, "you are too thoughtful sometimes. I agree with Vishvamitra. She was not a lady! You did nothing wrong in killing her."

Rama took a deep breath that came out like a sigh.

"And, no, I don't think it was easy for you to kill her," Lakshmana said. "But for your arrows, it was. Admit it. You were just playing. She never really was a threat to us."

Rama smiled a bit. "Well, she was really, really huge. Bigger than anything I've ever encountered."

"A larger target then," Lakshmana said confidently.

Again, Rama let out an exasperated sigh, but he wasn't affronted by his brother anymore. He knew his brother would face and overcome the same hurdle in his own time. Despite Vishvamitra's and Lakshmana's assurances, it was Rama who had today killed a woman, a monster, a creature, a blood-drinker. Whatever she was, she had been alive, and now she was in the land of Yama because of Rama. *So this is what it feels like to be a killer,* he thought. He had always known this day would come. Destroying his enemy was the clear goal of all his training since his first school day.

Unable to stop his pensive thoughts, Rama let the remorse wash through him. Once it filled his being completely, it was gone. And Rama knew he could bear the burden of what he had done.

CHAPTER 34

Revenge and Enlightenment

The next morning they rose before the sun did and, clad only in loincloths, dipped into the chilly water of the Ganga. Rama marveled at all these new sensations of sleeping on the bare earth and bathing unattended by servants. They sat on the ground, cross-legged, saying their prayers to the sun and the thirty gods. Soon the morning rays warmed their skin, drying their loincloths.

As their morning prayers concluded, Vishvamitra told them, "Though I had many unforgivable faults as a king, I was completely dedicated to weapon lore. Over the millennia of my life, I've perfected many of the mantras that invoke supernatural missiles. Aside from Parashuram, who notoriously hates warriors, I'm the only person who possesses this extensive knowledge on this subject."

Vishvamitra had their full attention. The brothers shared his fascination with weapons and warfare.

"My dear Rama, you passed the first test with excellence. You are a worthy recipient of this knowledge. Raise your palm and sip the holy water of the Ganga. Then I will begin the transmission of my knowledge to you. These missiles acknowledge only one master."

"But that means you won't have access to them!" Rama exclaimed.

"My dear boy, I'm not a warrior anymore. I've kept this weapon lore to myself far too long. It's time to pass it on. And I give you full permission to share what you deem appropriate with your brother."

Without delay, Vishvamitra took water from his vessel and poured it through his palm, onto Rama's hand.

The students sat in front of the sage, listening attentively.

"First, I will help you invoke Bala and Atibala," Vishvamitra said. "Bala will protect your body from fatigue and Atibala will heal your wounds."

As Vishvamitra taught Rama the mantra, Bala and Atibala appeared, two sisters holding hands. Their bodies were ethereal, more energy than matter, and constantly shifting.

"We will protect you when you call us," they promised Rama, momentarily surrounding him like a glowing shield and then vanishing completely from sight.

Rama absorbed the fact that his first weapon was in actuality a shield.

In this way, Rama had to memorize each weapon's mantra. When he spoke the mantra aloud, even in a whisper, the presiding deity of each weapon appeared before him and acknowledged him as its new master. Rama was astounded to see the power of sound, when a softly spoken mantra invoked Brahma, the creator. Rama could not even see him at first, the light of Brahma's body was so immense to his human eyes.

Even as Brahma's form became distinct, he intercepted Rama's obeisance by asking, "What is your command, Master?"

"When I think of you, appear in my hand," Rama instructed, prompted by Vishvamitra. His mentor seemed unmoved by the appearance of divine beings that Rama had only before imagined.

After Brahma left, Rama invoked Agni, the fire god; Vayu, the wind god; and Surya, the sun god. In this way, Rama mastered the entire range of earthly and celestial weapons. Coming into his possession through a true master, Rama's arsenal of weapons had grown to dizzying heights. The most astounding thing was that each weapon was actually a person.

Rama's mind was full of the mantras and the visions he had just seen.

His three favorites were the sister shields; Manu's weapon, which actively pursued a moving target; and the Chakra, a discus that would take any form he wished.

The three continued their journey through greener forests and arrived at Vishvamitra's hermitage, where all was ready for the fire sacrifice. Vishvamitra had told the brothers its purpose was enlightenment. The other hermits came out to greet Vishvamitra and the youths. The ascetics present were minimally clad in loincloths alone. The austere life they led was evident by the absence of fat on their bodies. Rama had never beheld such skeletal human bodies, yet they were formidable, with their piercing, intelligent eyes.

After brief introductions and instructions, the sacrifice began. Rama and Lakshmana took their bows out, stringing them carefully. Bow and arrow in hand, they began to circle the area, two panthers on the prowl. Vishvamitra's lips were now sealed in a vow of silence. He sat in the middle of the arena, in front of the fire pit, pouring clarified butter into the fire, the yellow liquid feeding the flames. He stared into the fire as the sages around him chanted the mantras in sonorous tones.

Nothing interfered with the sacrifice that day or the next. Six days passed, with no sign of disturbance. The sacrifice was blazing gloriously, and mantras poured out along with ladle upon ladle of ghee. Rama and Lakshmana remained on constant alert, but the sky was clouded only by smoke from the fire pit. The blood-drinkers were out of sight. Every muscle in Rama's body was tightly coiled, anticipating a battle that never came.

On the sixth day, the sacrifice was drawing to a close. It was then that the devious blood-drinkers made their calculated move. Cackling laughter and shrieks louder than thunder filled the sky. Blood and foul-smelling substances began to pour from the firmament. The only sign the sages showed of acknowledging that they were under attack was to chant louder.

"Lakshmana!" Rama called out, placing his first arrow against the bow.

Quick as thought, Rama invoked Manu's missile, aiming it at the foul substances raining from the clouds. The missile cleared the sky. When the downpour failed to disrupt the sacrifice, two blood-drinkers appeared, hovering like ghastly red comets.

Rama stood still, never taking his eyes off them. One of the drinkers looked familiar. They bared their fangs and dropped down toward Vishvamitra with great speed, their flaming red hair whirling through the air. Vishvamitra did not move an inch from his calm conduct of the fire ritual. Neither of the attackers spared Rama a glance, taking him for a mere boy.

"It's Marichi!" Rama hissed through clenched teeth. "Ayodhya's escaped prisoner!"

The former prisoner had not aged a day since Rama last saw him. In a flash, Rama was ten years old again, promising seven dead Ayodhyan children that he would avenge their deaths. Looking at the other blood-drinker, Rama recognized him too. He had the same wild eyes. So this was Marichi's accomplice, by all appearances his brother.

Rage twisted Marichi's face. "Look Subahu, it's the little prince from Ayodhya."

The demon brothers turned into birdlike creatures with fangs and red eyes.

"Invoke Agni, the fire god!" Rama called to Lakshmana, as he invoked Bala and Atibala, the sister shields.

Rama invoked the Chakra, which could take any form he wished. He sent it flying as a winged demon, the same form Marichi and Subahu had taken. The blood-drinkers were pursued by a creature just like them.

Lakshmana let loose his arrow, and sparks of fire shot from its tip. The blast set Subahu's wings on fire, and the blood-drinker resumed his original form, cursing loudly.

Rama wasted no time; he turned the Chakra into its original form of a discus and hurled it at the pretender's chest. With burning wings, and the discus sawing him in half, Subahu fell to the ground. Lakshmana's arrows showered on him relentlessly.

Marichi howled and flew through the sky like lightning. Rama followed his movements, an arrow drawn to his ear. Marichi was not a ray of light, as his name implied; he only usurped it, the way he drank blood, leaving no life behind.

Rama aimed at Marichi's heart. But the blood-drinker was very fast. Rama's arrow disappeared into a cloud, leaving Marichi unharmed. Baring his large fangs in mock salute,

Marichi was gone. Rama waited and watched, eyes focused on the sky. Subahu's soul left his body, and Rama recalled the Chakra from the corpse.

Rama felt a prickle in his neck and turned around just in time. Marichi rushed toward him, claws lifted. When their eyes met, Marichi froze for just a moment. His claws sunk into Rama's skin, pulling out large chunks of flesh. Bala and Atibala grew effulgent around Rama, who was instantly healed. Rama could have lunged forward and grabbed Marichi's long beard; the two were so close. Instead, Rama's arrow struck Marichi with explosive force, blasting him up and away, like a rag doll in the wind. He would not survive the impact of it, no matter where he landed. Rama felt his surge of anger pursue Marichi and disappear with him.

The air filled once again with sacred hymns. Vishvamitra's sacrifice continued unabated. On the seventh night, the fire accepted their bid for enlightenment. It accepted the last ladle of ghee and then died down instantly. The fire, which had roared for seven days and seven nights, let out one final crackle and then swallowed itself and was gone.

Rama noticed the sensation that something was pulled from him and drawn into the fire, to disappear with it. Lakshmana felt it too, for he took an involuntary step forward, his chest expanding, an invisible force tugging at him. The sages and Vishvamitra, who were chanting loud mantras, were sucked toward the fire, forced to lean forward, their crossed legs holding them to the ground. Whatever the fire was doing was so powerful the mortal frame could not resist it. Rama saw eyes rolling back in their sockets, limbs twitching, and faces contorting. Many sages were shaking from head to toe, as if what the fire demanded was too much.

"Rama," Lakshmana pleaded, like he was in pain.

Rama put his hand on Lakshmana's shoulder, and his brother relaxed.

Vishvamitra alone was undaunted. He broke his silence and chanted loudly, his hair and beard wild like the last flames of the fire. Rama felt totally free.

"Look," Lakshmana whispered.

The ascetics collectively raised their arms to the sky, and Rama and Lakshmana looked on as the spirit forms separated from the mortal bodies. It was like seeing an assembly that had suddenly doubled in size, only the new half was glowing so fiercely that it was difficult to see anything at all.

The fire hummed one last time and turned to embers. The sages were released from the fire's demand, and their spirits returned to their bodies. The sacrifice was complete.

Vishvamitra sat frozen, the wooden ladle hovering in the air and dripping with ghee. There no longer was a fire to offer the golden liquid to. Lakshmana's breath returned to normal. Rama kept his hand where it was. He could feel that Lakshmana needed that touch to remain standing. His brother was deeply shaken, and so was the entire assembly.

The silence was so vibrant that it was hardly a silence at all. They had been purified, for each and every one there was now glowing, just as their spirits had been. And now Rama could see, beyond a doubt, that the sacrifice had been successful.

He dropped his hand from Lakshmana's shoulder, full of awe. He was surrounded by enlightened beings. The assembled ascetics had been powerful enough to withstand the final cleanse of their mortal existence and still remain embodied. This was no ordinary feat. It was exceptional.

Just as Rama began to kneel in reverence to them, the assembly turned their eyes on him. Rama froze. Only his gaze moved across the gathering. They looked at Rama as if he was the strangest or most wonderful thing they had ever seen, as if they had not seen him at all these past seven days. Even Vishvamitra's eyes glowed with intense adoration. Rama could not understand it or what happened next.

Vishvamitra's eyes filled with tears, and he prostrated himself on the ground in Rama's direction. He was the first, but every other ascetic followed suit. Lakshmana, who had regained his composure, looked as puzzled as Rama. The brothers glanced at each other but had the sense not to move, not to disrupt this moment when the sages paid homage to them. Many of the sages were crying audibly and murmuring words of praise. They remained flat on the ground.

This continued so long that Lakshmana began to shuffle his feet. Even Vishvamitra's face was resting against the ground. He was as overcome as the others, so Rama was left to draw his own conclusions.

He pulled Lakshmana to his side and said, "They must be overcome with gratitude, that's all. We protected the sacrifice. They have been trying to complete it for the past seven years. They are enlightened beings now, Lakshmana."

Lakshmana nodded at first, but then whispered back, "But somehow I don't really feel like they are bowing to me."

Vishvamitra's voice rose above the murmurs. "I knew it! I knew it!" he cried.

Still, no one lifted their head from the ground, one hundred enlightened heads pointing directly at Rama.

Lakshmana turned and looked into Rama's eyes. "What did you feel?"

The sensation had been so subtle, Rama couldn't articulate it at once.

"Do you know what I felt?" Lakshmana asked. "I felt like my connection to you was pulled away from me, my reliance on you. The fire was ripping it from my body, telling me I didn't need it." He clutched his chest, as if the memory was too painful still. "But I do! I felt like I was dying, Rama." He patted his chest nervously. Then he gestured toward the prostrated sages. "I think they died too, in a manner of speaking."

"And you think they are bowing to me because of that?" Rama asked.

Lakshmana made big eyes and shrugged.

Just then Vishvamitra lifted his head from the ground and looked up at Rama. For a split second, Rama was enveloped by such an immense feeling of being worshipped that he had to close his eyes. The next moment, Vishvamitra was on his feet and congratulating the brothers on their victory. When Rama opened his eyes, Vishvamitra had resumed being the one he had been, their mentor. Rama quietly sighed in relief. Now he knew what was expected of him. He listened attentively to Vishvamitra's words.

"You were astounding," Vishvamitra said. "You allowed us to complete our sacrifice. We," his hand swept across the assembly of sages, "are so grateful."

As if on cue, they all began to make their way to their feet. Now Rama was no longer the target of their attention. They hardly looked at him, but Rama still felt that they were focused on him, aware of every action he took, so he stood still, allowing Vishvamitra and Lakshmana to carry the conversation. As they did, the sense of a normal day settled on them. Lakshmana described in some detail how they had kept the blood-drinkers at bay.

"Well done!" Vishvamitra said again. He embraced both of them. "Finally my sacrifice, seven years in the making, has come to completion because of your unrelenting skills as warriors. Tataka's vile sons have met a fitting end."

Rama and Lakshmana nodded at each other. It had not been easy to remain vigilant for seven days on end.

"Wait," Rama suddenly said, looking up at the sky. "Marichi is still alive."

Vishvamitra's eyes grew clouded. "You blasted him with such force, Rama, he was flung eight hundred miles away."

Rama peered into the sky too, wondering if he could shoot another arrow eight hundred miles away.

"He is drowning now," Vishvamitra said. "He fell into the middle of the ocean. Your work here is done. It is time I returned you to your father."

"Has it really been less than ten days since we left?" Lakshmana asked. "It feels like much longer!"

"Missing your home and your family? I'm sure King Dasharatha misses you."

"As long as I'm with Rama . . ." Lakshmana began.

"I miss Father," Rama said. Just thinking of his father made an achy feeling appear in his heart.

"Let us return then," Vishvamitra said. "But first these bodies of ours need some rewards."

Gratefully, the princes sat down, stretched their limbs, and accepted the fresh fruits they were offered. After such a long fast, the light meal was perfect.

"Sleep now," their mentor said. "In the morning we will return to your home."

Rama thought he would fall into a dreamless sleep, and he did for a time. But then his old dream came to him, only it was more vivid and lifelike than before. Kashi looked exactly like a blood-drinker with ten heads; he plucked up Shiva's bow as if it was a toy. Rama was hit by arrow after arrow as a woman cried into her hands, singing a heartbreaking song amid sobs. Rama woke up. It was still dark all around them. Lakshmana snored lightly on the ground next to him. Until sunrise, Rama lay awake, thinking about what he loved the most and how he would feel if it was lost.

CHAPTER 35

A Woman of Stone

When the sun rose, the princes left the ashram with Vishvamitra without even an informal farewell. In Ayodhya a decision to go anywhere entailed lengthy arrangements and extended formalities. Yet Rama did not have to turn around to know that the ascetics behind them had bowed to the ground again. Rama's chivalrous heart longed to walk among the sages and exchange words, and perhaps discern the reason for their behavior toward him.

Observing Vishvamitra's purposeful forward-moving steps, Rama could see how superfluous some of the palace's formalities were. It was rather efficient and appropriate to simply move on now that their work was done.

Rama adjusted his quiver and bow against his shoulder, his only possessions at present. Soon after, Rama turned his attention to their route; they were not returning the way they had come. Perhaps there were many ways to reach the same destination.

Vishvamitra took them through a lush mango grove, where they stopped to eat mangoes. They continued on a path that only Vishvamitra could see, passing by wild ponds teeming with waterfowl and a forest so thick they could see nothing but leaves and flowers. The princes' legs and arms were scratched by prickly vines, and they had to stop several times to dislodge thorns from their feet.

After a day's journey, Vishvamitra led them onto a path and pointed out the flags peeking out above the trees, which signaled the city of Mithila. Rama and Lakshmana knew this was the capital city of the province of Videha, and King Janaka's city. It was the home of Shiva's bow and the princess who would never marry. Rama felt a strong pulsation in his heart. He wanted to enter the city and discover its wonders.

"It so happens that tomorrow is the second contest for Sita's hand," Vishvamitra told them. "King Janaka invited every eligible king or prince to participate. Your father may have told you?"

The princes shook their heads, and Vishvamitra laughed. "Mayhap he wanted to spare you. It's widely known that no man can lift Shiva's bow. The bruised ego of a warrior is something to be aware of, as I certainly know."

The dazzling ivory towers disappeared from their view as Vishvamitra swerved off the main path to one that was narrow and overgrown with weeds and bushes.

"A shortcut," Lakshmana whispered to Rama.

Rama shrugged and smiled at his brother. Vishvamitra led them forward purposefully. Eventually the neglected path brought them to an empty hermitage. It was ancient and surprisingly solitary, considering its proximity to the city. The deserted dwelling was filled with a profound silence; every word and gesture seemed amplified. Responding to this, Rama lightly tapped Lakshmana's hand, cautioning him against another whisper.

As they slowly moved into the silent courtyard of the hermitage, the soft sand caressed their feet, and small whirls of dust flew up and settled down again. They left deep imprints behind with each step. When they stood inside the clearing, Rama observed that Vishvamitra's eyes were filled with an intense expectancy, penetrating every corner of the area with eyes like an eagle. Lakshmana also noted his heightened focus and was quiet. Rama began to look around with a puzzled feeling; he was aware of another presence, one that was gentle and so very sorrowful. Rama's eyes lingered on a shiny black stone, polished by time, the most noticeable feature in the clearing. Vishvamitra focused intently on the stone.

"The warrior-turned-sage will come," Vishvamitra said, and it sounded like a recitation. "He will stand here, in the shadow of the prince, son of the Sun dynasty."

Vishvamitra turned to Rama, his voice returned to normal but his expression was grave. "I will now broach a sensitive topic unfamiliar to a child: marriage vows betrayed. You are on the brink of manhood. Dissension and human anguish are facts of life. To be unaware is to be unwise."

Signaling them to come closer to him, Vishvamitra spoke. "Rama, Lakshmana, all sins committed do not have an immediate retribution. The punishment comes, but the laws of nature are not always clearly discernible. However, I have brought you to this place to talk to you of a sin committed by two people and the lightning-swift punishment that was meted out to them."

His gaze wandered from them and back to the rock. "This was once the ashram of the virtuous Gautama and his wife, Ahalya. They lived here, performing austerities and purifying their lives. Bound by the vows of marriage, they prospered together. However, Indra, king of the gods, became smitten by the lovely Ahalya. Even though she was the wife of Gautama, he started thinking of ways that he might enjoy her. One day when Gautama went for his daily bath, Indra seized his chance. He took the form and dress of Gautama himself and approached Ahalya. Speaking sweetly to her and praising her appearance, Indra made his intention clear. She yielded to his advance, forgetting all chastity and loyalty; she enjoyed with Indra as on a first wedding night, though she knew in her heart that he was not her husband.

"After the union, Indra became nervous and hurried out of the ashram to avoid Gautama. But Indra did not escape unnoticed. Gautama, wet from his bath and pure from his austerity, came face to face with Indra, still disguised as Gautama—one, rich in virtue and the other, with none. Indra immediately felt the full weight of his shameful act and turned into his own form again.

"When Gautama understood what his wife and Indra had done, his fury knew no bounds. His anger took shape in words, which he hurled like a weapon at Indra: 'May you be covered by the private parts of a thousand women!'

"Instantly, Indra's skin was transmuted.

"To his mortified wife, Gautama said, 'You, heartless woman, become a stone!'

"At once her body became rigid and turned into a solid rock."

While he told the story, Vishvamitra's eyes had not moved from the black stone before them.

When it dawned on them that this was that very stone, Lakshmana gasped, and Rama's eyes widened in disbelief. They looked at Vishvamitra for confirmation.

"Yes. This is that stone. Inside it, Ahalya's being has been trapped. Indra was not punished in the same way, but became a laughing stock to the world, his whole body proof of his decadence. It was impossible to conceal or misunderstand the nature of his transgression. Ahalya, at least, suffered her humiliation in privacy. Of course, this incident occurred a very long time ago."

"But how long must she be punished, trapped inside this stone?" Rama asked, moving closer to the stone. "Indra used trickery to deceive her."

"But she saw through Indra's disguise," Lakshmana said. "She knew in her heart it was not her husband, and still she accepted his advances."

Rama frowned at his brother.

"Gautama was a sage with great insight," Vishvamitra said. "After he overcame his anger, he agreed that Indra instead be covered by a thousand eyes. And Ahalya would be redeemed, he acquiesced, by the prince of Ayodhya, son of the Sun dynasty, by the name Rama."

Now Vishvamitra's gaze was on Rama, and Rama finally understood the cause of Vishvamitra's intensity. Rama stared back at the sage, astonished.

"They knew that we would be born and come here?" Lakshmana asked, his eyebrows nearly touching his hairline.

Vishvamitra could only shake his head. He too was perplexed. "The pattern of birth and death and the ultimate destination for all souls was set at the inception of the universe. Yet because each soul has freedom to choose otherwise at any moment, the accuracy of a prediction can be astonishing."

Rama was by this time more concerned for Ahalya, the woman whose one-time transgression had fixed her inside a stone, an eternity of immobility and loneliness touched only by the unrelenting hands of nature, wind, and rain. Rama's attention fixated on the rock, and he softly approached it. What his part was in her salvation, he did not know. It was his compassion that made him approach the woman of stone. As he did, the sand flew up in whirls from his feet and wafted onto the stone. As the dust particles settled down on it, something started melting inside the hard rock.

Rama could feel the soul in the stone emerging from her pall of darkness. Like a lost soul breaking through bondage and transforming the material carcass for the eternal body, Rama felt Ahalya reach out to him. The rigid stone gave way to a softer element, and Ahalya regained her form and vitality. Curled at Rama's feet, the last rigid covering melted from her heart. Ecstasy of relief emanated from her, and her tears were warm and reverent as she pressed her forehead to Rama's feet. Her long black hair draped around her body as she looked up at Rama with tear-filled eyes. She was naked as a newborn child and filled with the same innocence.

"Rama," she said, chanting his name with adoration.

Rama swept his shoulder cloth around her, and a deep compassion filled his entire being. She had suffered so long. Instinctively, he gently touched her shoulders and raised her up, his feelings of forgiveness and love transmitting through his hands. The rays of love reached her heart, melting away the last strands of shame and self-recrimination. Because he forgave her, she could free herself from any self-reproach. She had more than atoned for her transgression. Rama saw her bask in the pure glow of her salvation.

At that moment, Gautama, the disgraced husband, mystically appeared. He had the effulgence and bearing of a long-lived holy one. His long hair and beard were white like camphor, and his limbs glowed with acetic prowess. Ahalya fell at his feet before he could stop her. The moment Gautama touched her, she was draped in pure silk and adorned with jewels. Gautama embraced her, and Rama saw the intensity of their union. After an eternity of separation, Gautama welcomed Ahalya back to her rightful place beside him. Although Rama had not known this couple an hour before, he was deeply moved by the love between the sage and his wife. They belonged together, sharing a bond so strong that neither was whole without the other. Rama felt an awakening in his heart, a desire to belong to another being so completely. A sense of great satisfaction filled the air.

Rama bowed down at the feet of the timeless sage and the pure Ahalya. She placed her hand gently on his head in blessing and returned the cloth he had so thoughtfully draped around her. Her white garment shimmered with rainbow hues. Vishvamitra and Lakshmana, who had witnessed the miracle in stillness, came forth to offer their respect. After accepting their obeisance, Gautama and Ahalya disappeared.

The place that Ahalya had occupied was now empty. The entire episode seemed like a dream. The trio went forth from the deserted hermitage, leaving only their footprints behind in the sand.

CHAPTER 36

A Miracle of Creation

As they entered Mithila's city gate, a joyful mood greeted them. The citizens of Mithila were decorating the streets with flower garlands and strings of bilva leaves. Fragrant incense and camphor wafted from every corner, and Rama recognized all the signs of a massive celebration under way. Groups of girls sat in clusters on the ground painting colorful patterns with dyed rice flour. The patterns swirled with lotuses, paisleys, and peacocks, and, most prominent of all, a large ornate bow. Rama imagined Shiva's bow as the very center point of Mithila.

Reading his thoughts, Vishvamitra said, "The mighty bow has been in King Janaka's family for so many generations, it has become Mithila's most prized heirloom. The unkind say that the king is intent on making a spinster of his lovely daughter, for during the first contest, no man was able to lift it. Tomorrow, kings from far and wide will approach the bow again to prove their strength and win Sita's hand."

In the heart of the city, Rama and Lakshmana were wide-eyed with curiosity. Mithila was a beautiful city, and its people were happy. The festivities gave the city a warm glow, no matter what the outcome of the contest would be. On one side of the path was a clear pond full of blue, red, and white lotuses swarming with bees. On the other side of the path, Rama saw a garden grove full of trees laden with fruits. Colorful flower petals were scattered everywhere on the ground. The garden was full of young girls, whose cheeks were red from laughing, running, and playing among the trees and bushes.

Rama was happy to be enjoying himself in the merry city atmosphere and allowed his gaze to wander freely while walking. The large palace, dotted by arched windows and terraces, was impossible to miss. Rama's eyes were drawn to a girl standing on the largest terrace, looking out into the city. As they walked toward the palace, Rama's eyes were fixed on her, seeing more of her features with every step closer.

The sight of her stunned him and took his breath away. He had never felt the need to look twice at any girl, but he couldn't stop staring at the captivating form of this one. She was a miracle of creation. Every female had a particular beauty, but this girl was a composite of all the beautiful aspects possible in a woman. She was slender and graceful, with dainty feminine curves, a tapering waist, full hips, and round breasts. She looked like a lotus about to bloom, not a girl but not yet a woman.

The breeze made the curls of her hair caress her cheeks, and her long black hair lay in waves around her shoulders and hips. Rama's heart was lost in her splendor, and it seemed to him that everyone was staring at her as he was. If Lord Brahma, the creator, was asked to create another like her, he would have to say no, for he had used all his tricks in making this girl. Celestial damsels like Rambha, Menaka, and Urvasi, themselves paragons of beauty and the inspiration of poets, would bow their heads on seeing such stirring loveliness as this girl possessed.

Her hands were dainty and delicate, her pinkish palms resting gracefully on the terrace railing. Her eyes were unbelievably large and deep, sparkling, and exquisite with thick eyelashes curling up and framing their almond outline. Her mouth was as red and full as a ripe berry, and a small, ethereal smile played on her lips, making Rama eager to know why she was smiling. Her skin was so fair that one would be afraid to touch her, and the rosy blush on her cheeks resembled the color of sunset through a pure white cloud.

She stood, motionless, her right hand placed over her heart, and Rama saw why when he looked into her eyes. She was staring at him. She was a perfect statue, her breath suspended, and Rama saw his own emotions reflected in her eyes. A profound longing cried out to him from the deep black of her eyes, and Rama felt his eyes were crying out the same longing to her.

Vishvamitra kept marching forward purposefully, and within moments Rama lost sight of the girl. For the rest of the day and that night, he saw her again and again in his mind and wondered at her beauty and who she was. He had left his heart with her and felt incomplete and agitated in body and mind for the first time in his life.

Vishvamitra brought them to a residence provided for wandering holy ones. The clay huts were replicas of dwellings Rama has seen in Vishvamitra's ashram. Preferring to be incognito, Vishvamitra had not announced their presence to the king. Walking through the streets of Mithila, Rama had received curious glances, but since the princes were dressed simply and walking by foot alongside a sage, no one had openly recognized them as royalty.

As they settled down for the night, Lakshmana and Vishvamitra stretched out on the

straw mats. Vishvamitra's long matted hair doubled his length, as it extended behind him on the floor. Rama was unable to sit still and felt like an animal in a cage in the small room. While beholding Rama curiously, Vishvamitra combed through his black beard with his fingers.

Rama was aware of Lakshmana's and Vishvamitra's eyes following him from one side of the room to the other. Though the exchange with the girl on the terrace was momentous to Rama, he realized it had lasted only a few seconds. He did not know how to articulate what he felt.

"Aren't you exhausted?" Lakshmana asked. "I am." He didn't budge an inch from his reclining position, though his gaze moved with Rama.

"I think it's time I tell you a story," Vishvamitra said with a knowing look.

Rama sat down and leaned against the clay wall. Vishvamitra sat cross-legged, his matted locks pooling around him on the floor. The storytelling had its soothing effect. This was the tale Rama's mentor told:

Many thousands of years ago, or not so very long ago, the lord of lords, Vishnu, descended to the earthly realm in answer to the plea of the holy ones. Vishnu's eternal consort, Lakshmi, could not bear the distance and followed him to take birth on Earth. She appeared as a sage's daughter and lived isolated in the mountains of the Himalayas. No disguise, however, could conceal the presence of the goddess—the source of all opulence, wealth, and beauty—and the mountain sages worshipped her as Vedavati, the embodiment of the Vedas.

Sitting cross-legged and still, Vedavati could only think of her Lord Vishnu. She was like a diamond bereft of light, her sparkling dependent on Vishnu. Along with her breath, her life force rose and fell as she counted the moments until she would see her beloved lord again. Day after day, she sat immersed.

As fate would have it, Ravana, the king of blood-drinkers, was drawn to that sacred site, sensing the presence of the goddess.

Coming upon a well-kept ashram, Ravana felt a tingling sensation on the back of his neck, as if the most beautiful spirit had blessed him. Stopping in his tracks, he turned around. Then he saw her. Like a thief who had stumbled on an unguarded treasure, he could see only her. In that one instant he became one with his heart, passion his only purpose. Ravana fell to his knees in reverence, worshipping the ground where Vedavati sat in meditation. He wanted to wash her feet with his passionate tears. Most of all, he longed for her to open her eyes, to reciprocate his feelings. Her closed eyes were shutting him out of her world, and he knew he was glimpsing but a spark of her splendor.

To awaken her, he cleared his throat loudly. She remained absorbed in her own meditation. This only increased his fixation. She was like a magnet, and his hand was drawn to make contact. Without thinking, he reached his hand out to touch her. With his fingertips, he lightly traced the shape of her head, then stroked the hair that

cascaded down her back. Her black hair flowed through his fingers. He was stung by this woman's lack of reaction. She was not affected in the least by his proximity or presence. No woman had ever been indifferent to him before. Not all women loved him at once, but he always got a reaction. Ravana's pride was stung. He had thousands of women more attractive than her at his palace—women who fought for his attention. How did she dare ignore him!

With wasp-like thoughts stinging him, Ravana straightened, grasping Vedavati's long hair firmly in his fist. Determined that she acknowledge him, he yanked her hair sharply. For a few moments, nothing happened. He stared at her again, seeing nothing but her, his pride forgotten. Would she open her eyes? Would her passion match his?

Tension filled the air, but Vedavati did not respond. He yanked her hair once more.

This time she slowly opened her eyes.

He stumbled back as their eyes met.

Ravana, who had fought with the most ferocious beasts, who could not be killed by Yama, was scorched by the burning fire in her eyes. Shocked, he tightened his grip on her hair. Her anger only heightened her beauty and appeal.

Vedavati knew instantly who was standing before her and arrogantly holding her hair. She had prayed to see her lord, but instead his nemesis had appeared, the most evil being alive in the universe. He was so close to her that she felt the heat of his body and the threat of his demanding eyes.

As she returned his stare, Vedavati transformed the side of her hand into a sharp blade and severed the lock of hair he held, leaving it limp in his grip. The ever-present pain of separation in her heart now mingled with rage.

She spoke with a voice that crackled with anger: "My body has been defiled by your touch. How dare you covet that which can never belong to you. I cannot bear to live with this body any longer."

As if he did not hear her, Ravana stared at her with unabated fervor.

"But know this, lusty fool. I will not give up this life in vain, for I will take birth again, and I will be the weapon of your destruction."

Having pronounced this curse, Vedavati gazed inward, directing the burning rage toward the center of her forehead. She uttered her lord's name and was consumed by the flames that erupted between her brows and burned her entire body.

Within seconds, her ashes whirled around Ravana's feet. He stood there, holding the shank of hair in his clenched fist.

She was gone.

His body felt raw, and he choked down a sob.

How fragile and sweet she had looked with her eyes closed, so desirable, but the blazing comets of her eyes had emasculated him. He lifted his hand toward his chest as if to clasp her hair to his heart, but flung it to the earth instead, a black oblation falling into the gray of her ashes.

Then he quickly turned away and left the mountains, his demon associates following silently behind. He would try to forget her. But the red-hot rubies of her eyes scorched his dreams. He would never stop coveting that which wasn't his.

Vedavati's soul rested within the womb of the Earth as she bided her time to reappear.

In Mithila, King Janaka peacefully scattered seeds into freshly tilled furrows. No sooner had the seed hit the soil than life emerged. King Janaka saw the ground at his feet crumble and crack open. The Great Mother offered forth her daughter. A baby girl appeared, her limbs covered in dust. Lakshmi had chosen King Janaka as her father. No one could imagine that this delicate, dirt-smeared girl was the goddess herself. Lifting the child, his heart filling with affection, King Janaka spontaneously declared, "This shall be my daughter."

Because she came from the Earth, Janaka named her Sita, "Furrow."

"Traveling from lap to lap," Vishvamitra said, "Sita, who has no mother, received the love of many. She is the incomparable princess in whose honor the contest tomorrow is taking place."

Lakshmana had fallen deeply asleep while Rama sat rapt with attention. Was it possible that Lakshmi, who was Vedavati who was Sita, was the girl he had seen on the balcony?

CHAPTER 37

Sita's Visions

Sita knew she was a girl unlike others. She had strange dreams of walking in tunnels of fire but not being burned, dreams of a great woman whose color was like a freshly tilled field, dreams of being like the sky, knowing everything. Sita loved her dreams; they confirmed a deep knowing she had that she was not like other human beings. Only one recurring dream disturbed her. In this one, she stood waiting at an enormous black gate, unable to enter. It had a nightmarish element, and yet she was simply arrested in time, waiting for the gate to open. Sita did not share these dreams with anyone, for her sister and mother already had told her she was too imaginative. Her sister Urmila was the true daughter of Queen Sunayana and King Janaka, while Sita was adopted, her parentage unknown. Yes, she had appeared from the Earth; the Great Mother was her mother. But Sita had heard the whispers. Some said she was a mere foundling, an unwanted child, buried alive at birth. The possibility of this cruelty was therefore part of Sita's earliest legacy. The mystery of her origin made her both more valuable and less secure in her belonging to her family.

But when Sita saw *him*, looking up at her from the street, there were no secrets, no question of belonging. She belonged at once to him. He already knew everything there was to know. It was the strangest stirring within Sita, a deep inkling of the soul within her that was not just a fifteen-year-old princess.

The stunning bowman was the embodiment of masculine beauty, and Sita was shocked at her own audacity. Even before he returned her gaze, she had memorized his every feature. She worshipped every inch of his form. He was luminous like an emerald. His skin was smooth, his chest broad. His black hair curled at his neck. His hands were pink, like lotuses, and so were the soles of his feet. He was a work of art come alive. Sita had never before seen anyone so perfect.

Sita stood for a long time, watching for the young bowman who did not reappear. He had gazed up at her with a longing that was so sweet, Sita had thought her life was complete, right then and there. He was neither boy nor man, but exactly on that threshold where Sita stood, she who was neither girl nor woman. It was possible that she would never see the bowman again.

Before he disappeared in the crowd, Sita felt as if the bowman had pressed a key into her hand. The key to the gate in her dream! Long after he was gone, Sita stood stunned, amazed at the unraveling within and without. The moments with him had felt like an eternity, so much had unfolded within her. It had never dawned on her that the gate in her dream and the maze beyond it was a real place. It was only a dream. She knew she was prone to imagine things. Perhaps this was the case now too, for when she looked down at her hand, she saw no key. But she could swear it was there as long as she didn't look for it.

The sky whispered, "Come with me and we will find him." She felt her spirit grow beyond her frame but stilled the expansion at once. It frightened her, for she was reminded again how different she was. Yes, she strove to please her father and mother and to be a proper princess like her sister. But she had to always watch herself—check herself—especially the feelings that began deep in her belly, which felt like a fire burning. She knew how to quell those. She had seen the warning in her father's eyes well before she had acquired language.

So she shushed the sky and sighed deeply. She would not allow the sky to take her anywhere. For if she did, she might get lost in insanity and never know the real from the unreal.

Sita was startled by a voice behind her.

"Come inside," her maidservant Padmini said, beckoning with her hand. "What is the matter? You have been standing there for close to an hour. It's not like you."

Sita lifted her hands from the cold marble, noticing how stiff her fingers were, especially the hand that had held the little key. Sita shook her hands and flexed her fingers, flicking away the imaginary key and telling herself to end these silly fantasies. Tomorrow she might be wed—if anyone was strong enough to lift Shiva's bow.

"Come, Sita. Your sister is here for you."

Sita took Padmini's hand and went within. It was good to return inside. Here the whispers of wind and sky were more subdued, even silent, and she felt like herself again.

"Padmini," she hesitated. She was on the verge of speaking about the young bowman. But what truly could she say? How could she explain that one glance from a stranger had changed her profoundly? No, she wanted to savor this secret.

"Yes?" Padmini asked. "Is it because of tomorrow? Are you nervous?"

Sita sighed. "No. It's not that. But I begged Father not to call me into the arena."

"Why? Urmila is very excited. She can't wait to see it all with her own eyes."

Urmila had gone to the arena as often as she was allowed, to inspect the site and the decorations that were under way. Sita had not gone even once.

"Maybe my little sister would feel differently if it was her life at stake."

Padmini nodded, but glanced askance at Sita's choice of words.

Before she could reply, Urmila came rushing down the hall. Her vivacious face was flushed. "Sita! Come quickly. Mother sent me with the three final outfits. You are to choose the one you like the most."

Sita smiled at her sister, admiring her grand features. At fourteen, Urmila was already a grown woman and living up to her name, which meant "Enchantress." There was very little about Urmila that gave away her tender age. She had ample curves, dressed in bold colors, and spoke like an adult. She had something pert to say on any given topic and was always bursting with energy.

She was pulling Sita along impatiently, having no time for Sita's dreams today.

Urmila certainly was the wiser one when it came to the ways of the world. But there were other ways of knowing. There were shades beneath the colors that told other stories.

As promised, three elaborate silk gowns waited for Sita. Urmila, Padmini, and the potential bride-to-be gathered around the outfits, which were all very different in their beauty. One was crimson and bold. The other, lotus pink and demure. The third, green and lush, like a forest.

Padmini draped each one around Sita, and Urmila ordered her to walk about the room so that they might see which one suited Sita best. The other maidservants gathered around, chiming in with their opinions and admiration. Urmila favored the crimson; she had herself picked out the fabric. Padmini mooned over the forest-green silk, saying Sita looked like the goddess of Earth. In the end, Sita chose the lotus pink one. It had an iridescent veil that would trail behind her. It pleased her and as Sita had learned that a princess delighted in such creations of beauty.

Urmila began to describe in detail some of the kings she had glimpsed at the arena. Sita listened in silence, thinking that Urmila had been too young during the first contest. She hadn't really understood what was happening. Neither had she walked across the arena, a spectacle for the kings to see. *That* was what Sita dreaded. She knew she would have to face the eyes and hunger of many men. She did not like the way the kings stared at her, as if she was something delicious to eat. Though she had begged her father not to call her to the arena, it was unavoidable. The kings always wanted to see the promised bride.

"Oh, don't be scared," Urmila said, noticing Sita's pensive look. "No one old will have the strength to lift the bow."

Sita laughed. It was Urmila's deepest fear that *she* would be married off to someone old. Such things were done for political reasons. Both princesses knew that girls like them were pawns in political games.

"If I'm lucky," Sita said in a teasing voice, "my groom will be someone like Shigraga."

Padmini and the others laughed. Urmila covered her mouth, too shocked to laugh.

Shigraga was one of their distant uncles, who had long hair growing from his nose and ears—exactly the sort of old man Urmila dreaded marrying.

"Father would never—" Urmila's eyes were horrified.

The girls grew serious. Father was the kindest man they knew, but he was a king first, a father second. That was the price of kingship.

"I begged Father, you know," Urmila said, "to make my bride-price the same as yours."

"I see, since no hairy old man can hope to lift it."

"Exactly! But Father did not indulge me at all. He muttered that he had already lost one daughter to this bow."

The maidservants all looked at Sita.

"Is that what people say?" she asked.

"Yes," Padmini answered, with lowered eyes. "They say you will always remain a maiden, unmarried and unclaimed."

"They say the bow is impossible to lift," another girl added.

"They are right," Sita said.

"But then, why did your father—"

Sita looked away. The rumors would go on, no matter what she said or did.

On the morrow, she might be married. Sita was not worried. She trusted Shiva's bow.

"Thank you, Father," she whispered.

She was grateful to him for setting this as her bride-price. The ancient bow was impossible to lift. Sita had done the impossible once. She could only marry someone who could do the same. She hoped the green-hued bowman was the one. She hoped he would be bold enough to try and blessed enough to succeed. Sita sent this prayer out to Earth's elements. She wanted the green bowman or no one. The bow would make that decision. Sita was content.

Queen Sunayana came inside, and they all stood up. She looked at Sita's choice of dress and smiled with approval. She admonished Sita to rest early and sleep well, but negated her own words when she allowed Urmila to stay. Urmila was a talker. Sita did not know when she would again be able to spend the night with her sister and didn't disagree with their mother. As expected, Urmila could not help herself and wanted to talk into the night. Sita fell asleep while her sister was still talking, exhausted by the upheaval of the day.

That night Sita dreamed again about standing at the black gate and being shut out. It started off as usual. She stood by the barred gate alone, with growing unease. A swirling mist of golden light emanated from beneath the door. The edges of the light shimmered with darkness, one fighting the other. She knew without a doubt that beyond the closed gates there was a vast, dark maze she had to conquer. She heard women moaning, sobbing, and sighing; they were trapped within and she was trapped without because the gate was locked. Always locked. This time, Sita began to search the perimeters of the gates. She needed to find a way to enter. Even though, she was afraid of being trapped within it, like the others. Usually, Sita's unease would grow so large she would wake up with a palpitating heart.

On this night, though, the dream was different. She held a small golden key in her hand.

When she saw the key, her heart leaped with anticipation. Finally, she would gain entrance to the maze. But to her dismay, there was no keyhole! She searched and searched but found no opening for the little golden key. But when she pressed the key to her heart, it whispered:

I am the key to your heart. You have found me. Only you can find this gate. It's hidden in the most unlikely place, in a place so dark no one can find it. The gatekeeper has many heads and many minds. He is impossible to cheat. You can enter only if the gatekeeper asks you to enter. They are within, waiting for you. Help them.

Sita woke with her hand clutched to her heart. When she opened her hand, there was nothing in it, but for a moment she saw faint traces of a small key in her palm. Whether she would ever see the bowman again, he had given her the key to her heart. Now Sita knew that the black gates were inside the heart of a ten-headed gatekeeper. Sita didn't know why she must enter, only that the crying women within needed her. Their call was one of the strongest forces Sita had ever felt.

The rising sun brightened the new day, and Sita drew her legs to her chest and rested her forehead on her knees. The day had not yet started and already she felt confused. She was a silly girl. Sita took dreams more seriously than her own life, while all of Mithila was awake with the contest for her hand.

CHAPTER 38

The Bow and the Princess

Rama arose with the sun, stirring before Vishvamitra did. He had hardly slept. He rushed through his morning prayers and bath, which was unlike him. The whole city was bustling with life, engaged in the contest for the princess's hand. Mithila already celebrated as if the marriage was under way. Strings of colorful flags hung across the streets. Pillars were decorated with banana leaves and flower garlands. The ground was painted with intricate designs. The heightened energy all around Rama matched his restless heart.

Vishvamitra led them to the arena where the contest would be held. Because they were the emperor's sons, Vishvamitra brought them to meet King Janaka. The arena was elbow to elbow with kings from across the world. Sita's reputation had only grown since the first contest. As Rama made his way through the arena, he glanced at each of the kings, noticing that the contest had attracted the strongest of men. By now, every warrior knew that no man had ever lifted the bow.

Vishvamitra announced their presence, and King Janaka greeted them heartily. He touched Vishvamitra's feet and said, "You who are famous throughout the world, bless our endeavor today with success."

"Though I'm rather infamous," Vishvamitra answered, "I certainly bless the contest. May a worthy man master the bow and win the hand of your daughter today."

Turning to the princes, Janaka said, "What an honor to host King Dasharatha's sons!"

King Janaka was instantly likable; his smile radiated through his eyes. The king inquired about their ages and the welfare of Ayodhya. While Rama answered his questions, he felt the king's covert study of him. Rama was not entirely unused to this; he had been told his emerald color was unusual, even fascinating. Consciously, Rama relaxed, allowing the king to see him fully. Father had taught him to do that, saying, "People don't trust you when you hide from them. You have nothing to hide, Rama." And so Rama practiced his father's instructions, feeling the prickle of Janaka's gaze. After a few moments, the king's appraising eyes turned warm. Rama knew the king liked him.

"The emperor's oldest son is a handsome lad," Janaka said to Vishvamitra. "I have not seen the young princes since they were seven. But who can forget Prince Rama's epic victory at the archery contest?"

Rama felt like seven years old again, a child too young to be included in the musings of the elders. King Janaka's words evoked a memory of many kings and their reverence for Father.

"He has good muscle tone for a youngster," Janaka observed. "But I'm afraid Shiva's bow is in a league of its own."

"There is more to Rama than meets the eye," Vishvamitra said. "Like one who has found the answer to an impossible riddle, I feel deeply satisfied by what I have observed in Rama." Vishvamitra turned to Rama, including him in the conversation. "Your heart, Rama, is divided into two equal parts. The steely resolve you demonstrated while killing Tataka and her sons, Marichi and Subahu, is balanced by a loving, compassionate nature. Dear prince, when you battled with the blood-drinkers, I saw the prowess of your mind. You showed that you can kill when necessary, destroying evil. The uncompromising steel of a warrior was manifested through you. But the power to destroy is ruthless. It can be intoxicating. Destroying in itself is an incomplete act if you cannot also absolve and protect. When you absolved Ahalya, you showed me and yourself that you are a protector. You were spontaneously drawn toward Ahalya's suffering, and you touched her with a compassion so strong it went through the solid rock."

King Janaka's eyes expressed his amazement at these revelations.

A number of people crowded around the king wanting his attention; the contest was set to begin shortly. Vishvamitra continued, "That said, we are here only to observe, Your Highness. We are on our way back to Ayodhya but could not ignore the opportunity to witness this great contest."

Accepting Vishvamitra's words, King Janaka arranged elevated seats for the princes and the holy one, given their high rank. After Rama was seated, he surveyed the large arena. He had never been to a contest like this before. Unlike the Summit of Fifty Kings, this contest had only one purpose: to win Sita's hand. At the summit, the subordinate kings arrived with attendants and soldiers in the hundreds. Here, each king's entourage was considerably smaller, with just a handful of guards and servants. Rama thought he knew why. In the last contest for Sita's hand, Kashi had rallied together a formidable army to attack Mithila. King Janaka had taken precautions against that happening again by limiting the number of soldiers. Today the number of Mithilans far outnumbered the visitors. Behind the kings, thousands of spectators had gathered.

As the sun began to rise in the sky, King Janaka made a signal, and musical instruments started playing, including the blowing of conch shells. A pair of large doors opened on the south side of the arena, and two lines of men emerged, pulling a rope, moving forward arduously step by step. Rama counted over a hundred of them before he could see the large iron case with wheels. When the bow came into view, the kings cheered. The bow was mounted inside the case—a daunting sight. It shone, almost vibrated. It took the power of all five hundred men to propel it forward.

Lakshmana whispered, "That is the largest bow we have ever seen."

The ancient bow had become like a deity in Mithila and was treated with the same respect. When the bow was in the middle of the arena, the five hundred guards stepped away, moving to the sides of the arena. The throng quieted.

King Janaka rose to address the assembly of kings. "I welcome you all to this contest for my daughter's hand. I commend your courage. Some of you are here having heard about Sita's beauty and her supernatural birth. Others among you may be eager to prove your strength. You know that the task before you is of the highest challenge. Many men have tried before you and have failed. I have great hopes that today one of you will enter the legends of time and master this bow. This bow is Mithila's treasure, handed down through generations of Videha's kings. It was crafted by Vishvakarma, the divine architect for Shiva, the lord of transformation. May the thirty gods infuse the right man with power to lift this bow. May Shiva, for whom this bow was crafted, empower the worthiest one here. Whosoever proves his strength today by lifting and stringing this bow will win the hand of Sita, who is my pride and the daughter of the Earth."

As soon as Janaka finished speaking, a handsome prince stood up. His thick golden belt shone in the sun, and he wore bright purple silks draped around his hips. His hair was drawn into a topknot and hidden under a large golden crown. He walked down from his seat, trailed by his guards and flagbearer. The flag too was bright purple, and when the prince drew near, Rama saw the sigil, a trumpeting elephant. Just as Rama identified the sigil, Lakshmana leaned toward him and said, "The prince of Hastinapur."

The elephants from Hastinapur were just as famous as the horses from Kekaya. The king of Hastinapur, Jayasena, had evidently sent one of his sons to compete. When the prince of Hastinapur stepped onto the arena, his guards stood back. The prince approached the bow confidently, waving to the crowd.

"He looks like a baby elephant," Lakshmana commented, "approaching an enormous tree."

The prince waved one last time at the crowd and then planted his feet firmly on the ground. He placed both hands on the bow and made every effort to lift it. Nothing happened,

save for his face and neck turning red. After several long minutes of this, he stepped away in defeat, eyes lowered.

The next contestant, a king with thick arms, approached more cautiously, yet also appeared confident. His silk garments billowed in the wind as he strode toward the bow. He ambitiously attempted to lift the bow with only one hand. As he clamped both hands on it, he clenched his teeth as he willed the bow to lift. For several minutes, he strained this way and that way until, his strength spent, he collapsed, falling onto the bow.

Thinking he had fainted, the crowd's murmurs changed to chortles. Hearing the laughter, the king lifted his head. He too was stunned by his own failure; the laughter of the crowd did not make it easier to stand up and return to his seat.

What king after king discovered was that this was not so much a contest as a circus. The spectators could not contain their mirth at the failures; Rama could understand why a warrior would leave feeling humiliated. Nevertheless, the brothers also laughed, joining in the atmosphere of merriment. When a king approached the bow with humility, Rama would not laugh, even once he failed. But he did not spare the arrogant kings, laughing out loud and slapping his thighs, as Lakshmana did, no matter the countenance of the king. Many, in their eagerness to prove themselves, clamped their hands on the bow and tried to jerk it up as if they were champion weightlifters. One king actually jumped on the box, squatting astride the bow, struggling to pull the bow up. The Mithilan guards rushed to restrain him and escorted him back to his seat.

The sun was high in the sky. The kings sweated in their seats, their confidence visibly melting. Rama studied King Janaka where he sat, high on his throne. King Janaka did not laugh, not even once. As a father, this was not a light matter. His daughter's future lay in that bow.

When there was a lull in the action, King Janaka lifted his hand, sending forth refreshments to the participants. Rama and Lakshmana were offered both cool water and sugarcane juice with lime. Another brave soul stood up, drinking down his beverage. He approached the bow with a confidence that everyone could see was forced. His smile quivered and he sweated profusely. And why not? He had seen stronger kings fail. As he too failed to budge the bow, there was no laughter. The gravity of the situation began to dawn on the assembled crowd. Silence descended on the arena. About half the kings had tried their luck. The other half shrank into their seats.

King Janaka stood up. "Witnessing you today, my worst fears are coming true. I fear that there is no one on Earth who is a match to my daughter. You see, strength alone is not enough to lift this bow. But it can be lifted. I deliberated carefully before I set this bride-price. Many of you may have wondered why I chose this test. When Sita was but a girl of eight, she lifted this bow with only one hand. That settled the test."

"Do you really think an eight-year-old could lift that bow?" Lakshmana asked.

"Remember the missive we read with Father," Rama said. "In the last contest, Sita lifted the bow in front of all the kings. That's when they went mad, their egos crushed. She did not lift it with muscle power, as King Janaka pointed out."

Lakshmana settled back into his seat.

"I have reminded you of this," King Janaka said, "to give you hope. I encourage the remaining contestants to gather all your resources and approach the bow. Do not let the failures you've witnessed dishearten you. May the best man win!"

Rama looked at the remaining kings, but no one rose. The cloth of the bright flags flapped in the wind, the sigils obscure in the distance. Rama's gaze returned to King Janaka, who was still standing and looking out into the arena.

King Janaka then commanded, "Bring Princess Sita to the arena! Bring the garland that she will place around the neck of the winner!"

Rama smiled. King Janaka was an expert conductor. When the contestants had grown hopeless, he was reminding them of the prize. Rama leaned toward Lakshmana to speak of this, when the princess of Mithila entered the arena on a palanquin. Conch shells blew and the crowd went wild, chanting, "Sita! Sita!"

The princess stepped out from the palanquin.

Rama's heart stopped. It was the girl from the balcony. The girl who had kept him sleepless through the night, the girl who had stolen a piece of him, who had made a place for herself in his heart; he had not even known her name. Until this moment, Rama had only observed the contest. Now he whispered, "Sita." Knowing her name, he was closer to knowing her.

"They worship her," Lakshmana said. He seemed mesmerized by the reaction the princess provoked. Hence, he had not noticed Rama's. Rama unwillingly took his eyes from Sita to see that the other kings were leaning forward in their seats, swooning at the princess.

She belongs to me, Rama thought, with a possessiveness he had never felt.

Now she had turned her back to them, walking up the steps to join her father. Her long white veil trailed behind her, as did her maidservants. The veil was transparent, displaying Sita's long black hair and her shapely form.

Rama wanted to shield her from all their eyes. When Sita turned to face the arena again, there was a collective sigh of admiration. Her beauty was dazzling them all. For a moment, Rama was awestruck, feeling every emotion that had carried him away the previous day. His heart beat faster. His skin felt hot. His spirit danced, yet he was acutely aware of this moment. Of her.

That's when a giant of a man stood up. Rama's heart plummeted. It was Kashi, the king of Kashi. Rama had not expected to see Kashi here and had not recognized him earlier. Kashi seemed to have doubled in size since Rama last saw him. He was more menacing than Marichi, the blood-drinker. Just one arm was the size of two maces.

"If he can't lift it," Lakshmana said, "no one can."

"He looks like he could easily lift an elephant," Rama said. The words were hard to speak.

Rama's heart stood in his throat, his nightmare taking form. The king of Kashi was taller than most men and stronger than any man Rama had known. King Janaka's face was inscrutable, and Rama knew his hands were bound. Although an aggressor, Kashi had not strictly speaking violated the warrior codes in his previous siege of Mithila.

Kashi's glaring prowess raised a great anticipation in the air. Every eye followed the king of Kashi as he strode forth, marching toward the bow. He waved to the crowd and then clamped his hand on the bow. The crowd hushed, and Rama covered his eyes.

The king put both his hands on the bow. Slowly, the bow lifted up an inch. The crowd gasped. Kashi howled with victory. The bow hovered where it was. The king of Kashi's face turned red, the veins in his neck bulging. Thousands cheered him on. With a loud crack, the bow smacked back down into its place. The king's hands trembled as he backed away from the bow, but his ego remained intact. He spat on the ground and looked up at Sita.

The guards took a step toward him, and he returned to his seat.

Immediately Rama stood up, his heart alight with relief.

He raised his voice. "May I join the contest, Your Majesty?"

He felt Lakshmana's total surprise by his side but kept his eyes on King Janaka, who looked just as startled. Rama didn't dare look at Sita again. Not yet.

"You are most welcome, Prince Rama of Ayodhya," King Janaka said.

Rama turned to Vishvamitra, who encouraged him with a slight bow of his head. For extra luck, Rama touched Vishvamitra's feet and broke the solemn moment only when he smiled at Lakshmana. Until this moment, they had reached all their landmarks of growth together. But Rama was moving ahead now, into that sphere that made him absolutely a man.

As Rama made his way to the center of the arena, he felt every eye on him. There were as many reactions to him as there were people, and Rama felt them all around him: excitement, doubt, derision, admiration, hope. What did *she* feel? He still did not dare raise his eyes and seek her out. He kept his eyes on the bow, following his instincts. It was only him and the bow.

Nearing the bow, Rama felt something awakening within. Rama's hands went out to touch the dark wood and to feel the heavy fiber. Even at the narrowing ends, the circumference of the ancient bow was greater than Rama's upper arm. He reached out and stroked the smooth surface and, to his surprise, the bow was alive; Rama could feel it as a distinct presence.

The prince walked slowly around the bow. The people watched his every move. No one spoke at first, but then the murmurs began. Despite the forceful pressure of expectation, Rama was in no hurry. He let his hands explore the bow, gliding across the wood and under it, holding it but not lifting it. He studied it. Rama circled the bow a few times in this manner, feeling its power. Finally he stopped in the middle, where he would be able to put his hands on each side equally. Rama closed his eyes and started praying, hands palm to palm. The buzzing crowd quieted, intent on Rama. As he stood still, the crowd swelled with curiosity.

Rama stood in silent supplication seeing something through the darkness of his eyelids. A face appeared before him: the former owner of the bow. He was dark skinned and effulgent. Rama realized it must be Shiva, the lord of transformation, the last one to master the bow. He had guarded it ever since, not wishing anyone unworthy to use it. Rama's heart was pure and his intention clear.

"I do not mean to harm the bow," Rama murmured. "I will revere it as if it were my father's."

Rama saw a brief smile on Shiva's face before the vision disappeared. It was only then that he opened his eyes, for the smile had reassured him that his certainty was true: he would master the bow. Now seeing the bow with this knowledge, he noticed a change in its physical structure. It did not shine so brightly. Rather, it had begun to look like a normal bow, though unusually large. The presence that had infused the bow with so much power was gone.

Rama quickly took action. His hand slid under the bow and lifted it in one swift motion. Anyone slightly inattentive would have missed the feat. Rama heard loud gasps and cries fill the arena. He remained calm. He stood the bow upright, leaning one tip on the ground. Putting his foot on this tip to steady the bow, he gathered the string into his right hand. The bow was so large he had to stand on his toes to reach the other end of it. The old wood creaked as he shaped it to his will. Slowly it bent, Rama's muscles flexing to bring it into a proper shape. The bow was nearing a perfect arch when suddenly it exploded into a thousand pieces. The Earth almost shook with the explosion, or so it seemed to the people in attendance.

Rama had been as gentle as he could be with the bow. It had destroyed itself. The legend of its greatness had been shattered and lay in the pieces of wood scattered on the floor. Now a new legend—how the great bow finally broke—would replace the old one. The bow had fulfilled its final purpose.

Rama grinned, and the next moment everyone was cheering and clapping tumultuously. Rama was poised, but his heart beat in unison with the enthused claps of the people around him. They were bringing Sita to him. Lakshmana ran down from their seats and threw his arms around his brother. Vishvamitra's hand was raised in blessing.

Rama's mind took a leap away from boyhood, leaving Lakshmana behind. He lost all trace of boyishness in those moments when he stood waiting for Sita to approach, waiting for her to see him and to garland him as her husband.

Two thoughts struck Rama. First, a question: How did Sita feel about his victory?

And then a realization: He needed his father's blessings to marry.

CHAPTER 39

Sita's Soul

Sita had been instantly drawn to the rich, manly voice filling the arena: "May I join the contest, Your Majesty?"

As she turned her gaze to the speaker, her breath left her body. It was *him*.

"You are most welcome, Prince Rama of Ayodhya," her father had said.

She had to control her lips, which wanted to curve into a sunny smile. Her inner voice sang songs of love, warming her heart. Her happiness in those moments was so deep that she didn't know what to do with her eyes, which darted here and there like black bumblebees. She prayed every prayer she knew, wishing him success. Hardly breathing, she watched every minute move he made. When he lifted the bow, she was lifted into the sky. When the great bow shattered, she too fell at his feet.

Her father touched her elbow, waking her from her trance. "Prince Rama, son of the emperor, has won your hand," he said.

"Rama," she whispered, feeling so happy that pieces of herself were scattered across the sky like unseen stars. She blushed with joy as her father led her down to Rama, accompanied by all her jubilant friends.

When Sita stood in front of Rama, drops of perspiration lined the arches of her eyebrows. Teardrops clung to her eyelashes. Slowly, she looked up into his face. After that, she looked nowhere else.

Her eyelids fluttered, and the tears rolled down from her eyes. A light mist began to rain down on them, cooling the entire assembly. Sita's garland trembled, and she took deep, deep breaths. Whatever emotion was strong in her, she saw mirrored in him.

Her father put one hand on Rama's shoulder; the other was already resting on Sita's.

"Prince Rama, son of the Sun dynasty, you have conquered the bow and won the contest. Sita's hand is now yours. Will you accept my daughter as your wife?"

Rama suddenly looked stricken, as if he had made a mistake.

Sita turned to ice. The stars fell from the sky. She cast her gaze down.

Rama's voice was soft, apologetic. "I want nothing more than Sita's garland around my neck and to claim her as my own," Rama said. "But I cannot agree without my father's permission."

Sita's spirit rose; his hesitation was not directed toward her.

"We will send a message to your father at once," Janaka declared. "Today you will be promised to one another. The fires will be lit and the sacred vow made only with your father's blessings. Do you agree?"

"Yes." Rama smiled, looking intently at Sita.

"Sita," her father said, turning to her. "Place your garland on Rama if you consent to this betrothal." He was speaking the formal words, but there was no formality in his voice.

Sita lifted the flower garland to place it around Rama. As she stood on her toes, he bent his head so she could reach. With the flowers around his neck, Rama became shy. Sita wanted to touch his skin and garland him with her arms.

Flower petals showered on them from every direction, and the cheering grew louder. The bow was broken and their princess would marry!

After the momentous day, the moon illuminated the gardens at midnight. Sita sat by the lotus pond with Urmila dipping her toes in the water. Neither Sita nor her sister could sleep. The darkness of night was bright as a blessing. The silence was filled with Urmila's whispers; the success of the contest and Sita's dazzling prince only increased Urmila's loquaciousness. As Sita listened to her sister's happy chatter, she felt the waters in the lotus pond swirl up around her feet. The quiet wind and the sky above them were filled with Rama's name.

Another name appeared: Lakshmana. Rama's brother who seemed close like a twin.

"Did you see the way Lakshmana ran down from his seat?" Urmila said enthusiastically. "He couldn't wait to congratulate his brother. It was so sweet. Did you notice that he stood right by Rama the whole time, even when you garlanded Rama?"

Sita had not noticed any of those things. Her attention had been wholeheartedly on Rama, to the exclusion of common sense. A lucid part of her consciousness had of course noted Lakshmana's presence, but the one time Sita had glanced his way . . .

"I felt like a shield around Lakshmana deflected my very glance," Sita said. "I could not truly see him."

"Do you think he is jealous of you?"

"No!" The thought had not crossed Sita's mind.

"I have heard that sometimes even a father gets jealous," Urmila said, "if a mother dotes too much on her newborn. It could be the same with a brother. Lakshmana's eyes follow Rama everywhere he goes."

"And someone's eyes seem to follow Lakshmana wherever he goes." Sita raised her eyebrows at Urmila.

"No, no," Urmila shook her head vigorously, but Sita saw a blush appear on her cheeks.

Suddenly eager to turn the attention away from herself, Urmila said, "When you think of being with Rama forever, what do you really feel?"

Sita thought her joy was written in every word and gesture she made. She put her hands on her cheeks to contain the expansion of bliss she felt.

"The bow chose Rama for me, but I feel like I wandered the whole universe to find him."

"I told father to set the same bride-price for me! Then I would be as happy as you are. But now the bow is broken. There is no hope for me."

Urmila dropped her hands into her lap and sighed.

Sita thought of Rama's brother again. Everyone's life would change. Sita would go alone to Ayodhya. She reached for Urmila's hand. "I will miss you more than anything."

"We knew this day would come," Sita said in a soft voice. "We have to be brave."

Urmila leaned on her sister's shoulder. "You always accept everything so easily. You are grace personified."

Sita had to smile. That was their mother's phrase. In this case, Sita didn't have to struggle to find acceptance. She felt beyond lucky. This night would have been very different if someone else had broken Shiva's bow. Like the king of Kashi—a menacing brute. At the first contest when she was thirteen, Kashi had been the most repulsive of them all. During his second attempt, she had fervently prayed that he would once again fail. Kashi frightened her; he had been willing to snatch her away against her will. In his presence, she felt like a deer scrutinized by a tiger. Or worse, that he was a blood-drinker and she his prey.

"Why are you scared, Sister?" Urmila asked.

"Oh," Sita said, rippling the surface of the water with her hand. "I was just imagining how much I would grieve if someone else had lifted the bow."

Rama's gentle and powerful face loomed in her consciousness. Sita could ask for nothing more. She was so happy she could not imagine going to sleep.

A few moments later, however, Queen Sunayana came into the gardens. "Sita, your father seeks you."

The sisters rose from the lotus pond. Urmila looked at their mother, the question in her eyes. Was she too summoned to their father, the king?

Sunayana shook her head. "Father wants to speak with Sita in private."

A shadow crossed Urmila's face. She persisted in thinking that Sita was Father's favorite. Sita viewed it differently. There was something more, or simply something else, in Father's attention. Sita didn't quite understand it herself. If she had to describe it, she would name it fear. She saw it in her father's eyes, how it spread through his body like veins of blood.

Sita parted from her mother and sister in the courtyard. Padmini and Urmila's maid

stepped out of the shadows where they had quietly waited, and for a moment Sita felt ashamed. Just because *she* couldn't sleep, the maidservants were forced to stay awake. But there was no reproach in Padmini's eyes. As Sita walked into her father's chambers, Padmini once again took her place in a corner to wait.

All the candles and flames were lit in the room, sparkling like stars breathing in the darkness. Sita loved the sight of fire, and she was content to stand and wait for her father.

Father smiled when he saw her. He had taken off his crown and most of the jewels he wore. Flickering shadows from the flames danced across his face. His eyes sparkled with joy. Perhaps he only meant to share his delight in the success of the contest. He dismissed the two servants who stood at his beck and call. Like Padmini, they melted into the shadows, becoming unobtrusive in the large chamber. Janaka took Sita's elbow gently and guided her to the balcony so they truly could speak in private.

Sita's heartbeat quickened. It wasn't often that secrets were so secret that the trusted servants were kept at bay.

"Janaki, my daughter," he said, using the nickname, which simply meant daughter of Janaka. "I have never spoken to you openly regarding this. But being the perceptive girl you are, I'm sure you have noticed me keeping a watchful eye on you."

Sita nodded, looking at her father with a somber feeling. She knew it well. Her father's caution was her own. She had second-guessed her own thoughts and reactions ever since she understood that they were separate from her. She was not her sadness, her anger, her love, her confusion. She was the witness, very much like someone standing inside while a storm raged without. She could control and subdue her thoughts and feelings. She could walk away from those storms. That's what she had done all these years for the sake of her father. To please him. To be the one he expected. And because she did not want to be singular, a lone mind excluded from the resonance that bound all humans together.

"I don't fully understand your nature, Janaki. The thirty gods know I have tried. I even wrote a letter to King

Dasharatha once, asking for Vasishta's advice." Janaka laughed lightly. His teeth were white in the moonlight.

Rama's father knew about her, Sita thought. But what exactly was there to know?

"You were hardly three years old," Janaka said, "when I finally sent that missive to the emperor. My hands shook as I wrote. The tale I told was strange, even to me. There is something different about you, Sita. You know that, do you not?"

Sita nodded. But there was a big lump in her throat.

"No, no, no," her father said, noticing at once. "It is not a bad thing. Of that I'm certain. Janaki, listen to me." He put a gentle hand on her shoulder and lightly touched her chin, telling her to look up at him. "Listen to me, my girl. You are not an ordinary human like the rest of us. Your birth showed us that, and then when you easily lifted the bow, it was confirmed."

"Are you afraid of me?" Sita asked frankly. Her chin was trembling, but she knew she should not allow the upsurge of tears to spill out. *That* always increased her father's apprehension. No man could stand to see a woman cry. Urmila's wisdom words.

"I was afraid at first, my dear. That's why I sought Vasishta's help. Even now, when I must speak openly with you about it, I feel a tremor within. But it's not *you* that I'm afraid of!"

He let those words sink in. "From the very beginning, when I saw what you could do, I feared other humans. If I know anything as king, it's that people cannot accept anyone who differs from them. You saw how the kings reacted when you lifted the bow. They did not want to believe it. They called it sorcery, black magic. They wanted to possess you and subdue you."

Sita remembered well the uproar she had caused that time. Lifting the bow had seemed so easy. She hadn't truly understood that she was proving herself stronger than every man in the arena. Now, she would have never done it. In fact, she couldn't. She had tried to lift the bow once again after that, but it had become impossibly heavy.

"But Father, what is it that I can do?" Sita asked. "Why am I different than Urmila? Why don't you watch her the way you watch me?"

Janaka took a deep breath. He looked up at the moon, and then toward the ground. This was the portion of the conversation he had evidently feared, despite what he said. Sita watched him carefully.

"Actually, Sita, I want to ask you the same thing."

He looked at her then, as if she was capable of unimaginable things. There was awe and wonder in his eyes. Sita preferred his fearful concern to this worship!

"But I'm just a girl with strange dreams," Sita said. "That's all!"

"Don't you remember when you were a small child? In those years before you could speak. Do you remember anything from that time?"

She shook her head. Shrugged. Blinked. Shook her head some more.

"Before you could walk and talk, every display of emotion on your part would have a response or counterpart out here." He motioned to the sky, the wind, the fire, the earth.

Sita's mouth fell open. She blinked hard. She thought this was merely her deepest held fantasy.

"Yes, my child. When you cried, it rained. When you were angry, the fires crackled. When you screamed, the Earth trembled. No one could imagine that these occurrences were tied to a little child. But I observed it, many a time, and therefore took it upon myself to keep you appeased."

He looked carefully at Sita.

She remembered those days well. They were her sweetest childhood memories of wild joy, rolling on the ground, being underwater, singing to the wind. She rode on deer, gabbled with parrots, and felt one with the Earth.

"Then it stopped," Father said. "After you mastered language, you became reserved, even guarded. Mithila has never seen such a serious and mature child. Since then, I have never observed any elemental occurrences around you. What changed?"

Sita felt terribly exposed. She hugged herself as the memory returned. The large ones, the humans, had gathered around her, emanating big tangles in their energy. The one who was Father rushed to appease her, enveloping her in his protection. His energy vibrated with waves of anxiety. So she took farewell from the Earth and the sky and withdrew into herself, and for a time, she was paralyzed, denying her connection to the elements she was made of. It was a terrible pain, like having her limbs amputated.

Father drew her to his side. His hands were warm, her skin cold. "Hush, hush," he said, as though she was crying. Warmth returned to her limbs.

"I remember when Ananda came to live with us," she said.

"Shatananda. Our dear friend."

He had come with his matted hair, clay markings, and a boyish face with alert eyes. Sita had loved to pick bits of the dried clay off his forehead and eat them. It made Ananda laugh. He saw the fire at her core, but he was not afraid. He taught her to become the witness, to be free even with constraints. All this was done without words, and whatever Ananda told her father in words transformed the situation. Father's eyes grew less watchful, and his energy flowed naturally again, like a river to the sea.

"Did you know that Rama's father sent Ananda to us?"

Sita shook her head. She had not known that. It made her like Rama's father.

"Ayodhya is a very good place," Janaka said. "Flawless in reputation. In addition to his military prowess, King Dasharatha is widely known for his thoughtfulness. By all evidence, his son Rama has inherited that trait from his father. Over time, Rama will come to know you better than I do. But Sita, if a man is not prepared to see what's in front of his eyes, nothing can persuade him of the truth. I pray that Rama's love will be strong. I pray that the gods reveal your purpose here among us."

"You make it sound like I'm not one of you."

"I don't know if you are, child," he said.

But when he saw the expression on Sita's face, he amended. "You are the beloved of my heart. And now the beloved of Rama's heart. I treasure no one the way I treasure you. And I can see the same adoration in Rama's eyes. He will take care of you. He will do everything for you. But even he is but a man. Don't be afraid, my child. Just be careful. That's all. Now go."

The stars blinked above them. The fires shone within the room.

Sita had to be careful. She always had been. She hoped Ananda would come to Ayodhya with her. She wished Urmila would come too. She longed for anchors to keep her secure in this strange world. A sudden possibility dawned on Sita.

"Urmila is more than a sister to me, Father. She is my best friend and a natural leader. She is vivacious and does not shy away from being at the center of attention."

Her father nodded. He knew this too.

Sita hesitated, choosing her words. She had never before made a political suggestion.

"Urmila mentioned Lakshmana to me several times," she said. "If Sister marries Lakshmana, she and I could always be together."

With that, Sita turned and ran out. She couldn't bear to think of the farewells that stood between them all. What would her life become without her father's watchfulness? What would she do without Urmila's wise words?

As Sita walked to her chamber, the faithful Padmini held Sita's arm. She had sensed the anxiety of her mistress. It had been a tremendous day for them all, and especially for Sita. Padmini brought Sita a calming herbal tea, and moments later, Sita sank deep into her dreams.

This night, an entirely new dream came to her.

The entire Earth was trembling. No one was safe. The fires at the core burned too hot, pushing toward the surface, demanding more space to breathe. The Earth split apart and was no longer one. The ocean claimed the planet. Hungry waves swallowed the rich soil of the Earth, turning it into sea bottom. When the fires sighed in peace and the waves forgot to be hungry, the Earth had split into thousands of pieces, scattered across the ocean. All the while, Sita had been the silent witness. She might have been able to stop it once, but by the time it happened, it was too late.

When Urmila's eager hands shook Sita awake, she had forgotten the dream, but had a vague sense that she had been scattered into a million little pieces. Sita smiled at her sister and put the vision away. She could no longer be a dreamer. Her father had entrusted her fate into her own hands. She had to embrace her fate with a cautious but open heart.

CHAPTER 40

A Father's Blessings

While Rama waited for word from his father, he savored every moment with Sita. He woke early in the morning, leaving Lakshmana and Vishvamitra, to find Sita at the lotus pond. She always waited for him there. Nothing seemed more certain to him than this. Sita's attendants kept a thoughtful distance, and the new couple would sit together for hours and sometimes stroll about in the lush grooves. Rama was careful not to cross any lines of propriety, for he did not yet feel his claim on her was final. He did not reach for Sita's hand; he did not touch her cheek; he did not play with her hair or the curls around her face. But sometimes he had to clasp his hands together to stop them from seeking her nearness.

Lakshmana came to the lotus pond once but left rather quickly. Sita's sister came too and stayed longer but eventually noticed that neither Sita nor Rama paid full attention to her presence. When King Janaka visited, he waved at them from a distance with a contented smile. There was one unexpected visitor, a sage unknown to Rama. Sita's face lit up as the holy one arrived. His face was smooth and boyish, but his matted hair was long, and he was effulgent like Vasishta.

"Ananda," Sita said, "please come."

"Revered prince, you do not know me," Ananda said to Rama, "but I was present at your birth. I have longed to do this, and now I have a concrete reason."

He fell at Rama's feet, touching his forehead to Rama's toes. This was unusual, for with holy ones, it was the other way around. And yet not long ago, a woman of stone and rested her forehead on his feet in this exact manner.

"Ahalya is my mother," Ananda said, rising to his knees, tears streaming down his cheeks. "For over a thousand years, she was trapped in that stone, and your mercy released her. I thank you. I have not felt my mother's presence for a thousand years, and now I do. From deep within my soul, I thank you."

He placed his hand on Rama's feet and touched his hand to his forehead. For several long moments, no one spoke. Ananda was overcome with emotion, and both Sita and Rama held still, giving him time to release his sorrow. When Ananda's emotions were contained, Rama said, "Your mother is free now. She was reborn into purity and glowed like the sun. Your esteemed father embraced her with such affection that my own longing for love arose."

He looked at Sita, and she looked at him.

Ananda dried his last tears and folded his hands at his chest. "It is my great honor to be Sita's servant, and I will continue to serve you both."

"Will you return to Ayodhya with me?" Sita asked.

Ananda nodded once. The timeless young sage bowed, and Rama saw Ahalya's grace in him. As Ananda left, Rama recounted Ahalya's release from the stone to Sita. Remembering that moment, Rama became quiet and full of thought. It was easy to be himself around Sita. There had been no time for Rama to consider the feelings he had experienced when he freed Ahalya. Her son's gratitude had brought it back to him, and the empowering feelings reverberated within Rama.

"I cannot explain how I melted the stone," he told Sita, "but my feelings were so potent, I could not contain them within my physical frame. They emanated spontaneously from me, embracing the anguished Ahalya. I felt that each soul in the world was as near and dear to me as my own mother, brother, and father."

"As your name suggests, Rama, you are capable of pleasing by your presence alone. It appears that your capacity to take action is far vaster."

Rama appreciated that Sita did not make light of his experience, as perhaps Lakshmana or his brothers would have. There was a tragic solemnity in Sita's being that made him feel that the impossible was possible.

The next day, Rama expected a messenger from Ayodhya to arrive with Father's response, but he could not resist meeting Sita at the lotus pond as usual. What if this was his last day with her? King Dasharatha might object to the alliance. Rama knew that a prince was not always free to marry the one of his heart. The kingdom and its welfare came first.

Any other day and any other time, Rama would have heard the tumult in the streets of Mithila as the gates opened and the royal entourage from Ayodhya entered. But his mind was elsewhere. It was hardly present on Earth at all. It was on Sita's sparkling eyes, the breeze caught in her hair, the energy emanating from her soul. But when Rama heard his father's voice, he returned to the present. His heart skipped a beat; Father had personally come! He hadn't sent an envoy with an answer. This meant he approved, did it not?

Rama wanted to run to his father, but his feet were heavy. He was frightened of his father's decision; the feeling held his insides in a terrible grip. He had to speak to Dasharatha and make him see how important his blessings were. If Father said no, Rama would face an unprecedented situation, one wherein his and his father's wills diverged. It had not occurred before, but Rama knew that his duty as a son took precedent. Sita could be his only if Father said so.

Rama forced energy into his feet. His eyes lingered on Sita. He withheld his distress from her and said, "Wait here. I will bring my father to meet you."

Rama sprinted to meet his father on the garden path. Seeing Rama approach, King Dasharatha stopped and held out his hands to his son. The attendant from Mithila escorting him stepped aside. Father was regal, with strong arms and broad shoulders. The furrows lining his face and his silver hair gave him authority. Rama, who was now of height with his father, looked directly into his father's piercing eyes and then took his father's hands. The fragrant scent of sandalwood clung to his father. Rama bent down and touched the king's feet. Father was alone, save his two guards standing at a distance.

"Father," Rama began. "Please come with me. I must have a word with you in private."

Rama led his father away from where Sita waited.

Standing under a flowering tree, Rama spoke. "Something has happened to me, Father. I cannot explain it. I don't understand it. It's in here." Rama pointed to his heart. "I suddenly feel like I never truly existed before I met Sita."

Rama laughed. He knew it must sound crazy. "When I asked to join the contest, I followed a clear instinct. I didn't know if I could master the bow. But I wanted to lift it. I wanted to win her hand. I wanted to protect her. But Father"—Rama's voice became urgent—"I cannot marry her without your blessing, you know that. I'm so relieved that you are finally here."

Quickly Rama embraced his father and then steeled himself for his father's words. When his father simply stood back and beheld him, Rama's foolish actions dawned on him. He had not inquired about his father's well-being or his mothers. He had not asked if King Janaka and Father had met. He had not asked about his brothers. His actions said that he cared only for himself and Sita. Lakshmana might never forgive him for being so self-absorbed.

Rama took a deep breath and waited. Father said, "I can see that you are quite taken with the princess of Mithila. But are you prepared to accept my decision if I say no?"

Rama swallowed hard but nodded. The grip in his gut grew tighter.

"You depend so completely on my judgment?"

"Yes, Father."

"Very well. Your trust in me increases my trust in you. Allow me to meet her."

Unbearably tense, Rama led his father through the garden. In his heart, he could not imagine anyone objecting to Sita. She was so divine. But Rama had remained cautious in his expression of love; he could not take for granted that she would be his.

Sita was not on the cushioned seat in the pavilion where Rama had left her. She sat on the grass surrounded by a flock of animals: a peacock, two deer, several monkeys, and hares.

Where had they all come from suddenly? Each of them was fawning around Sita: the peacock danced, the deer licked her face, and the monkeys chirped in her ears.

Rama went to her side at once; he could not help himself. The animals scattered.

Sita stood up, letting go of a little hare in her hand.

Together they turned to Father. King Dasharatha looked awestruck.

"You did not tell me, Rama," he said, "that your bride was not a girl at all but a goddess!"

Rama looked at Sita.

"I have heard Vasishta and King Janaka say," Dasharatha said, "that you are the daughter of the Great Mother. The words meant little to me before this moment. Sita, I think you are the dream of Earth come true, just as Rama is mine. I have never met someone so young with such ancient wisdom in her being."

He placed his hand over his heart and looked at Sita with his fullest smile. Rama's tension melted away like frost under the sun.

"I see my son's awe of you, Sita. Well chosen, my son. May every god and goddess bless your union. My warmest blessings are with you now and forever."

Rama's face split into a grin so wide, Dasharatha couldn't help but match it.

Having received his father's blessing, Rama had eyes only for Sita. Respectful of their elders, neither of them showed their impatience. But Father knew Rama well. He backed away, signaling for Rama to stay. "Your mothers and brothers are all here. Come see us."

Rama reached for Sita's hand. Their fingers entwined. He did not place his lips on hers, for just feeling her slender palm in his hand created an unbearable ecstasy. He drew her close, speaking the words of love that were in his heart.

After some time, Rama became mindful of his duties as a son and brother. He bid Sita's leave and went in search of his mothers and brothers. The reunion with his family was joyful. All his mothers took turns kissing him, and he was glad that Sita was not there to see him so coddled. Though his mind was on his bride, Rama still relished sharing his adventures, the slaying of Tataka and freeing of Ahalya. Lakshmana filled in many details and kept his arm slung over Rama's shoulder. Rama had been missed.

As the brothers were in the midst of detailing the mantra missiles they had received, King Dasharatha joined them. The family imperceptibly split in half. Father sat down with Kaikeyi, and the two other queens retreated to another seat. The boys stood in the middle of this rift; perhaps only Rama noticed.

Father made a surprising announcement. The two kings and their ministers had come to an agreement: Lakshmana would marry Janaka's younger daughter, Urmila. Bharata and Shatrugna would marry Sita's cousins, Mandavi and Shrutakirti. Rama watched Lakshmana's face turn flaming red and understood that Urmila had not gone unnoticed. Soon after, Rama's brothers met their prospective brides and all agreed to the matches. With unanimous agreement on all sides, the quadruple marriage took place three days later at an hour known as Vijay, "Victory."

The four couples underwent all the marriage rituals and were adorned with sparkling gems, costly silks, and garlands of jasmine, rose, and lotus blooms. First the couples exchanged garlands, which in some circles was a marriage rite in itself. Here, it was one of many steps.

When Sita placed the marriage garland around Rama's neck, he took her hand and faced their elders. "I vow to marry only one woman in this lifetime. Sita is my heart and soul. No one will take her place in my life or in my heart."

Sita's eyes began to shine with bright tears. A mist of rain settled on them. Warm applause greeted Rama's vow. Rain on a wedding day was an auspicious sign. The fires were lit, and Shatananda, son of Gautama and Ahalya, presided over the ceremony. As the royal couples walked around the sacred fire with clasped hands, the fire blazed in approval.

When the ceremony concluded, Rama sought Vishvamitra, touching his feet first among the witnesses. Rama was filled with gratitude. "You had the foresight to bring me to the contest, holy one. You have taught me many valuable lessons. I will not fail to remember you when I invoke the missiles you transmitted to me. I will not fail to remember you when I wake in the mornings and see Sita by my side."

"That is not necessary, my dear boy." Vishvamitra's matted locks swayed as he shook his head. He was perhaps the only one dressed starkly in his usual bark cloth. "The honor of being your mentor these few days has been greater than you can imagine."

Vishvamitra blessed the newlyweds and then turned away with his characteristic forcefulness, departing to the Himalayas, the great mountain peaks of the north.

Sita and Rama touched the feet of all the elders, and the three other couples followed. A sumptuous feast was served, and Rama's new life as Sita's beloved began.

CHAPTER 41

Sita's Secret

Sita had impeccable training and knew the etiquette required of a princess. Ayodhya was not so different from Mithila in its customs. Each day was laid out meticulously. The royal family began their day at the golden altars in prayer and worship. This was a familiar and soothing place to Sita. The altars in Videha were not as golden and grand, but the same deities were worshipped. Sita knew what to do and how to behave, and Kausalya's gentle guidance settled the new brides into routines they understood well.

Sita observed quickly, however, that Kaikeyi never attended the morning prayers. She alone was absent from the royal family. Even Bharata and Mandavi were in attendance. This puzzled Sita, and as she was leaving the golden altars, she took hold of Urmila's hand and whispered her observation. Urmila always had her pulse on what was going on.

Sure enough, Urmila said, "She goes riding every morning and every evening. She has boldly declared this to be the tradition in Kekaya and insisted on maintaining it, even here."

The admiration shone in Urmila's eyes. She clearly longed to be bold like Kaikeyi. Sita had to admit that she too was impressed. It was not common for a woman to defy the norms.

"Of course, some say," Urmila said, lowering her voice, "that Queen Kausalya refused the younger queen entry, insisting she had to bathe first, since she stank like a horse. Understandably, Queen Kaikeyi never set foot here again."

Now this was some rich servant's gossip.

"How come they never tell me these things?" Sita asked, feeling slightly outraged.

Before Urmila could utter her smart reply, the sisters were pulled apart, swept away for their daily duties. Rani, the head maid assigned to Sita's palace, had a list ready of various tasks that needed Sita's attention. Rani was expert in the matters of the palace and came highly recommended by Queen Kausalya. Sita had liked her instantly; she was a tiny woman with boundless energy and authority. Rani took Padmini under her wing at once, for which Sita was doubly grateful. Sita had noted other servants looking at Rani with a mixture of awe and something else, another thing Urmila would probably know the reason for.

Each of the newlyweds had received an entire palace of their own. Sita's new home had a courtyard with a lotus pond. There were so many rooms and hallways, Sita still was not familiar with them all. Each chamber contained gifts from all over Ayodhya: bolts of silk fabric, brass statues of the gods, vases and lamps, artisan cushions, and clay sculptures and pots painted with intricate designs. On top of this, Sita's father had given her and Urmila immense wealth to bring with them, not to mention horses, cows, elephants, and maidservants.

Padmini took charge of arranging the clothing, jewelry, and bolts of fabric in the dressing room with its large mirrors. This was where Sita dressed in the mornings, a procedure that took well over two hours. After one of the maids oiled her limbs, she soaked in the bath scented with Sita's favorite fragrances: earthy khus and sandalwood, Rama's fragrances. They had become her favorite after she met him. Once her hair was washed, combed, and oiled, she sat before the large mirrors and was adorned from head to toe in fine silks, jewels, and fresh flowers. It was like creating a piece of art every day, and Sita knew that the women of the palace scrutinized each other, hopefully with admiration. All this was not new to Sita, but she found that a married princess was more highly adorned than an unmarried one. She appreciated now the time it took to look so elegant. Sita understood that Queen Kausalya had to rise very early each morning in order to look the way she did in time to oversee the morning rituals.

Sita and Rama's home quickly became a gathering place for Rama's friends and even his brothers, despite having palaces of their own. There was always someone who wanted a word with Rama, and he was generous with his time. Hence, they were surrounded at all times by friends and well-wishers. In being mistress of her own palace, Sita had her hands full. She had to make sure that all the dancers, singers, and other servants were fed and satisfied and doing their assigned duties. She quickly learned their names and identified those she could rely on to carry out the various household tasks. Kausalya helped her the first many days, but returned to her own duties the moment Sita understood what needed to be done. The life of a wedded princess was full indeed. Sita was both overwhelmed and pleased by the responsibilities expected of her. In the evening especially, the four brothers gathered for an evening of games, entertainment, debates, and sumptuous food.

These gatherings helped Sita get to know Rama's brothers. Bharata was the easiest to understand and gain liking toward, for he was very similar to Rama in his manners and disposition. Sita felt that she could ask him anything and receive a thoughtful and kind response. Shatrugna made her laugh, and so did Lakshmana. But Lakshmana was unpredictable, and sometimes laughed at things she said that were not a jest. She could not quite understand him and felt wary of provoking his temper. One thing was clear, Lakshmana spoke his mind and declared his opinions. He was not arrogant, however, and was always quick to accept his mistake if he made one. He was perfect for Urmila, who had just such a temperament of her own, and took pleasure in verbally sparring with her beloved. Sita sometimes had to cover her whole face with her hands when she saw Urmila's and Lakshmana's debates escalate. It was only when laughter erupted on both sides that Sita could breathe easily.

Sita thanked the thirty gods that Rama was who he was, the perfect match for her. She told him so every day, and he never tired of hearing those words from her. Truly, it was the most sublime, passionate, and blessed time in Sita's life.

One evening, only a few weeks after their arrival, Urmila came storming in, eyes shining with excitement. "She is riding in the ring next to here. Want to go see?"

There was no need to say whom Urmila meant, for she was endlessly fascinated by Queen Kaikeyi. Also, there was no other "she" who rode at all.

Sita glanced at Rama, who was engaged in a lengthy debate with his brothers regarding a political point. Lakshmana disagreed loudly. Rama disagreed quietly. Both were unyielding. Sita left a message with Padmini, saying where she had gone, and slipped away quietly with Urmila. Her sister led her forward, rushing down the hallways. Servants and guards bowed as they passed by.

The sisters stopped on the balcony overlooking the nearby field, fenced in with golden posts. Only royalty could use this area, and until now, Sita had seen only the four princes ride here.

"There she is!" Urmila pointed at the rider, whose hair was flying behind her like a dark cape. Sita saw Kaikeyi riding in furious circles, wreaking a dust storm in her wake. Sita and Urmila leaned over the balcony, following every move Kaikeyi made. For several minutes, the princesses merely watched as Kaikeyi demonstrated not just her skills on horseback but her penchant for tricks. She could slide down under the horse and come up on the other side without stopping the horse's gallop. She could stand on the horse's back while it flew forward. Urmila informed Sita that Kaikeyi could do all this *and* wield weapons at the same time. Sita held her breath as the queen did yet another acrobatic trick.

"It's said that she entreated the king to train all Ayodhya's girls in weaponry. But the maidservants told me that Queen Kausalya argued against it."

The girls looked at each other. One did not need to be a politician to sense the tension between the two queens—and that it was not openly discussed.

"I don't know if I would be of much use with a sword," Sita said, in defense of her mother-in-law.

"But if you were faced with a dire threat, would it not be good to know how to use a weapon?"

Sita's answer was cut short by Kaikeyi, who brought her horse to a halt, her hair and the horse's mane swaying forth. The queen waved energetically to them. They had not yet had a chance to speak to her outside the formal introductory greetings. The girls walked down from the balcony and toward the golden posts. The energy around Kaikeyi was vibrant. Her hair danced in the wind. She summoned them with one wave of a hand.

Urmila needed no more invitation and verily ran towards Kaikeyi. Sita followed her sister into the horse ring. She too was curious about the queen who was the king's favorite.

"Would you like to learn?" Kaikeyi said. She clapped the horse gently but firmly on the neck. Though she was a queen and their elder, she was slender and beautiful, immediately more a friend than a mother.

"Yes!" Urmila declared.

Sita looked around, noticing how many people were observing them. There were guards standing at the ready everywhere. It was easy to forget, standing within Kaikeyi's energy. Here was the sense that one could do anything, needing no permission from anyone. Sita could understand why Urmila was intoxicated by it. Kaikeyi seemed powerful.

"But we cannot do such a thing without the permission of our husbands," Sita said.

Kaikeyi waved her hand downward, as though such trivial things did not matter. "It's good to show men you have the upper hand," she said. "It keeps them on their toes."

Sita felt nervous laughter rise in her throat. She considered Kaikeyi's words carefully. What Kaikeyi was saying was opposite to everything she and Urmila had been taught. Urmila's public jesting with Lakshmana was already quite bold and unusual. But that was Urmila's expression of love towards Lakshmana, not a calculated attempt to gain the upper hand. Sita remembered that Kaikeyi had not been raised by a queen. Sita's gaze darted about, seeking Manthara, the old woman with the curved back who had mothered Kaikeyi. She seemed to cling to Kaikeyi like an invasive creeper on a tree. Rama had cautioned Sita to stay far from Manthara, and Sita had never spoken to the old one personally.

Urmila asked, "How is it that you acquired a man's skills? You can ride, fight, and even seem to think like a man!"

Kaikeyi laughed, a handsome laugh, throwing her head back and showing her teeth. Like a man would do. Sita was certain she had never laughed like that herself.

"Where I come from," Kaikeyi answered, "a skill belongs to the one who masters it. Not to a woman. Not to a man. And that is the way it should be."

Sita saw defiance flash in the queen's eyes, like she was haunted by something terrible. But the next moment it was gone, and she told the princesses that they could come to her whenever they wanted. She would be there to teach them to be warrior-queens like she was.

"Sita!" It was Padmini's soft voice, calling for her. "Rama is asking for you."

Sita smiled at the queen, thanking her for her kindness to them. Kaikeyi lifted one eyebrow in response. Sita left Urmila there, talking to the queen.

The torchlights and fire lamps were being lit all around Ayodhya. This was Sita's favorite time of day, the late evening when they finally closed the doors to their private chamber, and she had Rama to herself. She began to hurry. Rama would unbraid her hair and run his fingers through it. She would massage his callused hands. They would talk about anything and everything. Sita felt like their hearts were like two riverbanks, the water flowing back and forth between them naturally.

Sita passed Lakshmana in the hallway, and pointed him in the direction where Urmila was. They exchanged shy smiles. Perhaps he was just as unsure around her as she was around him. His purposeful steps belied the thought, but Sita clung to it as she entered the main hall of her new home. She had to understand Lakshmana; he was so important in Rama's life.

Rama held her eyes the moment she entered. A few friends lingered in the hall, but Rama led Sita within and closed the doors to their private chamber. No servants. No friends. No brothers. No sisters. Only the two of them.

It was heaven.

But this evening Rama cupped her face and said, "Beloved, why do you withhold from me?"

"My love," Sita replied, "I tell you everything. You know me better than I do."

"Yes, and I can feel that there is something you are keeping from me. Some secret you wish to conceal from me. Why?" His dark, gentle eyes probed her deeply.

Sita shook her head and looked away, not putting her answer into words.

When Sita wandered in her dreamlands, she understood many things, but she could not translate those truths into her daily life. Sita had always kept those dreams to herself, and although Rama was wise and mystical, Sita could not find a way to open up this part of herself.

When Rama fell asleep, Sita lay awake. Why didn't she tell him what her father had said? Or about the strange feelings that came and went within her?

Rama knew everything about her except for this. But what was there to know, really?

As her eyes began to flutter closed, Sita thought she might finally dream of the black barred gate again. She had not dreamed of it since she walked around the fire with Rama's hand in hers. The gate of her heart was open. She did *not* keep secrets.

And yet there were her father's words, his caution, which she had known long before he spoke them. She had seen it always in his loving eyes: the fear that she would do something, anything, to set herself apart from others.

As Sita's consciousness entered the twilight realm, the in-between place, her inner thoughts intensified and became vivid and clear. There were aspects of Mother Nature that were frightening, even repelling. If she was bold like Kaikeyi, this is what she would tell Rama: "I was born from the Earth and I am my mother's daughter. For if I close my eyes and seek the memory, I too know what blood tastes like, for I have tasted it through *her*, who drinks up the blood of the dead. I know what a decomposed body turning to dirt smells like and feels like, for I have sensed it through her, who decomposes everything in her rich soil. I know too that lesser creatures like worms and maggots, which a princess might run screaming from, are her treasured servants. *She* does not run screaming from anything. Only when the situation on Earth becomes too unbearable does she withdraw, leaving it all to wither and dry up. Sometimes it has been covered in ice, frozen and dead. Other times, dry and lifeless, a desert, another kind of death.

"There will come a time, my mother tells me, when Earth will no longer be one. Something will happen to split the world apart. The rich soil of the Earth will be scattered across the ocean. Only pieces of it will emerge from the bottom of the sea and become home for the creatures that survive. My mother looks at me when she says this, as if I will have something to do with it; her eyes of fire and water see far beyond time.

"I have never known anyone to be wiser than my mother. But this means that I also know that she can be frightening and ruthless. She is capable not only of birth and new life but of death, of drinking the blood of the dead."

Sita woke with a start, the taste of blood and dirt in her mouth. She looked over at Rama, her beautiful sleeping prince.

"The secrets I keep from you," she whispered, "are only the things I myself do not understand."

He stirred and drew her to him in his sleep. She curled up by his side, falling into a dreamless sleep, safe in his arms, with a feeling of timeless forever.

Rama's Second Summit

If Rama had not been a king's son, he would have forgotten himself in his love for Sita. But Father depended on him, not just emotionally but politically. Rama felt it keenly. Once Rama was married, Father's attitude had changed drastically. He treated Rama like an equal, like a grown man. Having recently turned seventeen, Rama knew he could not compete with Father's wisdom. At sixty-seven, Father was strong and swift. But the near-fatal wound on his chest had never fully healed, and he had recently aggravated it during a training session. Father could no longer match Rama's stamina or precision. Rama knew that in combat, he was superior to his father. So were Bharata and the twins, all skilled warriors. Thus, when the Summit of Fifty Kings approached, Rama had a notion of what his father would do.

The four princes were summoned. Along with his brothers, Rama faced the king and his eight trusted ministers, elders who had watched over Rama since his birth. Every one of them now had white hair, and several had grown fine beards.

"Welcome, princes of Ayodhya," the king said. "This is an official matter, but I ask you to speak freely." He looked at each of them in turn. "The ministers and I have decided to send you to represent me at the Summit of Fifty Kings."

This is what Rama had suspected. There was a momentary silence; then Lakshmana spoke. "But Father, the tributary kings come to see you!"

Bharata said, "You are the center point of it all, Father."

"And now the four of you will fill that place," Father assured his sons. "It is time to introduce them to your leadership."

"But why don't you want to go, Father?" Shatrugna asked.

The king shifted in his seat, unconsciously touching the injury on his chest.

"I do wish to go," Father said. "But we believe it is in the best interest of the state that you take my place. As you know, the emperor is not spared the challenges."

They nodded.

"You wrestled bare-chested, Father," Rama said. "You competed with swords and bow. You were the strongest one there." Rama remembered how awestruck they had been, seeing their father in action. Rama wanted to spare his father the humiliation of being defeated.

Turning to his brothers, he said, "Remember how Father beat every contender in verbal disputes and dice games."

If Rama hadn't worshipped his father already, the summit had cemented his adulation; there was nothing that his father was not expert at.

"Now it is your turn," Father said. "You will represent me at the summit this year."

Rama understood the undercurrent of his father's words. Only one of them would be consecrated as crown prince. Only one of them would ascend the throne after Father's rule. Manthara's hateful face rose in his mind, since this was the dead horse issue that she continued beating. Now, Father was offering the brothers and the fifty kings a chance to come to their own conclusions. That was the point of the summit, after all: to determine the centers of power. Rama felt his brothers' eyes bore into him; they also understood what was at stake.

"If any of you have objections or concerns," Father said, "voice them now."

Rama looked at Bharata, who got a stubborn look on his face, as if he had repeated his stance too many times. In fact, they had not spoken of it since that time when Bharata had declared that he wanted Rama to be king. Both of them knew, however, that the choice was between the two of them; Lakshmana and Shatrugna were content to be followers. It had always been like that. Besides, Manthara never let anyone forget Kaikeyi's bride-price.

Bharata stood up. "I agree to go if Rama takes the lead. We decided long ago, Great King, that Rama would ascend the throne after you."

"Is that so?" Father asked. He looked both surprised and amused by this declaration.

"If it pleases you, Father," Bharata answered.

To Rama's surprise, a tear appeared in the corner of Father's eye. "I'm deeply gratified that there is no rivalry among you, my sons. If Bharata speaks for you all, Rama will assume the lead at the summit."

"Yes, Father," the brothers affirmed.

All eyes were suddenly on Rama, waiting for him to speak. It was momentous, and yet Rama had expected this moment.

"It is my privilege to serve you, Father. Bharata is equally worthy of this honor. I am touched by his humility and his trust in me."

"Remember," Father cautioned, "your wives will not be allowed to accompany you. No women are allowed at the summit. A man's weakness is the woman he loves, and men's senses are too often clouded by wine and women, be they lawful wives or courtesans. At the summit, there is no room for weakness. These rules were set down from the day that the summit was established. You will be separated from your wives for at least two weeks."

Rama had not been separated from Sita even a day since their marriage. Because of this, he knew that the lawmakers were wise; if Sita was present at the summit, Rama's attention would naturally be divided. His first priority would be to protect her. Only a scheming, unrighteous king like Kashi would stoop so low, but such people walked the Earth. Sita would be safer in Ayodhya.

"Tomorrow you will receive detailed instructions from Sumantra," Father said. "He will be by your side throughout should any doubts arise. You will not be alone. Your guards, as well as many of mine, will be there to protect you. But you can never relax while you are there. You must be vigilant. You must display the full prowess of your intelligence. You must choose your challenges wisely. If you are too eager to prove your strength, you will weaken yourself and become vulnerable. And yet, you must not shy away from the fights that intimidate you," Dasharatha said. "Those are the fights you must engage in. Men smell fear, like animals do. Your foremost duty is to win their trust."

Rama understood that the summit would be a test for them and also a small taste of kingship.

"We will do everything to prepare you for success," Father assured him. "I would not send you into the lion's den if I did not know your claws were sharp." Father smiled, a menacing one. With those words, they were dismissed.

On their way out, Rama caught hold of Bharata's hand. "Brother, I do not hold you to the words you once said. We were only ten."

"Nothing has changed, Rama. If anything, I feel only more certain."

"You are an exemplary brother." Rama put his arm across Bharata's shoulder.

"Are you sure?" Bharata said, eyeing Rama with a side glance. "Even Father calls it a lion's den."

"On my way to sharpen my claws, as we speak."

The brothers parted. Rama immediately returned to his palace to inform Sita of his departure.

The summit would once again be held in the arena built on the banks of the Sarayu, the very place where Dasharatha had petitioned the gods for an heir. The fifty kings would bypass Ayodhya and go straight to the summit. Built to accommodate thousands, it was the perfect place for the kings with their armies, attendants, and horses.

As the four princes left Ayodhya, Rama felt a sudden trepidation. He was aware that most kings would resist acknowledging the authority of a seventeen-year-old. Many would look at Rama and see only a boy. Would he really be able to face fifty kings and be anything like a leader to them? Rama knew that his father-in-law, King Janaka, would be there, along with many elders to whom Rama was used to deferring.

With the arena in close proximity, Sumantra halted their party, instructing the princes to wait outside. As the emperor's chosen representatives, they would enter only after all fifty kings were seated. When Sumantra summoned Rama, his entry was announced with fanfare; his title was declared and conch shells blew. All the kings stood up. Even so, some had unwillingly stood; they were the ones who would do their best to squash him. No doubt certain kings longed to humiliate Ayodhya and undermine its authority. That was the way of politics. Rama could not be naive. His presence in place of the king was a golden opportunity for such opponents.

After Rama and his brothers sat in the reserved seats, Lakshmana leaned toward Rama and whispered, "Many of these kings saw you break Shiva's bow. They respect you for that."

Sumantra stood at their side, quietly informing them of each king's known strengths and weaknesses. While Rama listened to each king's report, he held their gaze, making his own assessment. Most kings were favorable toward him and his brothers. Among the inimical, Rama counted only nine. Not bad odds.

The long day ended in a feast, and the travel-weary kings retreated, readying themselves for the next day when the summit would begin in earnest.

Rama and Lakshmana had opted to stay in the same room. It was just like when they were children and they always slept together. As they prepared to rest, Sumantra visited. "As custom has it, tomorrow is the hunting expedition. If we provide an outlet for the kings' aggressions, they will choose their opponents for the personal combats in the evening with more care. Your father has taken an active part leading the hunt and also has declined to participate altogether. You may participate according to your own discretion, Prince Rama."

Rama wondered how Sita was faring in Ayodhya without him.

After Sumantra left, Lakshmana turned to look at Rama, leaning his head into his hand. "Remember the first time we went hunting?"

"As if I could forget," Rama said, and laughed.

It had been a disaster.

"I still don't know," Lakshmana said, "who started crying first."

Rama rubbed his eyes. "It was probably me. Though I fancied myself a grown man. At eight years old, I felt quite empowered. The crying . . . I would like to blame Shatrugna." Even though Lakshmana was only a few minutes older, Shatrugna always had more leeway as the youngest.

"I think it *was* Shatrugna, actually," Lakshmana said. "He couldn't bear to see the fawn without its mother. The lord knows how we all doted on that deer."

"Father didn't spare us, though," said Rama. "He said it was good that we felt kinship with the deer. The purpose of hunting was to prepare us to face humans in battle."

"It is a warrior's duty to kill," Lakshmana recited, a mantra they had learned long before they handled lethal weapons.

"A king's, to protect," Rama said.

Since then, Rama and his brothers had gone hunting regularly, as part of their training. Father had taught them to be aware of each life as it ended. The hides of the animals were harvested, and the meat offered to the goddess Kali.

The next morning as Rama strode out to greet the fifty kings, he decided to participate as an observer. The temptation was to use the hunting expedition to demonstrate one's prowess. Many of the kings certainly had that agenda. Not all the kings had joined the hunt; Rama counted thirty-nine who did. The kings rode through the forest in stealth, forming natural clusters.

The joy of riding always released Rama's spirit. He let his horse Tara move at her own pace; sometimes she cantered, other times she stopped to chew on leaves. Several of the kings watched him with disapproval, thinking no doubt that he could not control his own horse. Rama did not feel the need to join the fray. As the morning turned into day, the kings found plenty of game; Rama's participation was not required, until he heard the roar of a feline. Rama urged Tara toward the sound. Lakshmana came riding toward him, the mane of his horse flying in the wind.

"They have surrounded a pride of lions," Lakshmana cried.

When Rama and Lakshmana arrived on the scene, it was a battle of lions against men. The male lion was protecting his pride of eighteen females. Three already lay dead, pierced by spears and arrows. Rama couldn't count the cubs who were running about in distress. The lion was surrounded by several kings, who were slashing at it with their swords and spears. One man lay dead, crushed under his horse. Several other kings were engaged in shooting the females who were herding away their cubs.

Rama felt distaste rise in his throat. This was no hunt but a slaughter. The animals were not meted out the quick, merciful death they deserved. The lion king was bleeding profusely, his golden pelt soaked in red. Three kings continued to ride around him, goading him, laughing, and playing with him.

"Enough!" Rama roared, just as an arrow pierced one of the lion's eyes.

The great beast shook its mane and meowed pitifully. The surrounding kings backed away when they saw Rama approach. Rama beheld the dying lion, seeing its life leave its body like the rays of the sun disappearing on the horizon. Other arrows flew past Rama into the lion's neck. The lion collapsed onto the ground. His mates escaped, and several kings rode after them in pursuit.

Rama swung off Tara.

A low purr emanated from his own throat as he approached the dying beast. The lion scrutinized Rama unblinkingly with one yellow eye. With a swift tug, Rama pulled the arrow out of the other eye. He couldn't stand to see it there. Rama growled softly to the beast, in the language he had learnt, placing his hand on the lion's mane. The words he said were something like, "Go where the sun goes," the lion's way of farewell.

The lion's eyes filled with energy. He got onto his feet, and the arrows fell out from his hide as if they had never pierced his skin. Before Rama could blink, the lion opened its jaws wide, letting out a thundering roar, and bounded away. His two yellow eyes gave Rama a lively look. Rama and the company of kings stared after the disappearing lion, which should have been dead.

The power of life and death surged in Rama's fingertips. Rama did not roar out loud. But he had wanted the great beast to live, and it had. He knew that if he lifted his hand, whomsoever he pointed at would fall down dead. So he curled his hands tightly at his side as he turned around to the remaining kings.

"Who shot that arrow?" he asked.

He didn't have to raise his voice. He had their attention.

"I did," the king of Kashi said, with an arrogance that pulsated around him. "He was mine to kill."

"You foreswore your right to be his killer," Rama answered, "when you ignored his right to die with dignity."

Kashi sneered. "The boy talks as though the animal were a human. Only a weakling makes such foolish judgments."

Rama felt the hairs on his neck rise. Kashi had vowed to gain Shiva's bow and destroy the Sun dynasty. He had failed the former but was still intent on the latter. The desire to murder Rama shone in Kashi's eyes.

Kashi jumped off his horse, landing on the ground with an enormous thud. He smashed his fist against his palm. "Your blood is mine!"

"This is against the laws of the summit!" Lakshmana called out. "Challenges take place at the appointed time."

"Shut your mouth," Kashi called out without looking at Lakshmana.

There was a stir of unease among the kings. Lakshmana was right. None of Rama's guards were present; neither was Sumantra. Many things could go wrong. But Rama would not back down. He was staring into Kashi's eyes. The inimical king was barely human. Killing was his sport, which he meted out cruelly and indiscriminately. He had killed women. He had killed children. He had the smell of human blood on his lips, and he would not mind having a taste of Rama's. Rama glanced at his bow, which was slung across Tara's saddle.

"Don't even think about your bow," Kashi said. "I will smash your skull the moment you turn toward it."

He would not honor the warrior code that forbid attacking a man's back. Kashi gloated, smirking with satisfaction.

Rama understood. "You orchestrated this to separate me from my bow."

"Always so intelligent," Kashi said. "Always too late."

"Don't do this!" Lakshmana shouted—a telling sign of how menacing Kashi was. Lakshmana had not objected to his killing Tataka, a monster triple Kashi's size.

Rama spread his fingers like stars, the power he had felt was still alive there. He could raise his hand and destroy Kashi with one thought. The energy pulsated from his soul into his palms. His hands lifted slightly. A fury that was larger than his body began to fill his form. If he let this continue, his human form would shatter and in its place, another being would stand. Rama clenched his fists and clamped his arms to his side. He had to stay human at all costs. It was the strangest thought, the deepest conviction of his heart.

Kashi spat out insult after insult.

It gave Rama time. The prince took long, steadying breaths, quelling his anger. The energy in his hands disappeared, and his eyes darted to his bow. What could he do without it?

Kashi jabbed his fists through the air, aiming directly at Rama's skull. The fist flew by Rama's ear. Rama ducked quickly, avoiding the blow. The king had no qualms about killing Rama under the sun today. There was no spark of honor in him. He brought forth a knife in each hand and began slashing at Rama. Loud protests erupted, since Rama was unarmed. The prince invoked Bala and Atibala, who immediately wrapped around him protectively.

Lakshmana saw this and stopped protesting. Rama whistled for Tara.

"Coward!" Kashi howled.

Rama ran toward Tara and jumped onto her back, then stood up on her, a move that Kaikeyi had taught him. From there, he hurled himself against Kashi, toppling him to the ground. Rama quickly stood up, his foot on Kashi's neck. It was disdainful to touch a person with the foot, and Rama showed what he thought of the king as he pressed Kashi down with a near lethal pressure. Lakshmana cheered. No one else did.

The king did not beg to be released. Even a small movement could render him voiceless forever or break his windpipe. Rama addressed the crowd of kings.

"Imbued with the authority of my father, I have won the first challenge against Ayodhya's authority. Like my father, I will be kind and just. But I will not tolerate undue violence."

He removed his foot from Kashi's neck and mounted Tara again. He ignored Kashi and turned to the other kings. "I will meet you at the summit this evening. There, you may challenge me as you see fit."

"I will not play your child's games," Kashi said. "I will kill you. I will destroy your pathetic father. I will enjoy your wife. I will even take your mother."

Before Rama could respond to the insult, Kashi mounted his horse and galloped away.

When they returned to the summit, Kashi and his people were gone.

"Send scouts out in all four directions," Rama told Sumantra. "Keep a lookout for Kashi's return. Send a messenger to Father to have reinforcements ready."

As evening came, the summit continued and the combats began.

CHAPTER 43

The Future in the Past

The palace was incredibly quiet. Sita did not normally mind silence, but now the whispering echoes spoke only of Rama's absence. It was day ten without him. There were, of course, maidservants and attendants prepared to amuse her and fulfill any whims or desires she had. But she had few desires now that Rama was not here. She walked from chamber to chamber, her hands trailing across the walls and pillars, playing with the flowing silks of the curtains and canopies. She examined objects that she had never noticed before: a leaflet of prayers containing the thousand names of Vishnu, a mirror with gold carvings that magnified the features of the face, a small carved wooden box full of golden nose rings with multicolored gems. She lingered the longest at the statue of Kamadeva, his five arrows of love across his bow. She touched each of the tips, each one sharp to the touch, although they were depicted as flowers. Love had to be sharp, or it would never pierce its target.

Sita walked into her personal chamber, walking around the bed where she slept with Rama. She fluffed up the pillows and found a strand of Rama's hair: thick and curly, almost coarse, like Kausalya's. Sita's own hair was straight and silky. Even though hair that was separated from the body was considered unclean, Sita held Rama's strand of hair in her hand as she left the room.

Sita went to the gardens, feeling the welcome of the lush trees. Here, finally, she felt some measure of life return to her bleak heart. As she sat on one of the swings, the role of a princess and the idea of who she was floated away in the breeze. She left the attendants behind, to walk alone in the gardens. It was impossible to be here and not transform. Step by step, she felt solid like the Earth, expansive like the sky, flowing like the waters, and fierce like the fire that glowed within the heart of every living being. She planted her feet into the earth, digging them into the soil as though they were tree roots. She closed her eyes and held her arms to the sky.

"Sister!" Urmila's voice echoed through the trees, breaking Sita's reverie.

She drew her feet out from the earth, shaking off the dirt.

"I knew I would find you here somewhere," Urmila said.

She hooked her arm in Sita's and said, "I feel lonely too."

Together they walked through the gardens, Urmila guiding Sita back toward the palace.

"There is good news. Queen Kaikeyi has promised us riding lessons. She told me that I should not wait for Lakshmana's approval, but rather seize the opportunity now that he is gone."

Sita widened her eyes and smiled. It seemed like a harmless rebellion. Kaikeyi was a queen and their respected mother-in-law. Surely Lakshmana would not mind Urmila having that glorious skill.

"You will no doubt master it," Sita said.

"You too!"

Sita shook her head. "No, Urmila. I'm not meant to be on horseback. I felt it deep in my bones."

Urmila's restless fingers and eyes spoke of her desire to begin her adventure. "I will tell you every single detail when I return."

"Go, then," Sita said. "I will see you this evening."

One special treat that came with their husbands' absence was that the sisters got to sleep together, like they did before they were married. This made for long nights of talking and exchanging secrets. Sita now knew where Lakshmana was ticklish, though she could not imagine him rolling on the floor laughing, as Urmila promised he did. Some nights, even Mandavi and Shrutakirti joined. There had been unstoppable laughter among them as they spoke about the brothers they had married. It was a closeness of sisters that Sita could not hope to share with anyone else.

Urmila drew Sita back into the palace. Aimlessly, she walked along the palace hallways, allowing her fingers to trail along the marble, gems, and mosaic patterns. Through her fingers, she sensed the life present within the inanimate structures. The architects and builders of the magnificent buildings had left a little piece of themselves within. Even the marble was alive under her feet.

Sita found herself within the royal library, the place where many of Rama's lessons had taken place as a child. She sought Ayodhya's records of its own history. After a brief search, she found the public documents of Dasharatha's rule, beginning with his first epic battle when he had gained the name Dasharatha. Sita had read the records of her own father's rule

many times. It was fascinating to see the actions of a man documented, gaining a life of its own on the parchments. Dasharatha's long rule did not disappoint. It contained many, many battles, along with meticulous documentation of the warriors who had fought with him and who among them had returned. Sita scanned these pages, having little taste for war scenes.

What interested Sita more was when the queens appeared on the pages—Dasharatha's marriage records. Sita carefully read about Dasharatha's acquisition of Kaikeyi and the bride-price he had promised. Eager to learn more about this love story, Sita turned the page.

What she read next drew her breath away. Ice filled her veins. She clutched the book to her chest and left the library. She stalked through the hallways, heedless of etiquette. She carefully remained the witness of her emotion, but she did not stop until she reached her chamber. Ignoring Padmini's questions and walking past Rani, Sita hid herself in her chamber.

She sat on the bed, letting the book fall into her lap. She was stunned by what she'd learned. She curled up on the divan, hiding her face in her arms. The book lay open, the story continuing to whisper terrible truths into her mind.

A small hand touched her cheek briefly. The touch was cool and firm. A mist of rose-scented water settled on her skin, rousing her from her despondency.

Sita opened her eyes and saw Rani standing over her. Rani had not touched the book that lay open at Sita's feet. But she pointed at it and said in a quiet voice, "I was one of them."

"Maharani," Sita whispered back. The name stood out at once from the list she'd read.

Rani blinked rapidly but held Sita's gaze.

"You are the girl who first came to Ayodhya heralding the return of the abducted women."

Rani nodded. Sita's heart hammered against her chest.

"Shall I tell you my story?" Rani asked.

Sita sat up and drew the little woman into her arms. Rani was no longer a servant or a woman older than Sita, but a child whom Sita had to soothe and protect.

"Tell me," Sita said, releasing Rani. Tears ran down both their cheeks.

The two women looked at each other for a long time before Rani began.

CHAPTER 44

Kashi Attacks

Even though Kashi's desertion was a portentous breach of the law, the summit continued. Additional troops were called in from Ayodhya and stationed around the summit. Kashi's attempt to kill Rama was unforgivable. The emperor himself would decide Kashi's fate.

Rama was challenged to wrestle, debate, and battle with every kind of weapon—and even sing. Rama quickly learned that there were two kinds of challenges. Most of them were competitive, the opponent set on defeating Rama. Some challenges, however, had another quality altogether.

Guha, king of the Nishadas, the largest forest tribe, was dark as night and sleek as a panther. As Rama and Guha wrestled bare-chested, Rama's heart grew light. Guha's technique was impressive; when Rama had him in a tight lock, he found a way out. Soon both of them were laughing in each other's arms, until finally they rolled apart, tightly clasping each other's arms. The joy was in the technique of the martial arts and the competition to match offense with defense; neither of them had the thirst to win.

"You are the first kindred I have the pleasure to meet here," Rama said, pulling Guha up from the ground.

Like Rama, Guha had been sent in his father's place. This was his first summit as king.

"I am not king yet," Rama insisted.

"As you say, Your Majesty." Guha smiled, his teeth startlingly white against his night-dark skin. "But the Nishadas are your servants now that you have defeated me."

"But I didn't," Rama said.

"You did, in just the right way."

Guha was older than Rama by several years, but over the next few days, they wrestled their way to the most amicable friendship.

Such delightful challenges were rare. As the days passed and the kings feasted and fought, Sumantra was at Rama's side, advising him which challenges to accept. Rama had never before set his mind on proving his superiority. He was usually more intent on making his brothers shine. As he set his mind to win, however, he discovered that no one present was in his league at all. Not one among the fifty kings could match Rama's power, skills, or knowledge.

Though Rama had often sensed his innate powers, the summit put his prowess into the open for all to see. He understood and accepted that he had the makings of a true king. Lakshmana smiled from the sidelines, as though he'd always known this.

On the last day of the summit, Kashi attacked. The final feast and the celebration of champions were well under way, with the royal musicians and the voices of hundreds of people laughing and conversing creating a din. Kashi's first blast of soldiers was subdued by the archers along the walls, and the warnings stormed into the arena. Rama and every other king set down their cups and stood at once. Entire tables overturned and cups and platters crashed to the floor. The musicians paused, hands in the air. A split second of silence confirmed that an army was approaching. The noise in the hall doubled and tripled.

Oaths and calls of outrage filled the arena, and Rama roared his first order: "Send word to Ayodhya! Bring forth the troops!"

He pointed to Shatrugna, who bowed and ran out. Next, he turned to the kings and proclaimed, "In the name of my father, King Dasharatha, emperor of the world, I command you to fight with me or retreat with Shatrugna into the safety of Ayodhya's walls. The choice is yours. The time is now."

All but two elderly kings bowed their heads, placing their hands on their swords.

"We will bring you to safety within Ayodhya," Rama promised, looking at the two who abstained. "Bharata, you and Shatrugna will lead Ayodhya's troops. Those who will fight with me, arm yourself and your men. We meet in the courtyard as soon as you are armed. Lakshmana, come with me."

The kings and their men left in a hurry. Although they all carried arms at all times, a battle required armor and an arsenal of weapons. Even in a crisis like this, it would take several long minutes to don the necessary gear.

Rama and Lakshmana threw on their chain mail, arm guards, finger guards, and helmets emblazoned with the Sun dynasty crest. Their attendants gathered their swords, shields, quivers, bows, and assortment of other weapons, carrying them to the awaiting chariot.

Horses and chariots were made ready, and Rama beheld the men at his disposal. They were far outnumbered. The dust storm in the distance warned of a very large army advancing. Kashi was putting all his resources into this attack. Rama placed his hand on the ground and listened, as his father had taught him to do. Kashi's troops numbered in the thousands and would be upon them in less than an hour's time.

The summit was not prepared for a battle of this magnitude. Though Ayodhya's troops were close at hand, Rama knew that it would take at least two hours for them to mobilize and reach the summit. Rama took some solace in the presence of the mantra missiles Vishvamitra had imparted to him.

Rama quickly formed a plan. He could take on the army by himself, launching his arsenal of magical missiles, all of them lethal. But the strategist in him could not forsake the opportunity to rally the kings together under one umbrella. They could not, however, take a stance against the oncoming army at the summit. In quick words, he consulted Prince Yuddhajit and King Janaka, his closest relatives at the summit. They agreed with Rama's plan. Standing on his chariot, Rama called out his orders to the forty-seven remaining kings, splitting them into four divisions.

Rama took the reins of his chariot and led the way, heading out from the summit. As they reached the riverbanks of the Sarayu, Rama invoked Manu's missile and unleashed it on the Sarayu. Meekly, the river parted.

"Go!" Rama cried to his small army of kings. He did not know how long Manu's missile could uphold its feat. "I will cross last," he said, urging the others to proceed.

Prince Yuddhajit galloped across, and every man followed. Finally Guha crossed.

The wind greeted Rama as the chariot flew across the river bottom. Sprays of water splashed his face. On either side of him the water flowed ferociously.

Reaching the other shore, Rama recalled Manu's missile, and the path disappeared, as if it had never been. As the kings took their stance, they saw Kashi's troops surrounding the summit, discovering quickly that it was empty. Kashi's soldiers lined up on the banks of Sarayu, hurling insults across the water. Rama waited. Kashi's troops parted, letting their king through. Kashi rode an elephant and appeared gigantic next to the foot soldiers. Kashi gave his command, and his troops surged forward, headlong into the Sarayu. The current carried them away at once. Even the strongest swimmer would come to shore far downriver.

Rama smiled. His army patiently waited.

The horses began to nicker and paw at the ground with impatience. Still, Rama commanded them to wait. It was not pleasant to watch soldiers drown by the hundreds, but Rama would not have commanded his own troops to cross a swiftly flowing river. He had counted on Kashi's bloodthirst and impulsive thinking. Eventually Kashi, along with a score of warriors, emerged on the shore, drenched to the bone, hair plastered to their skulls. Now their numbers were more evenly matched. Ayodhya's troops on the other side would demolish the rest of Kashi's army.

Kashi had abandoned his elephant midstream and was mounting a horse while calling out orders to his soldiers. They organized into a protective formation around him, working as a human shield. The kings around Rama cursed Kashi. It was understood that if Kashi won this battle, every single person present would have to bow their heads at his feet.

Rama did not have to issue further commands to the veteran warriors. Weapons were launched and the two forces charged at each other. Kashi was as eager to kill Rama as Rama was to kill him. The two immediately found each other and began the dance of death. Kashi ignored Rama's body and shot Rama's bow out of his hands. Rama's shield caught the next volley of arrows as he reached for his other bow. Rama shot off Kashi's crown and his armor, and smashed all his weapons. Kashi did the same to Rama.

When Rama summoned one of his divine missiles, Kashi counteracted it with spells of his own. The air crackled with dark magic. Rama sent the missile of Agni, fire shooting from the tip of his arrow. Kashi's arrow released a dark shadow that swallowed and suffocated the fire. Divine missiles were subdued by demoniac ones, light swallowed by darkness. Eventually the battle was reduced to Rama and Kashi circling each other, swords in hand, as it should have been from the start. The surviving kings formed a circle around the two, witnessing the battle.

When Rama struck his death blow, Kashi did not fall to the ground like a common man. He exploded, spraying Rama with blood from head to toe. The form of Kashi's spirit body became visible, a dark mass that should have been invisible to the mortal eye. Whispering threats in a language not human, the spirit swept across them before slowly dissipating.

Had they harbored a demon in their midst?

"Victory," one of the kings called in a subdued voice.

Rama raised his sword in the air and repeated, "Victory!"

When he smiled, the dead man's blood seeped into his mouth. Rama spit it out and mounted his horse, picking up Kashi's crown. The battle on the other side of the bank was still going on. Rama could hear his brothers' voices across the Sarayu. Rama rode like a demon, invoking Manu's missile again, and galloped onto the other side, the dead king's crown held high.

Without their king, Kashi's troops had no reason to fight. The battle was over. Lakshmana herded together the defeated troops. The surviving kings rode behind Rama. Together the victorious entered Ayodhya, emitting cries of victory. King Dasharatha rode to meet them. Flowers rained down on them, bugles and conch shells blew, and drums resounded. Rama had led them to victory!

CHAPTER 45

Sita's Premonition

The celebration of Rama's victory extended over three days. Ayodhya reveled in his glory; the story was told and retold. Dancers enacted the scene; singers composed songs; actors created elaborate enactments. The queens and princesses were given lavish silks; the priests were given milk cows, and every citizen in Ayodhya received a gift suited to his or her needs. King Dasharatha spared no cost in celebrating Rama's success. Throughout this, Sita stood at Rama's side, thanking citizens, smiling, and receiving gifts on his behalf. She longed to be alone with Rama. Only he could thaw the ice that had been around her heart since she read that passage in Ayodhya's history. Rani's heartfelt sharing had only fueled Sita's anger.

Finally, finally, the hour came. On the third day of celebration, Sita and Rama retreated to their palace. The crowds of friends thinned from their quarters. Rama, eager to be with Sita, excused himself from his duties and social obligations.

The doors to their chamber closed. After the servants assisted them in untying and removing their luxurious silks and jewels, Sita dismissed them. The murmur of voices receded.

Sita asked Rama to sit and rubbed healing oil into his neck and shoulders. She enjoyed the feel of his smooth skin and strong muscles. For a few minutes, a sweet silence held them as Rama sighed and relaxed under her hands.

Then he asked, "What is it, my love?"

"How did you know, Rama?"

Sita looked at the curve of his ear and the curls of his black hair. Even from behind, he was alluring. She continued to massage his shoulders, but marveled that he knew her heart. She did not want to be anything but gracious and forthcoming to their friends and well-wishers. She had been careful to keep her private turmoil to herself.

"I know everything," Rama said in a light voice.

"I hoped you would say that."

Even though part of her simply wanted to revel in his company, she dried her hands of oil and brought forth the book that had chilled her so. Without words, she opened the pages and placed the book in Rama's lap.

"Ayodhya's history," Rama said, immediately recognizing the text. "My father's great deeds."

Sita was silent. She could see Rama's eyes quickly scanning the open pages. When he was done, he closed the book and looked up at her.

"I will *never* let that happen to you," he said, as if swearing a solemn promise.

Sita sank onto her knees and sought refuge in Rama's lap. Instead, she made contact with the book that had haunted her. She wanted to fling the book away or burn it. But that would not change the past or the feelings that exploded in Sita's heart.

"It's not what happened that scares me," she said. "The men on Earth had no power to stop Ravana. Your father says so clearly, in the passage. I can understand how helpless he felt from his words. Ravana is the *king of the blood-drinkers*. No one can stop him."

Rama clenched his jaw.

"It was this which really chilled my heart." She quickly flipped the pages to find what she was looking for. "Here."

Her finger rested on a letter from one of the citizens, a man named Lochana. She didn't look at the record. She had already memorized it. "'My wife is dead,' he writes. How could he say that! How could he swear before the fire to protect her and then dismiss her as dead!"

"Perhaps she was dead," Rama said, in a neutral voice.

"Perhaps she had been tortured and mistreated and needed nothing but her home and her husband's love!" Sita countered. "Did you know that Rani, our powerful little Rani, who knows how to do everything, was one of the victims? Her family shunned her, without even listening to her side of the story. She was only ten years old! I made her tell me everything. Every single detail. It's impossible to exonerate Ravana, ever. He must be held accountable. And Rani must be fully embraced."

Sita was so angry. She had been angry for days.

"You are angry," Rama stated.

"Yes! It is not fair! All these women were abducted. They were innocent. They did not ask Ravana to take them. They did not go of their own free will. The women were terrified and praying for their lives."

"Sita, Father and his ministers took all of this into account. It was a difficult time for everyone on Earth. Families were destroyed."

"King Dasharatha and Queen Kausalya did what they could to counteract the damage. But those families destroyed themselves the moment they closed the doors on their innocent wives!"

Rama lifted his hands, shielding himself from her accusations. She took a deep breath.

"Come here," he said, taking the book from her and pulling her into his lap.

She was enveloped by the comforting scent of Rama, with its intoxicating fragrance. She leaned her cheek against his, bringing forth the question that really haunted her. "Rama . . ." she hesitated.

"I told you," he said. "I will never allow this to happen to you."

"You cannot protect me from everything. I'm sure these women had valiant husbands too."

"I can and I will," he said stubbornly.

"But Rama, when I read this, I was overwhelmed by a strange feeling, as if I was one of these women in my last life. It was like looking into the future or the past. The feeling was so strong."

She turned to look into Rama's eyes. He shook his head. He didn't want to believe her premonition.

"What would you do, Rama, if I was taken by someone like Ravana and then escaped and came back to you?"

Rama's answer shocked Sita more than anything else.

"I don't know," he said—the first time Sita had heard him say those words. Rama always knew. He knew everything. He was a treasure house of knowledge, always knowing what to say and what to do. He made it his business to know the right words to say and the right questions to ask.

"You—you don't know?" Sita stammered, her eyes growing wide like never before.

For a long time silence wrapped itself around them, speaking to each of them privately. They both rose silently and moved to the alcove, with its night-blooming jasmine. The book was in Rama's hands still, the topic all but closed. Crickets chirped, and the stars twinkled in the night sky. Sita began to think Rama simply had no more to say on the topic, when his deep voice filled the emptiness.

"The night before our wedding, I could not sleep," he said. "I paced up and down in Videha's royal garden, below the rooms where my brothers slept soundly. The next day I would be married. The moon illuminated the starry sky. The stars twinkled, just like tonight. I had known you for only five days, but I knew more about myself already. I knew that I had become whole in a way that I had not been before. Every good quality I had was illuminated and highlighted in your presence. I wanted to be the best man on Earth for you. I had no misgivings, no apprehensions, no doubts about this union with you.

"When I saw all those kings ready to claim your hand, I was ready to battle every single king on Earth for you. I didn't even remember Father in those moments when I approached Shiva's bow. There was only me, the bow, and my unstoppable desire to protect you from the unwanted eyes that were on you. It was an irresistible urge."

Sita looked at Rama without smiling. The words were too life giving. She wanted to close her eyes and wrap herself in his words forever.

"Thinking of you," he said, "I was so content on that night before our wedding. Yet there was something that kept me awake. It evaded me at first, as far off as a star in the sky. I couldn't simply pluck it from its place and examine it. It was a puzzle, and every time I completed a round in the gardens, I had found another piece."

Rama took a deep breath. "The first piece was my mother's sadness, though she hid it from me, and still does, behind her kind demeanor. She has never spoken of it to me. But I have seen how Mother looks at Father, how she becomes nervous in his presence, how she always tries to stay in his company as long as she can. She would always look at the doorway after he was gone, as though she hoped he would return. If Kausalya was my only mother, I might have simply thought mothers were like this, having their secret sorrows. But I had seen Kaikeyi's zest for life, the way she enjoys everything she does. It did not escape my notice that Father favors Kaikeyi, that he seeks out only her company. I have never seen Kaikeyi sad. Father makes sure she never is. I had always thought that when I was a grown man, I would understand more. But now that day was here, and after several rounds in the garden I knew this: Mother was unhappy because Father did not love her the way he loved Kaikeyi. Kaikeyi was happy because Father loved her. Father felt torn about his own actions. Finally, I held the star in my hand. Standing there in your gardens, Sita, I held the final piece to the clarity I sought."

His luminous eyes settled on her. "Remember the vow I made on our wedding day before the sacred fires?"

"That you would love and marry only me?" she whispered.

He nodded. "That was the star I held in my hand. The knowing I received from deep within. I never want to subject you to torment, Sita. I never want to divide my affection between you and another woman. I never want any wife but you. My brothers might choose differently. They might, like Father and most other kings, marry several wives, for personal or political reasons. But I will not. And so I made that vow, then and there to the sky, the Earth, and the universe. I held the words close to my heart, and I longed for the opportunity to say the words to you. When we stood with the fire as a witness and I declared my intention, I was bound by my love and my vow. You will be my one and only love. If anything happened to you . . . if anything like this"—he swept his hand across the page—"happened to you . . ."

He closed the book with a snap. "Sita, I would be destroyed. If you die before I do, I will be a shadow of who I am. I know it's unmanly to say so. It's not a warrior's way to depend on anything external. But I cannot extricate my being from yours. I knew the moment I set eyes on you, and my heart leaped out of my soul to unite with yours, that there can be no life for me without you. You are the gatekeeper to my heart. If I ever lost you, I would lose the way to my own self."

Sita's hands covered her heart, holding their love within her chest. When he called her his gatekeeper, Sita thought of her long-standing dream of the black gate. She had received a key to the gate the moment she laid eyes on Rama. But that gate was not Rama's. She knew it as clearly as she knew Rama's heart lived within her. She could feel his love alive within her, the dance of their hearts, celebrating his tender words. Sita felt truth reverberate around every single word Rama said. The tide of her feelings turned, and suddenly she was more afraid for him than herself. What would become of Rama if something like this—she glanced at the book—ever happened to her?

After a while, Sita said, "I am safe here." The serene night and Rama's quiet presence melted the frost from her heart. "I don't know why I was so frightened and angry. The women in Ayodhya are safe. Ravana has never breached Ayodhya's walls. And I have you. No man or blood-drinker has ever stood a chance against you."

"Yes, the last three days Ayodhya has sung my glories, while my own wife has silently harbored doubts about her safety and future with me."

"All gone now," Sita said, and smiled.

The dark night settled around them, bringing them closer. Sita wanted to stay in this sweet darkness the rest of her life, and yet a part of her knew she wouldn't.

THE QUEEN'S PLOT

CHAPTER 46

A Brother's Memory

Ayodhya was still buzzing with Rama's victory when Kaikeyi received the summons from Kekaya. Her father longed to see his grandson, Bharata. One of Ashvapati's swans delivered the message to Kaikeyi, and she asked Dasharatha for his consent. Her father's health was not at its best; he had requested Bharata to come at the earliest. Yuddhajit offered to personally escort Bharata. It was the most practical solution since Yuddha was already in Ayodhya due to the recent summit. Still, Kaikeyi was moved by her brother's gesture; he could have appointed someone else to do it.

There had been no time during Rama's victory celebration to speak privately with Yuddha. Brother and sister had barely exchanged pleasantries. Kaikeyi was eager to speak to her brother and arranged to meet with Yuddha on the plains beyond Ayodhya. Yuddha would soon return to Kekaya with Bharata.

When Kaikeyi spied her dashing brother on his stallion, she felt the world as a vast place full of opportunities. Her mind felt energized, and she galloped toward him. Without a covert gesture, they slid off their horses at the same moment and strode toward one another.

Kaikeyi ran into his arms. Over the years, she had missed her brother more than she had expected, realizing their closeness only once it was gone.

"Sister," he said, squeezing her so tight she couldn't breathe. The moment she was locked in his arms, however, another feeling came upon her. A remembrance of why she rarely visited Kekaya. She literally could not breathe in her brother's arms, even after he had let her go. She looked up at him and recognized the resemblance others remarked upon. She was seeing herself as a man. They had the same piercing blue eyes, the same symmetrical features, and tall, almost lanky, builds. His skin had the sun-kissed glow that had faded from Kaikeyi's skin over the years. She was not constantly out in the fields on horseback as he was.

"You are as beautiful as ever," he said.

He had crinkles around his eyes when he smiled. Kaikeyi wondered if he noticed the signs of aging on her face. But then he pinched the tender skin under her arm and she grew still. If she tried to snatch her hand away, it would only hurt more; she knew this from long experience. It had been his favorite way to subdue her. Brother and sister looked at each other again, communicating in a way that could never be expressed in words. Instead of wanting to hurt her brother back, as she always did as a girl, she reached up and cupped his face. Yuddha dropped his hand, but not before smoothing the pinch with his thumb.

"I thought you would have grown out of teasing me," she said quietly.

"Never." He flashed his handsome grin at her, even if it wasn't a real one.

Kaikeyi wanted to rub the skin where he had pinched her to alleviate the throbbing. But she would not show him that she had grown weak.

"Maybe this is why Father dares not set you on the throne," she said. "He's afraid that you'll torture those weaker than you."

She meant it as a joke, but he answered seriously. "You know I would never be unjust. You are the only one I tease. You are not supposed to count yourself among the weak, remember."

And she did remember. The many hours spent pitted against Yuddha, who was so much stronger than she but showed her no mercy, none at all. It was to his credit that she knew how to fight like she did and how to withstand pain. Left to Manthara's care, she would have been spineless. Kaikeyi was grateful to her brother for his teasing, his pinching, his punching, and his fighting. He had "made a man" out of her, and she missed being that man just as much as she loved being Dasharatha's woman. Seeing her thoughts, Yuddha's smile grew real.

The horses nickered, communicating with each other.

"How is Father?" Kaikeyi asked. "You look more like him now, you know." It was in Yuddha's manner more than anything. His eyes had become quick and darting, never resting for long on anyone or anything.

"Looking forward to see Bharata," Yuddha said, "and otherwise well. The healthiest old king I've ever known."

Father had recently turned seventy, but showed no sign of stepping down from the throne. Yuddha had been crown prince of Kekaya for close to twenty years now. He took it gracefully, with more cheer than Kaikeyi had known him to possess. Then again, it was as he had pointed out: Kaikeyi was the sole victim of his cruelty. He would never admit to resenting their father's stronghold.

"I must come and visit sometime," she said.

"You are always welcome, Sister," he said with a hint of formality.

They both knew that Kaikeyi would not come. Dasharatha was loathe to part from her for even a day. At least that was the excuse Kaikeyi had often made.

"Why can't you stay here for a while?" she asked. She suddenly felt that she did not know her brother anymore. It made her heart jump in unease. How could this have happened?

Yuddha did not answer, but said, "We hope that Bharata will stay with us for a while."

"Bharata and Shatrugna," Kaikeyi amended. There was no way to part the two pairs, Bharata and Shatrugna, Rama and Lakshmana.

Yuddha inclined his head, assenting. That's what he had meant. In every previous visit, Shatrugna had been Bharata's shadow. "I was not sure if their wives had allowed them to be as close as before."

Kaikeyi frowned. "Does your wife interfere in your friendships?"

She did not know her brother's wife. He had married after her, which was not the usual way. But Dasharatha had swooped down on Kaikeyi unexpectedly, saving her when she did not even know she needed to be saved. Yuddha's silence on the matter was eloquent. Not every marriage was destined to be happy. Kaikeyi sent a silent prayer of thanks to the gods for Dasharatha's love.

Returning to the practical matter at hand, Kaikeyi said, "The boys and their wives will come—with the usual retinue, of course."

"And you?" Yuddha said, resting his gaze on her. "Will you be able to bear this separation from your beloved son?"

His pique hit its mark. Kaikeyi's eyes filled with tears—more because Yuddha mocked the love she felt as a mother. "He is my son," she said angrily, "the only thing that has ever been really and truly mine."

"He is lucky to have such a loving mother." A peace offering.

"Sometimes I feel I would do anything, even something completely irrational, to keep him safe," she said. "As long as he lives and beyond, my love will too. I tell him often, 'Land nor sea can part you from me.'"

The words were lightly spoken, but Yuddha's eyes darkened. "What did you just say?"

Kaikeyi repeated, "Land nor sea can part you from me."

She was puzzled by her brother's reaction, by his sudden intensity.

"Pleasant words," she assured. "I say them often to Bharata. He knew them by heart when he was hardly three."

Yuddha shook his head. "This is not possible." His eyes were darting here and there as he blinked through his emotions. "Come with me," he said, leaping onto his horse.

He signaled to his men to ride on, telling them, "We will meet you in my sister's courtyard."

Following her brother's lead, Kaikeyi signaled to her four guards to remain at a distance. She was safe with her brother.

She rode up close to him, placing her hand on her brother's arm. "What's wrong, Yuddha?"

"You were too young. How can you remember her last words to you?"

"Whose last words?" Kaikeyi felt her distress rise. She had not seen Yuddha so affected, not since they were young; even after a near-death battle he would restrain his emotions. She did not need to know the cause to be affected by her brother's anguish.

Yuddha dismounted, beckoning her to follow. Their horses stood between them and Ayodhya's fort. Kaikeyi's guards were hidden from view. She focused on her brother.

"Those words you said, that's what Mother said before she left." Yuddha shuddered. "Before she was *made* to leave."

"Our mother?" Kaikeyi could do nothing but echo her brother. She had no memory of her mother. None at all. All she knew were things she had been told. Or? She took a quick breath and then forgot to continue. A feeling of terror rose in her heart. A desperate need that was not heeded nor fulfilled.

"Our true mother, yes," Yuddha replied. "The mother we never speak of."

"You have no memory of her," Kaikeyi asserted. It was easy to forget a person you had never known. Kaikeyi was not interested in her mother anymore. Kaikeyi was close to forty now and her brother several years past it. He couldn't suddenly have a true memory of their mother. Of the emotions rising with Kaikeyi, one became dominant. A feeling that snaked around her inner organs, clamping them together.

"She loved us, you know," Yuddha said. "She didn't want to leave."

"You were hardly four when she left. You don't know anything!"

Instead of getting angry, Yuddha lifted his hand to his neck. "I remember how soft the skin of her neck was when I would rest my nose there. She always smelled so sweet, like jasmine and milk. Not like Father, with his unpredictable smells. When I sat in her lap, her hair sometimes covered both sides of my face, tickling my cheeks."

Her brother spoke quickly, as if catching the memories before they disappeared. Kaikeyi's eyes narrowed. She didn't believe him. Where did all these "memories" suddenly come from?

"I remember the day you were born," Yuddha said. This was more familiar ground. "How Mother said you had the lungs of an elephant. That you would be someone who would really be heard. 'My silly filly,' she called you. I didn't really like you at first. You woke me up at night. But Mother kept making me hold you, and admonished me to kiss you. 'She is yours too.' I never wanted to remember the night she left. Maybe that's why I remember it so well."

Kaikeyi was not breathing. Yuddha had dropped hints about their mother every so often through their childhood. But it was always things that were hearsay—about how beautiful she had been—things Kaikeyi had already heard from others. Her brother had never before spoken like this, with feeling. Their mother began to take form between them from the force of his emotions. Kaikeyi did not like it, not at all.

The horse snorted, blowing air through their nostrils. Yuddha's hand flew up automatically to pat his steed. But his eyes were clouded, and his voice grew more rounded, like a child's. Kaikeyi shifted on her feet, searching for a way to interrupt him.

Yuddha went on. "Sometimes the animals in my dreams made noises just like you, and I wouldn't even wake up. But that night, your cry was different. It didn't sound like you at all.

There were words in the cry—big people's words that I might not understand even if I tried. I sat up in my bed, looking at the darkness around me. It was Mother's voice. She sounded like you, the way you took huge deep breaths in between crying more. I scrambled out of my bed. The marble was cold and slippery, and the air too. I saw my wooden sword leaning by the door and grabbed it. Mother was crying. I had to go to her.

"I ran past the guard at my door and turned quickly toward Mother's rooms. If the guard couldn't hear Mother's cries, maybe I was in a nightmare. Maybe the guard would follow me and try to kill me. People act strangely in dreams. I heard his footsteps behind me and started running as fast as I could. Mother's cries grew louder. I thought someone was killing her! I ran so fast I could not even breathe anymore. When I saw the two shadows guarding Mother's door, I knew it was a dream. The guards were supposed to do everything to protect her. But they were just standing there, leaning on their spears. They could not hear her. Only I could. And so I knew I could do anything I set my mind to. I kept running straight toward the guards. They tried to stop me by saying my name, but I didn't listen. I jumped up high and slashed my sword across one guard's face. It was Soma, who would always smile and mock fight with me. Soma's face started bleeding and the other guard just stared at me, so I left him unharmed. As I continued into Mother's chamber, I could hear your cries too, growing louder than Mother's. If anyone dared to touch you, I would show no mercy! But I was glad it was a dream. I had to grow up more before I could be like Father, and protect you.

"I heard the guards behind me. I warned Soma with my sword. The guards quietly watched me. None of them smiled. 'You should go back to your room,' Soma said.

"Ahead of me, the light flickered from Mother's room. The shadows were like the tongues of blood-drinkers, licking the walls. Mother's voice had grown quiet as she hushed you. Everything was suddenly quiet. I could hear my own breathing. Mother might scold me for sleepwalking if she caught me. But then Mother's voice grew louder again. She was begging for something.

"I stepped into her room, clutching my sword tight. Mother sat on her bed with the baby in her arms. The curtains around the bed swayed like ghosts. Mother's hair was completely loose, hanging around her like black curtains. Father was there with his arms crossed. I wasn't so sure I was in a dream anymore. I was afraid to take another step because I'd never seen Father so angry.

"'Put her down,' Father said in his ordering voice. 'You have to leave now.'

"Neither of them had seen me yet. It had to be a dream; I was suddenly sure that a demon had taken over Father's body. I held my sword as tightly as I could. It was quiet all around me now, except for you sucking on Mother's breast. Mother's tears were running down her face, dripping down onto your cheeks. Mother's nose was pink.

"'Please,' Mother said, looking up at Father. 'She needs me. Let me take her, at least.'

"'Nonsense.' Father's voice was a bark.

"Mother said, 'If you ever loved me at all, please let me take my baby.'

"I was suddenly terrified of Mother leaving without me. 'Where are you going, Mother?'

"'She is not your mother anymore,' Father said. 'We will find someone else more suitable.'

"I didn't understand a word he said. Mother began crying again, softly, kissing your head again and again. She held out her free hand to me. I ran toward her.

"'Stay were you are!' Father ordered. He told me to go back to my rooms. I could see the flames flicker in his eyes as I disobeyed him. My stomach was a stone. I hid my face in her knees. I was afraid to let Father see my tears. Mother's hand rested on my head for a moment. Father's iron hand clamped around my arm. He started tugging me away. I clung to Mother's leg as Father pulled at me. A terror that was not mine alone began to fill me up. You felt it too. You forgot Mother's breast and gave out a wail. Because you did, I did too. I opened my mouth and howled. At first no words came out. But as Father's hand grew tight around my arm—I thought my arm would rip off—I cried, 'I'm going with Mother!'

"Father bent down, prying my fingers away. He even smelled different, stinking like one of the guards after they wrestled. I clung to Mother's leg. She was trying to get the baby quiet again, but you refused to drink any more. You knew something was terribly wrong. Father put his face to mine. His eyes were all wet. 'You are going to be the king of Kekaya. You have to stay.'

"I felt Mother kiss the top of my head. I thought she would tell Father to let me go with her, but instead she said, 'Let me take my daughter.'

"'They are *my* children,' Father said, yanking me away so hard I lost my arm at Mother's side. But when I looked down, it was still there, though I couldn't make it move. My sword was hidden under Mother's skirts. After a moment, she lifted her foot and kicked it toward me. It slid across the floor and gently hit my feet. I stopped crying. It was her way to tell me I had to be a big boy. I stared at her and you. Both of you looked almost the same, your mouths were open and your eyes squeezed closed. Tears were rolling down from your closed eyes. Father lifted me and held me to his chest. The next second, he called for Soma, ordering him to take me to my room. I was completely silent now. Mother didn't want me. She never begged Father to take me. She held the baby so close, I could not even see you at all. Soma backed out of Mother's room with me. I strained to see. Father pulled Mother up with his free hand. You had stopped crying, and you looked straight at me with your big eyes. I knew they were blue, like mine, but they looked black that night. Father reached forward to take you from Mother, but she turned away. Both of them fought over you, and I was afraid you would break or split in half. You started shrieking again, louder than an elephant.

"Mother cried. Father shouted. You wailed and wailed.

"I started squirming, trying to get away from Soma. I hit his legs with my sword. He didn't catch my hand or restrain me. But he didn't let me go.

"'Look at your mother,' he whispered into my ear. He continued walking backward.

"I felt his heart hammer against my back. Soma was upset. Everyone was. Mother most of all. Father had taken you. He held you with one hand; your arms and neck just dangled. With the other he pushed Mother away. Mother struggled against Father's hands, trying to take you back. It was like she thought she was in a dream too. She thought if she kept trying, she could get you back. Father still had the demon in him. He held Mother back. He didn't say anything to her. Soma paused for a moment in the doorway. His arms and body were warm around me. 'Look at your mother,' he repeated. 'You will never see her again.'

"I saw how Mother's hair shone and was like a black cape around her. But her face was not the one I knew, because it was so twisted and strange, the way she was crying. I shouted to Father to let her stay. Father looked toward the guards but not at me. 'Take this woman away. Now.'

"The other guards started moving toward Mother.

"'Land nor sea can part you from me,' Mother said. 'As long as you live, my heart lives too.'

"With his sternest voice, Father told her, 'This was supposed to be a quiet farewell, Chaya?'

"The guards started dragging her away. Soma whispered calming words into my ear. All I could say was, 'Mother, Mother, Mother.'

"The nightmare continued as it started. The air in the corridors was cold. Mother's cries hit my ears. She called my name. She called yours. Soma sat down with me on the bed. He let me curl up in his lap, even though I had made his nose bleed. I understood then that it had not been a dream at all. I knew Mother was gone because you kept crying and crying. You had never cried like that, not even when you were first born.

"Father was going to find a new mother for us. Father was making a big, big mistake. I knew that you would never stop crying."

Yuddha stopped speaking. His face was streaked with tears. So was Kaikeyi's. Her body trembled, her convictions shaken.

"This is *not* true," she said. "She did not care for us. She hated us. She wanted to feed us to the dogs."

Kaikeyi watched her brother straighten and look at her differently. "Is that what Manthara told you all these years?"

"At least she told me something," Kaikeyi cried. "How many times have I asked you about Mother? Now you tell me this. I don't believe you. It's too late."

She refused to notice how her brother had turned into a little boy as he spoke. She attributed the tears in his eyes to the wind in the air. Any excuse would suffice. Anything but accepting his sudden admission as the truth. Their mother had been selfish and self-serving, no mother at all.

"Do not speak about her ever again," Kaikeyi warned him.

"Or what? You'll set Manthara after me? Mother loved us!"

"I have no mother!" Kaikeyi shouted so loudly, the horses spooked and flattened their ears. She turned away from her brother, the liar. She was glad that he was leaving in the morning. She mounted her horse, turning it toward Ayodhya, her safe place. She ignored her brother.

He called after her, "Then why did you say her words, 'Land nor sea can part you from me'?"

"I don't know! Those are *my* words!"

Kaikeyi urged the horse to break into a gallop. It was *not* true. It couldn't be. Once within her courtyard, she ignored all Kekaya's people waiting there. Without looking, she ran past every single one of them. Even if it had been Dasharatha she wouldn't have stopped. An indescribable terror was taking hold of her and she could not run from it. But she would try. It was the ghost of her mother trying to sink her claws into Kaikeyi. It was the heart-eating witch. She told the shadow to leave her alone. She was brave now, not a helpless little girl. But of course, Yuddha sought her out again. He had no sense of privacy and entered her private chamber without asking.

She felt spent and tired. And tomorrow she had to send Bharata off. But Yuddha looked different, unburdened. Unbidden, he sat on the edge of her bed, soiling it with his horse smell.

"I've been jealous of you all these years," he said. He reached for her hand, grasping it firmly.

"You have?"

"Why else do you think I constantly pinched and tormented you?"

"I thought all brothers did that."

"Maybe every brother has a reason to be jealous. I don't know. But Mother wanted you, not me. I resented you for that. But I understand now that it was simply desperation. She knew Father would never let go of his only son. He would not let her take anything with her in exile. You know that part of the story."

Yes, she had heard it many times by now. The swans. Her father's laugh. Her mother's demand to know. The subsequent exile. It all seemed so crisp and clear, told like that. Yuddha was casting it in a darker light. Kaikeyi wanted to hear all of it and none of it.

"I would *never* do what she did and abandon my child," Kaikeyi said.

"That's what I'm telling you, Sister. Our mother didn't leave without a fight."

"She did not fight hard enough. If she truly loved us, she would have found a way."

Yuddha had no answer to that. Kaikeyi wished he had not come from Kekaya.

"I'm tired," she said to him. "You are right about one thing. It isn't easy for me to say farewell to Bharata."

"Despite my earlier words, I admire you for that."

"See you in the morning," she said, dismissing her brother.

She sought out Dasharatha, finding solace in his warm arms. He whispered many soothing words of love into her ear and caressed her cheek and back until she fell asleep.

The next morning, she clung to Bharata as if she would never see him again.

"What's wrong, Mother?" he asked, ever astute.

She would not take up his time now with the whole story. He already knew the salient parts. Instead she said, "You know that I love you, don't you? That I would do everything for you, that I would never let anyone hurt you."

Bharata's large eyes looked puzzled by her emotional display. But she needed him to know that she was not the kind of mother who abandoned her child. Not ever.

"Of course, Mother," Bharata replied. "I know you have my best at heart."

"You are my heart," she said. "As long as you live, my heart lives too."

She quelled her tears so that she could be a queen and bid them a proper farewell.

CHAPTER 47

Dasharatha's Haste

Bharata and Shatrugna were in the land of their grandfather. Dasharatha was haunted by dark omens, which followed him day and night. After Bharata's departure, Kaikeyi had clung to Dasharatha like a vine to a tree. Her passion dimmed his dread, but when the lovemaking was over, he was left with his sinister dreams: Dasharatha stared into the hypnotic eyes of the swaying snake. Beads of sweat stung his eyes as he tried not to blink. The cobra was ready to strike, hood lifted and fangs visible. Dasharatha stood frozen, his ability to remain motionless paramount to his survival. Suddenly the reptile changed tactics and slithered closer, intending to choke him, not bite. The giant snake began coiling itself around his body, suffocating him. The king was paralyzed with fear. He screamed silently, and the snake hissed in his ear while encircling his throat. Dasharatha gasped for air, for life, and suddenly found himself gazing upward toward a red canopy, silken sheets clinging to his sweaty body. A dream, he realized.

He was perspiring all over. Kaikeyi's thick braid lay heavily across his throat. Since when did she sleep with her hair braided? He sat up and irritably flung it aside, feeling the cool air against his throat. The dream left him with a feeling of imminent disaster that was harder to shake off, but he resisted the urge to quickly leave the bed. Instead, he steadied his mind, telling himself the cobra was an illusion.

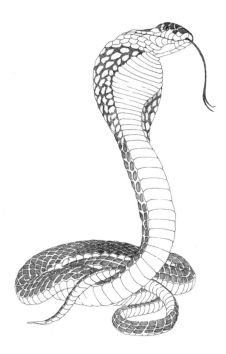

He reminded himself of the concrete facts of his life. He was sixty-seven years old. His sons would turn eighteen this month. Bharata and Shatrugna had gone to the land of Kekaya to visit King Ashvapati. Rama was excelling like the rising sun. As Dasharatha opened his mind to it, he counted an endless stream of facts and events that defined and grounded his life. Finally, there was the old curse, the crime he had committed at fifteen, which had haunted him ever since. He would die in grief torn from his son. There was no way around it; dreaming of a black cobra was a bad omen. This was not the first inauspicious portent he had recently observed, and Dasharatha was starting to feel acutely worried. But what was there to worry about?

Affairs of the state ran smoothly. Rama demonstrated real leadership, taking part in every decision. As always, Dasharatha's thoughts dwelled longer on Rama than on his other sons. Over the years, Rama had become more than a son. His instincts were razor-sharp, yet his way with people was kind, the delivery of his insights temperate—a rare combination. Dasharatha had come to rely on Rama's counsel. Indeed, he could no longer imagine running affairs of state without Rama. All this had unfolded naturally, thanks to Bharata's innate submission toward Rama.

Dasharatha looked at Kaikeyi again, who still slept like a child, unaware of her husband's morning thoughts. Ever since Bharata left for Kekaya, Kaikeyi had clung to Dasharatha with unusual need. She wanted to be by his side at all times. It was not unwelcome at all.

For years, he had dreaded the conflict that would arise once he announced his heir. Although Kaikeyi agreed that the terms had changed when she bore him no natural sons, Ashvapati remained resistant. But he had nothing to offer but innuendos as threats. Bharata insisted that he did not want the throne. Still, the minds of men were fickle. Dasharatha's dread returned, a snake in his gut.

He rose from his bed, flexing his unwilling limbs. He was still stronger than many men, but the gods knew his battle days were over. He had to consult Vasishta, seeking the preceptor's advice on how to proceed. Because of the urgency Dasharatha felt, he left the bedchamber and rushed through his morning ablutions. Kausalya was in the golden altars, as dependably there as the deities themselves. Soon after, Dasharatha sent a messenger to the holy one, informing Vasishta that he would visit before the day's duties commenced.

Vasishta sat cross-legged on a straw mat and had placed a cushion for the king to sit on. Vasishta listened attentively to Dasharatha's descriptions of the bad omens, the complexity of Kaikeyi's bride-price, and his growing desire to see Rama crowned as the king. Dasharatha said, "I carry a feeling of extreme dread with me wherever I go. I don't feel certain of the right path ahead."

"The path ahead is clear," Vasishta said. "The moment Rama was born as your first son, the path was made. But I understand the reasons for your turbulent mind. The decisions of a king may garner displeasure from some faction of the people. That is common. Still, I would like to examine the movement of your ruling stars and the planets that influence you. This may shed some light on your current anxiety."

Together, they studied the alignment of his ruling stars.

Vasishta grew graver than usual. "Great King," he said, "you have a very malignant star coming into activation. The formation of Sun, Mars, and the shadow planet Rahu appears only when a man is about to die or will suffer a terrible accident."

Dasharatha had known deep within that his anxiety wasn't unfounded. "Before it's too late," he said, "I must take action to consecrate Rama as prince-regent. Before I do so, you, whose advice can never steer me wrong, must tell me your opinion."

"Rama is undoubtedly the most extraordinary human being on this Earth. No one can compare to your firstborn son. The ministers will agree."

And they did. All eight ministers unanimously agreed that Rama, among all the princes, was the prime candidate. Still, Ayodhya was a democracy, and it was time to summon the leading citizens of Ayodhya. Dasharatha was so eager and so anxious that he called a meeting on the shortest notice, to be held on the succeeding day.

Dasharatha waited until the large retinue had settled into the court before he addressed them gravely with a resonant voice. "My dear people, you have allowed me to rule for many years now. I am no longer the vigorous man I was when I became your king. With your permission, I wish to appoint my eldest son Rama as my successor."

A great cry of approval rose from the crowd, invigorating Dasharatha. But to make sure they were not only trying to please him, he posed a question. "Why are you so eager to see my son rule in my place? Have I not worked for the welfare of all beings and ruled righteously?"

After conferring among themselves, a spokesperson addressed the king. "Your son Rama has enhanced the Sun dynasty's glory by his exemplary actions. We believe his words because we have seen that he is devoted to truth. He exemplifies nobility by his even temper, gentle speech, and love for righteousness. We trust his strength because he has never been defeated in battle. When he returns to the city after being away, he asks about our welfare as if we are his own family. He shares in our joys and sorrows as if he were our father. All of us remember Rama in our daily prayers. You fulfill our wishes by appointing him as your heir, for we already worship him. Crown him without any delay. That will give us great happiness!"

When the king heard these words, his heart swelled with a joy similar to the elation he felt when Rama was born.

"As you say," Dasharatha answered, joining them in their delight.

Since everyone was supremely pleased, Dasharatha decided to proceed immediately. He could not afford any mistakes or delays. The fact that Bharata was at his maternal home only made it more urgent. Dasharatha would let nothing stand in his way. They would consecrate Rama as prince-regent the very next day. He proclaimed, "Let the celebration begin!"

It would take a concerted effort of all Ayodhya's manpower to prepare for the grand coronation in such a short time.

CHAPTER 48

The Fateful Servant

Something was happening in Ayodhya without Manthara's knowing. All after-noon Manthara had heard an unusual amount of noise. Come evening, she heard loud cheers from the street and could not contain her curiosity. Leaning heav-ily on her cane, she made her way up the stairways. From there, she would have a good view of the courtyard and the streets beyond. Craning her neck up while the rest of her was pulled down by gravity, she would have appeared painfully humble were it not for her facial expression. She made no attempt to conceal her mind-set as her eyes darted here and there. The clunk of her walking stick was one of the only jarring sounds in the palace, outdone only by her hoarse, nagging voice.

After over twenty years in Ayodhya, Manthara was still an outcast. There were one or two people here and there whom she tolerated but none she trusted. Over the years, she had come to derive pleasure in spreading rumors and creating misery in the lives of others. She kept her ears sharp and her tongue wagging wherever in the palace she hobbled. It was a low pleasure, but it fueled something within her.

As she reached the rooftop, her breath wheezed through her lungs like a ghost. A few of the palace servants stood on the rooftop and chattered. Manthara caught a few of their words on the wind: "Rama's coronation!" and "The Great Queen's joy!"

Manthara's wheezing breaths stopped completely. It could not be! She had both dreaded and expected this day. The "righteous" Dasharatha was proving himself not only a hypocrite but a liar after all. Just to be certain, she sidled closer to them and overheard Rama's wet nurse boasting about Rama's rise to power—all because of her breast milk, of course. The cluster of idiots was standing and admiring their queen. Manthara peeked over the railing; Kausalya was out there in the streets, handing out gifts, as if she was a lavish person. Manthara could see the selfish motive behind that generosity.

Manthara had seen enough. She turned and hurried down the stairway, grabbing the hem of her silk sari so she wouldn't trip. Her spine jounced with every step, a stabbing knife in her back.

"Quiet," she hissed, to end the self-pity. She needed to be as sharp as she could be.

This was her moment.

This news about Rama's royal consecration was a shameful affair. Without exaggerating the facts, the sweet-talking king was betraying them after all. In truth, Manthara was shaken. A part of her felt a nasty thrill at having been right all these years. There was only one person who needed to see this as Manthara did: Kaikeyi.

She thumped her walking stick heavily on the ground and on the feet of people too slow to move. "Out of my way!" she brayed.

Her old face was scrunched up, and her mouth was a tight line of wrinkles. The cogs in her brain turned quickly, and alarming thoughts wound round and round. The gossip's thrill she had first felt dissipated and the real emotion appeared; she was afraid for her life.

Entering Kaikeyi's chamber, she found her mistress reclining on a luxurious throne.

"Kaikeyi! Get up! You will be thrown into the streets at any moment!"

Kaikeyi laughed and didn't move. When had she become so indolent?

"Kaikeyi, get up at once and realize the gravity of the situation!" Manthara waved her cane in the air in frustration.

"You forget, my dear, that I have no idea what grave situation you are so wild about, unless you are about to drop that cane on me."

Kaikeyi's calm was a wind on Manthara's fire, making her blaze up when she had promised herself to stay calm. How stupid Kaikeyi had become over the years, like a docile cow, drunk on that love poison the king kept feeding her. And yet in the past years, Manthara had become overly zealous and every week had a "grave" situation to be dealt with. She cursed herself, though she didn't have time for self-recrimination now. She had to make Kaikeyi see!

Banging her stick on the floor for emphasis, Manthara again commanded, "Get up, I say!"

"All right," Kaikeyi said, raising herself slightly. "I'm up."

"Listen carefully," Manthara implored.

The old woman looked Kaikeyi hard in the eyes, and in one breath she said, "Rama is going to be consecrated as prince-regent tomorrow morning, and he will be the next king of Ayodhya."

"Oh, Manthara!" Kaikeyi exclaimed, sitting up at once. "That is wonderful news."

Manthara stared at Kaikeyi with dismay. This was not the reaction she wanted.

"The installation is *tomorrow*," Manthara repeated.

"Today, tomorrow—what does it matter? Rama will make a perfect king. I'm so happy to hear this!"

A warm color spread across Kaikeyi's cheeks. Kaikeyi had gone from neutral to exulted within seconds. It didn't seem natural. For who's sake was she acting the part of a doting mother? Kaikeyi stood up and, with eager fingers, unfastened the largest gem she was wearing, presenting it to Manthara. "This is for bringing me such good news."

Her eyes glittered; she radiated joy.

"Have you gone completely and utterly mad?" Manthara asked.

It was either that or a theatrical act, as Kaikeyi stood there beaming, cheeks flushed. It was so well rehearsed, in fact, that Kaikeyi herself believed it.

"I know it's a priceless gem," Kaikeyi said, misunderstanding Manthara yet again. "You deserve nothing less for being the bearer of this news!"

"You are the biggest fool on Earth!" Manthara exclaimed. She threw the gem to the floor with all her might. Kaikeyi looked in shock at the gem that clattered against the floor, skidding away. Manthara glared at Kaikeyi.

"Manthara! How dare you behave like this? Get out of my sight at once! Or I will really regret what I'm about to say."

Undaunted, Manthara screamed back, "I do not care if you are angry at me or if you punish me. Soon we will both be begging in the streets. We will be thrown out of Ayodhya!"

"What is this madness about?"

"If only you weren't so invested in this theatrical act, you would already know!"

"Theatrical act?"

"Can't you see that Rama's coronation is the beginning of your downfall as Dasharatha's favored queen?"

"The king loves us all," Kaikeyi countered weakly.

"Please, play your game with others, but not with me. I've known you from your birth, don't forget that. You are Dasharatha's favorite queen and you know it."

"So what?" Kaikeyi said proudly.

"I can't believe I have to point out the obvious. The reality of the situation is—"

"I am a grown woman and a mother," Kaikeyi said. "Don't presume to lecture me anymore. The king's love for me will last beyond our deaths."

"That is all going to change when Rama becomes king."

"I *don't* understand. Rama is a son to me, and I am truly happy to see him crowned."

"But you are forgetting a crucial detail," Manthara said. "Rama is *not* your son. He is Kausalya's son. The son of your co-wife, who is jealous of you. Kausalya hates you."

Manthara's fear grew, as she whispered, "Bharata is in the most vulnerable position of all. If he is not put on the throne, then he is a threat, that's all. Why didn't Dasharatha, the so-called upholder of justice, simply do as he promised when taking your hand, Kaikeyi? Bharata should be king. If Rama becomes king, eliminating Bharata will be the first step. That's what any king would do!"

Manthara had Kaikeyi's attention.

"But Rama loves Bharata. He would never let harm befall us."

Manthara dug deep into her knowledge of her queen. Kaikeyi had to discard her fantasies and open her eyes to the reality before them.

"You are naive. Everyone changes when they taste power. Do you seriously think that Kausalya has no influence over her own son? The balance of power is about to tip toward the Great Queen. She will become the most valuable queen with her son on the throne."

Kaikeyi sat down heavily. "The king wouldn't listen to her. He has been faithful and devoted to me alone all these years."

"Listen to me, Kaikeyi, because your grief is my grief. Only if you prosper can I prosper; there is no doubt in this. I will not mislead you. Bharata and I completely depend on you. You must protect us."

"Rama loves—"

"Love again! Is that your best argument? I'm *tired* of this nonsense about *love*."

She spit out the words and had to wipe spittle from her chin. She sat down close to the queen. "Kausalya has envied your beauty since you arrived. In the past, you have openly disrespected her. Won't she finally take her revenge? Trust me, you will become her maidservant."

Kaikeyi beheld Manthara with narrowing eyes. "Kausalya did threaten me of this once," she said. "She threw clay pots at me and shouted that she was the queen, that everything I have was due to her permission. My hold on the king, she claimed, was only due to her benevolence."

"You see. You and Bharata will become slaves under the rule of Rama and his mother. Rama is a learned man in the affairs of state. His actions are timely and appropriate. A king in power must weed out anyone who threatens his throne, and Bharata is next in line among the brothers. He is the only brother who is in danger because Lakshmana is Rama's right-hand man. Rama protects Lakshmana. Shatrugna is the youngest, fourth in line to the throne. When I think of what will become of Bharata under Rama's rule, I'm overwhelmed with fear."

"Rama thinks of his brothers as his own self. He will be fair towards Bharata."

"Nonsense! Rama is his elder brother by only a day. Bharata's life is in danger. Better you advise him to stay in your father's house or send him far, far away. Rama will throw him in the dungeon at best. More likely he will kill him or have him executed. Be sure of that. And you—you can imagine what Kausalya will do to you."

Kaikeyi shook her head.

She clung to her foolish illusions, Manthara could see that.

"I will give you proof," Manthara said, unable to hide her satisfaction. "As I first emphasized, the installation is"—she paused dramatically—"*tomorrow*."

Kaikeyi shrugged and threw her hands up, as if this fact meant nothing. "How do you even know all this? I am the queen, and I have not been informed."

"Exactly! Everyone on Kausalya's team knows. You are being purposefully excluded. Even the lowly wet nurse knows. She is the one who told me."

Manthara watched in silence, as Kaikeyi's thoughts played across her face. The doubt spread itself across Kaikeyi's face, like stubborn insects crawling in where least welcome.

"Why is your dear king in such haste?" Manthara demanded, satisfied to see that Kaikeyi was holding her breath. "Because Bharata is not here! The king wants to finish everything before Bharata or your father comes to know of it, before they can stop it. Think, my dear, think! Why an installation all of a sudden? Why can't he wait for Bharata and Shatrugna to return? Why didn't he talk to you about all this? Even Rama's wet nurse, a mere servant, knows. And you, the so-called favorite queen, are left completely in the dark. Is it a coincidence? Neither your father, your son, nor you have been informed. Shouldn't your father be told that his grandson is being robbed of his throne?"

"When Dasharatha made that promise, he thought that my son would be his only son."

"On the contrary, your king knows he's on shaky ground. He is worried that you or Bharata will assert your rights to the throne. He is rushing through this entire procedure. Yuddhajit's coronation took months to prepare for!"

Kaikeyi looked shaken by Manthara's accusations.

"He has seemed worried lately," Kaikeyi muttered to herself. "Was it guilt? Has he been afraid I would disapprove? Has he been planning to abandon me?"

Manthara had heard enough. "I have not stood by you your entire life to watch this happen. Rama is not more qualified than Bharata. This throne was never meant for Rama. He must be displaced. Rama is nobody. He was not even born when it was decided that your son would be king."

Manthara put her face very close to Kaikeyi and said, "He . . . is . . . not . . . your . . . son. Come back to your senses."

Manthara sat down, as if the effort had cost her. "Listen to me. Just leave Rama out of this. It's not personal against him. It's not him we are against. We are against the king breaking his promise, neglecting the bride-price he made when he married you. That's one thing. The other factors to consider are our goals. We want our position in this kingdom to remain secure. We do not want to be exiled, do we? Do you want to be ruined and turn into wasteland?"

Here, Manthara paused. She waited until Kaikeyi shook her head. "Your brother told you what happened to your mother. She was torn away from her children. Discarded. Exiled. She disappeared. You don't want to turn out like your mother, do you?"

Kaikeyi stared at Manthara. She sat down, whispering almost imperceptibly, "No, no."

With every passing moment, Manthara felt that her own sense of impending doom was transferred to Kaikeyi. Manthara could tell that Kaikeyi was starting to see the world as Manthara saw it.

"If you don't want to be exiled," Manthara said, articulating each word slowly, "then Bharata *must* become king. That's the only way to protect him. That's the only way he can protect you. Do you understand?"

"I will not become a wasteland!" Kaikeyi said. "I must stop this. I will protect Bharata. I will protect myself."

"You will do what you are best at," Manthara said as she pulled Kaikeyi's head near and whispered into her ear. "Fight."

Two Old Boons

The day quickly became night. Since the decision to consecrate Rama, Dasharatha's hands had been full. It was not small feat to pull together a consecration in such short time. As the moon rose in the sky, Dasharatha finally disengaged himself from the preparations.

He headed straight to Kaikeyi's palace, eager to be with her and share the news. His mind buzzed with the urgency of the next day's event. Just placing Rama in front of the people and saying, "This is your new king" would be enough. The citizens had already roared their approval. But the formality of consecrating Rama was nevertheless necessary. A slight apprehension seized him again. But so much had changed. Manthara and Ashvapati's accusations had no bearings.

When he arrived at Kaikeyi's palace gate and passed the pond with swans, his heartbeat quickened. He laughed aloud when he realized why. What a joy to have a wife like her. He longed to relax in her proximity and to share his exhilaration with her. He was sure the news would delight her. She loved Rama so much. As he entered, she didn't greet him at the door as she usually did. He hurried into the bedroom.

"Kaikeyi," he said, "you won't believe the wonderful news I have to tell you."

The room was empty.

"Kaikeyi," he said, louder.

This was unusual. He stroked his beard thoughtfully. She was always here when he arrived. He looked around the luxurious chamber and heard musical instruments mingling with the sound of parrots and peacocks. He took in how charming the ornate ivory and silver thrones were, surrounded by creepers and flowers. The night-blooming jasmine, Kaikeyi's favorite scent, flowered in every corner, releasing its intoxicating perfume. Large champak flowers floated in ornate bowls of water, their citrus fragrance mingling with jasmine. Every corner of Kaikeyi's palace was created for intimacy and romance. These were all details he ordinarily did not notice when Kaikeyi was in front of him. Where was she?

Her absence agitated him significantly. Maybe all the bad omens he had been seeing of late were not about Rama at all. A vision of Kaikeyi lying in a pool of blood flashed through his mind. Heart pounding with unease, Dasharatha turned away from the desolate chamber and began to search for Kaikeyi. All the maidservants had been dismissed. Not even Manthara was in sight, one of the first times Dasharatha found himself wishing that the hunchback would appear.

To his great relief, he found Sukhi and Dukhi whispering in a corner. They jumped in fright when they saw Dasharatha approach and then began to bow and supplicate in an overly nervous manner. When he asked where Kaikeyi was, they answered both at the same time, speaking so fast, he understood nothing. They finally managed to convey that the queen had gone to the House of Wrath. Dasharatha did not ask why. He didn't think he could bear their circumspect manner of answering, not now when his nerves were stretched. He steeled himself for the encounter. A woman's wrath was a powerful thing.

As he hurried to the House of Wrath, he searched his mind for a cause of Kaikeyi's sudden displeasure. Pushing aside the black curtain, he ventured into the dimly lit room. The House did little to uplift anyone's mood, he thought, as he squinted into the dark corners to find Kaikeyi. He stepped on something and picked up an earring. It was one that he had given her last year. He found its match some distance away. Not a good sign, as the distance implied that she must have flung them. Dasharatha walked deeper into the dimly lit chamber, picking up discarded jewelry—a heavy necklace, a number of precious rings, and anklets. He saw a cascade of bangles and a small heap of flowers on the floor. He followed the trail into a secluded room to the side, his hands now weighed down by the solid gold ornaments that somehow did not look as heavy when they decorated Kaikeyi's lovely limbs.

Taking a few steps into the room, he suddenly dropped all that he had carefully gathered. So unprepared was he for the sight of Kaikeyi splayed out on the floor, her black hair scattered, half covering her face and snaking around her neck and arms. Her distress was clear, for she was convulsing with silent sobs. She hit her fists against the floor and shook her head from side to side. Dasharatha stumbled over the gold ornaments and ran to her, his heart in his throat.

"My love!" he exclaimed. He dropped to his knees and pulled her into his arms.

"No!" she cried, her voice hoarse. She went limp in his arms. She refused to look at him.

His heart was beating audibly, and as much to calm himself as her, he said, "All is well. I'm here now. I'm here."

He stroked her hair again and again and kissed the top of her head. What on earth could have happened? He couldn't recall ever seeing her like this. He continued questioning her while wiping the perspiration from her brow and hugging her tightly. But none of his questions hit the mark, for he was unsuccessful in eliciting a response from her or arousing her to animation.

Displaying the depth of his power and to what lengths he'd go to appease her, he said, "Is there a murderer I shall set free? Or is there an innocent man I shall execute? I will make a poor man rich, Kaikeyi, or if you like, a rich man poor!"

Still she remained inanimate, and the king started feeling sick with worry. "I swear on Rama, our son, that I will punish—"

"Leave me," she said, and rolled out of his startled arms, back onto the floor. "Leave!"

Then she closed her mouth and would say no more.

Dasharatha was dumbstruck. He scarcely recognized her as she stared up at the ceiling as if dead.

"Kaikeyi," he said, "what has happened to bring you to this state? I implore you, please, on the strength of the love we share, tell me what ails you."

He moved toward her again, but she rolled over several times, creating a clear gap between them. A tear rolled down the king's cheek. "I will not move from here until you speak to me. Speak. Please speak."

Silence ensued, and he listened to her breathing pattern, which was now steadier than his. He was about to voice his plea again, when she began to speak in an emotionless voice. "Do you remember when I served you on the battlefield as your charioteer?"

"Yes. You were a true warrior-queen."

A contemptuous laugh escaped from her mouth. "Do you remember that day you would have died if it wasn't for my intervention?"

"Of course," he said quietly.

He refrained from saying that he would never forget that time. It had become impossible to be apart from one another; they had bonded so intensely. His life was hers.

"Do you remember the two boons you offered me?"

So that's where she was going with this. He replied, "You said you had all you wanted now that I was alive."

"And you insisted that I keep them for later," she said, still speaking in a monotone. "Now that time has come."

"Is that all, my love?" he said with evident relief. "You did not have to conjure the past like this. Have I not always fulfilled your desires? I will give you anything."

"Anything?" she asked, with the first quiver of feeling.

"On the love I have for my eldest son, Rama," he answered, solemnly, "I promise to give you anything you ask for."

The words echoed ominously inside him. The solitary chambers were oppressive, haunted.

Kaikeyi's face lit up, but not in her usual beautiful and loving way. She sat up, unsmiling, and he perceived that there were yet miles to cover before she was reconciled to him. She stood to regain some of her majesty before proceeding. He also stood and, for the first time, she faced him squarely.

"King Dasharatha of the Sun dynasty, originating from the sun god," she said, formally. "You come from a line of kings renowned for keeping their word."

"Kaikeyi, what's the need for all this?"

"Do you promise me on the strength of your ancestral line to redeem the two boons you gave me?"

Dasharatha started perspiring. There could only be one answer, yet he found that he was afraid. His voice shook, but he renewed his promise.

Kaikeyi spoke. "First, I want you to honor your promise that my son, Bharata, will be king. This is my first wish. Second, I want you to exile Rama, banishing him from Ayodhya and every other kingdom on Earth, for fourteen years."

Dasharatha felt like laughing. Exile Rama? An overwhelming fear and hysteria overcame him. Everything became dim while Rama's beautiful features glowed like a fire before him. He sank down to the floor, unable to speak or think.

Broken Hearts

Kaikeyi grew worried when she saw Dasharatha's shock. His eyes were glazed over, and he made no response when she kneeled by his side. The hard shell around her heart made her stand up and move away from him. She refused to feel sympathy for the slumped figure of her husband. If it was true what Manthara had said—that he didn't truly love her but only loved Rama—then he deserved no sympathy.

She took shelter in her early warrior training, thinking only of her goal and never about how many she must kill to achieve it. Patiently, she sat down to wait for him to recover. If he said her name while coming to, it would be a sign of her victory. Exhausted by her own emotional upheaval, she soon fell into a light sleep, lying on the floor, her mind waiting for the first syllables from his mouth.

"Rama," he mumbled.

Kaikeyi opened her eyes at once and knew that no compromise would be possible in this war. The moment consciousness again descended upon Dasharatha, he sprang up like an arrow and had to steady himself against a pillar for a second.

"Kai—," he tried, but choked on her name.

"Don't tell me you are becoming weak in your old age," she said, anger rising. "I'm asking you to part with only one of your sons. You have three more, although you seem to care little for them by comparison. I'm not asking you to kill Rama! He can return after fourteen years, once Bharata's rule is established."

She could have demanded that Rama be exiled forever, as her own mother had been. Dasharatha's eyes brimmed with tears; he did not see the benevolence in her terms. Kaikeyi sat up, the curve of her hip more pronounced as she leaned on one arm. Her thick hair fell over her face so that only one eye looked up at the king. She did not feel quite like herself. But she had to be strong to see this through.

Dasharatha slowly approached her and knelt in front of her. He pushed her hair behind her ear and cupped her face gently with both hands. "My love, my queen, my sweet wife," he said. Tears streamed through his words. "Don't do this. You love Rama. Rama is a tiger among men, who advises and cares for all beings with a clear mind. He has captivated each and every one in the kingdom with his kind actions. He is endowed with honesty and is as splendorous as a sage. You have praised him yourself countless times. You have said that Rama's happiness is your happiness."

She grew hard as a stone. His words could not touch her.

"You have said that he is just like your own son."

"But he is *not* my son."

His hands tightened around her face.

For a second, she feared he would crush her skull. His hot breath moistened the curls around her face. She stared at him without blinking, her enmity toward him cementing. Her heart throbbed wildly and angrily with the knowledge that Rama meant so much more to the king than she did. Everything he said only made her more certain of his foul play. His love was not real.

She wanted to slap him and shout, but instead she whispered, hissing like a cobra, "What kind of man are you? You are obsessed with this one son of yours. We lived here happily without Rama before he was born."

"Remember the day Rama was born," Dasharatha begged. "You said you loved him instantly. What has our son done to deserve this sudden change of heart from you?"

"Bharata is my son. I want him to rule the world. Rama must live like a recluse with matted hair, wearing only deerskins, barred from entering any kingdom."

"Nothing makes sense anymore," he said, looking very tired. "You consider Rama and Bharata on an equal level. I know that because you have told me so many times. The words you are saying are not yours. This is Manthara's scheme. You are a puppet in her hands."

"What is the use of this talk, King? Are you going to fulfill your boons? Or are they as empty as the bride-price you promised my father?"

The king, who ruled the entire Earth with an iron hand, stooped in front of his wife. Thousands of valorous men had kissed his feet during his lifetime, and now he touched the feet of his wife, weeping piteously, begging. "Have pity on an old man. If not for your husband, who loves you, have mercy on a man at the end of his life. When I see Rama, supreme delight enters my heart. My very consciousness is lost if I don't see Rama. The world can exist without the sun, crops without water, but life cannot continue in my body without Rama. I beg you to let me die with my son at my side. Let me die in peace."

"How can you die in peace when you have not kept your word?"

Dasharatha clutched at his chest and cried louder. "I will give you the entire Earth," he said. "I agree to make Bharata king. I will gladly appoint him as my successor. But I will not banish Rama. He is faultless and has never hurt anyone. When Rama treats you as his own mother, why are you bent on harming him? What kind of wicked heart do you possess, wishing harm on one so pure, who is kind to every being? Has he ever said a single word that displeased you?"

"We are not here to discuss the qualities of your darling son, King. Stop temporizing and agree, as you must, to *both* of my wishes."

"Do you really think Bharata will accept this kingdom? He is devoted to Rama . . . or was. But he is, after all, your son. Maybe his greed will be like yours. How could I have been so blind to your defects? Where has all this hate come from? You are jealous of an innocent child who loves you. You have changed from my beloved wife into a fanged serpent."

For a few moments, Kaikeyi's determination evaporated. Couldn't her husband understand how badly she needed assurance? Couldn't he see how she ached for him to say the right words, to assure her that he loved her above all else, that he could live without Rama, that he had not meant to go behind her back with the sudden consecration, that he would protect her for all time.

Kaikeyi longed to hear words of assurance, to end up in his arms again. But he said nothing of the sort, obsessed only with Rama's exile. Her heart wrenched painfully as years of love transformed into something foul and nameless. The pain wracked her entire body, and it toughened her, like an actual wound did when it healed.

She forced a smile onto her lips. "I *will* have my boons."

"But at what cost?" he shouted. "I will die. You gave my life back so many years ago, it's true, but do you now wish me to die a broken man? This world will curse you, and my poor Rama will be exiled from a kingdom that is rightfully his. I see him wandering in a cold jungle, searching for something to eat, starving, my little prince, my boy. How can I let this happen to him? I will never agree to your evil plan. Never! Cruel woman of wicked nature, you are bent on exterminating my dynasty. What wrong have I or Rama done to you?"

Kaikeyi's heart was ice cold. All she felt was disgust for this old man who had promised so many sweet things in the solitude of her bedchambers, but when she finally asked something of him, he denied her desires. He was not a man of honor; he was not the man she had loved.

"Manthara was right," she said bitterly. "Other women who spoke to me about men's deception, they were right. Men are always promising, promising, but never giving what actually matters. I rejected those words as the bitter prattle of the unloved, but now I know they were true. All your love has been a joke, an illusion. The truth is that you have never loved me or my son. Only Rama matters to you. How could I ever have believed myself safe in Ayodhya?"

Dasharatha sat frozen, barely blinking.

As if thrashing a horse with a whip, Kaikeyi pressed her demands on Dasharatha again and again. He refused and she insisted. She knew that she would get her way. She always had. Two hearts, once one, separated that night.

The Honorable Son

Rama and Sita, dressed in the finest silks and jewelry, sat together in their private chamber, waiting for the auspicious day to begin. Rama played with a lotus flower that Sita had brought him. His other hand rested on Sita's knee. With her by his side, he felt like a king already. Sita's grace emphasized his feeling of power.

Sita looked at him with admiration; she had told him that his boyish slenderness had given way to a physique that reflected his maturation. He had grown into a man. The definition of his muscles and the calluses on his hands testified to his skill and dedication as a warrior.

"I am going to train all our children to become warriors," Rama said.

"Even the girls?"

"Even the girls. My mother, Kaikeyi, proves that women can fight just as skillfully as men. We never really dared ask her how many men she has killed."

"I cannot imagine killing anyone," Sita said.

"It gets easier over time." He had told Sita about Tataka. How remorseful he had felt, even though she was a giant monster. When he killed Kashi, he felt only triumph.

"Until we have children," Sita said, "I want to invite lots of animals to live in our gardens."

"We will have children soon," Rama said confidently. "Many kings in Sun dynasty had hundreds of children."

"Rama! Those kings also had many wives, each wife bearing them ten children."

"Alright, then we will have ten," Rama jested.

Sita sighed with a smile.

Just then, Sumantra approached. Rama and Sita both stood up respectfully, greeting the king's closest advisor.

"King Dasharatha wishes to see you privately, Rama." Sumantra said. "He waits in Queen Kaikeyi's quarters."

Sumantra kept his expression neutral, but Rama knew Sumantra so well, he heard the tone of anxiety in the minister's voice. Rama had not expected the summons. He turned to Sita. "Father and Kaikeyi must want to bless me personally before the ceremony begins. I will come back for you soon."

When Rama emerged from his palace, he was greeted by hundreds of cheering Ayodhyans. The previous night had not been an idle one for the citizens, who had decorated the city. Flower garlands were wrapped around every pillar, and colorful flags fluttered in the breeze. The fragrance of burning aloe wood enhanced the auspicious atmosphere. Rama noticed that they were dressed beautifully, equaling the sun in splendor. The uniformed soldiers lining the steps to the entrance looked fit to serve the gods.

Lakshmana stood at the outer gate with folded hands. Today really was a day of formalities. Rama hurried to his brother, greeting him with heightened affection. A chariot drawn by four horses stood waiting for Rama. Waving to the people who surrounded it, Rama mounted the chariot. Lakshmana jumped on behind as they sped off toward the king's palace. Driving through the clean streets, Rama saw how expectant the people were. When they saw him, the people shouted words of praise or shed tears of joy. The lionhearted roared their approval. Women adorned like queens sprinkled flowers from their balconies as he passed. Their love for him was as enormous as the ocean.

Glowing with their love, Rama entered Kaikeyi's chambers, followed by Sumantra. Since Lakshmana had not been summoned, he remained outside. Seeing Father and Kaikeyi, Rama smiled broadly and went forward toward them. His father's eyes were shut, but it was evident that he was not asleep.

"You called for me, Father?" Rama asked.

He bowed low, touching Father's feet respectfully and then Kaikeyi's. Kaikeyi was in an unusual state of disarray, hair loose and makeup smudged. Rama had not seen her like this before. Father opened his eyes and looked into Rama's, but instantly averted them, as they began to brim with tears. Rama felt a sharp alarm rise, as tears streamed down his father's cheeks. He had *never* seen his father like this. Rama turned to Kaikeyi.

"When seeing me, Father's face filled with anguish. Have I done something to displease him?"

Though Kaikeyi stood like a statue, Rama sensed her stumbling and regaining her

balance. She cleared her throat and blinked rapidly. She was not herself either, and she refused to look him in the eye as she spoke.

"Your father is not ill. He wants something from you but is afraid to tell you. He fears it will hurt you."

"Afraid?" Rama smiled in surprise. "I have never seen Father afraid. And when have I ever neglected to follow his orders in any way? If he does not speak, then you, Mother, must tell me on his behalf."

Kaikeyi smiled Manthara's smile, and Rama's heart went cold. "Your father has made several promises to me," she said, "promises he now wishes to forget and ignore. As you well know, your father agreed to a bride-price when he married me, which your father did not honor." Rama's eyes went back and forth between his silent father and his cold mother.

"As if that was not enough," Kaikeyi continued, "he gave me two boons to redeem at any time. Now that time has come. But because of his unmanly weakness, your father has taken refuge in silence. You, Rama, must heed your father's words."

Rama clenched his jaw. He did not like hearing his father criticized. "Father's promise is my promise," he said. "I will sacrifice my life for him. Please speak freely about what he has promised. I will carry out his wishes impeccably. You have my word."

Only then did Kaikeyi look into Rama's eyes. Rama started understanding the nature of Father's silence. Rama turned into a prince instead of a son, shielding his heart. He needed that distance to bear the way Kaikeyi looked at him.

"First, my son, Bharata, will be consecrated as prince regent, taking his rightful place on Ayodhya's throne." Kaikeyi spoke to him as if he was a stranger. "Second, you will be exiled to the forest for fourteen years, living as a recluse, banned from entering any kingdom or civilization. These are my two desires."

Rama looked at her steadily as she spoke and his demeanor did not change. But he heard Sumantra inhale sharply behind him, revealing the minister's shock. He had not known the depth of the king's predicament. Rama's heart hammered against his chest; he kept looking at the silent figure of his father. Would Father say nothing?

The king's agony was clear, but Rama did not yet comprehend his father's silence or his mother's sudden enmity. Was Father merely afraid to hurt Rama's feelings, as Kaikeyi had suggested? Perhaps Father wished for Bharata to become the crown prince. Rama would not question his change of heart. Rama kept his face neutral but his eyes were alert.

"Send messengers for Bharata," Rama said, "so that he may take my place at the consecration. I will leave Ayodhya at once."

A moan escaped Father's lips.

Suddenly animated, Kaikeyi exclaimed, "Yes! Send messengers on the swiftest horses to bring my son home. Rama, don't waste your time on farewells. Go at once. Your exile is effective immediately."

Rama's manner became formal. "Queen, be delighted, for I will without a doubt do as you say. However, do not become indignant if I stay for a moment by my father's side.

My heart aches because my father has not personally told me his wishes. Why is he gazing steadily at the floor? Why are tears flowing from his eyes?"

"It is because he is a coward and a hypocrite," Kaikeyi said, turning to the king. "Aren't you?"

How could she speak to Father like this! Rama wanted to protest, but Dasharatha did not defend himself.

He opened his eyes, black bottomless pits. His eyes were on Kaikeyi and he said in a deflated voice, "This is my punishment for loving you."

"How can you violate your pledge to me?" she demanded. "You are still alive because of me, and this is how you thank me!"

"Like a woman perverted by an evil spirit, you are not ashamed of speaking like this, making worthless things seem worthwhile."

"I agree that saving your life did not amount to much."

"How can you insist on righteousness when what you ask for is abominable?"

"How is putting Bharata, your own son, on the throne abominable?"

"If I agree with your scheme, the world will scorn me as an infatuated dog. But they will also scorn you, Kaikeyi. Can't you see this?"

"You speak of hate, but I speak of truth," Kaikeyi answered. "You are stubbornly avoiding your duty. You care only for Rama and Kausalya. Bharata and I are nothing to you."

Observing their heated exchange, Rama felt he was not even there. Their hate was as exclusive as their love once had been, and yet Rama was the vortex around which it all swirled, at a dizzying speed.

"How will I face Kausalya," Dasharatha asked, "after sending her son into the jungle? She deserves the kindest treatment, which I have failed to give, doting on you, serpent of a wife."

"Praising Kausalya will certainly not sway me."

"If I do as you say," Dasharatha said, "Kausalya, Sumitra, and our sons will feel tortured. Having thrown all of us into hell, you alone will be happy."

Kaikeyi said nothing. Father slumped in his seat.

Kaikeyi turned back to Rama, her eyes ablaze. "Do not concern yourself with your father or his words. He is just mortified because you are his pet son. I advise you to leave as soon as possible. Until you leave, he will not recover himself. I doubt he will be able to eat breakfast or bathe until you are out of the city."

The king crouched in his seat as if in pain. Rama ran forward to him; he understood clearly now that the exile was contrary to his father's desire. Rama had grown to manhood without ever seeing his father so vulnerable. He kept his arms around his father.

For the first time, he reproved Kaikeyi. "I am not a slave of passion or greed, Mother. I would gladly have given you the kingdom had you only asked. What was the need to trouble Father? You could have simply asked me. I will always obey you."

Kaikeyi's eyes filled with tears. But she clenched her jaw and said softly, as if she was asking him to stay, "Make haste, Rama. It's time. Go now."

Implored by his stepmother, Rama reluctantly let go of his feeble father and left.

Emerging from Kaikeyi's chamber, Rama saw Lakshmana pacing furiously. He obviously had not missed a single word from within. Lakshmana's fists were clenched, his knuckles white. His eyes were an explosion of red. While Rama was tightly withheld, Lakshmana was bursting with fury. "*We* will send *her* into exile!"

Rama quelled Lakshmana with one look and did not give his brother a chance to speak; he hurried to his mother's palace. Lakshmana silently followed Rama's rushed steps.

"I have to inform Mother personally about my exile," he told Lakshmana. "If she hears the news from someone else, I fear she will break down and never recover."

As Rama proceeded to his mother's chambers, he felt keenly how his mother's life revolved around him, how much she depended on him.

It was not his fault that he had to leave her, but it felt like it was. Rama schooled his face to calmness. He had to be prepared to see the shock of those close to him without compounding it with his own. The pain he felt came from Kaikeyi's transformation and his father's anguish. Rama realized that by carrying out the order, he was actually hurting his father, but there was no other choice. Rama did not want Kausalya to see his anguish, so he curtained off his mind as he walked into his mother's quarters.

A Mother's Sorrow

When Dasharatha had announced Rama as his heir, Kausalya had felt that all her years of observances had yielded their results. Although Rama was the firstborn son, Kausalya had not taken her son's rights for granted. The king's announcement and the explosive joy of Ayodhya felt like the crowning jewel making up for years of exclusion.

Kausalya had turned to the golden altar with joy, lighting every single flame, offering special oblations into the sacred fire, and offering an abundance of flowers. She had given gifts to every person that she knew, which numbered in the thousands. She had sent Rani and Divya and all the head maids to deliver the presents she could not personally see to. Now Kausalya sat by the altar in her private chamber, waiting to be summoned to her son's side. She was instrumental in the consecration ceremony, for a son could do nothing without the blessing of his mother.

Sitting with her hands folded and eyes closed, Kausalya felt the strength of her purity. Her body over the years had grown lean, almost ascetic, due to her observance of vows. Her hair was pure white. She wore a rich silk sari that shimmered with pure gold. The Great Queen felt happy and peaceful, and when Rama arrived, her heart lit up, like the sacred fire blazing up when fed. Before Kausalya could express her happiness, however, Rama took both her hands and told her in quick words of Kaikeyi's two wishes. Kausalya slowly lowered herself to the floor.

This was the final assault by Kaikeyi and Manthara, one so low, Kausalya had not seen it coming. She covered her eyes with her hands. She did not want Rama to see the bitterness drying up her face. That malicious Kaikeyi!

"This is unacceptable, my son," she said through her fingers. "On what grounds are you being exiled?"

When Rama was silent, Kausalya took a deep breath and removed her hands from her face. She knew how close Rama was to his father. She took hold of his hand and pulled herself up, looking into his sweet face. Yes, her son was deeply aggrieved, though he tried to hide it. Kausalya wanted to march out at once, pulling Rama by the hand, and confront Dasharatha and Kaikeyi. At the same time, a wave of remorse swept over her.

"This is all my fault," she whispered.

Rama's eyes widened. "Mother?"

"I warned them both," she said. "Your father and your third mother. I had such a strong feeling that their love affair would be destructive to Ayodhya. They did not listen. And I did nothing."

"Mother," Rama said, compassion in his eyes and voice. He was being thrown out of his home, like a base criminal, and yet his concern was for her.

Kausalya drew herself up. Her ascetic purity blazed up within her. "I will not let this happen. I will use all my resources as the Great Queen to stop this."

"Yes!" Lakshmana said, and Kausalya's eyes flickered to him for the first time. His fists were clenched, and his nostrils flared.

"No," Rama said quietly. "Give me your blessing so that I will return safely to Ayodhya once the fourteen years are complete."

Kausalya covered her mouth, tears rising in her throat. Rama had made up his mind.

"I cannot accept that Rama follows the orders of that vulgar woman," Lakshmana said, his breath laborious. "Mother, I want you to know that I am loyal to Rama and Rama alone. Father has clearly become senile, controlled by lust and old age, and he will now do anything Kaikeyi proposes. I will not stand by while my brother is robbed of what is rightfully his. I am ready to take up my sword and fight for the throne. If anyone tries to stop me, I will annihilate the entire city! I swear, if the king is against us, I am ready to kill even him!"

"Don't speak like that about Father," Rama said, still in a quiet voice. "I know your loyalty to me is unbreakable. But don't be so quick to turn against Father."

"I disagree, Rama! A guru or a father who has gone astray should be rejected. Father has proven beyond all doubt that he is not capable of following righteousness any longer. He should be rejected and overthrown."

Kausalya assessed Lakshmana with discerning eyes.

"Brother, you are angry," Rama said. "That's why you think like this."

"You should be angry too!"

"But has Father ever been unjust before this day? Have you ever seen him follow evil ways? He has taught us everything we know about goodness, and we should never forget this. He is not doing this out of misplaced attachment to Kaikeyi. I swear my life on it. You didn't see him, Lakshmana. He is suffering. He has been trapped by his own words. Don't forget the boons he gave Kaikeyi."

Lakshmana faced his brother squarely, Kausalya standing between them. "You are forgetting that you are a warrior. You should fight for what is yours. Destroy your enemies and reverse this injustice. My arrows itch to subdue this uprising. I am prepared to die for you, brother. Instruct me and I will claim the land under your control. I am your servant."

Kausalya's eyes rested on Rama. Lakshmana's words were aligned with a warrior's way.

Rama said, "Brother, we are not speaking of enemies, but of our father and mother. Check your anger, Lakshmana. Forget these insults and gather courage instead. Revenge is never a commendable path. Even if our father has wronged us, we must not wrong him in return. I have never consciously displeased any of my elders, and I will not begin today."

"Kaikeyi. That snake. She is no mother. I will have *her* exiled for fourteen years!"

"Do not work against me, Lakshmana. Fate has cast her web, and we are her pawns."

"Now is not the time for panic," Lakshmana insisted, "which is surely the source of your response. Could a man like you talk this way were he not fearful of losing people's respect? How can you blame Fate, a contemptible, feeble thing? I despise this righteousness, which is completely clouding your thinking. Today you will see fate checked by my arrows, just as your royal consecration was checked by so-called Fate. This is the only path to please Ayodhya and its people."

Rama's voice rose. "The people will become satisfied as soon as Bharata is on the throne and they see that he is a good king. I must be far away from here by then. The people will not accept Bharata while I am still here." Rama turned to his mother. "I insist, Mother, that you give me your blessing. Messengers have already been sent to bring Bharata home. I must leave as soon as possible."

Kausalya did not move. She looked at Lakshmana. If only his powerful arguments could sway Rama from his misplaced sense of duty. Like Lakshmana, Kausalya felt no righteousness in this exile. It was the mere whim of a power-hungry woman.

Rama became stern. "Mother, now you are joining sides with Lakshmana without considering my opinion. I will honor my father's promise. I will go to the forest wearing deerskin and matted hair for his sake. I will remain dutiful to my father's word." He took her hands again and said earnestly, "Mother, please do not make this hard for me. I am determined to protect my father's honor. I don't want to go without your blessing. Please grant it to me."

Kausalya had carefully watched the exchange between Rama and Lakshmana. She knew that Rama would not waver. Not ever. A fierce pride rose in her heart. She had not taken the easy path when it came to Kaikeyi, but it had been the righteous one. Her son was doing the same. How could she dissuade him from such conviction?

Quivering with unshed tears, she called out to the elements to protect her son. "May the sun and moon protect you, my son. May the day and night protect you. May the rivers you cross, the trees under which you walk, the flowers on your path, and the animals protect you.

May the path of righteousness protect you. May the knowledge of weapons you gained from Vishvamitra protect you. May the entire world protect you, and may you return safely. For the blessings of your mother protect you."

She pulled his head down, kissing the top of his head.

Rama touched her feet. His hand lingered on her cheek. It took immense self-control to simply watch him leave. She who had closed so many chapters in her life, would she have the power to endure this next one? The queen had blessed Rama's determination, it was true, but she could not silently stand by to see this farce go on. If she could stay the hand of Fate, she would. She would summon the eight ministers and face the king and his favorite. Furious with years of unspent words, Kausalya gathered her golden silks into her hands and departed for Kaikeyi's palace.

Sita's Destiny

When Rama returned alone, adorned the same way he had left, Sita knew something was wrong. Why had no one garlanded him or marked his forehead with auspicious pulp? Those questions disappeared when she saw the pallor of his face. At first Rama simply stood before her, his hands hanging by his sides. He looked like a tortured prisoner, pale and hopeless. Then Rama embraced her tightly. As soon as Sita's heart touched his, she knew what he meant to do. Rama was leaving her. Alarm rose in her like a volcanic tide, starting deep in her belly. She had not felt those tremors in a long time.

Then Rama spoke, confirming her deepest fear. He was leaving Ayodhya to honor his father's promise. He offered many arguments in favor of leaving her behind. The forest was dangerous; women did not live there; blood-drinkers and other predators abounded; he could never forgive himself if anything happened to her.

Sita cared for none of those arguments. A terrible and unspeakable anger took hold of her. She pushed it down, down, intuiting its power. She looked at her beloved and just the tip of her fury spilled out into words. "You are the cruelest, most hardhearted person I have ever met. Those who praise your kindness are fools. You have tied me to you with the deepest bonds of love. Now that I depend on you and need you, you abandon me."

It was unbearable. The spark at her core turned into fire. Sita trembled, but felt an immediate restraint and caution. Her emotions and thoughts had the power to transform the Earth. If she trembled like this, the Earth would quake in response. Sita severed her connection to her mortal frame and was cast away into darkness. Her frightened spirit flew up into the void.

The Great Mother rushed up toward her and caught hold of her spirit, bringing it back down to the Earth and then below its surface. The moment the goddess held her, Sita knew her mother.

Mother, Sita cried, but not in her earthly voice. She was not in that body. The mother here was not the mother Sita shared with Urmila, her little sister. This mother was more visceral to her; she was like Sita. They were one of a kind. Wrapped in the Great Mother's warmth, Sita felt all the elements within her harmonize and come alive. Goddess Bhumi was made of the natural elements. Earth, water, fire, air, and ether were her form, as was Sita. The elements were extensions of her being, as strong as arms, limbs, and thoughts were to a human body. It was not with human eyes that Sita looked at her mother. Those eyes were left behind on the surface of the Earth, where Sita knew that she had fainted, closing her eyes to the reality before her: a life without Rama.

Sita's soul blazed up when the name "Rama" grazed her consciousness.

He is yours and you are his, her mother's caressing hands told her. *And so it will be forever.*

The goddess held Sita and allowed her to crash, to rise, and then to fall again. Sita could not find her center point, her anchor, when Rama was walking away from her. As Sita became still in her elemental form, she rested in her mother's embrace. Until she faced the daylight and felt her mother's warm hands withdraw behind her, Sita had not known what it felt like to be alone.

It was Bhumi who had lifted Sita up from the center of the Earth and pushed the little baby girl through the opening in the field, to face the sun for the first time. Sita remembered those first moments, seeing through the eyes of a newborn infant, a hazy vision. The bright light of the day had made her close her eyes and cry. That's what her body needed to do to embrace the new embodied experience. Now she would be alone again when Rama left her and walked into the unknown.

The unknown took form on the horizon, growing from a dark mass into a vision Sita recognized the massive black gates. She stood by the gates and could not gain entrance. She remained frozen as the gates moved away from her, growing smaller and smaller. When they were a small speck on the horizon, the form containing the gates grew visible. A ripple of horror ran through Sita. She hid in her mother's bosom, but could not help looking up at the form, knowing him to be the gatekeeper: her archenemy. With every one of his ten heads and twenty eyes, he looked at her watchfully; then his attention fragmented. His heads scanned the universe, Bhumi's little daughter forgotten. The gates held his power; Sita would never gain entrance.

Bhumi claimed Sita's attention. There was a time her mother said, when Sita and Bhumi had been one body, one mind. Sita had grown in her womb, an intrinsic part of her. It was the way any child was nurtured in her mother's womb, only Sita's mother's womb was the entire Earth, and they had been connected to each other through the fires that shimmered at its core. Sita and Bhumi were connected through the great fire, through the water that covered her, through the mountain peaks, the wind within her sphere, and the force of gravity that contained it all. Sita experienced this truth with great wonder. She was kindred to every part of the Earth.

Why did I not remember you? Sita asked, wanting to keep this new wisdom with her always.

Bhumi's fire began to scorch Sita. *There are things you cannot remember when you are a human being. That is the price you pay. You, my daughter, must live that way too, veiled from knowing your true self. All you are and all that you know is always there beneath the surface. Just as I am. I walk with you in your dreams. Every time you touch the ground with your feet or any part of your body, I will rise up to greet you. I will be there.*

Bhumi's elements swirled around Sita, kissing her, embracing her, saying farewell.

Face your destiny bravely, my daughter. You are never alone.

With those words, she pushed Sita back up to the surface, as if she was being born again.

Sita's eyes snapped open. She blinked, focusing her eyes on Rama's beloved face.

Rama's arms held her; his concern was all for her. His love made Sita's pain and confusion disappear, as if it had never been.

"I cannot live without you," Sita told him, and she was merely speaking the words she saw in his eyes. He crushed Sita to his chest, and it was a long time before he let her go.

As long as the sun and Earth existed, they would not be separated.

"I may regret this decision as long as I live," he said, "but we will go together."

He held Sita's hand firmly and led her out.

Sita's spirit soared with triumph. The veil of consciousness had returned, and she could not recall in detail what had occurred below the Earth—neither the vision of the gatekeeper nor her mother's being. But deep within her heart, Sita knew that she was supported by her mother, the goddess. She knew that she had decided long ago that Rama's destiny was her own. Knowing Rama's firm nature, Sita had not expected Rama to give in at all. And so Sita followed her husband into his exile with a victorious heart, embracing his hardships as her own. She would walk with him past the boundaries of civilization, into worlds where few humans had dared to go.

The Departure

Rama led Sita out, leaving their home. He would bid his father farewell and inform the elders that he was taking Sita with him. Taking the exile to heart, Rama set out on foot to Dasharatha's palace, taking only his bow with him. Lakshmana stood waiting at the gate. Rama both expected and did not expect Lakshmana's decision. His brother's anger had, for the moment, been replaced by his absolute desire to accompany Rama. Like Sita, he would not be dissuaded from following Rama into exile. Rama reached for his brother's shoulder.

"Then bid Urmila farewell," Rama said. "Join us as soon as you can. I do not wish to tarry."

At the mention of Urmila's name, Sita's hand twitched. Rama pressed her hand and led her onward. The news had spread fast. The people of Ayodhya had expected a grand celebration; instead, hours of silence brought them only tragic news. The prince and princess were greeted by thousands of lamenting citizens. The older men stood together in groups, heads shaking in disbelief. The younger men were more agitated; shaking their fists in the air, they seemed uncertain how to react. Many women openly sobbed and consoled one another. The same beautiful women who had showered flowers on Rama from their balconies now hung from the balconies like wilted flowers. Ayodhya, the happy, spotless capital, was facing a dynastic collapse. When Rama and Sita passed by in the streets, the crowds grew silent. Then a cry arose: "Don't go! Don't go!"

The shout was heard from every corner. Rama gazed ahead steadily, but smiled now and then to the people as he passed. As they walked, the citizens began to follow, and by the time they reached King Dasharatha's palace, thousands of distressed citizens had amassed behind them. Lakshmana joined them at the king's palace, a grim expression across his face.

When the three entered, Dasharatha rose from his seat. Kausalya and the eight ministers stood on one side, Kaikeyi and Manthara on the other. Father's transformation was shocking. Halfway across the room to meet Rama, his knees buckled and he fell forward. Rama ran to catch him. The two brothers took their father's arms and lifted him. After seating their father, Lakshmana grabbed a fan from one of the servants and fanned his father, swallowing his tears.

With one arm around his father, Rama looked at Kaikeyi. During Rama's absence, Kaikeyi had taken the time to change her garb; she was decked in jewelry, hair done up, and draped in her signature red silks. Manthara stood next to the queen, leaning on her cane. Manthara's gaze darted across the room, settling on Rama. Sita nudged Rama, and whispered, "Manthara is pleased."

While every soul in the room grieved, Manthara celebrated. His stepmother had not invented this scheme alone. Who was the wicked soul, hiding inside the form of a hunchback?

The ministers spoke quietly among themselves, though Sumantra had left the room to compose himself. Kausalya spoke into one of the minister's ears; Rama caught his mother's eyes and shook his head. He did not want her to interfere; his course was set.

Kaikeyi avoided everyone but Manthara. But Rama noticed how often her gaze strayed to Dasharatha. She was not as immune to Father as she pretended. Why, then, was she hurting him with her desires? Rama probed into her soul, seeing layers of thoughts, a web of colors. But he found no answer. Kaikeyi's motives were so deeply buried within her, perhaps she did not know them herself. Rama looked once again at Manthara. He felt increasingly certain that Manthara held the key to Kaikeyi's mind.

Father regained his composure. He looked directly at Rama. "Rama, imprison me at once! Take the throne by force! Overthrow me! No one will stop you!"

Father's eyes were dark with desperation.

Rama knelt by his side, resting his hands on Father's knees. "Father, please. I do not covet the throne or the kingdom. Do not feel that you have hurt me. Honoring your promise is the only thing dear to me."

"Sumantra," the king called, searching for his trusted friend. Sumantra entered, eyes red. "Make arrangements for a portion of the army to accompany this honorable son of mine. Select the best servants and cooks. Let them arrange for large tents, soft blankets, and many cushions. If my son must go to the forest, let him go in royal comfort."

"You cannot do this!" Kaikeyi exclaimed.

She had been silent until then. "He is trying to trick me," she cried louder. Manthara seemed to be mouthing the words silently behind her. "You are taking what belongs to my son. Bharata will never accept a land robbed of its plenty."

"Be quiet!" Dasharatha roared. "Why do you poke a hot iron into the wounds you have made? If you wanted Rama bereft of comforts, you should have included that in your boons."

"I said I wanted him to dress in bark cloth and live as an ascetic!"

Manthara whispered something into Kaikeyi's ears. The queen's eyes grew cold, and she said, "King, there is a precedent in our dynasty for how a son should be exiled. King Sagara cast off his son, Asamanja, without anything. You should do the same to Rama."

The room became heavy with silence. Rama refused to defend himself.

Siddhartha, the oldest minister, spoke up, his white beard trembled as he shook with indignation. "Asamanja delighted in drowning his playmates in the river Sarayu. How dare you compare Asamanja to Rama, who has never spoken an ill word or harmed anyone. King Sagara acted in accordance with his people's wishes. Can you claim that you are doing the same? You should end this evil charade before it goes too far."

Kaikeyi stared at Siddhartha with disdain. Sumantra stepped forward.

"Ayodhya embraced you with open arms. Until this day we have never spoken about your mother or the legacy she left you. Do not prove yourself to be your mother's daughter. You can choose differently, Queen Kaikeyi. Rise above this petty ambition."

Kaikeyi looked at one after the other, blinking rapidly. Rama felt her waver. Again Manthara muttered something and Kaikeyi clenched her jaw. "I am merely enforcing the right course of action by returning my son's birthright to him."

Dasharatha stood up. "If you go on with this scheme, Kaikeyi, I will take all my people with me and accompany Rama to the forest. You can stay here and enjoy the kingdom with your son. The citizens will never follow you when their hearts are with Rama."

Kaikeyi opened her mouth, but Rama stepped forward. "No, Father. I will go to the forest alone, as my third mother has decreed. Sita and Lakshmana are determined to follow me. Please give us your blessings to proceed at once. Let Bharata hold absolute rule over the land I abdicate. The truth of your vow must be preserved."

Dasharatha sat down heavily, putting his head in his hands. Kaikeyi wasted no time.

"Here they come, finally," she said, pointing at the Kekayan twins who served her. "Rama, I have arranged the proper attire for you."

As if she was being helpful and kind, Kaikeyi took the bundles from Sukhi and Dukhi and presented them to Rama. He accepted the bundle without a word, seeing within it rough strips of bark cloth and deerskins.

First, Rama removed his crown, earrings, and his golden necklaces. Having been dressed for the coronation, he had extra adornments to remove: bracelets, armlets, belts, and rings. Lakshmana mirrored his movements. The heap of jewelry on the floor grew. No one said a word as the brothers stripped down to their loincloths and replaced their fine silk attire with the bark cloths. Still, Kaikeyi was not satisfied. "What about her?" she said, pointing to Sita. "She needs to divest herself of her royal garb."

Sumantra audibly cursed. Sita's hands went to her necklace.

"Stop," Rama said with authority. "The terms of this exile apply to me alone." He did not turn to face Kaikeyi, but his eyes found her and warned her that he too had an edge. "My brother is simply demonstrating his loyalty by following my example. Sita is free to leave or to stay, as the princess that she is."

Kaikeyi waved her hands, letting it go, but then said, "What of your signet ring?"

Kaikeyi pointed at the only thing Rama had not discarded on the floor. Now she merely acted the part of a spoiled, gloating child, wanting anything she pointed out. It was painful to experience her in this way.

Lakshmana stepped between them. "If you so much as say another word to Rama, I will not hold myself accountable for my actions."

Kaikeyi laughed as if he were harmless. But she did not press Rama further.

"Sumantra, prepare the chariot," she ordered. "It's time to send them off."

Sumantra looked at King Dasharatha, who neither nodded nor disagreed. Rama, Sita, and Lakshmana walked around the room, touching their elders' feet. When Sita reached out for Dasharatha's hand, he clasped both of hers to his chest and sobbed, saying, "Forgive me! Forgive me!"

His grief was terrible. Lakshmana hid his face at Father's knee. Dasharatha stroked Lakshmana's hair. Meanwhile, Rama brought forth his reluctant mother.

"Father, I have one request to make of you before I leave. Here is my mother, your faithful wife. Watch over her carefully and do not allow any harm to befall her from anyone, especially from her co-wife. She is now bereft of her only son, and I beg you to take care of her."

Mother held her head high, but tears rolled down her face. Father hung his head in shame and said, "Your mother is my only hope for shelter now, if she will have me. I have renounced that one as my wife."

He pointed at Kaikeyi without looking at her. Kaikeyi crossed her arms, keeping her face averted.

Rama went forward to embrace his father one last time, and Father took hold of him and refused to let go. Rama heard Sita's voice speaking to Kausalya. "Mother, will you please inform my father that it was my own wish to follow Rama into this exile. I want my father to know that I made the choice and that I'm content."

"Blessings upon you Sita," Kausalya answered. "Many are those who turn fickle in face of hardship, forgetting past prosperity. Your choice speaks of your strong character. Your sacrifice will be rewarded."

"Rama's love is the only reward I need," Sita said softly. And then, "Will Urmila not come to bid us farewell?"

Lakshmana's eyes did not seek anyone, and therefore Rama knew that Urmila would not come to bid them farewell. The time to leave had come. Father's arms were still tightly wrapped around him. Rama had to carefully extricate himself. Pain etched deep lines on Father's face.

Rama took Sita's hand and reached for Lakshmana's as well.

Without looking back, they went down the stairway to the waiting chariot. Everyone in Kaikeyi's chamber followed them out, even Kaikeyi.

They ascended the chariot. "Please start at once," Rama told Sumantra. He didn't want to see his father openly sobbing on the street as he left, but the Ayodhyans clung to his chariot, trying to detain their prince. The chariot's start was a slow one. As Rama spoke in a soothing tone, the people let go, and the chariot gradually picked up speed.

Just as the chariot horses began to gallop, a loud command reached their ears. "Stop the chariot!"

Sumantra's head whipped around when he heard the shout.

Rama turned around and saw his father running through the crowd. "Stop the chariot!"

Sumantra habitually heeded the king's command.

"What are you doing?" Rama cried. "Speed up!"

Confused by the contradictory instructions, Sumantra didn't know what to do. He had lived his life following the king's orders. He slowed the chariot. The king, who was weak and exhausted, ran pitifully behind. It was a heart-breaking sight.

"Can't you see that it is unbearable for me to see my aged father like this?" Rama shouted. "Speed up the chariot and end this at once!"

Sumantra cracked his whip and urged the horses on.

Sita took Rama's shoulder and firmly turned him back until he was facing the direction they were going, saving him from seeing his father stumble in the dust and fall.

The chariot sped forever out of Dasharatha's reach.

CHAPTER 55

Sunset

In the five days since Rama had left Ayodhya, Kausalya had kept vigil at her husband's bed. After exiling her only son, Dasharatha had taken residence in her inner apartment, a day of reunion that Kausalya had always longed for. How ironic it was now, when she ached to just spit out her anger and hurt. Every time she was on the brink of doing so, she was checked by the king's condition. He was not the husband she knew but a helpless man. Stripped of his power, Dasharatha's love for Rama had never been more exposed. He clung to the hope that Rama would return to them. But Sumantra had returned with an empty chariot. Rama had crossed Ayodhya's border along with his companions. As if Dasharatha's life was tied to Rama, he grew weaker before Kausalya's eyes.

"Kausalya, take my hands. I feel so cold."

She did as he asked, inching closer and massaging his hands. With a lifeless voice, Dasharatha spoke only of his firstborn. Rama was too obedient. Why had he listened, when he knew better than any of them? Rama should have revolted against the exile. Dasharatha had begged him to. But his words had come too late. Kaikeyi's cunning scheme had trapped Rama, just as she had snared in Dasharatha.

"As my love for Rama grew," Dasharatha said, "so did my certainty that one day I would lose him. I committed a great crime in my youth." Dasharatha told

Kausalya and Sumitra that he had murdered a boy on a moonless night, taking him for an animal at the river. "His parents cursed me to die in grief without my son. Now those words are coming true. I have been called the 'Great King.' I doubt I will be remembered that way. My last act will overshadow a lifetime of tireless action. The curse was there all along."

Despite the king's chilling confession, Kausalya blamed Kaikeyi for what had taken place. Manthara was involved, that was certain, but Kaikeyi was the queen. She had viciously shattered endless years of peace and destroyed a dynasty for her selfish reasons. Ayodhya was a broken city, the royal family in turmoil.

"Call Vasishta," Dasharatha whispered.

A messenger was sent to summon the preceptor. Kausalya brought water to Dasharatha's lips hoping to alleviate the tenor of his strained voice. When Vasishta entered, he let go of Kausalya's hands. "I need just a few moments," he said, almost apologetically, as if every moment with her now counted.

Kausalya stepped away from the bed unwillingly. His need had instantly bound her deeper to him than ever. Turning his cloudy eyes on the all-seeing preceptor, Dasharatha said, "You who are so wise, how did you let this happen?"

There was no accusation in Dasharatha's voice, only grief.

Vasishta was as silent as Death who comes to your door unannounced. The gravity of the ancient sage filled the room. Dasharatha's eyes closed. "Do you too shun me then?"

Still Vasishta was silent. His bright white hair was tied into a topknot on his head. His white garments shone with purity. Dasharatha struggled to sit up, cleared his throat, and then spoke, louder than necessary. "I call on you, Vasishta, to be the executor of my will when I die. Now that my righteous Rama is gone, you are the only one I can trust. I cannot retract my past with Kaikeyi, but I do hereby shun her as my wife. Do not allow her to touch my body ever again, in life or in death. She may not approach the sacred pyre or attend my last rites. From now on, I will be the husband of two queens alone."

Kausalya bit her lip. He was speaking of his death as though it was imminent.

"My relationship to my second son, Bharata," he continued, "is contingent on his innocence. If by even one word or thought he is complicit in his mother's scheme, I hereby shun him as my son. I will be the father of three, not four, sons. Vasishta, use your unequaled perceptive capacity to judge this errant son of mine. If you find him guilty, I bar him from any and all privileges or duties of a son. He may not come near me or touch me, in life or in death."

Kausalya reached for Sumitra's hand, feeling the ice of the king's declaration. Bharata, the absent prince, had been convicted for his mother's crime. Kausalya felt hot tears rise for the boy who was like a son to her. And yet the king's words resonated with truth. If Bharata was of his mother's heart, he would be cast out of theirs, hers and the king's. It was only fitting and fair.

"You can depend on me," Vasishta reassured his king, speaking for the first time.

As Vasishta left them, Kausalya stepped closer.

"Kausalya, come to me," he begged, as if he fully expected her to deny him. "Stay by my side until the end."

"I'm here," Kausalya said. She lay down by his side, resting her head on his shoulder, a place once so familiar to her. As Kausalya listened to his breathing and his endless murmurs, she prayed that his end was far, far away.

"Rama, Rama," Dasharatha mumbled.

Kausalya could not pacify him, for she too wondered where Rama was now. Were his feet bruised by rocky jungle paths? Was his form losing its strength bereft of sustenance? Was his back aching from sleeping on the bare ground? Would she ever see him again? Would she ever see Lakshmana or Sita again?

"Rama, can you ever forgive me?" Dasharatha called out.

Kausalya and Sumitra tried to soothe his ramblings, but he no longer seemed to be aware of them. He spoke only to Rama.

"Your feet must be walking over rocks and thorns. Crush my chest with your feet. My heart must be like a stone, for I allowed this to happen to you. Stay with your old father, Rama . . . Rama . . . Rama . . ."

Kausalya fell asleep with her ear to his chest, soothed by the murmurs of his heart.

Vasishta's face rose in her consciousness. He stood by her side with his bright hair and his pristine garments. She noticed now what she had not before: his face was serene. His loyalty to the Sun dynasty was beyond dispute, yet he was not devastated by the exile of the prince. He looked steadily ahead with shining eyes. He joined his palms at his heart. "We bless you with victory." He lifted his palms, emanating grace.

Kausalya lifted hers too. In the horizon, she saw the sun, glowing with emerald hues. But she could not tell if it was rising or setting.

CHAPTER 56

Kaikeyi's Only Hope

Only six days had passed since Rama's exile. Six days since the messengers left for Kekaya. It seemed like an eternity. Kaikeyi's heart hammered constantly against her chest. Even on the swiftest horses, it took two weeks to reach Kekaya. She had to wait, wait, wait for her son to return.

Sitting on her throne, Kaikeyi felt the waves of terror and excitement undulate within her body. She had reached out with her own hands and controlled the hands of destiny. She had never been more powerful, never more vulnerable. She could only look forward. She was utterly alone, save for Manthara, and it would be so until Bharata returned.

Over and over, she replayed Dasharatha's words. Dasharatha had been fixated on Rama. He could see nothing else. His behavior fortified her conviction that she had done the right thing. When it came to her child, a loving mother was capable of anything. She had put Bharata's future above her own. She had to keep doing that. Her own desires fought to speak, screaming in her ears so loud that she had a splitting headache. She wanted to take refuge in her husband's loving arms, but she had cut off those arms. Oh, what had she done, what had she done?

"What are you whispering?" Manthara asked, sneaking up on her. She had constantly been on Kaikeyi's back, demanding to know every thought Kaikeyi had. It

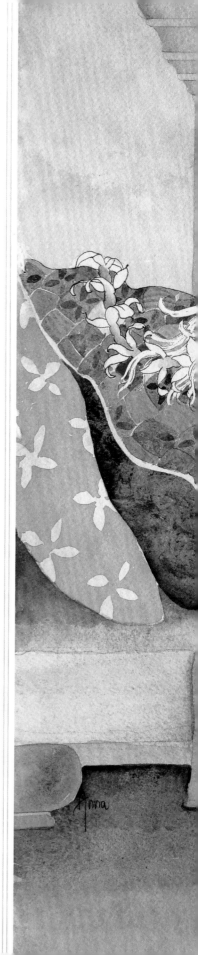

kept Kaikeyi on track. She glanced sideways at Manthara and said, "Nothing."

She felt nothing. That was it. The clamor in her head was subdued. Yet Kaikeyi resented Manthara's intrusion; all this was so easy for Manthara, who had never liked Dasharatha or Rama.

Kaikeyi felt the terror rush up her entrails, up, up, into her throat, her eyes. She tightly clasped her hands, digging her thumb into her girdle of Venus mound, massaging it, pushing the emotion down. "Breathe," she whispered, coaxing herself to calmness. She forced herself to think about Dasharatha's slumped figure, how he had repeatedly lost consciousness, proving himself weak, not a man of action at all. She did not need the love of such a man!

As she fought with her own thoughts, hiding them from Manthara, one of the king's servants approached timidly.

"What now?" Kaikeyi demanded, instantly alert.

"Your presence is requested in Kausalya's quarters."

To demonstrate her reluctance, Kaikeyi sighed loudly. Her heart drummed against her chest. She stood up, securing her red silks neatly around herself. Dasharatha had been cooped up in Kausalya's chambers. She had to face them both. It wasn't the place Kaikeyi would have chosen to face her husband. Nothing good had ever come to her through Kausalya's hands. Except for Rama. She quickly pushed that thought away. But it came back. Rama's innocent eyes, probing into her soul, asking her, *Why?*

"The king has summoned me," she said to Manthara. "You had better stay here. They will find any excuse to sink their claws into you."

Manthara eyed Kaikeyi and then agreed, staying in Kaikeyi's palace. Kaikeyi faced the corridors alone. The guards and attendants who usually followed her had thinned out. A handful of faithful ones remained. Kaikeyi made a note to reward them.

As Kaikeyi approached Kausalya's quarters, she heard wails from the inner chamber. Unconsciously, she quickened her steps and crossed into Kausalya's apartment. As she approached the inner chamber, the guards at the door crossed their spears in front of her. The sounds of women crying made shivers run up her legs and arms. Was that Kausalya wailing?

"How dare you!" Kaikeyi demanded, turning on one guard and then the other. "I have been summoned!" Her whole body began to shiver, and she wanted to grab one of the spears and stab the guards with it. They had no authority to stop her. The guards refused to

look at her, but the knuckles on their hands turned ghostly white, clenched around the spears in her path.

"You must wait for Vasishta," one of them said. "He summoned you. He will meet you here."

A female servant came up to her. "Please sit down, Queen Kaikeyi," she said, eyes lowered, indicating the cushioned seats with her hand.

Did they think she would just sit and wait? What would they do if she forced her way in? Before she had fully formed the thought, she ducked under their spears and rushed into the apartment. She felt their hands restraining her, dragging her back, but not before she saw the body on the bed. Dasharatha, eyes closed, mouth open, pale as a ghost.

The guards pulled her out roughly, her silken garment falling in disarray around her. She glimpsed her two co-wives on either side of the body. Sumitra cried into her hands while Kausalya wept openly. Kaikeyi and Kausalya locked eyes for a moment. There was pure hate in Kausalya's eyes. And then Kaikeyi was outside, the spears crossed before her. The steel was bright like silver, polished to a smooth surface. The red of her silks reflected in their surface, the color of blood mixed with water. One of the spears had a dent on its surface. She looked up and down the spears, first one and then the other. Dasharatha was dead. The X blurred in front of her eyes.

Her heart, which had been skipping so fast for days, slowed down, down, down. She reached into her chest. It was cold. Just like the king. She held her icy heart between her hands. It thumped one last time and fell quiet. And so she felt nothing. The dead body on the bed was a stranger. The man she loved was not there. He had disappeared before that body had died. When he turned away from her, when he denied her boons, when he loved Rama more than her. If she would mourn, she would mourn for that death, not the death of his body. Two tears rolled down her cheeks. Those would be her only.

Kaikeyi turned away, the X of the spears imprinted on her eyes. She left her heart on the floor. Every person who exited would trample it now and make a bloody trail to and from the dead body to whom the dead heart belonged. The wails continued, but they evoked nothing in Kaikeyi. Did those women think that men on the battlefield cried when their friends were slaughtered before their eyes?

Kaikeyi wanted to cover her ears and block out the shrieks. As if any of them had ever truly loved Dasharatha. They had not known him the way Kaikeyi had. And Kaikeyi had no more tears for this man, a hypocrite and a liar. His death was for the better. He had made all this painful for her, when *he* was the one who had promised it to her in the first place. His death made Bharata's life less complicated. He wouldn't have to feel torn between two parents who no longer loved one another. The gods were on her side, after all. Bharata's path to the throne was clearer now. Good. Good.

Kaikeyi's spine was straight and strong, like a sword. "I have more backbone than anyone here," she said to herself. She would not sob like those co-wives in there. They *should* cry. They were not on the winning side, as Kaikeyi was. Kaikeyi sank down on one of the couches. Just for a moment, then she would get up and leave.

"Queen Kaikeyi."

Vasishta's voice. Kaikeyi nodded without looking up. He informed her of the king's dying decree. Kaikeyi was not allowed near the king's body nor would she be allowed to attend his funeral rites. He had died as the husband of two queens. If Bharata was complicit in Kaikeyi's scheme, he would not be allowed to light the funeral pyre and send his father to heaven.

"Scheme?" Kaikeyi said. The word made no sense to her.

She had simply wanted Bharata to be king. That's all. Ayodhya had turned it into a scheme.

Kaikeyi stood up and escaped. The hallways were deserted. Ayodhya was a place of ghosts and dead bodies. Kausalya's wails echoed in every corner. Kaikeyi's legs were unsteady as she walked up the stairs to her palace. Manthara waited, tapping her cane.

"The king is dead," Kaikeyi said, purposely not saying his name. "Our victory is more complete now."

"You are relieved that the king has died?" Manthara's eyes were like hot iron rods.

"Yes," Kaikeyi said, taking a gulp of air. "Yes, yes, yes."

"Sit down," Manthara ordered. She called for Sukhi and Dukhi to bring fans.

The cool air wafted against Kaikeyi's skin. Not so very long ago, she had loved the king with all her heart. She had cared about the boy who was exiled. But like a warrior, like a strategist, like a diplomat, she severed her personal feelings from this completely. It was as Manthara said. This procedure was not personal against Rama. Bharata would see that. Had she been a true enemy, she could have called for Rama's execution. Because she loved Rama, she had simply made sure he was gone for some years. It was nothing but proper planning.

Manthara was gleeful. "Bharata will be king! Instead of a crown-prince in the shadows of his father, he will be king."

Her croaking voice was not soothing to Kaikeyi's ears. Manthara was most likely the only happy one in Ayodhya at this moment. Bent on feeling anything but what she truly felt, Kaikeyi caught the contagion of Manthara's glee. Bharata would be king! Her son would be the most powerful man on the Earth!

Kaikeyi felt hot, cold, happy, exhausted. If she had to bear the price of her son's success, so be it. Once the funeral rites were out of the way, Bharata would be Ayodhya's king. She would not sit idle and wait for her son's return. Kaikeyi summoned all her remaining servants.

"King Dasharatha is dead," she said. Their hostility turned to shock. "More than ever, it's important that you demonstrate loyalty to me and to Bharata. Some of you might be calling me names, but I'm here to tell you that I did this for the welfare of the kingdom, to protect not just my son but Ayodhya's honor.

"Remember when the king could not have sons, and we went to great lengths to petition the gods? We needed to restore balance and purify Ayodhya. I could not allow that imbalance to once again assert itself in our kingdom. If I had simply sat quiet and watched the king dishonor his promise to my father and to me, I fear a great calamity would befall our city. I could not let that happen."

The servants stood quiet, eyes lowered, showing no reaction to her words. She had to convince them of her sincerity. "Any one of you could witness to how truly I've loved Rama and served him through the eighteen years of his life. That has not changed. Please don't think I'm unfeeling or coldhearted. What you must know, however, is that I am a queen and a warrior before anything else. It's my duty to protect this land and its honor. It was with a heavy heart that I saw Rama leave. If there was a way to spare him, I would. But because of the king's lack of honor, he put Rama in an unfortunate position. The king knew he acted shamefully by surreptitiously crowning Rama while Bharata was not here. I believe the king's guilt consumed his life."

She paused, allowing a few moments for tears to shed. A few them looked at her now as she spoke. "I want each of you to know that Bharata will be a fair and just king. Your loyalty will be amply rewarded, starting now. Manthara." She gestured to Manthara to bring out her personal jewels. "These are heirlooms from my family treasure. To show how much I value each of you and your service over the years. Until my son arrives, we are standing against the powers of Ayodhya. When he becomes king, the tide will turn in our favor. Don't wait for that moment to show me your loyalty. It will be too late then."

Kaikeyi looked at each of them. She was glad to see that some of their hands closed around the jewels they were given. More were the eyes that refused to look into hers, but no one dared return or refuse the gifts. It was a good start.

"Thank you for your time," she said, dismissing them.

She felt drained and stood up, the blood rushing to her head. She had to think. Or not think. She wasn't sure which one it was. The king's dead eyes stared at her. She couldn't tell what he thought or what he felt. All she saw in his eyes was "nothing." That was all that was left between them.

Manthara had not left with the other servants. Kaikeyi felt those eyes bore into her.

"Out!" Kaikeyi said, as if Manthara was a dog. "Out of my sight. Now."

But as Manthara started walking away, Kaikeyi ran after her. "Wait, wait, wait . . ."

Manthara turned to her, for once showing nothing on her old face.

"I—I—" Kaikeyi shook her head, searching for words, searching for herself. Everything came back blank.

Manthara softened and patted Kaikeyi's cheek. "Don't worry, my dear girl. I know this isn't easy for you. You've done your part. Everything else will sort itself out now. Bharata will thank you for the rest of his life."

Kaikeyi felt her tears rise to her eyes again. She wasn't as sure as Manthara was. But *it had to be true.* The alternative was unthinkable. She knew the day would come when she would sit down in front of the mirror and, no matter how hard she tried, she wouldn't be able to see herself. The tears would blur her view. There was no telling who she would see in the mirror once the tears cleared up. Kaikeyi knew that day would come. She held Manthara's hand to her cheek for a moment, and then let the old woman go. Bharata would be her solace. Bharata would be to her what Rama was to the others. Her only hope.

CHAPTER 57

Manthara's End

Bharata had returned, but Manthara was uneasy. He had not come to see her. Something was not right. Manthara did not know what was happening in Ayodhya. She had heard nothing about a coronation, nothing about Bharata ascending the throne. Surely with the king dead, they would hurry to crown the new king. But, no, they were all imbeciles in Ayodhya. This was not new.

After Bharata's return, Manthara had found Kaikeyi sobbing hysterically. Manthara hadn't been able to get a sensible word out of her. No one else would tell her what was happening. No one would speak to her. No one. Sukhi and Dukhi, who didn't count, had muttered that Bharata was in the Great Queen's quarters. When Manthara pressed them, they said Bharata had bolted out of Kaikeyi's and run straight for the balcony, as if he meant to throw himself off. Dukhi maintained that Bharata's eyes had been bloodshot and full of tears. Sukhi said they had not dared approach him, for he had looked at them with toxic fury. None of this was like Bharata at all. Manthara wasn't sure Sukhi and Dukhi were to be trusted. But Kaikeyi had been crying since. This concerned Manthara. It looked as if she, as usual, would have to take charge of the situation and insert herself into the vortex of action.

Manthara pushed her hand against her thigh and got up, lumbering to the corner where her canes waited. A dark feeling grew in her heart, but she sharply reminded herself that her plans had always unfolded smoothly. She reached for a cane without looking. Agonizing prickles shot through her hand and up her arm. Yelping, she dropped the cane. With disbelief, she looked down at the splinters lodged under the skin of her gnarled hand. Thirty gods! She would have to get Sukhi and Dukhi to remove them. With her other hand, she carefully selected another cane, one with a smooth polished surface, one that would not think to attack the hand that cared for it. The splinters throbbed in her hand even though she held her fingers absolutely still, cradled to her chest.

With her strong hand on the cane, she put on every piece of jewelry she owned. Loyalty could and would be bought. Even before she was out of her room, she stared shouting, "Sukhi! Dukhi!"

The names echoed down the deserted corridor. No one answered.

"Curse them all!"

Now that Kaikeyi was indulging in her moods, Manthara had all the more to carry. As she shuffled along the corridors, she kept shouting for the twins. She had to have some support. After what felt like ages, the two imps appeared.

"How may we serve you, wise one?" they asked with the exaggerated manner they reserved for Manthara alone. At least that had not changed.

Manthara held out her hand. While Dukhi examined the injury, Sukhi tapped her foot against the ground. Manthara looked at the tap-tap, reminded of her cane. A feeling of stress squeezed Manthara's heart. She refused to wince as the twins used one of their pins to dislodge the thorns.

At that exact moment, Shatrugna turned the corner. But Manthara, in her agitated state, mistook him for Lakshmana. When the prince saw Manthara, he broke into a run. Manthara gasped and began backing away. The prince's usual hostility and anger was amplified a thousand fold. Manthara stumbled backward. Had Rama returned? Was everything falling apart?

The prince charged toward her. Sukhi and Dukhi jumped away, hands over their mouths. Before Manthara could cry for help, the twins turned their backs on her and ran as fast as they could. Manthara and her cane stood alone to face the demon charging toward her.

"I-am-going-to-kill-you!" the prince shouted, lifting his sword.

Fear squeezed Manthara's lungs such that she couldn't even scream.

With the dull side of the sword, the prince began beating her across her back. Manthara's spine sagged with every blow. She fell to the ground, her bones crunching.

"You are the cause of our family's destruction," he screamed.

The next moment, she was dragged across the ground, the cold marble slithering against her exposed skin. Her sari slipped from her chest, exposing her shriveled bosom. Her cane, her only ally, was quickly disappearing from sight. Her precious jewels scattered behind her, a trail of lost loyalties. The pillars rushed by Manthara as the prince dragged her by her hair, then her arm, all the while raging and cursing. She tried to think, but the world was spinning, her whole body convulsing. Wails erupted from her mouth against her will. Finally, she saw something she recognized: Kaikeyi's archway.

"Keyi, Keyi!" she screamed at the top of her lungs.

She felt the prince hesitate, and then Kaikeyi was there. "Release her!"

The prince only resumed smashing the sword against her, promising to kill her. Every blow felt like her last. Kaikeyi circled around him as if she was helpless. The prince grunted with every blow. Manthara shut her eyes, and the terrible humiliation brought her back to another time when she had been on the verge of death, beaten with stick and stones. The shock of being suddenly attacked hurled Manthara into the old trauma. "Slither out of this if you can," the leader had said, the very one she might have married, had she not been a Manthara.

Their insults rang in her ears:

"Worm!"

"Snake!"

"Witch!"

"A snail has more spine than you!"

"You leave a trail of slime wherever you go!"

"The spit of a lowborn is more clean than you!"

The death threat evaporated when Bharata appeared. Manthara lifted her hand toward him. His face was so like Ashvapati's. Manthara's windpipe emitted a low shriek as yet another lash fell across her back. Bharata would save her.

"Bharata, please," Kaikeyi begged. "End this. She is aged. She is weak."

"Shatrugna, enough!" Bharata said, intercepting the next blow.

Manthara looked up at them in confusion. Shatrugna? Manthara peered up at the one standing over her, red in the face with anger. Her whole body shivered with pain. Of course it was Shatrugna. How could she have been so mistaken? But all cruel people looked the same.

Bharata looked down at her without kindness. "If it wasn't for fear of Rama's displeasure," he said, "I would let Shatrugna kill you."

He pulled Shatrugna away. Manthara's mouth hung open. Kaikeyi knelt by Manthara's side, carefully examining Manthara's bruised back.

"Nothing is broken," she said soothingly.

"Everything is broken!" Manthara wheezed.

Bharata left her on the ground without a backward glance, just as those antagonists had years ago, leaving her to die. Hatred boiled up in Manthara's heart. Curse them all! Even the ones she tried to protect deserved no protection. Manthara had utterly miscalculated Bharata's reaction. She had led Kaikeyi to destruction; all her plotting would bring them only to ruin. The malicious part of Manthara's heart sighed in relief, satiated, having reached its aim. Kaikeyi would become a wasteland. Despite her beauty and erect back, Kaikeyi was ruined. Everyone in Ayodhya was ruined. But the ruined queen could see none of this. She was all love and concern, carefully arranging for Manthara to be taken back to her rooms. Manthara kept her eyes firmly shut, lest she reveal the utter contempt she now felt for every person around her. Kaikeyi's "love" was merely a selfish act, a respite from her own misfortune. In caring for the repulsive hunchback, she sought redemption from her own failures.

As the servants carefully lifted her up, Manthara moaned and cried. Kaikeyi firmly held Manthara's hand and walked with her the whole way.

"Careful," she admonished the carriers, as they placed Manthara, a sack of broken bones, on the bed. Liquids ran from Manthara's eyes and nose, and she could not even lift her hand to wipe it off. She was disgusting. Kaikeyi cleaned Manthara's face. Manthara still did not open her eyes. She breathed in shallow gasps; her life was over.

"Manthara," Kaikeyi gently prodded. "You are going to recover from this."

Manthara did not respond. She wanted Kaikeyi to leave. She wanted to be alone. Forever.

"I'm summoning the physician," Kaikeyi said. "I will return soon."

She felt Kaikeyi's soft lips press onto her brow. Her face twitched, repulsed by the false affection. The moment Kaikeyi left, Manthara peeked with one eye. She was alone. She slithered out of the bed, almost losing consciousness from the horrendous pain. Manthara dragged herself across the ground, as she had done once before, seeking the white teardrops dangling from her lily of the valley plants. Without hesitation, she ate the poisonous wild-flower, gaging on the leaves and stalks, swallowing every single piece of the plant. When Kaikeyi returned, the nausea had begun.

"You are so pale, Manthara," Kaikeyi said, bringing water to Manthara's lips.

Manthara pushed the cup away even though her tongue was dry. The tendrils of Manthara's mind reached across a vast desert to cast her final blow. "Come here," she ordered. She was unable to speak loudly, and she wanted Kaikeyi to hear every word she said. She grabbed hold of Kaikeyi's head and pulled the queen's ear to her mouth. "Did you know that I was the one who orchestrated your mother's exile?"

Kaikeyi pulled away, blue eyes filling with fear.

"Your mother, the beautiful Queen Chaya, was just as stupid as you are."

Manthara relished the description of her clever manipulation. It had been too easy.

"Did you learn the lesson now?" Manthara sneered. "Never give anyone the power to break your heart! How many times have I told you that? You should never have trusted me."

Tears began pouring from Kaikeyi's eyes. She was a weakling despite her warrior training.

"I do not regret loving," Kaikeyi said. "I should have loved Dasharatha more. Trusted him. I should have loved Rama more. None of this would have happened if I believed in their love. More love is the solution. Not less! My father should have loved my mother despite her demand. He should have never exiled her. If you trusted in love, Manthara, you would not have said or done any of these things!"

"You naive idiot! I gave my whole life to teach you, and still you have learned nothing!"

"Manthara, don't do this. Don't speak hurtful words. Don't push me away. Love me."

She pressed her cheek against Manthara. "Love me."

Manthara cringed away. Kaikeyi was beyond hope.

Manthara swallowed the bile that rose in her throat. She would not release the teardrops that were burning her insides. She slumped against the pillows, struggling to breathe. Her throat contracted, unable to take in the air. Her lungs twisted, her hands went numb, and her fingers and toes curled in on themselves. Kaikeyi's face morphed before her eyes, contorting into strange shapes. Manthara heard sounds but could not comprehend. Dogs barked, jackals howled. She squeezed her eyes shut and fell into the poisoned pit of suicide.

It was not the fast death she had hoped for. It was nothing like that first time, when she had embraced it, experiencing the end as soothing. Now she was pushed away by Yama himself, forced back into the body that was convulsing, foaming at the mouth, and turning blue. She existed in every strangled breath, every eternal moment of pain. Even in the halls of death, she was unwelcome. Rama's eyes haunted the darkness of her soul. The ghastly souls walking the halls of death had Rama's eyes. He was everywhere. He glowed in the hearts of the lost. He was in Manthara's soul, drinking up her poison. She clawed at her heart, tearing the flesh of her chest. "It's mine!" Her body convulsed violently. Foul liquids erupted from her mouth and bottom. Her eyes rolled in their sockets. Her final word was, "Rama!"

As her soul finally escaped its crooked form, it began to glow. It began to know. Despite herself, she had accomplished her purpose. She had been a devious but worthy instrument: the future of the world depended on Rama's exile. The poison in her heart was his nectar. Manthara had been the bow and Rama the arrow.

The human laws that Manthara had despised her whole life would influence Rama, and it was too soon to know whether those laws would ensure his victory or destroy it. Together, Kaikeyi and Manthara had propelled him far, but he was nowhere near his target yet. The secrecy of the scheme was its power, the lethal weapon still hidden. The archenemy would not see the weapon until it was firmly lodged in his heart. The woman who was destined to be Ravana's doom did not know her own power. Before Sita and Rama achieved their purpose, there would be many more bows, many more arrows, and many more servants like Manthara, playing unwitting parts in a scheme so grand that even the holy ones could see neither the beginning nor the end.

Acknowledgments

THANK YOU

Annapurna: My mamma, for doing your art no matter what and nurturing my creativity from day one, for being the backbone and the visionary of this project. That I ended up writing this is entirely due to you. Your approval and encouragement have blessed this work and give me the courage to trust my creativity and continue writing.

Visvambhar: My husband, for being my best friend, the one I can open my heart to in all circumstances, for being a loving father, for reading all my drafts, for being such a fierce and dedicated artist, for actively supporting me to dance and sing, and much much more.

Mirabai: Editor par excellence, for being the fairy godmother of this work, for going above and beyond, for pushing me and the trilogy to an entirely new horizon, for sharing your wealth of knowledge on craft and process, for having spot-on insights, for being an amazingly sweet person and soul sister.

Len: My bonus-dad, for being the generous patron of this work, for your enthusiasm, for always being there to mediate, and for being a loving grandfather and family member.

Yogindra: My pita, most recently for photocopying and handing me Diana Eck's article, "Following Rama: The Ramayana on the Landscape of India," from *India: A Sacred Geography*. For overseeing my growth since my birth, for setting such an outstanding example as a dedicated seeker of self-realization.

Ananga mama: For being the most selfless person I know, for loving us, sheltering us, feeding us. For lighting up our lives with your spirit, for choosing the bright side always, for being the transmitter of crucial memories.

Bhadra Das: For being a steady influence in your children's lives, for your smiles, and all your recent encouragement.

Gangi: For creating beauty wherever you go and for being sensitive and strong all at once.

Jambu: For being a poet and dedicated yogini, and for reading my first book.

My sacred women's circle: For being the ancient orchard of the feminine, for being the witness to my deepest self and allowing me to glimpse yours.

David B. Wolf and Marie Glasheen: For creating Satvatove and providing a space where all emotions are welcome.

Dhanya: For your inquisitive intellect, grounded spirituality, your voice, your music, your unfolding creative fire.

Kish & Bali: For including me in The Mayapuris project, for being goofballs, my brothers, and for having mad music talent.

Gaura Vani: For fearlessly spearheading your dreams and bringing them to manifestation.

Radhanatha Swami: For kindly endorsing this work with so much love, for being a fearless visionary and spiritual teacher.

Jai Uttal: For being the sweetest friend, inspired storyteller, and Rama-lover. For your effusive and heartwarming praise of book two, for bringing Nubia into my life.

Raoul Goff: Our publisher, for setting the standards high and welcoming us into your folds.

Courtney Andersson: For competently and cheerfully overseeing the project.

Beth Mansbridge and Beverly H. Miller: For your thorough copyediting.

Raghu Consbruck: For your beautiful design work, for being someone I can fully rely on.

Chaya Sharon Heller: For Ayurvedic treatment ideas for Manthara's kyphosis.

Julia Cameron: For writing *The Artist's Way*, which changed my life: "The refusal to be creative is self-will and is counter to our true nature."

Dr. Clarissa Pinkola Estes: For writing the incomparable *Women Who Run with Wolves*, a book every woman and man should read.

Rukmini Devi Arundale: For being a true pioneer, visionary, and creative powerhouse.

Robert P. Goldman and his team: For translating the Ramayana so expertly, and broadening my perspective through your scholarly introductions to each kanda.

Other references: Kamban Ramayana translated by P. S. Sundaram, *The Laws of Manu* by G. Buhler, *Many Ramayanas* by Paula Richman, *How to Think Like a Horse* by Cheryl Hill, Ram: *The Abduction of Sita into Darkness* by Yael Farber, Ramayana by C. Rajagopalachari.

The online resources: www.valmikiramayana.net, www.spine-health.com, mayoclinic.com, wikipedia's kyphosis page.

Special thanks to Philip Lutgendorf for his insightful suggestions and the beautiful foreword.

Characters and Terms

AYODHYA (CAPITAL CITY OF EARTH) / AYODHYANS

Aja – Dasharatha's father; king of Ayodhya before him

Anaranya – king of the Sun dynasty more than twenty-five generations before Rama; killed by Ravana in a famous battle

Asamanja – the only son of the Sun dynasty who disgraced his line; known for drowning his playmates in the river Sarayu

Bharata – Rama's half-brother, second in line to the throne; Kaikeyi's son

Chitra – a scout in Dasharatha's service who rescues and adopts Rani, one of Ravana's victims

Daksha – the head of Ayodhya's treasury

Dasharatha / Dasha – emperor of the Earth, Rama's father; known for his great skill in battle, hence his name "Ten Chariots"

Divya – Queen Kausalya's head maidservant

Guha – king of the Nishadas, Rama's friend; king of the Nishada forest tribe

Indumati – Dasharatha's mother, queen of Ayodhya

Jatayu – a giant vulture, king of his kind

Jayasena – king of Hastinapur, one of the fifty kings of Earth

Kaikeyi / Keyi – third and favorite wife of King Dasharatha; queen 3; mother of Bharata

Kashi – king of Kashi, one of the most persistently aggressive kings under Dasharatha's rule

Kausalya – first wife of King Dasharatha; queen 1; mother of Rama

Koshala – the land surrounding Ayodhya

Lakshmana – Rama's closest friend and half-brother; Shatrugna's twin brother; son of King Dasharatha and queen 2, Sumitra

Lochana – citizen of Ayodhya, whose wife and children are destroyed by Ravana

Manu – the first man; established Ayodhya and created the laws for mankind, known as *The Laws of Manu*

Rama / Rama Chandra – firstborn son of King Dasharatha; son of Kausalya, queen 1; next in line to the throne and wed to Sita

Rani / Maharani – one of the females Ravana abducts, who escapes and returns. She is eventually assigned to serve as Sita's head maid.

Sagara – Rama's ancestor, father of Asamanja

Senapati – the commander-in-chief of Ayodhya's army

Shanta – daughter of King Romapada, married to Rishyashringa

Shatrugna – Lakshmana's twin brother; Bharata's constant companion; son of King Dasharatha and queen 2, Sumitra

Siddhartha – one of the king's eight trusted ministers

Sumantra – one of King Dasharatha's eight ministers and a loyal friend

Sumitra – princess of Magadha, second wife of Dasharatha; mother of twins, Lakshmana and Shatrugna

Vasishta – the royal priest / preceptor of the Sun dynasty through countless generations, and one of the nine mind-born children of Brahma, the creator

RAJAGRIHA (CITY OF KEKAYA) / KEKAYANS

Ashvapati – "Lord of Horses," king of Kekaya, father of Kaikeyi and Yuddhajit

Chaya – "Shadow," the exiled queen, mother of Yuddhajit and Kaikeyi

Dukhi – a maidservant to Kaikeyi, twin of Sukhi

Dvi – one of Kaikeyi's suitors, whom she spurns and punishes

Indu – the mare who gives birth to Kaikeyi's first horse Surya

Manthara – "The Hunchback," Kaikeyi's hunchbacked confidante

Sukhi – a maidservant to Kaikeyi, twin of Dukhi

Surya – Kaikeyi's favorite horse, killed by Dvi

Rajagriha – the city of Kekaya

Yuddhajit / Yuddha – prince of Kekaya, brother to Kaikeyi

MITHILA (CITY OF VIDEHA) / MITHILANS

Bhumi – the goddess of Earth, considered to be Sita's real mother

Janaka – king of Mithila; Sita's adoptive father who found Sita in a furrow

Mandavi – wife of Bharata, Sita's cousin, Kushadvaja's daughter

Mithila – the capital city of Janaka's kingdom, and Sita's birthplace

Shrutakirti – Shatrugna's wife, Sita's cousin, Kushadvaja's daughter

Sita – "Furrow," Rama's wife who appeared from the earth, adopted by King Janaka as his own, also known as Janaki

Sunayana – King Janaka's wife, mother of Urmila and Sita

Urmila – Sita's sister, daughter of Janaka and Sunayana; wife of Lakshmana

OTHER BEINGS AND TERMS

Agni – lord of fire

Ahalya – the stone-woman, Gautama's beloved wife, a mind-born daughter of Brahma

Ananta-Sesha – thousand-headed serpent on whom Vishnu rests

Atibala – one of the sentient mantra-weapons Rama receives from Vishvamitra, healer of wounds, sister to Bala

Ayodhya – the indestructible capital city of Earth

Ayodhyan – citizen of Ayodhya, "the indestructible"

Bala – one of the sentient mantra-weapons Rama receives from Vishvamitra, reliever of fatigue, sister to Atibala

Bhagiratha – Rama's ancestor who brought down the sacred Ganga from the heavens

Bilva – a tree whose leaves are used in worship and for decoration

Brahma (Lord) – father of the universe, the creator of all, and granter of boons

Brahmin – a high priest deeply schooled in the sacred scriptures

Chakra – Vishnu's legendary discus, one of the weapons Rama receives from Vishvamitra

Dandaka – an uncivilized jungle considered a borderland full of supernatural creatures

Dashamukha – "Ten Heads," one of Ravana's original names

Dharma – one of Kaikeyi's favorite horses

Gautama – one of the *sapta-rishis*, or seven sages, recognized as supremely exalted; author of several ancient hymns found in the Rig and Sama Vedas

Indra – lord of Heaven

Indrajit – "Conqueror of Indra," Ravana's son and heir to Lanka

Jatamamsi ointment – an Ayurvedic remedy

Kajal – a black-colored cosmetic used around the eyes and sometimes on forehead

Kalinga – a province

Kamadeva – cupid, god of love

Kaushika – Vishvamitra's original name before transforming into a sage

Kekaya – Kaikeyi's birth kingdom

Khus – vetiver, Rama's favorite fragrance

Kuvera – treasurer to the gods, Ravana's half-brother

Nishadas – the forest tribe loyal to Ayodhya, ruled by Guha

Lakshmi – the goddess of wealth and prosperity, Vishnu's eternal consort

Mahisi – the Great Queen

Manu – the First Man, who built Ayodhya and fathered mankind

Marichi – Ayodhya's blood-drinker prisoner; son of Tataka

Menaka – a celestial damsel and dancer in Indra's court

Padmini – Sita's personal maidservant

Parashuram – the notorious warrior hater

Parivritti – the neglected woman

Rambha – a celestial damsel, one of the famous four

Rasatala – the hellish planet below Earth where the blood-drinkers were cursed to live

Ravana – King of the blood-drinkers; name means "loud wailing"

Rishyashringa – son of Vibhandaka, mysteriously conceived by a deer

Romapada – king of Anga, close friend of King Dasharatha

Rudraksha – spiky beads worn by holy ones for auspiciousness

Sandesh – the stallion King Dasharatha rides on when he first meets Kaikeyi

Sarayu – the river running alongside Ayodhya

Shabala – a celestial wish-fulfilling cow, who appeared from the milk ocean during the legendary churning

Shambara – the blood-drinker who causes King Dasharatha's near-fatal wound

Shatananda / Ananda – son of Gautama and Ahalya, Sita's mentor and King Janaka's chief priest

Shiva – lord of dissolution, who dances vigorously as the world comes to its end

Shigraga – one of Sita's distant relatives, an old man Urmila dreaded marrying

Soma – a plant with a moon-shaped bulb, addictive, intoxicating, used medicinally as a pain remedy

Subahu – the impersonator who sets Marichi free; son of Tataka, brother of Marichi

Surya – lord of the sun

Tara – Rama's horse

Tataka – the first blood-drinker Rama kills; a female monster

Tulsi – the holy basil plant, an essential component in the temple's rituals

Urvasi – a celestial damsel in Indra's court; often considered one of the four primary ones, along with Rambha, Menaka, and Tilottama

Uttar-kashi – a province above Kashi

Varuna – the ocean god

Vavata – the concubine

Vayu – lord of the wind

Vedas – the sacred ancient text, divided into four divisions: Rig, Sama, Yajur, and Atharva

Vedavati – incarnation of the goddess Lakshmi, who cursed Ravana when he accosted her

Vibhandaka – ascetic, grandson of Brahma, father of Rishyashringa

Videha – the province of King Janaka

Vishakanya – a strikingly beautiful maiden, poisonous to the touch; assassin of kings

Vishnu – the maintainer of the universe, present in every molecule of creation

Vishvakarma – the divine architect of the gods who made Shiva's bow

Vishvamitra – Rama's mentor, formerly King Kaushika, exalted from warrior to sage

Yama – lord of death

Artist's Note

The illustrations for this book began as a vision that never left me. Sita, Rama, Lakshmana, and Hanuman have been in my consciousness since I was a young adult living in Sweden. Like a seed that is put into fertile soil, the Ramayana has been growing daily. The fruit of that seed will be an illustrated trilogy based on India's ancient classic.

The origin of this project can be traced back to 1998 when my daughter left home at the age of fourteen to attend a boarding school in Florida. Needless to say, my life changed as she left Sweden and I had to adjust to living without her. The idea of working on a project together took birth at that time. Because of the vast distance between us, I thought that a joint project would keep our bond strong and I would perhaps feel less the pain of separation from her.

I dare say that this book is a product of love more than anything else: the love that my daughter and I share for each other and the love we have for the wisdom, beauty, and knowledge of the ancient Indian history and religion.

I am basically a self -taught artist in regards to book illustration and painting watercolors. It has been a continuous learning experience for me, a process that is still in progress. I am grateful and indebted to numerous artists, both earlier and contemporary, who have helped me on this journey. Without absorbing their skills and accomplishments I would not be where I am today as an artist. I am certainly aware of my limitations as an illustrator,

which helps me be humble and reminds me to experiment with new ways and to learn from the experts.

The illustrations do not entirely cohere with the text. There are several reasons for this. Primarily, the manuscript did not exist when I began to do the artwork. This was a new experience for me and my daughter. I knew next to nothing about illustrating a book as I embarked on this project. My daughter also began expanding the text to such an extent that I began a marathon to keep up. Much contemplation has gone into each illustration, and up until the publisher's deadline, I worked diligently, hoping to produce one painting per chapter.

The trilogy is the product of efforts by many people who are dear to me. Without their patience and support this work would never have fructified, like a plant that can't survive without water and nutrition. A special thanks goes to Vrinda, my daughter and co-worker. Her writing complements whatever I do graphically. I could never have done this book without her and it encourages me to see how she is so inspired by this writing and how she has brought it to a very personal level. Her writing has greatly enhanced both of our lives.

I also must extend a big hug and thanks to Len, my husband. He has always encouraged me in my artistic pursuits, even if, as a consequence, dinner was not always there on the table.

Sam Cohen, my late father-in-law deserves a mention here also. The accumulation of inheritance from his life's work helped to pay for the manufacture of this trilogy.

"From the inside out" is an expression that many of you have heard. That is what I want to welcome you to. My inside creative, fantastic world of art and illustration will be shared with you and the outside world. I hope you enjoy it.

Lastly, I am eternally indebted to my spiritual mentors, to Srila Prabhupada, and to the brilliant spiritual path of bhakti. I humbly offer my heart in their service.

Illustration Index

Look for Book Two

THE SITA'S FIRE TRILOGY: BOOK TWO

QUEEN OF THE ELEMENTS

AN ILLUSTRATED SERIES BASED ON THE RAMAYANA

VRINDA SHETH

ILLUSTRATED BY
ANNA JOHANSSON

Available Spring 2017